PLATO'S PHAEDO

PLATO'S PHAEDO

EDITED

WITH INTRODUCTION AND NOTES

BY

JOHN BURNET

OXFORD

AT THE CLARENDON PRESS

Oxford University Press, Ely House, London W. 1

GLASGOW NEW YORK TORONTO MELBOURNE WELLINGTON
CAPE TOWN IBADAN NAIROBI DAR ES SALAAM LUSAKA ADDIS ABABA
DELHI BOMBAY CALCUTTA MADRAS KARACHI LAHORE DACCA
KUALA LUMPUR SINGAPORE HONG KONG TOKYO

FIRST EDITION 1911
REPRINTED 1924, 1930, 1937, 1949, 1953, 1956, 1959,
1963, 1967, 1972

PRINTED IN GREAT BRITAIN

PREFACE

THE text of this edition is that prepared by me for the *Scriptorum Classicorum Bibliotheca Oxoniensis* with a few corrections and modifications. Such as it is, it is the only text based on the three archetypal MSS., the *Clarkianus* (B), the *Marcianus* (T), and the *Vindobonensis* (W). The readings of T are taken from a photograph in my possession, those of W from the collation of Professor Král of Prague.

In the Introduction and Notes I have chiefly endeavoured to elucidate the argument, and to show the importance of the *Phaedo* as an historical document. Grammatical points have only been dealt with when they seemed to have a direct bearing on these problems. The interpretation of an ancient document must always be based on grammar, but an edition of the *Phaedo* is not the place for a full discussion of general grammatical problems like the constructions of οὐ μή and μὴ οὐ.

I have given references throughout to the second edition of my *Early Greek Philosophy* (E. Gr. Ph.²), where I have discussed more fully the historical background of the dialogue. I hope to have an early opportunity of discussing certain textual problems in a more scientific way than is possible in an edition like the present.

The reader will see that I am under great obligations to the editions of Wyttenbach and Heindorf. Of more recent editions I owe most to that of the late Sir William Geddes.

J. B.

CONTENTS

INTRODUCTION

I

IF only we may take the *Phaedo* for what it professes to be, it surely stands quite by itself in European literature. It does not, indeed, claim to be a word for word report of all Socrates said to the inner circle of his followers on the day he drank the poison in prison. By letting us know incidentally (59b 10) that he was not present, Plato seems to decline responsibility for the literal exactitude of every detail. But, for all that, it does on the face of it bear to be such an account of that memorable day as its author could conceive a favourite disciple giving not long afterwards to a group of deeply interested listeners. That means a great deal. Though he was not present when the Master died, it is certain that Plato continued in close association with others who were,[1] and they must often have talked about Socrates together. Further, the narrative is put into the mouth of Phaedo of Elis, who was certainly still living when the dialogue called by his name was written. So, no doubt, were the chief interlocutors, Simmias and Cebes, and

---

[1] The statement in Diog. Laert. ii. 106, iii. 6 that, just after the death of Socrates, Plato retired with other Socratics to Megara, the home of Euclides (cp. 59 c 2 *n.*), rests on the authority of Hermodorus, who was a disciple of Plato and wrote a book about him. Even apart from this, it is certain that the Socratics kept together and remained in touch with Plato. Some of them, like Theaetetus and the younger Socrates, were subsequently members of the Academy.

probably others of the company.[1] In these circumstances, it is not easy to believe that Plato intended his readers to regard the *Phaedo* simply as an 'imaginary conversation'.

Of course, as has been indicated, he need not have meant every detail to be taken as historically exact. If we choose to suppose that he introduced into the *Phaedo* sayings and doings of Socrates which really belonged to other occasions, there is nothing to be said against that ; for such concentration of characteristic traits in a single scene is quite legitimate in dramatic composition. A certain idealization might also be allowed for; but we should expect the idealizing process to have taken place in the minds of Plato and the rest before the dialogue was written, and to have been in the main unconscious. We may say, then, that the *Phaedo* professes to be nothing less than a faithful picture of Socrates as Plato conceived him when he wrote it. It professes to be even more. We are certainly led to believe that it gives us a truthful record of the subjects on which Socrates discoursed on the last day of his life, and of his manner of treating them. No reader who made his first acquaintance with Socrates here could possibly suppose anything else. This, then, is what the *Phaedo* professes to be ; and if only it is this, it is the likeness of a great philosopher in the supreme crisis of his life, drawn by a philo-

---

[1] It is impossible to discuss the date of the *Phaedo* here ; for this would involve an inquiry into that of the *Republic*. I may say, however, that I regard it as proved that the *Phaedo* is earlier than the *Republic*, and as probable that it was written within ten years of the death of Socrates. But, in any case, Phaedo, who lived to found the school of Elis, is a mere lad in 399 B. c. (cp. 89 b 3), while Simmias and Cebes are νεανίσκοι (89 a 3). No one would assign the *Phaedo* to a date at which it is reasonable to suppose they were dead.

sopher who was greater still, and was also one of the most consummate dramatic artists the world has known. It would not be easy to find the match of such a work.

II

But are we entitled to take the *Phaedo* for what it professes to be? The general opinion apparently is that we are not.[1] It is admitted, indeed, that the narrative portion of the dialogue is historical, but most interpreters doubt whether Socrates talked about immortality at all, and many deny that he held the belief set forth in our dialogue. Hardly any one ventures to suppose that the reasons given for holding this belief could have been given by Socrates; it is assumed that they are based on doctrines formulated by Plato himself at least ten years after Socrates had passed away. I cannot accept this account of the matter. I cannot, indeed, feel sure that all the incidents of the narrative are strictly historical. These are, in my opinion, the very things for which a dramatic artist might fairly draw on his imagination. I have only an impression that they are, broadly speaking, true to life, and that they all serve to bring before us a picture of Socrates as he really was. But the religious and philosophical teaching of the *Phaedo* is on a very different footing. Whatever Plato may or may not have done in other dialogues—and I say nothing here about that [2]—I cannot bring myself to believe that he falsified

[1] I refer mainly to current opinion in this country. Some references to views of another character will be found below (p. xiv, *n.* 2).

[2] It is obvious that we must apply a somewhat different standard to a dialogue like the *Phaedo*, which is supposed to take place when Plato was twenty-eight years old, and to one like the *Parmenides*, which deals with a time at least twenty years before he was born. If it can be

the story of his master's last hours on earth by using him as a mere mouthpiece for novel doctrines of his own. That would have been an offence against good taste and an outrage on all natural piety ; for if Plato did this thing, he must have done it deliberately. There can be no question here of unconscious development ; he must have known quite well whether Socrates held these doctrines or not. I confess that I should regard the *Phaedo* as little better than a heartless mystification if half the things commonly believed about it were true.

III

The interpretation which finds nothing in the *Phaedo* but the speculations of Plato himself is based on the belief that ' the historical Socrates ', of whom we may get some idea from Xenophon, is quite a different person from ' the Platonic Socrates '. What the latter is made to say is treated as evidence for the philosophy of Plato, but not for that of Socrates himself. This does not mean merely that Plato's Socrates is idealized. That might be allowed, if it were admitted that Xenophon too idealized Socrates after his own fashion. If it were only meant that each of these men drew Socrates as he saw him, and that Socrates was, in fact, a different man for each of them, the truth of such a view would be self-evident. We should only have to ask which of the two had the better opportunity of seeing Socrates as he really was, and which was the more capable of understanding and portraying him. But very much more than this is meant.

shown, as I believe it can, that the latter dialogue is accurate in its historical setting (cp. E. Gr. Ph.[2] p. 192) and involves no philosophical anachronism, the *Phaedo* will *a fortiori* be a trustworthy document.

It is meant that Plato has used Socrates as a mask to conceal his own features, and that the Platonic 'Socrates' is, in fact, Plato.

The general acceptance of this view in recent times is apparently due to the authority of Hegel. Speaking of Socrates, he lays down that 'we must hold chiefly to Xenophon in regard to the content of his knowledge, and the degree in which his thought was developed ',[1] and this dictum became a sort of dogma with the Hegelian and semi-Hegelian writers to whom we owe so much of the best nineteenth-century work in the history of Greek philosophy. It can only be made plausible, however, by isolating the *Memorabilia* from Xenophon's other writings in a way which seems wholly illegitimate. We must certainly take the *Oeconomicus* and the *Symposium* into account as well ; and, in estimating Xenophon's claim to be regarded as a historian, we must never forget that he was the author of the *Cyropaedia.*

The *Apology of Socrates* which has come down to us under Xenophon's name raises another question. It is pretty clearly based on Plato's *Apology*, and it contains a rather clumsy plagiarism from the *Phaedo*.[2] This has led many scholars to deny the authenticity of the work ; but the more Xenophon's methods are studied the less cogent do such arguments appear, and there is now a growing disposition to regard the *Apology* as Xenophon's after all. If so, we have to face the possibility that he derived much of his knowledge of Socrates from the writings of Plato.

As for the *Memorabilia* itself, there is no doubt that it is a strangely constructed work, and the 'higher critics'

[1] *Gesch. der Phil.* ii. 69.   [2] Cp. 89 b a *n.*

have condemned whole chapters as interpolations.[1]   It is not necessary to discuss their theories here; I only mention them at all in order to show that the book presents a real problem, and that the time has gone by for speaking of its historical character as something beyond cavil.   If, however, we wish to avoid the conclusions of the critics, we can only do so by putting something better in their place.   The question we must ask is whether it is possible to give an account of Xenophon's Socratic writings which will explain them as they stand. I believe that it is; but I also believe that it is 'the historical Socrates' who will then appear as the fictitious character.[2]

IV

By his own account of the matter, Xenophon was quite young—hardly more than five and twenty—when he saw

[1] It has quite recently been argued that two of the most important conversations (i. 4 and iv. 3) are derived from Plato's *Timaeus*, and were inserted in their present place by Zeno, the founder of Stoicism (K. Lincke, *Xenophon und die Stoa*, Neue Jahrbücher, xvii (1906), pp. 673 sqq.).

[2] This view is gradually making its way. Raeder, while speaking of the distinction between the Platonic and the historical Socrates as 'a recognized truth', is equally emphatic in stating that the Platonic Socrates must be distinguished from Plato himself (*Platons philosophische Entwickelung*, p. 53). Ivo Bruns (*Das literarische Porträt der Griechen*, 1896) insists upon the fact that both Plato and Xenophon give faithful portraits of Socrates as they knew him, only it was a different Socrates that they knew. C. Ritter (*Platon*, i, p. 71) says that Plato's Socrates, 'even though poetically transfigured, is yet certainly the true one, truer not only than the Socrates of comedy, but also than that of Xenophon'. My colleague Professor Taylor's *Varia Socratica* (*St. Andrews University Publications, No. IX. Oxford, Parker*) came into my hands too late for me to refer to it in detail. Though I cannot accept all his conclusions, I am glad to find myself in substantial agreement with him.

Socrates for the last time.[1]   When he made his acquaintance we do not know ; but of course Socrates was a familiar figure to most Athenian lads.   We can see pretty clearly, however, that Xenophon cannot have associated regularly with Socrates after he reached the age of military service.   It is very significant that, as he tells us himself (*An.* iii. 1. 4), it was the Boeotian Proxenus who wrote to him suggesting that he should attach himself to the expedition of Cyrus.   That certainly looks as if he had already served a pretty serious military apprenticeship, and in these years most of the fighting was at a distance from Athens.   The fact that a Boeotian professional soldier knew him to be a likely man for an adventure of this kind seems to imply that he had already given proof of such inclinations ; and, if so, his intercourse with the teacher who had not left Athens for years must have been intermittent at best.

That Xenophon did know Socrates personally, I see, however, no reason to doubt.[2]   What he tells us on the subject in the *Anabasis* rings true, and is in complete harmony with what we know otherwise.   He says (*An.* iii. 1. 5) that, when he had read the letter of Proxenus,

[1] The youth of Xenophon at the time of the expedition of Cyrus was first pointed out clearly by Cobet (*Novae Lectiones*, pp. 539 and 543).   In the *Anabasis* (iii. 1. 14 and 23) he tells us himself that he hesitated to take command of the Ten Thousand because of his youth.   Now two of the generals who had been killed were thirty-five and Proxenus was thirty, so Xenophon must have been appreciably younger.   Cp. also iii. 2. 37, iii. 3 sq., and iv. 2 where he insists upon his youth.   As Croiset says (*Litt. grecque*, vol. iv, p. 340, *n.* 1), ' Si l'on se laissait aller à l'impression générale que donne l'*Anabase*, on attribuerait à Xénophon en 399 plutôt vingt-cinq ans que trente.'   The fact that Apollodorus gave his *floruit* as the archonship of Xenaenetus (401/0 B. C.) does not weigh against this ; for that is merely the date of the expedition.

[2] It has been doubted by E. Richter, whose work I have not seen.

he consulted Socrates the Athenian on the matter.
Socrates had misgivings. He was afraid—and the event
proved him right—that, if Xenophon attached himself to
Cyrus, it would damage his prospects at Athens, so he
advised him to consult the Delphic oracle. But Xenophon had already made up his mind, and only asked the
Pythia to what gods he should pray and sacrifice to en-
sure a prosperous issue to the journey he had in view and
a safe return. The oracle, of course, gave him the answer
he sought, but Socrates blamed him for not asking first
whether he should undertake the journey at all. As it
was, he bade him do as the god commanded. This story
throws great light on what Xenophon afterwards wrote in
the *Memorabilia*. We read there (i. 1. 4) that Socrates
used to warn his friends to do this and not to do that, on
the strength of premonitions from his 'divine sign', and
that for those who did as he told them it turned out well,
while those who did not repented of it later on. We are
also told that Socrates used to advise his friends to consult
oracles on difficult questions, but in matters within the
reach of human intelligence to use their own judgement.

It is not, surely, without significance that Xenophon
should tell us this at the very beginning of the *Memorabilia*, just as the story given above from the *Anabasis*
occurs at the precise point in the narrative where he introduces his own personality. It seems as if it had been
the centre round which his personal memories of Socrates
naturally grouped themselves. In those days, as we
know from other sources, Socrates struck many young
men chiefly as one possessed of a sort of 'second sight'.
In the *Theages* (wrongly included in the Platonic canon,
but still an early work) we read (128 d 8 sqq.) how

Charmides consulted Socrates before beginning to train for the foot-race at Nemea. He neglected the advice given him, 'and it is worth while to ask him what he got by that training!' So, too, Timarchus declared, when he was being led to execution, that he owed his plight to disregard of a warning given by Socrates. And there were others. A certain Sannio consulted Socrates, just like Xenophon, before starting for the wars, and Socrates is represented as saying that he expects him either to lose his life or come within an ace of doing so.

It was not his second sight alone, however, that attracted these young men to Socrates. If they had re-garded him as a mere *clairvoyant*, their feelings to him would not have been what they plainly were. No doubt it was Alcibiades who did most to make Socrates the fashion ; but we can see from the *Symposium* that Plato had good grounds for believing that his enthusiasm was based on a conviction that Socrates was a man of no common strength of character. In particular, all these young men knew him to be a brave soldier and a good citizen. His services at Potidaea, where he saved the life of Alcibiades, and at Amphipolis, and above all his personal courage in the field of Delium, were matter of common report. In the dialogue called by his name (181 a 7 sqq.), Plato makes Laches express the high esteem in which Socrates was held in military circles, and all that would appeal strongly to the group of young men I am trying to characterize. The close of the war with Sparta had left them without any very definite occupation, and they were very ready to try their luck as soldiers of fortune. They were not all Athenians—the Thessalian Meno was one of them—and in any case they had no local patriotism to speak of. They were willing to fight for any one who would employ them, and they were naturally attracted by a man who had not only given proof of bravery in the field, but had also a mysterious gift of foreseeing the chances of military adventures.

Nor would these young men think any the worse of Socrates because he was an object of suspicion to the leaders of the Athenian democracy. They were mostly hostile, if not actually disloyal, to the democracy themselves. They would certainly be impressed by the action of Socrates at the trial of the generals after Arginusae. Xenophon was very likely present on that occasion, and he mentions the matter with some emphasis in the *Hellenica* (i. 7. 15).

That Xenophon belonged to this group we may readily admit, without supposing him to have been a member of the more intimate Socratic circle. As we have seen, he can have had little time for that, and this makes his testimony to the existence of such an inner circle all the more valuable. In dealing with the charge that Critias and Alcibiades had been associates of Socrates, he points out that they were so only for a time and to serve their own ends. Besides these, and others like them, there were many who associated with Socrates in order to become good men, and not to further any political ambitions of their own. The names he gives—Crito, Chaerephon, Chaerecrates, Hermocrates, Simmias, Cebes, Phaedondas [1]—are all familiar to the readers of Plato.

[1] *Mem.* i. 2. 48. The mention of the Theban Phaedondas, of whom nothing is known (cp. 59 c 2 *n.*), might suggest the suspicion that Xenophon merely took his list from the *Phaedo*, were it not that Plato calls him *Phaedondes*, just as he calls Archytas *Archytes*. It almost seems as if Xenophon knew him personally by his Boeotian name.

With one doubtful exception,[1] they are those of men whom he represents as supporting Socrates at the trial or in the prison or both.

Now, if Xenophon is here speaking from his own personal knowledge, he confirms the statements of Plato in the most remarkable way; for he bears witness to the existence of a circle of true disciples which included the Theban Pythagoreans, Simmias and Cebes. If, on the other hand, he has merely taken his list of names from Plato's *Apology*, *Crito*, and *Phaedo*, he must mean at the very least that Plato's account of the matter is quite in keeping with the memories of his youth. The reference to Simmias and Cebes in the conversation with Theodote (*Mem.* iii. 11. 17) shows further that he knew they had been attracted to Athens from Thebes by their desire to associate with Socrates, or at least that he accepted this as a true account of the matter.

There is nothing so far to suggest that Xenophon had any special information about Socrates, or that he was in any real sense his follower. His behaviour in the matter of the Delphic oracle is highly characteristic, and he tells the story himself. It represents him as a self-willed lad who thought he might guard against the consequences of his actions by getting a favourable response, no matter

---

[1] Most editors follow Groen van Prinsterer in changing the MS. Ἑρμοκράτης to Ἑρμογένης, which would bring Xenophon and Plato into complete agreement. It is to be observed, however, that, in the *Timaeus* and *Critias*, Plato represents Hermocrates as present, and that he meant to make him the leading speaker in the third dialogue of the trilogy. I do not think it likely that Plato should have invented an impossible meeting, and Hermocrates may have come to Athens and made the acquaintance of Socrates during his exile. If he did, the fact would certainly interest Xenophon.

how, from the Pythia. That is quite human, and we need not be too severe upon him for it; but it hardly inspires confidence in him as a witness to the beliefs of Socrates about things unseen and eternal.

V

Turning a deaf ear to the warnings of Socrates, young Xenophon left Athens to join the expedition of Cyrus, and he never saw Socrates again. He had, therefore, no first-hand knowledge of his trial and death, while Plato was certainly present at the trial. Further, though it is just possible that Xenophon revisited Athens for a short time in the interval between his return from Asia and his fresh departure with Agesilaus, he spent practically all the rest of his life in exile. He was, therefore, far less favourably situated than Plato for increasing his knowledge of Socrates by conversation with others who had known him. Phaedo, indeed, was not far off at Elis, but he never mentions Phaedo at all. He might very easily have made inquiries among the Pythagoreans of Phlius; but, in spite of the exceptional sympathy he shows for Phlius in the *Hellenica*, he never says a word about Echecrates or any of them. We have seen that he does mention Simmias and Cebes twice (in both cases for a special purpose), but it is very significant that no conversations with them are reported in the *Memorabilia*. It seems to follow that Xenophon did not belong to the same circle as these men did, and we can very well believe his sympathy with them to have been imperfect. He does appear to have known Hermogenes, son of Hipponicus (*Phaed.* 59 b 7 *n.*), but that is apparently all.

Where, then, did he get the conversations recorded in

the *Memorabilia*? To a considerable extent they are discussions at which he cannot have been present, and which he had no opportunity of hearing about from oral tradition, as Plato may easily have done in similar cases. It does not seem probable that they are pure inventions, though he has given them an unmistakable colouring which is quite his own. In some cases they seem to be adaptations from Plato. It is difficult to believe that what he makes Socrates say about Anaxagoras, and the hazy account he gives of the method of hypothesis, have any other source than the *Phaedo*.[1] It is highly probable that some of the conversations come from Antisthenes, though I think it a mistake to regard Antisthenes as his main source. We must bear in mind that there were many 'Socratic discourses', of which we get a very fair idea from what Wilamowitz calls 'the Socratic Apocrypha'. If we take up the *Memorabilia* when we are fresh from the *Theages* or the *Clitopho* (to the latter of which there seems to be an allusion in the *Memorabilia*[2]) we shall find the book much easier to understand in many respects. If I mistake not, we shall have the feeling that Xenophon got the substance of many of his conversations from sources of this kind, and fitted these as well as he could into his own recollections of the

[1] For Anaxagoras cp. *Mem*. iv. 7. 6 with *Phaed*. 97 b 8, and for ὑπόθεσις cp. *Mem*. iv. 6. 13 and *Phaed*. 92 d 6 *n*. That both passages are misunderstood proves nothing against this view.

[2] *Clitopho* 408 d 2 πῶς ποτε νῦν ἀποδεχόμεθα τὴν Σωκράτους προτροπὴν ἡμῶν ἐπ' ἀρετήν; ὡς ὄντος μόνου τούτου, ἐπεξελθεῖν δὲ οὐκ ἔνι τῷ πράγματι καὶ λαβεῖν αὐτὸ τελέως; ... 410 b 4 νομίσας σε τὸ μὲν προτρέπειν εἰς ἀρετῆς ἐπιμέλειαν κάλλιστ' ἀνθρώπων δρᾶν ... μακρότερον δὲ οὐδέν. Cp. Xen. *Mem*. i. 4. 1 Εἰ δέ τινες Σωκράτην νομίζουσιν, ὡς ἔνιοι γράφουσί τε καὶ λέγουσι περὶ αὐτοῦ τεκμαιρόμενοι, προτρέψασθαι μὲν ἀνθρώπους ἐπ' ἀρετὴν κράτιστον γεγονέναι, προαγαγεῖν δ' ἐπ' αὐτὴν οὐχ ἱκανόν κτλ.

brave old man with the gift of second sight, whose advice he had sought in early life without any particular intention of taking it.

VI

It is not even necessary for our purpose to discuss the vexed question of Xenophon's veracity, though it is right to mention that, when he claims to have been an eye-witness, his statements are not to be trusted. At the beginning of his *Symposium* he says he was present at the banquet which he describes, though he must have been a child at the time.[1] He also claims in the *Oeconomicus* to have heard the conversation with Critobulus, in the course of which (4. 18 sqq.) Socrates discusses the battle of Cunaxa, though it is certain that Xenophon saw Socrates for the last time before that battle was fought. These things show clearly that we are not to take his claims to be a first-hand witness seriously, but the misstatements are so glaring that they can hardly have been intended to deceive. Xenophon was eager to defend the memory of Socrates ; for that was part of the case against the Athenian democracy. He had to eke out his own rather meagre recollections from such sources as appealed to him most, those which made much of the 'divine sign' and the hardiness of Socrates, and occasionally he has to invent, as is obviously the case in the passage of the *Oeconomicus* referred to. When Plato

---

[1] The banquet is supposed to take place in 421/0 B. C. In Athenaeus 216 d we are told that Xenophon was perhaps not born at that date, or was at any rate a mere child. It follows that Herodicus (a follower of Crates of Mallos), whom Athenaeus is here drawing upon, supposed Xenophon to have been only twenty years old at the time of the *Anabasis*. This is probably an exaggeration of his youth at that date.

reports conversations at which he cannot have been present, he is apt to insist upon the fact that he is speaking at second- or third-hand with what seems to us unnecessary elaboration,[1] but Xenophon's manner is different. He says ' I was there ', or ' I heard ', but that is only to make the narrative vivid. We are not supposed to believe it.

VII

In view of all this, it is now pretty generally admitted that Xenophon's Socrates must be distinguished from the historical Socrates quite as carefully as Plato's. That seems to leave us with two fictitious characters on our hands instead of one, though of course it is allowed that in both cases the fiction is founded upon fact. But how are we to distinguish the one from the other? We require, it would seem, a third witness, and such a witness has been found in Aristotle. It is pointed out that he was a philosopher, and therefore better able to appreciate the philosophical importance of Socrates than Xenophon was. On the other hand, he was far enough removed from Socrates to take a calm and impartial view of him, a thing which was impossible for Plato. Where, therefore, Aristotle confirms Plato or Xenophon, we may be sure we have at last got that elusive figure, ' the historical Socrates.'[2]

This method rests wholly, of course, on the assumption that Aristotle had access to independent sources of infor-

[1] Cp. especially the openings of the *Parmenides* and the *Symposium*.

[2] This is the distinctive feature of Joel's method in his work entitled *Der echte und der Xenophontische Sokrates.* Though I cannot accept his conclusions, I must not be understood to disparage Joel's learning and industry.

mation about Socrates. There can be no question of first-hand evidence ; for Socrates had been dead fifteen years when Aristotle was born, and a whole generation had passed away before he came to Athens for the first time. He might certainly have learnt something from conversation with Plato and the older members of the Academy, and he might have read Socratic dialogues no longer extant. It is impossible to suggest any other source from which he could have derived his information, and these do not come to much. It is to be supposed that Plato and his friends would represent Socrates much as he appears in the dialogues, while the lost Socratic writings would not take him far beyond Xenophon.

In practice, too, this criterion proves of little value. Aristotle himself does not tell us a great deal, and the Aristotelian Socrates has to be reconstructed with the help of the *Eudemian Ethics* and the *Magna Moralia*. This seriously vitiates the results of the method ; for the considerations urged in support of Aristotle's trustworthiness cannot be held to cover these later works. As to the remainder, Zeller is clearly right in his contention that Aristotle never says anything about Socrates which he might not have derived from works which are still extant.[1] There is no sign that he had even read the *Memorabilia*, and in fact the presumption is that, when Aristotle says ' Socrates ', he regularly means the Socrates of Plato's dialogues. No doubt, like all of us, he sometimes refers to the Platonic Socrates as Plato, but that is natural enough on any supposition ; the really significant fact is that he so often calls him Socrates. Indeed, he was so much in the habit of regarding the dialogues

[1] *Phil. der Griechen* [4] ii. 94, *n.* 4.

of Plato as 'discourses of Socrates' that he actually includes the *Laws* under this title.[1] It is surely quite impossible to suppose that he really meant to identify the Athenian Stranger with Socrates. If he was capable of making a blunder like that, it would not be worth while to consider his evidence on the subject at all. It is far simpler to assume that, for Aristotle, Socrates was just the Platonic Socrates, and that, in speaking of the *Laws* as 'discourses of Socrates', he has made a slip which would be intelligible enough on that supposition, but wholly inexplicable on any other. If that is so, and if 'discourses of Socrates' meant to Aristotle 'dialogues of Plato', we can make no use of what he says to check the statements of Xenophon, and still less to support the view that the Platonic Socrates is unhistorical. Aristotle is always ready to criticize Plato, and if he had been in a position to contrast the real Socrates with Plato's, we may be sure he would have done so somewhere in unmistakable language.

It cannot be said either that Aristotle's statements as to what 'Socrates' really meant are of much help to us. He is by no means a good interpreter of philosophical views with which he is not in sympathy. He is, for instance, demonstrably unfair to the Eleatics, and the Platonic Socrates is almost equally beyond his range.

---

[1] *Pol.* B. 6. 1265 a 11 τὸ μὲν οὖν περιττὸν ἔχουσι πάντες οἱ τοῦ Σωκράτους λόγοι καὶ τὸ κομψὸν καὶ τὸ καινοτόμον καὶ τὸ ζητητικὸν κτλ. Aristotle has just been speaking of the *Republic*, the paradoxes of which he also ascribes to Socrates, and he goes on to the *Laws* with these words (1265 a 1) τῶν δὲ Νόμων τὸ μὲν πλεῖστον μέρος νόμοι τυγχάνουσιν ὄντες, ὀλίγα δὲ περὶ τῆς πολιτείας εἴρηκεν (sc. ὁ Σωκράτης). The editors say that the Athenian Stranger is identified with Socrates, and seem to be unconscious of the absurdity of such an identification.

VIII

It looks after all as if our only chance of learning anything about Socrates was from Plato, but we must of
course subject his evidence to the same tests as we have
applied to Xenophon and Aristotle. In the first place
we must ask what opportunities he had of knowing the
true Socrates. He is singularly reticent on this point in
his dialogues. We learn from them that he was present
at the trial of Socrates but not at his death, and that is
all. He has completely effaced his own personality from
his writings. We may note, however, that he likes to
dwell on the fact that his kinsmen, Critias and Charmides,
and his brothers, Glaucon and Adimantus, were intimate
with Socrates.

Plato was twenty-eight years old when Socrates was
put to death,[1] and we cannot doubt that he had known
him from his boyhood. The idea that Plato first made
the acquaintance of Socrates when he was grown up may
be dismissed.[2] It is inconsistent with all we know about
Athenian society, and especially that section of it to
which Plato's family belonged. It was common for
parents and guardians to encourage boys to associate
with Socrates, and to beg Socrates to talk with them.
Plato was the nephew of Charmides, and we know that

[1] This rests on the authority of Hermodorus (ap. Diog. Laert. iii. 6).
Cp. p. ix, *n.* 1.

[2] The current story that Plato made the acquaintance of Socrates when
he was twenty does not rest on the authority of Hermodorus at all,
though it is quoted in Diogenes Laertius just before the statement referred to in *n.* 1. Others said that Plato associated with Socrates for ten
years. Both figures, I take it, are arrived at by a calculation based on
the solitary datum furnished by Hermodorus. Some counted from the
beginning and others from the end of Plato's two years as an ἔφηβος. If
that is so, there was no genuine tradition.

Charmides was warmly attached to Socrates when Plato was in his 'teens. Even later, as we know from Xenophon, Socrates prevented Glaucon from speaking in public before he was twenty, 'being well-disposed to him because of Charmides and Plato.'[1] In these circumstances, it is inconceivable that Plato did not meet Socrates over and over again in the *gymnasia* and elsewhere. Xenophon may have known Socrates in this way too, but the presumption is far stronger in the case of Plato. Moreover, the son of Ariston would certainly be a far cleverer boy than the son of Gryllus, while his artistic susceptibility and his keen eye for the characteristic would be early developed. The sketches he has left us of the Master's way with boys in the *gymnasia* are too vivid to be wholly imaginary.

When he grew up, Plato does not seem to have left Athens. No doubt he saw some service ; but he tells us himself that his ambitions were political,[2] and by his time the political and military careers were quite distinct. If he had qualified himself, like Xenophon, to be a professional soldier, we should have known something about it.

---

[1] We learn from the dialogue called by his name that Charmides came under the influence of Socrates as a boy, three or four years before the birth of Plato. We learn from Xenophon that he kept up the close relationship to him which began then. It was Socrates who did him the doubtful service of urging him to enter public life in spite of his shyness (*Mem.* iii. 7), and in the *Symposium* (1. 3) Xenophon represents him as associating with Socrates along with Critobulus, Hermogenes, and Antisthenes. He is made to say that he could associate more freely with Socrates when reduced to poverty by the war. For the conversation with Glaucon, cp. *Mem.* iii. 6. 1. These data cover the whole period of Plato's boyhood and early manhood.

[2] *Ep.* vii. 324 b 8 sqq.

Plato, then, had exceptional opportunities of knowing Socrates, but this does not prove that he belonged to the inner Socratic circle.[1] The evidence does not carry us beyond the probability that he belonged to the group of young men—'the sons of the richer citizens, who have most time to spare'[2]—who gathered round Socrates for the pleasure of hearing him expose the ignorance of pretenders to knowledge. That is a different group from the one to which Xenophon belonged, but it is equally well marked, and it is not the inner circle. We can infer no more from the passage in the *Apology* where Socrates offers to call Adimantus to prove that Plato had got no harm from associating with him.[3] The fact that Phaedo thinks it necessary to explain Plato's absence from the scene in the prison may mean a little more, but that refers to a later date.

If we regard the Seventh Epistle as Plato's—and I do not see who else could have written it—the matter appears in a clearer light. Plato does not say a word in it about having been a disciple of Socrates, though he speaks of him as an older friend for whose character he had a profound admiration.[4] His ambitions, as we have seen, were political, not scientific. He was in his twenty-fourth year when the Thirty were established, and his kinsmen urged him to take office under them; but the behaviour of Socrates in the affair of Leon of Salamis[5]

---

[1] We cannot draw any inference from Xenophon's omission of his name from the list. To mention the kinsman of Critias and Charmides would have spoilt the point he is trying to make.

[2] *Apol.* 23 c 2.   [3] *Apol.* 34 a 1.

[4] *Ep.* vii. 324 d 8 φίλον ἄνδρα ἐμοὶ πρεσβύτερον Σωκράτη, ὃν ἐγὼ σχεδὸν οὐκ ἂν αἰσχυνοίμην εἰπὼν δικαιότατον εἶναι τῶν τότε.

[5] *Ep.* vii. 324 e 2 ἐπί τινα τῶν πολιτῶν μεθ' ἑτέρων ἔπεμπον, βίᾳ ἄξοντα ὡς

opened his eyes to the real character of the oligarchy.
When the Thirty fell, he was at first impressed by the
moderation of the restored democracy, and once more
thought of entering public life, but the condemnation of
Socrates proved to him that there was no hope in that
direction either.[1] In fact, though his first awakening
went back to the year of the Thirty, his final conversion
dated only from the death of Socrates. He probably
rose a new man from the sick-bed on which he was then
lying. It would not be the only case of a man called to
be an apostle after the death of his Master.

Such seems to me the most probable account of the
relations between Socrates and Plato ; but, even if he was
not a disciple in the strict sense, his opportunities for
learning to know Socrates as he really was were vastly
greater than those of Xenophon. Above all, he was at
Athens during the last two years of his life, while Xenophon was in Asia. So far as the *Phaedo* is concerned,
the statement of our earliest authority, Hermodorus, that,
after the death of Socrates, Plato threw in his lot with the
Socratics and retired with them to Megara, the home of
Euclides and Terpsion, is of the first importance.[2] We
may be sure that he made it his business to hear every
detail of the Master's last words and actions from all who
had been present, and he makes Phaedo express the
delight they all took in speaking of him, while Echecrates

ἀποθανούμενον, ἵνα δὴ μετέχοι τῶν πραγμάτων αὐτοῖς, εἴτε βούλοιτο εἴτε μή·
ὁ δ' οὐκ ἐπείθετο, πᾶν δὲ παρεκινδύνευσεν παθεῖν πρὶν ἀνοσίων αὐτοῖς ἔργων
γενέσθαι κοινωνός. The story is told in *Apol.* 32 c 4 sqq., where the name
of Leon is given.

[1] *Ep.* vii. 325 a 5 sqq. Plato says that he was prevented from entering
public life by the impossibility of effecting anything without a party and
the proved impossibility of acting with either party.

[2] Cp. p. ix, *n.* 1.

voices the desire of all admirers of Socrates for exact information about him. That Plato was really in a position to give a full and true account of the day described in the *Phaedo* is not, therefore, open to doubt.

IX

Still, it will be said, the ancient idea of historical truth was so different from ours, that we cannot look for what is called an 'objective narrative' from such a writer as Plato. It is usual to refer to the speeches of Thucydides in support of this contention, and they are really rather to the point. It seems to me, however, that they prove something different from the position they are supposed to illustrate. Thucydides tells us that he has put into the mouth of each speaker the sentiments proper to the occasion, expressed as he thought he would be likely to express them, while at the same time endeavouring, as nearly as he could, to give the general purport of what was actually said.[1] Even that would carry us a considerable way in the case of the Platonic Socrates in the *Phaedo*. It would surely mean at the very least that Socrates discussed immortality with two Pythagoreans on his dying day, and that implies a good many other things.

But it is really the contrast between the speeches of Thucydides and the dialogues of Plato that is most instructive. Broadly speaking, all the orators in Thucydides speak in the same style. Even Pericles and Cleon can hardly be said to be characterized. In Plato

[1] Thuc. i. 22. Observe that he only professes to give τὰ δέοντα, what was called for by the occasion, not τὰ προσήκοντα, what was appropriate to the character of the speakers.

we find just the opposite. Even the Eleatic Stranger and the speakers in the *Laws* have a character of their own, and only seem shadowy by contrast with the rich personalities of the earlier dialogues. This realism is just one of the traits which distinguishes the literature of the fourth century from that of the fifth. Aristotle had observed the existence of the new literary *genre* and calls attention to the fact that it had not received a name. It had two distinctive marks, it used prose for its instrument and it was an imitation. It included the mimes of Sophron and Xenarchus and also 'the Socratic discourses'.[1] This classification of the Platonic dialogue with the mime is one of Aristotle's happiest thoughts. If the anecdotes which are told of Plato's delight in Sophron are historical,[2] we can see what suggested it; but in any case, it is true. Plato's dialogues really are mimes, but with this difference, that the characters are all real and well-known people. They are just the opposite of the speeches in Thucydides.

The critics have, no doubt, discovered a certain number of apparent anachronisms in the dialogues. It is said that, in the *Symposium* (193 a 2), Plato makes Aristophanes refer to the διοικισμός of Mantinea which took place in 385 B. C., and that, in the *Meno* (90 a 4), he makes Socrates refer to the enrichment of Ismenias by Persian gold as recent, whereas it happened after the death of Socrates. The latter instance, however, is extremely doubtful; for Ismenias was an important figure at Thebes considerably before the death of

[1] *Poet.* 1447 b 2 sqq.
[2] The story that Socrates was a student and imitator of Sophron rests on the authority of Duris of Samos (FHG. ii, p. 480).

Socrates,[1] and the former is probably a misunderstanding. Aristophanes does not mention Mantinea, and what he says about the διοικισμός of the Arcadians by Sparta may very well refer to the dissolution of the Arcadian Confederacy, which was quite recent when the banquet described in the *Symposium* is supposed to take place.[2] For my part, I am quite ready to accept the *dictum* of Wilamowitz that there are no anachronisms in Plato; but, even if there were one or two of the kind just mentioned, they would be of little account. They would have to be regarded as slips which no one would have noticed unless he had been looking for them, and which do not detract in the least from the historical character of the dialogues in which they occur.

On the other hand, we must note certain positive features which show that Plato was not only a realist in his character-drawing, but had also a strong sense of historical perspective and a genuine feeling for historical values. In particular, he has avoided completely a very subtle form of anachronism. He has a wonderful way of keeping up the illusion that his dialogues belong to the pre-revolutionary period. The Revolutions of 404 and

[1] Cp. E. Meyer, *Gesch. des Alterth.* v. §§ 854, 855. The chronology of the *Hellenica* is certainly at fault in regard to these transactions, and Persian gold may well have found its way to Thebes before the supposed date of the conversation described in the *Meno.*

[2] Wilamowitz-Moellendorff, *Die Xenophontische Apologie*, Hermes xxxvi (1897), p. 102, *n.* 1. He points out that Plato does not make Aristophanes mention Mantinea at all, and that the allusion does not correspond to what we know of the Spartan treatment of Mantinea in 385 B.C. The Arcadian League struck coins with the superscription 'Αρκαδικόν, and these coins cease after the battle of 418 B.C. As the *Symposium* is supposed to take place in 416 B.C., Aristophanes is alluding in a natural way to an event then recent.

403 B. C. made a complete break in the politics and literature of Athens. A new world had arisen, and the carry-over, so to speak, was far less than at the French Revolution. There is hardly a single statesman or writer of the fifth century whose activity was prolonged into the fourth. Aristophanes is the exception that proves the rule ; for the Aristophanes of the *Ecclesiazusae* and the *Plutus* is a different man from the Aristophanes of the *Lysistrata* and the *Birds*. It is important to realize this gap between the centuries and to keep it constantly in view if we wish to understand Plato's art.

The majority of the dialogues are supposed to take place before the Revolutions, and Plato never loses sight of this for a moment, though many of his personages came to play a leading part in the troubled times which he had cause to remember so vividly. Critias and Charmides were kinsmen of his own, and he must have been affected by the tragedy of the life of Alcibiades. Yet there is not the slightest hint of all this in the *Charmides* or the *Symposium*. Critias is still a cultured politician and poet; Charmides is still a modest and beautiful lad ; Alcibiades is still at the height of his wild career. Coming events are not even suffered to cast their shadows before, as an inferior artist would have made them do. Like the great dramatist he was, Plato has transported himself back to the age of Pericles and the age of Alcibiades, and portrayed them as they seemed to the men who lived in them, not as they must have appeared to his contemporaries and to himself, when the glamour of the great time had passed away.

Nowhere, perhaps, is Plato's self-restraint in this respect better seen than in the picture he has drawn of Aristophanes. It is almost the only one of his literary portraits which we can fully appreciate. We can form a fairly clear idea of Aristophanes from his comedies, and there can be no doubt that Plato's Aristophanes corresponds admirably to it. The Platonic Aristophanes is thoroughly Aristophanic, and this raises at least a presumption that the Platonic Socrates is Socratic. But, above all, what strikes us is the relation of good fellowship in which Socrates and Aristophanes stand to one another. The *Clouds* had been produced some years before, but they are still the best of friends. At that time, there was really no reason why Socrates should resent the brilliant caricature of Aristophanes, and Alcibiades does not hesitate to quote it in his encomium (*Symp.* 221 b 3). No one in these days would take a comedy too seriously. At a later date, things were rather different. Even if what Socrates is made to say about Aristophanes in the *Apology* is not to be taken quite literally, the Socratic circle must have felt some resentment against him after the condemnation. Yet Plato keeps all that out of sight; such thoughts belong to the fourth century and not to the fifth.

It seems to me that the reason why Plato's power of transporting himself back to an earlier time has met with such scant recognition is just the success with which he has done it. As we read him, we can hardly realize that he is calling up a time which was passing away when he himself was a boy. The picture is so actual that we feel it must be contemporary. That is why so many writers on Plato speak as if the first half of the fourth century ran concurrently with the second half of the fifth.[1] They

[1] It is no wonder that lesser writers should be deceived, seeing that

think of Plato as the adversary of the 'Sophists', though, when he wrote, there were no longer any sophists in the sense intended. They were merely memories in his day; for they had no successors. Even Thrasymachus belongs to the generation which flourished when Plato was a child.[1] So, too, the problems discussed in the dialogues

Eduard Meyer, who has done more than any one to make the historical background of Plato's life intelligible, falls under the illusion. He says (*Gesch. des Alterthums*, vol. iv, p. 429) that the *Symposium* ' proves nothing as to the relations of Socrates with Aristophanes, but only as to those of Plato. . . . Two such diametrically opposed natures as Socrates and Aristophanes could have no relations with one another, but it is quite natural that Plato and Aristophanes should have found and understood each other '. He finds a confirmation of this in the *Ecclesiazusae*, which he regards as a parody of Plato's *Republic*, but which he says is quite free from the bitterness and malice of the *Clouds*, so that Plato and Aristophanes may have been on excellent terms. Now Meyer also holds (*loc. cit.*) that Aristophanes was in earnest when he attacked Socrates, and that Plato was quite right in ascribing the chief responsibility for his master's death to him. We must apparently believe then that, some half-dozen years after the death of Socrates (the *Ecclesiazusae* was probably produced in 392 B.C.), and within a few years of the time he wrote the *Phaedo*, Plato 'found and understood' the man whom he rightly regarded as mainly responsible for the death of Socrates, and then thought it appropriate to write a dialogue in which he represents Socrates and Aristophanes as boon companions. If that can be true, anything may. The fact is that the Aristophanes whom Plato might very well have 'found and understood' is just the Aristophanes of the *Symposium*, not the *revenant* who wrote the *Ecclesiazusae* and the *Plutus*. But Plato was only a baby when the *Clouds* was produced, and a mere boy at the time the *Symposium* took place. What we may really infer is that the references to Aristophanes in the *Apology* are little more than Socratic *persiflage* like the similar allusion in the *Phaedo* itself (70 c 1), and that Plato knew very well that Aristophanes was not in earnest, and that no one supposed he was. Constantin Ritter has, in my opinion, put this matter in a truer light (*Platon*, i, p. 50, *n.* 1).

[1] Thrasymachus is about the last representative of the 'Sophists' (though Plato never gives him that name), and he was early enough to be satirized in the Δαιταλῆς, the first comedy which Aristophanes wrote. That was in 427 B.C., before Plato had learned to speak. It is improbable

are those which were of interest at the time they are supposed to take place. That of the Strong Man, for instance, which is the subject of the *Gorgias*, belongs to the end of the fifth century. It is also the theme of the *Herakles* of Euripides.

It naturally follows from this that, when Plato does wish to discuss questions which had come up in his own time, he is quite conscious of the impropriety of making Socrates the leading speaker. If we adopt the chronology of the dialogues now generally received, the *Theaetetus* is, with one striking exception, the latest in which Socrates leads the discussion. In the *Parmenides*, he is quite a youth, and the immature character of his views is shown by Parmenides and Zeno. In form, the *Sophist* and the *Statesman* are a sequel to the *Theaetetus*; but Socrates, though present, takes hardly any part in the argument, which is conducted by an anonymous stranger from Elea. The *Timaeus* and the *Critias* profess in the same way to continue the *Republic*, but here too Socrates is no more than an 'honorary president', as a recent writer puts it. We can see that the same was meant to be the case in the *Hermocrates*, a dialogue which Plato designed but never wrote. In the *Laws*, Socrates disappears altogether, and his place is taken by an 'Athenian Stranger' who seems really to be Plato himself. The only exception to this rule is the *Philebus*, and that exception is easily accounted for, as the dialogue deals with subjects which Plato makes Socrates discuss elsewhere. In fact the *Philebus* is the crucial case. It must

that he was still living when Plato began to write, and the theories which he is made to uphold in the *Republic* are not such as any one is likely to have maintained in the fourth century.

be later than some, at least, of the dialogues just mentioned, and the fact that Plato once more makes Socrates
take the lead shows that it was solely in the interests of
historical verisimilitude that he refrained from doing so
in other dialogues.

X

Of course, if we are to regard Plato as our best
authority, we shall have to revise our estimate of Socrates
as a philosopher.   The need for such a revision has long
been felt, though it has never been taken thoroughly in
hand.   Even before Hegel laid down that Xenophon
was our only authority for the philosophy of Socrates,
Schleiermacher had suggested a much more fruitful method
of studying the question.[1] He started from the consideration that, as Xenophon himself was no philosopher, and
as the *Memorabilia* does not profess to be anything more
than a defence of Socrates against certain definite accusa-
tions, we are entitled to assume that Socrates *may* have
been more than Xenophon is able to tell us, and that
there *may* have been other sides to his teaching than
Xenophon thinks it convenient to disclose in view of his
immediate purpose.   He goes on to show that Socrates
must have been more than Xenophon tells us, if he was
to exercise the attraction he did upon the ablest and
most speculative men of his time.   The question, then,
is : ' What *may* Socrates have been, besides what Xenophon tells us of him, without, however, contradicting the
traits of character and principles of life which Xenophon
definitely sets up as Socratic ; and what *must* he have

[1] *Ueber den Werth des Sokrates als Philosophen* (*Works*, Section III
vol. ii, pp. 287 sqq.).

been to give Plato the occasion and the right to represent
him as he does in his dialogues?' This is surely the
proper light in which to regard the question, and it was
formally acknowledged to be so by Zeller, though the
consequences of so regarding it have not been fully
recognized. I would only add one more question to
Schleiermacher's, and it is quite in harmony with his
method. We must ask, I think, very specially 'What
must Socrates have been to win the enthusiastic devotion
of the Pythagoreans of Thebes and Phlius and of the
Eleatics of Megara?' That question is forced upon us
by any serious study of the *Phaedo*, and the answer to it
reveals Socrates to us in a very different light from
Xenophon's *Memorabilia*.

XI

For one thing, this consideration suggests that Socrates
cannot have stood aloof from the scientific movement of
his time. Xenophon does not really say that he did.
He tells us, indeed, that Socrates dissuaded his friends
from spending their lives in the study of higher mathematics and astronomy, but he adds in both cases that
Socrates was not unversed in these subjects himself. It
would be quite like Socrates to tell a young man to leave
these things alone till he had learnt to know himself, and
that would account for all Xenophon says.[1] Nor does

[1] *Mem*. iv. 7. 3 καίτοι οὐκ ἄπειρός γε αὐτῶν ἦν (sc. τῶν δυσσυνέτων δια-
γραμμάτων, as Xenophon quaintly calls them), *ib.* 5 καίτοι οὐδὲ τούτων γε
ἀνήκοος ἦν (sc. the planetary orbits, their distances from the earth, the
times of their revolutions and their causes, i.e. the whole higher
astronomy of the Pythagoreans). Certainly Socrates held that there
was something more important than this knowledge, and what Xenophon
tells us as to his advice not to waste one's life in such studies would be
amply accounted for by the recollection of some such saying as that re-

Aristotle say anything inconsistent with the account given by Socrates of his intellectual development in the *Phaedo* (96 a 6 sqq.). He only says that he applied his new method of universal definitions to ethical subjects alone; and, as the *Phaedo* represents the discovery of the new method as subsequent to the scientific studies of Socrates, there is no contradiction at all.[1]   On the other hand, the narrative in the *Phaedo* is confirmed in a striking way by our earliest witness, Aristophanes. As was pointed out long ago by F. A. Wolf,[2] Socrates was only about forty-five years old, and Plato and Xenophon were babies, when the *Clouds* came out (423 B. C.), and it is quite possible that Socrates was still known chiefly as a student of natural science at that time.   The really decisive argument, however, is this, that, if we take the *Phaedo* and the *Clouds* seriously, making due allowance for comic exaggeration in the latter, we get an account of the scientific position of Socrates which fits exactly into what we know of the intellectual atmosphere of the middle of the fifth century B. C., and which would be inconceivable at any other date.

In the first place, the cosmological theories burlesqued in the *Clouds* are mainly those of Diogenes of Apollonia, who had revived the theory of Anaximenes that Air was

corded in the *Phaedrus* (229 e 5) οὐ δύναμαί πω κατὰ τὸ Δελφικὸν γράμμα γνῶναι ἐμαυτόν· γελοῖον δή μοι φαίνεται τοῦτο ἔτι ἀγνοοῦντα τὰ ἀλλότρια σκοπεῖν. Cp. *Mem.* i. 1. 12 καὶ πρῶτον μὲν αὐτῶν ἐσκόπει πότερά ποτε νομίσαντες ἱκανῶς ἤδη τἀνθρώπινα εἰδέναι ἔρχονται ἐπὶ τὸ περὶ τῶν τοιούτων φροντίζειν κτλ.

[1] Cp. *Met.* 987 b 1; 1078 b 17.   *Part. An.* 642 a 28.   These statements only mean that Socrates did not apply his special method to cosmological subjects. Aristotle nowhere denies that Socrates started from the science of his time.

[2] See his edition of the *Clouds* (1811), pp. ix sqq.

the primary substance.[1] Indeed, the whole comedy is based on this. According to Diogenes, Air condenses into Mist, and becomes visible in the form of Clouds. That is why the Clouds are the divinities of the Socratic school.[2] Further, Diogenes held that Air was 'what we think with', and that is why Socrates swings aloft in the air. The damp of the earth would clog his thought.[3] The theories of Diogenes were fashionable at Athens when Socrates was a young man, and it would only be natural for him to adopt them at that date.

Another influence with which we must reckon is that of the Anaxagorean Archelaus. The statement that Socrates was his disciple is far too well attested to be ignored. Ion of Chios apparently said that he visited Samos with Archelaus, and in any case the statement was known to Aristoxenus and (what is more important) to Theophrastus.[4] It is, therefore, no Alexandrian figment. Archelaus is not mentioned in the *Phaedo* by

[1] See Diels in *Rhein. Mus.* N.F. xlii, p. 12 sqq. and *Vors.*[2] pp. 340, 341. Cp. also E. Gr. Ph.[2] p. 408, *n.* 3.

[2] See E. Gr. Ph.[2] pp. 409 sqq.

[3] Cp. *Phaedo* 96 b 4 *n.* and *Clouds* 225 sqq. where Socrates explains that he could not rightly have discovered 'the things aloft', εἰ μὴ κρεμάσας τὸ νόημα καὶ τὴν φροντίδα | λεπτὴν καταμείξας ἐς τὸν ὅμοιον ἀέρα. If he had tried to do so on the ground, he would have failed οὐ γὰρ ἀλλ' ἡ γῆ βίᾳ | ἕλκει πρὸς αὑτὴν τὴν ἰκμάδα τῆς φροντίδος. Cp. Theophrastus, *de Sens.* 44 (of Diogenes) φρονεῖν δ', ὥσπερ ἐλέχθη, τῷ ἀέρι καθαρῷ καὶ ξηρῷ· κωλύειν γὰρ τὴν ἰκμάδα τὸν νοῦν.

[4] Diog. Laert. ii. 22 Ἴων δὲ ὁ Χῖος καὶ νέον ὄντα (sc. Σωκράτη) εἰς Σάμον σὺν Ἀρχελάῳ ἀποδημῆσαι. Ion may, however, have meant another Socrates, as Wilamowitz suggests (*Philol. Unters.* i. 24), viz. Socrates of Anagyrus, who was a colleague of Pericles and Sophocles in the Samian War. For the evidence of Aristoxenus, see Diels, *Vors.*[2] p. 323. 34 sqq. For Theophrastus, cp. Diels, *Dox.* p. 479. 17 Καὶ Ἀρχέλαος ὁ Ἀθηναῖος, ᾧ καὶ Σωκράτη συγγεγονέναι φασίν, Ἀναξαγόρου γενομένῳ μαθητῇ. See also Chiapelli in *Arch. f. Gesch. der Phil.* iv, pp. 369 sqq.

name, but Socrates says he had heard the book of Anaxagoras read aloud by 'some one' and had been deeply impressed by it (97 b 8 sqq.).

The narrative in the *Phaedo* goes on to tell us how Socrates grew dissatisfied with the doctrines of Anaxagoras. That also is characteristic of the time. Gorgias certainly, and Protagoras probably, had given up science in the same way. And we can see pretty clearly that the dialectic of the Eleatic Zeno was what shook the faith of all three.[1] In the *Parmenides*, Plato has told us this of Socrates in so many words, while the problem of the unit, which had been raised by Zeno, holds a prominent place in the enumeration of his doubts and difficulties in the *Phaedo* (96 e 7 sqq.).

But there is another influence at work and from a different quarter. In the *Phaedo* there are several references to the doctrines of Empedocles. Socrates was in doubt whether 'what we think with' was Air or Blood (96 b 4). The latter was the doctrine of Empedocles, and Aristotle tells us it was adopted by Critias.[2] What is more important still is that Socrates was troubled in his youth by the question whether the earth was flat or round (97 d 8), and that implies Pythagorean influence. The philosophers of Ionia all held that the earth was flat, and it was only from some Italian source that Socrates could have learned the other theory.[3]

[1] Cp. E. Gr. Ph.[2] p. 417. Gorgias had been an Empedoclean (*ib.* p. 234, *n.* 4), and Plato at least suggests that Protagoras had been a Heraclitean (*ib.* p. 188). The experience of Socrates was only one effect among others of the 'bankruptcy of science' in the middle of the fifth century (*ib.* 406).

[2] Arist. *de An.* A. 2. 405 b 6. As Empedocles joined the Athenian colony of Thurii in 444 B.C., his views may easily have become known at Athens. [3] Cp. 97 d 8 *n.*

This influence of Western cosmological ideas upon Socrates is confirmed in a curious way by Aristophanes. It is quite natural that Socrates should be classed with those who busy themselves with 'things aloft' (τὰ μετέωρα), but we regularly find that 'the things beneath the earth' (τὰ ὑπὸ γῆς) are associated with these in his case.[1] Now it was Empedocles who first paid much attention to the subterranean. The volcanic phenomena of Sicily and the Orphic interest in the House of Hades both led him to dwell upon the question of the earth's interior,[2] and this double interest is beautifully brought out in the closing myth of the *Phaedo*. Aristophanes knows this point too, and his words ἐρεβοδιφῶσιν ὑπὸ τὸν Τάρταρον[3] might have been written in ridicule of the very theories which Plato has put into the mouth of Socrates at the end of our dialogue.

Further details as to the science of the *Phaedo* will be found in the notes; here I only wish to point out that the curious fusion of Ionian and Western theories which characterizes it is inexplicable unless we regard it as belonging to Athens in the middle of the fifth century B.C. At no other date, and in no other place, could such a fusion well have taken place.[4]

[1] Cp. *Apol.* 18 b 7 τά τε μετέωρα φροντιστὴς καὶ τὰ ὑπὸ γῆς πάντα ἀνεζη-τηκώς, *Clouds* 188 ζητοῦσιν οὗτοι τὰ κατὰ γῆς.

[2] E. Gr. Ph.[2] p. 277, *n.* 2. Diels, *Vors.*[2] p. 164. 1.

[3] *Clouds* 192. The interest of the myth in the *Phaedo* is mainly eschatological, but it also gives us a complete theory of τὰ ὑπὸ γῆς, explaining incidentally tides, volcanoes, earthquakes, and the like. The subterranean rivers are specially Empedoclean.

[4] The Ionians remained unaffected by the more scientific cosmology of the West. Democritus still believed that the earth was a disk hollow in the centre. As explained in the note to *Phaedo* 109 b 3, the theory of Socrates represents an attempt to combine this view with the theory of a spherical earth. At any date earlier or later than that of Socrates,

XII

According to the *Phaedo*, when Socrates gave up natural science in despair, he found satisfaction in what is generally known as the Theory of Ideas. I have tried to explain this theory simply in the Notes, so far as such an explanation is necessary for a right understanding of the *Phaedo*; we have only to do here with the fact that it is represented in our dialogue as already familiar to Socrates and all his associates, whereas it is generally held to be a specifically Platonic doctrine, and one which was not even formulated by Plato in any dialogue earlier than the *Phaedo* itself. This is evidently a problem of the first magnitude and cannot be treated fully here. I can only restate the conclusion to which I have come elsewhere, namely, that the doctrine in question was not originated by Plato, or even by Socrates, but is essentially Pythagorean, as Aristotle tells us it was.[1] A few further considerations, which tend to confirm this view are, however, strictly pertinent to the present inquiry.

We have seen that there was a point beyond which Plato did not think it right to go in making Socrates the leader of his dialogues. Now, if the ' Ideal Theory' had originated with himself, and if, as is commonly believed, it was the central thing in his philosophy, we should certainly expect the point at which Socrates begins to take a subordinate place to be that at which the theory is introduced. What we do find is exactly the opposite.

such an attempt would have been an anachronism, and it is only at Athens that it would seem worth making. The Ionians did not trouble themselves about a spherical earth nor the Westerns about a flat one.

[1] E. Gr. Ph.[2] pp. 354 sqq.

The dialogues where Socrates falls into the background are just those in which the 'Ideal Theory' is criticized, or in which nothing at all is said about it; where it is assumed and affirmed, Plato has no hesitation in making Socrates its mouthpiece. Indeed, with one remarkable and significant exception, no speaker but Socrates is ever made to expound the doctrine at all, and the exception is the *Pythagorean* Timaeus.[1]

It has been said that to question Plato's authorship of the 'Ideal Theory' is 'to deprive him of his birthright'. It is at any rate a birthright he has never claimed; indeed, he has done everything in his power to bar any such claim on his part. He has made Socrates discuss the theory with Parmenides and Zeno almost a generation before his own birth, and he has indicated that it was not unknown to the Eleatics. Nor is it only Socrates who is represented as familiar with the theory. In the *Phaedo*, the Theban Pythagoreans, Simmias and Cebes, know all about it and are enthusiastic believers in it. Men of such divergent views as Antisthenes and Euclides of Megara are present, but no one asks for a proof of it, or even for an explanation. It is simply taken for granted. When Phaedo repeats all this to the Pythagoreans at Phlius, the same thing happens. Echecrates, who shows himself anxious for exact information on other points, asks no questions about this one. As I have argued elsewhere (E. Gr. Ph.[2] p. 355), it is surely incredible that any philosopher should introduce a novel

---

[1] *Tim.* 51 c 4 εἶναί τί φαμεν εἶδος ἑκάστου νοητόν. Here we have the 'we', which is such a marked feature of the discussions of the *Phaedo*, and this time it is used by a Pythagorean. The *Timaeus* was written years after the *Phaedo*, but it still preserves the old way of speaking.

theory of his own by representing it as already familiar to a number of distinguished living contemporaries, and that in reporting a conversation at which he distinctly states he was not present.

Plato's own contribution to philosophy is a great enough thing, quite apart from the theory of 'forms' expounded in the *Phaedo*. This is not the place to discuss it, but it seems worth while to consider how it has come about that in modern times the ' Ideal Theory ' of the *Phaedo* and the *Republic* has often been regarded as practically the whole of it. In the first place, about the middle of the nineteenth century, most of the dialogues from which we can learn anything of Plato's riper thought, the dialogues in which Socrates no longer takes the leading part, were declared to be spurious. In the second place, the importance of Plato's oral teaching in the Academy, which did not find full expression in his dialogues, was seriously underrated. This was due to a natural reaction against the theory of an 'esoteric doctrine', which had been much abused; but it cannot really be disputed that many of Plato's fundamental doctrines were only expounded orally. Aristotle over and over again attributes to him precise statements which may be implicit in the later dialogues, but are certainly not to be found there in so many words. The task of reconstructing Plato's mature philosophy from the unsympathetic criticisms of Aristotle is a delicate but not, I believe, an impossible one.

During the latter half of the nineteenth century, the later dialogues were reinstated one by one in the positions from which they had been thrust, and a serious attempt was made to understand Aristotle's criticism of Plato.

It was assumed that there was a ' later theory of Ideas ' [1] which in many respects contradicted that set forth in the *Phaedo* and the *Republic*, and this had one very salutary effect, that of directing attention once more to those dialogues which had always been held in antiquity to contain the genuine philosophy of Plato. At the same time, I am convinced that the theory of an earlier and later theory of Ideas is only a half-way house. Aristotle knows nothing of such a distinction, and he would have delighted to insist upon it if he had. The time has come, I believe, for a return to the older and better view. I prefer, accordingly, not to speak of ' Plato's earlier theory of Ideas ', because I do not believe the theory was Plato's at all ; and I prefer not to speak of ' Plato's later theory of Ideas ', because I am not clear that Platonism proper is adequately described as a ' theory of Ideas ', however true it may be that it is based on the Pythagorean doctrine to which alone that name is really appropriate.[2]

[1] This view is specially associated with the name of Professor Henry Jackson. Though I cannot accept all his results, I must not be taken to undervalue his great services to Platonic study. The genuineness of Plato's later dialogues was first clearly established by my predecessor, Professor Lewis Campbell.

[2] Aristotle is commonly said to have denied that Socrates held ' the theory of Ideas ', but there is really no such statement in all his writings. What he does say is that Socrates did not make universals ' separate ' ($\chi\omega\rho\iota\sigma\tau\acute{a}$) from particulars, and that is quite true of the Platonic Socrates. In the *Parmenides* he is represented as puzzled about the precise relation of the forms to particular things, and in the *Phaedo* (100 d 5) he is not sure whether $\pi\alpha\rho\upsilon\sigma\acute{\iota}\alpha$ or $\kappa\upsilon\iota\nu\omega\nu\acute{\iota}\alpha$ is the right term. So, too, particulars ' partake in ' or ' imitate ' the forms ; but always and everywhere the particular thing is what it is because the $\epsilon\tilde{\iota}\delta\upsilon s$ is immanent in it. We know from Plato's *Sophist* that there were ' friends of the $\epsilon\tilde{\iota}\delta\eta$ ' who did ' separate ' the intelligible from the sensible, and it is with these that Aristotle contrasts Socrates. The true Peripatetic interpretation is preserved

It remains to be added that I have only discussed in the notes that aspect of the theory of Ideas with which we are concerned in reading the *Phaedo*. So far as that dialogue goes, it is a purely logical and scientific doctrine. The possibility of science extends just as far as the theory of Ideas will carry us and no further. Where it can no longer be applied, the region of myth begins. I am well aware that the doctrine has another aspect, to which attention has been specially called by Professor Stewart In certain dialogues the Ideas are regarded as objects of ecstatic contemplation, and appear, to some extent, in a mythical setting. With that we have nothing to do at present. I may say, however, to avoid misunderstanding, that, while I quite agree with the demand for a ' psychological' explanation of this way of presenting the doctrine, I can by no means admit that the explanation is to be looked for in the ψυχή of Plato son of Ariston. The idea of ecstatic vision is most prominent in the *Symposium* and the *Phaedrus*, that is to say, in just those dialogues where Plato's dramatic art is at its best, and where, therefore, if my general principles of interpretation are sound, Socrates is most truly Socrates. The soul of the man who stood transfixed in silent, brooding thought for twenty-four hours in the camp at Potidaea is surely the soul to which we must look for a psychological explanation of the beatific vision described in the *Phaedrus*. On what else can his thoughts

by Aristocles the teacher of Alexander of Aphrodisias (fr. 1) Οὐχ ἥκιστα δὲ καὶ Σωκράτης, αὐτὸ δὴ τὸ λεγόμενον, ἐγένετο πῦρ ἐπὶ πυρί, καθάπερ αὐτὸς ἔφη Πλάτων. εὐφυέστατος γὰρ ὢν καὶ δεινὸς ἀπορῆσαι περὶ παντὸς ὁτουοῦν, ἐπεισήνεγκε τάς τε ἠθικὰς καὶ πολιτικὰς σκέψεις, ἔτι δὲ τὴν περὶ τῶν ἰδεῶν, πρῶτος ἐπιχειρήσας ὁρίζεσθαι· πάντα δὲ ἐγείρων λόγον καὶ περὶ πάντων ζητῶν, ἔφθη τελευτήσας.

have been concentrated during that day and night? Surely not on the things he discusses in the *Memorabilia*?

XIII

The best book on Greek beliefs about the soul has no chapter on Socrates. Even Plato, the writer says, had not clearly conceived the thought of immortality so long as he continued to regard the world from the standpoint of a slightly developed Socraticism.[1] This view is based on two considerations. It is said, in the first place, that in the *Apology* Plato makes Socrates treat the question of immortality as an open one, and that the *Apology* is more historical than the *Phaedo*. In the second place, it is pointed out that Xenophon does not make Socrates say anything about immortality in the *Memorabilia*. The inference is that the belief was foreign to 'the historical Socrates'.

When, however, we look a little closer at these facts, their significance is seen to be rather different. Plato's *Apology* professes to give us the speeches delivered by Socrates at his trial; and, though it would be absurd to treat it as a word for word report, it is doubtless historical in its main outlines.[2] Even if it is not, it is clear that Plato has taken pains to make it such a speech as might actually have been delivered in an Athenian court, and it is quite certain from the practice of the orators that, in addressing the judges, it was impossible to assume immortality as distinct from mere survival. The old belief in powerful and dangerous ghosts had disappeared, and nothing very definite had

[1] E. Rohde, *Psyche*, ii, p. 265 (557).
[2] As Gomperz puts it, the *Apology* is 'stilisierte Wahrheit'.

taken its place. No doubt the average Athenian would allow that the souls of the departed had some sort of existence—the religious observances connected with the dead imply that—but he had lost all faith in the primitive belief that they continued to interest themselves in the affairs of this world. ' If by any means,' says Demosthenes, 'the departed should be made aware of what is now taking place,' and that is the standing formula.[1] Nor is there any evidence that people thought of the next life as a better life, or of the house of Hades as a better world. It was believed, indeed, that those who had been initiated at Eleusis enjoyed a better lot than others. They alone could properly be said to live after death ; but even that was a shadowy sort of life, and as far removed as possible from the immortality preached by the Orphic sectaries and the Pythagoreans. According to them, the soul was divine and immortal in its own right, and it was only after separation from the body that it could become truly itself. The soul of the Orphic votary dwelt with God and the saints and attained to complete purity and wisdom, while the initiated of Eleusis were at best a class of privileged shades.

Had there been any real belief in a better life, it must have found expression in the Funeral Speeches, and especially in that part of them which was regularly devoted to the consolation of the survivors[2] ; but we

[1] Cp. Dem. *Lept.* 87 εἴ τινες τούτων τῶν τετελευτηκότων λάβοιεν τρόπῳ τινὶ τοῦ νυνὶ γιγνομένου πράγματος αἴσθησιν. At the end of his speech against Eratosthenes (100) Lysias goes so far as to say οἶμαι δ' αὐτοὺς (τοὺς τεθνεῶτας) ἡμῶν τε ἀκροᾶσθαι καὶ ὑμᾶς εἴσεσθαι τὴν ψῆφον φέροντας, which is the strongest statement in the orators. Cp. also Isocr. 19. 42 εἴ τίς ἐστιν αἴσθησις τοῖς τεθνεῶσι περὶ τῶν ἐνθάδε γιγνομένων, Plato, *Menex.* 248 b 7 εἴ τις ἔστι τοῖς τετελευτηκόσιν αἴσθησις τῶν ζώντων.

[2] Rohde, *Psyche*, ii, p. 203 (495), *n.* 3.

find nothing of the sort even in the *Menexenus*, which is put into the mouth of Socrates. The writer, whether Plato or another, has felt bound to conform to the usual practice in this respect. Nor is there any trace in Aeschylus or Sophocles of a belief in a blessed immortality. It is Euripides who says 'Who knows if life be death and death be life?', and is laughed at by Aristophanes for doing so. We see from this how foreign such a thought was to the Athenian mind. Euripides, like Socrates, had been influenced by strange doctrines, and he, like Socrates, was considered 'impious'.

In the *Apology*, then, Socrates only speaks as he was bound to speak. He wishes to show that death is no evil to a good man, even if the ordinary view of it is correct. At the worst, it is a dreamless sleep, and a night of dreamless sleep is better than most waking days. But that is only one possibility. There are certain 'sayings'[1] according to which death is really a migration of the soul to another world ; and, if these are true, we may hope after death to join the company of Orpheus and Musaeus and Hesiod and Homer. It is surely clear that Socrates himself is more in sympathy with this belief than the other, though he may not say so in as many words, and though he speaks with a certain reserve on the subject. Even in the *Phaedo* he makes certain reservations. He is sure that the soul is immortal, and that the purified soul only leaves the

----

[1] This, and not 'popular opinion', I take to be the meaning of τὰ λεγόμενα in *Apol.* 40 c 7, d 6. Cp. notes on *Phaedo* 63 c 6 and 70 c 5. The term belongs originally to the language of the mysteries, in which τὰ λεγόμενα are opposed to τὰ δρώμενα, and is used elsewhere in Plato of the mystic doctrine or ἱερὸς λόγος.

body to be with the wise and good God ; he is not sure
that it will enjoy the company of the saints and heroes
of old.[1] Both in the *Phaedo* and elsewhere he steadily
declines to commit himself to the details of the Orphic
doctrine. It is a 'probable tale ', and we may hope that
it, or something like it, is true. In this respect the
Phaedo does not go a step further than the *Apology*, and
the language of the *Apology* really implies the belief
explicitly stated in the *Phaedo*. Whatever concessions
he may make for the sake of argument, Socrates lets
it be clearly seen that his beliefs about the soul are not
those of the man in the street.

The same considerations help to explain the silence of
Xenophon in the *Memorabilia*. He is seeking to prove
that the belief of Socrates about the gods was just the
same as that of other pious people,[2] and it would never
have done to suggest that he held peculiar views about
the soul. The doctrine of the soul's immortality was,
and remained, a heresy. Even Plato's brother Glaucon
is represented in the *Republic* as startled when Socrates
propounds it as something he seriously believes and
thinks he can prove.[3] And yet Xenophon knew the
doctrine perfectly well. Even in the *Memorabilia*, he
lets slip the statement that the soul 'partakes in the
divine ', a phrase which really implies the whole theory.[4]

[1] *Phaed.* 63 c 1.

[2] *Mem.* i. 1. 3 ὁ μὲν δ' οὐδὲν καινότερον εἰσέφερε τῶν ἄλλων κτλ.

[3] *Rep.* 608 d 3 Οὐκ ᾔσθησαι, ἦν δ' ἐγώ, ὅτι ἀθάνατος ἡμῶν ἡ ψυχὴ καὶ οὐδέποτε ἀπόλλυται ;—Καὶ ὃς ἐμβλέψας μοι καὶ θαυμάσας εἶπε· Μὰ Δί', οὐκ ἔγωγε·
σὺ δὲ τοῦτ' ἔχεις λέγειν ;

[4] *Mem.* iv. 3. 14 ἀλλὰ μὴν καὶ ἀνθρώπου γε ψυχή, ᾗ, εἴπερ τι καὶ ἄλλο τῶν
ἀνθρωπίνων, τοῦ θείου μετέχει, ὅτι μὲν βασιλεύει ἐν ἡμῖν φανερόν, ὁρᾶται δὲ
οὐδ' αὐτή. The invisibility and divine nature of the soul are just the

Further, this view, which could not safely be developed in the *Memorabilia*, is worked out at considerable length in the *Cyropaedia*, where the dying Cyrus is made to formulate it in language almost identical with that of the *Phaedo*.[1] Of this fact there can only be two explanations. Either Xenophon is borrowing from the *Phaedo*, or Plato and Xenophon are drawing from a common source. Further, this source must be Socratic; for the kinship of the dying speech of Cyrus with the argument about the invisibility of the soul ascribed to Socrates in the *Memorabilia* is patent.[2] It is possible that Xenophon derived it from Hermogenes, from whom he professes to have heard what he knew of the trial and death of Socrates[3]; but, on the whole, it is more likely

points made in *Phaedo* 79 b 1 and 80 a 8, while βασιλεύει refers to the argument of *Phaedo* 79 e 8. Cp. Rohde, *Psyche*, ii, p. 2 (205). 'If the soul is immortal, it is in its essential property identical with God. Among the Greeks, whoever says *immortal* says *God*; these are interchangeable notions. Now in the religion of the Greek people the true fundamental proposition is that, in the divine order of the world, humanity and divinity are locally and essentially distinct and must remain so. A deep gulf separates the worlds of man and God.' Even so innocent-looking a phrase as τοῦ θείου μετέχει ignores this gulf, and therefore implies the mystic doctrine. There are some other passages about the ψυχή which seem to be reminiscences of the *Phaedo*. Cp. i. 2. 4 τὴν τῆς ψυχῆς ἐπιμέλειαν οὐκ ἐμποδίζειν (cp. *Phaed.* 65 a 10), i. 4. 13 τὴν ψυχὴν κρατίστην τῷ ἀνθρώπῳ ἐνέφυσε (ὁ θεός), i. 2. 53 τῆς ψυχῆς ἐξελθούσης, ἐν ᾗ μόνῃ γίγνεται φρόνησις. These go far beyond the popular use of the word ψυχή.

[1] Xen. *Cyr.* viii. 7. 17 sqq. Cp. especially 19 οὗτοι ἔγωγε, ὦ παῖδες, οὐδὲ τοῦτο πώποτε ἐπείσθην, ὡς ἡ ψυχὴ ἕως μὲν ἂν ἐν θνητῷ σώματι ᾖ, ζῇ, ὅταν δὲ τούτου ἀπαλλαγῇ, τέθνηκεν . . . οὐδέ γε ὅπως ἄφρων ἔσται ἡ ψυχή, ἐπειδὰν τοῦ ἄφρονος σώματος δίχα γένηται, οὐδὲ τοῦτο πέπεισμαι· ἀλλ' ὅταν ἄκρατος καὶ καθαρὸς ὁ νοῦς ἐκκριθῇ, τότε καὶ φρονιμώτατον αὐτὸν εἰκὸς εἶναι.

[2] Cp. *Cyr.* vii. 7. 17 οὐδὲ γὰρ νῦν τοι τήν γ' ἐμὴν ψυχὴν ἑωρᾶτε with the passage about the invisibility of the soul quoted p. li., *n.* 4.

[3] Xen. *Apol.* 2.

that he simply took it from the *Phaedo*, adding some touches of his own. If so, he at least knew nothing inconsistent with the ascription of such arguments to Socrates.

But we can go much further than this. We have positive evidence, dating from a time when Plato and Xenophon were children, that Socrates was commonly believed to hold strange doctrine about the soul. In the *Clouds* of Aristophanes (v. 94), Strepsiades says, pointing to the house of Socrates—

ψυχῶν σοφῶν τοῦτ' ἐστὶ φροντιστήριον,

and, however natural such a way of speaking may appear to us, it was not natural for an ordinary Greek in the fifth century B.C. It is sufficiently established that the use of the word ψυχή to express a living man's true personality is Orphic in its origin, and came into philosophy from mysticism. Properly speaking, the ψυχή of a man is a thing which only becomes important at the moment of death. In ordinary language it is only spoken of as something that may be lost; it is, in fact, 'the ghost' which a man 'gives up'.[1] Yet we find Aristophanes trying to raise a laugh by representing Socrates and his disciples as 'souls' or 'ghosts' even in their lifetime.[2]

---

[1] The φιλόψυχος is the man who clings to life. To risk one's life is θεῖν, τρέχειν, κινδυνεύειν περὶ ψυχῆς. Cp. Rohde, *Psyche*, i, p. 47 (43), *n.* 1; ii, p. 141 (432), *n.* 1. From Homer downwards, the ψυχή is so regarded; wherever it means more than this, we may trace the influence of mysticism or philosophy.

[2] Cp. van Leeuwen, *ad loc.* 'innuit non vivos vegetosque illic habitare homines sed mera εἴδωλα καμόντων, νεκύων quaedam ἀμενηνὰ κάρηνα quibus φρένες οὐκ ἔμπεδοί εἰσιν, Socrati ψυχαγωγῷ (Av. 1555 qui locus omnino est conferendus) obtemperantia. Cf. infra vs. 504, ubi unus ex eorum numero dicitur ἡμιθνής.' This is the popular view of the μελέτη θανάτου (81 a 1) See note on θανατῶσι, *Phaed.* 64 b 5.

The same point is made in the chorus of the *Birds* where Socrates is represented as calling up the souls of the dead.[1] This, at any rate, cannot be aimed at 'the Sophists', and the caricature would be wholly pointless unless the real Socrates taught even at that date something like the doctrine of immortality and the 'practice of death' (μελέτη θανάτου) which, as we know from the *Phaedo* itself, seemed so ridiculous to the mass of men.[2]

The truth is that, apart from the prejudice which insists on seeing Socrates as a 'rationalist', there is nothing to cause surprise in the fact that he was influenced by mystic doctrines. We have only to remember the character of the man and the times he lived in. The fusion of science and mysticism, to the great advantage of both, had been the characteristic feature of the generations immediately preceding his own, and his youth was passed at a time when it was much in evidence. He had even spoken with Parmenides at Athens,[3] and he was only about twenty years younger than Empedocles, who joined the Athenian colony of Thurii when Socrates was about five and twenty.[4] A little later, the Pythagoreans were expelled from the cities of Magna Graecia, and took refuge at Thebes, Phlius, and

[1] Cp. van Leeuwen, *ad loc.* 'Sic ridetur philosophus de animi immortalitate disputare solitus dum vitae lenocinia aspernatur'. The context makes it clear that ψυχαγωγεῖ is to be taken in the strict sense of ghost-raising. Chaerephon 'the bat' is represented as playing the part of the 'spirit'.

[2] *Phaed.* 64 b 1 sqq.

[3] E. Gr. Ph.[2] p. 192, and, for the connexion of Parmenides with Pythagoreanism, *ib.* pp. 194 and 221.

[4] E. Gr. Ph.[2] pp. 229 and 237. It is nowhere stated that Empedocles visited Athens, but it would be strange if he did not, seeing that he went to Thurii.

elsewhere.[1] All this could not but impress a young man who had a strong vein of mysticism in his own nature, as is shown by what we know of his ecstatic trances and the ' divine sign '. We are told expressly that he had the latter from boyhood.[2] It would be much more difficult to account for all this, if we were to suppose Plato rather than Socrates to have been the mystic. By his time Orphicism had degenerated into a mere superstition, and the barefooted Pythagorists who still maintained the original practices of their order would be quite un-sympathetic to him.[3] The Pythagoreans whom he knew had dropped all that, and busied themselves only with science and politics.[4] It is a fine historical touch in the *Phaedo* that the young Pythagoreans, Simmias and Cebes, are not very familiar with the mystic doctrine, and require to have it explained to them by Socrates.

XIV

But Socrates was no Orphic for all that. He had another characteristic which kept him from turning mystic out and out. That was the Attic εἰρωνεία, that shrewd, non-committal spirit, natural to a people of farmers and tradesmen, which Aristophanes has depicted for us in his typical Athenian figures, and which Demosthenes denounced.[5] Enthusiasm tempered by

[1] E. Gr. Ph.[2] p. 99.

[2] *Apol.* 31 d 2 ἐμοὶ δὲ τοῦτ' ἐστὶν ἐκ παιδὸς ἀρξάμενον. The twenty-four hours trance at Potidaea happened when Socrates was about thirty-seven, five years before Plato was born.

[3] E. Gr. Ph.[2] p. 103, *n.* 2.

[4] E. Gr. Ph.[2] p. 319 sq.

[5] The proper meaning of εἴρων is ' sly ', ' cunning ', *malin*, and εἰρωνεία is not regarded as exactly a good quality. In the Platonic dialogues, it is

irony (using both words in their Greek sense) may serve as a formula for the Socratic ἦθος.[1] Xenophon gives us too little enthusiasm and Aristophanes too little irony ; it is only in the Platonic Socrates that both elements are harmoniously combined in a character with a marked individuality of his own. The Platonic Socrates is no mere type, but a living man. That, above all, is our justification for believing that he is in truth ' the historical Socrates'.

---

only the opponents of Socrates who ascribe it to him. The Scots words ' canny' and ' pawky' express something similar. Demosthenes speaks of it as a bad trait in the Athenian character (*Phil.* i. 7, 37). At its worst, it leads people to shirk their responsibilities ; at its best, it is a salutary νᾶφε καὶ μέμνασ' ἀπιστεῖν. For the way in which Socrates refuses to commit himself to the positive details of the mystic theology cp. 63 c 1 *n*. It is clearly a personal trait.

[1] Or, as Gomperz puts it, ' a hot heart under a cool head.'

NOTE UPON THE TEXT

THE dialogues of Plato were arranged in nine tetralogies by the grammarian Thrasyllus in the reign of Tiberius. The first tetralogy comprised the *Euthyphro, Apology, Crito,* and *Phaedo,* i.e. those dialogues which deal specially with the trial and death of Socrates.

At some subsequent date the dialogues were edited in two volumes, the first of which contained tetralogies I–VII, the second, tetralogies VIII–IX, with some spurious works. As one or other of the two volumes was apt to be lost, the MS. authority for tetralogies I–VII is quite different from that for tetralogies VIII–IX and the spurious dialogues.

The leading representatives of the first volume are the Bodleian MS., E. D. Clarke 39 (B), the Venice MS. App. class. 4, 1 (T), and the Vienna MS. 54, suppl. phil. gr. 7 (W).

B. The Bodleian MS., commonly called the *Clarkianus* after E. D. Clarke, who discovered it in the island of Patmos, was written for Arethas in the year 895 A.D. It was held by Cobet and others that it was our sole independent authority, and all recent texts of the *Phaedo* are based more or less consistently on this hypothesis.

T. The Venice MS. or *Marcianus* (tenth century A. D. ?) is the original of the great majority of existing Plato MSS., and in particular of the MS. from which the Aldine text was derived. The text of Stephanus also goes back to the same source. These MSS. were arbitrarily classed by Cobet and at one time by Schanz as *deteriores,* and the chief work of Platonic critics down to the last quarter of the nineteenth century was to bring the text more and more into accordance with B, and to eliminate readings which came from other MSS.

The credit of inaugurating a better method belongs to Schanz himself. In 1877 he showed that T was of co-ordinate authority with B, and that we must take account of both. In some ways T represents the tradition even more faithfully than B. For instance, it contains the old *scholia*, while B has a new set composed in the ninth century A.D., probably by Arethas himself.

Unfortunately, Schanz had edited the *Phaedo* before he made this discovery, and he has not republished it since. The readings of T were first published by the present editor in 1899.

W. The importance of this MS. had been seen by Bast, and an imperfect collation of it was used to some extent by Stallbaum, but its omission from Bekker's *apparatus criticus* led to its being generally ignored till Professor Král of Prague once more called attention to it. Its claims to be regarded as a co-ordinate authority with B and T were warmly contested by Schanz, but on insufficient grounds. The publication of the anonymous commentary on the *Theaetetus* from a Berlin papyrus showed conclusively that W represented a very ancient tradition of the text. The MS. was brought to Vienna from Florence, and it seems to have come there from Sicily. The Latin version of the *Phaedo* made by Euericus Aristippus, Archdeacon of Catana, in the twelfth century, A.D., was made either from it or from a very similar MS. It is to be noted further that the corrections made by the second hand in the *Clarkianus* (B²), which is probably that of Arethas himself, are taken from a MS. closely resembling W, so that it must represent a tradition older than B.

A special feature of W is the number of ancient variants which it records in the margin. If all the other MSS. were lost, we could still construct a good text from W alone, and that is more than can be said either of B or of T.

In this edition, when W alone is quoted, it is to be understood that B and T have the reading adopted in the text; when B and T alone are quoted, it is to be understood that W agrees with B. Thus, on the first page, it may be inferred that B and T have τὸ φάρμακον ἔπιεν and ἀγγεῖλαι, while W has ἐγὼ ἀκούσαιμι, οἷός τ᾽ ἦν and τί οὖν ἦν.

An interesting addition to our knowledge of the text was made by the publication by Professor Flinders Petrie of some papyrus fragments which must have been written within a century of Plato's death (Ars. i.e. *papyrus Arsinoitica*). On the whole, their text is inferior to that of our MSS., though these are more than a thousand years later. The papyrus represents the cheap texts current in early times, while our costly MSS. are copied from careful editions.

The quotations in ancient writers, especially Eusebius and Stobaeus, sometimes preserve old readings, and often confirm TW as against B. They are, however, taken from MSS. of various degrees of authority and must be used with great caution.

ΠΛΑΤΩΝΟΣ ΦΑΙΔΩΝ

ΦΑΙΔΩΝ

ΕΧΕΚΡΑΤΗΣ ΦΑΙΔΩΝ

St. I
p. 57

ΕΧ. Αὐτός, ὦ Φαίδων, παρεγένου Σωκράτει ἐκείνῃ τῇ a
ἡμέρᾳ ᾗ τὸ φάρμακον ἔπιεν ἐν τῷ δεσμωτηρίῳ, ἢ ἄλλου του
ἤκουσας;

ΦΑΙΔ. Αὐτός, ὦ Ἐχέκρατες.

ΕΧ. Τί οὖν δή ἐστιν ἄττα εἶπεν ὁ ἀνὴρ πρὸ τοῦ θανά- 5
του; καὶ πῶς ἐτελεύτα; ἡδέως γὰρ ἂν ἐγὼ ἀκούσαιμι. καὶ
γὰρ οὔτε [τῶν πολιτῶν] Φλειασίων οὐδεὶς πάνυ τι ἐπιχωριάζει
τὰ νῦν Ἀθήναζε, οὔτε τις ξένος ἀφῖκται χρόνου συχνοῦ
ἐκεῖθεν ὅστις ἂν ἡμῖν σαφές τι ἀγγεῖλαι οἷός τ᾽ ἦν περὶ b
τούτων, πλήν γε δὴ ὅτι φάρμακον πιὼν ἀποθάνοι· τῶν δὲ
ἄλλων οὐδὲν εἶχεν φράζειν.

ΦΑΙΔ. Οὐδὲ τὰ περὶ τῆς δίκης ἄρα ἐπύθεσθε ὃν τρόπον 58
ἐγένετο;

ΕΧ. Ναί, ταῦτα μὲν ἡμῖν ἤγγειλέ τις, καὶ ἐθαυμάζομέν
γε ὅτι πάλαι γενομένης αὐτῆς πολλῷ ὕστερον φαίνεται
ἀποθανών. τί οὖν ἦν τοῦτο, ὦ Φαίδων; 5

ΦΑΙΔ. Τύχη τις αὐτῷ, ὦ Ἐχέκρατες, συνέβη· ἔτυχεν
γὰρ τῇ προτεραίᾳ τῆς δίκης ἡ πρύμνα ἐστεμμένη τοῦ πλοίου
ὃ εἰς Δῆλον Ἀθηναῖοι πέμπουσιν.

a 2 ἔπιεν τὸ φάρμακον W   a 6 ἐγὼ B : om. T   a 7 τῶν πολιτῶν secl. v. Bamberg : Φλιασίων secl. Schaefer   b 1 ἀπαγγεῖλαι W
ἦν B : ᾖ T   a 5 οὖν B : om. T   a 8 πέμπουσιν B T : πέμπουσιν
κατ᾽ ἔτος B² W

ΕΧ. Τοῦτο δὲ δὴ τί ἐστιν;

10 ΦΑΙΔ. Τοῦτ᾽ ἔστι τὸ πλοῖον, ὥς φασιν Ἀθηναῖοι, ἐν ᾧ
Θησεύς ποτε εἰς Κρήτην τοὺς "δὶς ἑπτὰ" ἐκείνους ᾤχετο
b ἄγων καὶ ἔσωσέ τε καὶ αὐτὸς ἐσώθη. τῷ οὖν Ἀπόλλωνι
ηὔξαντο ὡς λέγεται τότε, εἰ σωθεῖεν, ἑκάστου ἔτους θεωρίαν
ἀπάξειν εἰς Δῆλον· ἣν δὴ ἀεὶ καὶ ?ῦν ἔτι ἐξ ἐκείνου κατ᾽
ἐνιαυτὸν τῷ θεῷ πέμπουσιν. ἐπειδὰν οὖν ἄρξωνται τῆς
5 θεωρίας, νόμος ἐστὶν αὐτοῖς ἐν τῷ χρόνῳ τούτῳ καθαρεύειν
τὴν πόλιν καὶ δημοσίᾳ μηδένα ἀποκτεινύναι, πρὶν ἂν εἰς
Δῆλόν τε ἀφίκηται τὸ πλοῖον καὶ πάλιν δεῦρο· τοῦτο δ᾽
ἐνίοτε ἐν πολλῷ χρόνῳ γίγνεται, ὅταν τύχωσιν ἄνεμοι ἀπο-
c λαβόντες αὐτούς. ἀρχὴ δ᾽ ἐστὶ τῆς θεωρίας ἐπειδὰν ὁ
ἱερεὺς τοῦ Ἀπόλλωνος στέψῃ τὴν πρύμναν τοῦ πλοίου·
τοῦτο δ᾽ ἔτυχεν, ὥσπερ λέγω, τῇ προτεραίᾳ τῆς δίκης γεγονός. διὰ ταῦτα καὶ πολὺς χρόνος ἐγένετο τῷ Σωκράτει ἐν
5 τῷ δεσμωτηρίῳ ὁ μεταξὺ τῆς δίκης τε καὶ τοῦ θανάτου.

ΕΧ. Τί δὲ δὴ τὰ περὶ αὐτὸν τὸν θάνατον, ὦ Φαίδων; τί
ἦν τὰ λεχθέντα καὶ πραχθέντα, καὶ τίνες οἱ παραγενόμενοι
τῶν ἐπιτηδείων τῷ ἀνδρί; ἢ οὐκ εἴων οἱ ἄρχοντες παρεῖναι,
ἀλλ᾽ ἔρημος ἐτελεύτα φίλων;

d ΦΑΙΔ. Οὐδαμῶς, ἀλλὰ παρῆσάν τινες, καὶ πολλοί γε.

ΕΧ. Ταῦτα δὴ πάντα προθυμήθητι ὡς σαφέστατα ἡμῖν
ἀπαγγεῖλαι, εἰ μή τίς σοι ἀσχολία τυγχάνει οὖσα.

ΦΑΙΔ. Ἀλλὰ σχολάζω γε καὶ πειράσομαι ὑμῖν διηγή-
5 σασθαι· καὶ γὰρ τὸ μεμνῆσθαι Σωκράτους καὶ αὐτὸν λέγοντα
καὶ ἄλλου ἀκούοντα ἔμοιγε ἀεὶ πάντων ἥδιστον.

ΕΧ. Ἀλλὰ μήν, ὦ Φαίδων, καὶ τοὺς ἀκουσομένους γε
τοιούτους ἑτέρους ἔχεις· ἀλλὰ πειρῶ ὡς ἂν δύνῃ ἀκριβέστατα διεξελθεῖν πάν-α.

e ΦΑΙΔ. Καὶ μὴν ἔγωγε θαυμάσια ἔπαθον παραγενόμενος.
οὔτε γὰρ ὡς θανάτῳ παρόντα με ἀνδρὸς ἐπιτηδείου ἔλεος

a 11 ποτε θησεὺς W   b 7 τε Β: om. T   c 6 τί ἦν ΒΤ: τίνα
ἦν Β²W   d 4 γε Β: τε Τ   d 8 ἑτέρους ΒΤ: ἑταίρους W
d 9 διεξελθεῖν Β: διελθεῖν Τ

εἰσῄει· εὐδαίμων γάρ μοι ἀνὴρ ἐφαίνετο, ὦ Ἐχέκρατες, καὶ
τοῦ τρόπου καὶ τῶν λόγων, ὡς ἀδεῶς καὶ γενναίως ἐτελεύτα,
ὥστε μοι ἐκεῖνον παρίστασθαι μηδ᾽ εἰς Ἅιδου ἰόντα ἄνευ 5
θείας μοίρας ἰέναι, ἀλλὰ καὶ ἐκεῖσε ἀφικόμενον εὖ πράξειν
εἴπερ τις πώποτε καὶ ἄλλος. διὰ δὴ ταῦτα οὐδὲν πάνυ μοι 59
ἐλεινὸν εἰσῄει, ὡς εἰκὸς ἂν δόξειεν εἶναι παρόντι πένθει,
οὔτε αὖ ἡδονὴ ὡς ἐν φιλοσοφίᾳ ἡμῶν ὄντων ὥσπερ εἰώθεμεν
—καὶ γὰρ οἱ λόγοι τοιοῦτοί τινες ἦσαν—ἀλλ᾽ ἀτεχνῶς
ἄτοπόν τί μοι πάθος παρῆν καί τις ἀήθης κρᾶσις ἀπό τε τῆς 5
ἡδονῆς συγκεκραμένη ὁμοῦ καὶ ἀπὸ τῆς λύπης, ἐνθυμουμένῳ
ὅτι αὐτίκα ἐκεῖνος ἔμελλε τελευτᾶν. καὶ πάντες οἱ παρόντες
σχεδόν τι οὕτω διεκείμεθα, τοτὲ μὲν γελῶντες, ἐνίοτε δὲ
δακρύοντες, εἷς δὲ ἡμῶν καὶ διαφερόντως, Ἀπολλόδωρος—
οἶσθα γάρ που τὸν ἄνδρα καὶ τὸν τρόπον αὐτοῦ.   b
ΕΧ. Πῶς γὰρ οὔ;
ΦΑΙΔ. Ἐκεῖνός τε τοίνυν παντάπασιν οὕτως εἶχεν, καὶ
αὐτὸς ἔγωγε ἐτεταράγμην καὶ οἱ ἄλλοι.
ΕΧ. Ἔτυχον δέ, ὦ Φαίδων, τίνες παραγενόμενοι;   5
ΦΑΙΔ. Οὗτός τε δὴ ὁ Ἀπολλόδωρος τῶν ἐπιχωρίων
παρῆν καὶ Κριτόβουλος καὶ ὁ πατὴρ αὐτοῦ καὶ ἔτι Ἑρμογέ-
νης καὶ Ἐπιγένης καὶ Αἰσχίνης καὶ Ἀντισθένης· ἦν δὲ καὶ
Κτήσιππος ὁ Παιανιεὺς καὶ Μενέξενος καὶ ἄλλοι τινὲς τῶν
ἐπιχωρίων. Πλάτων δὲ οἶμαι ἠσθένει.   10.
ΕΧ. Ξένοι δέ τινες παρῆσαν;
ΦΑΙΔ. Ναί, Σιμμίας τέ γε ὁ Θηβαῖος καὶ Κέβης καὶ   c
Φαιδώνδης καὶ Μεγαρόθεν Εὐκλείδης τε καὶ Τερψίων.
ΕΧ. Τί δέ; Ἀρίστιππος καὶ Κλεόμβροτος παρεγένοντο;
ΦΑΙΔ. Οὐ δῆτα· ἐν Αἰγίνῃ γὰρ ἐλέγοντο εἶναι.

e 3 ἀνὴρ Β : ὁ ἀνὴρ Τ   e 4 τῶν λόγων Β² Τ W : τοῦ λόγου Β t
e 5 ὥστε μοι Β Τ : ὥστ᾽ ἔμοιγε W   παρίστασθαι ἐκεῖνον W et transp.
signis fecit Τ   a 6 ἀπὸ Β : om. Τ   a 8 τοτὲ Τ : ὁτὲ Β : τὸ W
b 7 κριτόβουλος Τ : ὁ κριτόβουλος Β   αὐτοῦ Β Τ : αὐτοῦ κρίτων Β² W
b 11 δέ om. pr. Τ   c 1 τε Β Τ : om. W   c 2 φαιδώνδης Β² Τ :
φαιδωνίδης Β W

5 ΕΧ. Ἄλλος δέ τις παρῆν;

ΦΑΙΔ. Σχεδόν τι οἶμαι τούτους παραγενέσθαι.

ΕΧ. Τί οὖν δή; τίνες φῂς ἦσαν οἱ λόγοι;

ΦΑΙΔ. Ἐγώ σοι ἐξ ἀρχῆς πάντα πειράσομαι διηγήσα-
d σθαι. ἀεὶ γὰρ δὴ καὶ τὰς πρόσθεν ἡμέρας εἰώθεμεν φοιτᾶν
καὶ ἐγὼ καὶ οἱ ἄλλοι παρὰ τὸν Σωκράτη, συλλεγόμενοι
ἕωθεν εἰς τὸ δικαστήριον ἐν ᾧ καὶ ἡ δίκη ἐγένετο· πλησίον
γὰρ ἦν τοῦ δεσμωτηρίου. περιεμένομεν οὖν ἑκάστοτε ἕως
5 ἀνοιχθείη τὸ δεσμωτήριον, διατρίβοντες μετ' ἀλλήλων, ἀνεῴγετο γὰρ οὐ πρῴ· ἐπειδὴ δὲ ἀνοιχθείη, εἰσῇμεν παρὰ τὸν
Σωκράτη καὶ τὰ πολλὰ διημερεύομεν μετ' αὐτοῦ. καὶ δὴ καὶ
τότε πρῳαίτερον συνελέγημεν· τῇ γὰρ προτεραίᾳ [ἡμέρᾳ]
e ἐπειδὴ ἐξήλθομεν ἐκ τοῦ δεσμωτηρίου ἑσπέρας, ἐπυθόμεθα
ὅτι τὸ πλοῖον ἐκ Δήλου ἀφιγμένον εἴη. παρηγγείλαμεν οὖν
ἀλλήλοις ἥκειν ὡς πρῳαίτατα εἰς τὸ εἰωθός. καὶ ἥκομεν καὶ
ἡμῖν ἐξελθὼν ὁ θυρωρός, ὅσπερ εἰώθει ὑπακούειν, εἶπεν περι-
5 μένειν καὶ μὴ πρότερον παριέναι ἕως ἂν αὐτὸς κελεύσῃ·
"Λύουσι γάρ," ἔφη, "οἱ ἕνδεκα Σωκράτη καὶ παραγγέλλουσιν
ὅπως ἂν τῇδε τῇ ἡμέρᾳ τελευτᾷ." οὐ πολὺν δ' οὖν χρόνον
ἐπισχὼν ἧκεν καὶ ἐκέλευεν ἡμᾶς εἰσιέναι. εἰσιόντες οὖν
60 κατελαμβάνομεν τὸν μὲν Σωκράτη ἄρτι λελυμένον, τὴν δὲ
Ξανθίππην—γιγνώσκεις γάρ—ἔχουσάν τε τὸ παιδίον αὐτοῦ
καὶ παρακαθημένην. ὡς οὖν εἶδεν ἡμᾶς ἡ Ξανθίππη, ἀνηυ-
φήμησέ τε καὶ τοιαῦτ' ἄττα εἶπεν, οἷα δὴ εἰώθασιν αἱ
5 γυναῖκες, ὅτι "Ὦ Σώκρατες, ὕστατον δή σε προσεροῦσι νῦν
οἱ ἐπιτήδειοι καὶ σὺ τούτους." καὶ ὁ Σωκράτης βλέψας εἰς
τὸν Κρίτωνα, "Ὦ Κρίτων," ἔφη, "ἀπαγέτω τις αὐτὴν
οἴκαδε."

Καὶ ἐκείνην μὲν ἀπῆγόν τινες τῶν τοῦ Κρίτωνος βοῶσάν
b τε καὶ κοπτομένην· ὁ δὲ Σωκράτης ἀνακαθιζόμενος εἰς τὴν

---

d 5 ἀνεῴγετο Β Τ : ἀνεῴγνυτο W   d 6 εἰσῄειμεν Β : ᾔμεν Τ
d 8 ἡμέρᾳ secl. Hermann   e 4 ὅσπερ Β Τ : ὅστις Β² W   περιμένειν Β : ἐπιμένειν Τ   e 7 τελευτᾷ Τ : τελευτήσῃ Β   e 9 ἐκέλευεν Β Τ : ἐκέλευσεν Β² W   εἰσιόντες Β Τ : εἰσελθόντες Β² W
a 7 αὐτὴν Ρ. : ταύτην Τ W   b 1 εἰς Β Τ et s. v. W : ἐπὶ Β² W t

κλίνην συνέκαμψέ τε τὸ σκέλος καὶ ἐξέτριψε τῇ χειρί, καὶ
τρίβων ἅμα, Ὡς ἄτοπον, ἔφη, ὦ ἄνδρες, ἔοικέ τι εἶναι
τοῦτο ὃ καλοῦσιν οἱ ἄνθρωποι ἡδύ· ὡς θαυμασίως πέφυκε
πρὸς τὸ δοκοῦν ἐναντίον εἶναι, τὸ λυπηρόν, τὸ ἅμα μὲν 5
αὐτὼ μὴ 'θέλειν παραγίγνεσθαι τῷ ἀνθρώπῳ, ἐὰν δέ τις
διώκῃ τὸ ἕτερον καὶ λαμβάνῃ, σχεδόν τι ἀναγκάζεσθαι ἀεὶ
λαμβάνειν καὶ τὸ ἕτερον, ὥσπερ ἐκ μιᾶς κορυφῆς ἡμμένω
δύ' ὄντε. καί μοι δοκεῖ, ἔφη, εἰ ἐνενόησεν αὐτὰ Αἴσωπος, c
μῦθον ἂν συνθεῖναι ὡς ὁ θεὸς βουλόμενος αὐτὰ διαλλάξαι
πολεμοῦντα, ἐπειδὴ οὐκ ἐδύνατο, συνῆψεν εἰς ταὐτὸν αὐτοῖς
τὰς κορυφάς, καὶ διὰ ταῦτα ᾧ ἂν τὸ ἕτερον παραγένηται
ἐπακολουθεῖ ὕστερον καὶ τὸ ἕτερον. ὥσπερ οὖν καὶ αὐτῷ μοι 5
ἔοικεν· ἐπειδὴ ὑπὸ τοῦ δεσμοῦ ἦν ἐν τῷ σκέλει τὸ ἀλγεινόν,
ἥκειν δὴ φαίνεται ἐπακολουθοῦν τὸ ἡδύ.

Ὁ οὖν Κέβης ὑπολαβών, Νὴ τὸν Δία, ὦ Σώκρατες,
ἔφη, εὖ γ' ἐποίησας ἀναμνήσας με. περὶ γάρ τοι τῶν
ποιημάτων ὧν πεποίηκας ἐντείνας τοὺς τοῦ Αἰσώπου λόγους d
καὶ τὸ εἰς τὸν Ἀπόλλω προοίμιον καὶ ἄλλοι τινές με ἤδη
ἤροντο, ἀτὰρ καὶ Εὔηνος πρῴην, ὅτι ποτὲ διανοηθείς, ἐπειδὴ
δεῦρο ἦλθες, ἐποίησας αὐτά, πρότερον οὐδὲν πώποτε ποιήσας.
εἰ οὖν τί σοι μέλει τοῦ ἔχειν ἐμὲ Εὐήνῳ ἀποκρίνασθαι ὅταν 5
με αὖθις ἐρωτᾷ—εὖ οἶδα γὰρ ὅτι ἐρήσεται—εἰπὲ τί χρὴ
λέγειν.

Λέγε τοίνυν, ἔφη, αὐτῷ, ὦ Κέβης, τἀληθῆ, ὅτι οὐκ
ἐκείνῳ βουλόμενος οὐδὲ τοῖς ποιήμασιν αὐτοῦ ἀντίτεχνος
εἶναι ἐποίησα ταῦτα—ᾔδη γὰρ ὡς οὐ ῥᾴδιον εἴη—ἀλλ' e
ἐνυπνίων τινῶν ἀποπειρώμενος τί λέγοι, καὶ ἀφοσιούμενος
εἰ ἄρα πολλάκις ταύτην τὴν μουσικήν μοι ἐπιτάττοι ποιεῖν.

b 2 ἐξέτριψε B : ἔτριψε T   b 3 ἔοικέ τι B T : ἔοικεν W Stob.
b 5 τὸ B T W : τῷ B² t Stob.   b 7 ἀεὶ T Stob. : om. B   b 8 ἡμμένω T Stob. : συνημμένω B   c 3 αὐτοῖς B : αὐτῶν T Stob.
c 5 αὐτό W   c 6 σκέλει B T Stob. : σκέλει πρότερον B² W   ἀλ-
γεινὸν B : ἀλγεῖν T Stob.   c 9 εὖ γε πεποίηκας W   d 5 ἀποκρίνασθαι B : ἀποκρίνεσθαι T   d 6 ἐρωτᾷ B T : ἔρηται B² T² W   χρὴ
B T : χρή με B² W   e 1 οὐ T W : ὅτι οὐ B   e 2 λέγοι ref. T :
λέγειν B : λέγει pr. T b   e 3 εἰ B : εἰ ἄρα B² T W
6*

ἦν γὰρ δὴ ἄττα τοιάδε· πολλάκις μοι φοιτῶν τὸ αὐτὸ ἐν-
5 ύπνιον ἐν τῷ παρελθόντι βίῳ, ἄλλοτ' ἐν ἄλλῃ ὄψει φαινό-
μενον, τὰ αὐτὰ δὲ λέγον, "῏Ω Σώκρατες," ἔφη, "μουσικὴν
ποίει καὶ ἐργάζου." καὶ ἐγὼ ἔν γε τῷ πρόσθεν χρόνῳ ὅπερ
ἔπραττον τοῦτο ὑπελάμβανον αὐτό μοι παρακελεύεσθαί τε
61 καὶ ἐπικελεύειν, ὥσπερ οἱ τοῖς θέουσι διακελευόμενοι, καὶ
ἐμοὶ οὕτω τὸ ἐνύπνιον ὅπερ ἔπραττον τοῦτο ἐπικελεύειν,
μουσικὴν ποιεῖν, ὡς φιλοσοφίας μὲν οὔσης μεγίστης μουσικῆς, ἐμοῦ δὲ τοῦτο πράττοντος. νῦν δ' ἐπειδὴ ἥ τε δίκη
5 ἐγένετο καὶ ἡ τοῦ θεοῦ ἑορτὴ διεκώλυέ με ἀποθνῄσκειν, ἔδοξε
χρῆναι, εἰ ἄρα πολλάκις μοι προστάττοι τὸ ἐνύπνιον ταύτην
τὴν δημώδη μουσικὴν ποιεῖν, μὴ ἀπειθῆσαι αὐτῷ ἀλλὰ
ποιεῖν· ἀσφαλέστερον γὰρ εἶναι μὴ ἀπιέναι πρὶν ἀφοσιώ-
b σασθαι ποιήσαντα ποιήματα [καὶ] πιθόμενον τῷ ἐνυπνίῳ.
οὕτω δὴ πρῶτον μὲν εἰς τὸν θεὸν ἐποίησα οὗ ἦν ἡ παροῦσα
θυσία· μετὰ δὲ τὸν θεόν, ἐννοήσας ὅτι τὸν ποιητὴν δέοι,
εἴπερ μέλλοι ποιητὴς εἶναι, ποιεῖν μύθους ἀλλ' οὐ λόγους,
5 καὶ αὐτὸς οὐκ ἦ μυθολογικός, διὰ ταῦτα δὴ οὓς προχείρους
εἶχον μύθους καὶ ἠπιστάμην τοὺς Αἰσώπου, τούτων ἐποίησα
οἷς πρώτοις ἐνέτυχον. ταῦτα οὖν, ὦ Κέβης, Εὐήνῳ φράζε,
καὶ ἐρρῶσθαι καί, ἂν σωφρονῇ, ἐμὲ διώκειν ὡς τάχιστα.
c ἄπειμι δέ, ὡς ἔοικε, τήμερον· κελεύουσι γὰρ Ἀθηναῖοι.

Καὶ ὁ Σιμμίας, Οἷον παρακελεύῃ, ἔφη, τοῦτο, ὦ Σώκρατες, Εὐήνῳ. πολλὰ γὰρ ἤδη ἐντετύχηκα τῷ ἀνδρί·
σχεδὸν οὖν ἐξ ὧν ἐγὼ ᾔσθημαι οὐδ' ὁπωστιοῦν σοι ἑκὼν
5 εἶναι πείσεται.

Τί δέ; ἦ δ' ὅς, οὐ φιλόσοφος Εὔηνος;

Ἔμοιγε δοκεῖ, ἔφη ὁ Σιμμίας.

Ἐθελήσει τοίνυν καὶ Εὔηνος καὶ πᾶς ὅτῳ ἀξίως τούτου
τοῦ πράγματος μέτεστιν. οὐ μέντοι ἴσως βιάσεται αὐτόν·

a 8 εἶναι B T : εἶναι ἐνόμιζον B² W   πρὶν B T : πρότερον πρὶν ἂν
B² W   b 1 καὶ B T w : om. W et punct. not. t   πειθόμενον
B T W sed ει ex ι T   b 5 δὴ B : om. T   b 6 καὶ ἠπιστάμην
μύθους B² T W   τούτων T : τούτους B   b 8 ὡς τάχιστα B : om.
T   c 4 σοι B : ἄν σοι T   c 9 μέντοι B T Olymp. : μέντοι γε
B² W

οὐ γάρ φασι θεμιτὸν εἶναι. Καὶ ἅμα λέγων ταῦτα καθῆκε 10
τὰ σκέλη ἐπὶ τὴν γῆν, καὶ καθεζόμενος οὕτως ἤδη τὰ λοιπὰ d
διελέγετο.

Ἤρετο οὖν αὐτὸν ὁ Κέβης· Πῶς τοῦτο λέγεις, ὦ
Σώκρατες, τὸ μὴ θεμιτὸν εἶναι ἑαυτὸν βιάζεσθαι, ἐθέλειν δ᾽
ἂν τῷ ἀποθνήσκοντι τὸν φιλόσοφον ἕπεσθαι; 5
Τί δέ, ὦ Κέβης; οὐκ ἀκηκόατε σύ τε καὶ Σιμμίας περὶ
τῶν τοιούτων Φιλολάῳ συγγεγονότες;
Οὐδέν γε σαφές, ὦ Σώκρατες.
Ἀλλὰ μὴν καὶ ἐγὼ ἐξ ἀκοῆς περὶ αὐτῶν λέγω· ἃ μὲν
οὖν τυγχάνω ἀκηκοὼς φθόνος οὐδεὶς λέγειν. καὶ γὰρ ἴσως 10
καὶ μάλιστα πρέπει μέλλοντα ἐκεῖσε ἀποδημεῖν διασκοπεῖν e
τε καὶ μυθολογεῖν περὶ τῆς ἀποδημίας τῆς ἐκεῖ, ποίαν τινὰ
αὐτὴν οἰόμεθα εἶναι· τί γὰρ ἄν τις καὶ ποιοῖ ἄλλο ἐν τῷ
μέχρι ἡλίου δυσμῶν χρόνῳ;
Κατὰ τί δὴ οὖν ποτε οὔ φασι θεμιτὸν εἶναι αὐτὸν ἑαυτὸν 5
ἀποκτεινύναι, ὦ Σώκρατες; ἤδη γὰρ ἔγωγε, ὅπερ νυνδὴ σὺ
ἤρου, καὶ Φιλολάου ἤκουσα, ὅτε παρ᾽ ἡμῖν διῃτᾶτο, ἤδη δὲ
καὶ ἄλλων τινῶν, ὡς οὐ δέοι τοῦτο ποιεῖν· σαφὲς δὲ περὶ
αὐτῶν οὐδενὸς πώποτε οὐδὲν ἀκήκοα.
Ἀλλὰ προθυμεῖσθαι χρή, ἔφη· τάχα γὰρ ἂν καὶ ἀκού- 62
σαις. ἴσως μέντοι θαυμαστόν σοι φανεῖται εἰ τοῦτο μόνον
τῶν ἄλλων ἁπάντων ἁπλοῦν ἐστιν, καὶ οὐδέποτε τυγχάνει τῷ
ἀνθρώπῳ, ὥσπερ καὶ τἆλλα, ἔστιν ὅτε καὶ οἷς βέλτιον ⟨ὂν⟩
τεθνάναι ἢ ζῆν, οἷς δὲ βέλτιον τεθνάναι, θαυμαστὸν ἴσως 5
σοι φαίνεται εἰ τούτοις τοῖς ἀνθρώποις μὴ ὅσιον αὐτοὺς
ἑαυτοὺς εὖ ποιεῖν, ἀλλὰ ἄλλον δεῖ περιμένειν εὐεργέτην.
Καὶ ὁ Κέβης ἠρέμα ἐπιγελάσας, Ἴττω Ζεύς, ἔφη, τῇ
αὑτοῦ φωνῇ εἰπών.

d 1 σκέλη B Olymp. : σκέλη ἀπὸ τῆς κλίνης W et marg. T   d 8 σαφές T W : σαφῶς B   e 6 νῦν δὴ B T : δὴ νῦν W   a 1 ἀκούσαις
B : ἀκούσαιο T   a 3 τῷ ἀνθρώπῳ B T : τῶν ἀνθρώπων t   a 4 ὂν
add. ci. Heindorf   a 6 ὅσιον B T : ὅσιόν ἐστιν B² W   a 8 ἴττω
s. v. W Olymp. : ἴττι ὦ B : ἰττίω b : ἴττιω T : εἰττίω W   ζεὺς B T :
ζεῦ W

b Καὶ γὰρ ἂν δόξειεν, ἔφη ὁ Σωκράτης, οὕτω γ' εἶναι
ἄλογον· οὐ μέντοι ἀλλ' ἴσως γ' ἔχει τινὰ λόγον. ὁ μὲν οὖν
ἐν ἀπορρήτοις λεγόμενος περὶ αὐτῶν λόγος, ὡς ἔν τινι
φρουρᾷ ἐσμεν οἱ ἄνθρωποι καὶ οὐ δεῖ δὴ ἑαυτὸν ἐκ ταύτης
5 λύειν οὐδ' ἀποδιδράσκειν, μέγας τέ τίς μοι φαίνεται καὶ οὐ
ῥᾴδιος διιδεῖν· οὐ μέντοι ἀλλὰ τόδε γέ μοι δοκεῖ, ὦ Κέβης,
εὖ λέγεσθαι, τὸ θεοὺς εἶναι ἡμῶν τοὺς ἐπιμελουμένους καὶ
ἡμᾶς τοὺς ἀνθρώπους ἓν τῶν κτημάτων τοῖς θεοῖς εἶναι. ἢ
σοὶ οὐ δοκεῖ οὕτως;
10 Ἔμοιγε, φησὶν ὁ Κέβης.

c Οὐκοῦν, ἦ δ' ὅς, καὶ σὺ ἂν τῶν σαυτοῦ κτημάτων εἴ
τι αὐτὸ ἑαυτὸ ἀποκτεινύοι, μὴ σημήναντός σου ὅτι βούλει
αὐτὸ τεθνάναι, χαλεπαίνοις ἂν αὐτῷ καί, εἴ τινα ἔχοις
τιμωρίαν, τιμωροῖο ἄν;
5 Πάνυ γ', ἔφη.
Ἴσως τοίνυν ταύτῃ οὐκ ἄλογον μὴ πρότερον αὐτὸν
ἀποκτεινύναι δεῖν, πρὶν ἀνάγκην τινὰ θεὸς ἐπιπέμψῃ,
ὥσπερ καὶ τὴν νῦν ἡμῖν παροῦσαν.
Ἀλλ' εἰκός, ἔφη ὁ Κέβης, τοῦτό γε φαίνεται. ὁ μέν-
10 τοι νυνδὴ ἔλεγες, τὸ τοὺς φιλοσόφους ῥᾳδίως ἂν ἐθέλειν
d ἀποθνῄσκειν, ἔοικεν τοῦτο, ὦ Σώκρατες, ἀτόπῳ, εἴπερ ὃ
νυνδὴ ἐλέγομεν εὐλόγως ἔχει, τὸ θεόν τε εἶναι τὸν ἐπιμε-
λούμενον ἡμῶν καὶ ἡμᾶς ἐκείνου κτήματα εἶναι. τὸ γὰρ μὴ
ἀγανακτεῖν τοὺς φρονιμωτάτους ἐκ ταύτης τῆς θεραπείας
5 ἀπιόντας, ἐν ᾗ ἐπιστατοῦσιν αὐτῶν οἵπερ ἄριστοί εἰσιν τῶν
ὄντων ἐπιστάται, θεοί, οὐκ ἔχει λόγον· οὐ γάρ που αὐτός γε
αὑτοῦ οἴεται ἄμεινον ἐπιμελήσεσθαι ἐλεύθερος γενόμενος.
ἀλλ' ἀνόητος μὲν ἄνθρωπος τάχ' ἂν οἰηθείη ταῦτα, φευκτέον
e εἶναι ἀπὸ τοῦ δεσπότου, καὶ οὐκ ἂν λογίζοιτο ὅτι οὐ δεῖ ἀπό
γε τοῦ ἀγαθοῦ φεύγειν ἀλλ' ὅτι μάλιστα παραμένειν, διὸ

b 2 γ' BT : om. W   b 4 post ἐσμεν add. πάντες B²   b 10 φησιν B : ἔφη TW   c 1 κτημάτων B : om. T   c 7 πρὶν ⟨ἂν⟩ Heindorf
θεὸς B : ὁ θεὸς B²TW Olymp.   c 8 παροῦσαν ἡμῖν W   d 2 ἔχει
B²TW : ἔχειν B   d 6 που B Olymp. : πω T   d 7 ἐπιμελήσεσθαι
B Olymp. : ἐπιμελεῖσθαι T

ἀλογίστως ἂν φεύγοι· ὁ δὲ νοῦν ἔχων ἐπιθυμοῖ που ἂν ἀεὶ
εἶναι παρὰ τῷ αὑτοῦ βελτίονι. καίτοι οὕτως, ὦ Σώκρατες,
τοὐναντίον εἶναι εἰκὸς ἢ ὃ νυνδὴ ἐλέγετο· τοὺς μὲν γὰρ 5
φρονίμους ἀγανακτεῖν ἀποθνήσκοντας πρέπει, τοὺς δὲ ἄφρονας
χαίρειν.

Ἀκούσας οὖν ὁ Σωκράτης ἡσθῆναί τέ μοι ἔδοξε τῇ τοῦ
Κέβητος πραγματείᾳ, καὶ ἐπιβλέψας εἰς ἡμᾶς, Ἀεί τοι, 63
ἔφη, [ὁ] Κέβης λόγους τινὰς ἀνερευνᾷ, καὶ οὐ πάνυ εὐθέως
ἐθέλει πείθεσθαι ὅτι ἄν τις εἴπῃ.

Καὶ ὁ Σιμμίας, Ἀλλὰ μήν, ἔφη, ὦ Σώκρατες, νῦν γέ μοι
δοκεῖ τι καὶ αὐτῷ λέγειν Κέβης· τί γὰρ ἂν βουλόμενοι 5
ἄνδρες σοφοὶ ὡς ἀληθῶς δεσπότας ἀμείνους αὑτῶν φεύγοιεν
καὶ ῥᾳδίως ἀπαλλάττοιντο αὑτῶν; καί μοι δοκεῖ Κέβης εἰς
σὲ τείνειν τὸν λόγον, ὅτι οὕτω ῥᾳδίως φέρεις καὶ ἡμᾶς
ἀπολείπων καὶ ἄρχοντας ἀγαθούς, ὡς αὐτὸς ὁμολογεῖς, θεούς.

Δίκαια, ἔφη, λέγετε· οἶμαι γὰρ ὑμᾶς λέγειν ὅτι χρή με b
πρὸς ταῦτα ἀπολογήσασθαι ὥσπερ ἐν δικαστηρίῳ.

Πάνυ μὲν οὖν, ἔφη ὁ Σιμμίας.

Φέρε δή, ἦ δ' ὅς, πειραθῶ πιθανώτερον πρὸς ὑμᾶς ἀπολογήσασθαι ἢ πρὸς τοὺς δικαστάς. ἐγὼ γάρ, ἔφη, ὦ Σιμμία 5
τε καὶ Κέβης, εἰ μὲν μὴ ᾤμην ἥξειν πρῶτον μὲν παρὰ
θεοὺς ἄλλους σοφούς τε καὶ ἀγαθούς, ἔπειτα καὶ παρ'
ἀνθρώπους τετελευτηκότας ἀμείνους τῶν ἐνθάδε, ἠδίκουν
ἂν οὐκ ἀγανακτῶν τῷ θανάτῳ· νῦν δὲ εὖ ἴστε ὅτι παρ'
ἄνδρας τε ἐλπίζω ἀφίξεσθαι ἀγαθούς—καὶ τοῦτο μὲν οὐκ ἂν c
πάνυ διισχυρισαίμην—ὅτι μέντοι παρὰ θεοὺς δεσπότας πάνυ
ἀγαθοὺς ἥξειν, εὖ ἴστε ὅτι εἴπερ τι ἄλλο τῶν τοιούτων
διισχυρισαίμην ἂν καὶ τοῦτο. ὥστε διὰ ταῦτα οὐχ ὁμοίως
ἀγανακτῶ, ἀλλ' εὔελπίς εἰμι εἶναί τι τοῖς τετελευτηκόσι καί, 5

e 5 εἰκὸς εἶναι T sed add. sign. transp.   a 2 ὃ om. pr. T
a 4 γέ μοι δοκεῖ τι B : γε δοκεῖ τί μοι T : τέ μοι δοκεῖ τι W   a 9 ἀπολείπων B² T W : ἀπολιπὼν B   b 2 πρὸς ταῦτα B : om. T   b 4 πρὸς
ὑμᾶς πιθανώτερον T W   b 7 καὶ παρ' B t : παρ' T Stob.   b 9 ὅτι
om. Stob.   c 2 ὅτι B : τὸ T (in ras.) Stob.   c 4 διϊσχυρισαίμην
B Stob. : ἰσχυρισαίμην T sed δι s. v.

ὥσπερ γε καὶ πάλαι λέγεται, πολὺ ἄμεινον τοῖς ἀγαθοῖς ἢ τοῖς κακοῖς.

Τί οὖν, ἔφη ὁ Σιμμίας, ὦ Σώκρατες; αὐτὸς ἔχων τὴν διάνοιαν ταύτην ἐν νῷ ἔχεις ἀπιέναι, ἢ κἂν ἡμῖν μεταδοίης;
d κοινὸν γὰρ δὴ ἔμοιγε δοκεῖ καὶ ἡμῖν εἶναι ἀγαθὸν τοῦτο, καὶ ἅμα σοι ἡ ἀπολογία ἔσται, ἐὰν ἅπερ λέγεις ἡμᾶς πείσῃς.

Ἀλλὰ πειράσομαι, ἔφη. πρῶτον δὲ Κρίτωνα τόνδε σκεψώμεθα τί ἐστιν ὃ βούλεσθαί μοι δοκεῖ πάλαι εἰπεῖν.

5 Τί δέ, ὦ Σώκρατες, ἔφη ὁ Κρίτων, ἄλλο γε ἢ πάλαι μοι λέγει ὁ μέλλων σοι δώσειν τὸ φάρμακον ὅτι χρή σοι φράζειν ὡς ἐλάχιστα διαλέγεσθαι; φησὶ γὰρ θερμαίνεσθαι μᾶλλον διαλεγομένους, δεῖν δὲ οὐδὲν τοιοῦτον προσφέρειν
e τῷ φαρμάκῳ· εἰ δὲ μή, ἐνίοτε ἀναγκάζεσθαι καὶ δὶς καὶ τρὶς πίνειν τούς τι τοιοῦτον ποιοῦντας.

Καὶ ὁ Σωκράτης, Ἔα, ἔφη, χαίρειν αὐτόν· ἀλλὰ μόνον τὸ ἑαυτοῦ παρασκευαζέτω ὡς καὶ δὶς δώσων, ἐὰν δὲ δέῃ,
5 καὶ τρίς.

Ἀλλὰ σχεδὸν μέν τι ἤδη, ἔφη ὁ Κρίτων· ἀλλά μοι πάλαι πράγματα παρέχει.

Ἔα αὐτόν, ἔφη. ἀλλ᾽ ὑμῖν δὴ τοῖς δικασταῖς βούλομαι ἤδη τὸν λόγον ἀποδοῦναι, ὥς μοι φαίνεται εἰκότως ἀνὴρ τῷ
10 ὄντι ἐν φιλοσοφίᾳ διατρίψας τὸν βίον θαρρεῖν μέλλων
64 ἀποθανεῖσθαι καὶ εὔελπις εἶναι ἐκεῖ μέγιστα οἴσεσθαι ἀγαθὰ ἐπειδὰν τελευτήσῃ. πῶς ἂν οὖν δὴ τοῦθ᾽ οὕτως ἔχοι, ὦ Σιμμία τε καὶ Κέβης, ἐγὼ πειράσομαι φράσαι.

Κινδυνεύουσι γὰρ ὅσοι τυγχάνουσιν ὀρθῶς ἁπτόμενοι
5 φιλοσοφίας λεληθέναι τοὺς ἄλλους ὅτι οὐδὲν ἄλλο αὐτοὶ ἐπιτηδεύουσιν ἢ ἀποθνήσκειν τε καὶ τεθνάναι. εἰ οὖν τοῦτο ἀληθές, ἄτοπον δήπου ἂν εἴη προθυμεῖσθαι μὲν ἐν παντὶ τῷ

c 8 αὐτὸς BT : πότερον αὐτὸς B² W   ἔχων B T : οὕτως ἔχων B² W
d 2 ἢ T : οὕτως ἢ W : om. B   ἔσται W : ἐστὶν B T   d 5 δὲ B² T :
δ᾽ W : om. B   d 6 prius σοι B T : om. W   d 7 φράζειν B² T W :
φροντίζειν B   d 8 μᾶλλον B T : μᾶλλον τοὺς B² W   e 6 μέν
τι T : μέντοι B   πάλαι πράγματα B : πράγματα πάλαι T   e 9 ἤδη
B : om. T   e 10 θαρρεῖν T : θαρρεῖ B

βίῳ μηδὲν ἄλλο ἢ τοῦτο, ἥκοντος δὲ δὴ αὐτοῦ ἀγανακτεῖν
ὃ πάλαι προυθυμοῦντό τε καὶ ἐπετήδευον.

Καὶ ὁ Σιμμίας γελάσας, Νὴ τὸν Δία, ἔφη, ὦ Σώκρατες,
οὐ πάνυ γέ με νυνδὴ γελασείοντα ἐποίησας γελάσαι. οἶμαι b
γὰρ ἂν τοὺς πολλοὺς αὐτὸ τοῦτο ἀκούσαντας δοκεῖν εὖ πάνυ
εἰρῆσθαι εἰς τοὺς φιλοσοφοῦντας—καὶ συμφάναι ἂν τοὺς μὲν
παρ' ἡμῖν ἀνθρώπους καὶ πάνυ—ὅτι τῷ ὄντι οἱ φιλοσοφοῦντες θανατῶσι, καὶ σφᾶς γε οὐ λελήθασιν ὅτι ἄξιοί εἰσιν 5
τοῦτο πάσχειν.

Καὶ ἀληθῆ γ' ἂν λέγοιεν, ὦ Σιμμία, πλήν γε τοῦ σφᾶς
μὴ λεληθέναι. λέληθεν γὰρ αὐτοὺς ᾗ τε θανατῶσι καὶ ᾗ ἄξιοί
εἰσιν θανάτου καὶ οἵου θανάτου οἱ ὡς ἀληθῶς φιλόσοφοι.
εἴπωμεν γάρ, ἔφη, πρὸς ἡμᾶς αὐτούς, χαίρειν εἰπόντες ἐκεί- c
νοις· ἡγούμεθά τι τὸν θάνατον εἶναι;

Πάνυ γε, ἔφη ὑπολαβὼν ὁ Σιμμίας.

Ἆρα μὴ ἄλλο τι ἢ τὴν τῆς ψυχῆς ἀπὸ τοῦ σώματος
ἀπαλλαγήν; καὶ εἶναι τοῦτο τὸ τεθνάναι, χωρὶς μὲν ἀπὸ τῆς 5
ψυχῆς ἀπαλλαγὲν αὐτὸ καθ' αὑτὸ τὸ σῶμα γεγονέναι, χωρὶς
δὲ τὴν ψυχὴν [ἀπὸ] τοῦ σώματος ἀπαλλαγεῖσαν αὐτὴν καθ'
αὑτὴν εἶναι; ἆρα μὴ ἄλλο τι ἢ ὁ θάνατος ἢ τοῦτο;

Οὔκ, ἀλλὰ τοῦτο, ἔφη.

Σκέψαι δή, ὠγαθέ, ἐὰν ἄρα καὶ σοὶ συνδοκῇ ἅπερ ἐμοί· 10
ἐκ γὰρ τούτων μᾶλλον οἶμαι ἡμᾶς εἴσεσθαι περὶ ὧν σκο- d
ποῦμεν. φαίνεταί σοι φιλοσόφου ἀνδρὸς εἶναι ἐσπουδακέναι
περὶ τὰς ἡδονὰς καλουμένας τὰς τοιάσδε, οἷον σιτίων [τε]
καὶ ποτῶν;

Ἥκιστα, ὦ Σώκρατες, ἔφη ὁ Σιμμίας. 5

Τί δὲ τὰς τῶν ἀφροδισίων;

Οὐδαμῶς.

a 9 ὃ B et s. v. t : ἃ T   b 3 ἂν BT Olymp. : ἂν δὴ B²W
b 7 γ' BT : τ' W   τοῦ BT : τοὺς W   b 9 καὶ οἵου θανάτου B
Iambl. Olymp. : om. T   c 5 τὸ TW Iambl. Olymp. : om. B
c 7 ἀπὸ B . om. T Iambl.   c 8 ἢ ὁ θάνατος ἢ T : ᾗ * θάνατος ἢ B :
ἢ ὁ θάνατος ἢ W   c 10 ἅπερ B T : ἅπερ καὶ B²   d 3 σιτίων τε
B² T : σίτων B W sed ί s. v. W : σίτων τε Iambl.   d 5 ἥκιστα B :
ἥκιστά γε B²T W

Τί δὲ τὰς ἄλλας τὰς περὶ τὸ σῶμα θεραπείας; δοκεῖ σοι
ἐντίμους ἡγεῖσθαι ὁ τοιοῦτος; οἷον ἱματίων διαφερόντων
10 κτήσεις καὶ ὑποδημάτων καὶ τοὺς ἄλλους καλλωπισμοὺς
τοὺς περὶ τὸ σῶμα πότερον τιμᾶν δοκεῖ σοι ἢ ἀτιμάζειν,
e καθ' ὅσον μὴ πολλὴ ἀνάγκη μετέχειν αὐτῶν;
Ἀτιμάζειν ἔμοιγε δοκεῖ, ἔφη, ὅ γε ὡς ἀληθῶς φιλόσοφος.

Οὐκοῦν ὅλως δοκεῖ σοι, ἔφη, ἡ τοῦ τοιούτου πραγ-
5 ματεία οὐ περὶ τὸ σῶμα εἶναι, ἀλλὰ καθ' ὅσον δύναται
ἀφεστάναι αὐτοῦ, πρὸς δὲ τὴν ψυχὴν τετράφθαι;
Ἔμοιγε.

Ἆρ' οὖν πρῶτον μὲν ἐν τοῖς τοιούτοις δῆλός ἐστιν ὁ
65 φιλόσοφος ἀπολύων ὅτι μάλιστα τὴν ψυχὴν ἀπὸ τῆς τοῦ
σώματος κοινωνίας διαφερόντως τῶν ἄλλων ἀνθρώπων;
Φαίνεται.

Καὶ δοκεῖ γέ που, ὦ Σιμμία, τοῖς πολλοῖς ἀνθρώποις
5 ᾧ μηδὲν ἡδὺ τῶν τοιούτων μηδὲ μετέχει αὐτῶν οὐκ ἄξιον
εἶναι ζῆν, ἀλλ' ἐγγύς τι τείνειν τοῦ τεθνάναι ὁ μηδὲν φρον-
τίζων τῶν ἡδονῶν αἳ διὰ τοῦ σώματός εἰσιν.
Πάνυ μὲν οὖν ἀληθῆ λέγεις.

Τί δὲ δὴ περὶ αὐτὴν τὴν τῆς φρονήσεως κτῆσιν; πό-
10 τερον ἐμπόδιον τὸ σῶμα ἢ οὔ, ἐάν τις αὐτὸ ἐν τῇ ζητήσει
b κοινωνὸν συμπαραλαμβάνῃ; οἷον τὸ τοιόνδε λέγω· ἆρα ἔχει
ἀλήθειάν τινα ὄψις τε καὶ ἀκοὴ τοῖς ἀνθρώποις, ἢ τά γε
τοιαῦτα καὶ οἱ ποιηταὶ ἡμῖν ἀεὶ θρυλοῦσιν, ὅτι οὔτ' ἀκούομεν
ἀκριβὲς οὐδὲν οὔτε ὁρῶμεν; καίτοι εἰ αὗται τῶν περὶ τὸ
5 σῶμα αἰσθήσεων μὴ ἀκριβεῖς εἰσιν μηδὲ σαφεῖς, σχολῇ
αἵ γε ἄλλαι· πᾶσαι γάρ που τούτων φαυλότεραί εἰσιν. ἢ
σοὶ οὐ δοκοῦσιν;
Πάνυ μὲν οὖν, ἔφη.

Πότε οὖν, ἦ δ' ὅς, ἡ ψυχὴ τῆς ἀληθείας ἅπτεται; ὅταν

d 9 διαφερόντων Β² T W : καὶ διαφερόντων Β   d 11 σοι δοκεῖ W
a 4 γέ που T W : γε δήπου Β   a 5 μετέχει C Iambl. : μετέχειν B T W
b 3 ἡμῖν ἀεὶ Β : ἀεὶ ἡμῖν T Iambl. Olymp.

μὲν γὰρ μετὰ τοῦ σώματος ἐπιχειρῇ τι σκοπεῖν, δῆλον ὅτι 10
τότε ἐξαπατᾶται ὑπ' αὐτοῦ.

Ἀληθῆ λέγεις. c

Ἆρ' οὖν οὐκ ἐν τῷ λογίζεσθαι εἴπερ που ἄλλοθι κατά-
δηλον αὐτῇ γίγνεταί τι τῶν ὄντων;

Ναί.

Λογίζεται δέ γέ που τότε κάλλιστα, ὅταν αὐτὴν τούτων 5
μηδὲν παραλυπῇ, μήτε ἀκοὴ μήτε ὄψις μήτε ἀλγηδὼν μηδέ
τις ἡδονή, ἀλλ' ὅτι μάλιστα αὐτὴ καθ' αὑτὴν γίγνηται ἐῶσα
χαίρειν τὸ σῶμα, καὶ καθ' ὅσον δύναται μὴ κοινωνοῦσα
αὐτῷ μηδ' ἁπτομένη ὀρέγηται τοῦ ὄντος.

Ἔστι ταῦτα. 10

Οὐκοῦν καὶ ἐνταῦθα ἡ τοῦ φιλοσόφου ψυχὴ μάλιστα
ἀτιμάζει τὸ σῶμα καὶ φεύγει ἀπ' αὐτοῦ, ζητεῖ δὲ αὐτὴ καθ' d
αὑτὴν γίγνεσθαι;

Φαίνεται.

Τί δὲ δὴ τὰ τοιάδε, ὦ Σιμμία; φαμέν τι εἶναι δίκαιον
αὐτὸ ἢ οὐδέν; 5

Φαμὲν μέντοι νὴ Δία.

Καὶ αὖ καλόν γέ τι καὶ ἀγαθόν;

Πῶς δ' οὔ;

Ἤδη οὖν πώποτέ τι τῶν τοιούτων τοῖς ὀφθαλμοῖς εἶδες;

Οὐδαμῶς, ἦ δ' ὅς. 10

Ἀλλ' ἄλλῃ τινὶ αἰσθήσει τῶν διὰ τοῦ σώματος ἐφήψω
αὐτῶν; λέγω δὲ περὶ πάντων, οἷον μεγέθους πέρι, ὑγιείας,
ἰσχύος, καὶ τῶν ἄλλων ἑνὶ λόγῳ ἁπάντων τῆς οὐσίας ὃ
τυγχάνει ἕκαστον ὄν· ἆρα διὰ τοῦ σώματος αὐτῶν τὸ e
ἀληθέστατον θεωρεῖται, ἢ ὧδε ἔχει· ὃς ἂν μάλιστα ἡμῶν
καὶ ἀκριβέστατα παρασκευάσηται αὐτὸ ἕκαστον διανοηθῆναι
περὶ οὗ σκοπεῖ, οὗτος ἂν ἐγγύτατα ἴοι τοῦ γνῶναι ἕκαστον;

Πάνυ μὲν οὖν. 5

c 5 τότε B²TW Iambl.: τοῦτό τε B   μηδὲν τούτων αὐτὴν W
c 6 μηδὲ B Iambl.: μήτε TW   d 6 μέντοι B: τοι TW Olymp.
d 7 αὖ Heindorf e Ficino: οὐ T: om. B   d 9 ἤδη B²TW: τί δὴ B
e 1 τἀληθέστατον αὐτῶν T Olymp.

Ἆρ' οὖν ἐκεῖνος ἂν τοῦτο ποιήσειεν καθαρώτατα ὅστις
ὅτι μάλιστα αὐτῇ τῇ διανοίᾳ ἴοι ἐφ' ἕκαστον, μήτε τιν'
ὄψιν παρατιθέμενος ἐν τῷ διανοεῖσθαι μήτε [τινὰ] ἄλλην
66 αἴσθησιν ἐφέλκων μηδεμίαν μετὰ τοῦ λογισμοῦ, ἀλλ' αὐτῇ
καθ' αὑτὴν εἰλικρινεῖ τῇ διανοίᾳ χρώμενος αὐτὸ καθ' αὑτὸ εἰλι-
κρινὲς ἕκαστον ἐπιχειροῖ θηρεύειν τῶν ὄντων, ἀπαλλαγεὶς
ὅτι μάλιστα ὀφθαλμῶν τε καὶ ὤτων καὶ ὡς ἔπος εἰπεῖν σύμ-
5 παντος τοῦ σώματος, ὡς ταράττοντος καὶ οὐκ ἐῶντος τὴν
ψυχὴν κτήσασθαι ἀλήθειάν τε καὶ φρόνησιν ὅταν κοινωνῇ;
ἆρ' οὐχ οὗτός ἐστιν, ὦ Σιμμία, εἴπερ τις [καὶ] ἄλλος ὁ
τευξόμενος τοῦ ὄντος;

Ὑπερφυῶς, ἔφη ὁ Σιμμίας, ὡς ἀληθῆ λέγεις, ὦ
10 Σώκρατες.

b Οὐκοῦν ἀνάγκη, ἔφη, ἐκ πάντων τούτων παρίστασθαι
δόξαν τοιάνδε τινὰ τοῖς γνησίως φιλοσόφοις, ὥστε καὶ πρὸς
ἀλλήλους τοιαῦτα ἄττα λέγειν, ὅτι " Κινδυνεύει τοι ὥσπερ
ἀτραπός τις ἐκφέρειν ἡμᾶς [μετὰ τοῦ λόγου ἐν τῇ σκέψει],
5 ὅτι, ἕως ἂν τὸ σῶμα ἔχωμεν καὶ συμπεφυρμένη ᾖ ἡμῶν ἡ
ψυχὴ μετὰ τοιούτου κακοῦ, οὐ μή ποτε κτησώμεθα ἱκανῶς
οὗ ἐπιθυμοῦμεν· φαμὲν δὲ τοῦτο εἶναι τὸ ἀληθές. μυρίας
μὲν γὰρ ἡμῖν ἀσχολίας παρέχει τὸ σῶμα διὰ τὴν ἀναγκαίαν
c τροφήν· ἔτι δέ, ἄν τινες νόσοι προσπέσωσιν, ἐμποδίζουσιν
ἡμῶν τὴν τοῦ ὄντος θήραν. ἐρώτων δὲ καὶ ἐπιθυμιῶν καὶ
φόβων καὶ εἰδώλων παντοδαπῶν καὶ φλυαρίας ἐμπίμπλησιν
ἡμᾶς πολλῆς, ὥστε τὸ λεγόμενον ὡς ἀληθῶς τῷ ὄντι ὑπ'
5 αὐτοῦ οὐδὲ φρονῆσαι ἡμῖν ἐγγίγνεται οὐδέποτε οὐδέν. καὶ
γὰρ πολέμους καὶ στάσεις καὶ μάχας οὐδὲν ἄλλο παρέχει ἢ
τὸ σῶμα καὶ αἱ τούτου ἐπιθυμίαι. διὰ γὰρ τὴν τῶν χρημάτων κτῆσιν πάντες οἱ πόλεμοι γίγνονται, τὰ δὲ χρήματα

e 6 ποιήσειε(ν) B²TW : ποιήσῃ B   e 7 μήτε BT : μήποτε W
τιν' scripsi : τὴν BTW   e 8 τινὰ B : om. T Iambl. Olymp.
a 7 οὗτός Bt : οὕτως T   καὶ B : om. T Iambl.   b 3 ἄττα Bt :
om. T   b 4 τις B : om. T Iambl. Olymp.   ἐκφέρειν ἡμᾶς BT
Iambl. Olymp. : ἡμᾶς ἐκφέρειν W   μετὰ . . . σκέψει secl. Christ :
post b 5 ἔχωμεν transp. ci. Schleiermacher   b 6 τοιούτου B
Iambl. : τοῦ τοιούτου B²TW Olymp.   c 2 δὲ B Iambl. Olymp. :
τε T   c 8 οἱ BT Iambl. Olymp. : ἡμῖν οἱ B²W

ἀναγκαζόμεθα κτᾶσθαι διὰ τὸ σῶμα, δουλεύοντες τῇ τούτου d
θεραπείᾳ· καὶ ἐκ τούτου ἀσχολίαν ἄγομεν φιλοσοφίας πέρι
διὰ πάντα ταῦτα. τὸ δ' ἔσχατον πάντων ὅτι, ἐάν τις
ἡμῖν καὶ σχολὴ γένηται ἀπ' αὐτοῦ καὶ τραπώμεθα πρὸς τὸ
σκοπεῖν τι, ἐν ταῖς ζητήσεσιν αὖ πανταχοῦ παραπῖπτον 5
θόρυβον παρέχει καὶ ταραχὴν καὶ ἐκπλήττει, ὥστε μὴ
δύνασθαι ὑπ' αὐτοῦ καθορᾶν τἀληθές. ἀλλὰ τῷ ὄντι ἡμῖν
δέδεικται ὅτι, εἰ μέλλομέν ποτε καθαρῶς τι εἴσεσθαι,
ἀπαλλακτέον αὐτοῦ καὶ αὐτῇ τῇ ψυχῇ θεατέον αὐτὰ τὰ e
πράγματα· καὶ τότε, ὡς ἔοικεν, ἡμῖν ἔσται οὗ ἐπιθυμοῦμέν
τε καί φαμεν ἐρασταὶ εἶναι, φρονήσεως, ἐπειδὰν τελευτή-
σωμεν, ὡς ὁ λόγος σημαίνει, ζῶσιν δὲ οὔ. εἰ γὰρ μὴ οἷόν
τε μετὰ τοῦ σώματος μηδὲν καθαρῶς γνῶναι, δυοῖν θάτερον, 5
ἢ οὐδαμοῦ ἔστιν κτήσασθαι τὸ εἰδέναι ἢ τελευτήσασιν· τότε
γὰρ αὐτὴ καθ' αὑτὴν ἡ ψυχὴ ἔσται χωρὶς τοῦ σώματος, 67
πρότερον δ' οὔ. καὶ ἐν ᾧ ἂν ζῶμεν, οὕτως, ὡς ἔοικεν,
ἐγγυτάτω ἐσόμεθα τοῦ εἰδέναι, ἐὰν ὅτι μάλιστα μηδὲν
ὁμιλῶμεν τῷ σώματι μηδὲ κοινωνῶμεν, ὅτι μὴ πᾶσα ἀνάγκη,
μηδὲ ἀναπιμπλώμεθα τῆς τούτου φύσεως, ἀλλὰ καθαρεύωμεν 5
ἀπ' αὐτοῦ, ἕως ἂν ὁ θεὸς αὐτὸς ἀπολύσῃ ἡμᾶς· καὶ οὕτω μὲν
καθαροὶ ἀπαλλαττόμενοι τῆς τοῦ σώματος ἀφροσύνης, ὡς τὸ
εἰκὸς μετὰ τοιούτων τε ἐσόμεθα καὶ γνωσόμεθα δι' ἡμῶν
αὐτῶν πᾶν τὸ εἰλικρινές, τοῦτο δ' ἐστὶν ἴσως τὸ ἀληθές· b
μὴ καθαρῷ γὰρ καθαροῦ ἐφάπτεσθαι μὴ οὐ θεμιτὸν ᾖ."
τοιαῦτα οἶμαι, ὦ Σιμμία, ἀναγκαῖον εἶναι πρὸς ἀλλήλους
λέγειν τε καὶ δοξάζειν πάντας τοὺς ὀρθῶς φιλομαθεῖς. ἢ οὐ
δοκεῖ σοι οὕτως; 5

Παντός γε μᾶλλον, ὦ Σώκρατες.

Οὐκοῦν, ἔφη ὁ Σωκράτης, εἰ ταῦτα ἀληθῆ, ὦ ἑταῖρε,
πολλὴ ἐλπὶς ἀφικομένῳ οἷ ἐγὼ πορεύομαι, ἐκεῖ ἱκανῶς,

d 6 παρέχει B Iambl. : παρέξει T   e 3 φρονήσεως] φρόνησις Iambl.
a 1 ἡ ψυχὴ ἔσται B T : ἔσται ἡ ψυχὴ B² W Plut. Iambl.   a 6 αὐτὸς
B² T W Plut. Iambl. Olymp. : om. B   a 8 τε om. Iambl. Olymp.
b 4 τε B : om. T   b 8 ἐκεῖ ἱκανῶς B : ἱκανῶς ἐκεῖ T W Olymp.

εἴπερ που ἄλλοθι, κτήσασθαι τοῦτο οὗ ἕνεκα ἡ πολλὴ
10 πραγματεία ἡμῖν ἐν τῷ παρελθόντι βίῳ γέγονεν, ὥστε ἥ γε
c ἀποδημία ἡ νῦν μοι προστεταγμένη μετὰ ἀγαθῆς ἐλπίδος
γίγνεται καὶ ἄλλῳ ἀνδρὶ ὃς ἡγεῖταί οἱ παρεσκευάσθαι τὴν
διάνοιαν ὥσπερ κεκαθαρμένην.
Πάνυ μὲν οὖν, ἔφη ὁ Σιμμίας.

5 Κάθαρσις δὲ εἶναι ἆρα οὐ τοῦτο συμβαίνει, ὅπερ πάλαι
ἐν τῷ λόγῳ λέγεται, τὸ χωρίζειν ὅτι μάλιστα ἀπὸ τοῦ
σώματος τὴν ψυχὴν καὶ ἐθίσαι αὐτὴν καθ᾽ αὑτὴν παντα-
χόθεν ἐκ τοῦ σώματος συναγείρεσθαί τε καὶ ἀθροίζεσθαι,
καὶ οἰκεῖν κατὰ τὸ δυνατὸν καὶ ἐν τῷ νῦν παρόντι καὶ ἐν τῷ
d ἔπειτα μόνην καθ᾽ αὑτήν, ἐκλυομένην ὥσπερ [ἐκ] δεσμῶν ἐκ
τοῦ σώματος;
Πάνυ μὲν οὖν, ἔφη.
Οὐκοῦν τοῦτό γε θάνατος ὀνομάζεται, λύσις καὶ χωρισμὸς
5 ψυχῆς ἀπὸ σώματος;
Παντάπασί γε, ἦ δ᾽ ὅς.

Λύειν δέ γε αὐτήν, ὥς φαμεν, προθυμοῦνται ἀεὶ μάλιστα
καὶ μόνοι οἱ φιλοσοφοῦντες ὀρθῶς, καὶ τὸ μελέτημα αὐτὸ
τοῦτό ἐστιν τῶν φιλοσόφων, λύσις καὶ χωρισμὸς ψυχῆς
10 ἀπὸ σώματος· ἢ οὔ;
Φαίνεται.

Οὐκοῦν, ὅπερ ἐν ἀρχῇ ἔλεγον, γελοῖον ἂν εἴη ἄνδρα
e παρασκευάζονθ᾽ ἑαυτὸν ἐν τῷ βίῳ ὅτι ἐγγυτάτω ὄντα τοῦ
τεθνάναι οὕτω ζῆν, κἄπειθ᾽ ἥκοντος αὐτῷ τούτου ἀγανακτεῖν;
Γελοῖον· πῶς δ᾽ οὔ;

Τῷ ὄντι ἄρα, ἔφη, ὦ Σιμμία, οἱ ὀρθῶς φιλοσοφοῦντες
5 ἀποθνῄσκειν μελετῶσι, καὶ τὸ τεθνάναι ἥκιστα αὐτοῖς
ἀνθρώπων φοβερόν. ἐκ τῶνδε δὲ σκόπει. εἰ γὰρ δια-

c 1 μοι B : ἐμοὶ B²T W   c 2 παρεσκευάσθαι B T : παρασκευά-
σασθαι W   d 1 prius ἐκ T Iambl. Protr. : om. B W : alterum ἐκ
B T W Iambl. Protr. : om. Iambl. v. Pyth.   d 4 θάνατος τοῦτό
γε W   d 5 ψυχῆς B²T W Iambl. Stob. : om. B   d 9 ψυχῆς
B²T W Iambl. : τῆς ψυχῆς B   e 3 γελοῖον scripsi : οὐ γελοῖον
B T W Socrati tribuentes : in Ars. spatium septem litterarum

βέβληνται μὲν πανταχῇ τῷ σώματι, αὐτὴν δὲ καθ' αὑτὴν
ἐπιθυμοῦσι τὴν ψυχὴν ἔχειν, τούτου δὲ γιγνομένου εἰ
φοβοῖντο καὶ ἀγανακτοῖεν, οὐ πολλὴ ἂν ἀλογία εἴη, εἰ μὴ
ἄσμενοι ἐκεῖσε ἴοιεν, οἷ ἀφικομένοις ἐλπίς ἐστιν οὗ διὰ βίου 68
ἤρων τυχεῖν—ἤρων δὲ φρονήσεως—ᾧ τε διεβέβληντο, τούτου
ἀπηλλάχθαι συνόντος αὐτοῖς; ἢ ἀνθρωπίνων μὲν παιδικῶν
καὶ γυναικῶν καὶ ὑέων ἀποθανόντων πολλοὶ δὴ ἑκόντες
ἠθέλησαν εἰς Ἅιδου μετελθεῖν, ὑπὸ ταύτης ἀγόμενοι τῆς 5
ἐλπίδος, τῆς τοῦ ὄψεσθαί τε ἐκεῖ ὧν ἐπεθύμουν καὶ συνέσε-
σθαι· φρονήσεως δὲ ἄρα τις τῷ ὄντι ἐρῶν, καὶ λαβὼν σφόδρα
τὴν αὐτὴν ταύτην ἐλπίδα, μηδαμοῦ ἄλλοθι ἐντεύξεσθαι αὐτῇ
ἀξίως λόγου ἢ ἐν Ἅιδου, ἀγανακτήσει τε ἀποθνῄσκων καὶ b
οὐχ ἄσμενος εἶσιν αὐτόσε; οἴεσθαί γε χρή, ἐὰν τῷ ὄντι γε
ᾖ, ὦ ἑταῖρε, φιλόσοφος· σφόδρα γὰρ αὐτῷ ταῦτα δόξει,
μηδαμοῦ ἄλλοθι καθαρῶς ἐντεύξεσθαι φρονήσει ἀλλ' ἢ ἐκεῖ.
εἰ δὲ τοῦτο οὕτως ἔχει, ὅπερ ἄρτι ἔλεγον, οὐ πολλὴ ἂν 5
ἀλογία εἴη εἰ φοβοῖτο τὸν θάνατον ὁ τοιοῦτος;

Πολλὴ μέντοι νὴ Δία, ἦ δ' ὅς.

Οὐκοῦν ἱκανόν σοι τεκμήριον, ἔφη, τοῦτο ἀνδρός, ὃν
ἂν ἴδῃς ἀγανακτοῦντα μέλλοντα ἀποθανεῖσθαι, ὅτι οὐκ ἄρ'
ἦν φιλόσοφος ἀλλά τις φιλοσώματος; ὁ αὐτὸς δέ που c
οὗτος τυγχάνει ὢν καὶ φιλοχρήματος καὶ φιλότιμος, ἤτοι τὰ
ἕτερα τούτων ἢ ἀμφότερα.

Πάνυ, ἔφη, ἔχει οὕτως ὡς λέγεις.

Ἆρ' οὖν, ἔφη, ὦ Σιμμία, οὐ καὶ ἡ ὀνομαζομένη ἀνδρεία 5
τοῖς οὕτω διακειμένοις μάλιστα προσήκει;

Πάντως δήπου, ἔφη.

e 8 ἔχειν B T et γρ. W : εἶναι W   εἰ B : om. T   a 4 καὶ
ὑέων] ἢ παίδων ἕνεκα Ars.   δὴ om. Ars.   a 5 μετελθεῖν B² T :
ἐλθεῖν B W t   a 6 τε C : τι B (in ras.) T W   b 2 εἶσιν B W t :
οἴσει T   γε ᾖ B Ars. : om. T W   b 3 δόξει B : δόξειν T
b 4 .. θαμου αλλοθι ...... θαρως φρονήσει εν Ars. : γρ. ἄλλοθι δυνατὸν
εἶναι καθαρῶς in marg. B (i. e. μηδαμοῦ ἄλλοθι δυνατὸν εἶναι καθαρῶς
φρονήσει ἐντυχεῖν)   b 5 ἀλογία ἂν Ars.   b 8 ἔφη τεκμήριον Ars.
ἀνδρὸς et μέλλοντα ἀποθανεῖσθαι om. ut vid Ars.   c 2 .. γχάνει
φιλο .. Ars.   c 4 πάνυ B T Stob. : πάνυ γ' W

Οὐκοῦν καὶ ἡ σωφροσύνη, ἣν καὶ οἱ πολλοὶ ὀνομάζουσι
σωφροσύνην, τὸ περὶ τὰς ἐπιθυμίας μὴ ἐπτοῆσθαι ἀλλ'
10 ὀλιγώρως ἔχειν καὶ κοσμίως, ἆρ' οὐ τούτοις μόνοις προσήκει,
τοῖς μάλιστα τοῦ σώματος ὀλιγωροῦσίν τε καὶ ἐν φιλοσοφίᾳ
ζῶσιν;
d Ἀνάγκη, ἔφη.
Εἰ γὰρ ἐθέλεις, ἦ δ' ὅς, ἐννοῆσαι τήν γε τῶν ἄλλων
ἀνδρείαν τε καὶ σωφροσύνην, δόξει σοι εἶναι ἄτοπος.
Πῶς δή, ὦ Σώκρατες;
5 Οἶσθα, ἦ δ' ὅς, ὅτι τὸν θάνατον ἡγοῦνται πάντες οἱ ἄλλοι
τῶν μεγάλων κακῶν;
Καὶ μάλ', ἔφη.
Οὐκοῦν φόβῳ μειζόνων κακῶν ὑπομένουσιν αὐτῶν οἱ
ἀνδρεῖοι τὸν θάνατον, ὅταν ὑπομένωσιν;
10 Ἔστι ταῦτα.
Τῷ δεδιέναι ἄρα καὶ δέει ἀνδρεῖοί εἰσι πάντες πλὴν οἱ
φιλόσοφοι· καίτοι ἄλογόν γε δέει τινὰ καὶ δειλίᾳ ἀνδρεῖον
εἶναι.
e Πάνυ μὲν οὖν.
Τί δὲ οἱ κόσμιοι αὐτῶν; οὐ ταὐτὸν τοῦτο πεπόνθασιν·
ἀκολασίᾳ τινὶ σώφρονές εἰσιν; καίτοι φαμέν γε ἀδύνατον
εἶναι, ἀλλ' ὅμως αὐτοῖς συμβαίνει τούτῳ ὅμοιον τὸ πάθος
5 τὸ περὶ ταύτην τὴν εὐήθη σωφροσύνην· φοβούμενοι γὰρ
ἑτέρων ἡδονῶν στερηθῆναι καὶ ἐπιθυμοῦντες ἐκείνων, ἄλλων
ἀπέχονται ὑπ' ἄλλων κρατούμενοι. καίτοι καλοῦσί γε ἀκο-
69 λασίαν τὸ ὑπὸ τῶν ἡδονῶν ἄρχεσθαι, ἀλλ' ὅμως συμβαίνει
αὐτοῖς κρατουμένοις ὑφ' ἡδονῶν κρατεῖν ἄλλων ἡδονῶν.

c 8 ἦ Β Τ Iambl. Stob.: om. W   c 10 μόνον Ars.   d 1 ἔφη
om. Ars.   d 2 ἐθέλεις Β Τ Iambl. Stob.: ἐθελήσεις W   γε Τ W
Iambl. Stob.: τε Β   d 6 μεγάλων Β γρ. Τ Iambl. Olymp. Stob.:
μεγίστων Β² Τ W   κακῶν Β t Iambl. Olymp.: κακῶν εἶναι Β² Τ W
Ars. Stob.   d 9 ὑπομένωσιν] ὑπομειμὼ .. Ars.   d 12 ἄλογον
Β Ars. Iambl. Stob.: ἄτοπον Β² Τ W   e 3 ⟨σωφρον⟩ουσιν Ars.
γε Β Iambl. Stob.: γέ που Β² Τ W   e 4 τοῦτο Ars.   ὅμοιον Β
Iambl. Stob.: ὅμοιον εἶναι Β² Τ W   e 5 τὸ περὶ ταύτην] τοι επ αυτην
Ars.   εὐήθη] ἀνδραποδώδη Ars.   e 6 στερηθῆναι ἑτέρων ἡδονῶν
Ars.   e 7 κρατούμενοι ὑπ' ἄλλων W   ἄλλων] ἐκείνων Ars.
a 1 τῶν om. Ars.   ἀλλ' ὅμως συμβαίνει] συμβαίνει δ' οὖν Ars.

τοῦτο δ' ὅμοιόν ἐστιν ᾧ νυνδὴ ἐλέγετο, τῷ τρόπον τινὰ δι'
ἀκολασίαν αὐτοὺς σεσωφρονίσθαι.

Ἔοικε γάρ.

Ὦ μακάριε Σιμμία, μὴ γὰρ οὐχ αὕτη ᾖ ἡ ὀρθὴ πρὸς
ἀρετὴν ἀλλαγή, ἡδονὰς πρὸς ἡδονὰς καὶ λύπας πρὸς λύπας
καὶ φόβον πρὸς φόβον καταλλάττεσθαι, [καὶ] μείζω πρὸς
ἐλάττω ὥσπερ νομίσματα, ἀλλ' ᾖ ἐκεῖνο μόνον τὸ νόμισμα
ὀρθόν, ἀντὶ οὗ δεῖ πάντα ταῦτα καταλλάττεσθαι, φρόνησις, 10
[καὶ τούτου μὲν πάντα] καὶ μετὰ τούτου [ὠνούμενά τε καὶ b
πιπρασκόμενα] τῷ ὄντι ᾖ καὶ ἀνδρεία καὶ σωφροσύνη καὶ
δικαιοσύνη καὶ συλλήβδην ἀληθὴς ἀρετή, μετὰ φρονήσεως,
καὶ προσγιγνομένων καὶ ἀπογιγνομένων καὶ ἡδονῶν καὶ
φόβων καὶ τῶν ἄλλων πάντων τῶν τοιούτων· χωριζόμενα 5
δὲ φρονήσεως [καὶ] ἀλλαττόμενα ἀντὶ ἀλλήλων μὴ σκιαγραφία τις ᾖ ἡ τοιαύτη ἀρετὴ καὶ τῷ ὄντι ἀνδραποδώδης τε
καὶ οὐδὲν ὑγιὲς οὐδ' ἀληθὲς ἔχῃ, τὸ δ' ἀληθὲς τῷ ὄντι ᾖ
κάθαρσίς τις τῶν τοιούτων πάντων καὶ ἡ σωφροσύνη καὶ c
ἡ δικαιοσύνη καὶ ἀνδρεία, καὶ αὐτὴ ἡ φρόνησις μὴ καθαρμός τις ᾖ. καὶ κινδυνεύουσι καὶ οἱ τὰς τελετὰς ἡμῖν
οὗτοι καταστήσαντες οὐ φαῦλοί τινες εἶναι, ἀλλὰ τῷ ὄντι
πάλαι αἰνίττεσθαι ὅτι ὃς ἂν ἀμύητος καὶ ἀτέλεστος εἰς 5
Ἅιδου ἀφίκηται ἐν βορβόρῳ κείσεται, ὁ δὲ κεκαθαρμένος
τε καὶ τετελεσμένος ἐκεῖσε ἀφικόμενος μετὰ θεῶν οἰκήσει.
εἰσὶν γὰρ δή, [ὥς] φασιν οἱ περὶ τὰς τελετάς, "ναρθηκοφόροι
μὲν πολλοί, βάκχοι δέ τε παῦροι·" οὗτοι δ' εἰσὶν κατὰ τὴν d
ἐμὴν δόξαν οὐκ ἄλλοι ἢ οἱ πεφιλοσοφηκότες ὀρθῶς. ὧν δὴ
καὶ ἐγὼ κατά γε τὸ δυνατὸν οὐδὲν ἀπέλιπον ἐν τῷ βίῳ

a 6 γὰρ B Ars. Olymp. Stob. : om. T   ᾖ ἥ] ᾖ B : ἡ T   a 7 ἀλλαγὴ
W Iambl. : ἀλλὰ B : * * * * T   a 8 καὶ om. Iambl. Stob.   a 9 ἀλλ'
ᾖ W : ἀλλὴ B T   a 10 ἀνθ' ὅτου W   πάντα T Iambl. Stob. : ἅπαντα B
b 1, 2 inclusa seclusi   δικαιοσύνη καὶ σωφροσύνη W   b 6 καὶ
B² T W Iambl. Stob. : om. B   ἀλλήλων B² T W Iambl. Stob. :
ἄλλων B   b 8 ὑγιὲς T W Iambl. Stob. : ὑγιὲς εἶναι B   ἔχῃ B T
Stob. : ἔχει W Iambl. : γρ. ἔχουσα W   κάθαρσις ᾖ W   c 2 ἀνδρεία
B : ἡ ἀνδρεία T W   c 3 κινδυνεύουσι B γρ. W Iambl. Olymp. : κινδυ-
νεύωσι B² T W   c 4 τινες B² T W : om. B Iambl. Stob.   c 7 τε
om. W   c 8 ὥς B Clem. Stob. : om. T Iambl.   d 3 ἐγὼ B :
ἔγωγε T W   γε B W : om. T

ἀλλὰ παντὶ τρόπῳ προυθυμήθην γενέσθαι· εἰ δ᾽ ὀρθῶς
5 προυθυμήθην καί τι ἠνύσαμεν, ἐκεῖσε ἐλθόντες τὸ σαφὲς
εἰσόμεθα, ἂν θεὸς ἐθέλῃ, ὀλίγον ὕστερον, ὡς ἐμοὶ δοκεῖ.
ταῦτ᾽ οὖν ἐγώ, ἔφη, ὦ Σιμμία τε καὶ Κέβης, ἀπολογοῦμαι,
ὡς εἰκότως ὑμᾶς τε ἀπολείπων καὶ τοὺς ἐνθάδε δεσπότας οὐ
e χαλεπῶς φέρω οὐδ᾽ ἀγανακτῶ, ἡγούμενος κἀκεῖ οὐδὲν ἧττον
ἢ ἐνθάδε δεσπόταις τε ἀγαθοῖς ἐντεύξεσθαι καὶ ἑταίροις·
[τοῖς δὲ πολλοῖς ἀπιστίαν παρέχει]· εἴ τι οὖν ὑμῖν πιθανώ-
τερός εἰμι ἐν τῇ ἀπολογίᾳ ἢ τοῖς Ἀθηναίων δικασταῖς, εὖ
5 ἂν ἔχοι.

Εἰπόντος δὴ τοῦ Σωκράτους ταῦτα, ὑπολαβὼν ὁ Κέβης
ἔφη· Ὦ Σώκρατες, τὰ μὲν ἄλλα ἔμοιγε δοκεῖ καλῶς λέγεσθαι,
70 τὰ δὲ περὶ τῆς ψυχῆς πολλὴν ἀπιστίαν παρέχει τοῖς ἀνθρώποις
μή, ἐπειδὰν ἀπαλλαγῇ τοῦ σώματος, οὐδαμοῦ ἔτι ᾖ, ἀλλ᾽ ἐκείνῃ
τῇ ἡμέρᾳ διαφθείρηταί τε καὶ ἀπολλύηται ᾗ ἂν ὁ ἄνθρωπος ἀπο-
θνῄσκῃ, εὐθὺς ἀπαλλαττομένη τοῦ σώματος, καὶ ἐκβαίνουσα
5 ὥσπερ πνεῦμα ἢ καπνὸς διασκεδασθεῖσα οἴχηται διαπτομένη
καὶ οὐδὲν ἔτι οὐδαμοῦ ᾖ. ἐπεί, εἴπερ εἴη που αὐτὴ καθ᾽
αὑτὴν συνηθροισμένη καὶ ἀπηλλαγμένη τούτων τῶν κακῶν
ὧν σὺ νυνδὴ διῆλθες, πολλὴ ἂν εἴη ἐλπὶς καὶ καλή, ὦ
b Σώκρατες, ὡς ἀληθῆ ἐστιν ἃ σὺ λέγεις· ἀλλὰ τοῦτο δὴ
ἴσως οὐκ ὀλίγης παραμυθίας δεῖται καὶ πίστεως, ὡς ἔστι τε
ψυχὴ ἀποθανόντος τοῦ ἀνθρώπου καί τινα δύναμιν ἔχει καὶ
φρόνησιν.

5 Ἀληθῆ, ἔφη, λέγεις, ὁ Σωκράτης, ὦ Κέβης· ἀλλὰ τί δὴ
ποιῶμεν; ἢ περὶ αὐτῶν τούτων βούλει διαμυθολογῶμεν, εἴτε
εἰκὸς οὕτως ἔχειν εἴτε μή;

d 8 ἀπολείπων T W : ἀπολιπὼν B   e 2 ἑταίροις B² T W : ἑτέροις B
e 3 τοῖς .. παρέχει secl. Ast   e 7 ἔμοιγε δοκεῖ B t Stob. : δοκεῖ
ἔμοιγε T W   a 2 ἔτι ᾖ] ἐστι Stob.   a 3 διαφθείρεται Stob.
ἀπόλλυται Stob.   ὁ B T Stob. : om. W   ἀποθνήσκη B² :
ἀποθνήσκει B : ἀποθάνῃ B² (marg.) T W Stob.   a 5 οἴχηται . . . ᾖ
secl. Schanz   οἴχεται Stob.   a 8 νῦν δὴ B² W : νῦν ἂν B : νῦν
T Stob.   ἐλπὶς εἴη T   b 2 ἴσως B T W Stob. : σαφῶς s. v. W
b 3 ψυχὴ T : ἡ ψυχὴ B W Stob.

Ἐγὼ γοῦν, ἔφη ὁ Κέβης, ἡδέως ἂν ἀκούσαιμι ἥντινα δόξαν ἔχεις περὶ αὐτῶν.

Οὔκουν γ᾽ ἂν οἶμαι, ἦ δ᾽ ὃς ὁ Σωκράτης, εἰπεῖν τινα νῦν 10 ἀκούσαντα, οὐδ᾽ εἰ κωμῳδοποιὸς εἴη, ὡς ἀδολεσχῶ καὶ οὐ c περὶ προσηκόντων τοὺς λόγους ποιοῦμαι. εἰ οὖν δοκεῖ, χρὴ διασκοπεῖσθαι.

Σκεψώμεθα δὲ αὐτὸ τῇδέ πῃ, εἴτ᾽ ἄρα ἐν Ἅιδου εἰσὶν αἱ ψυχαὶ τελευτησάντων τῶν ἀνθρώπων εἴτε καὶ οὔ. παλαιὸς 5 μὲν οὖν ἔστι τις λόγος οὗ μεμνήμεθα, ὡς εἰσὶν ἐνθένδε ἀφικόμεναι ἐκεῖ, καὶ πάλιν γε δεῦρο ἀφικνοῦνται καὶ γίγνονται ἐκ τῶν τεθνεώτων· καὶ εἰ τοῦθ᾽ οὕτως ἔχει, πάλιν γίγνεσθαι ἐκ τῶν ἀποθανόντων τοὺς ζῶντας, ἄλλο τι ἢ εἶεν ἂν αἱ ψυχαὶ ἡμῶν ἐκεῖ; οὐ γὰρ ἄν που πάλιν ἐγίγνοντο μὴ d οὖσαι, καὶ τοῦτο ἱκανὸν τεκμήριον τοῦ ταῦτ᾽ εἶναι, εἰ τῷ ὄντι φανερὸν γίγνοιτο ὅτι οὐδαμόθεν ἄλλοθεν γίγνονται οἱ ζῶντες ἢ ἐκ τῶν τεθνεώτων· εἰ δὲ μὴ ἔστι τοῦτο, ἄλλου ἄν του δέοι λόγου. 5

Πάνυ μὲν οὖν, ἔφη ὁ Κέβης.

Μὴ τοίνυν κατ᾽ ἀνθρώπων, ἦ δ᾽ ὅς, σκόπει μόνον τοῦτο, εἰ βούλει ῥᾷον μαθεῖν, ἀλλὰ καὶ κατὰ ζῴων πάντων καὶ φυτῶν, καὶ συλλήβδην ὅσαπερ ἔχει γένεσιν περὶ πάντων ἴδωμεν ἆρ᾽ οὑτωσὶ γίγνεται πάντα, οὐκ ἄλλοθεν ἢ ἐκ τῶν e ἐναντίων τὰ ἐναντία, ὅσοις τυγχάνει ὂν τοιοῦτόν τι, οἷον τὸ καλὸν τῷ αἰσχρῷ ἐναντίον που καὶ δίκαιον ἀδίκῳ, καὶ ἄλλα δὴ μυρία οὕτως ἔχει. τοῦτο οὖν σκεψώμεθα, ἆρα ἀναγκαῖον ὅσοις ἔστι τι ἐναντίον, μηδαμόθεν ἄλλοθεν αὐτὸ γίγνεσθαι 5 ἢ ἐκ τοῦ αὐτῷ ἐναντίου. οἷον ὅταν μεῖζόν τι γίγνηται, ἀνάγκη που ἐξ ἐλάττονος ὄντος πρότερον ἔπειτα μεῖζον γίγνεσθαι;

b 8 ἔγωγε οὖν B : ἐγωγοῦν T : ἔγωγ᾽ οὖν W   c 1 κωμῳδοποιὸς pr. T (ut vid.) W : κωμῳδιοποιὸς B t   c 4 δὲ B : om. T   c 6 λόγος B : ὁ λόγος οὗτος B² T W Olymp. : λόγος οὗτος Stob.   d 1 αἱ ψυχαὶ ἡμῶν B : ἡμῶν αἱ ψυχαὶ T W Stob.   d 3 γίγνοιτο B T : γένοιτο W Stob.   d 8 ῥᾷον B Stob. : ῥᾴδιον T W   e 1 ἴδωμεν Olymp. Stob. : εἰδῶμεν B T W   οὕτως W   πάντα B W Olymp. Stob. : ἅπαντα T   e 4 τοῦτο οὖν B W Stob. : om. T e 5 ἔστι τι B T Stob. : ἔστιν W   e 6 ἑαυτῷ W

7*

Ναί.

10 Οὐκοῦν κἂν ἔλαττον γίγνηται, ἐκ μείζονος ὄντος πρότερον
71 ὕστερον ἔλαττον γενήσεται;

Ἔστιν οὕτω, ἔφη.

Καὶ μὴν ἐξ ἰσχυροτέρου γε τὸ ἀσθενέστερον καὶ ἐκ βρα-
δυτέρου τὸ θᾶττον;

5 Πάνυ γε.

Τί δέ; ἄν τι χεῖρον γίγνηται, οὐκ ἐξ ἀμείνονος, καὶ ἂν
δικαιότερον, ἐξ ἀδικωτέρου;

Πῶς γὰρ οὔ;

Ἱκανῶς οὖν, ἔφη, ἔχομεν τοῦτο, ὅτι πάντα οὕτω γίγνεται,
10 ἐξ ἐναντίων τὰ ἐναντία πράγματα;

Πάνυ γε.

Τί δ᾽ αὖ; ἔστι τι καὶ τοιόνδε ἐν αὐτοῖς, οἷον μεταξὺ
ἀμφοτέρων πάντων τῶν ἐναντίων δυοῖν ὄντοιν δύο γενέσεις,
b ἀπὸ μὲν τοῦ ἑτέρου ἐπὶ τὸ ἕτερον, ἀπὸ δ᾽ αὖ τοῦ ἑτέρου
πάλιν ἐπὶ τὸ ἕτερον· μείζονος μὲν πράγματος καὶ ἐλάττονος
μεταξὺ αὔξησις καὶ φθίσις, καὶ καλοῦμεν οὕτω τὸ μὲν αὐξά-
νεσθαι, τὸ δὲ φθίνειν;

5 Ναί, ἔφη.

Οὐκοῦν καὶ διακρίνεσθαι καὶ συγκρίνεσθαι, καὶ ψύχεσθαι
καὶ θερμαίνεσθαι, καὶ πάντα οὕτω, κἂν εἰ μὴ χρώμεθα τοῖς
ὀνόμασιν ἐνιαχοῦ, ἀλλ᾽ ἔργῳ γοῦν πανταχοῦ οὕτως ἔχειν
ἀναγκαῖον, γίγνεσθαί τε αὐτὰ ἐξ ἀλλήλων γένεσίν τε εἶναι
10 ἑκατέρου εἰς ἄλληλα;

Πάνυ μὲν οὖν, ἦ δ᾽ ὅς.

c Τί οὖν; ἔφη, τῷ ζῆν ἐστί τι ἐναντίον, ὥσπερ τῷ
ἐγρηγορέναι τὸ καθεύδειν;

Πάνυ μὲν οὖν, ἔφη.

Τί;

a 2 οὕτω ἔφη B : ἔφη οὕτω T W Stob.   a 3 γε T Olymp. Stob. :
om. B   a 7 ἐξ B T : οὐκ ἐξ W t Stob.   a 12 ἔστι τι B T : ἔστιν
ἔτι B² : ἔστι W   b 2 μὲν B : γὰρ T : μὲν γὰρ B² W Olymp.
b 10 ἑκατέρου T : ἐξ ἑκατέρου B W   b 11 μὲν οὖν B : γε T W

Τὸ τεθνάναι, ἔφη. 5

Οὐκοῦν ἐξ ἀλλήλων τε γίγνεται ταῦτα, εἴπερ ἐναντία
ἐστιν, καὶ αἱ γενέσεις εἰσὶν αὐτοῖν μεταξὺ δύο δυοῖν ὄντοιν;
Πῶς γὰρ οὔ;

Τὴν μὲν τοίνυν ἑτέραν συζυγίαν ὧν νυνδὴ ἔλεγον ἐγώ
σοι, ἔφη, ἐρῶ, ὁ Σωκράτης, καὶ αὐτὴν καὶ τὰς γενέσεις· σὺ 10
δέ μοι τὴν ἑτέραν. λέγω δὲ τὸ μὲν καθεύδειν, τὸ δὲ ἐγρηγορέναι, καὶ ἐκ τοῦ καθεύδειν τὸ ἐγρηγορέναι γίγνεσθαι καὶ
ἐκ τοῦ ἐγρηγορέναι τὸ καθεύδειν, καὶ τὰς γενέσεις αὐτοῖν d
τὴν μὲν καταδαρθάνειν εἶναι, τὴν δ' ἀνεγείρεσθαι. ἱκανῶς
σοι, ἔφη, ἢ οὔ;

Πάνυ μὲν οὖν.

Λέγε δή μοι καὶ σύ, ἔφη, οὕτω περὶ ζωῆς καὶ θανάτου. 5
οὐκ ἐναντίον μὲν φὴς τῷ ζῆν τὸ τεθνάναι εἶναι;

Ἔγωγε.

Γίγνεσθαι δὲ ἐξ ἀλλήλων;

Ναί.

Ἐξ οὖν τοῦ ζῶντος τί τὸ γιγνόμενον; 10

Τὸ τεθνηκός, ἔφη.

Τί δέ, ἦ δ' ὅς, ἐκ τοῦ τεθνεῶτος;

Ἀναγκαῖον, ἔφη, ὁμολογεῖν ὅτι τὸ ζῶν.

Ἐκ τῶν τεθνεώτων ἄρα, ὦ Κέβης, τὰ ζῶντά τε καὶ οἱ
ζῶντες γίγνονται; 15

Φαίνεται, ἔφη. e

Εἰσὶν ἄρα, ἔφη, αἱ ψυχαὶ ἡμῶν ἐν Ἅιδου.

Ἔοικεν.

Οὐκοῦν καὶ τοῖν γενεσέοιν τοῖν περὶ ταῦτα ἥ γ' ἑτέρα
σαφὴς οὖσα τυγχάνει; τὸ γὰρ ἀποθνῄσκειν σαφὲς δήπου, 5
ἢ οὔ;

Πάνυ μὲν οὖν, ἔφη.

Πῶς οὖν, ἦ δ' ὅς, ποιήσομεν; οὐκ ἀνταποδώσομεν τὴν

c 7 αὐτοῖν B Stob. : αὐτῶν T   c 11 ἐγρηγορέναι . . . 12 καθεύδειν
B² T W Stob. : om. B   d 1 αὐτῶν Stob.   d 5 μοι καὶ σύ B : καὶ
σύ μοι B² T W Stob.   e 2 εἰσὶν ἄρα T W Stob. : ἄρα εἰσὶν B

ἐναντίαν γένεσιν, ἀλλὰ ταύτῃ χωλὴ ἔσται ἡ φύσις; ἢ ἀνάγκη
10 ἀποδοῦναι τῷ ἀποθνήσκειν ἐναντίαν τινὰ γένεσιν;

Πάντως που, ἔφη.

Τίνα ταύτην;

Τὸ ἀναβιώσκεσθαι.

Οὐκοῦν, ἦ δ᾽ ὅς, εἴπερ ἔστι τὸ ἀναβιώσκεσθαι, ἐκ τῶν
72 τεθνεώτων ἂν εἴη γένεσις εἰς τοὺς ζῶντας αὕτη, τὸ ἀναβιώσκεσθαι;

Πάνυ γε.

Ὁμολογεῖται ἄρα ἡμῖν καὶ ταύτῃ τοὺς ζῶντας ἐκ τῶν
5 τεθνεώτων γεγονέναι οὐδὲν ἧττον ἢ τοὺς τεθνεῶτας ἐκ τῶν
ζώντων, τούτου δὲ ὄντος ἱκανόν που ἐδόκει τεκμήριον εἶναι
ὅτι ἀναγκαῖον τὰς τῶν τεθνεώτων ψυχὰς εἶναί που, ὅθεν δὴ
πάλιν γίγνεσθαι.

Δοκεῖ μοι, ἔφη, ὦ Σώκρατες, ἐκ τῶν ὡμολογημένων
10 ἀναγκαῖον οὕτως ἔχειν.

Ἰδὲ τοίνυν οὕτως, ἔφη, ὦ Κέβης, ὅτι οὐδ᾽ ἀδίκως ὡμο-
λογήκαμεν, ὡς ἐμοὶ δοκεῖ. εἰ γὰρ μὴ ἀεὶ ἀνταποδιδοίη τὰ
b ἕτερα τοῖς ἑτέροις γιγνόμενα, ὡσπερεὶ κύκλῳ περιιόντα, ἀλλ᾽
εὐθεῖά τις εἴη ἡ γένεσις ἐκ τοῦ ἑτέρου μόνον εἰς τὸ καταντικρὺ καὶ μὴ ἀνακάμπτοι πάλιν ἐπὶ τὸ ἕτερον μηδὲ καμπὴν
ποιοῖτο, οἶσθ᾽ ὅτι πάντα τελευτῶντα τὸ αὐτὸ σχῆμα ἂν σχοίη
5 καὶ τὸ αὐτὸ πάθος ἂν πάθοι καὶ παύσαιτο γιγνόμενα;

Πῶς λέγεις; ἔφη.

Οὐδὲν χαλεπόν, ἦ δ᾽ ὅς, ἐννοῆσαι ὃ λέγω· ἀλλ᾽ οἶον εἰ
τὸ καταδαρθάνειν μὲν εἴη, τὸ δ᾽ ἀνεγείρεσθαι μὴ ἀνταποδιδοίη
γιγνόμενον ἐκ τοῦ καθεύδοντος, οἶσθ᾽ ὅτι τελευτῶντα πάντ᾽
c ⟨ἂν⟩ λῆρον τὸν Ἐνδυμίωνα ἀποδείξειεν καὶ οὐδαμοῦ ἂν
φαίνοιτο διὰ τὸ καὶ τἆλλα πάντα ταὐτὸν ἐκείνῳ πεπονθέναι,
καθεύδειν. κἂν εἰ συγκρίνοιτο μὲν πάντα, διακρίνοιτο δὲ

---

a 4 ἄρα ἡμῖν B T Stob. : ἡμῖν ἄρα W   a 6 ἐδόκει B Stob. : om. T
a 11 οὕτως B : om. T W   b 4 ποιοῖτο B : ποιοῖ T   b 7 ἐννοῆσαι
B² T W : ἐννοήσασιν B   b 9 πάντ᾽ ἂν Bekker : πάντα B T W
c 3 διακρίνοιτο T : διακρίναιτο B W

μή, ταχὺ ἂν τὸ τοῦ Ἀναξαγόρου γεγονὸς εἴη, " Ὁμοῦ πάντα χρήματα." ὡσαύτως δέ, ὦ φίλε Κέβης, καὶ εἰ ἀποθνήσκοι 5 μὲν πάντα ὅσα τοῦ ζῆν μεταλάβοι, ἐπειδὴ δὲ ἀποθάνοι, μένοι ἐν τούτῳ τῷ σχήματι τὰ τεθνεῶτα καὶ μὴ πάλιν ἀναβιώσκοιτο, ἆρ᾽ οὐ πολλὴ ἀνάγκη τελευτῶντα πάντα τεθνάναι καὶ μηδὲν ζῆν; εἰ γὰρ ἐκ μὲν τῶν ἄλλων τὰ d ζῶντα γίγνοιτο, τὰ δὲ ζῶντα θνῄσκοι, τίς μηχανὴ μὴ οὐχὶ πάντα καταναλωθῆναι εἰς τὸ τεθνάναι;

Οὐδὲ μία μοι δοκεῖ, ἔφη ὁ Κέβης, ὦ Σώκρατες, ἀλλά μοι δοκεῖς παντάπασιν ἀληθῆ λέγειν. 5

Ἔστιν γάρ, ἔφη, ὦ Κέβης, ὡς ἐμοὶ δοκεῖ, παντὸς μᾶλλον οὕτω, καὶ ἡμεῖς αὐτὰ ταῦτα οὐκ ἐξαπατώμενοι ὁμολογοῦμεν, ἀλλ᾽ ἔστι τῷ ὄντι καὶ τὸ ἀναβιώσκεσθαι καὶ ἐκ τῶν τεθνεώτων τοὺς ζῶντας γίγνεσθαι καὶ τὰς τῶν τεθνεώτων ψυχὰς εἶναι [καὶ ταῖς μέν γε ἀγαθαῖς ἄμεινον εἶναι, ταῖς δὲ κακαῖς e κάκιον].

Καὶ μήν, ἔφη ὁ Κέβης ὑπολαβών, καὶ κατ᾽ ἐκεῖνόν γε τὸν λόγον, ὦ Σώκρατες, εἰ ἀληθής ἐστιν, ὃν σὺ εἴωθας θαμὰ λέγειν, ὅτι ἡμῖν ἡ μάθησις οὐκ ἄλλο τι ἢ ἀνάμνησις 5 τυγχάνει οὖσα, καὶ κατὰ τοῦτον ἀνάγκη που ἡμᾶς ἐν προτέρῳ τινὶ χρόνῳ μεμαθηκέναι ἃ νῦν ἀναμιμνῃσκόμεθα. τοῦτο δὲ ἀδύνατον, εἰ μὴ ἦν που ἡμῖν ἡ ψυχὴ πρὶν ἐν τῷδε τῷ ἀν- 73 θρωπίνῳ εἴδει γενέσθαι· ὥστε καὶ ταύτῃ ἀθάνατον ἡ ψυχή τι ἔοικεν εἶναι.

Ἀλλά, ὦ Κέβης, ἔφη ὁ Σιμμίας ὑπολαβών, ποῖαι τούτων αἱ ἀποδείξεις; ὑπόμνησόν με· οὐ γὰρ σφόδρα ἐν τῷ παρόντι 5 μέμνημαι.

Ἑνὶ μὲν λόγῳ, ἔφη ὁ Κέβης, καλλίστῳ, ὅτι ἐρωτώμενοι οἱ ἄνθρωποι, ἐάν τις καλῶς ἐρωτᾷ, αὐτοὶ λέγουσιν πάντα ᾗ ἔχει—καίτοι εἰ μὴ ἐτύγχανεν αὐτοῖς ἐπιστήμη ἐνοῦσα καὶ

c 5 καὶ T W: om. B   d 2 οὐχὶ T b: οὐχ W: που B   d 7 αὐτὰ B: τὰ αὐτὰ T W   e 1–2 καὶ . . . κάκιον secl. Stallbaum   γε B: om. T Olymp.   e 6 τοῦτον B: τοῦτο T   a 1 ἡμῖν B: ἡμῶν T W a 2 ἢ B T: τι ἢ W   ἡ ψυχή τι ἔοικεν B (ut vid.) W: τι ἔοικεν ἡ ψυχὴ T b Olymp.

10 ὀρθὸς λόγος, οὐκ ἂν οἷοί τ' ἦσαν τοῦτο ποιῆσαι—ἔπειτα
b ἐάν τις ἐπὶ τὰ διαγράμματα ἄγῃ ἢ ἄλλο τι τῶν τοιούτων,
    ἐνταῦθα σαφέστατα κατηγορεῖ ὅτι τοῦτο οὕτως ἔχει.

    Εἰ δὲ μὴ ταύτῃ γε, ἔφη, πείθῃ, ὦ Σιμμία, ὁ Σωκράτης,
    σκέψαι ἂν τῇδέ πῃ σοι σκοπουμένῳ συνδόξῃ. ἀπιστεῖς γὰρ
5 δὴ πῶς ἡ καλουμένη μάθησις ἀνάμνησίς ἐστιν;
    Ἀπιστῶ μέν [σοι] ἔγωγε, ἦ δ' ὃς ὁ Σιμμίας, οὔ, αὐτὸ δὲ
    τοῦτο, ἔφη, δέομαι παθεῖν περὶ οὗ ὁ λόγος, ἀναμνησθῆναι.
    καὶ σχεδόν γε ἐξ ὧν Κέβης ἐπεχείρησε λέγειν ἤδη μέμνημαι
    καὶ πείθομαι· οὐδὲν μεντἂν ἧττον ἀκούοιμι νῦν πῇ σὺ ἐπ-
10 εχείρησας λέγειν.

c   Τῇδ' ἔγωγε, ἦ δ' ὅς. ὁμολογοῦμεν γὰρ δήπου, εἴ τίς τι
    ἀναμνησθήσεται, δεῖν αὐτὸν τοῦτο πρότερόν ποτε ἐπίστασθαι.
    Πάνυ γ', ἔφη.

    Ἆρ' οὖν καὶ τόδε ὁμολογοῦμεν, ὅταν ἐπιστήμη παρα-
5 γίγνηται τρόπῳ τοιούτῳ, ἀνάμνησιν εἶναι; λέγω δὲ τίνα
    τρόπον; τόνδε. ἐάν τίς τι ἕτερον ἢ ἰδὼν ἢ ἀκούσας ἤ τινα
    ἄλλην αἴσθησιν λαβὼν μὴ μόνον ἐκεῖνο γνῷ, ἀλλὰ καὶ
    ἕτερον ἐννοήσῃ οὗ μὴ ἡ αὐτὴ ἐπιστήμη ἀλλ' ἄλλη, ἆρα
    οὐχὶ τοῦτο δικαίως λέγομεν ὅτι ἀνεμνήσθη, οὗ τὴν ἔννοιαν
d   ἔλαβεν;
    Πῶς λέγεις;
    Οἷον τὰ τοιάδε· ἄλλη που ἐπιστήμη ἀνθρώπου καὶ λύρας.
    Πῶς γὰρ οὔ;
5   Οὐκοῦν οἶσθα ὅτι οἱ ἐρασταί, ὅταν ἴδωσιν λύραν ἢ ἱμάτιον
    ἢ ἄλλο τι οἷς τὰ παιδικὰ αὐτῶν εἴωθε χρῆσθαι, πάσχουσι
    τοῦτο· ἔγνωσάν τε τὴν λύραν καὶ ἐν τῇ διανοίᾳ ἔλαβον τὸ

a 10 ποιῆσαι Hirschig : ποιήσειν B : ποιεῖν T W   b 4 σοι T W : σοι
ἂν B (sed ἂν punct. not.)   b 6 σοι B : om. T W   b 7 παθεῖν
Heindorf : μαθεῖν B T W   b 9 μέντ' ἂν B² W : μὲν ἂν B T   πῇ
σὺ B T : σὺ πῇ B² W   c 1 τῇδ' B : τί δὲ T   c 6 τόνδε B :
τοῦτον T   ἕτερον T : πρότερον B Olymp.   ἢ (post ἕτερον) B Olymp. :
τι T   c 9 λέγομεν T W : ἐλέγομεν B   d 6 ἄλλο τι B : τι
ἄλλο T

εἶδος τοῦ παιδὸς οὗ ἦν ἡ λύρα; τοῦτο δέ ἐστιν ἀνάμνησις·
ὥσπερ γε καὶ Σιμμίαν τις ἰδὼν πολλάκις Κέβητος ἀνεμνήσθη,
καὶ ἄλλα που μυρία τοιαῦτ᾽ ἂν εἴη.   10

Μυρία μέντοι νὴ Δία, ἔφη ὁ Σιμμίας.

Οὐκοῦν, ἦ δ᾽ ὅς, τὸ τοιοῦτον ἀνάμνησίς τίς ἐστι; μάλιστα e
μέντοι ὅταν τις τοῦτο πάθῃ περὶ ἐκεῖνα ἃ ὑπὸ χρόνου καὶ τοῦ
μὴ ἐπισκοπεῖν ἤδη ἐπελέληστο;

Πάνυ μὲν οὖν, ἔφη.

Τί δέ; ἦ δ᾽ ὅς· ἔστιν ἵππον γεγραμμένον ἰδόντα καὶ 5
λύραν γεγραμμένην ἀνθρώπου ἀναμνησθῆναι, καὶ Σιμμίαν
ἰδόντα γεγραμμένον Κέβητος ἀναμνησθῆναι;

Πάνυ γε.

Οὐκοῦν καὶ Σιμμίαν ἰδόντα γεγραμμένον αὐτοῦ Σιμμίου
ἀναμνησθῆναι;   10

Ἔστι μέντοι, ἔφη.   74

Ἆρ᾽ οὖν οὐ κατὰ πάντα ταῦτα συμβαίνει τὴν ἀνάμνησιν
εἶναι μὲν ἀφ᾽ ὁμοίων, εἶναι δὲ καὶ ἀπὸ ἀνομοίων;

Συμβαίνει.

Ἀλλ᾽ ὅταν γε ἀπὸ τῶν ὁμοίων ἀναμιμνήσκηταί τίς τι, ἆρ᾽ 5
οὐκ ἀναγκαῖον τόδε προσπάσχειν, ἐννοεῖν εἴτε τι ἐλλείπει
τοῦτο κατὰ τὴν ὁμοιότητα εἴτε μὴ ἐκείνου οὗ ἀνεμνήσθη;

Ἀνάγκη, ἔφη.

Σκόπει δή, ἦ δ᾽ ὅς, εἰ ταῦτα οὕτως ἔχει. φαμέν πού τι
εἶναι ἴσον, οὐ ξύλον λέγω ξύλῳ οὐδὲ λίθον λίθῳ οὐδ᾽ ἄλλο 10
τῶν τοιούτων οὐδέν, ἀλλὰ παρὰ ταῦτα πάντα ἕτερόν τι, αὐτὸ
τὸ ἴσον· φῶμέν τι εἶναι ἢ μηδέν;

Φῶμεν μέντοι νὴ Δί᾽, ἔφη ὁ Σιμμίας, θαυμαστῶς γε.   b

Ἦ καὶ ἐπιστάμεθα αὐτὸ ὃ ἔστιν;

Πάνυ γε, ἦ δ᾽ ὅς.

Πόθεν λαβόντες αὐτοῦ τὴν ἐπιστήμην; ἆρ᾽ οὐκ ἐξ ὧν
νυνδὴ ἐλέγομεν, ἢ ξύλα ἢ λίθους ἢ ἄλλα ἄττα ἰδόντες 5

---

d 9 γε B T W : om. B   e 9 αὐτοῦ B : αὖ τοῦ T   a 10 ἄλλο
B T : ἄλλο τι B² W   a 11 ταῦτα πάντα B : πάντα ταῦτα T W
a 12 τὸ B T W : τε B   b 1 μέντοι B : τοίνυν T   b 2 ἐστιν B T :
ἐστιν ἴσον W : ἴσον in marg. B² T²

ἴσα, ἐκ τούτων ἐκεῖνο ἐνενοήσαμεν, ἕτερον ὂν τούτων; ἢ
οὐχ ἕτερόν σοι φαίνεται; σκόπει δὲ καὶ τῇδε. ἆρ' οὐ λίθοι
μὲν ἴσοι καὶ ξύλα ἐνίοτε ταὐτὰ ὄντα τῷ μὲν ἴσα φαίνεται,
τῷ δ' οὔ;

10 Πάνυ μὲν οὖν.

c Τί δέ; αὐτὰ τὰ ἴσα ἔστιν ὅτε ἄνισά σοι ἐφάνη, ἢ ἡ ἰσότης
ἀνισότης;

Οὐδεπώποτέ γε, ὦ Σώκρατες.

Οὐ ταὐτὸν ἄρα ἐστίν, ἢ δ' ὅς, ταῦτά τε τὰ ἴσα καὶ αὐτὸ
5 τὸ ἴσον.

Οὐδαμῶς μοι φαίνεται, ὦ Σώκρατες.

Ἀλλὰ μὴν ἐκ τούτων γ', ἔφη, τῶν ἴσων, ἑτέρων ὄντων
ἐκείνου τοῦ ἴσου, ὅμως αὐτοῦ τὴν ἐπιστήμην ἐννενόηκάς τε
καὶ εἴληφας;

10 Ἀληθέστατα, ἔφη, λέγεις.

Οὐκοῦν ἢ ὁμοίου ὄντος τούτοις ἢ ἀνομοίου;

Πάνυ γε.

Διαφέρει δέ γε, ἢ δ' ὅς, οὐδέν· ἕως ἂν ἄλλο ἰδὼν ἀπὸ
d ταύτης τῆς ὄψεως ἄλλο ἐννοήσῃς, εἴτε ὅμοιον εἴτε ἀνόμοιον,
ἀναγκαῖον, ἔφη, αὐτὸ ἀνάμνησιν γεγονέναι.

Πάνυ μὲν οὖν.

Τί δέ; ἢ δ' ὅς· ἢ πάσχομέν τι τοιοῦτον περὶ τὰ ἐν τοῖς
5 ξύλοις τε καὶ οἷς νυνδὴ ἐλέγομεν τοῖς ἴσοις; ἆρα φαίνεται
ἡμῖν οὕτως ἴσα εἶναι ὥσπερ αὐτὸ τὸ ὃ ἔστιν, ἢ ἐνδεῖ τι
ἐκείνου τῷ τοιοῦτον εἶναι οἷον τὸ ἴσον, ἢ οὐδέν;

Καὶ πολύ γε, ἔφη, ἐνδεῖ.

Οὐκοῦν ὁμολογοῦμεν, ὅταν τίς τι ἰδὼν ἐννοήσῃ ὅτι βού-
10 λεται μὲν τοῦτο ὃ νῦν ἐγὼ ὁρῶ εἶναι οἷον ἄλλο τι τῶν ὄντων,
e ἐνδεῖ δὲ καὶ οὐ δύναται τοιοῦτον εἶναι [ἴσον] οἷον ἐκεῖνο, ἀλλ'

b 6 ἴσα B : τὰ ἴσα T   b 8–9 τῷ . . . τῷ B γρ. W : τότε . . . τότε
T W γρ. B   c 13 ἂν B : γὰρ ἂν B² T W   d 1 ἀνόμοιον εἴτε ὅμοιον T
d 4 δέ ; B : δὲ τόδ' T   d 5 τοῖς W : ἐν τοῖς B T   d 6 τὸ ὃ W :
τὸ pr. B (ut vid.): ὃ T : om. B in ras.   ἐστιν B W : ἐστιν ἴσον T b
τι T W : τῷ B   d 7 τῷ] τοῦ Heindorf   e 1 ἴσον secl. Mudge
ἀλλ' ἔστιν] ἀλλ' ἀλλό ἐστιν in marg. B²

ἔστιν φαυλότερον, ἀναγκαῖόν που τὸν τοῦτο ἐννοοῦντα τυχεῖν
προειδότα ἐκεῖνο ᾧ φησιν αὐτὸ προσεοικέναι μέν, ἐνδεεστέρως
δὲ ἔχειν;

Ἀνάγκη.   5

Τί οὖν; τὸ τοιοῦτον πεπόνθαμεν καὶ ἡμεῖς ἢ οὒ περί τε
τὰ ἴσα καὶ αὐτὸ τὸ ἴσον;

Παντάπασί γε.

Ἀναγκαῖον ἄρα ἡμᾶς προειδέναι τὸ ἴσον πρὸ ἐκείνου τοῦ
χρόνου ὅτε τὸ πρῶτον ἰδόντες τὰ ἴσα ἐνενοήσαμεν ὅτι 75
ὀρέγεται μὲν πάντα ταῦτα εἶναι οἷον τὸ ἴσον, ἔχει δὲ
ἐνδεεστέρως.

Ἔστι ταῦτα.

Ἀλλὰ μὴν καὶ τόδε ὁμολογοῦμεν, μὴ ἄλλοθεν αὐτὸ ἐν- 5
νενοηκέναι μηδὲ δυνατὸν εἶναι ἐννοῆσαι ἀλλ᾽ ἢ ἐκ τοῦ ἰδεῖν
ἢ ἅψασθαι ἢ ἔκ τινος ἄλλης τῶν αἰσθήσεων· ταὐτὸν δὲ
πάντα ταῦτα λέγω.

Ταὐτὸν γὰρ ἔστιν, ὦ Σώκρατες, πρός γε ὃ βούλεται
δηλῶσαι ὁ λόγος.   10

Ἀλλὰ μὲν δὴ ἔκ γε τῶν αἰσθήσεων δεῖ ἐννοῆσαι ὅτι
πάντα τὰ ἐν ταῖς αἰσθήσεσιν ἐκείνου τε ὀρέγεται τοῦ ὃ b
ἔστιν ἴσον, καὶ αὐτοῦ ἐνδεέστερά ἐστιν· ἢ πῶς λέγομεν;

Οὕτως.

Πρὸ τοῦ ἄρα ἄρξασθαι ἡμᾶς ὁρᾶν καὶ ἀκούειν καὶ τἆλλα
αἰσθάνεσθαι τυχεῖν ἔδει που εἰληφότας ἐπιστήμην αὐτοῦ 5
τοῦ ἴσου ὅτι ἔστιν, εἰ ἐμέλλομεν τὰ ἐκ τῶν αἰσθήσεων ἴσα
ἐκεῖσε ἀνοίσειν, ὅτι προθυμεῖται μὲν πάντα τοιαῦτ᾽ εἶναι οἷον
ἐκεῖνο, ἔστιν δὲ αὐτοῦ φαυλότερα.

Ἀνάγκη ἐκ τῶν προειρημένων, ὦ Σώκρατες.

Οὐκοῦν γενόμενοι εὐθὺς ἑωρῶμέν τε καὶ ἠκούομεν καὶ τὰς 10
ἄλλας αἰσθήσεις εἴχομεν;

Πάνυ γε.

e 2 τυχεῖν Β Τ : τυγχάνειν Β² W   e 6 τὸ Τ b : om. Β   ἢ Β²
Τ W : om. Β   a 9 γὰρ in marg. Τ   a 11 γε Τ W : om. Β
b 1 τε Β Τ : γε W   τοῦ Β : τοῦθ᾽ Τ   b 4 τοῦ ἄρα Β : γὰρ τοῦ Τ
prius καὶ Β : ἢ Τ   b 7 τοιαῦτ᾽ Β : τὰ τοιαῦτα Τ

c Ἔδει δέ γε, φαμέν, πρὸ τούτων τὴν τοῦ ἴσου ἐπιστήμην
εἰληφέναι;

Ναί.

Πρὶν γενέσθαι ἄρα, ὡς ἔοικεν, ἀνάγκη ἡμῖν αὐτὴν εἰλη-
5 φέναι.

Ἔοικεν.

Οὐκοῦν εἰ μὲν λαβόντες αὐτὴν πρὸ τοῦ γενέσθαι ἔχοντες
ἐγενόμεθα, ἠπιστάμεθα καὶ πρὶν γενέσθαι καὶ εὐθὺς γενόμενοι οὐ μόνον τὸ ἴσον καὶ τὸ μεῖζον καὶ τὸ ἔλαττον ἀλλὰ
10 καὶ σύμπαντα τὰ τοιαῦτα; οὐ γὰρ περὶ τοῦ ἴσου νῦν ὁ λόγος
ἡμῖν μᾶλλόν τι ἢ καὶ περὶ αὐτοῦ τοῦ καλοῦ καὶ αὐτοῦ τοῦ
d ἀγαθοῦ καὶ δικαίου καὶ ὁσίου καί, ὅπερ λέγω, περὶ ἁπάντων
οἷς ἐπισφραγιζόμεθα τὸ " αὐτὸ ὃ ἔστι " καὶ ἐν ταῖς ἐρωτήσεσιν ἐρωτῶντες καὶ ἐν ταῖς ἀποκρίσεσιν ἀποκρινόμενοι.
ὥστε ἀναγκαῖον ἡμῖν τούτων πάντων τὰς ἐπιστήμας πρὸ τοῦ
5 γενέσθαι εἰληφέναι.

Ἔστι ταῦτα.

Καὶ εἰ μέν γε λαβόντες ἑκάστοτε μὴ ἐπιλελήσμεθα,
εἰδότας ἀεὶ γίγνεσθαι καὶ ἀεὶ διὰ βίου εἰδέναι· τὸ γὰρ
εἰδέναι τοῦτ᾽ ἔστιν, λαβόντα του ἐπιστήμην ἔχειν καὶ μὴ
10 ἀπολωλεκέναι· ἢ οὐ τοῦτο λήθην λέγομεν, ὦ Σιμμία, ἐπιστήμης ἀποβολήν;

e Πάντως δήπου, ἔφη, ὦ Σώκρατες.

Εἰ δέ γε οἶμαι λαβόντες πρὶν γενέσθαι γιγνόμενοι ἀπωλέσαμεν, ὕστερον δὲ ταῖς αἰσθήσεσι χρώμενοι περὶ αὐτὰ
ἐκείνας ἀναλαμβάνομεν τὰς ἐπιστήμας ἅς ποτε καὶ πρὶν
5 εἴχομεν, ἆρ᾽ οὐχ ὃ καλοῦμεν μανθάνειν οἰκείαν ἂν ἐπιστήμην
ἀναλαμβάνειν εἴη; τοῦτο δέ που ἀναμιμνήσκεσθαι λέγοντες
ὀρθῶς ἂν λέγοιμεν;

Πάνυ γε.

c 1 τούτων BT : τούτου B² c 11 ἢ TW : om. B d 2 τὸ αὐτὸ
scripsi : τοῦτο BTW : τὸ Iambl. d 4 ἡμῖν B : ἡμῖν εἶναι B²TW
πάντων B : ἁπάντων B²TW d 7 μὴ ἑκάστοτε B²TW d 8 εἰδότας BWt : εἰδότες Tb καὶ ἀεὶ TW : καὶ B d 10 ὦ Σιμμία
om. T e 1 πάντως BT : παντελῶς B²W e 3 αὐτὰ BT : ταῦτα
W e 5 ἂν T : om. B e 6 εἴη T : ἂν εἴη B

Δυνατὸν γὰρ δὴ τοῦτό γε ἐφάνη, αἰσθόμενόν τι ἢ ἰδόντα 76
ἢ ἀκούσαντα ἤ τινα ἄλλην αἴσθησιν λαβόντα ἕτερόν τι ἀπὸ
τούτου ἐννοῆσαι ὃ ἐπελέληστο, ᾧ τοῦτο ἐπλησίαζεν ἀνόμοιον
ὂν ἢ ᾧ ὅμοιον· ὥστε, ὅπερ λέγω, δυοῖν θάτερα, ἤτοι ἐπι-
στάμενοί γε αὐτὰ γεγόναμεν καὶ ἐπιστάμεθα διὰ βίου πάντες, 5
ἢ ὕστερον, οὕς φαμεν μανθάνειν, οὐδὲν ἀλλ' ἢ ἀναμιμνή-
σκονται οὗτοι, καὶ ἡ μάθησις ἀνάμνησις ἂν εἴη.

Καὶ μάλα δὴ οὕτως ἔχει, ὦ Σώκρατες.

Πότερον οὖν αἱρῇ, ὦ Σιμμία; ἐπισταμένους ἡμᾶς γεγονέναι, ἢ ἀναμιμνῄσκεσθαι ὕστερον ὧν πρότερον ἐπιστήμην b
εἰληφότες ἦμεν;

Οὐκ ἔχω, ὦ Σώκρατες, ἐν τῷ παρόντι ἑλέσθαι.

Τί δέ; τόδε ἔχεις ἑλέσθαι, καὶ πῇ σοι δοκεῖ περὶ αὐτοῦ;
ἀνὴρ ἐπιστάμενος περὶ ὧν ἐπίσταται ἔχοι ἂν δοῦναι λόγον 5
ἢ οὔ;

Πολλὴ ἀνάγκη, ἔφη, ὦ Σώκρατες.

Ἦ καὶ δοκοῦσί σοι πάντες ἔχειν διδόναι λόγον περὶ τούτων ὧν νυνδὴ ἐλέγομεν;

Βουλοίμην μεντἂν, ἔφη ὁ Σιμμίας· ἀλλὰ πολὺ μᾶλλον 10
φοβοῦμαι μὴ αὔριον τηνικάδε οὐκέτι ᾖ ἀνθρώπων οὐδεὶς
ἀξίως οἷός τε τοῦτο ποιῆσαι.

Οὐκ ἄρα δοκοῦσί σοι ἐπίστασθαί γε, ἔφη, ὦ Σιμμία, c
πάντες αὐτά;

Οὐδαμῶς.

Ἀναμιμνῄσκονται ἄρα ἅ ποτε ἔμαθον;

Ἀνάγκη. 5

Πότε λαβοῦσαι αἱ ψυχαὶ ἡμῶν τὴν ἐπιστήμην αὐτῶν; οὐ
γὰρ δὴ ἀφ' οὗ γε ἄνθρωποι γεγόναμεν.

Οὐ δῆτα.

Πρότερον ἄρα.

Ναί. 10

a 1 αἰσθανόμενόν W   a 4 θάτερον B² T W : τὰ ἕτερα B   b 4 τόδε
W : om. B T   c 4 ἅ ποτε B : ποτε ἃ T   c 6 αὐτῶν B · om. T

Ἦσαν ἄρα, ὦ Σιμμία, αἱ ψυχαὶ καὶ πρότερον, πρὶν εἶναι ἐν ἀνθρώπου εἴδει, χωρὶς σωμάτων, καὶ φρόνησιν εἶχον.

Εἰ μὴ ἄρα ἅμα γιγνόμενοι λαμβάνομεν, ὦ Σώκρατες, 15 ταύτας τὰς ἐπιστήμας· οὗτος γὰρ λείπεται ἔτι ὁ χρόνος.

d Εἶεν, ὦ ἑταῖρε· ἀπόλλυμεν δὲ αὐτὰς ἐν ποίῳ ἄλλῳ χρόνῳ; —οὐ γὰρ δὴ ἔχοντές γε αὐτὰς γιγνόμεθα, ὡς ἄρτι ὡμολογήσαμεν—ἢ ἐν τούτῳ ἀπόλλυμεν ἐν ᾧπερ καὶ λαμβάνομεν; ἢ ἔχεις ἄλλον τινὰ εἰπεῖν χρόνον;

5 Οὐδαμῶς, ὦ Σώκρατες, ἀλλὰ ἔλαθον ἐμαυτὸν οὐδὲν εἰπών.

Ἆρ᾽ οὖν οὕτως ἔχει, ἔφη, ἡμῖν, ὦ Σιμμία; εἰ μὲν ἔστιν ἃ θρυλοῦμεν ἀεί, καλόν τέ τι καὶ ἀγαθὸν καὶ πᾶσα ἡ τοιαύτη οὐσία, καὶ ἐπὶ ταύτην τὰ ἐκ τῶν αἰσθήσεων πάντα ἀνα-
e φέρομεν, ὑπάρχουσαν πρότερον ἀνευρίσκοντες ἡμετέραν οὖσαν, καὶ ταῦτα ἐκείνῃ ἀπεικάζομεν, ἀναγκαῖον, οὕτως ὥσπερ καὶ ταῦτα ἔστιν, οὕτως καὶ τὴν ἡμετέραν ψυχὴν εἶναι καὶ πρὶν γεγονέναι ἡμᾶς· εἰ δὲ μὴ ἔστι ταῦτα, ἄλλως ἂν ὁ λόγος
5 οὗτος εἰρημένος εἴη; ἆρ᾽ οὕτως ἔχει, καὶ ἴση ἀνάγκη ταῦτά τε εἶναι καὶ τὰς ἡμετέρας ψυχὰς πρὶν καὶ ἡμᾶς γεγονέναι, καὶ εἰ μὴ ταῦτα, οὐδὲ τάδε;

Ὑπερφυῶς, ὦ Σώκρατες, ἔφη ὁ Σιμμίας, δοκεῖ μοι ἡ αὐτὴ ἀνάγκη εἶναι, καὶ εἰς καλόν γε καταφεύγει ὁ λόγος εἰς
77 τὸ ὁμοίως εἶναι τήν τε ψυχὴν ἡμῶν πρὶν γενέσθαι ἡμᾶς καὶ τὴν οὐσίαν ἣν σὺ νῦν λέγεις. οὐ γὰρ ἔχω ἔγωγε οὐδὲν οὕτω μοι ἐναργὲς ὂν ὡς τοῦτο, τὸ πάντα τὰ τοιαῦτ᾽ εἶναι ὡς οἷόν τε μάλιστα, καλόν τε καὶ ἀγαθὸν καὶ τἆλλα πάντα ἃ
5 σὺ νυνδὴ ἔλεγες· καὶ ἔμοιγε δοκεῖ ἱκανῶς ἀποδέδεικται.

Τί δὲ δὴ Κέβητι; ἔφη ὁ Σωκράτης· δεῖ γὰρ καὶ Κέβητα πείθειν.

Ἱκανῶς, ἔφη ὁ Σιμμίας, ὡς ἔγωγε οἶμαι· καίτοι καρτερώ-

c 11 πρὶν ἂν W   c 14 ἅμα W: om. BT   c 15 ὁ om. W
d 3 ἐν ᾧπερ B: ᾧπερ T   d 7 ἔφη ἡμῖν ἔχει W   d 8 τι B²TW:
om. B   e 8 ἔφη ὦ σώκρατες W   a 4 πάντα BT: ἅπαντα B²W
a 5 ἐμοὶ ἐδόκει B: ἔμοιγε B²T: μοί γε W

τατος ἀνθρώπων ἐστὶν πρὸς τὸ ἀπιστεῖν τοῖς λόγοις. ἀλλ᾽
οἶμαι οὐκ ἐνδεῶς τοῦτο πεπεῖσθαι αὐτόν, ὅτι πρὶν γενέσθαι
ἡμᾶς ἦν ἡμῶν ἡ ψυχή· εἰ μέντοι καὶ ἐπειδὰν ἀποθάνωμεν b
ἔτι ἔσται, οὐδὲ αὐτῷ μοι δοκεῖ, ἔφη, ὦ Σώκρατες, ἀποδεδεῖχθαι, ἀλλ᾽ ἔτι ἐνέστηκεν ὁ νυνδὴ Κέβης ἔλεγε, τὸ τῶν
πολλῶν, ὅπως μὴ ἅμα ἀποθνήσκοντος τοῦ ἀνθρώπου διασκεδάννυται ἡ ψυχὴ καὶ αὐτῇ τοῦ εἶναι τοῦτο τέλος ᾖ. τί 5
γὰρ κωλύει γίγνεσθαι μὲν αὐτὴν καὶ συνίστασθαι ἄλλοθέν
ποθεν καὶ εἶναι πρὶν καὶ εἰς ἀνθρώπειον σῶμα ἀφικέσθαι,
ἐπειδὰν δὲ ἀφίκηται καὶ ἀπαλλάττηται τούτου, τότε καὶ αὐτὴν
τελευτᾶν καὶ διαφθείρεσθαι;

Εὖ λέγεις, ἔφη, ὦ Σιμμία, ὁ Κέβης. φαίνεται γὰρ c
ὥσπερ ἥμισυ ἀποδεδεῖχθαι οὗ δεῖ, ὅτι πρὶν γενέσθαι ἡμᾶς
ἦν ἡμῶν ἡ ψυχή, δεῖ δὲ προσαποδεῖξαι ὅτι καὶ ἐπειδὰν
ἀποθάνωμεν οὐδὲν ἧττον ἔσται ἢ πρὶν γενέσθαι, εἰ μέλλει
τέλος ἡ ἀπόδειξις ἕξειν. 5

Ἀποδέδεικται μέν, ἔφη, ὦ Σιμμία τε καὶ Κέβης, ὁ
Σωκράτης, καὶ νῦν, εἰ ᾽θέλετε συνθεῖναι τοῦτό τε τὸν
λόγον εἰς ταὐτὸν καὶ ὃν πρὸ τούτου ὡμολογήσαμεν, τὸ
γίγνεσθαι πᾶν τὸ ζῶν ἐκ τοῦ τεθνεῶτος. εἰ γὰρ ἔστιν μὲν
ἡ ψυχὴ καὶ πρότερον, ἀνάγκη δὲ αὐτῇ εἰς τὸ ζῆν ἰούσῃ τε d
καὶ γιγνομένῃ μηδαμόθεν ἄλλοθεν ἢ ἐκ θανάτου καὶ τοῦ
τεθνάναι γίγνεσθαι, πῶς οὐκ ἀνάγκη αὐτὴν καὶ ἐπειδὰν
ἀποθάνῃ εἶναι, ἐπειδή γε δεῖ αὖθις αὐτὴν γίγνεσθαι; ἀποδέδεικται μὲν οὖν ὅπερ λέγετε καὶ νῦν. ὅμως δέ μοι δοκεῖς 5
σύ τε καὶ Σιμμίας ἡδέως ἂν καὶ τοῦτον διαπραγματεύσασθαι
τὸν λόγον ἔτι μᾶλλον, καὶ δεδιέναι τὸ τῶν παίδων, μὴ ὡς
ἀληθῶς ὁ ἄνεμος αὐτὴν ἐκβαίνουσαν ἐκ τοῦ σώματος δια-

a 9 ἐστὶν ... ἀπιστεῖν in marg. T   τοῖς in ras T   b 2 δοκεῖ
om. pr. W   ὦ σώκρατες ἔφη T   b 4 ἅμα B² T W : om. B   δια-
σκεδαννῦται Matthiae   b 6 ἀμόθεν Bekker : ἄλλοθεν B T W   c 3 δει
B : δεῖν T   ὅτι B : ἔτι εἰ T (εἰ s. v.) W   c 5 ἕξειν T : ἔχειν B
c 9 μὲν B : om. T W   d 2 καὶ B : τε καὶ ἐκ T   d 3 αὐτὴν T b :
αὐτῇ B (ut vid.) W   d 4 γε B : δὲ T sed punct. not.   αὐτὴν
αὖθις W   d 5 λέγετε Par. 1811 : λέγεται B T W

e   φυσᾷ καὶ διασκεδάννυσιν, ἄλλως τε καὶ ὅταν τύχῃ τις μὴ ἐν
νηνεμίᾳ ἀλλ' ἐν μεγάλῳ τινὶ πνεύματι ἀποθνῄσκων.

Καὶ ὁ Κέβης ἐπιγελάσας, Ὡς δεδιότων, ἔφη, ὦ Σώκρατες,
πειρῶ ἀναπείθειν· μᾶλλον δὲ μὴ ὡς ἡμῶν δεδιότων, ἀλλ'
5 ἴσως ἔνι τις καὶ ἐν ἡμῖν παῖς ὅστις τὰ τοιαῦτα φοβεῖται.
τοῦτον οὖν πειρῶ μεταπείθειν μὴ δεδιέναι τὸν θάνατον ὥσπερ
τὰ μορμολύκεια.

Ἀλλὰ χρή, ἔφη ὁ Σωκράτης, ἐπᾴδειν αὐτῷ ἑκάστης ἡμέρας
ἕως ἂν ἐξεπᾴσητε.

78   Πόθεν οὖν, ἔφη, ὦ Σώκρατες, τῶν τοιούτων ἀγαθὸν ἐπῳδὸν
ληψόμεθα, ἐπειδὴ σύ, ἔφη, ἡμᾶς ἀπολείπεις;

Πολλὴ μὲν ἡ Ἑλλάς, ἔφη, ὦ Κέβης, ἐν ᾗ ἔνεισί που
ἀγαθοὶ ἄνδρες, πολλὰ δὲ καὶ τὰ τῶν βαρβάρων γένη, οὓς
5 πάντας χρὴ διερευνᾶσθαι ζητοῦντας τοιοῦτον ἐπῳδόν, μήτε
χρημάτων φειδομένους μήτε πόνων, ὡς οὐκ ἔστιν εἰς ὅτι
ἂν εὐκαιρότερον ἀναλίσκοιτε χρήματα. ζητεῖν δὲ χρὴ καὶ
αὐτοὺς μετ' ἀλλήλων· ἴσως γὰρ ἂν οὐδὲ ῥᾳδίως εὕροιτε
μᾶλλον ὑμῶν δυναμένους τοῦτο ποιεῖν.

10   Ἀλλὰ ταῦτα μὲν δή, ἔφη, ὑπάρξει, ὁ Κέβης· ὅθεν δὲ
b   ἀπελίπομεν ἐπανέλθωμεν, εἴ σοι ἡδομένῳ ἐστίν.

Ἀλλὰ μὴν ἡδομένῳ γε· πῶς γὰρ οὐ μέλλει;

Καλῶς, ἔφη, λέγεις.

Οὐκοῦν τοιόνδε τι, ἦ δ' ὃς ὁ Σωκράτης, δεῖ ἡμᾶς ἀνερέσθαι
5 ἑαυτούς, τῷ ποίῳ τινὶ ἄρα προσήκει τοῦτο τὸ πάθος πάσχειν,
τὸ διασκεδάννυσθαι, καὶ ὑπὲρ τοῦ ποίου τινὸς δεδιέναι μὴ
πάθῃ αὐτό, καὶ τῷ ποίῳ τινὶ ⟨οὔ⟩· καὶ μετὰ τοῦτο αὖ
ἐπισκέψασθαι πότερον [ἦ] ψυχή ἐστιν, καὶ ἐκ τούτων
θαρρεῖν ἢ δεδιέναι ὑπὲρ τῆς ἡμετέρας ψυχῆς;

10   Ἀληθῆ, ἔφη, λέγεις.

c   Ἆρ' οὖν τῷ μὲν συντεθέντι τε καὶ συνθέτῳ ὄντι φύσει

e 6 πειρῶ μεταπείθειν W : πειρώμεθα πείθειν B T   e 9 ἐξεπᾴσητε
Vind. 21 T² : ἐξαπᾴσητε T : ἐξεπᾴσηται W : ἐξιάσηται B γρ. W et in
marg. t   a 1 ἀγαθῶν pr. T   a 7 ἂν εὐκαιρότερον T : ἀναγκαιότερον
B W γρ. T   a 10 ὑπάρξει ἔφη B² T W   b 1 ἀπελείπομεν T W
b 4 ἀνερέσθαι T W Olymp. : ἐρέσθαι B   b 6 τὸ T W Olymp. : τοῦ B
b 7 οὔ add. Heindorf   b 8 ἦ B : om. T W

προσήκει τοῦτο πάσχειν, διαιρεθῆναι ταύτῃ ᾗπερ συνετέθη·
εἰ δέ τι τυγχάνει ὂν ἀσύνθετον, τούτῳ μόνῳ προσήκει μὴ
πάσχειν ταῦτα, εἴπερ τῳ ἄλλῳ;

Δοκεῖ μοι, ἔφη, οὕτως ἔχειν, ὁ Κέβης. 5

Οὐκοῦν ἅπερ ἀεὶ κατὰ ταὐτὰ καὶ ὡσαύτως ἔχει, ταῦτα
μάλιστα εἰκὸς εἶναι τὰ ἀσύνθετα, τὰ δὲ ἄλλοτ' ἄλλως καὶ
μηδέποτε κατὰ ταὐτά, ταῦτα δὲ σύνθετα;

Ἔμοιγε δοκεῖ οὕτως.

Ἴωμεν δή, ἔφη, ἐπὶ ταὐτὰ ἐφ' ἅπερ ἐν τῷ ἔμπροσθεν 10
λόγῳ. αὐτὴ ἡ οὐσία ἧς λόγον δίδομεν τοῦ εἶναι καὶ ἐρω- d
τῶντες καὶ ἀποκρινόμενοι, πότερον ὡσαύτως ἀεὶ ἔχει κατὰ
ταὐτὰ ἢ ἄλλοτ' ἄλλως; αὐτὸ τὸ ἴσον, αὐτὸ τὸ καλόν, αὐτὸ
ἕκαστον ὃ ἔστιν, τὸ ὄν, μή ποτε μεταβολὴν καὶ ἡντινοῦν
ἐνδέχεται; ἢ ἀεὶ αὐτῶν ἕκαστον ὃ ἔστι, μονοειδὲς ὂν αὐτὸ 5
καθ' αὑτό, ὡσαύτως κατὰ ταὐτὰ ἔχει καὶ οὐδέποτε οὐδαμῇ
οὐδαμῶς ἀλλοίωσιν οὐδεμίαν ἐνδέχεται;

Ὡσαύτως, ἔφη, ἀνάγκη, ὁ Κέβης, κατὰ ταὐτὰ ἔχειν, ὦ
Σώκρατες.

Τί δὲ τῶν πολλῶν καλῶν, οἷον ἀνθρώπων ἢ ἵππων ἢ 10
ἱματίων ἢ ἄλλων ὡντινωνοῦν τοιούτων, ἢ ἴσων [ἢ καλῶν] ἢ e
πάντων τῶν ἐκείνοις ὁμωνύμων; ἆρα κατὰ ταὐτὰ ἔχει, ἢ πᾶν
τοὐναντίον ἐκείνοις οὔτε αὐτὰ αὑτοῖς οὔτε ἀλλήλοις οὐδέποτε
ὡς ἔπος εἰπεῖν οὐδαμῶς κατὰ ταὐτά;

Οὕτως αὖ, ἔφη ὁ Κέβης, ταῦτα· οὐδέποτε ὡσαύτως ἔχει. 5

Οὐκοῦν τούτων μὲν κἂν ἅψαιο κἂν ἴδοις κἂν ταῖς ἄλλαις 79
αἰσθήσεσιν αἴσθοιο, τῶν δὲ κατὰ ταὐτὰ ἐχόντων οὐκ ἔστιν
ὅτῳ ποτ' ἂν ἄλλῳ ἐπιλάβοιο ἢ τῷ τῆς διανοίας λογισμῷ,
ἀλλ' ἔστιν ἀιδῆ τὰ τοιαῦτα καὶ οὐχ ὁρατά;

c 4 ταῦτα Β (sed punct. not.): τὰ αὐτὰ Τ   c 7 τὰ] ἃ Heindorf
c 8 δὲ Β Τ : δὲ εἶναι Β² W t   d 2 κατὰ ταὐτὰ Β² Τ : κατὰ τὰ
αὐτὰ W : κατ αυτὰ Β   d 10 καλῶν secl. Classen   e 1 ἢ ante
ἴσων om. Τ   ἢ καλῶν seclusi   e 3 οὔτε Β Τ : καὶ οὔτε Β² W
οὐδεπώποτε Β² W   e 4 ταὐτά Β : ταῦτά ἐστιν Β² Τ W   e 5 αὖ
Τ b: om. Β   ταῦτα Β² Τ : om. Β   a 4 ἀιδῆ] ἀιδές, ἀιδῆ constanter
pr. Τ Ars. : ἀειδές, ἀειδῆ Β   ὁρατά Β : ὁρᾶται Τ (sed ex emend.) W

5 Παντάπασιν, ἔφη, ἀληθῆ λέγεις.

Θῶμεν οὖν βούλει, ἔφη, δύο εἴδη τῶν ὄντων, τὸ μὲν ὁρατόν, τὸ δὲ ἀιδές;

Θῶμεν, ἔφη.

Καὶ τὸ μὲν ἀιδὲς ἀεὶ κατὰ ταὐτὰ ἔχον, τὸ δὲ ὁρατὸν 10 μηδέποτε κατὰ ταὐτά;

Καὶ τοῦτο, ἔφη, θῶμεν.

b Φέρε δή, ἦ δ' ὅς, ἄλλο τι ἡμῶν αὐτῶν τὸ μὲν σῶμά ἐστι, τὸ δὲ ψυχή;

Οὐδὲν ἄλλο, ἔφη.

Ποτέρῳ οὖν ὁμοιότερον τῷ εἴδει φαμὲν ἂν εἶναι καὶ 5 συγγενέστερον τὸ σῶμα;

Παντί, ἔφη, τοῦτό γε δῆλον, ὅτι τῷ ὁρατῷ.

Τί δὲ ἡ ψυχή; ὁρατὸν ἢ ἀιδές;

Οὐχ ὑπ' ἀνθρώπων γε, ὦ Σώκρατες, ἔφη.

Ἀλλὰ μὴν ἡμεῖς γε τὰ ὁρατὰ καὶ τὰ μὴ τῇ τῶν ἀνθρώπων 10 φύσει ἐλέγομεν· ἢ ἄλλῃ τινὶ οἴει;

Τῇ τῶν ἀνθρώπων.

Τί οὖν περὶ ψυχῆς λέγομεν; ὁρατὸν ἢ ἀόρατον εἶναι;

Οὐχ ὁρατόν.

Ἀιδὲς ἄρα;

15 Ναί.

Ὁμοιότερον ἄρα ψυχὴ σώματός ἐστιν τῷ ἀιδεῖ, τὸ δὲ τῷ ὁρατῷ.

c Πᾶσα ἀνάγκη, ὦ Σώκρατες.

Οὐκοῦν καὶ τόδε πάλαι ἐλέγομεν, ὅτι ἡ ψυχή, ὅταν μὲν τῷ σώματι προσχρῆται εἰς τὸ σκοπεῖν τι ἢ διὰ τοῦ ὁρᾶν ἢ διὰ τοῦ ἀκούειν ἢ δι' ἄλλης τινὸς αἰσθήσεως—τοῦτο γάρ 5 ἐστιν τὸ διὰ τοῦ σώματος, τὸ δι' αἰσθήσεως σκοπεῖν τι—

---

a 6 βούλει B T Stob. : εἰ βούλει B W   b 4 φαμὲν T Stob. : φαῖμεν B Eus.   b 9 μὴν T W Eus. Stob. : om. B   b 10 ἐλέγομεν B² T W (ante φύσει) Eus. Stob. : λέγομεν B   b 12 λέγομεν B T Eus. Stob. : ἐλέγομεν B² W t   ἢ ἀόρατον B Eus. Stob.: om. T   c 2 ἐλέγομεν B T W Eus. Stob. : λέγομεν Theodoretus   c 5 αἰσθήσεως B² T W Stob. : αἰσθήσεων B

τότε μὲν ἕλκεται ὑπὸ τοῦ σώματος εἰς τὰ οὐδέποτε κατὰ
ταὐτὰ ἔχοντα, καὶ αὐτὴ πλανᾶται καὶ ταράττεται καὶ εἰλιγγιᾷ
ὥσπερ μεθύουσα, ἅτε τοιούτων ἐφαπτομένη;

Πάνυ γε.

῞Οταν δέ γε αὐτὴ καθ᾽ αὑτὴν σκοπῇ, ἐκεῖσε οἴχεται εἰς d
τὸ καθαρόν τε καὶ ἀεὶ ὂν καὶ ἀθάνατον καὶ ὡσαύτως ἔχον,
καὶ ὡς συγγενὴς οὖσα αὐτοῦ ἀεὶ μετ᾽ ἐκείνου τε γίγνεται,
ὅτανπερ αὐτὴ καθ᾽ αὑτὴν γένηται καὶ ἐξῇ αὐτῇ, καὶ πέπαυταί
τε τοῦ πλάνου καὶ περὶ ἐκεῖνα ἀεὶ κατὰ ταὐτὰ ὡσαύτως ἔχει, 5
ἅτε τοιούτων ἐφαπτομένη· καὶ τοῦτο αὐτῆς τὸ πάθημα φρόνησις κέκληται;

Παντάπασιν, ἔφη, καλῶς καὶ ἀληθῆ λέγεις, ὦ Σώκρατες.

Ποτέρῳ οὖν αὖ σοι δοκεῖ τῷ εἴδει καὶ ἐκ τῶν πρόσθεν καὶ ἐκ
τῶν νῦν λεγομένων ψυχὴ ὁμοιότερον εἶναι καὶ συγγενέστερον; e

Πᾶς ἄν μοι δοκεῖ, ἦ δ᾽ ὅς, συγχωρῆσαι, ὦ Σώκρατες, ἐκ
ταύτης τῆς μεθόδου, καὶ ὁ δυσμαθέστατος, ὅτι ὅλῳ καὶ
παντὶ ὁμοιότερόν ἐστι ψυχὴ τῷ ἀεὶ ὡσαύτως ἔχοντι μᾶλλον
ἢ τῷ μή. 5

Τί δὲ τὸ σῶμα;

Τῷ ἑτέρῳ.

῞Ορα δὴ καὶ τῇδε ὅτι ἐπειδὰν ἐν τῷ αὐτῷ ὦσι ψυχὴ καὶ
σῶμα, τῷ μὲν δουλεύειν καὶ ἄρχεσθαι ἡ φύσις προστάττει, 80
τῇ δὲ ἄρχειν καὶ δεσπόζειν· καὶ κατὰ ταῦτα αὖ πότερόν σοι
δοκεῖ ὅμοιον τῷ θείῳ εἶναι καὶ πότερον τῷ θνητῷ; ἢ οὐ
δοκεῖ σοι τὸ μὲν θεῖον οἷον ἄρχειν τε καὶ ἡγεμονεύειν πεφυκέναι, τὸ δὲ θνητὸν ἄρχεσθαί τε καὶ δουλεύειν; 5

Ἔμοιγε.

Ποτέρῳ οὖν ἡ ψυχὴ ἔοικεν;

Δῆλα δή, ὦ Σώκρατες, ὅτι ἡ μὲν ψυχὴ τῷ θείῳ, τὸ δὲ
σῶμα τῷ θνητῷ.

c 6 τότε B² T Eus. : τὸ B Stob. : ὅτε W   d 3 τε in ras. B
d 4 γένηται B T Eus. Stob. : γίγνηται B² W   d 5 τε B T : γε W t
d 8 ἀληθῆ B T Stob. : ἀληθῶς B² W   d 9 πρόσθεν B² T W Eus.
Stob. : ἔμπροσθεν B   e 2 μοι B : ἔμοιγε B² T W Eus. Stob.   e 8 δὴ
B T Eus. Olymp. : δὲ W Stob.   a 2 τῇ ex τῷ T   κατὰ ταὐτὸ
B² T W : καταυτὰ B

10 Σκόπει δή, ἔφη, ὦ Κέβης, εἰ ἐκ πάντων τῶν εἰρημένων
b τάδε ἡμῖν συμβαίνει, τῷ μὲν θείῳ καὶ ἀθανάτῳ καὶ νοητῷ
καὶ μονοειδεῖ καὶ ἀδιαλύτῳ καὶ ἀεὶ ὡσαύτως κατὰ ταὐτὰ
ἔχοντι ἑαυτῷ ὁμοιότατον εἶναι ψυχή, τῷ δὲ ἀνθρωπίνῳ καὶ
θνητῷ καὶ πολυειδεῖ καὶ ἀνοήτῳ καὶ διαλυτῷ καὶ μηδέποτε
5 κατὰ ταὐτὰ ἔχοντι ἑαυτῷ ὁμοιότατον αὖ εἶναι σῶμα. ἔχομέν
τι παρὰ ταῦτα ἄλλο λέγειν, ὦ φίλε Κέβης, ᾗ οὐχ οὕτως ἔχει;
Οὐκ ἔχομεν.

Τί οὖν; τούτων οὕτως ἐχόντων ἆρ' οὐχὶ σώματι μὲν
ταχὺ διαλύεσθαι προσήκει, ψυχῇ δὲ αὖ τὸ παράπαν ἀδια-
10 λύτῳ εἶναι ἢ ἐγγύς τι τούτου;
c Πῶς γὰρ οὔ;

Ἐννοεῖς οὖν, ἔφη, ἐπειδὰν ἀποθάνῃ ὁ ἄνθρωπος, τὸ μὲν
ὁρατὸν αὐτοῦ, τὸ σῶμα, καὶ ἐν ὁρατῷ κείμενον, ὃ δὴ νεκρὸν
καλοῦμεν, ᾧ προσήκει διαλύεσθαι καὶ διαπίπτειν καὶ δια-
5 πνεῖσθαι, οὐκ εὐθὺς τούτων οὐδὲν πέπονθεν, ἀλλ' ἐπιεικῶς
συχνὸν ἐπιμένει χρόνον, ἐὰν μέν τις καὶ χαριέντως ἔχων τὸ
σῶμα τελευτήσῃ καὶ ἐν τοιαύτῃ ὥρᾳ, καὶ πάνυ μάλα· συμ-
πεσὸν γὰρ τὸ σῶμα καὶ ταριχευθέν, ὥσπερ οἱ ἐν Αἰγύπτῳ
ταριχευθέντες, ὀλίγου ὅλον μένει ἀμήχανον ὅσον χρόνον,
d ἔνια δὲ μέρη τοῦ σώματος, καὶ ἂν σαπῇ, ὀστᾶ τε καὶ νεῦρα
καὶ τὰ τοιαῦτα πάντα, ὅμως ὡς ἔπος εἰπεῖν ἀθάνατά ἐστιν·
ἢ οὔ;
Ναί.

5 Ἡ δὲ ψυχὴ ἄρα, τὸ ἀιδές, τὸ εἰς τοιοῦτον τόπον ἕτερον
οἰχόμενον γενναῖον καὶ καθαρὸν καὶ ἀιδῆ, εἰς Ἅιδου ὡς
ἀληθῶς, παρὰ τὸν ἀγαθὸν καὶ φρόνιμον θεόν, οἷ, ἂν θεὸς

b 2 κατὰ B Eus. Stob. : καὶ κατὰ T   b 4 ἀνοήτῳ καὶ πολυειδεῖ
T W Eus. Stob.   b 6 ᾗ Schanz : ἢ B : ᾗ W : ὡς T Eus. Stob. : ἢ
marg. t : ἢ ὡς marg. b   c 2 ἐπειδὰν B: ὅτι ἐπειδὰν B T W Eus. Stob.
c 3 αὐτοῦ τὸ B Eus. : αὐτοῦ T Stob.   c 4 καὶ διαπνεῖσθαι T W b
Eus. Stob. : om. B   c 7 ὥρᾳ T W b Eus. Stob. : ἡμέρᾳ B
d 5 ἕτερον τόπον Ars.   d 6 τὸν γενναῖον Ars.   d 7 τὸν ἀγαθὸν
θεὸν ⟨καὶ φρόνιμον⟩ Ars. (ut vid.)   οἷ δὴ Ars. (ut vid.)

θέλῃ, αὐτίκα καὶ τῇ ἐμῇ ψυχῇ ἰτέον, αὕτη δὲ δὴ ἡμῖν ἡ
τοιαύτη καὶ οὕτω πεφυκυῖα ἀπαλλαττομένη τοῦ σώματος
εὐθὺς διαπεφύσηται καὶ ἀπόλωλεν, ὥς φασιν οἱ πολλοὶ 10
ἄνθρωποι; πολλοῦ γε δεῖ, ὦ φίλε Κέβης τε καὶ Σιμμία, e
ἀλλὰ πολλῷ μᾶλλον ὧδ' ἔχει· ἐὰν μὲν καθαρὰ ἀπαλλάττηται,
μηδὲν τοῦ σώματος συνεφέλκουσα, ἅτε οὐδὲν κοινωνοῦσα
αὐτῷ ἐν τῷ βίῳ ἑκοῦσα εἶναι, ἀλλὰ φεύγουσα αὐτὸ καὶ
συνηθροισμένη αὐτὴ εἰς ἑαυτήν, ἅτε μελετῶσα ἀεὶ τοῦτο— 5
τὸ δὲ οὐδὲν ἄλλο ἐστὶν ἢ ὀρθῶς φιλοσοφοῦσα καὶ τῷ ὄντι
τεθνάναι μελετῶσα ῥᾳδίως· ἢ οὐ τοῦτ' ἂν εἴη μελέτη 81
θανάτου;

Παντάπασί γε.

Οὐκοῦν οὕτω μὲν ἔχουσα εἰς τὸ ὅμοιον αὐτῇ τὸ ἀιδὲς
ἀπέρχεται, τὸ θεῖόν τε καὶ ἀθάνατον καὶ φρόνιμον, οἷ 5
ἀφικομένῃ ὑπάρχει αὐτῇ εὐδαίμονι εἶναι, πλάνης καὶ ἀνοίας
καὶ φόβων καὶ ἀγρίων ἐρώτων καὶ τῶν ἄλλων κακῶν τῶν
ἀνθρωπείων ἀπηλλαγμένη, ὥσπερ δὲ λέγεται κατὰ τῶν με-
μνημένων, ὡς ἀληθῶς τὸν λοιπὸν χρόνον μετὰ θεῶν διάγουσα;
οὕτω φῶμεν, ὦ Κέβης, ἢ ἄλλως; 10

Οὕτω νὴ Δία, ἔφη ὁ Κέβης.

Ἐὰν δέ γε οἶμαι μεμιασμένη καὶ ἀκάθαρτος τοῦ σώματος b
ἀπαλλάττηται, ἅτε τῷ σώματι ἀεὶ συνοῦσα καὶ τοῦτο θερα-
πεύουσα καὶ ἐρῶσα καὶ γοητευομένη ὑπ' αὐτοῦ ὑπό τε τῶν
ἐπιθυμιῶν καὶ ἡδονῶν, ὥστε μηδὲν ἄλλο δοκεῖν εἶναι ἀληθὲς
ἀλλ' ἢ τὸ σωματοειδές, οὗ τις ἂν ἅψαιτο καὶ ἴδοι καὶ πίοι 5
καὶ φάγοι καὶ πρὸς τὰ ἀφροδίσια χρήσαιτο, τὸ δὲ τοῖς
ὄμμασι σκοτῶδες καὶ ἀιδές, νοητὸν δὲ καὶ φιλοσοφίᾳ αἱρετόν,

d 8 θέλει Ars. : ἐθέλῃ Β Τ W Eus. Stob.   e 5 αὐτὴ εἰς ἑαυτὴν
(αὐτὴν) Β² Τ W Eus. Stob. : om. Β   e 6 τὸ Ars. : τοῦτο Β Τ W
Eus. Stob.   a 1 ῥᾳδίως Β Τ W Ars. Eus. Stob. : secl. Hirschig
a 8 ἀνθρωπείων Β Τ (sed ει ex ι) W : ἀνθρωπίνων C Ars.   a 9 θεῶν
Β² Τ Ars. Eus. Stob. : τῶν θεῶν Β   b 1 οἶμαι] οι Ars.
b 3 γοητευομένη pr. Τ Ars. : γεγοητευμένη Β t Eus. Stob.   ὑπ' αὐτοῦ
om. Ars.   τε om. Ars.   b 4 ἡδονῶν καὶ ἐπιθυμιῶν W   b 5 ἀλλ']
ἄλλο Ars.   ἄν τις Ars.   φάγοι καὶ πίοι W   b 7 σοφίᾳ Ars.

τοῦτο δὲ εἰθισμένη μισεῖν τε καὶ τρέμειν καὶ φεύγειν, οὕτω
c δὴ ἔχουσαν οἴει ψυχὴν αὐτὴν καθ' αὑτὴν εἰλικρινῆ ἀπαλ-
λάξεσθαι;

Οὐδ' ὁπωστιοῦν, ἔφη.

Ἀλλὰ [καὶ] διειλημμένην γε οἶμαι ὑπὸ τοῦ σωματοειδοῦς,
5 ὃ αὐτῇ ἡ ὁμιλία τε καὶ συνουσία τοῦ σώματος διὰ τὸ ἀεὶ
συνεῖναι καὶ διὰ τὴν πολλὴν μελέτην ἐνεποίησε σύμφυτον;

Πάνυ γε.

Ἐμβριθὲς δέ γε, ὦ φίλε, τοῦτο οἴεσθαι χρὴ εἶναι καὶ
βαρὺ καὶ γεῶδες καὶ ὁρατόν· ὃ δὴ καὶ ἔχουσα ἡ τοιαύτη
10 ψυχὴ βαρύνεταί τε καὶ ἕλκεται πάλιν εἰς τὸν ὁρατὸν τόπον
φόβῳ τοῦ ἀιδοῦς τε καὶ Ἅιδου, ὥσπερ λέγεται, περὶ τὰ
d μνήματά τε καὶ τοὺς τάφους κυλινδουμένη, περὶ ἃ δὴ καὶ
ὤφθη ἄττα ψυχῶν σκιοειδῆ φαντάσματα, οἷα παρέχονται αἱ
τοιαῦται ψυχαὶ εἴδωλα, αἱ μὴ καθαρῶς ἀπολυθεῖσαι ἀλλὰ
τοῦ ὁρατοῦ μετέχουσαι, διὸ καὶ ὁρῶνται.

5 Εἰκός γε, ὦ Σώκρατες.

Εἰκὸς μέντοι, ὦ Κέβης· καὶ οὔ τί γε τὰς τῶν ἀγαθῶν
αὐτὰς εἶναι, ἀλλὰ τὰς τῶν φαύλων, αἳ περὶ τὰ τοιαῦτα
ἀναγκάζονται πλανᾶσθαι δίκην τίνουσαι τῆς προτέρας τροφῆς κακῆς οὔσης. καὶ μέχρι γε τούτου πλανῶνται, ἕως ἂν τῇ
e τοῦ συνεπακολουθοῦντος, τοῦ σωματοειδοῦς, ἐπιθυμίᾳ πάλιν
ἐνδεθῶσιν εἰς σῶμα· ἐνδοῦνται δέ, ὥσπερ εἰκός, εἰς τοιαῦτα
ἤθη ὁποῖ' ἄττ' ἂν καὶ μεμελετηκυῖαι τύχωσιν ἐν τῷ βίῳ.

Τὰ ποῖα δὴ ταῦτα λέγεις, ὦ Σώκρατες;

5 Οἷον τοὺς μὲν γαστριμαργίας τε καὶ ὕβρεις καὶ φιλοποσίας
μεμελετηκότας καὶ μὴ διηυλαβημένους εἰς τὰ τῶν ὄνων γένη
82 καὶ τῶν τοιούτων θηρίων εἰκὸς ἐνδύεσθαι. ἢ οὐκ οἴει;

Πάνυ μὲν οὖν εἰκὸς λέγεις.

c 4 καὶ B : om. B² T Ars. Stob.   διειλημμένη pr. B   c 5 τε
om. W   c 8 δέ γε τοῦτο ⟨ὦ φίλε⟩ ? Ars.   οἴεσθαί γε W   c 9 δὴ
καὶ B T Stob. : δὴ W   d 2 . . . χων φαν . . . Ars. et mox ω ταφ . . .
σθένει   d 5 εἰκότως Ars.   ὦ Σώκρατες] ἔφη Ars.   d 7 αὐτὰς
Ars. : ταύτας B T W Stob.   d 8 τροφῆς B Stob : τρυφῆς T
e 2 τοιαῦτα B T Stob. : τὰ τοιαῦτα W Eus.   e 6 διευλαβημένους
T (sed η punct. not.) b : διευλαβουμένους B Stob.

Τοὺς δέ γε ἀδικίας τε καὶ τυραννίδας καὶ ἁρπαγὰς προτετιμηκότας εἰς τὰ τῶν λύκων τε καὶ ἱεράκων καὶ ἰκτίνων
γένη· ἢ ποῖ ἂν ἄλλοσέ φαμεν τὰς τοιαύτας ἰέναι;   5
Ἀμέλει, ἔφη ὁ Κέβης, εἰς τὰ τοιαῦτα.

Οὐκοῦν, ἦ δ' ὅς, δῆλα δὴ καὶ τἆλλα ᾗ ἂν ἕκαστα ἴοι
κατὰ τὰς αὐτῶν ὁμοιότητας τῆς μελέτης;
Δῆλον δή, ἔφη· πῶς δ' οὔ;
Οὐκοῦν εὐδαιμονέστατοι, ἔφη, καὶ τούτων εἰσὶ καὶ εἰς   10
βέλτιστον τόπον ἰόντες οἱ τὴν δημοτικὴν καὶ πολιτικὴν
ἀρετὴν ἐπιτετηδευκότες, ἣν δὴ καλοῦσι σωφροσύνην τε καὶ   b
δικαιοσύνην, ἐξ ἔθους τε καὶ μελέτης γεγονυῖαν ἄνευ φιλοσοφίας τε καὶ νοῦ;
Πῇ δὴ οὗτοι εὐδαιμονέστατοι;
Ὅτι τούτους εἰκός ἐστιν εἰς τοιοῦτον πάλιν ἀφικνεῖσθαι   5
πολιτικὸν καὶ ἥμερον γένος, ἤ που μελιττῶν ἢ σφηκῶν ἢ
μυρμήκων, καὶ εἰς ταὐτόν γε πάλιν τὸ ἀνθρώπινον γένος,
καὶ γίγνεσθαι ἐξ αὐτῶν ἄνδρας μετρίους.
Εἰκός.

Εἰς δέ γε θεῶν γένος μὴ φιλοσοφήσαντι καὶ παντελῶς   10
καθαρῷ ἀπιόντι οὐ θέμις ἀφικνεῖσθαι ἀλλ' ἢ τῷ φιλομαθεῖ·   c
ἀλλὰ τούτων ἕνεκα, ὦ ἑταῖρε Σιμμία τε καὶ Κέβης, οἱ
ὀρθῶς φιλόσοφοι ἀπέχονται τῶν κατὰ τὸ σῶμα ἐπιθυμιῶν
ἁπασῶν καὶ καρτεροῦσι καὶ οὐ παραδιδόασιν αὐταῖς ἑαυτούς,
οὔ τι οἰκοφθορίαν τε καὶ πενίαν φοβούμενοι, ὥσπερ οἱ   5
πολλοὶ καὶ φιλοχρήματοι· οὐδὲ αὖ ἀτιμίαν τε καὶ ἀδοξίαν
μοχθηρίας δεδιότες, ὥσπερ οἱ φίλαρχοί τε καὶ φιλότιμοι,
ἔπειτα ἀπέχονται αὐτῶν.
Οὐ γὰρ ἂν πρέποι, ἔφη, ὦ Σώκρατες, ὁ Κέβης.
Οὐ μέντοι μὰ Δία, ἦ δ' ὅς. τοιγάρτοι τούτοις μὲν   d

a 3 γε om. W   a 4 τε om. W   a 5 ἰέναι B² T : εἶναι B
a 7 ᾗ B T W Eus. : ἦ Stob. : οἳ recc.   ἕκαστα B W Stob. : ἑκάστῃ
T Eus.   a 11 καὶ B Eus. : τε καὶ T Stob.   b 5 ὅτι B² T W Eus.
Stob. : ὅτι οὐ B   ἐστιν om. Ars.   ἀφικέσθαι Ars.   b 6 καὶ
T Eus. Stob. : τε καὶ B   ⟨ἡμέ⟩τερον Ars. (ut vid.)   b 7 καὶ
T : ἢ W : ἢ καὶ B w Eus. Stob.   c 1 ἀλλ' B : ἄλλῳ B² T W Iambl.
Stob.   c 3 φιλόσοφοι T Ars. Iambl. : φιλοσοφοῦντες B   ἀπέχονται
T W Ars. Iambl. : ἔχονται B   c 4 πασῶν W   c 5 οὔτι B² T W :
οὐχὶ Iambl. : ὅτι B

ἄπασιν, ὦ Κέβης, ἐκεῖνοι οἷς τι μέλει τῆς ἑαυτῶν ψυχῆς
ἀλλὰ μὴ σώματι πλάττοντες ζῶσι, χαίρειν εἰπόντες, οὐ
κατὰ ταὐτὰ πορεύονται αὐτοῖς ὡς οὐκ εἰδόσιν ὅπη ἔρχονται,
5 αὐτοὶ δὲ ἡγούμενοι οὐ δεῖν ἐναντία τῇ φιλοσοφίᾳ πράττειν
καὶ τῇ ἐκείνης λύσει τε καὶ καθαρμῷ ταύτῃ δὴ τρέπονται
ἐκείνῃ ἑπόμενοι, ᾗ ἐκείνη ὑφηγεῖται.

Πῶς, ὦ Σώκρατες;

e Ἐγὼ ἐρῶ, ἔφη. γιγνώσκουσι γάρ, ᾗ δ' ὅς, οἱ φιλομαθεῖς
ὅτι παραλαβοῦσα αὐτῶν τὴν ψυχὴν ἡ φιλοσοφία ἀτεχνῶς
διαδεδεμένην ἐν τῷ σώματι καὶ προσκεκολλημένην, ἀναγκα-
ζομένην δὲ ὥσπερ διὰ εἱργμοῦ διὰ τούτου σκοπεῖσθαι τὰ
ὄντα ἀλλὰ μὴ αὐτὴν δι' αὑτῆς, καὶ ἐν πάσῃ ἀμαθίᾳ κυλιν-
5 δουμένην, καὶ τοῦ εἱργμοῦ τὴν δεινότητα κατιδοῦσα ὅτι δι'
ἐπιθυμίας ἐστίν, ὡς ἂν μάλιστα αὐτὸς ὁ δεδεμένος συλλήπτωρ
83 εἴη τοῦ δεδέσθαι,—ὅπερ οὖν λέγω, γιγνώσκουσιν οἱ φιλομαθεῖς ὅτι οὕτω παραλαβοῦσα ἡ φιλοσοφία ἔχουσαν αὐτῶν
τὴν ψυχὴν ἠρέμα παραμυθεῖται καὶ λύειν ἐπιχειρεῖ, ἐνδεικνυ-
μένη ὅτι ἀπάτης μὲν μεστὴ ἡ διὰ τῶν ὀμμάτων σκέψις,
5 ἀπάτης δὲ ἡ διὰ τῶν ὤτων καὶ τῶν ἄλλων αἰσθήσεων,
πείθουσα δὲ ἐκ τούτων μὲν ἀναχωρεῖν, ὅσον μὴ ἀνάγκη
αὐτοῖς χρῆσθαι, αὐτὴν δὲ εἰς αὑτὴν συλλέγεσθαι καὶ
ἀθροίζεσθαι παρακελευομένη, πιστεύειν δὲ μηδενὶ ἄλλῳ ἀλλ'
b ἢ αὐτὴν αὑτῇ, ὅτι ἂν νοήσῃ αὐτὴ καθ' αὑτὴν αὐτὸ καθ'
αὑτὸ τῶν ὄντων· ὅτι δ' ἂν δι' ἄλλων σκοπῇ ἐν ἄλλοις ὂν
ἄλλο, μηδὲν ἡγεῖσθαι ἀληθές· εἶναι δὲ τὸ μὲν τοιοῦτον
αἰσθητόν τε καὶ ὁρατόν, ὃ δὲ αὐτὴ ὁρᾷ νοητόν τε καὶ ἀιδές.
5 ταύτῃ οὖν τῇ λύσει οὐκ οἰομένη δεῖν ἐναντιοῦσθαι ἡ τοῦ ὡς

d 2 ὦ B : ἔφη ὦ B²TW   d 3 σώματι B : σώματα B²TW
d 4 πορεύσονται Ars.   d 6 καὶ τῷ καθαρμῷ Ars.   δὴ Ars. : om.
BT   d 7 ἐκείνη om. Ars.   d 8 πῶς] πῶς λέγεις ἔφη Ars.
d 9 ἔφη om. Ars.   e 1 ἢ BT : om. W   e 2 δεδεμένην
W   a 1 τοῦ Heindorf : τῷ B T W Ars.   a 5 ὤτων
BT Iambl. : ἀκοῶν W   καὶ] ἢ Ars.   a 6 ἀποχωρεῖν W   a 7 αὑτοῖς om. Ars.   a 8 ἀλλ' et mox αὐτὴν om. Ars.   b 1 ὅτι ἂν]
ὅταν Ars. et mox αὐτὸ καθ' αὐτό τι (ut vid.)   b 2 ὂν om. Ars.
b 4 τε om. Ars.   ὃ . . . ὁρᾷ] ᾧ . . . προσέχει Ars.   b 5 οὖν] δὲ b

ἀληθῶς φιλοσόφου ψυχὴ οὕτως ἀπέχεται τῶν ἡδονῶν τε
καὶ ἐπιθυμιῶν καὶ λυπῶν [καὶ φόβων] καθ' ὅσον δύναται,
λογιζομένη ὅτι, ἐπειδάν τις σφόδρα ἡσθῇ ἢ φοβηθῇ [ἢ
λυπηθῇ] ἢ ἐπιθυμήσῃ, οὐδὲν τοσοῦτον κακὸν ἔπαθεν ἀπ'
αὐτῶν ὧν ἄν τις οἰηθείη, οἷον ἢ νοσήσας ἤ τι ἀναλώσας c
διὰ τὰς ἐπιθυμίας, ἀλλ' ὃ πάντων μέγιστόν τε κακῶν καὶ
ἔσχατόν ἐστι, τοῦτο πάσχει καὶ οὐ λογίζεται αὐτό.

Τί τοῦτο, ὦ Σώκρατες; ἔφη ὁ Κέβης.

Ὅτι ψυχὴ παντὸς ἀνθρώπου ἀναγκάζεται ἅμα τε ἡσθῆναι 5
σφόδρα ἢ λυπηθῆναι ἐπί τῳ καὶ ἡγεῖσθαι περὶ ὃ ἂν μάλιστα
τοῦτο πάσχῃ, τοῦτο ἐναργέστατόν τε εἶναι καὶ ἀληθέστατον,
οὐχ οὕτως ἔχον· ταῦτα δὲ μάλιστα ⟨τὰ⟩ ὁρατά· ἢ οὔ;

Πάνυ γε.

Οὐκοῦν ἐν τούτῳ τῷ πάθει μάλιστα καταδεῖται ψυχὴ ὑπὸ d
σώματος;

Πῶς δή;

Ὅτι ἑκάστη ἡδονὴ καὶ λύπη ὥσπερ ἧλον ἔχουσα προσηλοῖ
αὐτὴν πρὸς τὸ σῶμα καὶ προσπερονᾷ καὶ ποιεῖ σωματοειδῆ, 5
δοξάζουσαν ταῦτα ἀληθῆ εἶναι ἅπερ ἂν καὶ τὸ σῶμα φῇ.
ἐκ γὰρ τοῦ ὁμοδοξεῖν τῷ σώματι καὶ τοῖς αὐτοῖς χαίρειν
ἀναγκάζεται οἶμαι ὁμότροπός τε καὶ ὁμότροφος γίγνεσθαι
καὶ οἵα μηδέποτε εἰς Ἅιδου καθαρῶς ἀφικέσθαι, ἀλλὰ ἀεὶ
τοῦ σώματος ἀναπλέα ἐξιέναι, ὥστε ταχὺ πάλιν πίπτειν εἰς 10
ἄλλο σῶμα καὶ ὥσπερ σπειρομένη ἐμφύεσθαι, καὶ ἐκ τούτων e
ἄμοιρος εἶναι τῆς τοῦ θείου τε καὶ καθαροῦ καὶ μονοειδοῦς
συνουσίας.

b 7 λυπῶν καὶ ἐπιθυμιῶν W   καὶ φόβων B et in marg. T : om. T
Ars. Iambl.   b 8 τις] τίς τι Ars.   ἢ λυπηθῇ T : post ἡσθῇ B² W
(sed καὶ pro ἢ W) Ars. Iambl. : om. B   c 1 ὧν B T W : ὡς Iambl.
τις οἰηθείη ἂν Ars.   c 2 κακῶν T Iambl. : κακὸν B   c 3 ἐστι om. W
c 6 σφόδρα ἢ λυπηθῆναι Ars. Iambl. : ἢ λυπηθῆναι σφόδρα B et marg.
T : om. T   δ] οὗ Ars.   c 7 τοῦτο . . . ἀληθέστατον] μάλιστα δὲ
(δὴ) εἶναι τοῦτο Ars.   c 8 τὰ add. Heindorf   d 1 ὑπὸ B T Iambl. :
ὑπὸ τοῦ B² W   d 6 καὶ om. Ars.   d 8 ὁμότροφος καὶ ὁμότροπος
B² W Ars.   d 9 καθαρῶς εἰς ἅιδου W Ars.   μηδέποτε post ἅιδου
Ars.   d 10 ἀναπλέα τοῦ σώματος T W Ars. Iambl.

Ἀληθέστατα, ἔφη, λέγεις, ὁ Κέβης, ὦ Σώκρατες.

5 Τούτων τοίνυν ἕνεκα, ὦ Κέβης, οἱ δικαίως φιλομαθεῖς
κόσμιοί εἰσι καὶ ἀνδρεῖοι, οὐχ ὧν οἱ πολλοὶ ἕνεκά φασιν·
ἢ σὺ οἴει;

84 Οὐ δῆτα ἔγωγε.

Οὐ γάρ· ἀλλ' οὕτω λογίσαιτ' ἂν ψυχὴ ἀνδρὸς φιλοσόφου,
καὶ οὐκ ἂν οἰηθείη τὴν μὲν φιλοσοφίαν χρῆναι αὐτὴν λύειν,
λυούσης δὲ ἐκείνης, αὐτὴν παραδιδόναι ταῖς ἡδοναῖς καὶ
5 λύπαις ἑαυτὴν πάλιν αὖ ἐγκαταδεῖν καὶ ἀνήνυτον ἔργον πράττειν Πηνελόπης τινὰ ἐναντίως ἱστὸν μεταχειριζομένης, ἀλλὰ
γαλήνην τούτων παρασκευάζουσα, ἑπομένη τῷ λογισμῷ καὶ
ἀεὶ ἐν τούτῳ οὖσα, τὸ ἀληθὲς καὶ τὸ θεῖον καὶ τὸ ἀδόξαστον
b θεωμένη καὶ ὑπ' ἐκείνου τρεφομένη, ζῆν τε οἴεται οὕτω
δεῖν ἕως ἂν ζῇ, καὶ ἐπειδὰν τελευτήσῃ, εἰς τὸ συγγενὲς
καὶ εἰς τὸ τοιοῦτον ἀφικομένη ἀπηλλάχθαι τῶν ἀνθρωπίνων
κακῶν. ἐκ δὴ τῆς τοιαύτης τροφῆς οὐδὲν δεινὸν μὴ φοβηθῇ,
5 [ταῦτα δ' ἐπιτηδεύσασα,] ὦ Σιμμία τε καὶ Κέβης, ὅπως μὴ
διασπασθεῖσα ἐν τῇ ἀπαλλαγῇ τοῦ σώματος ὑπὸ τῶν ἀνέμων διαφυσηθεῖσα καὶ διαπτομένη οἴχηται καὶ οὐδὲν ἔτι
οὐδαμοῦ ᾖ.

c Σιγὴ οὖν ἐγένετο ταῦτα εἰπόντος τοῦ Σωκράτους ἐπὶ
πολὺν χρόνον, καὶ αὐτός τε πρὸς τῷ εἰρημένῳ λόγῳ ἦν ὁ
Σωκράτης, ὡς ἰδεῖν ἐφαίνετο, καὶ ἡμῶν οἱ πλεῖστοι· Κέβης
δὲ καὶ Σιμμίας σμικρὸν πρὸς ἀλλήλω διελεγέσθην. καὶ ὁ
5 Σωκράτης ἰδὼν αὐτὼ ἤρετο, Τί; ἔφη, ὑμῖν τὰ λεχθέντα μῶν
μὴ δοκεῖ ἐνδεῶς λέγεσθαι; πολλὰς γὰρ δὴ ἔτι ἔχει ὑποψίας
καὶ ἀντιλαβάς, εἴ γε δή τις αὐτὰ μέλλει ἱκανῶς διεξιέναι. εἰ
μὲν οὖν τι ἄλλο σκοπεῖσθον, οὐδὲν λέγω· εἰ δέ τι περὶ

e 5 ὦ Κέβης om. Ars.   e 6 καὶ Β Τ : τε καὶ Β² W   φασιν
om. Ars.   a 3 αὐτὴν Ars. : ἑαυτὴν Β Τ Iambl.   a 4 αὐτὴ
Ars.   a 5 αὖ Β Τ Iambl. : om. W   ἐγκαταδεῖν] ἐπι in marg. Β²
a 6 μεταχειριζομένης Β Τ W Ars. Iambl. : μεταχειριζομένην vulg.
a 8 τὸ alterum et tertium om. Ars.   b 1 οἴεται οὕτως δεῖν Β Iambl. :
οἴεται δεῖν οὕτω Τ Ars. : οὕτως οἴεται δεῖν W   b 4 δὴ Β² Τ W
Iambl. : δὲ Β   b 5 δ'] γ' ci. Stephanus : inclusa secl. Ast
c 6 λέγεσθαι Β Τ : λελέχθαι Β² W t   c 8 δέ τι Β : δὲ Τ

τούτων ἀπορεῖτον, μηδὲν ἀποκνήσητε καὶ αὐτοὶ εἰπεῖν καὶ
διελθεῖν, εἴ πη ὑμῖν φαίνεται βέλτιον ⟨ἂν⟩ λεχθῆναι, καὶ d
αὖ καὶ ἐμὲ συμπαραλαβεῖν, εἴ τι μᾶλλον οἴεσθε μετ' ἐμοῦ
εὐπορήσειν.

Καὶ ὁ Σιμμίας ἔφη· Καὶ μήν, ὦ Σώκρατες, τἀληθῆ σοι
ἐρῶ. πάλαι γὰρ ἡμῶν ἑκάτερος ἀπορῶν τὸν ἕτερον προωθεῖ 5
καὶ κελεύει ἐρέσθαι διὰ τὸ ἐπιθυμεῖν μὲν ἀκοῦσαι, ὀκνεῖν δὲ
ὄχλον παρέχειν, μή σοι ἀηδὲς ᾖ διὰ τὴν παροῦσαν συμφοράν.

Καὶ ὃς ἀκούσας ἐγέλασέν τε ἠρέμα καί φησιν· Βαβαί,
ὦ Σιμμία· ἦ που χαλεπῶς ἂν τοὺς ἄλλους ἀνθρώπους πεί-
σαιμι ὡς οὐ συμφορὰν ἡγοῦμαι τὴν παροῦσαν τύχην, ὅτε e
γε μηδ' ὑμᾶς δύναμαι πείθειν, ἀλλὰ φοβεῖσθε μὴ δυσκολώ-
τερόν τι νῦν διάκειμαι ἢ ἐν τῷ πρόσθεν βίῳ· καί, ὡς ἔοικε,
τῶν κύκνων δοκῶ φαυλότερος ὑμῖν εἶναι τὴν μαντικήν, οἳ
ἐπειδὰν αἴσθωνται ὅτι δεῖ αὐτοὺς ἀποθανεῖν, ᾄδοντες καὶ ἐν 5
τῷ πρόσθεν χρόνῳ, τότε δὴ πλεῖστα καὶ κάλλιστα ᾄδουσι, 85
γεγηθότες ὅτι μέλλουσι παρὰ τὸν θεὸν ἀπιέναι οὗπέρ εἰσι
θεράποντες. οἱ δ' ἄνθρωποι διὰ τὸ αὑτῶν δέος τοῦ θανάτου
καὶ τῶν κύκνων καταψεύδονται, καί φασιν αὐτοὺς θρηνοῦντας
τὸν θάνατον ὑπὸ λύπης ἐξᾴδειν, καὶ οὐ λογίζονται ὅτι οὐδὲν 5
ὄρνεον ᾄδει ὅταν πεινῇ ἢ ῥιγῷ ἤ τινα ἄλλην λύπην λυπῆται,
οὐδὲ αὐτὴ ἥ τε ἀηδὼν καὶ χελιδὼν καὶ ὁ ἔποψ, ἃ δή φασι
διὰ λύπην θρηνοῦντα ᾄδειν. ἀλλ' οὔτε ταῦτά μοι φαίνεται
λυπούμενα ᾄδειν οὔτε οἱ κύκνοι, ἀλλ' ἅτε οἶμαι τοῦ Ἀπόλ- b
λωνος ὄντες, μαντικοί τέ εἰσι καὶ προειδότες τὰ ἐν Ἅιδου
ἀγαθὰ ᾄδουσι καὶ τέρπονται ἐκείνην τὴν ἡμέραν διαφερόντως
ἢ ἐν τῷ ἔμπροσθεν χρόνῳ. ἐγὼ δὲ καὶ αὐτὸς ἡγοῦμαι
ὁμόδουλός τε εἶναι τῶν κύκνων καὶ ἱερὸς τοῦ αὐτοῦ θεοῦ, 5
καὶ οὐ χεῖρον ἐκείνων τὴν μαντικὴν ἔχειν παρὰ τοῦ δεσπότου,

c 9 τούτων B : τούτω T   d 1 διελθεῖν B T : διεξελθεῖν B² W t
ἂν add. ci. Heindorf   e 3 τι om. Stob.   a 1 κάλλιστα W (conie-
cerat Blomfield) : μάλιστα B T Stob. et s. v. W   a 6 ῥιγοῖ B T W
a 7 ὁ om. W   b 3 καὶ B : τε καὶ T W   b 4 ἡγοῦμαι T b Stob. :
που οἶμαι B (ut vid.) W   b 5 τε T W Stob. : γε B   b 6 χεῖρον'
Hermann

οὐδὲ δυσθυμότερον αὐτῶν τοῦ βίου ἀπαλλάττεσθαι. ἀλλὰ
τούτου γ' ἕνεκα λέγειν τε χρὴ καὶ ἐρωτᾶν ὅτι ἂν βούλησθε,
ἕως ἂν Ἀθηναίων ἐῶσιν ἄνδρες ἕνδεκα.

10 Καλῶς, ἔφη, λέγεις, ὁ Σιμμίας· καὶ ἐγώ τέ σοι ἐρῶ ὃ
c ἀπορῶ, καὶ αὖ ὅδε, ᾗ οὐκ ἀποδέχεται τὰ εἰρημένα. ἐμοὶ
γὰρ δοκεῖ, ὦ Σώκρατες, περὶ τῶν τοιούτων ἴσως ὥσπερ καὶ
σοὶ τὸ μὲν σαφὲς εἰδέναι ἐν τῷ νῦν βίῳ ἢ ἀδύνατον εἶναι
ἢ παγχάλεπόν τι, τὸ μέντοι αὖ τὰ λεγόμενα περὶ αὐτῶν μὴ
5 οὐχὶ παντὶ τρόπῳ ἐλέγχειν καὶ μὴ προαφίστασθαι πρὶν ἂν
πανταχῇ σκοπῶν ἀπείπῃ τις, πάνυ μαλθακοῦ εἶναι ἀνδρός·
δεῖν γὰρ περὶ αὐτὰ ἕν γέ τι τούτων διαπράξασθαι, ἢ μαθεῖν
ὅπῃ ἔχει ἢ εὑρεῖν ἤ, εἰ ταῦτα ἀδύνατον, τὸν γοῦν βέλτιστον τῶν ἀνθρωπίνων λόγων λαβόντα καὶ δυσεξελεγκτό-
d τατον, ἐπὶ τούτου ὀχούμενον ὥσπερ ἐπὶ σχεδίας κινδυνεύοντα
διαπλεῦσαι τὸν βίον, εἰ μή τις δύναιτο ἀσφαλέστερον καὶ
ἀκινδυνότερον ἐπὶ βεβαιοτέρου ὀχήματος, [ἢ] λόγου θείου
τινός, διαπορευθῆναι. καὶ δὴ καὶ νῦν ἔγωγε οὐκ ἐπαισχυν-
5 θήσομαι ἐρέσθαι, ἐπειδὴ καὶ σὺ ταῦτα λέγεις, οὐδ' ἐμαυτὸν αἰτιάσομαι ἐν ὑστέρῳ χρόνῳ ὅτι νῦν οὐκ εἶπον ἅ μοι
δοκεῖ. ἐμοὶ γάρ, ὦ Σώκρατες, ἐπειδὴ καὶ πρὸς ἐμαυτὸν
καὶ πρὸς τόνδε σκοπῶ τὰ εἰρημένα, οὐ πάνυ φαίνεται ἱκανῶς
10 εἰρῆσθαι.

e Καὶ ὁ Σωκράτης, Ἴσως γάρ, ἔφη, ὦ ἑταῖρε, ἀληθῆ σοι
φαίνεται· ἀλλὰ λέγε ὅπῃ δὴ οὐχ ἱκανῶς.

Ταύτῃ ἔμοιγε, ἦ δ' ὅς, ᾗ δὴ καὶ περὶ ἁρμονίας ἄν τις καὶ
λύρας τε καὶ χορδῶν τὸν αὐτὸν τοῦτον λόγον εἴποι, ὡς ἡ
5 μὲν ἁρμονία ἀόρατον καὶ ἀσώματον καὶ πάγκαλόν τι καὶ
86 θεῖόν ἐστιν ἐν τῇ ἡρμοσμένῃ λύρᾳ, αὐτὴ δ' ἡ λύρα καὶ

b 9 ἕως ἂν T W : ἕως B   b 10 ἐγώ τε T W : ἔγωγε B t   c 1 ἐμοὶ
γὰρ T b : ἔμοιγε B (ut vid.) W   c 4 μέντοι αὖ τὰ B : τὸ μέντοι τὰ T :
τὸ δὲ τοιαῦτα ex emend. W   c 5 οὐχὶ B T : οὐ W   c 8 ἢ εἰ B t :
εἰ T   c 9 λόγον W   δυσελεγκτότατον W   d 3 ἢ secl.
Heindorf   d 6 ἅ μοι δοκεῖ B T : ἅ μοι ἐδόκει B² W   e 3 ᾗ δὴ
W : ἤδη B T   e 4 λόγον τοῦτον W   e 5 ἀόρατον T : ἀόρατόν
τι B

ΦΑΙΔΩΝ 86 a

αἱ χορδαὶ σώματά τε καὶ σωματοειδῆ καὶ σύνθετα καὶ
γεώδη ἐστὶ καὶ τοῦ θνητοῦ συγγενῆ. ἐπειδὰν οὖν ἢ κατάξῃ
τις τὴν λύραν ἢ διατέμῃ καὶ διαρρήξῃ τὰς χορδάς, εἴ τις
διισχυρίζοιτο τῷ αὐτῷ λόγῳ ὥσπερ σύ, ὡς ἀνάγκη ἔτι εἶναι 5
τὴν ἁρμονίαν ἐκείνην καὶ μὴ ἀπολωλέναι—οὐδεμία γὰρ
μηχανὴ ἂν εἴη τὴν μὲν λύραν ἔτι εἶναι διερρωγυιῶν τῶν
χορδῶν καὶ τὰς χορδὰς θνητοειδεῖς οὔσας, τὴν δὲ ἁρμονίαν
ἀπολωλέναι τὴν τοῦ θείου τε καὶ ἀθανάτου ὁμοφυῆ τε καὶ b
συγγενῆ, προτέραν τοῦ θνητοῦ ἀπολομένην—ἀλλὰ φαίη
ἀνάγκη ἔτι που εἶναι αὐτὴν τὴν ἁρμονίαν, καὶ πρότερον τὰ
ξύλα καὶ τὰς χορδὰς κατασαπήσεσθαι πρίν τι ἐκείνην
παθεῖν—καὶ γὰρ οὖν, ὦ Σώκρατες, οἶμαι ἔγωγε καὶ αὐτόν 5
σε τοῦτο ἐντεθυμῆσθαι, ὅτι τοιοῦτόν τι μάλιστα ὑπολαμβάνομεν τὴν ψυχὴν εἶναι, ὥσπερ ἐντεταμένου τοῦ σώματος
ἡμῶν καὶ συνεχομένου ὑπὸ θερμοῦ καὶ ψυχροῦ καὶ ξηροῦ
καὶ ὑγροῦ καὶ τοιούτων τινῶν, κρᾶσιν εἶναι καὶ ἁρμονίαν
αὐτῶν τούτων τὴν ψυχὴν ἡμῶν, ἐπειδὰν ταῦτα καλῶς καὶ c
μετρίως κραθῇ πρὸς ἄλληλα—εἰ οὖν τυγχάνει ἡ ψυχὴ οὖσα
ἁρμονία τις, δῆλον ὅτι, ὅταν χαλασθῇ τὸ σῶμα ἡμῶν
ἀμέτρως ἢ ἐπιταθῇ ὑπὸ νόσων καὶ ἄλλων κακῶν, τὴν μὲν
ψυχὴν ἀνάγκη εὐθὺς ὑπάρχει ἀπολωλέναι, καίπερ οὖσαν 5
θειοτάτην, ὥσπερ καὶ αἱ ἄλλαι ἁρμονίαι αἵ τ᾽ ἐν τοῖς
φθόγγοις καὶ ἐν τοῖς τῶν δημιουργῶν ἔργοις πᾶσι, τὰ δὲ
λείψανα τοῦ σώματος ἑκάστου πολὺν χρόνον παραμένειν,
ἕως ἂν ἢ κατακαυθῇ ἢ κατασαπῇ—ὅρα οὖν πρὸς τοῦτον τὸν d
λόγον τί φήσομεν, ἐάν τις ἀξιοῖ κρᾶσιν οὖσαν τὴν ψυχὴν
τῶν ἐν τῷ σώματι ἐν τῷ καλουμένῳ θανάτῳ πρώτην ἀπόλλυσθαι.

Διαβλέψας οὖν ὁ Σωκράτης, ὥσπερ τὰ πολλὰ εἰώθει, 5

a 2 σώματα B : σῶμα T   σύνθετα B : σύνθετά τε T   a 4 καὶ
B : ἢ T   a 7 ἂν secl. Bekker   b 1 ὁμοφυῆ καὶ ξυμφυῆ W
b 3 ἀνάγκη Baiter   b 4 καὶ B : τε καὶ B² T W   c 1 μετρίως
καὶ καλῶς W   c 3 ἡμῶν B : om. T   c 4 ἐπιταθῇ T W : ὑποταθῇ
B et ὑπο s. v. W in marg. t   c 5 ἀνάγκη B T W : ἀνάγκην t   ὑπάρχειν B T W   c 7 ἐν T : αἱ ἐν B   d 1 κατακαυθῇ] καταθῇ pr. W
d 5 διαβλεψάμενος in marg. B²

καὶ μειδιάσας, Δίκαια μέντοι, ἔφη, λέγει ὁ Σιμμίας. εἰ
οὖν τις ὑμῶν εὐπορώτερος ἐμοῦ, τί οὐκ ἀπεκρίνατο; καὶ γὰρ
οὐ φαύλως ἔοικεν ἁπτομένῳ τοῦ λόγου. δοκεῖ μέντοι μοι
χρῆναι πρὸ τῆς ἀποκρίσεως ἔτι πρότερον Κέβητος ἀκοῦσαι
e τί αὖ ὅδε ἐγκαλεῖ τῷ λόγῳ, ἵνα χρόνου ἐγγενομένου βου-
λευσώμεθα τί ἐροῦμεν, ἔπειτα [δὲ] ἀκούσαντας ἢ συγχωρεῖν
αὐτοῖς ἐάν τι δοκῶσι προσᾴδειν, ἐὰν δὲ μή, οὕτως ἤδη
ὑπερδικεῖν τοῦ λόγου. ἀλλ᾽ ἄγε, ἦ δ᾽ ὅς, ὦ Κέβης, λέγε,
5 τί ἦν τὸ σὲ αὖ θρᾶττον [ἀπιστίαν παρέχει].

Λέγω δή, ἦ δ᾽ ὃς ὁ Κέβης. ἐμοὶ γὰρ φαίνεται ἔτι ἐν
τῷ αὐτῷ ὁ λόγος εἶναι, καί, ὅπερ ἐν τοῖς πρόσθεν ἐλέγομεν,
87 ταὐτὸν ἔγκλημα ἔχειν. ὅτι μὲν γὰρ ἦν ἡμῶν ἡ ψυχὴ καὶ
πρὶν εἰς τόδε τὸ εἶδος ἐλθεῖν, οὐκ ἀνατίθεμαι μὴ οὐχὶ πάνυ
χαριέντως καί, εἰ μὴ ἐπαχθές ἐστιν εἰπεῖν, πάνυ ἱκανῶς
ἀποδεδεῖχθαι· ὡς δὲ καὶ ἀποθανόντων ἡμῶν ἔτι που ἔστιν,
5 οὔ μοι δοκεῖ τῇδε. ὡς μὲν οὐκ ἰσχυρότερον καὶ πολυ-
χρονιώτερον ψυχὴ σώματος, οὐ συγχωρῶ τῇ Σιμμίου ἀντι-
λήψει· δοκεῖ γάρ μοι πᾶσι τούτοις πάνυ πολὺ διαφέρειν. τί
οὖν, ἂν φαίη ὁ λόγος, ἔτι ἀπιστεῖς, ἐπειδὴ ὁρᾷς ἀποθανόντος
τοῦ ἀνθρώπου τό γε ἀσθενέστερον ἔτι ὄν; τὸ δὲ πολυ-
b χρονιώτερον οὐ δοκεῖ σοι ἀναγκαῖον εἶναι ἔτι σῴζεσθαι ἐν
τούτῳ τῷ χρόνῳ; πρὸς δὴ τοῦτο τόδε ἐπίσκεψαι, εἴ τι λέγω·
εἰκόνος γάρ τινος, ὡς ἔοικεν, κἀγὼ ὥσπερ Σιμμίας δέομαι.
ἐμοὶ γὰρ δοκεῖ ὁμοίως λέγεσθαι ταῦτα ὥσπερ ἄν τις περὶ
5 ἀνθρώπου ὑφάντου πρεσβύτου ἀποθανόντος λέγοι τοῦτον
τὸν λόγον, ὅτι οὐκ ἀπόλωλεν ὁ ἄνθρωπος ἀλλ᾽ ἔστι που
σῶς, τεκμήριον δὲ παρέχοιτο θοἰμάτιον ὃ ἠμπείχετο αὐτὸς
ὑφηνάμενος ὅτι ἐστὶ σῶν καὶ οὐκ ἀπόλωλεν, καὶ εἴ τις
c ἀπιστοίη αὐτῷ, ἀνερωτῴη πότερον πολυχρονιώτερόν ἐστι

d 6 ὁ Σιμμίας λέγει W   ὁ B : om. T   e 2 δὲ B : om. T W
e 4 ἀλλά γε B T W   e 5 τὸ B T W : δ al.   ἀπιστίαν παρέχει secl.
Hermann   e 7 ἔμπροσθεν W   a 2 ἀνατίθεμαι W Olymp.: ἀντι-
τίθεμαι B T   a 4 ἔστιν B² T : ἔσται B W   a 8 ἐπειδὴ B : ἐπειδή
γε B² T W   b 7 σῶς Forster : ἴσως B T W   c 1 ἀπιστοίη
Heindorf : ἀπιστῶν B T W

τὸ γένος ἀνθρώπου ἢ ἱματίου ἐν χρείᾳ τε ὄντος καὶ φορου-
μένου, ἀποκριναμένου δή [τινος] ὅτι πολὺ τὸ τοῦ ἀνθρώπου,
οἴοιτο ἀποδεδεῖχθαι ὅτι παντὸς ἄρα μᾶλλον ὅ γε ἄνθρωπος
σῶς ἐστιν, ἐπειδὴ τό γε ὀλιγοχρονιώτερον οὐκ ἀπόλωλεν. 5
τὸ δ' οἶμαι, ὦ Σιμμία, οὐχ οὕτως ἔχει· σκόπει γὰρ καὶ σὺ
ἃ λέγω. πᾶς [γὰρ] ἂν ὑπολάβοι ὅτι εὔηθες λέγει ὁ τοῦτο
λέγων· ὁ γὰρ ὑφάντης οὗτος πολλὰ κατατρίψας τοιαῦτα
ἱμάτια καὶ ὑφηνάμενος ἐκείνων μὲν ὕστερος ἀπόλωλεν πολλῶν ὄντων, τοῦ δὲ τελευταίου οἶμαι πρότερος, καὶ οὐδέν τι d
μᾶλλον τούτου ἕνεκα ἄνθρωπός ἐστιν ἱματίου φαυλότερον
οὐδ' ἀσθενέστερον. τὴν αὐτὴν δὲ ταύτην οἶμαι εἰκόνα
δέξαιτ' ἂν ψυχὴ πρὸς σῶμα, καί τις λέγων αὐτὰ ταῦτα περὶ
αὐτῶν μέτρι' ἄν μοι φαίνοιτο λέγειν, ὡς ἡ μὲν ψυχὴ 5
πολυχρόνιόν ἐστι, τὸ δὲ σῶμα ἀσθενέστερον καὶ ὀλιγο-
χρονιώτερον· ἀλλὰ γὰρ ἂν φαίη ἑκάστην τῶν ψυχῶν πολλὰ
σώματα κατατρίβειν, ἄλλως τε κἂν πολλὰ ἔτη βιῷ—εἰ γὰρ
ῥέοι τὸ σῶμα καὶ ἀπολλύοιτο ἔτι ζῶντος τοῦ ἀνθρώπου,
ἀλλ' ἡ ψυχὴ ἀεὶ τὸ κατατριβόμενον ἀνυφαίνοι—ἀναγκαῖον e
μεντἂν εἴη, ὁπότε ἀπολλύοιτο ἡ ψυχή, τὸ τελευταῖον ὕφασμα
τυχεῖν αὐτὴν ἔχουσαν καὶ τούτου μόνου προτέραν ἀπόλλυσθαι, ἀπολομένης δὲ τῆς ψυχῆς τότ' ἤδη τὴν φύσιν τῆς
ἀσθενείας ἐπιδεικνύοι τὸ σῶμα καὶ ταχὺ σαπὲν διοίχοιτο. 5
ὥστε τούτῳ τῷ λόγῳ οὔπω ἄξιον πιστεύσαντα θαρρεῖν ὡς
ἐπειδὰν ἀποθάνωμεν ἔτι που ἡμῶν ἡ ψυχὴ ἔστιν. εἰ γάρ 88
τις καὶ πλέον ἔτι τῷ λέγοντι ἢ ἃ σὺ λέγεις συγχωρήσειεν,
δοὺς αὐτῷ μὴ μόνον ἐν τῷ πρὶν καὶ γενέσθαι ἡμᾶς χρόνῳ
εἶναι ἡμῶν τὰς ψυχάς, ἀλλὰ μηδὲν κωλύειν καὶ ἐπειδὰν
ἀποθάνωμεν ἐνίων ἔτι εἶναι καὶ ἔσεσθαι καὶ πολλάκις γενή- 5
σεσθαι καὶ ἀποθανεῖσθαι αὖθις—οὕτω γὰρ αὐτὸ φύσει

c 3 ἀποκρινομένου T   δή om. W   τινος seclusi   c 7 γὰρ
B : om. T W   c 9 ὕστερος B T et σ s. v. W : ὕστερον B² W
d 3 ταύτην B² T W : om. B   d 5 αὐτῶν B² T W : τῶν αὐτῶν B
μὲν ψυχὴ B : ψυχὴ μὲν T W   d 8 κἂν B² T W : καὶ εἰ B   βιῷ T :
βιῴη B W   a 1 ἡ ψυχὴ ἡμῶν T W   a 4 τὰς ψυχὰς B : τὴν
ψυχὴν T W

ἰσχυρὸν εἶναι, ὥστε πολλάκις γιγνομένην ψυχὴν ἀντέχειν
—δοὺς δὲ ταῦτα ἐκεῖνο μηκέτι συγχωροῖ, μὴ οὐ πονεῖν
αὐτὴν ἐν ταῖς πολλαῖς γενέσεσιν καὶ τελευτῶσάν γε ἔν
10 τινι τῶν θανάτων παντάπασιν ἀπόλλυσθαι, τοῦτον δὲ τὸν
b θάνατον καὶ ταύτην τὴν διάλυσιν τοῦ σώματος ἢ τῇ ψυχῇ
φέρει ὄλεθρον μηδένα φαίη εἰδέναι—ἀδύνατον γὰρ εἶναι
ὁτῳοῦν αἰσθέσθαι ἡμῶν—εἰ δὲ τοῦτο οὕτως ἔχει, οὐδενὶ
προσήκει θάνατον θαρροῦντι μὴ οὐκ ἀνοήτως θαρρεῖν, ὃς ἂν
5 μὴ ἔχῃ ἀποδεῖξαι ὅτι ἔστι ψυχὴ παντάπασιν ἀθάνατόν τε
καὶ ἀνώλεθρον· εἰ δὲ μή, ἀνάγκην εἶναι ἀεὶ τὸν μέλλοντα
ἀποθανεῖσθαι δεδιέναι ὑπὲρ τῆς αὑτοῦ ψυχῆς μὴ ἐν τῇ νῦν
τοῦ σώματος διαζεύξει παντάπασιν ἀπόληται.

c   Πάντες οὖν ἀκούσαντες εἰπόντων αὐτῶν ἀηδῶς διετέθη-
μεν, ὡς ὕστερον ἐλέγομεν πρὸς ἀλλήλους, ὅτι ὑπὸ τοῦ
ἔμπροσθεν λόγου σφόδρα πεπεισμένους ἡμᾶς πάλιν ἐδόκουν
ἀναταράξαι καὶ εἰς ἀπιστίαν καταβαλεῖν οὐ μόνον τοῖς
5 προειρημένοις λόγοις, ἀλλὰ καὶ εἰς τὰ ὕστερον μέλλοντα
ῥηθήσεσθαι, μὴ οὐδενὸς ἄξιοι εἶμεν κριταὶ ἢ καὶ τὰ πράγματα αὐτὰ ἄπιστα ᾖ.

ΕΧ. Νὴ τοὺς θεούς, ὦ Φαίδων, συγγνώμην γε ἔχω ὑμῖν.
καὶ γὰρ αὐτόν με νῦν ἀκούσαντά σου τοιοῦτόν τι λέγειν
d πρὸς ἐμαυτὸν ἐπέρχεται· "Τίνι οὖν ἔτι πιστεύσομεν λόγῳ;
ὡς γὰρ σφόδρα πιθανὸς ὤν, ὃν ὁ Σωκράτης ἔλεγε λόγον,
νῦν εἰς ἀπιστίαν καταπέπτωκεν." θαυμαστῶς γάρ μου ὁ
λόγος οὗτος ἀντιλαμβάνεται καὶ νῦν καὶ ἀεί, τὸ ἁρμονίαν
5 τινὰ ἡμῶν εἶναι τὴν ψυχήν, καὶ ὥσπερ ὑπέμνησέν με ῥηθεὶς
ὅτι καὶ αὐτῷ μοι ταῦτα προυδέδοκτο. καὶ πάνυ δέομαι
πάλιν ὥσπερ ἐξ ἀρχῆς ἄλλου τινὸς λόγου ὅς με πείσει ὡς
τοῦ ἀποθανόντος οὐ συναποθνῄσκει ἡ ψυχή. λέγε οὖν πρὸς

---

a 7 τὴν ψυχὴν W   a 8 μηκέτι ἐκεῖνο T   b 1 ἢ T W :
εἰ B   b 3 αἰσθέσθαι T : αἰσθάνεσθαι B   b 4 προσήκειν Stephanus
b 6 ἀνάγκην BW t : ἀνάγκη T   c 3 πάλιν T : πάλαι B   c 5 ὕστερον
W sed α supra ον   c 6 εἴημεν T W : ἦμεν B   c 7 αὐτὰ B² T W :
om. B   ᾖ] εἴη Heindorf   d 1 πιστεύσομεν B : πιστεύσωμεν T

Διὸς πῇ ὁ Σωκράτης μετῆλθε τὸν λόγον; καὶ πότερον
κἀκεῖνος, ὥσπερ ὑμᾶς φής, ἔνδηλός τι ἐγένετο ἀχθόμενος ἢ e
οὔ, ἀλλὰ πράως ἐβοήθει τῷ λόγῳ; [ἢ] καὶ ἱκανῶς ἐβοήθησεν
ἢ ἐνδεῶς; πάντα ἡμῖν δίελθε ὡς δύνασαι ἀκριβέστατα.

ΦΑΙΔ. Καὶ μήν, ὦ Ἐχέκρατες, πολλάκις θαυμάσας
Σωκράτη οὐ πώποτε μᾶλλον ἠγάσθην ἢ τότε παραγενόμενος. 5
τὸ μὲν οὖν ἔχειν ὅτι λέγοι ἐκεῖνος ἴσως οὐδὲν ἄτοπον· ἀλλὰ 89
ἔγωγε μάλιστα ἐθαύμασα αὐτοῦ πρῶτον μὲν τοῦτο, ὡς ἡδέως
καὶ εὐμενῶς καὶ ἀγαμένως τῶν νεανίσκων τὸν λόγον ἀπ-
εδέξατο, ἔπειτα ἡμῶν ὡς ὀξέως ᾔσθετο ὃ 'πεπόνθεμεν ὑπὸ
τῶν λόγων, ἔπειτα ὡς εὖ ἡμᾶς ἰάσατο καὶ ὥσπερ πεφευγότας 5
καὶ ἡττημένους ἀνεκαλέσατο καὶ προύτρεψεν πρὸς τὸ παρ-
έπεσθαί τε καὶ συσκοπεῖν τὸν λόγον.

ΕΧ. Πῶς δή;

ΦΑΙΔ. Ἐγὼ ἐρῶ. ἔτυχον γὰρ ἐν δεξιᾷ αὐτοῦ καθήμενος παρὰ τὴν κλίνην ἐπὶ χαμαιζήλου τινός, ὁ δὲ ἐπὶ πολὺ b
ὑψηλοτέρου ἢ ἐγώ. καταψήσας οὖν μου τὴν κεφαλὴν καὶ
συμπιέσας τὰς ἐπὶ τῷ αὐχένι τρίχας—εἰώθει γάρ, ὁπότε
τύχοι, παίζειν μου εἰς τὰς τρίχας—Αὔριον δή, ἔφη, ἴσως, ὦ
Φαίδων, τὰς καλὰς ταύτας κόμας ἀποκερῇ. 5

Ἔοικεν, ἦν δ' ἐγώ, ὦ Σώκρατες.

Οὔκ, ἄν γε ἐμοὶ πείθῃ.

Ἀλλὰ τί; ἦν δ' ἐγώ.

Τήμερον, ἔφη, κἀγὼ τὰς ἐμὰς καὶ σὺ ταύτας, ἐάνπερ γε
ἡμῖν ὁ λόγος τελευτήσῃ καὶ μὴ δυνώμεθα αὐτὸν ἀναβιώ- 10
σασθαι. καὶ ἔγωγ' ἄν, εἰ σὺ εἴην καί με διαφεύγοι ὁ c
λόγος, ἔνορκον ἂν ποιησαίμην ὥσπερ Ἀργεῖοι, μὴ πρότερον
κομήσειν, πρὶν ἂν νικήσω ἀναμαχόμενος τὸν Σιμμίου τε καὶ
Κέβητος λόγον.

e 1 τι B : om. T   e 2 ἢ B : ἢ T : om. al. Heindorf   e 5 τότε
B² T W : ποτε B   a 9 καθήμενος ἐν δεξιᾷ αὐτοῦ T W   b 1 πολὺ
B : πολλῷ T b   b 5 ταύτας B² T W : om. B   b 7 γε ἐμοὶ B T :
ἔμοιγε W   b 10 δυνώμεθα B² T W : δυνάμεθα B   c 1 διαφύγοι T W
c 3 ἀναμαχόμενος in marg. T

5 Ἀλλ', ἦν δ' ἐγώ, πρὸς δύο λέγεται οὐδ' ὁ Ἡρακλῆς οἷός τε εἶναι.

Ἀλλὰ καὶ ἐμέ, ἔφη, τὸν Ἰόλεων παρακάλει, ἕως ἔτι φῶς ἐστιν.

Παρακαλῶ τοίνυν, ἔφην, οὐχ ὡς Ἡρακλῆς, ἀλλ' ὡς
10 Ἰόλεως τὸν Ἡρακλῆ.

Οὐδὲν διοίσει, ἔφη. ἀλλὰ πρῶτον εὐλαβηθῶμέν τι πάθος μὴ πάθωμεν.

Τὸ ποῖον; ἦν δ' ἐγώ.

d Μὴ γενώμεθα, ἦ δ' ὅς, μισόλογοι, ὥσπερ οἱ μισάνθρωποι γιγνόμενοι· ὡς οὐκ ἔστιν, ἔφη, ὅτι ἄν τις μεῖζον τούτου κακὸν πάθοι ἢ λόγους μισήσας. γίγνεται δὲ ἐκ τοῦ αὐτοῦ τρόπου μισολογία τε καὶ μισανθρωπία. ἥ τε γὰρ μισαν-
5 θρωπία ἐνδύεται ἐκ τοῦ σφόδρα τινὶ πιστεῦσαι ἄνευ τέχνης, καὶ ἡγήσασθαι παντάπασί γε ἀληθῆ εἶναι καὶ ὑγιῆ καὶ πιστὸν τὸν ἄνθρωπον, ἔπειτα ὀλίγον ὕστερον εὑρεῖν τοῦτον πονηρόν τε καὶ ἄπιστον, καὶ αὖθις ἕτερον· καὶ ὅταν τοῦτο πολλάκις πάθῃ τις καὶ ὑπὸ τούτων μάλιστα οὓς ἂν ἡγήσαιτο
e οἰκειοτάτους τε καὶ ἑταιροτάτους, τελευτῶν δὴ θαμὰ προσ-κρούων μισεῖ τε πάντας καὶ ἡγεῖται οὐδενὸς οὐδὲν ὑγιὲς εἶναι τὸ παράπαν. ἢ οὐκ ᾔσθησαι σύ πω τοῦτο γιγνόμενον;

Πάνυ γε, ἦν δ' ἐγώ.

5 Οὐκοῦν, ἦ δ' ὅς, αἰσχρόν, καὶ δῆλον ὅτι ἄνευ τέχνης τῆς περὶ τἀνθρώπεια ὁ τοιοῦτος χρῆσθαι ἐπεχείρει τοῖς ἀνθρώ-ποις; εἰ γάρ που μετὰ τέχνης ἐχρῆτο, ὥσπερ ἔχει οὕτως
90 ἂν ἡγήσατο, τοὺς μὲν χρηστοὺς καὶ πονηροὺς σφόδρα ὀλίγους εἶναι ἑκατέρους, τοὺς δὲ μεταξὺ πλείστους.

Πῶς λέγεις; ἔφην ἐγώ.

Ὥσπερ, ἦ δ' ὅς, περὶ τῶν σφόδρα σμικρῶν καὶ μεγάλων·

---

c 5 οὐδ' ὁ ἡρακλῆς λέγεται B²TW   c 9 τοίνυν ἔφην B²W : τοίνυν ἔφη B : ἔφην τοίνυν T   ὡς B : ὡς ὁ T   c 11 ἔφη B : om. T d 6 γε B²TW : τε B   e 3 σύ πω] σὺ B et in marg. γρ. W : οὔπω TW : οὕτω Stob.   e 6 ἐπεχείρει Stob. : ἐπιχειρεῖ BTW   ἀνθρώ-ποις B²TW : ἀνθρωπείοις B   a 1 ἡγήσατο B Stob. : ἡγήσαιτο Tb a 3 ἔφην B : ἦν δ' TW

οἴει τι σπανιώτερον εἶναι ἢ σφόδρα μέγαν ἢ σφόδρα σμικρὸν 5
ἐξευρεῖν ἄνθρωπον ἢ κύνα ἢ ἄλλο ὁτιοῦν; ἢ αὖ ταχὺν ἢ
βραδὺν ἢ αἰσχρὸν ἢ καλὸν ἢ λευκὸν ἢ μέλανα; ἢ οὐχὶ
ᾔσθησαι ὅτι πάντων τῶν τοιούτων τὰ μὲν ἄκρα τῶν ἐσχάτων
σπάνια καὶ ὀλίγα, τὰ δὲ μεταξὺ ἄφθονα καὶ πολλά;
Πάνυ γε, ἦν δ᾽ ἐγώ. 10
Οὐκοῦν οἴει, ἔφη, εἰ πονηρίας ἀγὼν προτεθείη, πάνυ ἂν b
ὀλίγους καὶ ἐνταῦθα τοὺς πρώτους φανῆναι;
Εἰκός γε, ἦν δ᾽ ἐγώ.
Εἰκὸς γάρ, ἔφη. ἀλλὰ ταύτῃ μὲν οὐχ ὅμοιοι οἱ λόγοι
τοῖς ἀνθρώποις, ἀλλὰ σοῦ νυνδὴ προάγοντος ἐγὼ ἐφεσπόμην, 5
ἀλλ᾽ ἐκείνῃ, ᾗ, ἐπειδάν τις πιστεύσῃ λόγῳ τινὶ ἀληθεῖ
εἶναι ἄνευ τῆς περὶ τοὺς λόγους τέχνης, κἄπειτα ὀλίγον
ὕστερον αὐτῷ δόξῃ ψευδὴς εἶναι, ἐνίοτε μὲν ὤν, ἐνίοτε δ᾽
οὐκ ὤν, καὶ αὖθις ἕτερος καὶ ἕτερος·—καὶ μάλιστα δὴ οἱ
περὶ τοὺς ἀντιλογικοὺς λόγους διατρίψαντες οἶσθ᾽ ὅτι τελευ- c
τῶντες οἴονται σοφώτατοι γεγονέναι καὶ κατανενοηκέναι
μόνοι ὅτι οὔτε τῶν πραγμάτων οὐδενὸς οὐδὲν ὑγιὲς οὐδὲ
βέβαιον οὔτε τῶν λόγων, ἀλλὰ πάντα τὰ ὄντα ἀτεχνῶς ὥσπερ
ἐν Εὐρίπῳ ἄνω κάτω στρέφεται καὶ χρόνον οὐδένα ἐν 5
οὐδενὶ μένει.
Πάνυ μὲν οὖν, ἔφην ἐγώ, ἀληθῆ λέγεις.
Οὐκοῦν, ὦ Φαίδων, ἔφη, οἰκτρὸν ἂν εἴη τὸ πάθος, εἰ
ὄντος δή τινος ἀληθοῦς καὶ βεβαίου λόγου καὶ δυνατοῦ
κατανοῆσαι, ἔπειτα διὰ τὸ παραγίγνεσθαι τοιούτοις τισὶ d
λόγοις, τοῖς αὐτοῖς τοτὲ μὲν δοκοῦσιν ἀληθέσιν εἶναι, τοτὲ
δὲ μή, μὴ ἑαυτόν τις αἰτιῷτο μηδὲ τὴν ἑαυτοῦ ἀτεχνίαν,
ἀλλὰ τελευτῶν διὰ τὸ ἀλγεῖν ἄσμενος ἐπὶ τοὺς λόγους ἀφ᾽

a 7 καλὸν ἢ αἰσχρὸν T W   οὐχὶ T W : οὐκ B   a 10 γε B :
om. W   b 3 γε W : δὲ B T   b 4 οἱ B T : om. W   b 5 ἀνθρώποις B : ἀνθρώποις εἰσίν T W   ἐφεσπόμην T : ἐφεσποίμην B W
b 6 ᾗ secl. Madvig   b 7 ὕστερον ὀλίγον T W   b 8 δόξει W
c 2 καὶ T W : τε καὶ B   c 4 οὔτε τῶν λόγων] οὐδὲν τῶν ὄντων in
marg. B²   τὰ B² W : om. B T   c 5 κάτω T W : καὶ κάτω B
c 7 ἔφη B T : om. B² W   c 9 δὴ B : γε T W   d 1 τοιουτοισὶ
τισὶ T : τοιουτοισὶ B t   d 2 ἀληθέσιν B : ἀληθῆ λέγειν T   d 3 μὴ
alterum om. pr. T   τις om. W

9*

5 ἑαυτοῦ τὴν αἰτίαν ἀπώσαιτο καὶ ἤδη τὸν λοιπὸν βίον μισῶν
τε καὶ λοιδορῶν τοὺς λόγους διατελοῖ, τῶν δὲ ὄντων τῆς
ἀληθείας τε καὶ ἐπιστήμης στερηθείη.
Νὴ τὸν Δία, ἦν δ' ἐγώ, οἰκτρὸν δῆτα.

Πρῶτον μὲν τοίνυν, ἔφη, τοῦτο εὐλαβηθῶμεν, καὶ μὴ
e παρίωμεν εἰς τὴν ψυχὴν ὡς τῶν λόγων κινδυνεύει οὐδὲν
ὑγιὲς εἶναι, ἀλλὰ πολὺ μᾶλλον ὅτι ἡμεῖς οὔπω ὑγιῶς ἔχομεν,
ἀλλὰ ἀνδριστέον καὶ προθυμητέον ὑγιῶς ἔχειν, σοὶ μὲν οὖν
καὶ τοῖς ἄλλοις καὶ τοῦ ἔπειτα βίου παντὸς ἕνεκα, ἐμοὶ δὲ
91 αὐτοῦ ἕνεκα τοῦ θανάτου, ὡς κινδυνεύω ἔγωγε ἐν τῷ παρόντι
περὶ αὐτοῦ τούτου οὐ φιλοσόφως ἔχειν ἀλλ' ὥσπερ οἱ πάνυ
ἀπαίδευτοι φιλονίκως. καὶ γὰρ ἐκεῖνοι ὅταν περί του ἀμ-
φισβητῶσιν, ὅπῃ μὲν ἔχει περὶ ὧν ἂν ὁ λόγος ᾖ οὐ φροντί-
5 ζουσιν, ὅπως δὲ ἃ αὐτοὶ ἔθεντο ταῦτα δόξει τοῖς παροῦσιν,
τοῦτο προθυμοῦνται. καὶ ἐγώ μοι δοκῶ ἐν τῷ παρόντι
τοσοῦτον μόνον ἐκείνων διοίσειν· οὐ γὰρ ὅπως τοῖς παροῦσιν
ἃ ἐγὼ λέγω δόξει ἀληθῆ εἶναι προθυμήσομαι, εἰ μὴ εἴη
πάρεργον, ἀλλ' ὅπως αὐτῷ ἐμοὶ ὅτι μάλιστα δόξει οὕτως
b ἔχειν. λογίζομαι γάρ, ὦ φίλε ἑταῖρε—θέασαι ὡς πλεονεκτικῶς—εἰ μὲν τυγχάνει ἀληθῆ ὄντα ἃ λέγω, καλῶς δὴ
ἔχει τὸ πεισθῆναι· εἰ δὲ μηδέν ἐστι τελευτήσαντι, ἀλλ' οὖν
τοῦτόν γε τὸν χρόνον αὐτὸν τὸν πρὸ τοῦ θανάτου ἧττον τοῖς
5 παροῦσιν ἀηδὴς ἔσομαι ὀδυρόμενος, ἡ δὲ ἄνοιά μοι αὕτη οὐ
συνδιατελεῖ—κακὸν γὰρ ἂν ἦν—ἀλλ' ὀλίγον ὕστερον ἀπο-
λεῖται. παρεσκευασμένος δή, ἔφη, ὦ Σιμμία τε καὶ Κέβης,
οὑτωσὶ ἔρχομαι ἐπὶ τὸν λόγον· ὑμεῖς μέντοι, ἂν ἐμοὶ πεί-
c θησθε, σμικρὸν φροντίσαντες Σωκράτους, τῆς δὲ ἀληθείας
πολὺ μᾶλλον, ἐὰν μέν τι ὑμῖν δοκῶ ἀληθὲς λέγειν, συνομο-
λογήσατε, εἰ δὲ μή, παντὶ λόγῳ ἀντιτείνετε, εὐλαβούμενοι

d 6 τοὺς λόγους B² T W : om. B   d 9 εὐλαβηθῶμεν B T : εὐλε-
βηθητέον B² W (sed θῶμεν s. v.)   a 3 φιλονείκως B t : φιλονεικῶσιν T
ἀμφισβητήσωσιν T W   a 8-9 δόξει T : δόξῃ B   a 8 προθυμήσομαι T :
προθυμηθήσομαι B   b 1 ὡς B T : ὥσπερ W   b 4 γε B² T W :
δὲ B   b 5 ἄνοια B² T W : διάνοια B   b 7 δή B : μὲν δὴ T b
c 2 λέγειν ἀληθές T   c 3 εὐλαβούμενοι B² T W : om. B

ὅπως μὴ ἐγὼ ὑπὸ προθυμίας ἅμα ἐμαυτόν τε καὶ ὑμᾶς ἐξα-
πατήσας, ὥσπερ μέλιττα τὸ κέντρον ἐγκαταλιπὼν οἰχήσομαι. 5
Ἀλλ᾽ ἰτέον, ἔφη. πρῶτόν με ὑπομνήσατε ἃ ἐλέγετε, ἐὰν
μὴ φαίνωμαι μεμνημένος. Σιμμίας μὲν γάρ, ὡς ἐγῷμαι,
ἀπιστεῖ τε καὶ φοβεῖται μὴ ἡ ψυχὴ ὅμως καὶ θειότερον καὶ
κάλλιον ὂν τοῦ σώματος προαπολλύηται ἐν ἁρμονίας εἴδει d
οὖσα· Κέβης δέ μοι ἔδοξε τοῦτο μὲν ἐμοὶ συγχωρεῖν,
πολυχρονιώτερόν γε εἶναι ψυχὴν σώματος, ἀλλὰ τόδε
ἄδηλον παντί, μὴ πολλὰ δὴ σώματα καὶ πολλάκις κατα-
τρίψασα ἡ ψυχὴ τὸ τελευταῖον σῶμα καταλιποῦσα νῦν 5
αὐτὴ ἀπολλύηται, καὶ ᾖ αὐτὸ τοῦτο θάνατος, ψυχῆς ὄλε-
θρος, ἐπεὶ σῶμά γε ἀεὶ ἀπολλύμενον οὐδὲν παύεται. ἆρα
ἄλλ᾽ ἢ ταῦτ᾽ ἐστίν, ὦ Σιμμία τε καὶ Κέβης, ἃ δεῖ ἡμᾶς
ἐπισκοπεῖσθαι;

Συνωμολογείτην δὴ ταῦτ᾽ εἶναι ἄμφω.   e

Πότερον οὖν, ἔφη, πάντας τοὺς ἔμπροσθε λόγους οὐκ
ἀποδέχεσθε, ἢ τοὺς μέν, τοὺς δ᾽ οὔ;

Τοὺς μέν, ἐφάτην, τοὺς δ᾽ οὔ.

Τί οὖν, ἦ δ᾽ ὅς, περὶ ἐκείνου τοῦ λόγου λέγετε ἐν ᾧ 5
ἔφαμεν τὴν μάθησιν ἀνάμνησιν εἶναι, καὶ τούτου οὕτως
ἔχοντος ἀναγκαίως ἔχειν ἄλλοθι πρότερον ἡμῶν εἶναι τὴν
ψυχήν, πρὶν ἐν τῷ σώματι ἐνδεθῆναι;   92

Ἐγὼ μέν, ἔφη ὁ Κέβης, καὶ τότε θαυμαστῶς ὡς ἐπείσθην
ὑπ᾽ αὐτοῦ καὶ νῦν ἐμμένω ὡς οὐδενὶ λόγῳ.

Καὶ μήν, ἔφη ὁ Σιμμίας, καὶ αὐτὸς οὕτως ἔχω, καὶ πάνυ
ἂν θαυμάζοιμι εἴ μοι περί γε τούτου ἄλλο ποτέ τι δόξειεν. 5

Καὶ ὁ Σωκράτης, Ἀλλὰ ἀνάγκη σοι, ἔφη, ὦ ξένε Θηβαῖε,
ἄλλα δόξαι, ἐάνπερ μείνῃ ἥδε ἡ οἴησις, τὸ ἁρμονίαν μὲν εἶναι
σύνθετον πρᾶγμα, ψυχὴν δὲ ἁρμονίαν τινὰ ἐκ τῶν κατὰ τὸ

---

c 7 γὰρ B : om. T   ὡς ἐγῷμαι om. W : ἐγῷμαι s. v. w   d 1 κάλ-
λιστον W   d 5 νῦν ante τὸ τελευταῖον transp. T   d 8 δεῖ e
δὴ T   e 4 ἐφάτην T b Stob. : φάτην B W   e 5 λέγετε T Stob. :
λέγεται B W   e 7 ἄλλοθι T : ἄλλο τι B Stob. : ἄλλοθί που W
a 3 ἐμμενῶ W   a 5 ἄλλο T b : ἄλλα B W Stob.   ποτέ τι scripsi :
ποτὲ ἔτι T Stob. : ποτὲ B W   a 7 ἄλλα] ἄλλο Stob.   δόξαι T
Stob. (sed δοξαι εν pr. T) : δοξάσαι B W

σῶμα ἐντεταμένων συγκεῖσθαι· οὐ γάρ που ἀποδέξῃ γε
b σαυτοῦ λέγοντος ὡς πρότερον ἦν ἁρμονία συγκειμένη, πρὶν
ἐκεῖνα εἶναι ἐξ ὧν ἔδει αὐτὴν συντεθῆναι. ἢ ἀποδέξῃ;
Οὐδαμῶς, ἔφη, ὦ Σώκρατες.

Αἰσθάνῃ οὖν, ἦ δ' ὅς, ὅτι ταῦτά σοι συμβαίνει λέγειν,
5 ὅταν φῇς μὲν εἶναι τὴν ψυχὴν πρὶν καὶ εἰς ἀνθρώπου εἶδός
τε καὶ σῶμα ἀφικέσθαι, εἶναι δὲ αὐτὴν συγκειμένην ἐκ τῶν
οὐδέπω ὄντων; οὐ γὰρ δὴ ἁρμονία γέ σοι τοιοῦτόν ἐστιν
ᾧ ἀπεικάζεις, ἀλλὰ πρότερον καὶ ἡ λύρα καὶ αἱ χορδαὶ καὶ
c οἱ φθόγγοι ἔτι ἀνάρμοστοι ὄντες γίγνονται, τελευταῖον δὲ
πάντων συνίσταται ἡ ἁρμονία καὶ πρῶτον ἀπόλλυται. οὗτος
οὖν σοι ὁ λόγος ἐκείνῳ πῶς συνᾴσεται;
Οὐδαμῶς, ἔφη ὁ Σιμμίας.

5 Καὶ μήν, ἦ δ' ὅς, πρέπει γε εἴπερ τῳ ἄλλῳ λόγῳ συνῳδῷ
εἶναι καὶ τῷ περὶ ἁρμονίας.

Πρέπει γάρ, ἔφη ὁ Σιμμίας.

Οὗτος τοίνυν, ἔφη, σοὶ οὐ συνῳδός· ἀλλ' ὅρα πότερον
αἱρῇ τῶν λόγων, τὴν μάθησιν ἀνάμνησιν εἶναι ἢ ψυχὴν
10 ἁρμονίαν;

Πολὺ μᾶλλον, ἔφη, ἐκεῖνον, ὦ Σώκρατες. ὅδε μὲν γάρ
d μοι γέγονεν ἄνευ ἀποδείξεως μετὰ εἰκότος τινὸς καὶ εὐπρεπείας, ὅθεν καὶ τοῖς πολλοῖς δοκεῖ ἀνθρώποις· ἐγὼ δὲ τοῖς
διὰ τῶν εἰκότων τὰς ἀποδείξεις ποιουμένοις λόγοις σύνοιδα
οὖσιν ἀλαζόσιν, καὶ ἄν τις αὐτοὺς μὴ φυλάττηται, εὖ μάλα
5 ἐξαπατῶσι, καὶ ἐν γεωμετρίᾳ καὶ ἐν τοῖς ἄλλοις ἅπασιν.
ὁ δὲ περὶ τῆς ἀναμνήσεως καὶ μαθήσεως λόγος δι' ὑποθέσεως
ἀξίας ἀποδέξασθαι εἴρηται. ἐρρήθη γάρ που οὕτως ἡμῶν
εἶναι ἡ ψυχὴ καὶ πρὶν εἰς σῶμα ἀφικέσθαι, ὥσπερ αὐτῆς
ἐστιν ἡ οὐσία ἔχουσα τὴν ἐπωνυμίαν τὴν τοῦ "ὃ ἔστιν"

b 1 σαυτοῦ B² T W Stob. : αὐτοῦ B   b 4 ὅτι B T Stob. : ὅτι οὐ W
b 6 τε B² T W : γε B : om. Stob.   b 8 ᾧ B² T W Stob. : ᛞ B
c 3 ξυνάσεται B² T W : ξυνέσεται B : ξυναινέσεται Stob.   c 8 σοὶ
οὐ B² T W Stob : οἴου B   c 9 ψυχὴν B² T W Stob. : ψυχὴ B
c 11 ἔφη ἐκεῖνο B (ἐκεῖνον B²): ἐκεῖνον ἔφη T W Stob.   d 7 ὑποδέ-
ξασθαι W sed ὰ supra ύ   d 8 αὐτῆς] αὐτὴ Mudge

ἐγὼ δὲ ταύτην, ὡς ἐμαυτὸν πείθω, ἱκανῶς τε καὶ ὀρθῶς ἀπο- e
δέδεγμαι. ἀνάγκη οὖν μοι, ὡς ἔοικε, διὰ ταῦτα μήτε ἐμαυτοῦ
μήτε ἄλλου ἀποδέχεσθαι λέγοντος ὡς ψυχή ἐστιν ἁρμονία.

Τί δέ, ἦ δ' ὅς, ὦ Σιμμία, τῇδε; δοκεῖ σοι ἁρμονίᾳ ἢ ἄλλῃ
τινὶ συνθέσει προσήκειν ἄλλως πως ἔχειν ἢ ὡς ἂν ἐκεῖνα 93
ἔχῃ ἐξ ὧν ἂν συγκέηται;

Οὐδαμῶς.

Οὐδὲ μὴν ποιεῖν τι, ὡς ἐγῷμαι, οὐδέ τι πάσχειν ἄλλο
παρ' ἃ ἂν ἐκεῖνα ἢ ποιῇ ἢ πάσχῃ; Συνέφη. 5

Οὐκ ἄρα ἡγεῖσθαί γε προσήκει ἁρμονίαν τούτων ἐξ ὧν ἂν
συντεθῇ, ἀλλ' ἕπεσθαι. Συνεδόκει.

Πολλοῦ ἄρα δεῖ ἐναντία γε ἁρμονία κινηθῆναι ἂν ἢ
φθέγξασθαι ἤ τι ἄλλο ἐναντιωθῆναι τοῖς αὑτῆς μέρεσιν.

Πολλοῦ μέντοι, ἔφη. 10

Τί δέ; οὐχ οὕτως ἁρμονία πέφυκεν εἶναι ἑκάστη ἁρμονία
ὡς ἂν ἁρμοσθῇ;

Οὐ μανθάνω, ἔφη.

Ἦ οὐχί, ἦ δ' ὅς, ἂν μὲν μᾶλλον ἁρμοσθῇ καὶ ἐπὶ πλέον,
εἴπερ ἐνδέχεται τοῦτο γίγνεσθαι, μᾶλλόν τε ἂν ἁρμονία εἴη καὶ b
πλείων, εἰ δ' ἧττόν τε καὶ ἐπ' ἔλαττον, ἥττων τε καὶ ἐλάττων;

Πάνυ γε.

Ἦ οὖν ἔστι τοῦτο περὶ ψυχήν, ὥστε καὶ κατὰ τὸ σμικρό-
τατον μᾶλλον ἑτέραν ἑτέρας ψυχῆς ἐπὶ πλέον καὶ μᾶλλον 5
ἢ ἐπ' ἔλαττον καὶ ἧττον αὐτὸ τοῦτο εἶναι, ψυχήν;

Οὐδ' ὁπωστιοῦν, ἔφη.

Φέρε δή, ἔφη, πρὸς Διός· λέγεται ψυχὴ ἡ μὲν νοῦν τε
ἔχειν καὶ ἀρετὴν καὶ εἶναι ἀγαθή, ἡ δὲ ἄνοιάν τε καὶ μοχθηρίαν
καὶ εἶναι κακή; καὶ ταῦτα ἀληθῶς λέγεται; c

Ἀληθῶς μέντοι.

a 1 ἂν ἐκεῖνα B Stob. : ἐκεῖνα ἂν T   a 2 ἐξ B T : τὰ ἐξ W
a 8 ἂν Stob. : om. B T W   a 14 ἢ om. Heusde   b 1 ἂν B Stob. :
om. T   b 2 ἥττων B T W Stob. : ἥττον al.   b 4 ἢ T b : ἢ B² et
s. v. W : εἰ B W   b 5 μᾶλλον secl. Heusde   ψυχὴν Stob.
b 6 ἐπ(ὶ) B T Stob. : om. W   b 8 ἔφη B Stob. : om. T   τε
B Stob. : om. T W

Τῶν οὖν θεμένων ψυχὴν ἁρμονίαν εἶναι τί τις φήσει
ταῦτα ὄντα εἶναι ἐν ταῖς ψυχαῖς, τήν τε ἀρετὴν καὶ τὴν
5 κακίαν; πότερον ἁρμονίαν αὖ τινα ἄλλην καὶ ἀναρμοστίαν;
καὶ τὴν μὲν ἡρμόσθαι, τὴν ἀγαθήν, καὶ ἔχειν ἐν αὐτῇ
ἁρμονίᾳ οὔσῃ ἄλλην ἁρμονίαν, τὴν δὲ ἀνάρμοστον αὐτήν τε
εἶναι καὶ οὐκ ἔχειν ἐν αὐτῇ ἄλλην;
    Οὐκ ἔχω ἔγωγ', ἔφη ὁ Σιμμίας, εἰπεῖν· δῆλον δ' ὅτι
10 τοιαῦτ' ἄττ' ἂν λέγοι ὁ ἐκεῖνο ὑποθέμενος.

d   Ἀλλὰ προωμολόγηται, ἔφη, μηδὲν μᾶλλον μηο' ἧττον
ἑτέραν ἑτέρας ψυχὴν ψυχῆς εἶναι· τοῦτο δ' ἔστι τὸ ὁμολόγημα, μηδὲν μᾶλλον μηδ' ἐπὶ πλέον μηδ' ἧττον μηδ' ἐπ'
ἔλαττον ἑτέραν ἑτέρας ἁρμονίαν ἁρμονίας εἶναι. ἦ γάρ;
5   Πάνυ γε.
    Τὴν δέ γε μηδὲν μᾶλλον μηδὲ ἧττον ἁρμονίαν οὖσαν μήτε
μᾶλλον μήτε ἧττον ἡρμόσθαι· ἔστιν οὕτως;
    Ἔστιν.
    Ἡ δὲ μήτε μᾶλλον μήτε ἧττον ἡρμοσμένη ἔστιν ὅτι πλέον
10 ἢ ἔλαττον ἁρμονίας μετέχει, ἢ τὸ ἴσον;
    Τὸ ἴσον.
    Οὐκοῦν ψυχὴ ἐπειδὴ οὐδὲν μᾶλλον οὐδ' ἧττον ἄλλη
e ἄλλης αὐτὸ τοῦτο, ψυχή, ἐστίν, οὐδὲ δὴ μᾶλλον οὐδὲ ἧττον
ἥρμοσται;
    Οὕτω.
    Τοῦτο δέ γε πεπονθυῖα οὐδὲν πλέον ἀναρμοστίας οὐδὲ
5 ἁρμονίας μετέχοι ἄν;
    Οὐ γὰρ οὖν.
    Τοῦτο δ' αὖ πεπονθυῖα ἆρ' ἄν τι πλέον κακίας ἢ ἀρετῆς
μετέχοι ἑτέρα ἑτέρας, εἴπερ ἡ μὲν κακία ἀναρμοστία, ἡ δὲ
ἀρετὴ ἁρμονία εἴη;

c 3 θεμένων B : τιθεμένων T b Stob.   c 5 πότερον B : πότερα T
Stob.   αὖ τινα B Stob. : τινὰ αὖ T   ἄλλην] καλὴν in marg. B²
c 9 ἔγωγε, φησὶν Stob.   ὁ B² T W : ὦ B   d 4 ἁρμονίας secl.
Schmidt   d 6-7 μήτε ... μήτε Stallbaum : μηδὲ ... μηδὲ B T W
Stob.   d 9 ἢ T : η W : εἰ B Stob.   d 12 ἐπειδὴ om. Stob.
e 1 οὐδὲ] οὐδὲν Bekker

Οὐδὲν πλέον. 10

Μᾶλλον δέ γέ που, ὦ Σιμμία, κατὰ τὸν ὀρθὸν λόγον 94
κακίας οὐδεμία ψυχὴ μεθέξει, εἴπερ ἁρμονία ἐστίν· ἁρμονία
γὰρ δήπου παντελῶς αὐτὸ τοῦτο οὖσα, ἁρμονία, ἀναρμοστίας
οὔποτ᾽ ἂν μετάσχοι.

Οὐ μέντοι. 5

Οὐδέ γε δήπου ψυχή, οὖσα παντελῶς ψυχή, κακίας.

Πῶς γὰρ ἔκ γε τῶν προειρημένων;

Ἐκ τούτου ἄρα τοῦ λόγου ἡμῖν πᾶσαι ψυχαὶ πάντων
ζῴων ὁμοίως ἀγαθαὶ ἔσονται, εἴπερ ὁμοίως ψυχαὶ πεφύκασιν
αὐτὸ τοῦτο, ψυχαί, εἶναι. 10

Ἔμοιγε δοκεῖ, ἔφη, ὦ Σώκρατες.

Ἦ καὶ καλῶς δοκεῖ, ἦ δ᾽ ὅς, οὕτω λέγεσθαι, καὶ πάσχειν
ἂν ταῦτα ὁ λόγος εἰ ὀρθὴ ἡ ὑπόθεσις ἦν, τὸ ψυχὴν ἁρμονίαν b
εἶναι;

Οὐδ᾽ ὁπωστιοῦν, ἔφη.

Τί δέ; ἦ δ᾽ ὅς· τῶν ἐν ἀνθρώπῳ πάντων ἔσθ᾽ ὅτι ἄλλο
λέγεις ἄρχειν ἢ ψυχὴν ἄλλως τε καὶ φρόνιμον; 5

Οὐκ ἔγωγε.

Πότερον συγχωροῦσαν τοῖς κατὰ τὸ σῶμα πάθεσιν ἢ καὶ
ἐναντιουμένην; λέγω δὲ τὸ τοιόνδε, οἷον καύματος ἐνόντος
καὶ δίψους ἐπὶ τοὐναντίον ἕλκειν, τὸ μὴ πίνειν, καὶ πείνης
ἐνούσης ἐπὶ τὸ μὴ ἐσθίειν, καὶ ἄλλα μυρία που ὁρῶμεν 10
ἐναντιουμένην τὴν ψυχὴν τοῖς κατὰ τὸ σῶμα· ἢ οὔ; c

Πάνυ μὲν οὖν.

Οὐκοῦν αὖ ὡμολογήσαμεν ἐν τοῖς πρόσθεν μήποτ᾽ ἂν
αὐτήν, ἁρμονίαν γε οὖσαν, ἐναντία ᾄδειν οἷς ἐπιτείνοιτο

---

a 9 ψυχαὶ secl. ci. Heindorf   a 10 τοῦτο T W Stob. :   τοῦτο
τὸ B t   εἶναι ψυχαὶ Stob.   b 1 ἂν Stob. : om. B T W   ἢ T W
Stob. : om. B   b 7 πάθεσιν B T : παθήμασιν W Stob.   ἢ καὶ
B² T W Stob. : om. B   b 8 ἐναντιουμένην T (sed add. in marg.
παθήμασιν) W Stob. : ἐναντιουμένην παθήμασι B   τὸ B T Stob. :
om. W   οἷον T W Stob. : ὡς εἰ B : ὡσεὶ et ὡς καύματος in marg. b
b 9 τὸ B T : τοῦ W   b 10 που μυρία Stob.   c 3 πρόσθεν B T
Stob. : ἔμπροσθεν W   μήποτ᾽ ἂν αὐτὴν B² T W : μήποτε ταύτην
B Stob.

5 καὶ χαλῷτο καὶ ψάλλοιτο καὶ ἄλλο ὁτιοῦν πάθος πάσχοι
ἐκεῖνα ἐξ ὧν τυγχάνοι οὖσα, ἀλλ' ἕπεσθαι ἐκείνοις καὶ οὔποτ'
ἂν ἡγεμονεύειν;
Ὡμολογήσαμεν, ἔφη· πῶς γὰρ οὔ;
Τί οὖν; νῦν οὐ πᾶν τοὐναντίον ἡμῖν φαίνεται ἐργαζομένη,
10 ἡγεμονεύουσά τε ἐκείνων πάντων ἐξ ὧν φησί τις αὐτὴν
d εἶναι, καὶ ἐναντιουμένη ὀλίγου πάντα διὰ παντὸς τοῦ βίου
καὶ δεσπόζουσα πάντας τρόπους, τὰ μὲν χαλεπώτερον κολά-
ζουσα καὶ μετ' ἀλγηδόνων, τά τε κατὰ τὴν γυμναστικὴν καὶ
τὴν ἰατρικήν, τὰ δὲ πρᾳότερον, καὶ τὰ μὲν ἀπειλοῦσα, τὰ δὲ
5 νουθετοῦσα, ταῖς ἐπιθυμίαις καὶ ὀργαῖς καὶ φόβοις ὡς ἄλλη
οὖσα ἄλλῳ πράγματι διαλεγομένη; οἷόν που καὶ Ὅμηρος ἐν
Ὀδυσσείᾳ πεποίηκεν, οὗ λέγει τὸν Ὀδυσσέα·

στῆθος δὲ πλήξας κραδίην ἠνίπαπε μύθῳ·
e   τέτλαθι δή, κραδίη· καὶ κύντερον ἄλλο ποτ' ἔτλης.

ἆρ' οἴει αὐτὸν ταῦτα ποιῆσαι διανοούμενον ὡς ἁρμονίας
αὐτῆς οὔσης καὶ οἵας ἄγεσθαι ὑπὸ τῶν τοῦ σώματος παθημάτων, ἀλλ' οὐχ οἵας ἄγειν τε ταῦτα καὶ δεσπόζειν, καὶ
5 οὔσης αὐτῆς πολὺ θειοτέρου τινὸς πράγματος ἢ καθ'
ἁρμονίαν;
Νὴ Δία, ὦ Σώκρατες, ἔμοιγε δοκεῖ.
Οὐκ ἄρα, ὦ ἄριστε, ἡμῖν οὐδαμῇ καλῶς ἔχει ψυχὴν
95 ἁρμονίαν τινὰ φάναι εἶναι· οὔτε γὰρ ἄν, ὡς ἔοικεν, Ὁμήρῳ
θείῳ ποιητῇ ὁμολογοῖμεν οὔτε αὐτοὶ ἡμῖν αὐτοῖς.
Ἔχει οὕτως, ἔφη.
Εἶεν δή, ἦ δ' ὃς ὁ Σωκράτης, τὰ μὲν Ἁρμονίας ἡμῖν τῆς
5 Θηβαϊκῆς ἵλεά πως, ὡς ἔοικε, μετρίως γέγονεν· τί δὲ δὴ τὰ
Κάδμου, ἔφη, ὦ Κέβης, πῶς ἱλασόμεθα καὶ τίνι λόγῳ;
Σύ μοι δοκεῖς, ἔφη ὁ Κέβης, ἐξευρήσειν· τουτονὶ γοῦν

---

c 5 ψάλλοιτο pr. T (ut vid.) Stob. : πάλλοιτο B T W   c 6 τυγχάνοι
T : τυγχάνει B Stob.   c 9 νῦν B T Stob. : om. W   d 1 ἐνατιου-
μένη B² T W Stob. : ἐναντιουμένην B   d 3 τε B T Stob. : δὲ W
e 3 παθημάτων B² T W Stob. : παθῶν B   e 5 πράγματος B : om. T
Stob.   e 7 ἔμοιγε B Stob. : ἐμοὶ T   a 3 ἔχει T W Stob. :
ἔχειν B t   a 7 τουτονὶ B : τοῦτον T

τὸν λόγον τὸν πρὸς τὴν ἁρμονίαν θαυμαστῶς μοι εἶπες ὡς
παρὰ δόξαν. Σιμμίου γὰρ λέγοντος ὅτε ἠπόρει, πάνυ ἐθαύ-
μαζον εἴ τι ἕξει τις χρήσασθαι τῷ λόγῳ αὐτοῦ· πάνυ οὖν b
μοι ἀτόπως ἔδοξεν εὐθὺς τὴν πρώτην ἔφοδον οὐ δέξασθαι
τοῦ σοῦ λόγου. ταὐτὰ δὴ οὐκ ἂν θαυμάσαιμι καὶ τὸν τοῦ
Κάδμου λόγον εἰ πάθοι.

Ὠγαθέ, ἔφη ὁ Σωκράτης, μὴ μέγα λέγε, μή τις ἡμῖν 5
βασκανία περιτρέψῃ τὸν λόγον τὸν μέλλοντα ἔσεσθαι.
ἀλλὰ δὴ ταῦτα μὲν τῷ θεῷ μελήσει, ἡμεῖς δὲ Ὁμηρικῶς
ἐγγὺς ἰόντες πειρώμεθα εἰ ἄρα τι λέγεις. ἔστι δὲ δὴ τὸ
κεφάλαιον ὧν ζητεῖς· ἀξιοῖς ἐπιδειχθῆναι ἡμῶν τὴν ψυχὴν
ἀνώλεθρόν τε καὶ ἀθάνατον οὖσαν, εἰ φιλόσοφος ἀνὴρ μέλ- c
λων ἀποθανεῖσθαι, θαρρῶν τε καὶ ἡγούμενος ἀποθανὼν ἐκεῖ
εὖ πράξειν διαφερόντως ἢ εἰ ἐν ἄλλῳ βίῳ βιοὺς ἐτελεύτα,
μὴ ἀνόητόν τε καὶ ἠλίθιον θάρρος θαρρήσει. τὸ δὲ ἀπο-
φαίνειν ὅτι ἰσχυρόν τί ἐστιν ἡ ψυχὴ καὶ θεοειδὲς καὶ ἦν ἔτι 5
πρότερον, πρὶν ἡμᾶς ἀνθρώπους γενέσθαι, οὐδὲν κωλύειν
φῂς πάντα ταῦτα μηνύειν ἀθανασίαν μὲν μή, ὅτι δὲ πολυχρόνιόν τέ ἐστιν ψυχὴ καὶ ἦν που πρότερον ἀμήχανον ὅσον
χρόνον καὶ ᾔδει τε καὶ ἔπραττεν πολλὰ ἄττα· ἀλλὰ γὰρ
οὐδέν τι μᾶλλον ἦν ἀθάνατον, ἀλλὰ καὶ αὐτὸ τὸ εἰς ἀν- d
θρώπου σῶμα ἐλθεῖν ἀρχὴ ἦν αὐτῇ ὀλέθρου, ὥσπερ νόσος·
καὶ ταλαιπωρουμένη τε δὴ τοῦτον τὸν βίον ζῴη καὶ τελευτῶσά
γε ἐν τῷ καλουμένῳ θανάτῳ ἀπολλύοιτο. διαφέρειν δὲ δὴ
φῂς οὐδὲν εἴτε ἅπαξ εἰς σῶμα ἔρχεται εἴτε πολλάκις, πρός 5
γε τὸ ἕκαστον ἡμῶν φοβεῖσθαι· προσήκει γὰρ φοβεῖσθαι,
εἰ μὴ ἀνόητος εἴη, τῷ μὴ εἰδότι μηδὲ ἔχοντι λόγον διδόναι
ὡς ἀθάνατόν ἐστι. τοιαῦτ' ἄττα ἐστίν, οἶμαι, ὦ Κέβης, ἃ e

a 9 ὅτε] ὅ τι ci. Forster   b 1 χρήσασθαι B : χρῆσθαι T   οὖν T :
μὲν οὖν B   b 5 ἡμῖν W : ἡμῶν B T   b 6 ἔσεσθαι B T : λέγεσθαι
B² W t   c 3 εἰ B : om. T   c 5 ἦν B T : ὅτι ἦν B² W   c 7 φῂς
ἂν in marg. b   πολυχρονιώτερόν W   c 8 ὅσον χρόνον B : om. T
d 4 διαφέρει al. Heindorf   d 6 προσήκειν Baiter   e 1 τοιαῦτ'
ἄττα B : τοιαῦτα T

λέγεις· καὶ ἐξεπίτηδες πολλάκις ἀναλαμβάνω, ἵνα μή τι
διαφύγῃ ἡμᾶς, εἴ τέ τι βούλει, προσθῇς ἢ ἀφέλῃς.

Καὶ ὁ Κέβης, 'Αλλ' οὐδὲν ἔγωγε ἐν τῷ παρόντι, ἔφη,
5 οὔτε ἀφελεῖν οὔτε προσθεῖναι δέομαι· ἔστι δὲ ταῦτα ἃ
λέγω.

Ὁ οὖν Σωκράτης συχνὸν χρόνον ἐπισχὼν καὶ πρὸς ἑαυτόν
τι σκεψάμενος, Οὐ φαῦλον πρᾶγμα, ἔφη, ὦ Κέβης, ζητεῖς·
ὅλως γὰρ δεῖ περὶ γενέσεως καὶ φθορᾶς τὴν αἰτίαν δια-
96 πραγματεύσασθαι. ἐγὼ οὖν σοι δίειμι περὶ αὐτῶν, ἐὰν
βούλῃ, τά γε ἐμὰ πάθη· ἔπειτα ἄν τί σοι χρήσιμον
φαίνηται ὧν ἂν λέγω, πρὸς τὴν πειθὼ περὶ ὧν δὴ λέγεις
χρήσῃ.

5 'Αλλὰ μήν, ἔφη ὁ Κέβης, βούλομαί γε.

"Ακουε τοίνυν ὡς ἐροῦντος. ἐγὼ γάρ, ἔφη, ὦ Κέβης,
νέος ὢν θαυμαστῶς ὡς ἐπεθύμησα ταύτης τῆς σοφίας ἣν
δὴ καλοῦσι περὶ φύσεως ἱστορίαν· ὑπερήφανος γάρ μοι
ἐδόκει εἶναι, εἰδέναι τὰς αἰτίας ἑκάστου, διὰ τί γίγνεται
10 ἕκαστον καὶ διὰ τί ἀπόλλυται καὶ διὰ τί ἔστι. καὶ πολλάκις
b ἐμαυτὸν ἄνω κάτω μετέβαλλον σκοπῶν πρῶτον τὰ τοιάδε·
"'Αρ' ἐπειδὰν τὸ θερμὸν καὶ τὸ ψυχρὸν σηπεδόνα τινὰ
λάβῃ, ὥς τινες ἔλεγον, τότε δὴ τὰ ζῷα συντρέφεται; καὶ
πότερον τὸ αἷμά ἐστιν ᾧ φρονοῦμεν, ἢ ὁ ἀὴρ ἢ τὸ πῦρ; ἢ
5 τούτων μὲν οὐδέν, ὁ δ' ἐγκέφαλός ἐστιν ὁ τὰς αἰσθήσεις
παρέχων τοῦ ἀκούειν καὶ ὁρᾶν καὶ ὀσφραίνεσθαι, ἐκ τούτων
δὲ γίγνοιτο μνήμη καὶ δόξα, ἐκ δὲ μνήμης καὶ δόξης λα-
βούσης τὸ ἠρεμεῖν, κατὰ ταῦτα γίγνεσθαι ἐπιστήμην; καὶ
αὖ τούτων τὰς φθορὰς σκοπῶν, καὶ τὰ περὶ τὸν οὐρανόν

e 3 διαφύγῃ W : διαφεύγοι Β Τ   e 9 δεῖ Β Τ Stob. : δὴ W
a 3 φανεῖται Τ   δὴ λέγεις Baumann : ἂν λέγῃς Β : λέγεις Τ Stob.
a 5-6 βούλομαι ... Κέβης om. Β : add. in marg. Β²   a 5 γε Β² W t :
τε Τ   a 8 ὑπερήφανος Β Τ W (ὑπέρφρων schol.) : ὑπερήφανον Eus.
Stob.   a 9 εἰδέναι Β² Τ W Eus. Stob. : om. B   αἰτίας Β W
Eus. Stob. et in marg. γρ. Τ : ἱστορίας Τ : ὁ ι πρῶτον Β² Τ W
Eus. Stob. : om. B   b 2 καὶ τὸ ψυχρὸν Τ Eus. Stob. : καὶ ψυχρὸν
Β W : secl. Schanz : καὶ τὸ ὑγρὸν Sprengel   b 8 κατὰ ταῦτα Β W
Eus. Stob. : καὶ ταῦτα Τ : κατὰ ταὐτὰ Heindorf

τε καὶ τὴν γῆν πάθη, τελευτῶν οὕτως ἐμαυτῷ ἔδοξα πρὸς c
ταύτην τὴν σκέψιν ἀφυὴς εἶναι ὡς οὐδὲν χρῆμα. τεκμήριον δέ σοι ἐρῶ ἱκανόν· ἐγὼ γὰρ ἃ καὶ πρότερον σαφῶς
ἠπιστάμην, ὥς γε ἐμαυτῷ καὶ τοῖς ἄλλοις ἐδόκουν, τότε
ὑπὸ ταύτης τῆς σκέψεως οὕτω σφόδρα ἐτυφλώθην, ὥστε 5
ἀπέμαθον καὶ ταῦτα ἃ πρὸ τοῦ ᾤμην εἰδέναι, περὶ ἄλλων τε
πολλῶν καὶ διὰ τί ἄνθρωπος αὐξάνεται. τοῦτο γὰρ ᾤμην
πρὸ τοῦ παντὶ δῆλον εἶναι, ὅτι διὰ τὸ ἐσθίειν καὶ πίνειν·
ἐπειδὰν γὰρ ἐκ τῶν σιτίων ταῖς μὲν σαρξὶ σάρκες προσ- d
γένωνται, τοῖς δὲ ὀστοῖς ὀστᾶ, καὶ οὕτω κατὰ τὸν αὐτὸν
λόγον καὶ τοῖς ἄλλοις τὰ αὐτῶν οἰκεῖα ἑκάστοις προσγένηται,
τότε δὴ τὸν ὀλίγον ὄγκον ὄντα ὕστερον πολὺν γεγονέναι,
καὶ οὕτω γίγνεσθαι τὸν σμικρὸν ἄνθρωπον μέγαν. οὕτως 5
τότε ᾤμην· οὐ δοκῶ σοι μετρίως;
Ἔμοιγε, ἔφη ὁ Κέβης.
Σκέψαι δὴ καὶ τάδε ἔτι. ᾤμην γὰρ ἱκανῶς μοι δοκεῖν,
ὁπότε τις φαίνοιτο ἄνθρωπος παραστὰς μέγας σμικρῷ μείζων
εἶναι αὐτῇ τῇ κεφαλῇ, καὶ ἵππος ἵππου· καὶ ἔτι γε τούτων e
ἐναργέστερα, τὰ δέκα μοι ἐδόκει τῶν ὀκτὼ πλέονα εἶναι διὰ
τὸ δύο αὐτοῖς προσεῖναι, καὶ τὸ δίπηχυ τοῦ πηχυαίου μεῖζον
εἶναι διὰ τὸ ἡμίσει αὐτοῦ ὑπερέχειν.
Νῦν δὲ δή, ἔφη ὁ Κέβης, τί σοι δοκεῖ περὶ αὐτῶν; 5
Πόρρω που, ἔφη, νὴ Δία ἐμὲ εἶναι τοῦ οἴεσθαι περὶ
τούτων του τὴν αἰτίαν εἰδέναι, ὅς γε οὐκ ἀποδέχομαι ἐμαυτοῦ
οὐδὲ ὡς ἐπειδὰν ἑνί τις προσθῇ ἕν, ἢ τὸ ἓν ᾧ προσετέθη
δύο γέγονεν, ⟨ἢ τὸ προστεθέν⟩, ἢ τὸ προστεθὲν καὶ ᾧ προσετέθη διὰ τὴν πρόσθεσιν τοῦ ἑτέρου τῷ ἑτέρῳ δύο ἐγένετο· 97
θαυμάζω γὰρ εἰ ὅτε μὲν ἑκάτερον αὐτῶν χωρὶς ἀλλήλων
ἦν, ἓν ἄρα ἑκάτερον ἦν καὶ οὐκ ἤστην τότε δύο, ἐπεὶ δ'

c 1 τε Β² Τ W Eus. Stob. : om. B   c 5 ὑπὸ ταύτης Β Τ : ὑπ' αὐτῆς W Eus.   c 6 ἀπέμαθον καὶ ταῦτα Β² (in marg.) T W Eus.
Stob. : ἄποτ' ἔμαθον B   c 8 τὸ Β : τοῦ Τ   d 1 προσγένωνται
Β² Τ W : προσγεννῶνται B   d 8 γὰρ Β : γὰρ ἐγὼ Τ : γὰρ ἔγωγε b
d 9 παραστὰς ἄνθρωπος W   e 1 αὐτῇ] αὐτοῦ Wyttenbach   ἵππου
Β : ἵππῳ Τ b   e 3 τὸ Β Τ : τὸ τὰ W   προσεῖναι Β² Τ W :
προσθεῖναι B   e 4 ἡμίσει Β² Τ W : ἥμισυ B   e 7 του W t :
τοῦ Β Τ   e 9 ἢ τὸ προστεθὲν add. Wyttenbach

ἐπλησίασαν ἀλλήλοις, αὕτη ἄρα αἰτία αὐτοῖς ἐγένετο τοῦ δύο
5 γενέσθαι, ἡ σύνοδος τοῦ πλησίον ἀλλήλων τεθῆναι. οὐδέ
γε ὡς ἐάν τις ἓν διασχίσῃ, δύναμαι ἔτι πείθεσθαι ὡς αὕτη
αὖ αἰτία γέγονεν, ἡ σχίσις, τοῦ δύο γεγονέναι· ἐναντία γὰρ
b γίγνεται ἢ τότε αἰτία τοῦ δύο γίγνεσθαι. τότε μὲν γὰρ ὅτι
συνήγετο πλησίον ἀλλήλων καὶ προσετίθετο ἕτερον ἑτέρῳ,
νῦν δ᾽ ὅτι ἀπάγεται καὶ χωρίζεται ἕτερον ἀφ᾽ ἑτέρου. οὐδέ
γε δι᾽ ὅτι ἓν γίγνεται ὡς ἐπίσταμαι, ἔτι πείθω ἐμαυτόν,
5 οὐδ᾽ ἄλλο οὐδὲν ἑνὶ λόγῳ δι᾽ ὅτι γίγνεται ἢ ἀπόλλυται ἢ
ἔστι, κατὰ τοῦτον τὸν τρόπον τῆς μεθόδου, ἀλλά τιν᾽ ἄλλον
τρόπον αὐτὸς εἰκῇ φύρω, τοῦτον δὲ οὐδαμῇ προσίεμαι.

Ἀλλ᾽ ἀκούσας μέν ποτε ἐκ βιβλίου τινός, ὡς ἔφη, Ἀναξ-
c αγόρου ἀναγιγνώσκοντος, καὶ λέγοντος ὡς ἄρα νοῦς ἐστιν ὁ
διακοσμῶν τε καὶ πάντων αἴτιος, ταύτῃ δὴ τῇ αἰτίᾳ ἥσθην τε
καὶ ἔδοξέ μοι τρόπον τινὰ εὖ ἔχειν τὸ τὸν νοῦν εἶναι πάντων
αἴτιον, καὶ ἡγησάμην, εἰ τοῦθ᾽ οὕτως ἔχει, τόν γε νοῦν
5 κοσμοῦντα πάντα κοσμεῖν καὶ ἕκαστον τιθέναι ταύτῃ ὅπῃ
ἂν βέλτιστα ἔχῃ· εἰ οὖν τις βούλοιτο τὴν αἰτίαν εὑρεῖν
περὶ ἑκάστου ὅπῃ γίγνεται ἢ ἀπόλλυται ἢ ἔστι, τοῦτο δεῖν
περὶ αὐτοῦ εὑρεῖν, ὅπῃ βέλτιστον αὐτῷ ἐστιν ἢ εἶναι ἢ
d ἄλλο ὁτιοῦν πάσχειν ἢ ποιεῖν· ἐκ δὲ δὴ τοῦ λόγου τούτου
οὐδὲν ἄλλο σκοπεῖν προσήκειν ἀνθρώπῳ καὶ περὶ αὐτοῦ ἐκείνου καὶ περὶ τῶν ἄλλων ἀλλ᾽ ἢ τὸ ἄριστον καὶ τὸ βέλτιστον.
ἀναγκαῖον δὲ εἶναι τὸν αὐτὸν τοῦτον καὶ τὸ χεῖρον εἰδέναι·
5 τὴν αὐτὴν γὰρ εἶναι ἐπιστήμην περὶ αὐτῶν. ταῦτα δὴ
λογιζόμενος ἅσμενος ηὑρηκέναι ᾤμην διδάσκαλον τῆς αἰτίας
περὶ τῶν ὄντων κατὰ νοῦν ἐμαυτῷ, τὸν Ἀναξαγόραν, καί
μοι φράσειν πρῶτον μὲν πότερον ἡ γῆ πλατεῖά ἐστιν ἢ
e στρογγύλη, ἐπειδὴ δὲ φράσειεν, ἐπεκδιηγήσεσθαι τὴν αἰτίαν

a 4 αὐτοῖς αἰτία T   τοῦ δύο W : δύο B : δυοῖν T   a 6 διχάσῃ W
a 7 αὖ om. T   b 1 ἢ W : ἡ B T   μὲν om. W   b 2 τὸ πλησίον
et mox τὸ ἕτερον W   b 3 ὑφ᾽ W   b 5 ἑνὶ λόγῳ B : ἐν
ὀλίγῳ T   ἢ γίγνεται W   c 2 δὴ B Eus. : ἤδη T   τε B
Eus. : om. T   c 7 ὅπῃ ἢ Eus.   c 8 αὐτῷ B² T W Eus. : αὐτῶν B   d 2 προσήκειν B² T W : προσήκει B w   ἐκείνου B : om.
T W Eus.   d 3 τῶν B² T W Eus. : om. B   d 8 ἐστιν om. W
e 1 ἐπεκδιηγήσασθαι W (et mox e 4, b 3)

καὶ τὴν ἀνάγκην, λέγοντα τὸ ἄμεινον καὶ ὅτι αὐτὴν ἄμεινον
ἦν τοιαύτην εἶναι· καὶ εἰ ἐν μέσῳ φαίη εἶναι αὐτήν, ἐπεκδιηγήσεσθαι ὡς ἄμεινον ἦν αὐτὴν ἐν μέσῳ εἶναι· καὶ εἴ μοι
ταῦτα ἀποφαίνοι, παρεσκευάσμην ὡς οὐκέτι ποθεσόμενος 98
αἰτίας ἄλλο εἶδος. καὶ δὴ καὶ περὶ ἡλίου οὕτω παρεσκευάσμην ὡσαύτως πευσόμενος, καὶ σελήνης καὶ τῶν ἄλλων
ἄστρων, τάχους τε πέρι πρὸς ἄλληλα καὶ τροπῶν καὶ τῶν
ἄλλων παθημάτων, πῇ ποτε ταῦτ' ἄμεινόν ἐστιν ἕκαστον 5
καὶ ποιεῖν καὶ πάσχειν ἃ πάσχει. οὐ γὰρ ἄν ποτε αὐτὸν
ᾤμην, φάσκοντά γε ὑπὸ νοῦ αὐτὰ κεκοσμῆσθαι, ἄλλην τινὰ
αὐτοῖς αἰτίαν ἐπενεγκεῖν ἢ ὅτι βέλτιστον αὐτὰ οὕτως ἔχειν
ἐστὶν ὥσπερ ἔχει· ἑκάστῳ οὖν αὐτῶν ἀποδιδόντα τὴν αἰτίαν b
καὶ κοινῇ πᾶσι τὸ ἑκάστῳ βέλτιστον ᾤμην καὶ τὸ κοινὸν
πᾶσιν ἐπεκδιηγήσεσθαι ἀγαθόν· καὶ οὐκ ἂν ἀπεδόμην πολλοῦ
τὰς ἐλπίδας, ἀλλὰ πάνυ σπουδῇ λαβὼν τὰς βίβλους ὡς
τάχιστα οἷός τ' ἦ ἀνεγίγνωσκον, ἵν' ὡς τάχιστα εἰδείην τὸ 5
βέλτιστον καὶ τὸ χεῖρον.

Ἀπὸ δὴ θαυμαστῆς ἐλπίδος, ὦ ἑταῖρε, ᾠχόμην φερόμενος,
ἐπειδὴ προϊὼν καὶ ἀναγιγνώσκων ὁρῶ ἄνδρα τῷ μὲν νῷ
οὐδὲν χρώμενον οὐδέ τινας αἰτίας ἐπαιτιώμενον εἰς τὸ
διακοσμεῖν τὰ πράγματα, ἀέρας δὲ καὶ αἰθέρας καὶ ὕδατα c
αἰτιώμενον καὶ ἄλλα πολλὰ καὶ ἄτοπα. καί μοι ἔδοξεν
ὁμοιότατον πεπονθέναι ὥσπερ ἂν εἴ τις λέγων ὅτι Σωκράτης
πάντα ὅσα πράττει νῷ πράττει, κἄπειτα ἐπιχειρήσας λέγειν
τὰς αἰτίας ἑκάστων ὧν πράττω, λέγοι πρῶτον μὲν ὅτι διὰ 5
ταῦτα νῦν ἐνθάδε κάθημαι, ὅτι σύγκειταί μου τὸ σῶμα ἐξ
ὀστῶν καὶ νεύρων, καὶ τὰ μὲν ὀστᾶ ἐστιν στερεὰ καὶ
διαφυὰς ἔχει χωρὶς ἀπ' ἀλλήλων, τὰ δὲ νεῦρα οἷα ἐπι-
τείνεσθαι καὶ ἀνίεσθαι, περιαμπέχοντα τὰ ὀστᾶ μετὰ τῶν d
σαρκῶν καὶ δέρματος ὃ συνέχει αὐτά· αἰωρουμένων οὖν τῶν
ὀστῶν ἐν ταῖς αὐτῶν συμβολαῖς χαλῶντα καὶ συντείνοντα

a 1 ἀποφαίνοι T b : ἀποφαίνοιτο B   παρεσκευασάμην W (et mox)
ποθεσόμενος T Eus. : ὑποθέμενος B et γρ. T : ὑποθησόμενος W   a 8 αἰτίαν αὐτοῖς B² W   βέλτιον W   b 1 αὐτῶν B Eus. : αὐτὸν T
b 7 ὦ ἑταῖρε ἐλπίδος T W Eus.   c 3 λέγοι pr. W

τὰ νεῦρα κάμπτεσθαί που ποιεῖ οἷόν τ' εἶναι ἐμὲ νῦν τὰ
5 μέλη, καὶ διὰ ταύτην τὴν αἰτίαν συγκαμφθεὶς ἐνθάδε κά-
θημαι· καὶ αὖ περὶ τοῦ διαλέγεσθαι ὑμῖν ἑτέρας τοιαύτας
αἰτίας λέγοι, φωνάς τε καὶ ἀέρας καὶ ἀκοὰς καὶ ἄλλα μυρία
e τοιαῦτα αἰτιώμενος, ἀμελήσας τὰς ὡς ἀληθῶς αἰτίας λέγειν,
ὅτι, ἐπειδὴ Ἀθηναίοις ἔδοξε βέλτιον εἶναι ἐμοῦ καταψη-
φίσασθαι, διὰ ταῦτα δὴ καὶ ἐμοὶ βέλτιον αὖ δέδοκται ἐνθάδε
καθῆσθαι, καὶ δικαιότερον παραμένοντα ὑπέχειν τὴν δίκην
5 ἣν ἂν κελεύσωσιν· ἐπεὶ νὴ τὸν κύνα, ὡς ἐγῷμαι, πάλαι ἂν
99 ταῦτα τὰ νεῦρα καὶ τὰ ὀστᾶ ἢ περὶ Μέγαρα ἢ Βοιωτοὺς ἦν,
ὑπὸ δόξης φερόμενα τοῦ βελτίστου, εἰ μὴ δικαιότερον ᾤμην
καὶ κάλλιον εἶναι πρὸ τοῦ φεύγειν τε καὶ ἀποδιδράσκειν
ὑπέχειν τῇ πόλει δίκην ἥντιν' ἂν τάττῃ. ἀλλ' αἴτια μὲν
5 τὰ τοιαῦτα καλεῖν λίαν ἄτοπον· εἰ δέ τις λέγοι ὅτι ἄνευ
τοῦ τὰ τοιαῦτα ἔχειν καὶ ὀστᾶ καὶ νεῦρα καὶ ὅσα ἄλλα ἔχω
οὐκ ἂν οἷός τ' ἦ ποιεῖν τὰ δόξαντά μοι, ἀληθῆ ἂν λέγοι· ὡς
μέντοι διὰ ταῦτα ποιῶ ἃ ποιῶ, καὶ ταῦτα νῷ πράττων, ἀλλ' οὐ
b τῇ τοῦ βελτίστου αἱρέσει, πολλὴ ἂν καὶ μακρὰ ῥᾳθυμία εἴη
τοῦ λόγου. τὸ γὰρ μὴ διελέσθαι οἷόν τ' εἶναι ὅτι ἄλλο μέν
τί ἐστι τὸ αἴτιον τῷ ὄντι, ἄλλο δὲ ἐκεῖνο ἄνευ οὗ τὸ αἴτιον
οὐκ ἄν ποτ' εἴη αἴτιον· ὃ δή μοι φαίνονται ψηλαφῶντες οἱ
5 πολλοὶ ὥσπερ ἐν σκότει, ἀλλοτρίῳ ὀνόματι προσχρώμενοι,
ὡς αἴτιον αὐτὸ προσαγορεύειν. διὸ δὴ καὶ ὁ μέν τις δίνην
περιτιθεὶς τῇ γῇ ὑπὸ τοῦ οὐρανοῦ μένειν δὴ ποιεῖ τὴν γῆν,
ὁ δὲ ὥσπερ καρδόπῳ πλατείᾳ βάθρον τὸν ἀέρα ὑπερείδει·
c τὴν δὲ τοῦ ὡς οἷόν τε βέλτιστα αὐτὰ τεθῆναι δύναμιν οὕτω
νῦν κεῖσθαι, ταύτην οὔτε ζητοῦσιν οὔτε τινὰ οἴονται δαιμονίαν ἰσχὺν ἔχειν, ἀλλὰ ἡγοῦνται τούτου Ἄτλαντα ἄν
ποτε ἰσχυρότερον καὶ ἀθανατώτερον καὶ μᾶλλον ἅπαντα

---

d 4 που om. W   e 1 ὡς om. pr. T   e 5 κελεύωσιν T   a 1 καὶ
T W Eus. : τε καὶ B   a 6 ἄλλα ὅσα W   a 7 ἀληθῆ ἂν λέγοι om. T
a 8 ποιῶ ἃ B² T W Eus. : ποιῶν ἃ B   πράττων Heindorf : πράττω
B T W Eus.   b 1 ἂν T W Eus. : om. B (post ῥᾳθυμία recc.)
b 3 ἐστι τι T   ἐκεῖνο B T Simpl. Stob. : ἐκεῖνο ὃ B² W t   b 5 σκότῳ
W   ὀνόματι T Simpl. Stob. : ὄμματι B W   b 8 ἀέρα B T
Simpl. Eus. Stob. : ἀέρα κάτω W   c 1 βέλτιστα αὐτὰ T Simpl. Eus.
Stob. : αὐτὰ βέλτιστα B² W : βέλτιστον αὐτὰ B   c 3 ἂν ποτε
ἄτλαντα T W Eus. Stob.

συνέχοντα ἐξευρεῖν, καὶ ὡς ἀληθῶς τὸ ἀγαθὸν καὶ δέον 5
συνδεῖν καὶ συνέχειν οὐδὲν οἴονται. ἐγὼ μὲν οὖν τῆς
τοιαύτης αἰτίας ὅπῃ ποτὲ ἔχει μαθητὴς ὁτουοῦν ἥδιστ' ἂν
γενοίμην· ἐπειδὴ δὲ ταύτης ἐστερήθην καὶ οὔτ' αὐτὸς εὑρεῖν
οὔτε παρ' ἄλλου μαθεῖν οἷός τε ἐγενόμην, τὸν δεύτερον
πλοῦν ἐπὶ τὴν τῆς αἰτίας ζήτησιν ᾗ πεπραγμάτευμαι βούλει d
σοι, ἔφη, ἐπίδειξιν ποιήσωμαι, ὦ Κέβης;
Ὑπερφυῶς μὲν οὖν, ἔφη, ὡς βούλομαι.

Ἔδοξε τοίνυν μοι, ἦ δ' ὅς, μετὰ ταῦτα, ἐπειδὴ ἀπειρήκη
τὰ ὄντα σκοπῶν, δεῖν εὐλαβηθῆναι μὴ πάθοιμι ὅπερ οἱ τὸν 5
ἥλιον ἐκλείποντα θεωροῦντες καὶ σκοπούμενοι πάσχουσιν·
διαφθείρονται γάρ που ἔνιοι τὰ ὄμματα, ἐὰν μὴ ἐν ὕδατι ἤ
τινι τοιούτῳ σκοπῶνται τὴν εἰκόνα αὐτοῦ. τοιοῦτόν τι καὶ e
ἐγὼ διενοήθην, καὶ ἔδεισα μὴ παντάπασι τὴν ψυχὴν τυφλω-
θείην βλέπων πρὸς τὰ πράγματα τοῖς ὄμμασι καὶ ἑκάστῃ
τῶν αἰσθήσεων ἐπιχειρῶν ἅπτεσθαι αὐτῶν. ἔδοξε δή μοι
χρῆναι εἰς τοὺς λόγους καταφυγόντα ἐν ἐκείνοις σκοπεῖν 5
τῶν ὄντων τὴν ἀλήθειαν. ἴσως μὲν οὖν ᾧ εἰκάζω τρόπον
τινὰ οὐκ ἔοικεν· οὐ γὰρ πάνυ συγχωρῶ τὸν ἐν [τοῖς] λόγοις 100
σκοπούμενον τὰ ὄντα ἐν εἰκόσι μᾶλλον σκοπεῖν ἢ τὸν ἐν
[τοῖς] ἔργοις. ἀλλ' οὖν δὴ ταύτῃ γε ὥρμησα, καὶ ὑποθέμενος
ἑκάστοτε λόγον ὃν ἂν κρίνω ἐρρωμενέστατον εἶναι, ἃ μὲν
ἄν μοι δοκῇ τούτῳ συμφωνεῖν τίθημι ὡς ἀληθῆ ὄντα, καὶ 5
περὶ αἰτίας καὶ περὶ τῶν ἄλλων ἁπάντων [ὄντων], ἃ δ' ἂν
μή, ὡς οὐκ ἀληθῆ. βούλομαι δέ σοι σαφέστερον εἰπεῖν
ἃ λέγω· οἶμαι γάρ σε νῦν οὐ μανθάνειν.
Οὐ μὰ τὸν Δία, ἔφη ὁ Κέβης, οὐ σφόδρα.
Ἀλλ', ἦ δ' ὅς, ὧδε λέγω, οὐδὲν καινόν, ἀλλ' ἅπερ ἀεί b

c 7 τοιαύτης B Stob. : αὐτῆς T   d 1 ᾗ T W b Stob. : ἤ B :
ἦν b   d 2 ποιήσωμαι recc. : ποιήσομαι B T W Stob.   d 3 οὖν
om. W   d 4 ἀπειρήκη T (η ex ει) : ἀπειρήκει Stob. : ἀπείρηκα
B W t   d 6 ἐκλιπόντα T   πάσχουσιν B² T W Stob. : om. B
d 7 ἔνιοι B T Stob. : ἐνίοτε B² W t   e 1 ᾗ ἔν τινι T   e 6 ᾧ T b :
ὡς B W t Stob.   a 1 τοῖς B W : om. T W   a 2 ἐν om. W
a 3 τοῖς B Stob. : om. T W   a 4 ὂν B² T W Stob. : om. B
a 6 ὄντων B W : om. T Stob. : τῶν ὄντων vulg.

τε ἄλλοτε καὶ ἐν τῷ παρεληλυθότι λόγῳ οὐδὲν πέπαυμαι
λέγων. ἔρχομαι [γὰρ] δὴ ἐπιχειρῶν σοι ἐπιδείξασθαι τῆς
αἰτίας τὸ εἶδος ὃ πεπραγμάτευμαι, καὶ εἶμι πάλιν ἐπ' ἐκεῖνα
5 τὰ πολυθρύλητα καὶ ἄρχομαι ἀπ' ἐκείνων, ὑποθέμενος εἶναί
τι καλὸν αὐτὸ καθ' αὑτὸ καὶ ἀγαθὸν καὶ μέγα καὶ τἆλλα
πάντα· ἃ εἴ μοι δίδως τε καὶ συγχωρεῖς εἶναι ταῦτα, ἐλπίζω
σοι ἐκ τούτων τὴν αἰτίαν ἐπιδείξειν καὶ ἀνευρήσειν ὡς
ἀθάνατον [ἡ] ψυχή.

c Ἀλλὰ μήν, ἔφη ὁ Κέβης, ὡς διδόντος σοι οὐκ ἂν
φθάνοις περαίνων.

Σκόπει δή, ἔφη, τὰ ἑξῆς ἐκείνοις ἐάν σοι συνδοκῇ ὥσπερ
ἐμοί. φαίνεται γάρ μοι, εἴ τί ἐστιν ἄλλο καλὸν πλὴν αὐτὸ
5 τὸ καλόν, οὐδὲ δι' ἓν ἄλλο καλὸν εἶναι ἢ διότι μετέχει
ἐκείνου τοῦ καλοῦ· καὶ πάντα δὴ οὕτως λέγω. τῇ τοιᾷδε
αἰτίᾳ συγχωρεῖς;

Συγχωρῶ, ἔφη.

Οὐ τοίνυν, ἦ δ' ὅς, ἔτι μανθάνω οὐδὲ δύναμαι τὰς ἄλλας
10 αἰτίας τὰς σοφὰς ταύτας γιγνώσκειν· ἀλλ' ἐάν τίς μοι λέγῃ
d δι' ὅτι καλόν ἐστιν ὁτιοῦν, ἢ χρῶμα εὐανθὲς ἔχον ἢ σχῆμα
ἢ ἄλλο ὁτιοῦν τῶν τοιούτων, τὰ μὲν ἄλλα χαίρειν ἐῶ,
—ταράττομαι γὰρ ἐν τοῖς ἄλλοις πᾶσι—τοῦτο δὲ ἁπλῶς καὶ
ἀτέχνως καὶ ἴσως εὐήθως ἔχω παρ' ἐμαυτῷ, ὅτι οὐκ ἄλλο τι
5 ποιεῖ αὐτὸ καλὸν ἢ ἡ ἐκείνου τοῦ καλοῦ εἴτε παρουσία εἴτε
κοινωνία εἴτε ὅπῃ δὴ καὶ ὅπως †προσγενομένη· οὐ γὰρ ἔτι
τοῦτο διισχυρίζομαι, ἀλλ' ὅτι τῷ καλῷ πάντα τὰ καλὰ
[γίγνεται] καλά. τοῦτο γάρ μοι δοκεῖ ἀσφαλέστατον εἶναι
καὶ ἐμαυτῷ ἀποκρίνασθαι καὶ ἄλλῳ, καὶ τούτου ἐχόμενος
e ἡγοῦμαι οὐκ ἄν ποτε πεσεῖν, ἀλλ' ἀσφαλὲς εἶναι καὶ ἐμοὶ
καὶ ὁτῳοῦν ἄλλῳ ἀποκρίνασθαι ὅτι τῷ καλῷ τὰ καλὰ
[γίγνεται] καλά· ἢ οὐ καὶ σοὶ δοκεῖ;

b 2 τε B²TW : καὶ B   b 3 γὰρ B : om. T   b 8 σοι B : σε T
τὴν BT : τήν τε W   b 9 ἡ om. pr. T   c 4, 5 πλὴν . . . καλόν
B²TW : om. B   d 1 ἢ (bis) B : ἢ ὅτι B²TW   d 4 εὐήθες W
d 6 προσγενομένη] προσαγορευομένη Wyttenbach   d 7 πάντα TW b :
om. B   d 8 γίγνεται Tb : om. BW   d 9 ἀποκρίνεσθα· T
e 3 γίγνεται T et (post καλὰ) W : om. B

Δοκεῖ.

Καὶ μεγέθει ἄρα τὰ μεγάλα μεγάλα καὶ τὰ μείζω μείζω, 5
καὶ σμικρότητι τὰ ἐλάττω ἐλάττω;

Ναί.

Οὐδὲ σὺ ἄρ' ἂν ἀποδέχοιο εἴ τίς τινα φαίη ἕτερον ἑτέρου
τῇ κεφαλῇ μείζω εἶναι, καὶ τὸν ἐλάττω τῷ αὐτῷ τούτῳ
ἐλάττω, ἀλλὰ διαμαρτύροιο ἂν ὅτι σὺ μὲν οὐδὲν ἄλλο λέγεις 101
ἢ ὅτι τὸ μεῖζον πᾶν ἕτερον ἑτέρου οὐδενὶ ἄλλῳ μεῖζόν ἐστιν
ἢ μεγέθει, καὶ διὰ τοῦτο μεῖζον, διὰ τὸ μέγεθος, τὸ δὲ
ἔλαττον οὐδενὶ ἄλλῳ ἔλαττον ἢ σμικρότητι, καὶ διὰ τοῦτο
ἔλαττον, διὰ τὴν σμικρότητα, φοβούμενος οἶμαι μή τίς σοι 5
ἐναντίος λόγος ἀπαντήσῃ, ἐὰν τῇ κεφαλῇ μείζονά τινα φῇς
εἶναι καὶ ἐλάττω, πρῶτον μὲν τῷ αὐτῷ τὸ μεῖζον μεῖζον εἶναι
καὶ τὸ ἔλαττον ἔλαττον, ἔπειτα τῇ κεφαλῇ σμικρᾷ οὔσῃ τὸν
μείζω μείζω εἶναι, καὶ τοῦτο δὴ τέρας εἶναι, τὸ σμικρῷ τινι b
μέγαν τινὰ εἶναι· ἢ οὐκ ἂν φοβοῖο ταῦτα;

Καὶ ὁ Κέβης γελάσας, Ἔγωγε, ἔφη.

Οὐκοῦν, ἦ δ' ὅς, τὰ δέκα τῶν ὀκτὼ δυοῖν πλείω εἶναι, καὶ
διὰ ταύτην τὴν αἰτίαν ὑπερβάλλειν, φοβοῖο ἂν λέγειν, ἀλλὰ 5
μὴ πλήθει καὶ διὰ τὸ πλῆθος; καὶ τὸ δίπηχυ τοῦ πηχυαίου
ἡμίσει μεῖζον εἶναι ἀλλ' οὐ μεγέθει; ὁ αὐτὸς γάρ που φόβος.

Πάνυ γ', ἔφη.

Τί δέ; ἑνὶ ἑνὸς προστεθέντος τὴν πρόσθεσιν αἰτίαν εἶναι
τοῦ δύο γενέσθαι ἢ διασχισθέντος τὴν σχίσιν οὐκ εὐλαβοῖο c
ἂν λέγειν; καὶ μέγα ἂν βοῴης ὅτι οὐκ οἶσθα ἄλλως πως
ἕκαστον γιγνόμενον ἢ μετασχὸν τῆς ἰδίας οὐσίας ἑκάστου
οὗ ἂν μετάσχῃ, καὶ ἐν τούτοις οὐκ ἔχεις ἄλλην τινὰ αἰτίαν
τοῦ δύο γενέσθαι ἀλλ' ἢ τὴν τῆς δυάδος μετάσχεσιν, καὶ 5
δεῖν τούτου μετασχεῖν τὰ μέλλοντα δύο ἔσεσθαι, καὶ μονάδος
ὃ ἂν μέλλῃ ἓν ἔσεσθαι, τὰς δὲ σχίσεις ταύτας καὶ προσθέσεις
καὶ τὰς ἄλλας τὰς τοιαύτας κομψείας ἐῴης ἂν χαίρειν, παρεὶς

e 6 ἐλάττω alterum in marg. t   e 8 ἄρα ἂν Τ W : ἄρα Β
a 2 τὸ Β Τ : τὸ μὲν W   a 4 ἔλαττον (ante ἢ) om. Τ   b 2 εἶναι
Β : εἰδέναι Τ   c 2 μέγα Β² Τ W : μεγάλα Β   οἶσθα Τ :
οἰόμεθα Β : οἰώμεθα W   c 4 μετάσχῃ Τ et η s. v. W : μετάσχοι Β W
10*

ἀποκρίνασθαι τοῖς σεαυτοῦ σοφωτέροις· σὺ δὲ δεδιὼς ἄν, τὸ
d λεγόμενον, τὴν σαυτοῦ σκιὰν καὶ τὴν ἀπειρίαν, ἐχόμενος
ἐκείνου τοῦ ἀσφαλοῦς τῆς ὑποθέσεως, οὕτως ἀποκρίναιο ἄν.
εἰ δέ τις αὐτῆς τῆς ὑποθέσεως ἔχοιτο, χαίρειν ἐῴης ἂν καὶ
οὐκ ἀποκρίναιο ἕως ἂν τὰ ἀπ' ἐκείνης ὁρμηθέντα σκέψαιο
5 εἴ σοι ἀλλήλοις συμφωνεῖ ἢ διαφωνεῖ· ἐπειδὴ δὲ ἐκείνης
αὐτῆς δέοι σε διδόναι λόγον, ὡσαύτως ἂν διδοίης, ἄλλην αὖ
ὑπόθεσιν ὑποθέμενος ἥτις τῶν ἄνωθεν βελτίστη φαίνοιτο,
e ἕως ἐπί τι ἱκανὸν ἔλθοις, ἅμα δὲ οὐκ ἂν φύροιο ὥσπερ οἱ
ἀντιλογικοὶ περί τε τῆς ἀρχῆς διαλεγόμενος καὶ τῶν ἐξ
ἐκείνης ὡρμημένων, εἴπερ βούλοιό τι τῶν ὄντων εὑρεῖν;
ἐκείνοις μὲν γὰρ ἴσως οὐδὲ εἷς περὶ τούτου λόγος οὐδὲ
5 φροντίς· ἱκανοὶ γὰρ ὑπὸ σοφίας ὁμοῦ πάντα κυκῶντες ὅμως
δύνασθαι αὐτοὶ αὑτοῖς ἀρέσκειν· σὺ δ', εἴπερ εἶ τῶν φιλοσόφων,
102 οἶμαι ἂν ὡς ἐγὼ λέγω ποιοῖς.

Ἀληθέστατα, ἔφη, λέγεις, ὅ τε Σιμμίας ἅμα καὶ ὁ Κέβης.

ΕΧ. Νὴ Δία, ὦ Φαίδων, εἰκότως γε· θαυμαστῶς γάρ
μοι δοκεῖ ὡς ἐναργῶς τῷ καὶ σμικρὸν νοῦν ἔχοντι εἰπεῖν
5 ἐκεῖνος ταῦτα.

ΦΑΙΔ. Πάνυ μὲν οὖν, ὦ Ἐχέκρατες, καὶ πᾶσι τοῖς
παροῦσιν ἔδοξεν.

ΕΧ. Καὶ γὰρ ἡμῖν τοῖς ἀποῦσι, νῦν δὲ ἀκούουσιν. ἀλλὰ
τίνα δὴ ἦν τὰ μετὰ ταῦτα λεχθέντα;

10 ΦΑΙΔ. Ὡς μὲν ἐγὼ οἶμαι, ἐπεὶ αὐτῷ ταῦτα συνεχωρήθη,
b καὶ ὡμολογεῖτο εἶναί τι ἕκαστον τῶν εἰδῶν καὶ τούτων
τἆλλα μεταλαμβάνοντα αὐτῶν τούτων τὴν ἐπωνυμίαν ἴσχειν,
τὸ δὴ μετὰ ταῦτα ἠρώτα, Εἰ δή, ἦ δ' ὅς, ταῦτα οὕτως λέγεις,
ἆρ' οὐχ, ὅταν Σιμμίαν Σωκράτους φῇς μείζω εἶναι, Φαίδωνος
5 δὲ ἐλάττω, λέγεις τότ' εἶναι ἐν τῷ Σιμμίᾳ ἀμφότερα, καὶ
μέγεθος καὶ σμικρότητα;

c 9 σεαυτοῦ B² T W : ἑαυτοῦ B   d 1 σαυτοῦ B² T W : ἑαυτοῦ B
d 2 ἀποκρίνοιο pr. T W   d 3 ἔφοιτο Madvig   d 6 αὖ B : δ' T
e 3 ὁρμωμένων pr. T   e 4 οὐδὲ εἷς B : οὐδεὶς T W b   e 5 ὅμως
B² T W : ὅπως B   b 5 τότ' B : τότε W : ταῦτ' T

Ἔγωγε.

Ἀλλὰ γάρ, ἦ δ' ὅς, ὁμολογεῖς τὸ τὸν Σιμμίαν ὑπερέχειν Σωκράτους οὐχ ὡς τοῖς ῥήμασι λέγεται οὕτω καὶ τὸ ἀληθὲς ἔχειν; οὐ γάρ που πεφυκέναι Σιμμίαν ὑπερέχειν τούτῳ, τῷ c Σιμμίαν εἶναι, ἀλλὰ τῷ μεγέθει ὃ τυγχάνει ἔχων· οὐδ' αὖ Σωκράτους ὑπερέχειν ὅτι Σωκράτης ὁ Σωκράτης ἐστίν, ἀλλ' ὅτι σμικρότητα ἔχει ὁ Σωκράτης πρὸς τὸ ἐκείνου μέγεθος; Ἀληθῆ. 5

Οὐδέ γε αὖ ὑπὸ Φαίδωνος ὑπερέχεσθαι τῷ ὅτι Φαίδων ὁ Φαίδων ἐστίν, ἀλλ' ὅτι μέγεθος ἔχει ὁ Φαίδων πρὸς τὴν Σιμμίου σμικρότητα; Ἔστι ταῦτα.

Οὕτως ἄρα ὁ Σιμμίας ἐπωνυμίαν ἔχει σμικρός τε καὶ 10 μέγας εἶναι, ἐν μέσῳ ὢν ἀμφοτέρων, τοῦ μὲν τῷ μεγέθει ὑπερέχειν τὴν σμικρότητα ὑπέχων, τῷ δὲ τὸ μέγεθος τῆς d σμικρότητος παρέχων ὑπερέχον. Καὶ ἅμα μειδιάσας, Ἔοικα, ἔφη, καὶ συγγραφικῶς ἐρεῖν, ἀλλ' οὖν ἔχει γέ που ὡς λέγω. Συνέφη.

Λέγω δὴ τοῦδ' ἕνεκα, βουλόμενος δόξαι σοὶ ὅπερ ἐμοί. 5 ἐμοὶ γὰρ φαίνεται οὐ μόνον αὐτὸ τὸ μέγεθος οὐδέποτ' ἐθέλειν ἅμα μέγα καὶ σμικρὸν εἶναι, ἀλλὰ καὶ τὸ ἐν ἡμῖν μέγεθος οὐδέποτε προσδέχεσθαι τὸ σμικρὸν οὐδ' ἐθέλειν ὑπερέχεσθαι, ἀλλὰ δυοῖν τὸ ἕτερον, ἢ φεύγειν καὶ ὑπεκχωρεῖν ὅταν αὐτῷ προσίῃ τὸ ἐναντίον, τὸ σμικρόν, ἢ προσελθόντος ἐκείνου e ἀπολωλέναι· ὑπομένον δὲ καὶ δεξάμενον τὴν σμικρότητα οὐκ ἐθέλειν εἶναι ἕτερον ἢ ὅπερ ἦν. ὥσπερ ἐγὼ δεξάμενος καὶ ὑπομείνας τὴν σμικρότητα, καὶ ἔτι ὢν ὅσπερ εἰμί, οὗτος ὁ αὐτὸς σμικρός εἰμι· ἐκεῖνο δὲ οὐ τετόλμηκεν μέγα ὂν 5 σμικρὸν εἶναι· ὡς δ' αὕτως καὶ τὸ σμικρὸν τὸ ἐν ἡμῖν οὐκ ἐθέλει ποτὲ μέγα γίγνεσθαι οὐδὲ εἶναι, οὐδ' ἄλλο οὐδὲν τῶν

c 6 τῷ Β Τ : τούτῳ W   d 1 ὑπέχων Τ W : ὑπερέχων Β t   τῷ δὲ ex τὸ δὲ Τ et mox om. τὸ   d 5 δὴ Τ b : δὲ W   d 6 οὐδέποτ(ε) Β W : οὔποτε Τ   e 1 προσίῃ Τ b : προσείη Β : προσήει W   e 4 ὥσπερ W   e 5 ἐκεῖνο Β² Τ W : ἐκεῖνος Β   οὐ Β² Τ W : om. Β   e 6 ὡσαύτως Τ   e 7 γενέσθαι W   οὐδὲ Β Τ : οὔτε Β² W t

ἐναντίων, ἔτι ὂν ὅπερ ἦν, ἅμα τοὐναντίον γίγνεσθαί τε
103 καὶ εἶναι, ἀλλ' ἤτοι ἀπέρχεται ἢ ἀπόλλυται ἐν τούτῳ τῷ
παθήματι.

Παντάπασιν, ἔφη ὁ Κέβης, οὕτω φαίνεταί μοι.

Καί τις εἶπε τῶν παρόντων ἀκούσας—ὅστις δ' ἦν, οὐ
5 σαφῶς μέμνημαι—Πρὸς θεῶν, οὐκ ἐν τοῖς πρόσθεν ἡμῖν
λόγοις αὐτὸ τὸ ἐναντίον τῶν νυνὶ λεγομένων ὡμολογεῖτο, ἐκ
τοῦ ἐλάττονος τὸ μεῖζον γίγνεσθαι καὶ ἐκ τοῦ μείζονος τὸ
ἔλαττον, καὶ ἀτεχνῶς αὕτη εἶναι ἡ γένεσις τοῖς ἐναντίοις,
ἐκ τῶν ἐναντίων; νῦν δέ μοι δοκεῖ λέγεσθαι ὅτι τοῦτο οὐκ
10 ἄν ποτε γένοιτο.

Καὶ ὁ Σωκράτης παραβαλὼν τὴν κεφαλὴν καὶ ἀκούσας,
b Ἀνδρικῶς, ἔφη, ἀπεμνημόνευκας, οὐ μέντοι ἐννοεῖς τὸ
διαφέρον τοῦ τε νῦν λεγομένου καὶ τοῦ τότε. τότε μὲν
γὰρ ἐλέγετο ἐκ τοῦ ἐναντίου πράγματος τὸ ἐναντίον πρᾶγμα
γίγνεσθαι, νῦν δέ, ὅτι αὐτὸ τὸ ἐναντίον ἑαυτῷ ἐναντίον οὐκ
5 ἄν ποτε γένοιτο, οὔτε τὸ ἐν ἡμῖν οὔτε τὸ ἐν τῇ φύσει.
τότε μὲν γάρ, ὦ φίλε, περὶ τῶν ἐχόντων τὰ ἐναντία ἐλέγομεν, ἐπονομάζοντες αὐτὰ τῇ ἐκείνων ἐπωνυμίᾳ, νῦν δὲ περὶ
ἐκείνων αὐτῶν ὧν ἐνόντων ἔχει τὴν ἐπωνυμίαν τὰ ὀνομαζό-
c μενα· αὐτὰ δ' ἐκεῖνα οὐκ ἄν ποτέ φαμεν ἐθελῆσαι γένεσιν
ἀλλήλων δέξασθαι. Καὶ ἅμα βλέψας πρὸς τὸν Κέβητα
εἶπεν, Ἆρα μή που, ὦ Κέβης, ἔφη, καὶ σέ τι τούτων
ἐτάραξεν ὧν ὅδε εἶπεν;

5 Οὐδ' αὖ, ἔφη ὁ Κέβης, οὕτως ἔχω· καίτοι οὔτι λέγω
ὡς οὐ πολλά με ταράττει.

Συνωμολογήκαμεν ἄρα, ἦ δ' ὅς, ἁπλῶς τοῦτο, μηδέποτε
ἐναντίον ἑαυτῷ τὸ ἐναντίον ἔσεσθαι.

Παντάπασιν, ἔφη.

e 8 ἔτι ὂν T W : αἴτιον B et γρ. W   a 5 ἡμῖν W : ὑμῖν B T
a 11 παραλαβὼν W   b 5 ποτε om. T   c 2 πρὸς B : εἰς B² T W
c 3 ἔφη ᾧ Κέβης T W   c 5 οὐδ' αὖ W t : ὁ δ' αὖ B T et γρ. W
καίτοι οὔτι B² : καὶ τοιοῦτό τι B T W   c 8 ἔσεσθαι ante ἑαυτῷ T

Ἔτι δή μοι καὶ τόδε σκέψαι, ἔφη, εἰ ἄρα συνομολογήσεις. 10
θερμόν τι καλεῖς καὶ ψυχρόν;

Ἔγωγε.

Ἆρ' ὅπερ χιόνα καὶ πῦρ;

Μὰ Δί' οὐκ ἔγωγε.   d

Ἀλλ' ἕτερόν τι πυρὸς τὸ θερμὸν καὶ ἕτερόν τι χιόνος τὸ
ψυχρόν;

Ναί.

Ἀλλὰ τόδε γ' οἶμαι δοκεῖ σοι, οὐδέποτε χιόνα γ' οὖσαν 5
δεξαμένην τὸ θερμόν, ὥσπερ ἐν τοῖς πρόσθεν ἐλέγομεν,
ἔτι ἔσεσθαι ὅπερ ἦν, χιόνα καὶ θερμόν, ἀλλὰ προσιόντος
τοῦ θερμοῦ ἢ ὑπεκχωρήσειν αὐτῷ ἢ ἀπολεῖσθαι.

Πάνυ γε.

Καὶ τὸ πῦρ γε αὖ προσιόντος τοῦ ψυχροῦ αὐτῷ ἢ 10
ὑπεξιέναι ἢ ἀπολεῖσθαι, οὐ μέντοι ποτὲ τολμήσειν δεξάμενον τὴν ψυχρότητα ἔτι εἶναι ὅπερ ἦν, πῦρ καὶ ψυχρόν.

Ἀληθῆ, ἔφη, λέγεις.   e

Ἔστιν ἄρα, ἦ δ' ὅς, περὶ ἔνια τῶν τοιούτων, ὥστε μὴ
μόνον αὐτὸ τὸ εἶδος ἀξιοῦσθαι τοῦ αὐτοῦ ὀνόματος εἰς τὸν
ἀεὶ χρόνον, ἀλλὰ καὶ ἄλλο τι ὃ ἔστι μὲν οὐκ ἐκεῖνο, ἔχει
δὲ τὴν ἐκείνου μορφὴν ἀεί, ὅτανπερ ᾖ. ἔτι δὲ ἐν τῷδε 5
ἴσως ἔσται σαφέστερον ὃ λέγω· τὸ γὰρ περιττὸν ἀεί που
δεῖ τούτου τοῦ ὀνόματος τυγχάνειν ὅπερ νῦν λέγομεν· ἢ οὔ;

Πάνυ γε.

Ἆρα μόνον τῶν ὄντων—τοῦτο γὰρ ἐρωτῶ—ἢ καὶ ἄλλο
τι ὃ ἔστι μὲν οὐχ ὅπερ τὸ περιττόν, ὅμως δὲ δεῖ αὐτὸ 104
μετὰ τοῦ ἑαυτοῦ ὀνόματος καὶ τοῦτο καλεῖν ἀεὶ διὰ τὸ οὕτω
πεφυκέναι ὥστε τοῦ περιττοῦ μηδέποτε ἀπολείπεσθαι; λέγω
δὲ αὐτὸ εἶναι οἷον καὶ ἡ τριὰς πέπονθε καὶ ἄλλα πολλά.
σκόπει δὲ περὶ τῆς τριάδος. ἆρα οὐ δοκεῖ σοι τῷ τε αὐτῆς 5

c 13 χιόνα B : χιὼν T   d 5 χιόνα γ' W : χιόνα B T   d 6 πρόσθεν T : ἔμπροσθεν B   d 8 αὐτῷ T W : αὐτὸ B   d 9-11 πάνυ ...
ἀπολεῖσθαι om. T   d 11 τολμήσειν B² T W : τολμήσειεν B
e 5 τῷδε T : τοῖσδε B

ὀνόματι ἀεὶ προσαγορευτέα εἶναι καὶ τῷ τοῦ περιττοῦ, ὄντος
οὐχ ὅπερ τῆς τριάδος; ἀλλ' ὅμως οὕτως πέφυκε καὶ ἡ
τριὰς καὶ ἡ πεμπτὰς καὶ ὁ ἥμισυς τοῦ ἀριθμοῦ ἅπας, ὥστε
b οὐκ ὢν ὅπερ τὸ περιττὸν ἀεὶ ἕκαστος αὐτῶν ἐστι περιττός·
καὶ αὖ τὰ δύο καὶ [τὰ] τέτταρα καὶ ἅπας ὁ ἕτερος αὖ στίχος
τοῦ ἀριθμοῦ οὐκ ὢν ὅπερ τὸ ἄρτιον ὅμως ἕκαστος αὐτῶν
ἄρτιός ἐστιν ἀεί· συγχωρεῖς ἢ οὔ;

5 Πῶς γὰρ οὔκ; ἔφη.

Ὁ τοίνυν, ἔφη, βούλομαι δηλῶσαι, ἄθρει. ἔστιν δὲ
τόδε, ὅτι φαίνεται οὐ μόνον ἐκεῖνα τὰ ἐναντία ἄλληλα οὐ
δεχόμενα, ἀλλὰ καὶ ὅσα οὐκ ὄντ' ἀλλήλοις ἐναντία ἔχει ἀεὶ
τἀναντία, οὐδὲ ταῦτα ἔοικε δεχομένοις ἐκείνην τὴν ἰδέαν ἢ
10 ἂν τῇ ἐν αὐτοῖς οὔσῃ ἐναντία ᾖ, ἀλλ' ἐπιούσης αὐτῆς ἤτοι
c ἀπολλύμενα ἢ ὑπεκχωροῦντα. ἢ οὐ φήσομεν τὰ τρία καὶ
ἀπολεῖσθαι πρότερον καὶ ἄλλο ὁτιοῦν πείσεσθαι, πρὶν ὑπομεῖναι ἔτι τρία ὄντα ἄρτια γενέσθαι;

Πάνυ μὲν οὖν, ἔφη ὁ Κέβης.

5 Οὐδὲ μήν, ἦ δ' ὅς, ἐναντίον γέ ἐστι δυὰς τριάδι.

Οὐ γὰρ οὖν.

Οὐκ ἄρα μόνον τὰ εἴδη τὰ ἐναντία οὐχ ὑπομένει ἐπιόντα
ἄλληλα, ἀλλὰ καὶ ἄλλ' ἄττα τὰ ἐναντία οὐχ ὑπομένει
ἐπιόντα.

10 Ἀληθέστατα, ἔφη, λέγεις.

Βούλει οὖν, ἦ δ' ὅς, ἐὰν οἷοί τ' ὦμεν, ὁρισώμεθα ὁποῖα
ταῦτά ἐστιν;

Πάνυ γε.

d Ἆρ' οὖν, ἔφη, ὦ Κέβης, τάδε εἴη ἄν, ἃ ὅτι ἂν κατάσχῃ
μὴ μόνον ἀναγκάζει τὴν αὐτοῦ ἰδέαν αὐτὸ ἴσχειν, ἀλλὰ καὶ
ἐναντίου αὐτῷ ἀεί τινος;

a 7 οὗπερ Heindorf   οὕτως T : οὕτω πως B t   b 2 τὰ om. T
b 4 ἀεὶ om. T   b 8 ἀεὶ ἔχει T   b 10 αὐτοῖς recc. : αὐτῇ B T W
c 2 πρὶν T W : πρὶν ἢ B   c 5 οὐδὲ B² T W : οὐ δὴ B et ἢ s. v. W
c 8 τὰ om. T   c 11 ἢ δ' ὅς] ἔφη W   d 1 ἃ B² W : om. B T
d 2 ἀναγκάζει B² T W : ἀναγκάζειν B   αὐτὸ B T : αὐτοῖς W   ἴσχειν
T W : σχεῖν B   d 3 αὐτῷ ἀεί τινος B : ἀεί τινος αὐτῷ W : δεῖ
αὐτῷ τινος T

Πῶς λέγεις;

Ὥσπερ ἄρτι ἐλέγομεν. οἶσθα γὰρ δήπου ὅτι ἃ ἂν ἡ τῶν 5
τριῶν ἰδέα κατάσχῃ, ἀνάγκη αὐτοῖς οὐ μόνον τρισὶν εἶναι
ἀλλὰ καὶ περιττοῖς.

Πάνυ γε.

Ἐπὶ τὸ τοιοῦτον δή, φαμέν, ἡ ἐναντία ἰδέα ἐκείνῃ τῇ
μορφῇ ἣ ἂν τοῦτο ἀπεργάζηται οὐδέποτ' ἂν ἔλθοι.   10

Οὐ γάρ.

Εἰργάζετο δέ γε ἡ περιττή;

Ναί.

Ἐναντία δὲ ταύτῃ ἡ τοῦ ἀρτίου;

Ναί.   15

Ἐπὶ τὰ τρία ἄρα ἡ τοῦ ἀρτίου ἰδέα οὐδέποτε ἥξει.   e

Οὐ δῆτα.

Ἄμοιρα δὴ τοῦ ἀρτίου τὰ τρία.

Ἄμοιρα.

Ἀνάρτιος ἄρα ἡ τριάς.   5

Ναί.

Ὃ τοίνυν ἔλεγον ὁρίσασθαι, ποῖα οὐκ ἐναντία τινὶ ὄντα
ὅμως οὐ δέχεται αὐτό, τὸ ἐναντίον—οἷον νῦν ἡ τριὰς τῷ
ἀρτίῳ οὐκ οὖσα ἐναντία οὐδέν τι μᾶλλον αὐτὸ δέχεται, τὸ
γὰρ ἐναντίον ἀεὶ αὐτῷ ἐπιφέρει, καὶ ἡ δυὰς τῷ περιττῷ καὶ   10
τὸ πῦρ τῷ ψυχρῷ καὶ ἄλλα πάμπολλα—ἀλλ' ὅρα δὴ εἰ   105
οὕτως ὁρίζῃ, μὴ μόνον τὸ ἐναντίον τὸ ἐναντίον μὴ δέχεσθαι,
ἀλλὰ καὶ ἐκεῖνο, ὃ ἂν ἐπιφέρῃ τι ἐναντίον ἐκείνῳ, ἐφ' ὅτι
ἂν αὐτὸ ἴῃ, αὐτὸ τὸ ἐπιφέρον τὴν τοῦ ἐπιφερομένου ἐναντιότητα μηδέποτε δέξασθαι. πάλιν δὲ ἀναμιμνῄσκου· οὐ   5
γὰρ χεῖρον πολλάκις ἀκούειν. τὰ πέντε τὴν τοῦ ἀρτίου
οὐ δέξεται, οὐδὲ τὰ δέκα τὴν τοῦ περιττοῦ, τὸ διπλάσιον.
τοῦτο μὲν οὖν καὶ αὐτὸ ἄλλῳ ἐναντίον, ὅμως δὲ τὴν

d 9 ἐπὶ Β : ἐπεὶ Τ   d 10 ἢ W : ἦ Β Τ   e 7 ὁρίσασθαι Β Τ :
ὁρίσασθαι δεῖν W   e 10 αὐτῷ ἀεὶ Τ W   a 2 μὴ δέχεσθαι τὸ
ἐναντίον Τ (add. sign. transp.)   a 3 ὅτι Β Τ : ὅτῳ Β² W   a 4 ἴῃ
Τ : ἦ Β : εἴη W   a 5 δέξεσθαι Madvig   a 8 αὐτὸ Τ W : αὐτῷ Β
et ᾧ s. v. W

b τοῦ περιττοῦ οὐ δέξεται· οὐδὲ δὴ τὸ ἡμιόλιον οὐδὲ τἆλλα
τὰ τοιαῦτα, τὸ ἥμισυ, τὴν τοῦ ὅλου, καὶ τριτημόριον αὖ
καὶ πάντα τὰ τοιαῦτα, εἴπερ ἔπῃ τε καὶ συνδοκεῖ σοι οὕτως.
Πάνυ σφόδρα καὶ συνδοκεῖ, ἔφη, καὶ ἕπομαι.

5   Πάλιν δή μοι, ἔφη, ἐξ ἀρχῆς λέγε. καὶ μή μοι ὃ ἂν
ἐρωτῶ ἀποκρίνου, ἀλλὰ μιμούμενος ἐμέ. λέγω δὴ παρ' ἣν
τὸ πρῶτον ἔλεγον ἀπόκρισιν, τὴν ἀσφαλῆ ἐκείνην, ἐκ τῶν
νῦν λεγομένων ἄλλην ὁρῶν ἀσφάλειαν. εἰ γὰρ ἔροιό με
ᾧ ἂν τί ἐν τῷ σώματι ἐγγένηται θερμὸν ἔσται, οὐ τὴν
c ἀσφαλῆ σοι ἐρῶ ἀπόκρισιν ἐκείνην τὴν ἀμαθῆ, ὅτι ᾧ ἂν
θερμότης, ἀλλὰ κομψοτέραν ἐκ τῶν νῦν, ὅτι ᾧ ἂν πῦρ· οὐδὲ
ἂν ἔρῃ ᾧ ἂν σώματι τί ἐγγένηται νοσήσει, οὐκ ἐρῶ ὅτι
ᾧ ἂν νόσος, ἀλλ' ᾧ ἂν πυρετός· οὐδ' ᾧ ἂν ἀριθμῷ τί
5 ἐγγένηται περιττὸς ἔσται, οὐκ ἐρῶ ᾧ ἂν περιττότης, ἀλλ'
ᾧ ἂν μονάς, καὶ τἆλλα οὕτως. ἀλλ' ὅρα εἰ ἤδη ἱκανῶς
οἶσθ' ὅτι βούλομαι.

'Αλλὰ πάνυ ἱκανῶς, ἔφη.

'Αποκρίνου δή, ἦ δ' ὅς, ᾧ ἂν τί ἐγγένηται σώματι ζῶν
10 ἔσται;

Ὧι ἂν ψυχή, ἔφη.

d   Οὐκοῦν ἀεὶ τοῦτο οὕτως ἔχει;
Πῶς γὰρ οὐχί; ἦ δ' ὅς.
Ψυχὴ ἄρα ὅτι ἂν αὐτὴ κατάσχῃ, ἀεὶ ἥκει ἐπ' ἐκεῖνο
φέρουσα ζωήν;

5   Ἥκει μέντοι, ἔφη.
Πότερον δ' ἔστι τι ζωῇ ἐναντίον ἢ οὐδέν;
Ἔστιν, ἔφη.
Τί;

---

b 1 δὴ T : om. B   b 5 μοι μὴ T   ὃ ἂν ἐρωτῶ B W : ᾧ ἂν ἐρωτῶ
T : ἣν ἂν ἐρωτῶ ἀπόκρισιν γρ W   b 6 ἀλλὰ B W : ἀλλὰ ἄλλῳ T :
ἀλλ' ἄλλην γρ. W   δὴ B² T W : δὲ B   b 7 ἐκ B T : ἀλλ' ἣν ἐκ
W   b 8 ὁρῶν T b : ὁρῶ B   b 9 ᾧ T : ὃ B W et mox   ἐν τῷ
secl. ci. Stephanus   ἔστιν W sed αι s. v.   c 3 ᾧ ἂν] ὃ ἂν B W :
ᾧ δὲ T   τί om. W   νοσήσει . . . c 5 ἐγγένηται B² T W : om. B
c 4 ᾧ T : ὃ B² W   c 5 περιττὸν pr. T   c 9 ᾧ T Stob. : ὃ B
(et mox c 11)   c 11 ἔφη B Stob. : ἔφη ἔσται T   d 3 ψυχὴ T :
ἡ ψυχὴ B Stob.

Θάνατος.

Οὐκοῦν ψυχὴ τὸ ἐναντίον ᾧ αὐτὴ ἐπιφέρει ἀεὶ οὐ μή 10
ποτε δέξηται, ὡς ἐκ τῶν πρόσθεν ὡμολόγηται;
Καὶ μάλα σφόδρα, ἔφη ὁ Κέβης.

Τί οὖν; τὸ μὴ δεχόμενον τὴν τοῦ ἀρτίου ἰδέαν τί νυνδὴ
ὠνομάζομεν;

᾿Ανάρτιον, ἔφη.   15

Τὸ δὲ δίκαιον μὴ δεχόμενον καὶ ὃ ἂν μουσικὸν μὴ δέχηται;

῎Αμουσον, ἔφη, τὸ δὲ ἄδικον.   e

Εἶεν· ὃ δ᾽ ἂν θάνατον μὴ δέχηται τί καλοῦμεν;
᾿Αθάνατον, ἔφη.

Οὐκοῦν ψυχὴ οὐ δέχεται θάνατον;

Οὔ.   5

᾿Αθάνατον ἄρα ψυχή.

᾿Αθάνατον.

Εἶεν, ἔφη· τοῦτο μὲν δὴ ἀποδεδεῖχθαι φῶμεν; ἢ πῶς δοκεῖ;
Καὶ μάλα γε ἱκανῶς, ὦ Σώκρατες.

Τί οὖν, ἦ δ᾽ ὅς, ὦ Κέβης; εἰ τῷ ἀναρτίῳ ἀναγκαῖον ἦν 10
ἀνωλέθρῳ εἶναι, ἄλλο τι τὰ τρία ἢ ἀνώλεθρα ἂν ἦν;   106

Πῶς γὰρ οὔ;

Οὐκοῦν εἰ καὶ τὸ ἄθερμον ἀναγκαῖον ἦν ἀνώλεθρον εἶναι,
ὁπότε τις ἐπὶ χιόνα θερμὸν ἐπάγοι, ὑπεξήει ἂν ἡ χιὼν οὖσα
σῶς καὶ ἄτηκτος; οὐ γὰρ ἂν ἀπώλετό γε, οὐδ᾽ αὖ ὑπο- 5
μένουσα ἐδέξατο ἂν τὴν θερμότητα.

᾿Αληθῆ, ἔφη, λέγεις.

῍Ως δ᾽ αὔτως οἶμαι κἂν εἰ τὸ ἄψυκτον ἀνώλεθρον ἦν,
ὁπότε ἐπὶ τὸ πῦρ ψυχρόν τι ἐπήει, οὔποτ᾽ ἂν ἀπεσβέννυτο
οὐδ᾽ ἀπώλλυτο, ἀλλὰ σῶν ἂν ἀπελθὸν ᾤχετο.   10

d 10 ψυχὴ B Stob. : ἡ ψυχὴ T W   d 13 νῦν δὴ B² T W Stob. :
νυνδὴ ταῦτα B   d 14 ὠνομάζομεν B et in marg. T : ὠμολογήσαμεν
T : ὀνομάζομεν W Stob.   e 4 ψυχὴ T W Stob. : ἡ ψυχὴ B
e 6 ψυχὴ T Stob. : ἡ ψυχὴ B W   e 10 ἀναρτίῳ B t Stob. : ἀρτίῳ T
a 1 ἢ B et post τι t Stob. : om. T   a 3 ἄθερμον t : θερμὸν B T W
Stob.   a 4 ἐπάγοι T W : ἐπάγει Stob. : ἐπαγάγοι B   οὖσα σῶς
καὶ] μένουσα Stob.   a 8 ὡς δ᾽ αὔτως T W Stob. : ὡσαύτως B
ἄψυκτον B T W : ψυχρὸν Stob. : ἄψυχρον Wyttenbach

Ἀνάγκη, ἔφη.

b Οὐκοῦν καὶ ὧδε, ἔφη, ἀνάγκη περὶ τοῦ ἀθανάτου εἰπεῖν; εἰ μὲν τὸ ἀθάνατον καὶ ἀνώλεθρόν ἐστιν, ἀδύνατον ψυχῇ, ὅταν θάνατος ἐπ' αὐτὴν ἴῃ, ἀπόλλυσθαι· θάνατον μὲν γὰρ δὴ ἐκ τῶν προειρημένων οὐ δέξεται οὐδ' ἔσται τεθνηκυῖα, 5 ὥσπερ τὰ τρία οὐκ ἔσται, ἔφαμεν, ἄρτιον, οὐδέ γ' αὖ τὸ περιττόν, οὐδὲ δὴ πῦρ ψυχρόν, οὐδέ γε ἡ ἐν τῷ πυρὶ θερμότης. "Ἀλλὰ τί κωλύει," φαίη ἄν τις, "ἄρτιον μὲν τὸ περιττὸν μὴ γίγνεσθαι ἐπιόντος τοῦ ἀρτίου, ὥσπερ ὡμολόγη-
c ται, ἀπολομένου δὲ αὐτοῦ ἀντ' ἐκείνου ἄρτιον γεγονέναι;" τῷ ταῦτα λέγοντι οὐκ ἂν ἔχοιμεν διαμαχέσασθαι ὅτι οὐκ ἀπόλλυται· τὸ γὰρ ἀνάρτιον οὐκ ἀνώλεθρόν ἐστιν· ἐπεὶ εἰ τοῦτο ὡμολόγητο ἡμῖν, ῥᾳδίως ἂν διεμαχόμεθα ὅτι ἐπελ-
5 θόντος τοῦ ἀρτίου τὸ περιττὸν καὶ τὰ τρία οἴχεται ἀπιόντα· καὶ περὶ πυρὸς καὶ θερμοῦ καὶ τῶν ἄλλων οὕτως ἂν διεμαχόμεθα. ἢ οὔ;

Πάνυ μὲν οὖν.

Οὐκοῦν καὶ νῦν περὶ τοῦ ἀθανάτου, εἰ μὲν ἡμῖν ὁμολογεῖται 10 καὶ ἀνώλεθρον εἶναι, ψυχὴ ἂν εἴη πρὸς τῷ ἀθάνατος εἶναι
d καὶ ἀνώλεθρος· εἰ δὲ μή, ἄλλου ἂν δέοι λόγου.

Ἀλλ' οὐδὲν δεῖ, ἔφη, τούτου γε ἕνεκα· σχολῇ γὰρ ἄν τι ἄλλο φθορὰν μὴ δέχοιτο, εἰ τό γε ἀθάνατον ἀίδιον ὂν φθορὰν δέξεται.

5 Ὁ δέ γε θεὸς οἶμαι, ἔφη ὁ Σωκράτης, καὶ αὐτὸ τὸ τῆς ζωῆς εἶδος καὶ εἴ τι ἄλλο ἀθάνατόν ἐστιν, παρὰ πάντων ἂν ὁμολογηθείη μηδέποτε ἀπόλλυσθαι.

Παρὰ πάντων μέντοι νὴ Δί', ἔφη, ἀνθρώπων τέ γε καὶ ἔτι μᾶλλον, ὡς ἐγῷμαι, παρὰ θεῶν.

e Ὁπότε δὴ τὸ ἀθάνατον καὶ ἀδιάφθορόν ἐστιν, ἄλλο

b 1 εἰπεῖν B : om. T Stob.   b 6 πῦρ B : τὸ πῦρ T Stob.
c 1 ἀπολομένου B T : ἀπολλυμένου W Stob.   c 2 διαμαχέσασθαι
T W : διαμάχεσθαι B Stob.   c 4 ὡμολόγητο B : ὡμολογεῖτο T Stob.
c 8 πάνυ μὲν οὖν B t : om. T   c 9 θανάτου pr. T Stob.   ἡμῖν
om. W   c 10 τῷ B² T W Stob. : τὸ B   d 3 εἰ τό γε B² T W :
εἰ τό τε Stob. : εἴ γε τὸ B   ἀίδιον ὂν B Stob. : καὶ ἀίδιον T
d 4 δέξεται B Stob. et ε, αι s. v. W : δέξαιτο T W   d 8 τέ γε B
Stob. : τε T W sed γ s. v. W

τι ψυχὴ ᾖ, εἰ ἀθάνατος τυγχάνει οὖσα, καὶ ἀνώλεθρος
ἂν εἴη;

Πολλὴ ἀνάγκη.

Ἐπιόντος ἄρα θανάτου ἐπὶ τὸν ἄνθρωπον τὸ μὲν θνητόν, 5
ὡς ἔοικεν, αὐτοῦ ἀποθνήσκει, τὸ δ' ἀθάνατον σῶν καὶ
ἀδιάφθορον οἴχεται ἀπιόν, ὑπεκχωρῆσαν τῷ θανάτῳ.

Φαίνεται.

Παντὸς μᾶλλον ἄρα, ἔφη, ὦ Κέβης, ψυχὴ ἀθάνατον καὶ
ἀνώλεθρον, καὶ τῷ ὄντι ἔσονται ἡμῶν αἱ ψυχαὶ ἐν Ἅιδου. 107

Οὔκουν ἔγωγε, ὦ Σώκρατες, ἔφη, ἔχω παρὰ ταῦτα ἄλλο
τι λέγειν οὐδέ πῃ ἀπιστεῖν τοῖς λόγοις. ἀλλ' εἰ δή τι
Σιμμίας ὅδε ἤ τις ἄλλος ἔχει λέγειν, εὖ ἔχει μὴ κατασιγῆ-
σαι· ὡς οὐκ οἶδα εἰς ὅντινά τις ἄλλον καιρὸν ἀναβάλλοιτο 5
ἢ τὸν νῦν παρόντα, περὶ τῶν τοιούτων βουλόμενος ἤ τι
εἰπεῖν ἢ ἀκοῦσαι.

Ἀλλὰ μήν, ἦ δ' ὃς ὁ Σιμμίας, οὐδ' αὐτὸς ἔχω ἔτι ὅπῃ
ἀπιστῶ ἔκ γε τῶν λεγομένων· ὑπὸ μέντοι τοῦ μεγέθους περὶ
ὧν οἱ λόγοι εἰσίν, καὶ τὴν ἀνθρωπίνην ἀσθένειαν ἀτιμάζων, b
ἀναγκάζομαι ἀπιστίαν ἔτι ἔχειν παρ' ἐμαυτῷ περὶ τῶν
εἰρημένων.

Οὐ μόνον γ', ἔφη, ὦ Σιμμία, ὁ Σωκράτης, ἀλλὰ ταῦτά
τε εὖ λέγεις καὶ τάς γε ὑποθέσεις τὰς πρώτας, καὶ εἰ 5
πισταὶ ὑμῖν εἰσιν, ὅμως ἐπισκεπτέαι σαφέστερον· καὶ ἐὰν
αὐτὰς ἱκανῶς διέλητε, ὡς ἐγᾦμαι, ἀκολουθήσετε τῷ λόγῳ,
καθ' ὅσον δυνατὸν μάλιστ' ἀνθρώπῳ ἐπακολουθῆσαι· κἂν
τοῦτο αὐτὸ σαφὲς γένηται, οὐδὲν ζητήσετε περαιτέρω.

Ἀληθῆ, ἔφη, λέγεις. 10

Ἀλλὰ τόδε γ', ἔφη, ὦ ἄνδρες, δίκαιον διανοηθῆναι, ὅτι, c
εἴπερ ἡ ψυχὴ ἀθάνατος, ἐπιμελείας δὴ δεῖται οὐχ ὑπὲρ τοῦ

e 2 ψυχὴ B T Stob. : ἡ ψυχὴ W   ἢ B : post τι Stob. : om. T
a 3 οὐδέ πῃ B T : οὐδέτι W   a 4 ὅδε B² T W : om. B   a 5 τις
B T : τις ἂν W   ἀναβάλλοιτο W (in marg. ἀνακρούοιτο)   a 6 ἤ τι
B T : ἤτοι W   a 8 ἔτι T W : om. B   b 1 οὐκ ἀτιμάζων in marg.
B²   b 5 γε B² T W : om. B   b 6 ἐπισκεπτέα Seager   b 7 διέλητε B² W : διέληται B : ἔληται T (ε s. v. t)   ἀκολουθήσετε B² W :
ἀκολουθήσεται B T (ε s. v. t)   b 8 κἂν B W t : καὶ T   c 1 τόδε
γ' B T : τόδε W : τό γ' Stob.   c 2 ἀθάνατος B T Iambl. Stob. :
ἀθάνατός ἐστιν B² W

χρόνου τούτου μόνον ἐν ᾧ καλοῦμεν τὸ ζῆν, ἀλλ' ὑπὲρ τοῦ
παντός, καὶ ὁ κίνδυνος νῦν δὴ καὶ δόξειεν ἂν δεινὸς εἶναι,
5 εἴ τις αὐτῆς ἀμελήσει. εἰ μὲν γὰρ ἦν ὁ θάνατος τοῦ παντὸς
ἀπαλλαγή, ἕρμαιον ἂν ἦν τοῖς κακοῖς ἀποθανοῦσι τοῦ τε
σώματος ἅμ' ἀπηλλάχθαι καὶ τῆς αὐτῶν κακίας μετὰ τῆς
ψυχῆς· νῦν δ' ἐπειδὴ ἀθάνατος φαίνεται οὖσα, οὐδεμία ἂν
d εἴη αὐτῇ ἄλλη ἀποφυγὴ κακῶν οὐδὲ σωτηρία πλὴν τοῦ ὡς
βελτίστην τε καὶ φρονιμωτάτην γενέσθαι. οὐδὲν γὰρ ἄλλο
ἔχουσα εἰς Ἅιδου ἡ ψυχὴ ἔρχεται πλὴν τῆς παιδείας τε καὶ
τροφῆς, ἃ δὴ καὶ μέγιστα λέγεται ὠφελεῖν ἢ βλάπτειν τὸν
5 τελευτήσαντα εὐθὺς ἐν ἀρχῇ τῆς ἐκεῖσε πορείας. λέγεται
δὲ οὕτως, ὡς ἄρα τελευτήσαντα ἕκαστον ὁ ἑκάστου δαίμων,
ὅσπερ ζῶντα εἰλήχει, οὗτος ἄγειν ἐπιχειρεῖ εἰς δή τινα
τόπον, οἷ δεῖ τοὺς συλλεγέντας διαδικασαμένους εἰς Ἅιδου
e πορεύεσθαι μετὰ ἡγεμόνος ἐκείνου ᾧ δὴ προστέτακται τοὺς
ἐνθένδε ἐκεῖσε πορεῦσαι· τυχόντας δὲ ἐκεῖ ὧν δὴ τυχεῖν
καὶ μείναντας ὃν χρὴ χρόνον ἄλλος δεῦρο πάλιν ἡγεμὼν
κομίζει ἐν πολλαῖς χρόνου καὶ μακραῖς περιόδοις. ἔστι δὲ
ἄρα ἡ πορεία οὐχ ὡς ὁ Αἰσχύλου Τήλεφος λέγει· ἐκεῖνος
108 μὲν γὰρ ἁπλῆν οἶμόν φησιν εἰς Ἅιδου φέρειν, ἡ δ' οὔτε
ἁπλῆ οὔτε μία φαίνεταί μοι εἶναι. οὐδὲ γὰρ ἂν ἡγεμόνων
ἔδει· οὐ γάρ πού τις ἂν διαμάρτοι οὐδαμόσε μιᾶς ὁδοῦ
οὔσης. νῦν δὲ ἔοικε σχίσεις τε καὶ τριόδους πολλὰς ἔχειν·
5 ἀπὸ τῶν θυσιῶν τε καὶ νομίμων τῶν ἐνθάδε τεκμαιρόμενος
λέγω. ἡ μὲν οὖν κοσμία τε καὶ φρόνιμος ψυχὴ ἕπεταί τε
καὶ οὐκ ἀγνοεῖ τὰ παρόντα· ἡ δ' ἐπιθυμητικῶς τοῦ σώματος
ἔχουσα, ὅπερ ἐν τῷ ἔμπροσθεν εἶπον, περὶ ἐκεῖνο πολὺν

---

c 5 ἀμελήσει B T Iambl. Stob. : ἀμελήσειεν B² W   c 6 ἂν B t
Iambl. : om. T Stob.   κακοῖς] κακῶς Stob.   d 4 μέγιστα λέγεται
B : λέγεται μέγιστα T W Iambl. Stob.   d 7 ὅσπερ . . . οὗτος] ὥσπερ
. . . οὕτως Stob.   e 2 ἐνθένδε B Stob. : ἐνθάδε T   πορεῦσαι B
Stob. : πορεύεσθαι T   ἐκεῖ ὧν T : ἐκείνων ὧν B : ἐκείνων Stob.   δὴ
Stob. : δεῖ B T W   a 2 οὐδὲ] οὐδὲν Stob.   ἂν B Stob. : om. T
sed add. post ἔδει   a 3 οὐ B T Stob. : οὐδὲ B² W   διαμάρτοι B :
ἁμάρτοι T W Stob.   a 4 τριόδους Olymp. Proclus : περιόδους B T W
Stob.   a 5 θυσιῶν T W Stob. : ὁσίων B et γρ. W t   a 6 οὖν
B² T W Stob. : om. B   a 8 ἔμπροσθεν B Stob. : πρόσθεν T

χρόνον ἐπτοημένη καὶ περὶ τὸν ὁρατὸν τόπον, πολλὰ b
ἀντιτείνασα καὶ πολλὰ παθοῦσα, βίᾳ καὶ μόγις ὑπὸ τοῦ
προστεταγμένου δαίμονος οἴχεται ἀγομένη. ἀφικομένην δὲ
ὅθιπερ αἱ ἄλλαι, τὴν μὲν ἀκάθαρτον καί τι πεποιηκυῖαν
τοιοῦτον, ἢ φόνων ἀδίκων ἡμμένην ἢ ἄλλ' ἄττα τοιαῦτα 5
εἰργασμένην, ἃ τούτων ἀδελφά τε καὶ ἀδελφῶν ψυχῶν ἔργα
τυγχάνει ὄντα, ταύτην μὲν ἅπας φεύγει τε καὶ ὑπεκτρέπεται
καὶ οὔτε συνέμπορος οὔτε ἡγεμὼν ἐθέλει γίγνεσθαι, αὐτὴ
δὲ πλανᾶται ἐν πάσῃ ἐχομένη ἀπορίᾳ ἕως ἂν δή τινες c
χρόνοι γένωνται, ὧν ἐλθόντων ὑπ' ἀνάγκης φέρεται εἰς τὴν
αὐτῇ πρέπουσαν οἴκησιν· ἡ δὲ καθαρῶς τε καὶ μετρίως τὸν
βίον διεξελθοῦσα, καὶ συνεμπόρων καὶ ἡγεμόνων θεῶν
τυχοῦσα, ᾤκησεν τὸν αὐτῇ ἑκάστη τόπον προσήκοντα. εἰσὶν 5
δὲ πολλοὶ καὶ θαυμαστοὶ τῆς γῆς τόποι, καὶ αὐτὴ οὔτε οἵα
οὔτε ὅση δοξάζεται ὑπὸ τῶν περὶ γῆς εἰωθότων λέγειν, ὡς
ἐγὼ ὑπό τινος πέπεισμαι.

Καὶ ὁ Σιμμίας, Πῶς ταῦτα, ἔφη, λέγεις, ὦ Σώκρατες; d
περὶ γάρ τοι γῆς καὶ αὐτὸς πολλὰ δὴ ἀκήκοα, οὐ μέντοι
ταῦτα ἃ σὲ πείθει· ἡδέως οὖν ἂν ἀκούσαιμι.

Ἀλλὰ μέντοι, ὦ Σιμμία, οὐχ ἡ Γλαύκου τέχνη γέ μοι
δοκεῖ εἶναι διηγήσασθαι ἅ γ' ἐστίν· ὡς μέντοι ἀληθῆ, 5
χαλεπώτερόν μοι φαίνεται ἢ κατὰ τὴν Γλαύκου τέχνην, καὶ
ἅμα μὲν ἐγὼ ἴσως οὐδ' ἂν οἷός τε εἴην, ἅμα δέ, εἰ καὶ
ἠπιστάμην, ὁ βίος μοι δοκεῖ ὁ ἐμός, ὦ Σιμμία, τῷ μήκει
τοῦ λόγου οὐκ ἐξαρκεῖν. τὴν μέντοι ἰδέαν τῆς γῆς οἵαν
πέπεισμαι εἶναι, καὶ τοὺς τόπους αὐτῆς οὐδέν με κωλύει e
λέγειν.

Ἀλλ', ἔφη ὁ Σιμμίας, καὶ ταῦτα ἀρκεῖ.

b 1 πολλὰ] ἄλλα Stob.   b 2 μόλις T Stob.   D 4 οἷπερ Cobet
b 7 ὑπεκτρέπεται] ὑποκρύπτεται Stob.   c 4 θεῶν B² T W Stob. :
ὅσων B   c 5 ἑκάστῃ T   c 8 τινος B T W : δέ τινος Stob. (fort.
δή τινος)   d 2 γῆς B Stob.: τῆς γῆς B² T   d 3 οὖν ἂν B : ἂν οὖν T :
οὖν Stob.   d 4 οὐχ ἡ B T W Stob. : οὐχὶ ἡ Eus. : οὐχὶ Heindorf
τέχνη γέ μοι B T Eus. Stob. : γέ μοι τέχνη W   d 5 ἅ γ' T Eus. :
ἅ γε W : ἅ τε Stob. : δέ γ' B   d 7 οὐδ' B T Eus. Stob. : οὐκ W
καὶ εἰ Eus.   d 9 ἐξαρκεῖν T W Eus. Stob. : ἐξαρκεῖ B

Πέπεισμαι τοίνυν, ἦ δ' ὅς, ἐγὼ ὡς πρῶτον μέν, εἰ ἔστιν
5 ἐν μέσῳ τῷ οὐρανῷ περιφερὴς οὖσα, μηδὲν αὐτῇ δεῖν μήτε
109 ἀέρος πρὸς τὸ μὴ πεσεῖν μήτε ἄλλης ἀνάγκης μηδεμιᾶς
τοιαύτης, ἀλλὰ ἱκανὴν εἶναι αὐτὴν ἴσχειν τὴν ὁμοιότητα
τοῦ οὐρανοῦ αὐτοῦ ἑαυτῷ πάντῃ καὶ τῆς γῆς αὐτῆς τὴν
ἰσορροπίαν· ἰσόρροπον γὰρ πρᾶγμα ὁμοίου τινὸς ἐν μέσῳ
5 τεθὲν οὐχ ἕξει μᾶλλον οὐδ' ἧττον οὐδαμόσε κλιθῆναι,
ὁμοίως δ' ἔχον ἀκλινὲς μενεῖ. πρῶτον μὲν τοίνυν, ἦ δ' ὅς,
τοῦτο πέπεισμαι.

Καὶ ὀρθῶς γε, ἔφη ὁ Σιμμίας.

Ἔτι τοίνυν, ἔφη, πάμμεγά τι εἶναι αὐτό, καὶ ἡμᾶς οἰκεῖν
b τοὺς μέχρι Ἡρακλείων στηλῶν ἀπὸ Φάσιδος ἐν σμικρῷ
τινι μορίῳ, ὥσπερ περὶ τέλμα μύρμηκας ἢ βατράχους περὶ
τὴν θάλατταν οἰκοῦντας, καὶ ἄλλους ἄλλοθι πολλοὺς ἐν
πολλοῖσι τοιούτοις τόποις οἰκεῖν. εἶναι γὰρ πανταχῇ περὶ
5 τὴν γῆν πολλὰ κοῖλα καὶ παντοδαπὰ καὶ τὰς ἰδέας καὶ τὰ
μεγέθη, εἰς ἃ συνερρυηκέναι τό τε ὕδωρ καὶ τὴν ὁμίχλην
καὶ τὸν ἀέρα· αὐτὴν δὲ τὴν γῆν καθαρὰν ἐν καθαρῷ κεῖσθαι
τῷ οὐρανῷ ἐν ᾧπέρ ἐστι τὰ ἄστρα, ὃν δὴ αἰθέρα ὀνομάζειν
c τοὺς πολλοὺς τῶν περὶ τὰ τοιαῦτα εἰωθότων λέγειν· οὗ δὴ
ὑποστάθμην ταῦτα εἶναι καὶ συρρεῖν ἀεὶ εἰς τὰ κοῖλα τῆς
γῆς. ἡμᾶς οὖν οἰκοῦντας ἐν τοῖς κοίλοις αὐτῆς λεληθέναι
καὶ οἴεσθαι ἄνω ἐπὶ τῆς γῆς οἰκεῖν, ὥσπερ ἂν εἴ τις ἐν
5 μέσῳ τῷ πυθμένι τοῦ πελάγους οἰκῶν οἴοιτό τε ἐπὶ τῆς
θαλάττης οἰκεῖν καὶ διὰ τοῦ ὕδατος ὁρῶν τὸν ἥλιον καὶ τὰ
ἄλλα ἄστρα τὴν θάλατταν ἡγοῖτο οὐρανὸν εἶναι, διὰ δὲ
d βραδυτῆτά τε καὶ ἀσθένειαν μηδεπώποτε ἐπὶ τὰ ἄκρα τῆς
θαλάττης ἀφιγμένος μηδὲ ἑωρακὼς εἴη, ἐκδὺς καὶ ἀνακύψας
ἐκ τῆς θαλάττης εἰς τὸν ἐνθάδε τόπον, ὅσῳ καθαρώτερος
καὶ καλλίων τυγχάνει ὢν τοῦ παρὰ σφίσι, μηδὲ ἄλλου

e 4 εἰ] γῆ Stob.   e 5 τοῦ οὐρανοῦ Stob.   a 3 αὐτῆς B t Stob. :
αὐτὴν T Eus.   a 6 μένει B T W   τοίνυν T W : δὴ Eus. : om.
B Stob.   ἢ δ' ὃς B Eus. Stob. : om. T (add. in marg.) W   b 4 πολλοῖσι T : πολλοῖς B Eus. Stob.   c 4 τῆς B T Eus. : om. Stob.
d 1 οὐδεπώποτε W   d 4 καλλίω pr. T

ἀκηκοὼς εἴη τοῦ ἑωρακότος. ταὐτὸν δὴ τοῦτο καὶ ἡμᾶς 5
πεπονθέναι· οἰκοῦντας γὰρ ἔν τινι κοίλῳ τῆς γῆς οἴεσθαι
ἐπάνω αὐτῆς οἰκεῖν, καὶ τὸν ἀέρα οὐρανὸν καλεῖν, ὡς διὰ
τούτου οὐρανοῦ ὄντος τὰ ἄστρα χωροῦντα· τὸ δὲ εἶναι ταὐτόν, ὑπ' ἀσθενείας καὶ βραδυτῆτος οὐχ οἵους τε εἶναι ἡμᾶς e
διεξελθεῖν ἐπ' ἔσχατον τὸν ἀέρα· ἐπεί, εἴ τις αὐτοῦ ἐπ' ἄκρα
ἔλθοι ἢ πτηνὸς γενόμενος ἀνάπτοιτο, κατιδεῖν ⟨ἂν⟩ ἀνακύ-
ψαντα, ὥσπερ ἐνθάδε οἱ ἐκ τῆς θαλάττης ἰχθύες ἀνακύπτοντες ὁρῶσι τὰ ἐνθάδε, οὕτως ἄν τινα καὶ τὰ ἐκεῖ κατιδεῖν, 5
καὶ εἰ ἡ φύσις ἱκανὴ εἴη ἀνασχέσθαι θεωροῦσα, γνῶναι ἂν
ὅτι ἐκεῖνός ἐστιν ὁ ἀληθῶς οὐρανὸς καὶ τὸ ἀληθινὸν φῶς
καὶ ἡ ὡς ἀληθῶς γῆ. ἥδε μὲν γὰρ ἡ γῆ καὶ οἱ λίθοι καὶ 110
ἅπας ὁ τόπος ὁ ἐνθάδε διεφθαρμένα ἐστὶν καὶ καταβεβρω-
μένα, ὥσπερ τὰ ἐν τῇ θαλάττῃ ὑπὸ τῆς ἅλμης, καὶ οὔτε
φύεται ἄξιον λόγου οὐδὲν ἐν τῇ θαλάττῃ, οὔτε τέλειον ὡς
ἔπος εἰπεῖν οὐδέν ἐστι, σήραγγες δὲ καὶ ἄμμος καὶ πηλὸς 5
ἀμήχανος καὶ βόρβοροί εἰσιν, ὅπου ἂν καὶ [ἡ] γῆ ᾖ, καὶ
πρὸς τὰ παρ' ἡμῖν κάλλη κρίνεσθαι οὐδ' ὁπωστιοῦν ἄξια.
ἐκεῖνα δὲ αὖ τῶν παρ' ἡμῖν πολὺ ἂν ἔτι πλέον φανείη δια-
φέρειν· εἰ γὰρ δὴ καὶ μῦθον λέγειν καλόν, ἄξιον ἀκοῦσαι, ὦ b
Σιμμία, οἷα τυγχάνει τὰ ἐπὶ τῆς γῆς ὑπὸ τῷ οὐρανῷ ὄντα.

Ἀλλὰ μήν, ἔφη ὁ Σιμμίας, ὦ Σώκρατες, ἡμεῖς γε τούτου
τοῦ μύθου ἡδέως ἂν ἀκούσαιμεν.

Λέγεται τοίνυν, ἔφη, ὦ ἑταῖρε, πρῶτον μὲν εἶναι τοιαύτη 5
ἡ γῆ αὐτὴ ἰδεῖν, εἴ τις ἄνωθεν θεῷτο, ὥσπερ αἱ δωδεκάσκυτοι σφαῖραι, ποικίλη, χρώμασιν διειλημμένη, ὧν καὶ τὰ
ἐνθάδε εἶναι χρώματα ὥσπερ δείγματα, οἷς δὴ οἱ γραφῆς

e 2 ἄκρα B T Eus. Stob. : ἄκρον W   e 3 ἂν Stephanus : δὴ Eus. :
om. B T W Stob.   e 6 ἀνασχέσθαι W t : ἂν ἀνασχέσθαι T Stob. :
ἀνέχεσθαι B Eus. et ε s. v. W   e 7 ἀληθινὸν B² T W Eus. Stob. :
ἀληθῶς B   a 1 ἥδε B² T W Eus. Stob. : ἤδη B   a 4 οὐδὲν
post λόγου T Eus. Stob. : ante ἄξιον B : utrobique W   a 6 καὶ
om. Stob. : ἡ om. recc.   a 8 πολὺ T W Eus. Stob. : πολλοῦ B t
b 1 δὴ T (e δεῖ) W Eus. Stob. : δεῖ B   καλόν B² T W Eus. Stob. :
om. B   ἄξιον B T Eus. Stob. : καὶ ἄξιον B² W   b 2 τῆς om.
Stob.   b 6 εἴ τις B² T W Eus. : ἥτις B Stob.   θεῷτο T Eus.
Stob. : θεῷτο ἂν B : θεῷτο αὐτὴν B² W

c καταχρῶνται. ἐκεῖ δὲ πᾶσαν τὴν γῆν ἐκ τοιούτων εἶναι, καὶ
πολὺ ἔτι ἐκ λαμπροτέρων καὶ καθαρωτέρων ἢ τούτων· τὴν
μὲν γὰρ ἁλουργῆ εἶναι [καὶ] θαυμαστὴν τὸ κάλλος, τὴν δὲ
χρυσοειδῆ, τὴν δὲ ὅση λευκὴ γύψου ἢ χιόνος λευκοτέραν,
5 καὶ ἐκ τῶν ἄλλων χρωμάτων συγκειμένην ὡσαύτως, καὶ ἔτι
πλειόνων καὶ καλλιόνων ἢ ὅσα ἡμεῖς ἑωράκαμεν. καὶ γὰρ
αὐτὰ ταῦτα τὰ κοῖλα αὐτῆς, ὕδατός τε καὶ ἀέρος ἔκπλεα
d ὄντα, χρώματός τι εἶδος παρέχεσθαι στίλβοντα ἐν τῇ τῶν
ἄλλων χρωμάτων ποικιλίᾳ, ὥστε ἕν τι αὐτῆς εἶδος συνεχὲς
ποικίλον φαντάζεσθαι. ἐν δὲ ταύτῃ οὔσῃ τοιαύτῃ ἀνὰ
λόγον τὰ φυόμενα φύεσθαι, δένδρα τε καὶ ἄνθη καὶ τοὺς
5 καρπούς· καὶ αὖ τὰ ὄρη ὡσαύτως καὶ τοὺς λίθους ἔχειν ἀνὰ
τὸν αὐτὸν λόγον τήν τε λειότητα καὶ τὴν διαφάνειαν καὶ τὰ
χρώματα καλλίω· ὧν καὶ τὰ ἐνθάδε λιθίδια εἶναι ταῦτα τὰ
ἀγαπώμενα μόρια, σάρδιά τε καὶ ἰάσπιδας καὶ σμαράγδους
e καὶ πάντα τὰ τοιαῦτα· ἐκεῖ δὲ οὐδὲν ὅτι οὐ τοιοῦτον εἶναι καὶ
ἔτι τούτων καλλίω. τὸ δ' αἴτιον τούτου εἶναι ὅτι ἐκεῖνοι οἱ
λίθοι εἰσὶ καθαροὶ καὶ οὐ κατεδηδεσμένοι οὐδὲ διεφθαρμένοι
ὥσπερ οἱ ἐνθάδε ὑπὸ σηπεδόνος καὶ ἅλμης ὑπὸ τῶν δεῦρο
5 συνερρυηκότων, ἃ καὶ λίθοις καὶ γῇ καὶ τοῖς ἄλλοις ζῴοις τε
καὶ φυτοῖς αἴσχη τε καὶ νόσους παρέχει. τὴν δὲ γῆν αὐτὴν
κεκοσμῆσθαι τούτοις τε ἅπασι καὶ ἔτι χρυσῷ τε καὶ ἀργύρῳ καὶ
III τοῖς ἄλλοις αὖ τοῖς τοιούτοις. ἐκφανῆ γὰρ αὐτὰ πεφυκέναι,
ὄντα πολλὰ πλήθει καὶ μεγάλα καὶ πανταχοῦ τῆς γῆς, ὥστε
αὐτὴν ἰδεῖν εἶναι θέαμα εὐδαιμόνων θεατῶν. ζῷα δ' ἐπ'
αὐτῇ εἶναι ἄλλα τε πολλὰ καὶ ἀνθρώπους, τοὺς μὲν ἐν
5 μεσογαίᾳ οἰκοῦντας, τοὺς δὲ περὶ τὸν ἀέρα ὥσπερ ἡμεῖς

---

c 3 καὶ B Stob. : om. T Eus.   c 5 ἐγκειμένην W   ἔτι B² T W :
ἐπὶ B   c 7 ἔκπλεα B T W Eus. Stob. : ἔμπλεα al.   d 1 παρέχεσθαι B² T W Eus. : παρέχεται B Stob.   d 4 ἄνθη B T Eus. Stob. :
ἄλση B² W   d 6 * * * * * * * * τήν τε λειότητα T (τελειότητα B
Stob.)   e 1 ὅτι οὐ B T : ὅτιοῦν Eus. (et mox οὐκ εἶναι) : ὅτι μὴ B² W :
ὃ μὴ Stob.   e 3 εἰσὶ καθαροὶ B : καθεροί εἰσιν T W Eus. Stob.
e 5 & s. v. T : om. Stob.   λίθοις] τοῖς in marg. B²   e 7 ἅπασι
B Eus. Stob. : πᾶσιν T   τε καὶ T Eus. Stob. : καὶ B   a 2 πανταχοῦ T W : πολλαχοῦ B Eus. Stob.   a 3 θεατῶν om. Stob.
a 4 αὐτῇ B · αὐτὴν T W : αὐτῆς Stob.

περὶ τὴν θάλατταν, τοὺς δ' ἐν νήσοις ἃς περιρρεῖν τὸν ἀέρα
πρὸς τῇ ἠπείρῳ οὔσας· καὶ ἑνὶ λόγῳ, ὅπερ ἡμῖν τὸ ὕδωρ τε
καὶ ἡ θάλαττά ἐστι πρὸς τὴν ἡμετέραν χρείαν, τοῦτο ἐκεῖ
τὸν ἀέρα, ὃ δὲ ἡμῖν ἀήρ, ἐκείνοις τὸν αἰθέρα. τὰς δὲ ὥρας b
αὐτοῖς κρᾶσιν ἔχειν τοιαύτην ὥστε ἐκείνους ἀνόσους εἶναι καὶ
χρόνον τε ζῆν πολὺ πλείω τῶν ἐνθάδε, καὶ ὄψει καὶ ἀκοῇ καὶ
φρονήσει καὶ πᾶσι τοῖς τοιούτοις ἡμῶν ἀφεστάναι τῇ αὐτῇ
ἀποστάσει ᾗπερ ἀήρ τε ὕδατος ἀφέστηκεν καὶ αἰθὴρ ἀέρος 5
πρὸς καθαρότητα. καὶ δὴ καὶ θεῶν ἄλση τε καὶ ἱερὰ αὐτοῖς
εἶναι, ἐν οἷς τῷ ὄντι οἰκητὰς θεοὺς εἶναι, καὶ φήμας τε καὶ
μαντείας καὶ αἰσθήσεις τῶν θεῶν καὶ τοιαύτας συνουσίας
γίγνεσθαι αὐτοῖς πρὸς αὐτούς· καὶ τόν γε ἥλιον καὶ σελήνην c
καὶ ἄστρα ὁρᾶσθαι ὑπ' αὐτῶν οἷα τυγχάνει ὄντα, καὶ τὴν
ἄλλην εὐδαιμονίαν τούτων ἀκόλουθον εἶναι.

Καὶ ὅλην μὲν δὴ τὴν γῆν οὕτω πεφυκέναι καὶ τὰ περὶ
τὴν γῆν· τόπους δ' ἐν αὐτῇ εἶναι κατὰ τὰ ἔγκοιλα αὐτῆς 5
κύκλῳ περὶ ὅλην πολλούς, τοὺς μὲν βαθυτέρους καὶ ἀνα-
πεπταμένους μᾶλλον ἢ ἐν ᾧ ἡμεῖς οἰκοῦμεν, τοὺς δὲ βαθυτέρους ὄντας τὸ χάσμα αὐτοὺς ἔλαττον ἔχειν τοῦ παρ' ἡμῖν
τόπου, ἔστι δ' οὓς καὶ βραχυτέρους τῷ βάθει τοῦ ἐνθάδε d
εἶναι καὶ πλατυτέρους. τούτους δὲ πάντας ὑπὸ γῆν εἰς
ἀλλήλους συντετρῆσθαί τε πολλαχῇ καὶ κατὰ στενότερα καὶ
εὐρύτερα καὶ διεξόδους ἔχειν, ᾗ πολὺ μὲν ὕδωρ ῥεῖν ἐξ
ἀλλήλων εἰς ἀλλήλους ὥσπερ εἰς κρατῆρας, καὶ ἀενάων 5
ποταμῶν ἀμήχανα μεγέθη ὑπὸ τὴν γῆν καὶ θερμῶν ὑδάτων
καὶ ψυχρῶν, πολὺ δὲ πῦρ καὶ πυρὸς μεγάλους ποταμούς,
πολλοὺς δὲ ὑγροῦ πηλοῦ καὶ καθαρωτέρου καὶ βορβορωδε-
στέρου, ὥσπερ ἐν Σικελίᾳ οἱ πρὸ τοῦ ῥύακος πηλοῦ ῥέοντες e
ποταμοὶ καὶ αὐτὸς ὁ ῥύαξ· ὧν δὴ καὶ ἑκάστους τοὺς τόπους

a 7 τε om. Stob.   b 2 αὐτοῖς T Stob. : αὐτῆς B   b 6 ἄλση
B Stob. : ἔδη T et ut vid. Timaeus   c 2 ὁρᾶσθαι Β Τ : θεωρεῖσθαι
Β² W   c 3 τούτων B Stob. : om. T   d 1 οὓς B Stob. : οὗ
pr. T   d 3 καὶ κατὰ Β Τ W : καὶ addubitavit Heindorf: καὶ τὰ
Stob.   d 5 καὶ T W Stob. : ἐξ in ras. B   d 8 δὲ Β Τ Stob. :
τε Β² W   καθαρωδεστέρου in marg. Β²   e 1 ἐν B Stob. : οἱ ἐν T
11*

πληροῦσθαι, ὡς ἂν ἑκάστοις τύχῃ ἑκάστοτε ἡ περιρροὴ γιγνο-
μένη. ταῦτα δὲ πάντα κινεῖν ἄνω καὶ κάτω ὥσπερ αἰώραν
5 τινὰ ἐνοῦσαν ἐν τῇ γῇ· ἔστι δὲ ἄρα αὕτη ἡ αἰώρα διὰ φύσιν
τοιάνδε τινά. ἔν τι τῶν χασμάτων τῆς γῆς ἄλλως τε
112 μέγιστον τυγχάνει ὂν καὶ διαμπερὲς τετρημένον δι' ὅλης τῆς
γῆς, τοῦτο ὅπερ Ὅμηρος εἶπε, λέγων αὐτό

τῆλε μάλ', ἧχι βάθιστον ὑπὸ χθονός ἐστι βέρεθρον·

ὃ καὶ ἄλλοθι καὶ ἐκεῖνος καὶ ἄλλοι πολλοὶ τῶν ποιητῶν Τάρ-
5 ταρον κεκλήκασιν. εἰς γὰρ τοῦτο τὸ χάσμα συρρέουσί τε
πάντες οἱ ποταμοὶ καὶ ἐκ τούτου πάλιν ἐκρέουσιν· γίγνονται
δὲ ἕκαστοι τοιοῦτοι δι' οἵας ἂν καὶ τῆς γῆς ῥέωσιν. ἡ δὲ
b αἰτία ἐστὶν τοῦ ἐκρεῖν τε ἐντεῦθεν καὶ εἰσρεῖν πάντα τὰ
ῥεύματα, ὅτι πυθμένα οὐκ ἔχει οὐδὲ βάσιν τὸ ὑγρὸν τοῦτο.
αἰωρεῖται δὴ καὶ κυμαίνει ἄνω καὶ κάτω, καὶ ὁ ἀὴρ καὶ τὸ
πνεῦμα τὸ περὶ αὐτὸ ταὐτὸν ποιεῖ· συνέπεται γὰρ αὐτῷ καὶ
5 ὅταν εἰς τὸ ἐπ' ἐκεῖνα τῆς γῆς ὁρμήσῃ καὶ ὅταν εἰς τὸ ἐπὶ
τάδε, καὶ ὥσπερ τῶν ἀναπνεόντων ἀεὶ ἐκπνεῖ τε καὶ ἀναπνεῖ
ῥέον τὸ πνεῦμα, οὕτω καὶ ἐκεῖ συναιωρούμενον τῷ ὑγρῷ τὸ
πνεῦμα δεινούς τινας ἀνέμους καὶ ἀμηχάνους παρέχεται καὶ
c εἰσιὸν καὶ ἐξιόν. ὅταν τε οὖν ὑποχωρήσῃ τὸ ὕδωρ εἰς τὸν
τόπον τὸν δὴ κάτω καλούμενον, τοῖς κατ' ἐκεῖνα τὰ ῥεύματα
[διὰ] τῆς γῆς εἰσρεῖ τε καὶ πληροῖ αὐτὰ ὥσπερ οἱ ἐπαν-
τλοῦντες· ὅταν τε αὖ ἐκεῖθεν μὲν ἀπολίπῃ, δεῦρο δὲ ὁρμήσῃ,
5 τὰ ἐνθάδε πληροῖ αὖθις, τὰ δὲ πληρωθέντα ῥεῖ διὰ τῶν
ὀχετῶν καὶ διὰ τῆς γῆς, καὶ εἰς τοὺς τόπους ἕκαστα ἀφικνού-
μενα, εἰς οὓς ἑκάστοις ὡδοποίηται, θαλάττας τε καὶ λίμνας
καὶ ποταμοὺς καὶ κρήνας ποιεῖ· ἐντεῦθεν δὲ πάλιν δυόμενα
d κατὰ τῆς γῆς, τὰ μὲν μακροτέρους τόπους περιελθόντα καὶ
πλείους, τὰ δὲ ἐλάττους καὶ βραχυτέρους, πάλιν εἰς τὸν

e 3 ὡς Stob. : ὧν Β Τ   a 5 τε Β Τ Stob. : om. W   b 4 αὐτὸ
Heindorf: αὐτὸν Β Τ Stob.   c 1 οὖν Β Τ Stob. : οὖν ὁρμῆσαν
Β² W   c 3 διὰ Β Τ : om. Stob.   c 4 ἀπολείπῃ W   c 6 καὶ
ὃιὰ om. W   c 7 ἑκάστοις Τ Stob. : ἑκάστους Β   ὡδοποίηται
Stob : ὁδοποιεῖται Β Τ : εἰδοποιεῖται W (sed ὁ s. v.)   d 2 ἐλάττω W
βραχυτέρους Β Stob. : βραδυτέρους Τ

Τάρταρον ἐμβάλλει, τὰ μὲν πολὺ κατωτέρω ⟨ἢ⟩ ᾗ ἐπην-
τλεῖτο, τὰ δὲ ὀλίγον· πάντα δὲ ὑποκάτω εἰσρεῖ τῆς ἐκροῆς,
καὶ ἔνια μὲν καταντικρὺ ⟨ἢ⟩ ᾗ [εἰσρεῖ] ἐξέπεσεν, ἔνια δὲ 5
κατὰ τὸ αὐτὸ μέρος· ἔστι δὲ ἃ παντάπασιν κύκλῳ περιελθόντα, ἢ ἅπαξ ἢ καὶ πλεονάκις περιελιχθέντα περὶ τὴν γῆν
ὥσπερ οἱ ὄφεις, εἰς τὸ δυνατὸν κάτω καθέντα πάλιν ἐμβάλλει.
δυνατὸν δέ ἐστιν ἑκατέρωσε μέχρι τοῦ μέσου καθιέναι, πέρα e
δ' οὔ· ἄναντες γὰρ ἀμφοτέροις τοῖς ῥεύμασι τὸ ἑκατέρωθεν
γίγνεται μέρος.

Τὰ μὲν οὖν δὴ ἄλλα πολλά τε καὶ μεγάλα καὶ παντοδαπὰ
ῥεύματά ἐστι· τυγχάνει δ' ἄρα ὄντα ἐν τούτοις τοῖς πολλοῖς 5
τέτταρ' ἄττα ῥεύματα, ὧν τὸ μὲν μέγιστον καὶ ἐξωτάτω ῥέον
περὶ κύκλῳ ὁ καλούμενος Ὠκεανός ἐστιν, τούτου δὲ καταντικρὺ καὶ ἐναντίως ῥέων Ἀχέρων, ὃς δι' ἐρήμων τε τόπων
ῥεῖ ἄλλων καὶ δὴ καὶ ὑπὸ γῆν ῥέων εἰς τὴν λίμνην ἀφικνεῖται 113
τὴν Ἀχερουσιάδα, οὗ αἱ τῶν τετελευτηκότων ψυχαὶ τῶν
πολλῶν ἀφικνοῦνται καί τινας εἱμαρμένους χρόνους μείνασαι,
αἱ μὲν μακροτέρους, αἱ δὲ βραχυτέρους, πάλιν ἐκπέμπονται
εἰς τὰς τῶν ζῴων γενέσεις. τρίτος δὲ ποταμὸς τούτων κατὰ 5
μέσον ἐκβάλλει, καὶ ἐγγὺς τῆς ἐκβολῆς ἐκπίπτει εἰς τόπον
μέγαν πυρὶ πολλῷ καόμενον, καὶ λίμνην ποιεῖ μείζω τῆς
παρ' ἡμῖν θαλάττης, ζέουσαν ὕδατος καὶ πηλοῦ· ἐντεῦθεν δὲ
χωρεῖ κύκλῳ θολερὸς καὶ πηλώδης, περιελιττόμενος δὲ τῇ b
γῇ ἄλλοσέ τε ἀφικνεῖται καὶ παρ' ἔσχατα τῆς Ἀχερουσιάδος
λίμνης, οὐ συμμειγνύμενος τῷ ὕδατι· περιελιχθεὶς δὲ πολλάκις
ὑπὸ γῆς ἐμβάλλει κατωτέρω τοῦ Ταρτάρου· οὗτος δ' ἐστὶν
ὃν ἐπονομάζουσιν Πυριφλεγέθοντα, οὗ καὶ οἱ ῥύακες ἀπο- 5

d 3 ἢ ᾗ] ᾗ Β Τ : ἢ W   d 5 ἢ ᾗ] ᾗ Β Τ W   εἰσρεῖ om. Stob.
e 2 γὰρ ἀμφοτέροις Τ Stob. : γὰρ πρὸς ἀμφοτέροις Β t : πρὸς γὰρ ἀμφοτέροις Β² W : γὰρ πρὸς ἀμφότερα in marg. W (error ortus e v. l.
πρόσαντες)   e 5 τυγχάνειν W   e 6 ἄττα Β : om. Τ Stob. : ὄντα
in marg. Β²   e 7 περὶ κύκλῳ Τ : περικύκλῳ Β : τὰ περὶ κύκλῳ Stob.
e 8 ἐναντίως Τ Stob. : ἐναντίος Β   a 2 οὗ] οἱ Schanz   a 5 τούτων
Β Τ Eus. Stob. : διὰ τούτων W   a 7 μέγα Τ   b 1 τῇ γῇ Β Τ W
Stob. : om. Theodoretus (habet Eus)   b 5 ἐπονομάζουσι Τ W Eus.
Stob. : ἔτι ὀνομάζουσιν Β

σπάσματα ἀναφυσῶσιν ὅπῃ ἂν τύχωσι τῆς γῆς. τούτου δὲ
αὖ καταντικρὺ ὁ τέταρτος ἐκπίπτει εἰς τόπον πρῶτον δεινόν
τε καὶ ἄγριον, ὡς λέγεται, χρῶμα δ' ἔχοντα ὅλον οἷον ὁ
c κυανός, ὃν δὴ ἐπονομάζουσι Στύγιον, καὶ τὴν λίμνην ἣν
ποιεῖ ὁ ποταμὸς ἐμβάλλων, Στύγα· ὁ δ' ἐμπεσὼν ἐνταῦθα
καὶ δεινὰς δυνάμεις λαβὼν ἐν τῷ ὕδατι, δὺς κατὰ τῆς γῆς,
περιελιττόμενος χωρεῖ ἐναντίος τῷ Πυριφλεγέθοντι καὶ
5 ἀπαντᾷ ἐν τῇ Ἀχερουσιάδι λίμνῃ ἐξ ἐναντίας· καὶ οὐδὲ τὸ
τούτου ὕδωρ οὐδενὶ μείγνυται, ἀλλὰ καὶ οὗτος κύκλῳ περιελ-
θὼν ἐμβάλλει εἰς τὸν Τάρταρον ἐναντίος τῷ Πυριφλεγέθοντι·
ὄνομα δὲ τούτῳ ἐστίν, ὡς οἱ ποιηταὶ λέγουσιν, Κωκυτός.

d Τούτων δὲ οὕτως πεφυκότων, ἐπειδὰν ἀφίκωνται οἱ τετε-
λευτηκότες εἰς τὸν τόπον οἷ ὁ δαίμων ἕκαστον κομίζει,
πρῶτον μὲν διεδικάσαντο οἵ τε καλῶς καὶ ὁσίως βιώσαντες
καὶ οἱ μή. καὶ οἳ μὲν ἂν δόξωσι μέσως βεβιωκέναι, πορευ-
5 θέντες ἐπὶ τὸν Ἀχέροντα, ἀναβάντες ἃ δὴ αὐτοῖς ὀχήματά
ἐστιν, ἐπὶ τούτων ἀφικνοῦνται εἰς τὴν λίμνην, καὶ ἐκεῖ
οἰκοῦσί τε καὶ καθαιρόμενοι τῶν τε ἀδικημάτων διδόντες
δίκας ἀπολύονται, εἴ τίς τι ἠδίκηκεν, τῶν τε εὐεργεσιῶν
e τιμὰς φέρονται κατὰ τὴν ἀξίαν ἕκαστος· οἳ δ' ἂν δόξωσιν
ἀνιάτως ἔχειν διὰ τὰ μεγέθη τῶν ἁμαρτημάτων, ἢ ἱερο-
συλίας πολλὰς καὶ μεγάλας ἢ φόνους ἀδίκους καὶ παρανόμους
πολλοὺς ἐξειργασμένοι ἢ ἄλλα ὅσα τοιαῦτα τυγχάνει ὄντα,
5 τούτους δὲ ἡ προσήκουσα μοῖρα ῥίπτει εἰς τὸν Τάρταρον,
ὅθεν οὔποτε ἐκβαίνουσιν. οἳ δ' ἂν ἰάσιμα μὲν μεγάλα δὲ
δόξωσιν ἡμαρτηκέναι ἁμαρτήματα, οἷον πρὸς πατέρα ἢ μη-
114 τέρα ὑπ' ὀργῆς βίαιόν τι πράξαντες, καὶ μεταμέλον αὐτοῖς
τὸν ἄλλον βίον βιῶσιν, ἢ ἀνδροφόνοι τοιούτῳ τινὶ ἄλλῳ
τρόπῳ γένωνται, τούτους δὲ ἐμπεσεῖν μὲν εἰς τὸν Τάρταρον

b 6 ὅπῃ B T Stob.: ὅπου Eus.   b 7 αὖ B² T W Eus. Stob.: αὐτοῦ B
c 1 ἣν al. Theodoretus: om. B T W Eus. Stob.   c 4 ἐναντίως Stob.
c 7 ἐναντίως W Stob.   e 2 ἢ B² T W Eus. Stob.: om. B
e 4 τυγχάνει τοιαῦτα W   a 3 τούτους B Stob.: τούτοις T Eus.

ἀνάγκη, ἐμπεσόντας δὲ αὐτοὺς καὶ ἐνιαυτὸν ἐκεῖ γενομένους
ἐκβάλλει τὸ κῦμα, τοὺς μὲν ἀνδροφόνους κατὰ τὸν Κωκυτόν, 5
τοὺς δὲ πατραλοίας καὶ μητραλοίας κατὰ τὸν Πυριφλεγ-
έθοντα· ἐπειδὰν δὲ φερόμενοι γένωνται κατὰ τὴν λίμνην τὴν
Ἀχερουσιάδα, ἐνταῦθα βοῶσί τε καὶ καλοῦσιν, οἱ μὲν οὓς
ἀπέκτειναν, οἱ δὲ οὓς ὕβρισαν, καλέσαντες δ' ἱκετεύουσι
καὶ δέονται ἐᾶσαι σφᾶς ἐκβῆναι εἰς τὴν λίμνην καὶ δέξασθαι, b
καὶ ἐὰν μὲν πείσωσιν, ἐκβαίνουσί τε καὶ λήγουσι τῶν
κακῶν, εἰ δὲ μή, φέρονται αὖθις εἰς τὸν Τάρταρον καὶ
ἐκεῖθεν πάλιν εἰς τοὺς ποταμούς, καὶ ταῦτα πάσχοντες οὐ
πρότερον παύονται πρὶν ἂν πείσωσιν οὓς ἠδίκησαν· αὕτη γὰρ 5
ἡ δίκη ὑπὸ τῶν δικαστῶν αὐτοῖς ἐτάχθη. οἱ δὲ δὴ ἂν δόξωσι
διαφερόντως πρὸς τὸ ὁσίως βιῶναι, οὗτοί εἰσιν οἱ τῶνδε μὲν
τῶν τόπων τῶν ἐν τῇ γῇ ἐλευθερούμενοί τε καὶ ἀπαλλαττόμενοι ὥσπερ δεσμωτηρίων, ἄνω δὲ εἰς τὴν καθαρὰν οἴκησιν c
ἀφικνούμενοι καὶ ἐπὶ γῆς οἰκιζόμενοι. τούτων δὲ αὐτῶν οἱ
φιλοσοφίᾳ ἱκανῶς καθηράμενοι ἄνευ τε σωμάτων ζῶσι τὸ
παράπαν εἰς τὸν ἔπειτα χρόνον, καὶ εἰς οἰκήσεις ἔτι τούτων
καλλίους ἀφικνοῦνται, ἃς οὔτε ῥᾴδιον δηλῶσαι οὔτε ὁ χρόνος 5
ἱκανὸς ἐν τῷ παρόντι. ἀλλὰ τούτων δὴ ἕνεκα χρὴ ὧν διεληλύθαμεν, ὦ Σιμμία, πᾶν ποιεῖν ὥστε ἀρετῆς καὶ φρονήσεως ἐν
τῷ βίῳ μετασχεῖν· καλὸν γὰρ τὸ ἆθλον καὶ ἡ ἐλπὶς μεγάλη.

Τὸ μὲν οὖν ταῦτα διισχυρίσασθαι οὕτως ἔχειν ὡς ἐγὼ d
διελήλυθα, οὐ πρέπει νοῦν ἔχοντι ἀνδρί· ὅτι μέντοι ἢ ταῦτ'
ἐστὶν ἢ τοιαῦτ' ἄττα περὶ τὰς ψυχὰς ἡμῶν καὶ τὰς οἰκήσεις,
ἐπείπερ ἀθάνατόν γε ἡ ψυχὴ φαίνεται οὖσα, τοῦτο καὶ
πρέπειν μοι δοκεῖ καὶ ἄξιον κινδυνεῦσαι οἰομένῳ οὕτως 5
ἔχειν—καλὸς γὰρ ὁ κίνδυνος—καὶ χρὴ τὰ τοιαῦτα ὥσπερ
ἐπᾴδειν ἑαυτῷ, διὸ δὴ ἔγωγε καὶ πάλαι μηκύνω τὸν μῦθον.

a 5 κῦμα B T Eus. : ῥεῦμα Stob.   b 2 ἐκβαίνουσι B² W Eus. :
ἀποβαίνουσι B T Stob.   b 5 ἠδικήκασιν W   b 7 βιῶναι B T W
Eus. Stob. : βιῶναι προσκεκλῆσθαι Clem. : βιῶναι προκεκρίσθαι Theodoretus   c 2 ἀφικόμενοι W   ἐπὶ τῆς γῆς Euseb. Stob.   οἰκ . . .
ζόμενοι T   c 3 σωμάτων] καμάτων Eus.   c 4 καλλίους τούτων W
d 1 ταῦτα B² T W Stob.: τοιαῦτα B   διισχυρίζεσθαι W   d 5 μοι
B Stob. : ἐμοὶ T

ἀλλὰ τούτων δὴ ἕνεκα θαρρεῖν χρὴ περὶ τῇ ἑαυτοῦ ψυχῇ
e ἄνδρα ὅστις ἐν τῷ βίῳ τὰς μὲν ἄλλας ἡδονὰς τὰς περὶ τὸ
σῶμα καὶ τοὺς κόσμους εἴασε χαίρειν, ὡς ἀλλοτρίους τε
ὄντας, καὶ πλέον θάτερον ἡγησάμενος ἀπεργάζεσθαι, τὰς δὲ
περὶ τὸ μανθάνειν ἐσπούδασέ τε καὶ κοσμήσας τὴν ψυχὴν
5 οὐκ ἀλλοτρίῳ ἀλλὰ τῷ αὐτῆς κόσμῳ, σωφροσύνῃ τε καὶ
115 δικαιοσύνῃ καὶ ἀνδρείᾳ καὶ ἐλευθερίᾳ καὶ ἀληθείᾳ, οὕτω
περιμένει τὴν εἰς Ἅιδου πορείαν [ὡς πορευσόμενος ὅταν ἡ
εἱμαρμένη καλῇ]. ὑμεῖς μὲν οὖν, ἔφη, ὦ Σιμμία τε καὶ
Κέβης καὶ οἱ ἄλλοι, εἰς αὖθις ἔν τινι χρόνῳ ἕκαστοι πορεύ-
5 σεσθε· ἐμὲ δὲ νῦν ἤδη καλεῖ, φαίη ἂν ἀνὴρ τραγικός, ἡ
εἱμαρμένη, καὶ σχεδόν τί μοι ὥρα τραπέσθαι πρὸς τὸ λουτρόν·
δοκεῖ γὰρ δὴ βέλτιον εἶναι λουσάμενον πιεῖν τὸ φάρμακον
καὶ μὴ πράγματα ταῖς γυναιξὶ παρέχειν νεκρὸν λούειν.

b Ταῦτα δὴ εἰπόντος αὐτοῦ ὁ Κρίτων, Εἶεν, ἔφη, ὦ
Σώκρατες· τί δὲ τούτοις ἢ ἐμοὶ ἐπιστέλλεις ἢ περὶ τῶν
παίδων ἢ περὶ ἄλλου του, ὅτι ἄν σοι ποιοῦντες ἡμεῖς ἐν
χάριτι μάλιστα ποιοῖμεν;
5 Ἅπερ ἀεὶ λέγω, ἔφη, ὦ Κρίτων, οὐδὲν καινότερον· ὅτι
ὑμῶν αὐτῶν ἐπιμελούμενοι ὑμεῖς καὶ ἐμοὶ καὶ τοῖς ἐμοῖς
καὶ ὑμῖν αὐτοῖς ἐν χάριτι ποιήσετε ἅττ' ἂν ποιῆτε, κἂν μὴ
νῦν ὁμολογήσητε· ἐὰν δὲ ὑμῶν [μὲν] αὐτῶν ἀμελῆτε καὶ
μὴ 'θέλητε ὥσπερ κατ' ἴχνη κατὰ τὰ νῦν τε εἰρημένα
10 καὶ τὰ ἐν τῷ ἔμπροσθεν χρόνῳ ζῆν, οὐδὲ ἐὰν πολλὰ ὁμολο-
c γήσητε ἐν τῷ παρόντι καὶ σφόδρα, οὐδὲν πλέον ποιήσετε.

Ταῦτα μὲν τοίνυν προθυμησόμεθα, ἔφη, οὕτω ποιεῖν·
θάπτωμεν δέ σε τίνα τρόπον;

Ὅπως ἄν, ἔφη, βούλησθε, ἐάνπερ γε λάβητέ με καὶ
5 μὴ ἐκφύγω ὑμᾶς. Γελάσας δὲ ἅμα ἡσυχῇ καὶ πρὸς ἡμᾶς
ἀποβλέψας εἶπεν· Οὐ πείθω, ὦ ἄνδρες, Κρίτωνα, ὡς

d 8 τῆς αὐτοῦ ψυχῆς W   e 2 τε om. W   a 7 δὴ Β Τ :
ἤδη Β² W   b 2 ἐπιστέλλεις Coisl. : ἐπιτέλλεις Τ : ἐπιτέλλει Β :
ἐπιτέλλῃ Β² W   b 4 ποιῶμεν Β² W   b 5 ἔφη λέγω W
b 6 καὶ τοῖς ἐμοῖς om. Τ   b 8 μὲν Β : om. Τ W   c 2 προθυμησόμεθα Τ W : προθυμηθησόμεθα Β   c 3 θάπτωμεν Β : θάπτομεν Τ W
σε τίνα Β : τίνα σε Τ   c 4 με Β : om. Τ   c 6 ὦ Τ : ἔφη ὦ
Β² W : om. Β

ἐγώ εἰμι οὗτος Σωκράτης, ὁ νυνὶ διαλεγόμενος καὶ δια-
τάττων ἕκαστον τῶν λεγομένων, ἀλλ᾽ οἴεταί με ἐκεῖνον εἶναι
ὃν ὄψεται ὀλίγον ὕστερον νεκρόν, καὶ ἐρωτᾷ δὴ πῶς με d
θάπτῃ. ὅτι δὲ ἐγὼ πάλαι πολὺν λόγον πεποίημαι, ὡς,
ἐπειδὰν πίω τὸ φάρμακον, οὐκέτι ὑμῖν παραμενῶ, ἀλλ᾽
οἰχήσομαι ἀπιὼν εἰς μακάρων δή τινας εὐδαιμονίας, ταῦτά
μοι δοκῶ αὐτῷ ἄλλως λέγειν, παραμυθούμενος ἅμα μὲν 5
ὑμᾶς, ἅμα δ᾽ ἐμαυτόν. ἐγγυήσασθε οὖν με πρὸς Κρίτωνα,
ἔφη, τὴν ἐναντίαν ἐγγύην ἢ ἣν οὗτος πρὸς τοὺς δικαστὰς
ἠγγυᾶτο. οὗτος μὲν γὰρ ἦ μὴν παραμενεῖν· ὑμεῖς δὲ ἦ μὴν
μὴ παραμενεῖν ἐγγυήσασθε ἐπειδὰν ἀποθάνω, ἀλλὰ οἰχή-
σεσθαι ἀπιόντα, ἵνα Κρίτων ῥᾷον φέρῃ, καὶ μὴ ὁρῶν μου τὸ e
σῶμα ἢ καόμενον ἢ κατορυττόμενον ἀγανακτῇ ὑπὲρ ἐμοῦ
ὡς δεινὰ πάσχοντος, μηδὲ λέγῃ ἐν τῇ ταφῇ ὡς ἢ προτίθεται
Σωκράτη ἢ ἐκφέρει ἢ κατορύττει. εὖ γὰρ ἴσθι, ἦ δ᾽ ὅς, ὦ
ἄριστε Κρίτων, τὸ μὴ καλῶς λέγειν οὐ μόνον εἰς αὐτὸ τοῦτο 5
πλημμελές, ἀλλὰ καὶ κακόν τι ἐμποιεῖ ταῖς ψυχαῖς. ἀλλὰ
θαρρεῖν τε χρὴ καὶ φάναι τοὐμὸν σῶμα θάπτειν, καὶ θάπτειν
οὕτως ὅπως ἄν σοι φίλον ᾖ καὶ μάλιστα ἡγῇ νόμιμον εἶναι. 116
Ταῦτ᾽ εἰπὼν ἐκεῖνος μὲν ἀνίστατο εἰς οἴκημά τι ὡς λουσό-
μενος, καὶ ὁ Κρίτων εἵπετο αὐτῷ, ἡμᾶς δ᾽ ἐκέλευε περιμένειν.
περιεμένομεν οὖν πρὸς ἡμᾶς αὐτοὺς διαλεγόμενοι περὶ τῶν
εἰρημένων καὶ ἀνασκοποῦντες, τοτὲ δ᾽ αὖ περὶ τῆς συμφορᾶς 5
διεξιόντες ὅση ἡμῖν γεγονυῖα εἴη, ἀτεχνῶς ἡγούμενοι ὥσπερ
πατρὸς στερηθέντες διάξειν ὀρφανοὶ τὸν ἔπειτα βίον. ἐπειδὴ
δὲ ἐλούσατο καὶ ἠνέχθη παρ᾽ αὐτὸν τὰ παιδία—δύο γὰρ αὐτῷ b
ὑεῖς σμικροὶ ἦσαν, εἷς δὲ μέγας—καὶ αἱ οἰκεῖαι γυναῖκες
ἀφίκοντο ἐκεῖναι, ἐναντίον τοῦ Κρίτωνος διαλεχθείς τε καὶ
ἐπιστείλας ἅττα ἐβούλετο, τὰς μὲν γυναῖκας καὶ τὰ παιδία

c 7 οὗτος B: οὗτος ὁ T W   d 2 θάπτῃ B: θάπτει T W: θάψει
fecit W (ψ s. v.)   d 8 ἠγγυᾶτο B T et γρ. W: ἠγγυήσατο B² W
d 9 οὖν post ἐγγυήσασθε add. t   e 1 ῥᾷον T: ῥάδιον B   e 3 δεινὰ
πάσχοντος B t: δεινὰ ἄττα σχόντος T   e 7 θάπτειν καὶ om. pr. T
b 3 ἐκεῖναι ἐναντίον T W: ἐναντίον ἐκεῖναι B (ἐκείναις fecit B⁴)

5 ἀπιέναι ἐκέλευσεν, αὐτὸς δὲ ἧκε παρ' ἡμᾶς. καὶ ἦν ἤδη
ἐγγὺς ἡλίου δυσμῶν· χρόνον γὰρ πολὺν διέτριψεν ἔνδον.
ἐλθὼν δ' ἐκαθέζετο λελουμένος καὶ οὐ πολλὰ ἄττα μετὰ
ταῦτα διελέχθη, καὶ ἧκεν ὁ τῶν ἕνδεκα ὑπηρέτης καὶ στὰς
c παρ' αὐτόν, Ὦ Σώκρατες, ἔφη, οὐ καταγνώσομαί γε σοῦ
ὅπερ ἄλλων καταγιγνώσκω, ὅτι μοι χαλεπαίνουσι καὶ κατα-
ρῶνται ἐπειδὰν αὐτοῖς παραγγείλω πίνειν τὸ φάρμακον
ἀναγκαζόντων τῶν ἀρχόντων. σὲ δὲ ἐγὼ καὶ ἄλλως
5 ἔγνωκα ἐν τούτῳ τῷ χρόνῳ γενναιότατον καὶ πρᾳότατον
καὶ ἄριστον ἄνδρα ὄντα τῶν πώποτε δεῦρο ἀφικομένων, καὶ
δὴ καὶ νῦν εὖ οἶδ' ὅτι οὐκ ἐμοὶ χαλεπαίνεις, γιγνώσκεις γὰρ
τοὺς αἰτίους, ἀλλὰ ἐκείνοις. νῦν οὖν, οἶσθα γὰρ ἃ ἦλθον
d ἀγγέλλων, χαῖρέ τε καὶ πειρῶ ὡς ῥᾷστα φέρειν τὰ ἀναγκαῖα.
Καὶ ἅμα δακρύσας μεταστρεφόμενος ἀπῄει.
Καὶ ὁ Σωκράτης ἀναβλέψας πρὸς αὐτόν, Καὶ σύ, ἔφη,
χαῖρε, καὶ ἡμεῖς ταῦτα ποιήσομεν. Καὶ ἅμα πρὸς ἡμᾶς,
5 Ὡς ἀστεῖος, ἔφη, ὁ ἄνθρωπος· καὶ παρὰ πάντα μοι τὸν
χρόνον προσῄει καὶ διελέγετο ἐνίοτε καὶ ἦν ἀνδρῶν λῷστος,
καὶ νῦν ὡς γενναίως με ἀποδακρύει. ἀλλ' ἄγε δή, ὦ
Κρίτων, πειθώμεθα αὐτῷ, καὶ ἐνεγκάτω τις τὸ φάρμακον, εἰ
τέτριπται· εἰ δὲ μή, τριψάτω ὁ ἄνθρωπος.
e Καὶ ὁ Κρίτων, Ἀλλ' οἶμαι, ἔφη, ἔγωγε, ὦ Σώκρατες, ἔτι
ἥλιον εἶναι ἐπὶ τοῖς ὄρεσιν καὶ οὔπω δεδυκέναι. καὶ ἅμα
ἐγὼ οἶδα καὶ ἄλλους πάνυ ὀψὲ πίνοντας, ἐπειδὰν παραγγελθῇ
αὐτοῖς, δειπνήσαντάς τε καὶ πιόντας εὖ μάλα, καὶ συγγενο-
5 μένους γ' ἐνίους ὧν ἂν τύχωσιν ἐπιθυμοῦντες. ἀλλὰ μηδὲν
ἐπείγου· ἔτι γὰρ ἐγχωρεῖ.
Καὶ ὁ Σωκράτης, Εἰκότως γε, ἔφη, ὦ Κρίτων, ἐκεῖνοί τε
ταῦτα ποιοῦσιν, οὓς σὺ λέγεις—οἴονται γὰρ κερδαίνειν ταῦτα
ποιήσαντες—καὶ ἔγωγε ταῦτα εἰκότως οὐ ποιήσω· οὐδὲν γὰρ

b 7 ἄττα B² T W : om. B   c 1 γε T W : om. B   c 3 παραγγείλω Τ : παραγγέλλω B   c 8 οὖν Τ: om. B   ὰ 🔧 : om. T
d 1 ῥᾷστα B² T W : ἄριστα B   e 5 ἂν T W : om. Ḃ   ⊖ ⊛ εἰκότως
ταῦτα Τ

οἶμαι κερδανεῖν ὀλίγον ὕστερον πιὼν ἄλλο γε ἢ γέλωτα 117
ὀφλήσειν παρ' ἐμαυτῷ, γλιχόμενος τοῦ ζῆν καὶ φειδόμενος οὐδενὸς ἔτι ἐνόντος. ἀλλ' ἴθι, ἔφη, πείθου καὶ μὴ ἄλλως ποίει.
Καὶ ὁ Κρίτων ἀκούσας ἔνευσε τῷ παιδὶ πλησίον ἑστῶτι.
καὶ ὁ παῖς ἐξελθὼν καὶ συχνὸν χρόνον διατρίψας ἧκεν ἄγων 5
τὸν μέλλοντα δώσειν τὸ φάρμακον, ἐν κύλικι φέροντα τετριμ-
μένον. ἰδὼν δὲ ὁ Σωκράτης τὸν ἄνθρωπον, Εἶεν, ἔφη, ὦ
βέλτιστε, σὺ γὰρ τούτων ἐπιστήμων, τί χρὴ ποιεῖν;
Οὐδὲν ἄλλο, ἔφη, ἢ πιόντα περιιέναι, ἕως ἄν σου βάρος
ἐν τοῖς σκέλεσι γένηται, ἔπειτα κατακεῖσθαι· καὶ οὕτως αὐτὸ b
ποιήσει. Καὶ ἅμα ὤρεξε τὴν κύλικα τῷ Σωκράτει.
Καὶ ὃς λαβὼν καὶ μάλα ἵλεως, ὦ Ἐχέκρατες, οὐδὲν
τρέσας οὐδὲ διαφθείρας οὔτε τοῦ χρώματος οὔτε τοῦ προσ-
ώπου, ἀλλ' ὥσπερ εἰώθει ταυρηδὸν ὑποβλέψας πρὸς τὸν 5
ἄνθρωπον, Τί λέγεις, ἔφη, περὶ τοῦδε τοῦ πώματος πρὸς τὸ
ἀποσπεῖσαί τινι; ἔξεστιν ἢ οὔ;
Τοσοῦτον, ἔφη, ὦ Σώκρατες, τρίβομεν ὅσον οἰόμεθα
μέτριον εἶναι πιεῖν.
Μανθάνω, ἦ δ' ὅς· ἀλλ' εὔχεσθαί γέ που τοῖς θεοῖς ἔξεστί c
τε καὶ χρή, τὴν μετοίκησιν τὴν ἐνθένδε ἐκεῖσε εὐτυχῆ γενέ-
σθαι· ἃ δὴ καὶ ἐγὼ εὔχομαί τε καὶ γένοιτο ταύτῃ. Καὶ ἅμ'
εἰπὼν ταῦτα ἐπισχόμενος καὶ μάλα εὐχερῶς καὶ εὐκόλως
ἐξέπιεν. καὶ ἡμῶν οἱ πολλοὶ τέως μὲν ἐπιεικῶς οἷοί τε 5
ἦσαν κατέχειν τὸ μὴ δακρύειν, ὡς δὲ εἴδομεν πίνοντά τε καὶ
πεπωκότα, οὐκέτι, ἀλλ' ἐμοῦ γε βίᾳ καὶ αὐτοῦ ἀστακτὶ ἐχώρει
τὰ δάκρυα, ὥστε ἐγκαλυψάμενος ἀπέκλαον ἐμαυτόν—οὐ
γὰρ δὴ ἐκεῖνόν γε, ἀλλὰ τὴν ἐμαυτοῦ τύχην, οἵου ἀνδρὸς
ἑταίρου ἐστερημένος εἴην. ὁ δὲ Κρίτων ἔτι πρότερος ἐμοῦ, d
ἐπειδὴ οὐχ οἷός τ' ἦν κατέχειν τὰ δάκρυα, ἐξανέστη.
Ἀπολλόδωρος δὲ καὶ ἐν τῷ ἔμπροσθεν χρόνῳ οὐδὲν ἐπαύετο
δακρύων, καὶ δὴ καὶ τότε ἀναβρυχησάμενος κλάων καὶ

a 1 κερδανεῖν Β² : κερδαίνειν Β Τ   πιὼν Β² t : ποιῶν Β Τ : ἀπιὼν W
a 3 πείθου Τ W : πιθοῦ Β   a 6 δώσειν Β² Τ W : διδόναι Β   a 8 τί
Β Τ : εἰπὲ τί W   b 4 post διαφθείρας add. οὔτε τοῦ σώματος W
c 3 ἅμα λέγων W   c 7 γε βίᾳ καὶ αὐτοῦ Β : αὐτοῦ βίᾳ καὶ Τ : τε καὶ
αὐτοῦ βίᾳ W   ἀστακτ(ε ὶ Β Τ : ἀσταλακτὶ W : γρ. καὶ ἀβαστακι)
καὶ βίᾳ W   d 1 πρότερον pr. W   ἐμοῦ Β : μου Τ

5 ἀγανακτῶν οὐδένα ὅντινα οὐ κατέκλασε τῶν παρόντων πλήν
γε αὑτοῦ Σωκράτους.

Ἐκεῖνος δέ, Οἷα, ἔφη, ποιεῖτε, ὦ θαυμάσιοι. ἐγὼ μέντοι
οὐχ ἥκιστα τούτου ἕνεκα τὰς γυναῖκας ἀπέπεμψα, ἵνα μὴ
e τοιαῦτα πλημμελοῖεν· καὶ γὰρ ἀκήκοα ὅτι ἐν εὐφημίᾳ χρὴ
τελευτᾶν. ἀλλ' ἡσυχίαν τε ἄγετε καὶ καρτερεῖτε.
Καὶ ἡμεῖς ἀκούσαντες ᾐσχύνθημέν τε καὶ ἐπέσχομεν τοῦ
δακρύειν. ὁ δὲ περιελθών, ἐπειδή οἱ βαρύνεσθαι ἔφη τὰ
5 σκέλη, κατεκλίνη ὕπτιος—οὕτω γὰρ ἐκέλευεν ὁ ἄνθρωπος—
καὶ ἅμα ἐφαπτόμενος αὐτοῦ οὗτος ὁ δοὺς τὸ φάρμακον,
διαλιπὼν χρόνον ἐπεσκόπει τοὺς πόδας καὶ τὰ σκέλη,
κἄπειτα σφόδρα πιέσας αὐτοῦ τὸν πόδα ἤρετο εἰ αἰσθάνοιτο,
118 ὁ δ' οὐκ ἔφη. καὶ μετὰ τοῦτο αὖθις τὰς κνήμας· καὶ ἐπανιὼν
οὕτως ἡμῖν ἐπεδείκνυτο ὅτι ψύχοιτό τε καὶ πήγνυτο. καὶ
αὐτὸς ἥπτετο καὶ εἶπεν ὅτι, ἐπειδὰν πρὸς τῇ καρδίᾳ γένηται
αὐτῷ, τότε οἰχήσεται.
5 Ἤδη οὖν σχεδόν τι αὐτοῦ ἦν τὰ περὶ τὸ ἦτρον ψυχόμενα,
καὶ ἐκκαλυψάμενος—ἐνεκεκάλυπτο γάρ—εἶπεν—ὃ δὴ τελευταῖον ἐφθέγξατο—Ὦ Κρίτων, ἔφη, τῷ Ἀσκληπιῷ ὀφείλομεν
ἀλεκτρυόνα· ἀλλὰ ἀπόδοτε καὶ μὴ ἀμελήσητε.
Ἀλλὰ ταῦτα, ἔφη, ἔσται, ὁ Κρίτων· ἀλλ' ὅρα εἴ τι ἄλλο
10 λέγεις.
Ταῦτα ἐρομένου αὐτοῦ οὐδὲν ἔτι ἀπεκρίνατο, ἀλλ' ὀλίγον
χρόνον διαλιπὼν ἐκινήθη τε καὶ ὁ ἄνθρωπος ἐξεκάλυψεν
αὐτόν, καὶ ὃς τὰ ὄμματα ἔστησεν· ἰδὼν δὲ ὁ Κρίτων συνέλαβε
τὸ στόμα καὶ τοὺς ὀφθαλμούς.
15 Ἥδε ἡ τελευτή, ὦ Ἐχέκρατες, τοῦ ἑταίρου ἡμῖν ἐγένετο,
ἀνδρός, ὡς ἡμεῖς φαῖμεν ἄν, τῶν τότε ὧν ἐπειράθημεν ἀρίστου
καὶ ἄλλως φρονιμωτάτου καὶ δικαιοτάτου.

d 5 κατέκλασε Τ : κατέκλαυσε Β   e 3 τε Β Τ : γε W   ἐπ-
έχομεν pr. Τ   e 5 κατεκλίθη Β Τ W   a 2 οὕτως ἡμῖν Β :
ἡμῖν οὕτως ἡμῖν Τ : οὕτως ἡμῖν αὐτοῖς Β² W   πήγνυτο Β Τ W
a 8 διαμελήσητε W   a 9 ταῦτα ἔσται ἔφη Τ   a 14 καὶ Β : τε
καὶ Τ

NOTES

Introductory dialogue in dramatic form, 57 a 1—59 c 7.

The scene is the Pythagorean συνέδριον at Phlius. The only Pythagorean who speaks is Echecrates, but the presence of the others is implied (cp. especially 58 d 7 and 102 a 8). The time is not long after the death of Socrates; for the Pythagoreans have not yet heard any details. As Geddes first pointed out, it would be natural for Phaedo to visit the Pythagoreans of Phlius on his way home from Athens to Elis. It is not far off the road.

For the Pythagoreans of Phlius, cp. Diog. Laert. viii. 46 τελευταῖοι γὰρ ἐγένοντο τῶν Πυθαγορείων, οὓς καὶ Ἀριστόξενος εἶδε, Ξενόφιλός τε ὁ Χαλκιδεὺς ἀπὸ Θρᾴκης καὶ Φάντων ὁ Φλιάσιος καὶ Ἐχεκράτης καὶ Διοκλῆς καὶ Πολύμναστος, Φλιάσιοι καὶ αὐτοί. ἦσαν δ᾽ ἀκροαταὶ Φιλολάου καὶ Εὐρύτου τῶν Ταραντίνων (cp. E. Gr. Ph.² p. 320).

Phlius lay in the upper valley of the Asopus (893 ft. above sea-level), where Argolis, Arcadia, and the territory of Sicyon meet. It was surrounded by mountains 4,000 to 5,000 feet high, ' under whose immemorial shadow' (δασκίοις Φλειοῦντος ἐν ὠγυγίοις ὄρεσιν, Pind. *Nem*. vi. 45) 'the high discourse is supposed to be held' (Geddes). The territory of Phlius, which was only a few miles square, con-sisted of a triangular valley with its apex to the north. The town was on the eastern side of the valley and built in the form of an amphitheatre. A few ruins are still left. The people were Dorians and faithful allies of Sparta.

Tradition connected Pythagoras himself with the place (E. Gr. Ph.² p. 94, *n.* 1), and he is said to have assumed the name of φιλόσοφος for the first time there or in the neighbouring Sicyon (E. Gr. Ph.² p. 321, *n.* 2).

Phaedo of Elis is said (Diog. Laert. ii. 105) to have been a prisoner of war brought as a slave to Athens, where he attracted the notice of Socrates, who secured his liberation. At the time of this dialogue he is quite a youth and still wears his hair long (89 b 5). At a later date he founded the school of Elis. We know nothing of his teaching; but, as the school of Eretria was an offshoot from that of Elis, and as both are commonly mentioned along with that of Megara, it is probable that he busied himself chiefly with the difficulties which beset early Logic. For us, as Wilamowitz says, he chiefly represents the conquest of the most unlikely parts of the Peloponnese by Athenian culture, which is the distinguishing feature of the fourth century B.C.

57 a 1 Αὐτὸς κτλ. We seem to be breaking in on a conversation already begun; for ἤκουσας has no expressed object. Perhaps Phaedo has already spoken of something Socrates said or did on the day of his death.

παρεγένου: the verbs παρεῖναι and παραγίγνεσθαι are specially used of *being at hand* to support any one in times of trouble or rejoicing. So in Lat. *adesse alicui*. We should say, 'Were you *with* Socrates?' Cp. also παρακαλεῖν, *advocare*.

a 2 τὸ φάρμακον, SC. τὸ κώνειον. It is nowhere expressly stated in the *Phaedo* that it was hemlock; but that was the drug commonly employed, and the symptoms described at the end of the dialogue (117 e sqq.) correspond to those elsewhere ascribed to it. It has been doubted whether hemlock-juice would really produce these symptoms, but see Appendix I.

a 5 Τί ... ἐστιν ἄττα: this is the regular construction (cp. 58 c 6), though in 102 a 9 we have τίνα ... ἦν ... τὰ ... λεχθέντα.

ὁ ἀνήρ is an emphatic αὐτός or ἐκεῖνος. Cp. 85 c 8; 61 c 3, and note on 58 e 3 ἀνήρ.

a 7 [τῶν πολιτῶν] Φλειασίων: Riddell (Dig. § 36) defends this by making Φλειασίων depend on οὐδεὶς τῶν πολιτῶν, 'for neither of the Phliasians does any citizen,' which seems unnatural. Most editors bracket Φλειασίων, but I think v. Bamberg is right in suspecting rather τῶν πολιτῶν. In Stephanus of Byzantium and elsewhere we regularly find notices like Οἷος· οἱ πολῖται, Οἰαῖοι· καὶ τὸ ἐθνικὸν ὁμοίως, and we can understand how, in the absence of capital letters, such an explanation might seem desirable. Further, the form Φλειάσιοι is exceptional (cp. however Ἀναγυράσιοι), and Cicero tells us (*ad Att.* vi. 2) that he himself wrote *Phliuntii* by mistake. A similar case

2

is possibly *Meno* 70 b 2 οἱ τοῦ σοῦ ἑταίρου [πολῖται] Λαρισαῖοι. The absence of the article with the ἐθνικόν is normal, and the form Φλειάσιοι (Φλιάσιοι MSS.) is guaranteed by inscriptions and coins.

a 7 οὐδεὶς πάνυ τι, 'no one to speak of.' The phrase does not necessarily mean 'no one at all', though it tends to acquire that sense. Cp. οὐ πάνυ (Riddell, Dig. § 139) and the English 'not very'. It is unnecessary to discuss, as most editors do, why communications between Athens and Phlius were interrupted. There is no statement that they were, and it must often have happened that no Phliasian had business in Athens and no Athenian at Phlius. There was, however, at least one such (58 a 3).

ἐπιχωριάζει . . . 'Αθήναζε: there seems to be no other instance of ἐπιχωριάζειν in this sense. It usually means 'to be native', and is used of local dialects, customs, &c. Here apparently it is equivalent to ἐπιδημεῖν and takes the construction of that verb. Cp. *Parm.* 126 b 3 ἐπεδήμησα δεῦρο ἐκ Κλαζομενῶν.

b 1 σαφές τι: in such expressions σαφής means 'sure', 'trustworthy' (not 'clear'). So σαφὴς φίλος, σαφὴς μάντις.

b 3 εἶχεν, sc. ὁ ἀγγείλας. He has not been mentioned, but he has been implied.

a 1 τὰ περὶ τῆς δίκης: the normal construction would be τὰ περὶ τὴν δίκην (cp. 58 c 6 τὰ περὶ αὐτὸν τὸν θάνατον), but the prepositional phrase is influenced by ἐπύθεσθε. Heindorf compares Xen. *Cyr.* v. 3. 26 ἐπεὶ πύθοιτο τὰ περὶ τοῦ φρουρίου, *Anab.* ii. 5. 37 ὅπως μάθοι τὰ περὶ Προξένου.

a 4 πολλῷ ὕστερον: Xen. *Mem.* iv. 8. 2 ἀνάγκη μὲν γὰρ ἐγένετο αὐτῷ μετὰ τὴν κρίσιν τριάκοντα ἡμέρας βιῶναι.

a 6 Τύχη has always the implication of *coincidence*, which is here made explicit by the cognate verb ἔτυχεν. In most of its uses, the meaning of τυγχάνειν is best brought out in English by using the adverb 'just'.

ἔτυχεν . . . ἐστεμμένη, 'had just been crowned.' The Ionic στέφειν is only used in a ritual sense in Attic prose. So, with mock solemnity, in *Rep.* 398 a 7 ἐρίῳ στέψαντες. The common word is στεφανοῦν.

a 8 πέμπουσιν. In the Bodleian (Clarke) MS. (B) Bishop Arethas, for whom the MS. was written, has added κατ' ἔτος in his own hand (B²). These words are also found in the Vienna MS. (W). The corrections of B² were taken throughout from a MS. very closely resembling W. The additional words may well be an ancient variant.

a 10 τὸ πλοῖον: i.e. the θεωρίς. For the Delian θεωρία, cp. Aristotle, Ἀθ. πολ. 56 καθίστησι δὲ καὶ (ὁ ἄρχων) εἰς Δῆλον χορηγοὺς καὶ ἀρχιθέωρον τῷ τριακοντορίῳ τῷ τοὺς ἠθέους ἄγοντι. The seven youths and seven maids were technically called the ἤθεοι (masc. and comm. of παρθένοι). The story is told in Bacchylides xvi (xvii), a dithyramb entitled Ἠἴθεοι. Cp. also Plut. *Thes.* 23 τὸ δὲ πλοῖον ἐν ᾧ μετὰ τῶν ἠἴθέων ἔπλευσε καὶ πάλιν ἐσώθη, τὴν τριακόντορον, ἄχρι τοῦ Δημητρίου τοῦ Φαληρέως χρόνου διεφύλαττον οἱ Ἀθηναῖοι. Of course none of the original timbers were left, and Plutarch tells us the philosophers took it as their stock example in discussing the question of identity. Was it the same ship or not?

a 11 τοὺς "δὶς ἑπτὰ" ἐκείνους: this was also a traditional name. Cp. Bacchyl. xvi. (xvii.) 1 Κυανόπρῳρα μὲν ναῦς μενέκτυπον | Θησέα δὶς ἑπτά τ' ἀγλαοὺς ἄγουσα | κούρους Ἰαόνων | Κρητικὸν τάμνε πέλαγος. In the *Laws* (706 b 7) Plato says it would have been better for the Athenians to lose πλεονάκις ἑπτὰ ... παῖδας than to become ναυτικοί.

b 2 θεωρίαν, 'pilgrimage', 'mission'. A θεωρός is simply a 'spectator' (θεαϝόρος, Dor. θεᾱρός), but the word was specialized in the meaning of an envoy sent by the State to the Great Games, to Delphi or to Delos. The θεωρίαι were λῃτουργίαι (cp. Dict. Ant., s. v. *Theoria*).

b 3 ἀπάξειν: the ἀπο- has the same force as in ἀποδιδόναι and ἀποφέρειν, that of rendering what is *due*. Cp. the technical ἀπάγειν τὸν φόρον, φόρου ἀπαγωγή, and Ditt. Syll. p. 43 τὴν ἀπαρχὴν ἀπήγαγον.

b 5 καθαρεύειν, sc. φόνου, 'to be clean from bloodshed.' Cp. Plut. *Phocion* 37 καθαρεῦσαι δημοσίου φόνου τὴν πόλιν ἑορτάζουσαν. So Xen. *Mem.* iv. 8. 2 διὰ τὸ Δήλια μὲν ἐκείνου τοῦ μηνὸς εἶναι, τὸν δὲ νόμον μηδένα ἐᾶν δημοσίᾳ ἀποθνῄσκειν ἕως ἂν ἡ θεωρία ἐκ Δήλου ἐπανέλθῃ.

b 7 δεῦρο, 'to Athens.' It is true that Phaedo is speaking at Phlius, but he is quoting the Athenian νόμος.

b 8 ἐν πολλῷ χρόνῳ γίγνεται, 'takes a long time.' This meaning of ἐν, which is not clearly explained in most grammars, is well brought out by an anecdote Plutarch tells of Zeuxis (Περὶ πολυφιλίας 94 f): ὁ Ζεῦξις αἰτιωμένων αὐτόν τινων ὅτι ζωγραφεῖ βραδέως, Ὁμολογῶ, εἶπεν, ἐν πολλῷ χρόνῳ γράφειν, καὶ γὰρ εἰς πολύν.

b 8 ὅταν τύχωσιν ... ἀπολαβόντες, 'at times when the winds detain them' (synchronous aor. pcp.). The regular term for 'cut off', 'intercept', is ἀπολαμβάνειν, especially of ships 'detained' by contrary winds. Cp. Hdt. ii. 115 ὑπ' ἀνέμων ἤδη ἀπολαμφθέντες, Thuc. vi. 22 ἤν που ὑπὸ ἀπλοίας ἀπολαμβανώμεθα, Dem. *Chers.* 35 νόσῳ καὶ χειμῶνι καὶ πολέμοις ἀποληφθέντος, Plato, *Menex.* 243 c 2 ἀπειλημμένων ἐν Μυτιλήνῃ τῶν νεῶν.

c 1 αὐτούς: the Greek thinks of the crew rather than the ship. In Thucydides and elsewhere a plural pronoun often stands for πόλις, ναῦς, and the like.

c 3 ἔτυχεν ... γεγονός, 'had just been done.' Cp. a 6 *n.*

c 6 τὰ περὶ αὐτὸν τὸν θάνατον : cp. a 1 *n.*

τί ἦν : cp. 57 a 5 *n.* W has τίνα here also, and B² corrects accordingly.

c 7 οἱ παραγενόμενοι: cp. 57 a 1 *n.* So παρεῖναι just below.

c 8 οὐκ εἴων, 'would they not allow?' 'Did they not allow?' is οὐκ εἴασαν. The difference between a negatived imperfect and a negatived aorist may generally be brought out in some such way as this.

οἱ ἄρχοντες, οἱ ἔνδεκα, as we shall see.

d 1 καὶ πολλοί γε, 'quite a number in fact.' There is something to be said, however, for the division indicated in some MSS., ΦΑΙ. Οὐδαμῶς. ΕΧ. Ἀλλὰ παρῆσάν τινες ; ΦΑΙ. Καὶ πολλοί γε. Cp. *Euthyphro* 2 b ΣΩ. Οὐ γὰρ οὖν. ΕΥΘ. Ἀλλὰ σὲ ἄλλος ; ΣΩ. Πάνυ γε.

d 3 εἰ μή ... τυγχάνει οὖσα, 'unless you are engaged *just now*.'

d 5 τὸ μεμνῆσθαι Σωκράτους: cp. Xen. *Mem.* iv. 1. 1 ἐπεὶ καὶ τὸ ἐκείνου μεμνῆσθαι μὴ παρόντος οὐ μικρὰ ὠφέλει (a characteristic Xenophontean touch) τοὺς εἰωθότας τε αὐτῷ συνεῖναι καὶ ἀποδεχομένους ἐκεῖνον.

d 8 τοιούτους ἑτέρους, 'just such others' (pred.), cp. 80 d 5, 'Well, you will find your hearers of the same mind.' The enthusiasm of the Pythagoreans for Socrates can hardly be an invention of Plato's.

ὡς ... ἀκριβέστατα, 'as minutely as you can.'

e 1 παραγενόμενος (synchronous aor. pcp.), cp. 57 a 1 *n.* and παρόντα just below.

e 2 οὔτε : the second οὔτε does not occur till 59 a 3 after this sentence has been resumed by διὰ δὴ ταῦτα κτλ.

με ... εἰσῄει : we can say δέος, ἔλεος, ἐλπὶς εἰσέρχεταί με, as here, or εἰσέρχεταί μοι, as at 59 a 1.

e 3 ἀνήρ : cp. 57 a 5 *n.* The MSS. have nowhere preserved this form.

but write either ἀνήρ or ὁ ἀνήρ, though we see from examples in the oblique cases (e. g. 58 c 8 ; 61 c 3) that the article is required. The existence of the *crasis* is proved by the metre in Aristophanes.

e 3 καὶ τοῦ τρόπου καὶ τῶν λόγων, 'both in his bearing and his words' (Church). Here εὐδαίμων ἐφαίνετο takes the construction of εὐδαιμονίζειν, for which see *Crito* 43 b 6 quoted in the next note. (The reading τῶν λόγων (TW) is better attested than τοῦ λόγου, which is a mere slip in B corrected by Arethas.)

e 4 ὡς ἀδεῶς ... ἐτελεύτα, 'so fearlessly and nobly did he pass away.' Such clauses are best regarded as dependent exclamations. Cp. *Crito* 43 b 6 πολλάκις ... σε ... ηὐδαιμόνισα τοῦ τρόπου, ... ὡς ῥᾳδίως αὐτὴν (sc. τὴν παρεστῶσαν συμφορὰν) φέρεις. Cp. below 89 a 2 ; 117 c 9.

e 5 ὥστε μοι ... παρίστασθαι, 'so that I was made to feel', 'so that I realized'. In the act. παριστάναι τί τινι is 'to impress a thing on some one's mind'. Cp. Dem. *Cor.* I τοῦτο παραστῆσαι τοὺς θεοὺς ὑμῖν, 'that the gods may put it into your hearts,' *Mid.* 72 τὸ δεινὸν παραστῆσαι τοῖς ἀκούουσιν, 'to make the audience realize the outrage.' In the mid. we can say δόξα μοι παρίσταται, 'the belief impresses itself upon me,' 'the thought comes home to me' (cp. 66 b 1), or the verb may be used impersonally as here and *Alc.*[2] 143 e 8 εἴ σοι αὐτίκα μάλα παρεσταίη, 'if it should come into your head.'

ἄνευ θείας μοίρας, lit. 'without a divine dispensation'. The meaning is that 'Providence' would watch over him on his way. The phrase θεία μοῖρα is common in Plato and Xenophon as the religious equivalent of τύχη. Hdt. iii. 139 says θείῃ τύχῃ. Cp. Xen. *Apol.* 32 ἐμοὶ μὲν οὖν δοκεῖ θεοφιλοῦς μοίρας τετυχηκέναι (Σωκράτης).

59 a 2 παρόντι πένθει, 'one who takes part in a scene of mourning.' The meaning of παρεῖναι was so fixed in this connexion (57 a 1 *n.*) that no Greek would be tempted to take it as neuter in agreement with πένθει. It is dependent on εἰσιέναι to be supplied from εἰσῄει, and governs πένθει.

a 3 οὔτε αὖ : the first οὔτε is at 58 e 2.

ἐν φιλοσοφίᾳ ὄντων, 'occupied with philosophy.' Heindorf compares Xen. *Cyr.* iii. 1. 1 ὁ μὲν δὴ Κῦρος ἐν τούτοις ἦν, iv. 3. 23 οἱ μὲν δὴ ἐν τούτοις τοῖς λόγοις ἦσαν. See below 84 a 8 ἀεὶ ἐν τούτῳ (τῷ λογισμῷ) οὖσα.

a 4 τοιοῦτοί τινες, i. e. philosophical.

6

a 4 ἀτεχνῶς, 'just.' The phrase is equivalent to ἀτεχνῶς ἄτοπόν τι ἔπαθον, for which cp. *Symp.* 198 c 2 ὥστε ἀτεχνῶς τὸ τοῦ Ὁμήρου ἐπεπόνθη, Arist. *Clouds* 408 νὴ Δί᾽ ἐγὼ γοῦν ἀτεχνῶς ἔπαθον τουτί ποτε Διασίοισιν. In this connexion the adverb means that the description of the πάθος is to be taken 'literally', as we say.

a 8 γελῶντες ... δακρύοντες: the participles explain οὕτω, and are not dependent on διεκείμεθα.

ἐνίοτε δέ: a variation of the usual τοτὲ δέ. Cp. *Theaet.* 150 a 9 ἐνίοτε μὲν ... ἔστι δ᾽ ὅτε ..., *Soph.* 242 d 1 ἐνίοτε ... τοτὲ δὲ ... Plato avoids formal symmetry with μέν and δέ.

a 9 καὶ διαφερόντως, 'quite exceptionally' (καί as in καὶ μάλα). Cp. 61e 1; 117 c 4.

Ἀπολλόδωρος is mentioned as a disciple in *Apol.* 34 a 2, and Plato has chosen him as the narrator of the *Symposium*. In that dialogue, the friend to whom he narrates it says (173 d 4) Ἀεὶ ὅμοιος εἶ, ὦ Ἀπολλόδωρε· ἀεὶ γὰρ σαυτόν τε κακηγορεῖς καὶ τοὺς ἄλλους, καὶ δοκεῖς μοι ἀτεχνῶς πάντας ἀθλίους ἡγεῖσθαι πλὴν Σωκράτους, ἀπὸ σαυτοῦ ἀρξάμενος. Xenophon mentions him along with Antisthenes (*Mem.* iii. 11. 17) Ἀπολλόδωρόν τε τόνδε καὶ Ἀντισθένην οὐδέποτέ μου ἀπολείπεσθαι), so he seems to have belonged to the Cynic section of the Socratic circle, which agrees very well with the tendency to κακηγορία and with other traits mentioned in the *Symposium*. In the Xenophontean *Apology* 28 we are told that he was ἐπιθυμητὴς μὲν ἰσχυρῶς αὐτοῦ (Σωκράτους), ἄλλως δ᾽ εὐήθης (*naif*, 'silly'). In most editions of the *Symposium* we read that he had the nickname (ἐπωνυμία) of μανικός (173 d 8), but μαλακός has better MS. authority and suits the context better. His friend says he does not know how Apollodorus got the name of 'soft'; for he is always savage with himself and every one but Socrates. Certainly his conduct here and at 117 d 3 is μαλακία rather than μανία.

b 6 τῶν ἐπιχωρίων, 'of native Athenians.' Cp. *Prot.* 315 b 2 ἦσαν δέ τινες καὶ τῶν ἐπιχωρίων ἐν τῷ χορῷ (as opposed to the ξένοι, whom Protagoras brought in his train), *Rep.* 327 a 4 ἡ τῶν ἐπιχωρίων πομπή (as opposed to the Thracian procession).

b 7 Κριτόβουλος, son of Crito, was chiefly known for his beauty. In Xenophon's *Symposium* Socrates undertakes to prove himself to be more beautiful than Critobulus.

ὁ πατὴρ αὐτοῦ: W adds the name Κρίτων, and so B²; but he was

so well known that this is unnecessary. Crito was of the same age
and deme ('Ἀλωπεκῆθεν) as Socrates (*Apol.* 33 d 9 ἡλικιώτης καὶ
δημότης), and Plato has drawn a touching picture of his devotion
here and in the *Crito*. We gather that he watched over his friend
and master's worldly interests without fully understanding his
philosophy.

b 7 Ἑρμογένης, brother of Callias son of Hipponicus, who had
spent more money on 'sophists' than any man of his time (*Apol.*
20 a 4), and in whose house the scene of the *Protagoras* is laid.
Hermogenes is one of the speakers in the *Cratylus*, where the
poverty into which he had fallen is alluded to (*Crat.* 384 c 5), and he
is included in Xenophon's list of the inner Socratic circle (*Mem.* i. 2.
48). In *Mem.* ii. 10 Socrates persuades his friend Diodorus to
assist him, and in iv. 8. 4 he is quoted as the authority for the trial
of Socrates, which took place after Xenophon left Athens.

b 8 Ἐπιγένης : cp. *Apol.* 33 e 2 Ἀντιφῶν ὁ Κηφισιεὺς οὑτοσί, Ἐπιγένους
πατήρ. This Antiphon must not be confused with the orator, who
was τῶν δήμων Ῥαμνούσιος. There is a conversation with Epigenes
in Xen. *Mem.* iii. 12, where Socrates says to him ὡς ἰδιωτικῶς ('in
bad training') τὸ σῶμα ἔχεις, ὦ Ἐπίγενες, and urges him to take
more exercise.

Αἰσχίνης : i. e. *Aeschines Socraticus,* so called to distinguish him
from the orator. Cp. *Apol.* 33 e 1 Λυσανίας ὁ Σφήττιος, Αἰσχίνου
τοῦδε πατήρ. After the death of Socrates, he appears to have fallen
into great poverty, but was given some place at the court of Diony-
sius II on the recommendation of Plato (or Aristippus). He was
one of the most highly appreciated writers of Socratic dialogues.
The *Axiochus,* the *Eryxias,* and the Περὶ ἀρετῆς were at one time
ascribed to him and have been edited under his name, but are
certainly of later date.

Ἀντισθένης is the well-known founder of the Cynic school. The
date of his birth is uncertain, but he certainly belonged to the
generation before Plato. He is probably the source of a good many
things in Xenophon's account of Socrates. It has been held in
recent times that many of Plato's dialogues were directed against
Antisthenes, and references to him have been discovered in a great
many places. It is well, however, to be sceptical regarding these.
We really know very little about Antisthenes, and it is not safe to

reconstruct him from doubtful allusions. So far as the *Phaedo* is concerned, we may be sure there are no attacks upon him in it, seeing that he is supposed to be present.

b 8   ἦν, 'there was also.' Though it is true that compound verbs are repeated by the simple (**60** b 3 *n*.), it is not necessary to take ἦν here as equivalent to παρῆν. Cp. *Prot.* **315** e 3 τοῦτό τ' ἦν τὸ μειράκιον, καὶ τὼ 'Αδειμάντω ἀμφοτέρω, *Rep.* **615** d 7 ἦσαν δὲ καὶ ἰδιῶταί τινες.

b 9   Κτήσιππος: in the *Euthydemus* he is called (**273** a 7) νεανίσκος τις Παιανιεύς, μάλα καλός τε κἀγαθὸς τὴν φύσιν, ὅσον μὴ ὑβριστὴς διὰ τὸ νέος εἶναι. He also appears in the *Lysis*.

Μενέξενος: the same after whom the *Menexenus* is called. He was son of Demopho and cousin of the Ctesippus just mentioned, as we learn from the *Lysis* (**206** d 3), in which dialogue he plays a leading part as the young friend of Lysis. He must not be confused with his namesake, the son of Socrates (**60** a 2 *n*.).

10   Πλάτων δὲ οἶμαι ἠσθένει. Many strange things have been written about this simple statement. Of course, it is an advantage from a dramatic point of view for Plato to keep himself out of his dialogues ; and, as a matter of fact, he only mentions his own name in two other places (*Apol.* **34** a 1 and **38** b 6). At the same time, it is hardly credible that he should represent himself as absent on this occasion unless he had actually been so. It has been said that, had Plato really been ill, he would have had no occasion to make the reservation implied by οἶμαι. He must have known whether he was ill or not. That is so ; but it does not follow that Phaedo was equally well informed, and he is the speaker, not Plato.

c 1   Σιμμίας . . . καὶ Κέβης. These are the chief interlocutors in the *Phaedo*. We shall see presently that they were disciples of Philolaus at Thebes, which, like Phlius, was a city of refuge for the Pythagoreans (E. Gr. Ph.[2] p. 99). From the *Crito* (**45** b 3) we learn that they had brought a sum of money from Thebes to aid the escape of Socrates, another case of Pythagorean devotion to him. It is all the more important to observe that Xenophon confirms this by including Simmias and Cebes in his list of true Socratics (*Mem.* i. **2.** 48). Cp. also *Mem.* iii. **11.** 17 (immediately after the mention of Antisthenes and Apollodorus) διὰ τί δὲ (οἴει) καὶ Κέβητα καὶ Σιμμίαν Θήβηθεν παραγίγνεσθαι ; It is probable that Σιμίας is the correct form of the name (from σιμός), but I have not ventured to introduce it.

c 2 Φαιδώνδης: the MSS. vary between this form and Φαιδωνίδης. Xenophon (*Mem.* 1. 2. 48) mentions him along with Simmias and Cebes as a true Socratic, giving the correct Boeotian form of his name, Φαιδώνδας.

Εὐκλείδης: Euclides was the head of a philosophical school at Megara, which held a form of the Eleatic doctrine. He is also represented in the *Theaetetus* as devoted to the memory of Socrates.

Τερψίων. All we know of Terpsion is that he is associated with Euclides in the dramatic introduction to the *Theaetetus*, which serves to dedicate that dialogue to the Megarians just as the *Phaedo* is dedicated to the Pythagoreans.

c 3 Ἀρίστιππος. Many anecdotes are told of Aristippus of Cyrene, which may be apocryphal, but agree in representing him as a versatile cosmopolitan (*omnis Aristippum decuit color et status et res*, Horace, *Ep.* i. 17. 23). Many allusions to his doctrine have been found in Plato's writings; but the same caution applies here (cp. b 8 *n.*) as in the case of Antisthenes.

Κλεόμβροτος : Callimachus has an epigram (24) on Cleombrotus of Ambracia who threw himself into the sea after reading the *Phaedo*, and he has often been identified with the Cleombrotus mentioned here. Nothing, however, is known of him.

c 4 ἐν Αἰγίνῃ γὰρ κτλ. In antiquity this was supposed to be an *innuendo*. Demetrius says (Περὶ ἑρμηνείας 288) that Socrates had been in prison for a number of days and they did not take the trouble to sail across, though they were not 200 stades from Athens. To make this more pointed, Cobet inserted οὐ before παρεγένοντο, and took the clause as a question, which only proves that the *innuendo* is not very apparent in the text as it stands. We must be very careful in reading such covert meanings into Plato's words. Athenaeus (504 f) makes it a grievance that he does not mention Xenophon here, though Xenophon had left Athens two years before. If the words Πλάτων δὲ οἶμαι ἠσθένει had been used of any one else, that would have been set down to malice. As we shall see, it had only become known the day before that the ship had returned from Delos, and we learn from the *Crito* (43 d 3) that the news came from

Sunium where she had touched. Aristippus and Cleombrotus could hardly have heard this in time, if they were in Aegina. There is no evidence that they had been there during the whole of the thirty days, as Demetrius suggests.

Introductory Narrative.—The attitude of Socrates towards death (59 c 8—70 c 3).

(1) *Preliminary Narrative* (59 c 8—63 e 8).

d 8   τῇ ... προτεραίᾳ : Attic usage seems to require either τῇ προτέρᾳ ἡμέρᾳ or τῇ προτεραίᾳ. I have therefore followed Hermann in bracketing ἡμέρᾳ.

e 4   ὑπακούειν, 'to answer the door.' Cp. *Crito* 43 a 5 θαυμάζω ὅπως ἠθέλησέ σοι ὁ τοῦ δεσμωτηρίου φύλαξ ὑπακοῦσαι.

εἶπεν περιμένειν, 'told us to wait.' T has ἐπιμένειν, which seems less suitable. It would mean 'to stay as we were' (Riddell, Dig. § 127).

e 5   ἕως ἄν: we should expect πρὶν ἄν after πρότερον, but καὶ μὴ πρότερον παριέναι is merely a 'polar' antithesis placed διὰ μέσου and does not affect the construction.

e 6   οἱ ἕνδεκα : on the Eleven and their functions, see Arist. 'Αθ. πολ. 52, where we are told that the people elected them *inter alia* ἐπιμελησομένους τῶν ἐν τῷ δεσμωτηρίῳ.

e 7   ὅπως ἄν ... τελευτᾷ, 'are giving instructions for his death to-day.' For this rare construction after verbs of commanding, where the dependent clause contains the substance of the order, cp. *Gorg.* 523 d 7 τοῦτο μὲν οὖν καὶ δὴ εἴρηται ('instructions have been given') τῷ Προμηθεῖ ὅπως ἄν παύσῃ, Isaeus 7. 27 διεκελεύεσθ' ὅπως ἄν, εἴ τι πάθοι πρότερον, ἐγγράφωσί με. The present τελευτᾷ (T) is more likely to have been altered to τελευτήσῃ (B) than *vice versa*.

οὐ πολὺν ... χρόνον ἐπισχών, lit. 'after waiting (ἐπέχω intrans.) no long time '. Cf. 95 e 7 συχνὸν χρόνον ἐπισχών. Similarly 117 e 7 διαλιπὼν χρόνον, 118 11 ὀλίγον χρόνον διαλιπών, 'after a short interval.'

e 8   ἐκέλευεν : W has ἐκέλευσεν (and so, accordingly, B²), but this is less idiomatic. The English verbs 'send' and 'bid' refer to the starting of the action, but πέμπειν and κελεύειν operate throughout the action. 'The thought follows the motion' (Gildersleeve). The imperfect is therefore natural where we should expect the aorist.

It is for the same reason that πέμπειν can mean 'convey', 'escort', and κελεύειν, 'urge on', 'incite'.

e 8 εἰσιόντες: W has εἰσελθόντες (and so B²), but the present pcp. goes better with κατελαμβάνομεν. There were a number of them, so the action is resolved into successive parts ('as we entered, we found ...').

60 a 1 κατελαμβάνομεν, 'we found.' When καταλαμβάνειν is used in this sense, it takes the construction of verbs of knowing.

a 2 Ξανθίππην. There is no hint in the *Phaedo*, or anywhere else in Plato, that Xanthippe was a shrew. Xenophon makes her son Lamprocles say of her (*Mem.* ii. 2. 7) οὐδεὶς ἂν δύναιτο αὐτῆς ἀνασχέσθαι τὴν χαλεπότητα, and in Xen. *Symp.* 2. 10 Antisthenes says she was the most 'difficult' (χαλεπωτάτη) of all wives, past, present, or future. The traditional stories about her appear to be of Cynic origin.

τὸ παιδίον. Socrates had three sons (*Apol.* 34 d 6 εἷς μὲν μειράκιον ἤδη, δύο δὲ παιδία). The μειράκιον must be the Lamprocles mentioned by Xenophon (see last note). There was one called Sophroniscus after his paternal grandfather, so he would be the second. The child here mentioned must accordingly be Menexenus (not to be confused with Menexenus, son of Demopho, cp. 59 b 9 *n*.). It is worthy of note that the names Xanthippe and Lamprocles suggest aristocratic connexions, and possibly Lamprocles was called after his maternal grandfather (cp. Arist. *Clouds* 62 sqq.). Socrates was not always a poor man ; for he had served as a hoplite, and in *Apol.* 23 b 9 he ascribes his poverty to his service of Apollo (ἐν πενίᾳ μυρίᾳ εἰμὶ διὰ τὴν τοῦ θεοῦ λατρείαν). This may explain the χαλεπότης of Xanthippe, if such there was.

a 3 ἀνηυφήμησε ought to mean 'raised a cry of εὐφημεῖτε' (*bona verba, favete linguis*), and that gives a perfectly good sense. The rule was ἐν εὐφημίᾳ χρὴ τελευτᾶν (117 e 1), and εὐφημεῖτε was therefore a natural address to people approaching a scene of death. That she should use it and then break the εὐφημία herself is only human—and feminine. Byzantine scholars took, however, another view. In the recently discovered portion of the Lexicon of the Patriarch Photius (ninth cent. A.D.) we read ἀνευφήμησεν· ἀντὶ τοῦ ἐθρήνησεν (Reitzenstein, *Anf. des Phot.* p. 135), and the rest follow suit. It was explained κατ' ἀντίφρασιν, i.e. by a curious figure of

speech which consisted in saying the opposite of what you meant
(*lucus a non lucendo*). Very similar is Soph. *Trach.* 783 ἅπας
δ' ἀνηυφήμησεν οἰμωγῇ λεώς (where G. Hermann took the word in its
natural sense) and Eur. *Or.* 1335 ἐπ' ἀξίοισί τἄρ' ἀνευφημεῖ δόμος.
In both these cases death is imminent. It may be said that the
οἰμωγή itself is δύσφημον, but that is not necessarily so ; at any rate
εὐφήμοις γόοις is quoted from Aeschylus (fr. 40 Sidgwick).

a 4 οἷα δή : these words might have been used even without εἰώθασιν,
in the sense of 'just like'. Cp. Xen. *Cyr.* i. 3. 2 οἷα δὴ παῖς (' just like
a boy'), Thuc. viii. 84. 3 οἷα δὴ ναῦται.

a 5 ὕστατον δή, ' so this is the last time that . . .' Cp. 89 b 4 αὔριον δή.

a 7 ἀπαγέτω τις αὐτήν κτλ. With this reading (that of B : TW have
ταύτην) the words are kindly and considerate. Xanthippe had apparently passed the night with Socrates and their child (at any rate
she was found there when the doors were opened), and it was only
right she should go home and rest. She is sent for again just before
the end to say farewell. I do not see any ground for the remarks
which some editors take occasion to make here on the Athenians'
treatment of their wives. Would it have been right to keep
Xanthippe there all day, in her overwrought condition, and allow her
to witness the actual agony ? Some women would have insisted on
staying, but we can find no fault with the behaviour of Socrates
in the matter.

a 9 τινες τῶν τοῦ Κρίτωνος, ' some of Crito's people.'

b 1 κοπτομένην : the original meaning of κόπτεσθαι was ' to beat the
breasts ', but it came to mean simply ' to lament ' (cp. the κομμός
in tragedy). The history of the Lat. *plango* (whence *planctus*,
' plaint ') is similar.

ἀνακαθιζόμενος : the use of this verb in the medical writers shows
that the meaning is ' sitting up '. Cp. Hippocrates, *Progn.* 37
ἀνακαθίζειν βούλεσθαι τὸν νοσέοντα τῆς νόσου ἀκμαζούσης πονηρόν. We
might expect ἐν τῇ κλίνῃ, but (ἵζεσθαι) καθίζεσθαι sometimes retain
the construction of (ἵζω) καθίζω, which are verbs of motion. The
variant ἐπὶ τὴν κλίνην (W and B²) may be due to the idea that the
verb means *residens*, ' sitting down.' Wohlrab argues that Socrates
must have got up to welcome his friends, and adopts ἐπί accordingly ; but this would spoil the picture. We are led to understand
that he put his feet on the ground for the first time at **61 c 10**. The

fetters had just been struck off, and at first he would be too stiff to get up.

b 2 συνέκαμψε: this verb is specially used of bending the joints. Cp. Arist. *Hist. An.* 502 b 11 πίθηκος πόδας συγκάμπτει, ὥσπερ χείρας. It is opposed to ἐκτείνω.

ἐξέτριψε, 'rubbed down,' as with a towel. Athenaeus (409 e) quotes Philoxenos for ἔκτριμμα in the sense of χειρόμακτρον.

b 3 τρίβων: the compound verb is regularly repeated by the simple. Cp. 71 e 8 ἀνταποδώσομεν ... ἀποδοῦναι, 84 c 7 διεξιέναι ... διελθεῖν, 104 d 10 ἀπεργάζηται ... εἰργάζετο.

ὡς ἄτοπον ... τι: the unemphatic τις is often postponed by hyperbaton (Riddell, Dig. § 290 c).

b 4 ὡς θαυμασίως πέφυκε πρός, 'how strangely it is related to —.' *Relation* is expressed by πεφυκέναι πρὸς ..., *design* or *adaptation* by πεφυκέναι ἐπὶ ...

b 5 τὸ ἅμα μὲν κτλ., 'to think that they will not —.' The exclamatory infinitive is often used after some expression of feeling (in the present case ὡς θαυμασίως) which it serves to justify. Cp. Eur. *Alc.* 832 ἀλλὰ σοῦ, τὸ μὴ φράσαι, 'Out on thee! to think thou didst not tell!', *Med.* 1051 ἀλλὰ τῆς ἐμῆς κάκης, τὸ καὶ προέσθαι κτλ., Arist. *Clouds* 819 τῆς μωρίας, τὸ Δία νομίζειν ὄντα τηλικουτονί. This explanation, which is due to Riddell (Dig. § 85), makes it unnecessary to read τῷ with inferior MS. authority and Stobaeus.

b 6 μὴ 'θέλειν: editors speak of personification and 'the lively fancy of the Greeks' here, but even we say 'won't' in such cases.

b 7 σχεδόν τι ... ἀεί, 'in almost every case.' The omission of ἀεί in B is probably accidental. The relativity of pain and pleasure is a Heraclitean doctrine, cp. fr. 104 Bywater νοῦσος ὑγιείην ἐποίησεν ἡδύ, κακὸν ἀγαθόν, λιμὸς κόρον, κάματος ἀνάπαυσιν, and it is not, perhaps, fanciful to suppose that this is intended to prepare us for the Heraclitean arguments as to the relativity of life and death below (70 d 7 sqq.).

b 8 ἐκ μιᾶς κορυφῆς ἡμμένω, 'fastened to (Greek says 'fastened from') a single head,' a grotesque imagination like those of Empedocles and of Aristophanes in the *Symposium*. B has συνημμένω, but that seems to be an anticipation of c 3 συνῆψεν.

c 1 Αἴσωπος: Aesop was a Phrygian slave of whom many odd tales were told (cp. Wilamowitz-Marchant, *Greek Reader*, ii, p. 1), and the Athenians attributed to him the beast-fables which play so large a part in all popular literature. The prose collection which has come down to us under the title of Αἰσώπου μῦθοι is of Byzantine date; but many of the fables were well known from popular verses and Archilochus.

3 αὐτοῖς : this is rather neater than the variant αὐτῶν. 'He fastened their heads together for them.'

5 αὐτῷ μοι ἔοικεν, sc. ἐπακολουθεῖν. The clause ἐπειδὴ κτλ. is in apposition (asyndeton explicativum), and the original statement is, as usual, restated more fully after the explanation (a b a).

6 ὑπὸ τοῦ δεσμοῦ : cp. ὑπὸ τοῦ δέους, prae metu.

8 ὑπολαβὼν ... ἔφη, 'rejoined' (synchronous aor. pcp.). The meaning of ὑπολαμβάνειν is not 'to interrupt', but 'to rejoin' or 'retort'. Cp. Lat. suscipere (Aen. vi. 723 suscipit Anchises) and contrast παραλαμβάνειν (τὸν λόγον) excipere.

9 εὖ γ' ἐποίησας ἀναμνήσας με, 'thank you for reminding me' (synchronous aor. pcp.). So Euthyd. 282 c 6 εὖ ἐποίησας ἀπαλλάξας με σκέψεως πολλῆς. Cp. Hdt. v. 24 εὖ ἐποίησας ἀπικόμενος, Eur. Med. 472 εὖ δ' ἐποίησας μολών.

1 ἐντείνας, 'setting to music.' Cp. Prot. 326 b 1 ποιήματα ... εἰς τὰ κιθαρίσματα ἐντείνοντες. This seems to come from the geometrical use of the term which we find in Meno 87 a 1 εἰ οἷόν τε εἰς τόνδε τὸν κύκλον τόδε τὸ χωρίον ... ἐνταθῆναι, where it refers to the 'inscription' of rectangular figures in a circle (for which Euclid uses ἐγγράφειν). That in turn, like many geometrical terms (e. g. arc, chord, subtend, hypotenuse, cp. E. Gr. Ph.² p. 116 n. 1), comes from the use of ropes or strings in geometrical constructions. The Pythagoreans were much concerned with the inscription of polygons in circles and polyhedra in spheres (cp. 110 b 6 n.), and it was natural that the same word should be used of making words fit into a musical scheme. Cp. also Phileb. 38 e 2 ἐντείνας εἰς φωνήν of putting thought into words.

λόγους, 'tales.' This was the usual name (cp. Ar. Birds 651 ἐν Αἰσώπου λόγοις, Herodotus ii. 134 Αἰσώπου τοῦ λογοποιοῦ); but, when it is important to mark their fictitious character, they are called μῦθοι and opposed to λόγοι (61 b 4). In Ionic μῦθος means the same as λόγος in Attic; the Ionic for 'fable' is αἶνος (cp. Archil. fr. 96 ἐρέω τιν' ὑμῖν αἶνον, ὦ Κηρυκίδη).

d 2 τὸ εἰs τὸν 'Απόλλω προοίμιον: Thucydides (iii. 104) gives this name to the Homeric 'Hymn' to Apollo. Properly speaking, προοίμια are 'preludes' intended to attach the rhapsode's epic recitations to the praise of the god at whose πανήγυρις they were delivered. This instance shows that ἐντείνας is 'setting to music', not merely 'versifying'; for no προοίμιον could have been in prose. In the *Phaedo*, Socrates is represented throughout as the servant of Apollo (cp. esp. 85 b 4 sqq.). Apollo Hyperboreus of Delos was in a special sense the god of the Pythagoreans (E. Gr. Ph.² p. 97, *n.* 3), and there would be no difficulty in identifying him with the Pythian Apollo who had given the famous oracle, and to whose service, as we know from the *Apology*, Socrates regarded himself as consecrated. They were identified in the public religion of Athens (Farnell, *Cults of the Greek States*, iv, p. 110). Geddes's suggestions about 'the God of Day' must be rejected. Apollo was not a sun-god at this date (Farnell, ib., p. 136 sq.).

καὶ ἄλλοι τινές ... ἀτὰρ καὶ ... So we find ἀεὶ μὲν ... ἀτὰρ καὶ νῦν (τότε) ... In these uses ἀτὰρ καὶ ... is equivalent to καὶ δὴ καὶ ...

d 3 Εὔηνος: from *Apol.* 20 b 8 we learn that Evenus was a Parian who taught 'human goodness' for 5 minae. In *Phaedr.* 267 a 3 we are told that he invented certain rhetorical devices such as ὑποδήλωσις and παρέπαινος. Some said he even composed παράψογοι in metre μνήμης χάριν. He was also an elegiac poet.

πρῴην, 'the other day.' We know from the *Apology* 20 a 3 that Evenus was at Athens about the time of the trial of Socrates.

d 9 ἀντίτεχνος, 'competitor', 'rival'. So in Ar. *Frogs* 816 Euripides is the ἀντίτεχνος of Aeschylus.

e 2 ἀποπειρώμενος: cp. Hdt. i. 46 τῶν μαντηίων ἀποπειρώμενος. Plato makes Socrates confess his belief in dreams elsewhere. Cp. *Apol.* 33 c 5 and *Crito* 44 a.

ἀφοσιούμενος: the verb ἀφοσιοῦμαι means *facio aliquid animi religione solvendi causa*. Tr. 'to satisfy my conscience'.

e 3 εἰ ἄρα πολλάκις, 'on the chance that,' *si forte*. This use of πολλάκις is fairly common after εἰ (ἐὰν) ἄρα and μή. Cp. 61 a 6.

ταύτην τὴν μουσικήν, 'music in the ordinary sense.' The pronoun οὗτος is often depreciatory like *iste*.

e 7 καὶ ἐργάζου, sc. μουσικήν. As distinguished from ποιεῖν, 'compose,'

16

ἐργάζεσθαι means 'to make a business of', 'practise', and is regularly used of arts and trades (L. S., *s. v.* II. 5, 6).

e 8 παρακελεύεσθαι *hortari aliquem ut aliquid faciat*; ἐπικελεύειν *incitare facientem* (Fischer). *Comparatio autem ducta est ex proverbio currentem incitare* (Wyttenbach). Cf. Xen. *Cyr.* vi. 3. 27 τοῖς . . . τὸ δέον ποιοῦσιν ἐπικελεύειν.

a 1 ὥσπερ . . . καὶ ἐμοὶ οὕτω: the simile brings out the meaning of ἐπικελεύειν and is therefore added appositively (*asyndeton explicativum*), after which the original fact is more fully restated (*a b a*). For this regular Platonic structure, cp. **109 e 4** (Riddell, Dig. § 209).

διακελευόμενοι: the proper meaning of διακελεύεσθαι is 'to exhort one another'. Cp. Hdt. ix. 5 διακελευσαμένη δὲ γυνὴ γυναικί, but Plato often uses the word as equivalent to παρακελεύεσθαι. Here, I think, it is merely employed for variety; it could hardly refer to the partisans of different runners exhorting their favourites.

a 3 φιλοσοφίας . . . οὔσης μεγίστης μουσικῆς: this is a distinctively Pythagorean doctrine. We have the authority of Aristoxenus for saying that the Pythagoreans used medicine to purge the body and music to purge the soul (E. Gr. Ph.² p. 107), and Aristotle's doctrine of the tragic κάθαρσις seems to be ultimately derived from this source. We shall see that philosophy is the true soul-purge. Strabo, who had access to Italiote and Siceliote historians now lost, says, in discussing the orgiastic dances of the Curetes (x. 468) καὶ διὰ τοῦτο μουσικὴν ἐκάλεσεν ὁ Πλάτων, καὶ ἔτι πρότερον οἱ Πυθαγόρειοι, τὴν φιλοσοφίαν. Cp. also *Rep.* 548 b 8 τῆς ἀληθινῆς Μούσης τῆς μετὰ λόγων τε καὶ φιλοσοφίας, *Laws* 689 d 6 ἡ καλλίστη καὶ μεγίστη τῶν συμφωνιῶν ('harmonies') μεγίστη δικαιότατ' ἂν λέγοιτο σοφία. This is quite different from the metaphor put into the mouth of Laches in *Lach.* 188 d 3. There the μουσικὸς ἀνήρ is he whose character is tuned in a noble key. Any educated Athenian might have said that; but here we have a definite doctrine, which is further developed in the sequel.

a 6 εἰ ἄρα πολλάκις: cp. **60 e 3** *n.*

b 1 πιθόμενον: this was originally the reading of T and should, I think, be preferred to πειθόμενον if καί is deleted and the participle made dependent on ποιήσαντα. Tr. 'by composing poems in obedience to the dream'. We often find καί interpolated between two participles, one of which is subordinated to the other. It is omitted here by W, and Schanz had bracketed it without knowing this.

b 4   μύθους ἀλλ' οὐ λόγους: cp. 60 d 1 *n.*   Cp. *Gorg.* 523 a 1 ἄκουε . . . λόγου, ὃν σὺ μὲν ἡγήσῃ μῦθον, . . . ἐγὼ δὲ λόγον, *Prot.* 324 d 6 τούτου . . . πέρι . . . οὐκέτι μῦθόν σοι ἐρῶ ἀλλὰ λόγον, *Tim.* 26 e 4 μὴ πλασθέντα μῦθον ἀλλ' ἀληθινὸν λόγον. The distinction is almost the same as ours between 'fiction' and 'fact'.

b 5   καὶ αὐτὸς οὐκ ᾖ: the construction ceases to be indirect, as if ἐπειδή, not ἐννοήσας ὅτι had preceded.

b 6   ἠπιστάμην, 'knew off by heart.' Cp. *Prot.* 339 b 4 τοῦτο ἐπίστασαι τὸ ᾆσμα ; *Gorg.* 484 b 10 τὸ γὰρ ᾆσμα οὐκ ἐπίσταμαι.

τοὺς Αἰσώπου: the antecedent is incorporated in the relative clause (Riddell, Dig. § 218).

b 7   οἷς πρώτοις ἐνέτυχον: the clause οὓς προχείρους εἶχον is restated after the explanation (*a b a*) (Riddell, Dig. § 218).

b 8   ἐρρῶσθαι, sc. φράζε. 'Bid him farewell from me.' The regular word for delivering messages is φράζειν, and ἔρρωσο (perf. imper. mid. of ῥώννυμι) means 'farewell' and was regularly used in ending letters, whence Lat. *vale*.

ἂν σωφρονῇ, 'if he is wise,' the regular phrase in this sense, σωφρονεῖν being used in its originally sense of *sapere*, 'to be in one's right mind.' The more common meaning of σωφρονεῖν is an extension of the idea of 'sanity' to a wider sphere.

ὡς τάχιστα: the omission of these words in T spoils the sense. Cp. *Theaet.* 176 a 8 πειρᾶσθαι χρὴ ἐνθένδε ἐκεῖσε ('from this world to the other') φεύγειν ὅτι τάχιστα.

c 2   οἷον: an exclamation, not a question. Cf. 117 d 7 οἷα . . . ποιεῖτε.

c 3   πολλὰ . . . ἐντετύχηκα, 'I have had many dealings with him.' Cp. *Lach.* 197 d 3 ὁ δὲ Δάμων τῷ Προδίκῳ πολλὰ πλησιάζει, *Crat.* 396 d 5 ἔωθεν . . . πολλὰ αὐτῷ συνῇ, *Parm.* 126 b 9 Πυθοδώρῳ . . . πολλὰ ἐντετύχηκε.

c 4   σχεδόν: used as in the phrase σχεδόν (τι) οἶδα. Tr. 'I am pretty sure that —'.

ἑκὼν εἶναι: always with a negative, 'if he can (could) help it.'

c 6   οὐ φιλόσοφος: as addressed to Pythagoreans, the word has a special sense (E. Gr. Ph.² p. 321), that of a man who follows a certain 'way of life'. It is much as if we should ask: 'Is he not a religious man ?

8 ἐθελήσει, 'will be willing', 'will be ready', not 'will wish'.

τούτου τοῦ πράγματος, sc. φιλοσοφίας, regarded as an occupation. Cp. *Apol.* 20 c 5 τὸ σὸν τί ἐστι πρᾶγμα; The term is natural if we remember that 'philosophy' is a life.

7 Φιλολάῳ : Philolaus was one of the most distinguished of the later Pythagoreans, and had taken refuge at Thebes when the community was expelled from Magna Graecia (E. Gr. Ph.² p. 99). There seems to have been a regular συνέδριον at Thebes as well as at Phlius. The Pythagorean Lysis was the teacher of Epaminondas.

8 οὐδέν . . . σαφές, 'nothing certain' rather than 'nothing clear' (cp. 57 b 1 *n.*). We shall see that there were good reasons for the teaching of Philolaus about the soul being doubtful (86 b 6 *n.*). I do not think there is any reference to the Pythagoreans' custom of speaking δι' αἰνιγμάτων, as Olympiodorus fancies.

10 φθόνος οὐδεὶς λέγειν, ' I don't mind telling you.'

1 καὶ μάλιστα, *vel maxime.* Cp. 59 a 9 *n.*

ἐκεῖσε . . . τῆς ἐκεῖ: the adverbs ἐνθάδε and ἐκεῖ are regularly used of 'this life and the next', 'this world and the other'. Cp. 64 a 1 ; 117 c 2. So *Theaet.* 176 a 8 quoted in 61 b 8 *n.*, and Aristophanes, *Frogs* 82 ὁ δ' εὔκολος μὲν ἐνθάδ' εὔκολος δ' ἐκεῖ. There is no need to read τῆς ἐκεῖσε for τῆς ἐκεῖ, for ἀποδημία means a residence abroad as well as a journey abroad. Tr. ' our sojourn in the other world'.

2 μυθολογεῖν, 'to tell tales.' Socrates regards all definite statements with regard to the next life as μῦθοι. Cp. *Apol.* 39 e 4 where he introduces what he has to say about it by οὐδὲν γὰρ κωλύει διαμυθολογῆσαι πρὸς ἀλλήλους. The immortality of the soul is capable of scientific proof; the details of the ἀποδημία are not. Cp. below 110 b 1 *n.* and 114 d 1.

4 μέχρι ἡλίου δυσμῶν : executions could not take place till sunset. Cp. 89 c 7 ἕως ἔτι φῶς ἐστιν, 116 e 1 ἔτι ἥλιον εἶναι ἐπὶ τοῖς ὄρεσιν καὶ οὔπω δεδυκέναι.

6 νυνδή, 'just now,' i. e. 'a little ago' (ὀλίγον πρόσθεν). In this sense, the grammarians accent as in the text, to distinguish the adverb from νῦν δή, 'now indeed ', ' now at last' (cp. 107 c 4). As a rule the MSS. have νῦν δή in both senses.

7 ὅτε παρ' ἡμῖν διῃτᾶτο : it appears from these words that Philolaus had left Thebes some time before 399 B.C. We hear of him at Tarentum (Taras), which was the chief seat of scientific Pythagoreanism

in the fourth century B.C. The leading man then was Archytas (E. Gr. Ph.² p. 319).

62 a 2 ἴσως μέντοι κτλ. As the construction of this sentence has been much disputed, I will first give what I take to be the right translation. This will be justified in the following notes, from which it will also appear how it differs from other interpretations. I render: 'I dare say, however, it will strike you as strange if this is the solitary case of a thing which admits of no distinctions— I mean, if it never turns out, as in other cases, that for man (that is at certain times and for certain men) it is better to die than to live —and, in such cases, I dare say it further strikes you as strange that it is not lawful for those for whom it is better to die to do this good office for themselves, but that they have to wait for some one else to do it for them.' This comes nearest to Bonitz's interpretation (*Plat. Stud.*, ed. 3 (1886), pp. 315 sqq.), and I shall note specially the points in which it differs.

εἰ τοῦτο ... ἁπλοῦν ἐστιν : I take this clause as the expression in a positive form of what is stated negatively in the next. If we must say what τοῦτο means, it will be τὸ βέλτιον εἶναι ζῆν ἢ τεθνάναι, but the pronoun is really anticipatory and only acquires a definite meaning as the sentence proceeds. Bonitz once took τοῦτο as meaning τὸ τεθνάναι, but in his latest discussion of the passage he substitutes τὸ αὐτὸν ἑαυτὸν ἀποκτεινύναι. I do not think it necessary to look backwards for a definite reference, and I think Bonitz does not do justice to the clearly marked antithesis of μόνον τῶν ἄλλων ἁπάντων and ὥσπερ καὶ τἄλλα. The ἄλλα must surely be the same in both clauses, and if so these must be positive and negative expressions of the same thought. I hold, with Bonitz, that the interpretation of most recent editors (τοῦτο = τὸ μὴ θεμιτὸν εἶναι αὐτὸν αὑτὸν ἀποκτεινύναι) is untenable, if only because it gives an impossible meaning to ἁπλοῦν. Further, no one has suggested that the lawlessness of suicide is the only rule which is absolute, and the suggestion would be absurd. On the other hand, many people would say that life is always better than death. It may be added that τοῦτο is the proper anticipatory pronoun ; it is constantly used *praeparative*, as the older grammars say.

a 3 τῶν ἄλλων ἁπάντων : Riddell, Dig. § 172.

ἁπλοῦν : that is ἁπλοῦν which has no διαφοραί (cp. *Polit.* 306 c 3 πότερον ἁπλοῦν ἐστι τοῦτο, ἢ ... ἔχει διαφοράν). It is what admits of no distinctions such as ἔστιν ὅτε καὶ οἷς. Cp. *Symp.* 183 d 4 οὐχ ἁπλοῦν ἐστιν ... οὔτε καλὸν εἶναι αὐτὸ καθ' αὑτὸ οὔτε αἰσχρόν, ἀλλὰ καλῶς μὲν πραττόμενον καλόν, αἰσχρῶς δὲ αἰσχρόν, *Phaedr.* 244 a 5 εἰ μὲν γὰρ ἦν ἁπλοῦν τὸ μανίαν κακὸν εἶναι (where Socrates immediately proceeds to enumerate the different kinds of madness), *Prot.* 331 b 8 οὐ πάνυ μοι δοκεῖ ... οὕτως ἁπλοῦν εἶναι ... ἀλλά τί μοι δοκεῖ ἐν αὐτῷ διάφορον εἶναι. This is the origin of the Aristotelian use of ἁπλῶς. Bonitz has shown once for all that ἁπλοῦν does not mean *simpliciter verum*, as many editors say after Heindorf.

a 3 οὐδέποτε τυγχάνει ... βέλτιον ⟨ὄν⟩ : these words must be taken together, whether we add ὄν, as suggested by Heindorf, or not. It is, I think, safer to add it; for the certain instances of the poetical use of τυγχάνω without a participle come from later dialogues where poetical idioms are commoner.

τῷ ἀνθρώπῳ, 'for man' generally. The dative is governed by βέλτιον, not by τυγχάνει, as some editors suppose.

a 4 ὥσπερ καὶ τἆλλα, 'as other things do.' Olympiodorus rightly says: ἐπαμφοτεριζόντων τῶν ἄλλων καὶ ἀγαθῶν καὶ κακῶν δυναμένων εἶναι (the rest of his interpretation is wrong). The phrase is an abbreviation of some such clause as this : ὥσπερ ἐνίοτε ἐνίοις βέλτιον ὂν τυγχάνει νοσεῖν, πένεσθαι κτλ., ἢ ὑγιαίνειν, πλουτεῖν κτλ.

ἔστιν ὅτε καὶ οἷς: i. e. ἔστιν ὅτε καὶ ἔστιν οἷς, ἐνίοτε καὶ ἐνίοις. Bonitz's proposal to delete the comma at τἆλλα and take ὥσπερ καὶ τἆλλα ἔστιν ὅτε καὶ οἷς together is at first sight attractive. It gets rid of the pleonasm of ἔστιν ὅτε after οὐδέποτε and the change from singular to plural involved in taking ἔστιν οἷς with τῷ ἀνθρώπῳ. These are not, however, insuperable difficulties, and I feel that the ellipse involved in ὥσπερ καὶ τἆλλα is easier if it is total than if it is partial.

a 5 τεθνάναι : in such phrases τεθνάναι may properly be translated 'to die'; for ἀποθνήσκειν lays stress on the process of dying, of which τεθνάναι is the completion. The translation 'to be dead' is clearly inadmissible in such common phrases as πολλάκις, μυριάκις τεθνάναι. Cp. also *Crito* 43 d 1 οὗ δεῖ ἀφικομένου (sc. τοῦ πλοίου) τεθνάναι με, 52 c 6 οὐκ ἀγανακτῶν εἰ δέοι τεθνάναι σε, *Apol.* 30 c 1 οὐδ' εἰ μέλλω πολλάκις τεθνάναι, 38 e 4 πολὺ μᾶλλον αἱροῦμαι ὧδε ἀπολογησάμενος τεθνάναι ἢ ἐκείνως ζῆν, 39 e 3 οὔπω ἔρχομαι οἳ ἐλθόντα με δεῖ τεθνάναι, 41 a 8 πολλάκις ἐθέλω τεθνάναι εἰ ταῦτ' ἔστιν ἀληθῆ. So below 62 c 3 ὅτι βούλει αὐτὸ τεθνάναι, 64 a 6; c 5, 67 e 2; 81 a 1. Cp. the similar use of ἀπολωλέναι and that of τεθνάτω in criminal law, and see Vahlen, *Opuscula*, ii. 211 on the whole subject.

a 8 ἴττω Ζεύς: Schol. τὸ ἴττω ἐπιχωριάζοντός ἐστι. In Ar. *Ach.* 911 the Boeotian says ἴττω Δεύς, 'let Zeus know' (ἴττω = Ϝίδτω = Att. ἴστω), 'Zeus be my witness.' The meaning is much attenuated, and the French *Parbleu!* comes nearest to it. *Epist.* vii. 345 a 3 ἴττω Ζεύς, φησὶν ὁ Θηβαῖος may or may not be a reminiscence of this passage. It is more likely that the phrase struck Athenian ears as a quaint one. The expletives of a language generally strike foreigners in this way.

a 9 φωνῇ, 'dialect.' Cp. *Apol.* 17 d 5 and *Crat.* 398 d 8 ἐν τῇ Ἀττικῇ φωνῇ. So we say βοιωτιάζειν, δωρίζειν, ἑλληνίζειν, ξενίζειν τῇ φωνῇ. In classical Greek διάλεκτος means 'conversation', 'manner of speech'. Aristotle uses it (*Poet.* 1458 b 32) for 'everyday language' as opposed to the diction of poetry. It only acquires the meaning of 'dialect' at a later date.

b 1 οὕτω γ', 'put in that way.'

b 2 ἔχει τινὰ λόγον: lit. 'it admits of something being said for it', i.e. 'is justifiable' or 'intelligible' (opp. ἄλογόν ἐστιν, 'it is unjustifiable', 'inexplicable', syn. εὔλογόν ἐστιν). For the sense of ἔχειν cp. συγγνώμην ἔχει, *excusationem habet*, 'it admits of excuse', 'is excusable'. The phrase is sometimes personal as in *Apol.* 31 b 7 εἶχον ἄν τινα λόγον, 'my conduct would be intelligible,' 34 b 1 τάχ' ἂν λόγον ἔχοιεν βοηθοῦντες, 'their conduct would be explicable.' That λόγος does not mean 'reason' in this phrase is shown by the words which immediately follow in the last of these passages: τίνα ἄλλον ἔχουσι λόγον . . . ἀλλ' ἢ τὸν ὀρθόν τε καὶ δίκαιον; 'what explanation can be given except the straight and honest one?'

b 3 ἐν ἀπορρήτοις, 'in a mystery.' Cp. Eur. *Rhes.* 943 μυστηρίων τε τῶν ἀπορρήτων φανὰς | ἔδειξεν Ὀρφεύς. The doctrine of the immortality of the soul is Orphic in origin (cp. 70 c 5 *n.*). There is not the slightest reason for doubting that Socrates held it, or that he derived it from this source (cp. Introd. XIII). At the same time, he always refers to the details of Orphic theology with a touch of ironical deference as here. Cp. below 69 c 4 *n.*

ἔν τινι φρουρᾷ, 'in ward.' This is Archer-Hind's translation, and

conveniently retains the ambiguity of the original, which was sometimes understood to mean (1) 'watch', and sometimes (2) 'prison'.
Cicero took it in the first sense. Cp. *de Senectute* 20, *vetatque
Pythagoras iniussu imperatoris, id est dei, de praesidio et statione
vitae decedere.* In the *Somnium Scipionis* (3. 10) he uses the word
custodia, clearly a translation of φρουρά: *piis omnibus retinendus
est animus in custodia corporis, nec iniussu eius a quo ille est vobis
datus ex hominum vita migrandum est.* Antiphon the Sophist,
a contemporary of Socrates, says τὸ ζῆν ἔοικε φρουρᾷ ἐφημέρῳ, but
that may be merely a simile like the Psalmist's 'watch in the night'.
The Stoic formula that we must live ἕως ἂν ὁ θεὸς σημήνῃ τὸ ἀνακλη-
τικόν (*dum receptui canat*) seems to be derived from an interpretation of this kind, and we must remember that φρουρά is the
Peloponnesian word for στρατεία. The other view, however, that
φρουρά means 'prison', is strongly supported by the *Axiochus,* an
Academic dialogue of the third century B. C., where we read
(365 e 6) ἡμεῖς μὲν γάρ ἐσμεν ψυχή, ζῷον ἀθάνατον ἐν θνητῷ καθειργ-
μένον φρουρίῳ. There is no doubt that the Orphics did speak of the
body as the prison of the soul. The Christian apologist Athenagoras
says (Diels, *Vors.*[2] p. 245. 19) καὶ Φιλόλαος δὲ ὥσπερ ἐν φρουρᾷ πάντα
ὑπὸ τοῦ θεοῦ περιειλῆφθαι λέγων, with which we may compare Plato,
Crat. 400 c 4 δοκοῦσι μέντοι μοι μάλιστα θέσθαι οἱ ἀμφὶ Ὀρφέα τοῦτο
τὸ ὄνομα (σῶμα), ὡς δίκην διδούσης τῆς ψυχῆς ὧν δὴ ἕνεκα δίδωσιν, τοῦτον
δὲ περίβολον ἔχειν, ἵνα σῴζηται, δεσμωτηρίου εἰκόνα. Cp. also the use
of ἐνδεῖσθαι 'to be imprisoned' below 81 e 1 (ἕως ἂν) πάλιν ἐνδεθῶσιν
εἰς σῶμα, 92 a 1 πρὶν ἐν τῷ σώματι ἐνδεθῆναι. So too *Tim.* 43 a 5
ἐνέδουν εἰς ἐπίρρυτον σῶμα καὶ ἀπόρρυτον, 44 b 1 ὅταν (ψυχή) εἰς σῶμα
ἐνδεθῇ θνητόν. Cp. also ἐνδεδέσθαι in the fragment of Euxitheus
quoted in the next note. The φρουρά in *Gorg.* 525 a 7 is the
'prison-house' of the other world, not the body.

b 4 **καὶ οὐ δεῖ δὴ κτλ.** The genuinely Pythagorean origin of this is
vouched for by a passage from an unknown Pythagorean called
Euxitheus, quoted by Athenaeus from the Peripatetic Clearchus
(Diels, *Vors.*[2] p. 245. 8), Εὐξίθεος ὁ Πυθαγορικός, ὦ Νίκιον, ὥς φησι
Κλέαρχος ὁ Περιπατητικὸς ἐν δευτέρῳ Βίων, ἔλεγεν ἐνδεδέσθαι (cp. preceding note) τῷ σώματι καὶ τῷ δεῦρο βίῳ τὰς ἁπάντων ψυχὰς τιμωρίας
χάριν· καὶ διείπασθαι τὸν θεὸν ὡς, εἰ μὴ μενοῦσιν ἐπὶ τούτοις, ἕως ἂν ἑκὼν
αὐτοὺς λύσῃ, πλείοσι καὶ μείζοσιν ἐμπεσοῦνται τότε λύμαις· διὸ πάντας

εὐλαβουμένους τὴν τῶν κυρίων (i.e. δεσποτῶν, ἐπιστατῶν) ἀνάτασιν ('threat') φοβεῖσθαι τοῦ ζῆν ἑκόντας ἐκβῆναι, μόνον τε τὸν ἐν τῷ γήρᾳ θάνατον ἀσπασίως προσίεσθαι, πεπεισμένους τὴν ἀπόλυσιν τῆς ψυχῆς μετὰ τῆς τῶν κυρίων γίγνεσθαι γνώμης. As Clearchus of Soli wrote about 300 B.C., this fragment is almost certainly genuine.

b 5 μέγας, 'high.' Cp. *Gorg.* 493 c 3, where Socrates says of the most characteristic of the Orphic doctrines ταῦτ' ἐπιεικῶς μέν ἐστιν ὑπό τι ἄτοπα ('rather queer').

b 8 κτημάτων, 'chattels.' The word is often used of flocks and herds, in which sense it is opposed to χρήματα. This doctrine of the divine herdsman appears more than once in Plato's later dialogues. Cp. esp. *Laws* 906 a 6 σύμμαχοι δὲ ἡμῖν θεοί τε ἅμα καὶ δαίμονες, ἡμεῖς δ' αὖ κτῆμα (*v. l.* κτήματα) θεῶν καὶ δαιμόνων. In describing the *Saturnia regna* he says (*Polit.* 271 e 5) θεὸς ἔνεμεν αὐτοὺς αὐτὸς ἐπιστατῶν, 'God was their shepherd and tended them himself.' Again, in *Laws* 902 b 8 we have Θεῶν γε μὴν κτήματά φαμεν εἶναι πάντα ὁπόσα θνητὰ ζῷα, ὥσπερ καὶ τὸν οὐρανὸν ὅλον.—Πῶς γὰρ οὔ;—Ἤδη τοίνυν σμικρὰ ἢ μεγάλα τις φάτω ταῦτα εἶναι τοῖς θεοῖς· οὐδετέρως γὰρ τοῖς κεκτημένοις ἡμᾶς (i. e. τοῖς δεσπόταις ἡμῶν) ἀμελεῖν ἂν εἴη προσῆκον, ἐπιμελεστάτοις γε οὖσι καὶ ἀρίστοις. The similarity of phrase here points to a common Orphic-Pythagorean origin for the two passages. Cp. also *Critias* 109 b 6 κατοικίσαντες, οἷον νομῆς ποίμνια, κτήματα καὶ θρέμματα ἑαυτῶν ἡμᾶς ἔτρεφον.

c 3 τεθνάναι: cp. 62 a 5 *n.*

c 7 πρὶν ... ἐπιπέμψῃ: it is easy to insert ἄν before ἀνάγκην with Heindorf, but it is more likely that this archaic and poetical construction is used to give solemnity to the sentence. Unless we are prepared to emend a large number of passages, we must admit that Plato sometimes used it to produce a particular effect. It is especially common in the solemn, formal diction of the *Laws*, cp. 872 e 10 οὐδὲ ἔκπλυτον ἐθέλειν γίγνεσθαι τὸ μιανθὲν πρὶν φόνον φόνῳ ὁμοίῳ ὅμοιον ἡ δράσασα ψυχὴ τείσῃ.

c 10 ῥᾳδίως, 'lightly', 'without complaining', as in ῥᾳδίως φέρειν. Cp. 63 a 7.

d 2 εὐλόγως ἔχει: a frequent equivalent of εὐλογόν ἐστι (cf. supra b 2). That which it is easy to explain or justify is εὔλογον.

θεόν: the transition from the popular θεούς to the philosophic θεόν seems quite unconscious.

d 4 τοὺς φρονιμωτάτους: in Plato φρόνιμος and σοφός mean exactly the same thing. Aristotle distinguished φρόνησις from σοφία as practical from theoretical wisdom, a distinction which he shows to be in conformity with popular usage. See my edition of the *Ethics*, p. 261 sq.

d 5 ἐπιστατοῦσιν . . . ἐπιστάται: these are the regular terms in this connexion. Cp. *Polit.* 271 e 5 θεὸς ἔνεμεν αὐτοὺς αὐτὸς ἐπιστατῶν.

d 6 οὐκ ἔχει λόγον, i. e. ἄλογόν ἐστι, οὐκ εὐλόγως ἔχει (cp. b 2 ; d 2).

αὐτός: the shift from plural to singular is not uncommon. Cp. esp. 104 d 1 *n.*

e 2 παραμένειν, 'not to run away,' the regular opposite of ἀποδιδράσκειν.

e 4 οὕτως, 'putting it that way,' more often οὕτω γ' as above b 1.

e 5 τοὐναντίον . . . ἤ: we say 'opposite to'. We cannot always render ἤ by 'or' or 'than'; for its meaning is wider than either. Cp. especially the common διαφέρειν ἤ . . .

e 6 ἄφρονας : as φρόνιμος = σοφός, so ἄφρων = ἀμαθής (ἄσοφος is not in ordinary use).

a 1 πραγματεία, 'diligence', 'painstaking', the noun of πραγματεύομαι, which is equivalent to πράγματα ἔχω, 'take pains', 'take trouble'. In late Greek πολυπραγμοσύνη is 'curiosity' in a good sense, and the meaning here is similar.

a 2 [ὁ] Κέβης: it is Plato's almost uniform practice to insert the article with proper names in the narrative (cp. τοῦ Κέβητος just above) and to omit it in the dialogue when directly reported (cp. Κέβης twice in the next speech, introduced by καὶ ὁ Σιμμίας). See Beare in *Hermathena*, 1895, vol. ix, pp. 197 sqq. As ὁ was omitted by the first hand of T, I have ventured to bracket it.

λόγους τινὰς ἀνερευνᾷ, 'is always on the track of some argument.' Metaphors from hunting are often used by Socrates in speaking of arguments, and the λόγος is regularly the game which is hunted. Cp. μετιέναι τὸν λόγον (88 d 9 *n.*) and μέθοδος (79 e 3 *n.*). This metaphor has survived in the word 'investigation'. (Cp. κατ' ἴχνη 115 b 9 *n.*)

οὐ πάνυ . . . ἐθέλει, 'is not very ready to believe at once.' Note the interlaced order (*a b a b*); οὐ πάνυ belongs to ἐθέλει and εὐθέως to πείθεσθαι.

a 4 'Αλλὰ μὴν . . . γε: the emphasis is on νῦν. 'Even I think that *this* time ('for once') there is something in what Cebes says.'

a 6 ὡς ἀληθῶς belongs to σοφοί.

a 7 ῥᾳδίως, 'lightly.' Cp. 62 c 10.

εἰς σὲ τείνειν τὸν λόγον, 'to be aiming his words at you.' For an elaboration of the same metaphor, cp. *Symp.* 219 b 3 ταῦτα ... εἰπὼν καὶ ἀφεὶς ὥσπερ βέλη, τετρῶσθαι αὐτὸν ᾤμην.

b 6 παρὰ θεοὺς ἄλλους, sc. τοὺς χθονίους. Archer-Hind compares *Laws* 959 b 4 παρὰ θεοὺς ἄλλους ἀπιέναι δώσοντα λόγον. Geddes refers to Aesch. *Suppl.* 230 κἀκεῖ δικάζει τἀμπλακήμαθ', ὡς λόγος, | Ζεὺς ἄλλος ἐν καμοῦσιν ὑστάτας δίκας.

b 7 παρ' ἀνθρώπους : who these were, appears from *Apol.* 41 a 6, where Socrates mentions Orpheus, Musaeus, Hesiod, and Homer (in that order) as persons whom one would give anything to meet after death.

c 1 οὐκ ἂν πάνυ ... διισχυρισαίμην : another touch of the Socratic irony which Plato has reproduced elsewhere. Cp. above 62 b 5 *n.*, 114 d 1 *n.*, and *Meno* 86 b 6, where, after explaining the doctrine of ἀνάμνησις, Socrates says : καὶ τὰ μέν γε ἄλλα οὐκ ἂν πάνυ ὑπὲρ τοῦ λόγου διισχυρισαίμην, ὅτι δὲ κτλ.

c 2 ὅτι ... ἥξειν : the sentence begins as if it were to end ἥξειν ἐλπίζω (ἐλπίς is Orphic for 'faith' and quite in place here) εὖ ἴστε. Instead of that, it takes a fresh start at εὖ ἴστε, and the remainder of it is accommodated to the parenthesis καὶ τοῦτο μὲν οὐκ ἂν πάνυ διισχυρισαίμην. In T and Stobaeus the construction is regularized by writing τό for ὅτι, but this looks suspiciously like an 'emendation'.

c 4 οὐχ ὁμοίως, *non perinde* (Heindorf), 'not to the same extent,' as if I were without this hope.

c 5 εἶναί τι : cp. 91 b 3 εἰ δὲ μηδέν ἐστι τελευτήσαντι.

c 6 πάλαι λέγεται : we must interpret this in the light of the παλαιὸς λόγος at 70 c 5, where the reference is certainly to Orphic doctrine. Such a belief as is here mentioned formed no part of ordinary Greek religion. According to that, only a few great sinners (Sisyphus, Tantalus, Ixion) were punished in the other world, while only a few favourites of heaven (Menelaus, Diomede, Achilles, and, in Athenian belief, Harmodius and Aristogiton) were carried off to the Isles of the Blessed.

c 8 αὐτὸς ἔχων, 'keeping to yourself' ('αὐτός *h. l. est solus*,' Heindorf).

d 1 κοινόν, 'to be shared' (as in κοινὸς Ἑρμῆς). Cp. *Phaedr.* 279 c 6 κοινὰ γὰρ τὰ τῶν φίλων, which is a Pythagorean rule.

d 2 ἡ ἀπολογία, 'the defence' (of which you spoke a little ago, 63 b). The article should be kept, though omitted in B.

d 3 πρῶτον δὲ κτλ. This interlude marks the end of the preliminary narrative.

d 4 πάλαι, 'for some time past.' The adverb does not necessarily refer to a *long* time.

d 5 Τί δέ... ἄλλο γε ἤ... 'Why, simply that...' The first hand of B omits δέ, but the weight of MS. authority is in its favour. Cp. *Hipp. ma.* 281 c 9 Τί δ' οἴει, ὦ Σώκρατες, ἄλλο γε ἤ...

d 8 προσφέρειν τῷ φαρμάκῳ : as προσφέρειν means 'to apply', especially in a medical sense, the usual construction is that seen in *Charm.* 157 c 4 προσοίσω τὸ φάρμακον τῇ κεφαλῇ.

e 1 ἐνίοτε ἀναγκάζεσθαι κτλ. In Plut. *Phocion* 36 we have this story : Πεπωκότων δ' ἤδη πάντων, τὸ φάρμακον ἐπέλιπε, καὶ ὁ δημόσιος οὐκ ἔφη τρίψειν ἕτερον εἰ μὴ λάβοι δώδεκα δραχμάς, ὅσου τὴν ὁλκὴν ὠνεῖται. χρόνου δὲ διαγενομένου καὶ διατριβῆς, ὁ Φωκίων καλέσας τινὰ τῶν φίλων καὶ εἰπών· Ἦ μηδὲ ἀποθανεῖν Ἀθήνῃσι δωρεὰν ἔστιν, ἐκέλευσε τῷ ἀνθρώπῳ δοῦναι τὸ κερμάτιον. The suggestion has accordingly been made that the δημόσιος or δήμιος here was thinking less of Socrates than his own pocket.

e 3 ἔα... χαίρειν αὐτόν, 'never mind him.' The phrases χαίρειν ἐᾶν, and χαίρειν εἰπεῖν ('to bid farewell to') are used of dismissing anything from one's mind. Cp. 64 c 1 ; 65 c 7.

e 6 σχεδὸν μέν τι ἤδη : σχεδόν τι go together and μέν is *solitarium*. Cp. *Lach.* 192 c 5 σχεδὸν γάρ τι οἶδα.

(2) *The ἀπολογία of Socrates. The philosopher will not fear death; for his whole life has been a rehearsal of death.* 63 e 8—69 e 5.

e 8 δή marks these words as a reference to 63 b 2 sqq.

e 9 τὸν λόγον ἀποδοῦναι, 'to render my account' (*rationem reddere*) to the persons who are entitled to demand it (λόγον ἀπαιτεῖν) and to get it (λόγον λαμβάνειν, ἀπολαμβάνειν) from me (παρ' ἐμοῦ). For the article τόν cp. ἡ ἀπολογία above d 2.

ἀνὴρ... διατρίψας, 'a man who has spent,' quite general, and only a more emphatic form of ὁ διατρίψας.

τῷ ὄντι : in his earlier dialogues Plato uses only τῷ ὄντι, in his latest only ὄντως. The dialogues in which both occur are *Rep.*, *Phaedr.*, *Theaet.* In *Soph.* there are twenty-one cases of ὄντως to one of τῷ ὄντι. The absence of ὄντως from the *Phaedo* is one reason among others for dating it before the *Republic*.

e 10 θαρρεῖν, 'not to fear', 'to have no fear of' (opp. δεδιέναι and φοβεῖσθαι). We have no single word for this in English. See 88 b 4 *n.*

64 a 1 ἐκεῖ : cp. 61 e 1 *n.*

a 4 ὅσοι τυγχάνουσιν ... ἁπτομένοι, 'all who really engage in'. So commonly ἅπτεσθαι γεωμετρίας, μουσικῆς, γυμναστικῆς, 'to go in for', 'to study'. For ὀρθῶς 'in the true sense of the word', cp. below 67 b 4 *n.*

a 5 λεληθέναι τοὺς ἄλλους ὅτι ..., 'it looks as if men did not know that —.' As the negative of verbs of knowing, λανθάνειν may take ὅτι as well as a participial complement.

αὐτοί, ' of themselves ', ' of their own accord '.

a 6 ἐπιτηδεύουσιν, 'practise.' Cp. Cicero, *Tusc.* i. 30 *tota enim philosophorum vita, ut ait idem* (sc. Socrates), *commentatio mortis est,* ib. 31 *secernere autem a corpore animum ecquid aliud est quam mori discere?* Seneca, *Ep.* xxvi *egregia res est mortem condiscere ... meditare mortem.* The phrase *meditatio mortis* means the 'practising' or 'rehearsal' of death; for *meditatio* is a translation of μελέτημα, 67 d 8.

ἀποθνῄσκειν τε καὶ τεθνάναι, 'dying' (the process) 'and death' (its completion). Cp. 62 a 5 *n.*

a 9 ὃ ... προυθυμοῦντο: Plato often restates the first member of a period with emphasis at the end (*Palindromia of the period*, Schanz, *Nov. Comm.*, p. 10). A good instance is *Apol.* 27 d Οὐκοῦν εἴπερ δαίμονας ἡγοῦμαι ... ἐπειδήπερ γε δαίμονας ἡγοῦμαι. As the first member here is προθυμεῖσθαι ... μηδὲν ἄλλο ἢ τοῦτο, ὃ must be the object of προυθυμοῦντο, and not of ἀγανακτεῖν.

b 1 οὐ πάνυ ... γελασείοντα, 'not very inclined to laugh', 'in no laughing mood'. In prose only the participle of desideratives in -σειω is used, though Sophocles says τί δ' ἐργασείεις; (*Philoct.* 1001) and Euripides φευξείω (*Herc.* 628). Aristophanes has δρασείει in parody (*Wasps* 168).

b 2 ἂν ... δοκεῖν, 'would think.'

b 3 εἰρῆσθαι goes closely with b 5 ὅτι. That the words καὶ συμφάναι ... καὶ πάνυ are parenthetical is clear; for φημί and its compounds do not take ὅτι.

ɔ 3　τοὺς ... παρ' ἡμῖν ἀνθρώπους: i. e. the Thebans (not the Athenians, as Schleiermacher held). Olympiodorus says εἰκότως· Θηβαῖος γὰρ ἦν ὁ Σιμμίας, παρ' οἷς καὶ ἡ Βοιωτία ὗς. That, however, is hardly adequate; for Simmias was not likely to share Athenian prejudice on this subject. More probably we have here a reflexion of the impression made by the Pythagorean refugees on the *bons vivants* of Thebes. The φιλόσοφοι would not appreciate Copaic eels and ducks. In any case, it is distinctly implied that the word φιλόσοφος in its technical sense was well known at Thebes before the end of the fifth century, and this confirms the view that it was originally Pythagorean (E. Gr. Ph.[2] p. 321 *n.* 2).

b 5　θανατῶσι, 'are moribund', 'are ripe for death'. The scholium is θανάτου ἐπιθυμοῦσι, and late writers certainly use the word (or θανατιᾶν) in this sense. But it is not the meaning required here, and a glance at the list in Rutherford, *New Phrynichus*, p. 153, will show that verbs in -άω (-ιάω) express morbid states of body or mind, and are only occasionally and secondarily desiderative. Thus ναυτιᾶν is not 'to long to go to sea', but 'to have passenger-sickness', i.e. 'to be sea-sick'. For the real meaning of οἱ πολλοί cp. below ἐγγύς τι τείνειν τοῦ τεθνάναι (65 a 6 *n.*). They think philosophers 'as good as dead', and look upon them as 'living corpses' (cp. Sophocles quoted *l. c.*). They do not trouble about their desires. 'The picture of the pale-faced students in the φροντιστήριον of the *Clouds* is the best commentary on this popular impression' (Geddes). Cp. v. 103 τοὺς ὠχριῶντας, τοὺς ἀνυποδήτους λέγεις, 504 ἡμιθνὴς γενήσομαι (if I become like Chaerephon).

　　σφᾶς, sc. τοὺς πολλούς.

b 6　τοῦτο πάσχειν, sc. τεθνάναι. Tr. 'It would serve them right'.

c 1　χαίρειν εἰπόντες ἐκείνοις, 'dismissing them from our thoughts.' Tr. 'Never mind them, but let us discuss among ourselves'. Cp. 63 e 3 *n.*

c 2　ἡγούμεθά τι τὸν θάνατον εἶναι: Socrates regularly begins a dialectical argument by asking whether we attach a definite meaning to the name of the thing under discussion. Cp. *Gorg.* 464 a 1 σῶμά που καλεῖς τι καὶ ψυχήν, *Prot.* 358 d 5 καλεῖτέ τι δέος καὶ φόβον; *Meno*, 75 e 1 τελευτὴν καλεῖς τι; 76 a 1 ἐπίπεδον καλεῖς τι; so below 103 c 11 θερμόν τι καλεῖς καὶ ψυχρόν;

c 4　ἄλλο τι ἤ, 'anything else than.' Here the words have their full

29

sense ; but, if we suppress the ἆρα μή which introduces them, we see how ἄλλο τι ἤ came to be used as an interrogative = *nonne.*

c 5 τοῦτο: pred. 'that death is this', which is further explained by χωρὶς μὲν κτλ. The same definition is given in *Gorg.* 524 b 2 ὁ θάνατος τυγχάνει ὤν, ὡς ἐμοὶ δοκεῖ, οὐδὲν ἄλλο ἢ δυοῖν πραγμάτοιν διάλυσις, τῆς ψυχῆς καὶ τοῦ σώματος, ἀπ' ἀλλήλων. For τὸ τεθνάναι cp. 62 a 5 *n.*

c 6 αὐτὸ καθ' αὑτό, 'alone by itself.' The emphatic αὐτός often acquires a shade of meaning which we can only render by 'alone'. So ἐν αὐτοῖς ἡμῖν εἰρῆσθαι, αὐτοὶ γάρ ἐσμεν. Observe especially the substitution of μόνην καθ' αὑτήν, 67 d 1.

c 8 ἆρα μὴ . . . ᾖ; 'surely it can be nothing else than this, can it ?' The interrogative form of the idiomatic ' μή in cautious assertions' is very rare, and occurs only four times in Plato (Goodwin, *M. T.,* § 268).

c 10 Σκέψαι δὴ κτλ. Three arguments are given (1) the philosopher holds bodily pleasures cheap, (2) the body impedes the search for truth, (3) the things which the philosopher seeks to know cannot be perceived by the bodily senses.

ἐάν does not mean 'whether' like εἰ, but 'on the chance that', ' if haply', *si forte.* Goodwin, *M. T.,* §§ 489–93.

d 3 οἷον has become purely adverbial and always stands outside the construction of the sentence. Cp. 73 d 3 ; 78 d 10 ; 83 c 1.

d 6 Τί δὲ τὰς τῶν ἀφροδισίων; 'what of the pleasures of love?' Riddell (Dig. § 21) seems to be right in regarding this as a case where τί δέ stands for a sentence, or part of a sentence, unexpressed, but hinted at in a following interrogation (here δοκεῖ σοι κτλ., d 8). Cp. e.g. *Phileb.* 27 e 1 τί δὲ ὁ σὸς (βίος) ; ἐν τίνι γένει . . . ὀρθῶς ἂν ποτε λέγοιτο ; and below 78 d 10.

d 8 τὰς περὶ τὸ σῶμα θεραπείας, *cultus corporis.* We see here how περί *c. acc.* comes to be used as equivalent to a genitive. So just below, d 11.

d 9 ἐντίμους ἡγεῖσθαι, i.e. τιμᾶν, 'to value', 'esteem', 'appreciate' (τιμή, ' price'), opp. ἀτιμάζειν, 'to hold cheap.'
διαφερόντων, 'better than other people's.'

e 4 πραγματεία, 'business ', ' concern ', rather different from 63 a 1 above.

65 a 5 ᾧ μηδὲν . . . μηδὲ μετέχει αὐτῶν, ' that, for the man *to whom* none

of these things is pleasant, *and who* takes no part in them.' The rule is that, when the second relative would be in a different case from the first, it is either omitted (cp. 81 b 5; 82 d 2) or replaced by a demonstrative. Not understanding the construction BTW give μετέχειν, but the true reading is preserved by Iamblichus (fourth cent. A.D.).

6 ἐγγύς τι τείνειν τοῦ τεθνάναι, 'that he runs death hard.' Cp. *Rep.* 548 d 8 ἐγγύς τι αὐτὸν Γλαύκωνος τουτουὶ τείνειν ἕνεκά γε φιλονικίας, *Theaet.* 169 a 9 σὺ δέ μοι δοκεῖς πρὸς τὸν Σκίρωνα μᾶλλον τείνειν. It seems to me that this 'objectless' use of τείνειν is derived from racing (τείνειν δρόμον, *cursum tendere*), and that the meaning is 'to run hard', 'to run close'. This view is confirmed by a comparison of *Crat.* 402 c 2 (ταῦτα) πρὸς τὰ τοῦ Ἡρακλείτου πάντα τείνει with *ib.* 409 a 7 τοῦτο . . . φαίνεται τὸν Ἀναξαγόραν πιέζειν, where πιέζειν may very well mean *premere*, 'to press hard.' The use of τείνειν in this sense, 'to hold one's course' in a certain direction, 'to be bound for,' 'tend' points to the same interpretation. So also ἐγγύς, ὁμοῦ τι ἐλαύνειν. For the thought, cp. Soph. *Ant.* 1165 τὰς γὰρ ἡδονὰς | ὅταν προδῶσιν ἄνδρες, οὐ τίθημ' ἐγὼ | ζῆν τοῦτον, ἀλλ' ἔμψυχον ἡγοῦμαι νεκρόν. This is a good commentary on 64 b 6 θανατῶσι.

9 Τί δὲ κτλ. The second argument. The body impedes the search for truth.

τῆς φρονήσεως, syn. τῆς σοφίας. Cp. 62 d 4 *n.*

3 καὶ οἱ ποιηταί : this cannot, I think, refer to Parmenides and Empedocles, as Olympiodorus suggests and most editors repeat. They would hardly be spoken of as 'even the poets'. Epicharmus, whom he also mentions, is more possible (cp. fr. 249 νοῦς ὁρῇ καὶ νοῦς ἀκούει· τἆλλα κωφὰ καὶ τυφλά). More likely still, the reference is, as Olympiodorus also suggests, to Hom. *Il.* v. 127 ἀχλὺν δ' αὖ τοι ἀπ' ὀφθαλμῶν ἕλον, ἣ πρὶν ἐπῆεν, | ὄφρ' εὖ γιγνώσκῃς ἠμὲν θεὸν ἠδὲ καὶ ἄνδρα. At any rate, the ἀχλύς of this passage is often referred to by later Platonists as an allegory of the infirmity of sense-perception, and such allegorizing interpretation was already common in the fifth cent. B.C.

4 περὶ τὸ σῶμα, i. e. τοῦ σώματος. Cp. 64 d 8 *n.*

5 σαφεῖς, 'trustworthy.' Cp. 57 b 1 *n.*

σχολῇ, *vix.* Cp. our phrase ' It will take him all his time '.

2 ἐν τῷ λογίζεσθαι, 'in mathematical reasoning.' The primary sense of the word is arithmetical 'calculation' (ψήφοις λογίζεσθαι), from which it was extended to geometrical demonstration, and finally to all exact and scientific reasoning. It is no paradox, but an obvious fact, that in mathematics the sense of sight only misleads, and yet we are sure that there we reach the truth. The sense of hearing is mentioned with reference to the science of 'harmonics', which was just the mathematical treatment of the octave, and is more exact than tuning 'by ear' can ever be. To take the stock instance, 'the ear' does not reveal to us the impossibility of dividing a tone into two equal semitones; we only discover that by means of τὸ λογίζεσθαι.

c 3 τῶν ὄντων: the term τὰ ὄντα is used very vaguely in Plato, and may generally be rendered 'things'. Here, however, it is equivalent to τῶν ἀληθῶν. The verb εἶναι often means 'to be true', especially in Herodotus and Thucydides (cp. L. S., *s. v.* εἰμί A. III).

c 6 παραλυπῇ, 'annoys', 'irritates'. For the force of παρα-, cp. παρ-ενοχλεῖν.

μηδέ τις ἡδονή, 'nor any pleasure either.' This is preferable to the μήτε τις ἡδονή of TW.

c 7 αὐτὴ καθ' αὑτήν, 'alone by itself.' Cp. 64 c 6 *n.*

ἐῶσα χαίρειν, cp. 63 e 3 *n.*

c 9 τοῦ ὄντος, i. e. τοῦ ἀληθοῦς. Cp. above **c 3** *n.*

c 11 καὶ ἐνταῦθα, 'in this case too,' i. e. ἐν τῇ τῆς φρονήσεως κτήσει (65 a 9). The καί refers to πρῶτον μὲν ἐν τοῖς τοιούτοις (64 e 8).

d 4 Τί δὲ δὴ τὰ τοιάδε κτλ. The third argument. The things the philosopher seeks to know are not perceptible by the bodily senses, but can only be apprehended by thought.

The present passage introduces us to what is generally called the 'Theory of Ideas'. The name is unfortunate; for in English 'idea' means something which is 'in the mind', and an 'idea' is often opposed to a 'reality', whereas the 'forms' (μορφαί, εἴδη, ἰδέαι) are more real than anything else.

On the other hand, the 'forms' are not 'things' in time or space.

If we will only translate literally, and avoid loose 'philosophical' terminology, there is nothing in the doctrine here set forth which should be unintelligible to any one who understands a few propositions of Euclid and recognizes a standard of right conduct.

Let us begin with a mathematical instance. The geometer makes a number of statements about 'the triangle', as, for instance, that its interior angles are equal to two right angles, and we know that his statements are true. Of what is he speaking? Certainly not of any triangle which we can perceive by our senses (for all these are only approximately triangles), nor even of any we can imagine. He is speaking of what is 'just a triangle' (αὐτὸ τρίγωνον) and nothing more. Now, if geometry is true, that triangle must be the true triangle. It is from this consideration that the theory seems to have arisen.

The next step is to extend it to such things as 'right' (δίκαιον) and 'beautiful' (καλόν). We seem to be able to make true statements about these too; and, if so, it follows that τὸ δίκαιον and τὸ καλόν must be real in the same sense as 'the triangle'. We have never had experience of a perfectly right action or a perfectly beautiful thing, yet we judge actions and things by their greater or less conformity to what is 'just right' (αὐτὸ δίκαιον) and 'just beautiful' (αὐτὸ καλόν).

The 'forms', then, are what we really *mean* by 'triangle', 'right', 'beautiful', and it will be found helpful to think of them in the first place as *meanings*. There are, of course, further difficulties, but these can be dealt with as they arise. On the whole subject see A. E. Taylor, *Plato*, Chap. II.

d 4   φαμέν τι εἶναι . . . ἢ οὐδέν; 'Do we say there is such a thing . . . or not?' It is to be noticed that, in introducing the doctrine, Socrates says 'we', and Simmias, to whom it is apparently familiar, accepts it enthusiastically, also using the first person plural. The suggestion clearly is that Socrates and Simmias are using the language of a school to which both belong. The same phenomenon recurs whenever the doctrine is mentioned. Cp. E. Gr. Ph.² p. 354 sq.

d 5   αὐτό, 'by itself.' In this technical sense αὐτό is a development of αὐτός, 'alone.' It has become almost adverbial, as we see from such expressions as αὐτὸ ἡ ἀρετή, αὐτὸ δικαιοσύνη (Riddell, Dig. § 47). We come nearest the meaning by rendering it 'just'. The translation '*in* itself' is highly misleading; for it suggests the modern doctrine that we cannot know the 'thing in itself', whereas the αὐτὸ τρίγωνον is just the only triangle we can know.

d 6 Φαμὲν μέντοι νὴ Δία, 'I should think we do!' The particle μέντοι is used when the emphatic word of a question is repeated in an affirmative answer (cp. 81 d 6; 93 c 2), and may be further strengthened by νὴ Δία (cp. 68 b 7; 73 d 11). Olympiodorus gives us the orthodox Platonist interpretation of this remark: ὁ Σιμμίας ἑτοίμως συγκατατίθεται ('assents') τῷ περὶ τῶν ἰδεῶν λόγῳ ὡς συνήθης ('familiar') Πυθαγορείοις.

d 12 ὑγιείας, ἰσχύος: the addition of medical εἴδη like health and strength is significant. It has quite recently become known that Philolaus played an important part in the history of medicine (E. Gr. Ph.² p. 322). If medicine is a true science, its objects must be real like those of geometry.

d 13 καὶ τῶν ἄλλων κτλ. The construction is καὶ ἑνὶ λόγῳ περὶ τῆς οὐσίας τῶν ἄλλων ἁπάντων, i. e. τῶν ἄλλων ἁπάντων is governed by οὐσίας, which is governed by περί understood. Tr. 'And, to sum up, I am speaking of the reality of all the rest, i. e. of what each of them really is'.

ἑνὶ λόγῳ: this phrase is not quite accurately rendered by 'in one word'; for λόγος does not mean 'a word', nor is there any Greek word for 'a word'. A λόγος is always a statement, and in the great majority of cases consists of several 'words'.

τῆς οὐσίας, 'the reality.' In this sense the term οὐσία was not familiar at Athens (where it meant 'property', 'estate'), and it is explained by ὃ τυγχάνει ἕκαστον ὄν, 'what a given thing really is' (cp. *Meno* 72 b 1 μελίττης περὶ οὐσίας ὅτι ποτ' ἐστίν). It was not, however, invented by Socrates, and still less by Plato. In *Crat.* 401 c 3 we read ὃ ἡμεῖς " οὐσίαν " καλοῦμεν, εἰσὶν οἳ " ἐσσίαν " καλοῦσιν, οἱ δ' αὖ " ὡσίαν ", and we see from 401 d 3 that Socrates there means τὴν πάντων οὐσίαν, just as he does here. We could hardly be told more plainly that the term is Pythagorean. The fem. pcp. ἔσσα = οὖσα is genuine Doric, and ἐσσία is therefore a correct Doric form, while ὡσία, though only found now in pseudo-Pythagorean writings, may be justified by the Boeotian ἰῶσα.

e 3 αὐτὸ ἕκαστον, 'any given thing by itself,' generalizing αὐτὸ δίκαιον, αὐτὸ καλόν, αὐτὸ μέγεθος, &c. If we wish to know a thing, we must think 'just that', e. g. 'just the triangle', leaving out of account its material, colour, &c., and even its particular shape (equilateral, isosceles, or scalene).

e 6   καθαρώτατα, 'most cleanly.' To the mathematical mind irrelevancy suggests dirt. Later mathematicians speak of the 'elegance' of a demonstration in a similar sense.

e 7   αὐτῇ τῇ διανοίᾳ, 'with thought alone.'

    μήτε . . . παρατιθέμενος, 'without taking into account.' As τιθέναι is used of 'setting down' an item in an account, it is probable that παρατιθέναι is here equivalent to *apponere* (cp. Hor. *Carm.* i. 9. 15 *lucro appone*), though I can find no exact parallel. The middle, as often, would give the sense 'setting down to his own account'. If this is correct, we must understand τᾷ λογισμῷ from the context.

    τιν' ὄψιν: I have written τιν' for τήν as being more idiomatic, and because B has a superfluous τινά in the next line, which I take to be a correction of τήν added after the wrong μήτε.

a 1   ἐφέλκων, 'trailing after him.'

    αὐτῇ καθ' αὑτήν . . . αὐτὸ καθ' αὑτό: thought 'alone by itself' apprehends its object 'alone by itself'. Cp. 64 c 6 *n.*

a 2   εἰλικρινεῖ . . . εἰλικρινές: Cicero (*Off.* i. 4) translates *sincerum*, Tertullian (*de An.* 41) *germanum*. The etymology is uncertain, but the meaning is 'unmixed', 'unadulterated'. Valckenaer (quoted by Stallbaum) says : *proprie significat volvendo s. volubili agitatione secretum, atque adeo cribro purgatum,* and 'sifted clean' would certainly suit very well.

a 3   θηρεύειν: the favourite metaphor of Socrates. Cp. above 63 a 2 *n.*, and 66 c 2 τὴν τοῦ ὄντος θήραν, 115 b 9 ὥσπερ κατ' ἴχνη.

    τῶν ὄντων, 'things,' apparently, but at a 8 τοῦ ὄντος is 'the truth'.

b 1   ἐκ πάντων τούτων, as a conclusion from the three arguments just given.

    παρίστασθαι δόξαν, 'that a belief like this should be brought home to —.' Cp. 58 e 5 *n.*

b 2   γνησίως, 'genuinely,' much the same as ὀρθῶς (64 a 4 ; 67 e 4) and δικαίως (83 e 5).

b 3   ὥσπερ ἀτραπός [τις], 'it looks as if a sort of by-way', 'a short cut as it were'. The weight of evidence is slightly against the addition of τις (W omits it in the text, and adds it in the margin) ; but, whether it is added or not, the phrase is the subject of κινδυνεύει (cp. *Meno* 70 c 4 ὥσπερ αὐχμός τις, 'a sort of drought'), and there is no reason for inserting ὁ θάνατος after it with Tournier. Further, the short cut is not death—the γνησίως φιλόσοφοι know there is no thoroughfare that way—but the μελέτη θανάτου or philosophy itself. An ἀτραπός is properly a 'track' over hills or through woods (*semita, sentier*), which does not follow the turnings of the high road. The mountain-path taken by the Persians at Thermopylae is so called (Hdt. vii. 215, Thuc. iv. 36). There was a Pythagorean precept τὰς λεωφόρους μὴ βαδίζειν, 'not to walk on highways,' and Olympiodorus supposes a reference to this here. Though no doubt originally a mere taboo, it may quite possibly have received some such application as this by the end of the fifth century B. C. (E. Gr. Ph.² p. 105). The Pythagorean idea of the 'Way' (ὁδὸς βίου) would naturally suggest the idea of the Narrow Path.

b 4 ἐκφέρειν ἡμᾶς: as the metaphor of hunting dominates the whole passage (cp. 66 a 3 *n*. and c 2 τὴν τοῦ ὄντος θήραν), the meaning is really settled by Soph. *Ai.* 7 εὖ δέ σ' ἐκφέρει | κυνὸς Λακαίνης ὥς τις εὔρινος βάσις. 'The by-way brings us on to the trail in our hunt after truth.' It will be seen that the metaphor of the ἀτραπός gains very much when we bring it into close connexion with the hunt.

μετὰ τοῦ λόγου ἐν τῇ σκέψει: these words have been variously interpreted. There is no difficulty about ἐν τῇ σκέψει except that the phrase is superfluous. As to μετὰ τοῦ λόγου it must mean the same thing as μετὰ τοῦ λογισμοῦ above (66 a 1). Schleiermacher transposed the words, placing them after ἔχωμεν, where they make excellent sense; but, on the whole, it seems more likely that they are a marginal note on ἔχωμεν which has got into the wrong place.

b 5 ὅτι, 'because.'

συμπεφυρμένη : the word suggests the opposite of καθαρώτατα (65 e 6).

b 7 μυρίας ... ἀσχολίας, 'countless distractions.'

c 2 τοῦ ὄντος: i. e. τοῦ ἀληθοῦς (cp. b 7).

c 3 εἰδώλων, 'imaginations.'

c 4 τὸ λεγόμενον, 'as the saying is.' This must refer to the phrase οὐδὲ φρονῆσαι ἐγγίγνεται, 'we don't even get a chance of thinking for it.' We do not know what quotation or proverb Socrates refers to.

ὡς ἀληθῶς τῷ ὄντι, 'in very truth.' The two phrases are placed ἐκ παραλλήλου, as the grammarians say, and their effect is cumulative. Both (and in later dialogues ὄντως) are used to emphasize the

appositeness of quotations. We also find ἀτεχνῶς in the same sense. Cp. 90 c 4.

c 7 διὰ γὰρ κτλ. The same account of the origin of war is put into the mouth of Socrates in *Rep.* 373 e 6. The dialogue of the *Republic* is supposed to take place during the Peloponnesian War, and that of the *Phaedo* while the memory of it was still fresh, and it was clearly recognized, especially by opponents of the war like Aristophanes, that commercial interests had a great deal to do with it. (Cp. the *Acharnians* on the Megarian decree.)

d 3 τὸ δ' ἔσχατον, 'and the worst of all is that —.' Cp. τὸ δὲ μέγιστον ὅτι (followed also by γάρ).

d 5 παραπῖπτον, 'turning up,' when you least expect it. Cp. *Rep.* 561 b 3 τῇ παραπιπτούσῃ ἀεὶ (ἡδονῇ), *Laws* 832 b 6 τῷ παραπεπτωκότι λόγῳ.

e 1 αὐτὰ τὰ πράγματα, 'things by themselves', 'just the things themselves'. There is no distinction between πράγματα and ὄντα.

e 3 φρονήσεως is assimilated in case to the preceding relative (Riddell, Dig. § 192). The phrase φρονήσεως ἐρασταί is an explication of the name φιλόσοφοι.

e 4 ὡς ὁ λόγος σημαίνει, 'as the argument signifies.' This is the only rendering which will suit all the passages where this phrase occurs, so we must not think of the ἱερὸς λόγος here.

e 5 δυοῖν θάτερον : the regular way of introducing a dilemma.

a 4 ὅτι μὴ πᾶσα ἀνάγκη : cp. 64 e 1 καθ' ὅσον μὴ πολλὴ ἀνάγκη μετέχειν αὐτῶν, 83 a 6 ὅσον μὴ ἀνάγκη αὐτοῖς χρῆσθαι.

a 5 μηδὲ ἀναπιμπλώμεθα, 'nor suffer the contagion of.' Cp. Thuc. ii. 51 (in the description of the Plague) ἕτερος ἀφ' ἑτέρου θεραπείας ἀναπιμπλάμενοι ('one catching the infection from tending another') ὥσπερ πρόβατα ἔθνῃσκον. So also 83 d 10 τοῦ σώματος ἀναπλέα.

a 8 μετὰ τοιούτων : sc. καθαρῶν (Riddell, Dig. § 54). Some suppose this to be neuter and refer it to αὐτὰ τὰ πράγματα or ὄντα, but it is far better to take it of the 'great company' of which Socrates speaks above (63 b 8). The καθαροί are in Orphic language 'the saints'.

δι' ἡμῶν αὐτῶν : no longer 'through a glass darkly'.

b 1 τοῦτο δ' ἐστὶν ἴσως τὸ ἀληθές, 'and that, I take it, is the truth.' Cp. 66 b 7 φαμὲν δὲ τοῦτο εἶναι τὸ ἀληθές. No real doubt is expressed by ἴσως. Cp. *opinor*.

b 2 μὴ οὐ . . . ᾖ, 'I fear it is not.' For this characteristically

Platonic idiom (he has it thirty-five times) see Goodwin, *M. T.*, § 265.

b 4 τοὺς ὀρθῶς φιλομαθεῖς, equivalent to τοὺς γνησίως φιλοσόφους (cp. 66 b 2) ; for φιλομαθής is freely used as an equivalent of φιλόσοφος, and ὀρθῶς refers to the ὀρθότης ὀνομάτων. It means those who are φιλόσοφοι ' in the true sense of the word ', those who ' have a right to the name '. So in 82 c 2 οἱ ὀρθῶς φιλόσοφοι are the same as οἱ δικαίως φιλομαθεῖς 83 e 5. For this sense of ὀρθῶς cp. Eur. *Alc.* 636 οὐκ ἦσθ᾽ ἄρ᾽ ὀρθῶς τοῦδε σώματος πατήρ; *Hipp.* 1169 ὡς ἄρ᾽ ἦσθ᾽ ἡμὸς πατὴρ | ὀρθῶς, *Androm.* 376 οἵτινες φίλοι | ὀρθῶς πεφύκασ(ι).

b 8 ἐλπὶς . . . κτήσασθαι : the aor. inf. is preferred after ἐλπίς ἐστιν (cp. 68 a 1 ἐλπίς ἐστιν . . . τυχεῖν).

b 10 πραγματεία : cp. 64 e 4.

ἡμῖν : i. e. the Socratic circle.

c 2 ἄλλῳ ἀνδρί, ' for any one else,' a more emphatic ἄλλῳ τινί.

c 5 Κάθαρσις : this is the central idea of Orphicism (cp. 61 a 3 *n.*). The Pythagoreans seem to have added the practice of κάθαρσις by science to the original κάθαρσις by abstinence and the like (E. Gr. Ph.² p. 107).

τοῦτο is the predicate, and is used *praeparative*. Cp. 62 a 2 *n.*

συμβαίνει is here personal. For the other construction cp. 74 a 2.

ὅπερ πάλαι . . . λέγεται : this has not been said in the course of the present argument, and must, I think, be understood in the light of 63 c 6 ὥσπερ . . . πάλαι λέγεται and the παλαιὸς λόγος of 70 c 5. Cp. also 69 c 5 πάλαι αἰνίττεσθαι. It seems to be the regular way of referring to the Orphic ἱερὸς λόγος, ' as is said by those of old in the Word ' (cp. E. Gr. Ph.² p. 146, *n.* 3).

c 6 τὸ χωρίζειν κτλ. As Wohlrab justly remarked, this is to be understood in the light of the account given in *Symp.* 174 c and 220 c of Socrates standing still and silent for hours at a time. The religious term for this was ἔκστασις, ' stepping outside ' the body.

d 1 μόνην καθ᾽ αὑτήν : syn. αὐτὴν καθ᾽ αὑτήν. Cp. 64 c 6 *n.*

ὥσπερ [ἐκ] δεσμῶν κτλ. There is considerable uncertainty about the reading. The commonest idiom is ὥσπερ ἐκ δεσμῶν τοῦ σώματος, but sometimes the preposition is repeated (cp. 82 e 3 ; 115 b 9). In *Tim.* 79 a 3 we have ὥσπερ αὐλῶνος διὰ τοῦ σώματος.

d 8 ὀρθῶς : cp. 67 b 4 *n.*

e 3 Γελοῖον· πῶς δ' οὔ ; The MSS. have οὐ γελοῖον ; and give the words to Socrates, but we should then expect ἢ οὐ γελοῖον ; The Petrie papyrus has only room for seven letters, so I have deleted οὐ and given γελοῖον to Simmias.

e 6 εἰ . . . διαβέβληνται, 'if they are at variance with', 'estranged from' the body. The original sense of διαβάλλειν is 'to set at variance', εἰς ἔχθραν καθιστάναι.

e 8 εἰ φοβοῖντο : T omits εἰ, but its repetition is natural in a binary protasis like this, especially as there is a change of mood, and εἰ has a slightly different meaning in the two clauses.

e 9 εἰ μὴ . . . ἴοιειν : this simply repeats εἰ φοβοῖντο in a negative form (a b a). Cp. *Apol.* 20 c σοῦ γε οὐδὲν τῶν ἄλλων περιττότερον πραγματευομένου . . . εἰ μή τι ἔπραττες ἀλλοῖον ἢ οἱ πολλοί.

a 3 ἢ ἀνθρωπίνων μὲν κτλ. A good instance of the disjunctive question, in which two statements are bound together in a single interrogation to signify that they cannot or should not both be true at once. In such questions ἆρα (a 7) is regular in the second clause. We must subordinate the first to the second ('Can it be that, whereas . . . ?') or use two sentences. In *Symp.* 179 b sqq. Alcestis, Eurydice, and Patroclus are given as examples of 'human loves' whom men have gone to seek beyond the grave. Such loves are contrasted with the 'divine beloved' of which Socrates speaks in the *Gorgias* (482 a 4 φιλοσοφίαν, τὰ ἐμὰ παιδικά).

a 5 μετελθεῖν, 'to go in quest of.' The MS. authority is in favour of ἐλθεῖν, but the μετελθεῖν of T is too good for a mere error.

a 7 φρονήσεως . . . ἐρῶν : syn. φιλόσοφος. Cp. 66 e 3 *n.*

b 2 οἴεσθαί γε χρή, 'I should think so ! '

b 4 μηδαμοῦ ἄλλοθι κτλ. It is noteworthy that the reading which the original scribe (B, not B²) has added in the margin (with the monogram for γράφεται) is that of the Petrie papyrus, which was written within a hundred years of Plato's death. This shows how old some of those variants are.

b 5 ὅπερ ἄρτι ἔλεγον, sc. 67 e 9. The antecedent to the relative is the following question.

b 7 μέντοι νὴ Δία : cp. 65 d 6 *n.*

b 8 τοῦτο is used *praeparative* (cp. 62 a 2 *n.*) and refers to the relative clause ὃν ἂν ἴδῃς κτλ. This construction is as old as Homer (*Il.* xiv. 81 βέλτερον ὃς φεύγων προφύγῃ κακὸν ἠὲ ἁλώῃ). Cp. Thuc. vi

14 τὸ καλῶς ἄρξαι τοῦτ' εἶναι ὃς ἂν τὴν πατρίδα ὠφελήσῃ, Xen. *Oec.* 4. 19 ἐγὼ δὲ τοῦτο ἡγοῦμαι μέγα τεκμήριον ἄρχοντος ἀρετῆς εἶναι, ᾧ ἂν ἑκόντες ἔπωνται.

b 9   οὐκ ἄρ' ἦν: the use of the imperfect of something just realized was first explained by Heindorf in his note on this passage. With this imperfect ἄρα represents our 'So!' of surprise. 'So he isn't a philosopher after all!'

c 2   φιλοχρήματος καὶ φιλότιμος: the tripartite division of the soul which plays so great a part in the *Republic* is here implied; for χρήματα are the object of ἐπιθυμία and τιμή of θυμός. We find φιλοχρήματος as a synonym of ἐπιθυμητικός in *Rep.* 436 a 1; 549 b 2; 580 e 2 ἐπιθυμητικὸν γὰρ αὐτὸ κεκλήκαμεν . . . καὶ φιλοχρήματον δή, ὅτι διὰ χρημάτων μάλιστα ἀποτελοῦνται αἱ τοιαῦται ἐπιθυμίαι, 581 a 5 τοῦτο τῆς ψυχῆς τὸ μέρος . . . καλοῦντες φιλοχρήματον καὶ φιλοκερδὲς ὀρθῶς ἂν καλοῖμεν. So φιλότιμος is a regular synonym of θυμοειδής, e. g. 551 a 7 ἀντὶ δὴ φιλονίκων καὶ φιλοτίμων ἀνδρῶν φιλοχρηματισταὶ καὶ φιλοχρήματοι τελευτῶντες ἐγένοντο. This somewhat primitive psychology is doubtless older than Socrates; for it stands in close relation to the Pythagorean doctrine of the 'Three Lives' (E. Gr. Ph.[2] pp. 108, 109, *n.* 1). To Plato the soul is really one and indivisible, in spite of the use he makes of the older view. Cp. Galen, *de Hipp. et Plat.*, p. 425 ὡς καὶ ὁ Ποσειδώνιός φησιν ἐκείνου (Πυθαγόρου) πρώτου μὲν εἶναι λέγων τὸ δόγμα, Πλάτωνα δὲ ἐξεργάσασθαι καὶ κατασκευάσαι τελεώτερον αὐτό, *ib.* 478 Ποσειδώνιος δὲ καὶ Πυθαγόραν φησίν, αὐτοῦ μὲν τοῦ Πυθαγόρου συγγράμματος οὐδενὸς εἰς ἡμᾶς διασῳζομένου, τεκμαιρόμενος δὲ ἐξ ὧν ἔνιοι τῶν μαθητῶν αὐτοῦ γεγράφασιν. Iamblichus, ap. Stob. *Ecl.* i, p. 369 (Wachsmuth) Οἱ δὲ περὶ Πλάτωνα καὶ Ἀρχύτας καὶ οἱ λοιποὶ Πυθαγόρειοι τὴν ψυχὴν τριμερῆ ἀποφαίνονται, διαιροῦντες εἰς λογισμὸν καὶ θυμὸν καὶ ἐπιθυμίαν. Posidonius is not likely to have been mistaken on such a point.

τὰ ἕτερα . . . ἀμφότερα: for the plural pronouns referring to a single fact see Riddell, *Dig.* § 42.

c 5   καὶ ἡ ὀνομαζομένη: this is more clearly expressed at c 8 ἦν καὶ οἱ πολλοὶ ὀνομάζουσι.

c 6   τοῖς οὕτω διακειμένοις: this is made more explicit below, c 11.

c 8   Οὐκοῦν is repeated by c 10 ἆρ' οὔ.

ἦν καὶ οἱ πολλοὶ κτλ. This is best explained by *Laws* 710 a 5 τὴν δημώδη γε (σωφροσύνην) . . . καὶ οὐχ ἥν τις σεμνύνων ἂν λέγοι, φρόνησιν προσαναγκάζων εἶναι τὸ σωφρονεῖν. We are not speaking here of courage and σωφροσύνη in the high Socratic sense in which they are identical with knowledge.

c 9 ἐπτοῆσθαι, 'to be excited.' This verb suggests primarily the quickened heartbeat of fear or desire. Cp. Hom. *Od.* xxii. 298 φρένες ἐπτοίηθεν, Sappho 2. 6 τό μοι μὰν | καρδίαν ἐν στήθεσιν ἐπτόασεν.

11 ἐν φιλοσοφίᾳ ζῶσιν : Philosophy is a life. Cp. *Theaet.* 174 b 1 ἐν φιλοσοφίᾳ διάγουσι and 61 a 3 *n.*

d 2 εἰ . . . ἐθέλεις, 'if you care.' Cp. *Prot.* 324 a 3; 342 d 6. *Meno* 71 a 1.

d 6 τῶν μεγάλων κακῶν : it is unnecessary to add εἶναι to the partitive genitive, but there was evidently an ancient variant τῶν μεγίστων κακῶν εἶναι which is hardly consistent with μειζόνων κακῶν just below, by which phrase such things as dishonour and slavery are intended.

d 9 ὅταν ὑπομένωσιν: the addition of such phrases is almost a mannerism. There is no emphasis, and the meaning is merely ἑκάστοτε, ὅταν τύχῃ, 'on occasion.' Cp. *Euthyphro* 7 d 4 ἐχθροὶ ἀλλήλοις γιγνόμεθα, ὅταν γιγνώμεθα.

12 ἄλογον : cp. 62 b 2 *n.*

e 2 οἱ κόσμιοι : syn. οἱ σώφρονες. Cp. 83 e 6. Attic tends to substitute less emphatic words for adjectives implying praise. So ἀγαθός is represented by σπουδαῖος, ἐπιεικής, χρηστός, μέτριος, and σοφός by χαρίεις, κομψός, &c. There is the same tendency in English; cp. 'decent', 'respectable' as substitutes for 'good'.

e 3 ἀκολασίᾳ τινὶ κτλ., 'it is immorality that makes them moral.' The appositive structure is regular after τοῦτο πάσχειν. Cp. below 73 d 7 (Riddell, Dig. § 207). The regular opposite of σωφροσύνη (the virtue of moral sanity, for which English has no name) is ἀκολασία. The literal meaning of ἀκόλαστος is 'unchastened'.

καίτοι φαμέν γε . . . ἀλλ' ὅμως . . ., 'we say, indeed . . . but yet . . .' For this combination of particles, which marks a concession afterwards partially retracted, cp. below e 7 and *Euthyphro* 3 c 2 καίτοι οὐδὲν ὅτι οὐκ ἀληθὲς εἴρηκα ὧν προεῖπον, ἀλλ' ὅμως . . .

e 4 συμβαίνει . . . ὅμοιον, 'turns out in their case to be like this.' TW add εἶναι, but cp. *Gorg.* 479 c 8 συμβαίνει μέγιστον κακὸν ἡ ἀδικία.

τὸ πάθος τὸ περὶ κτλ., 'the condition of —' (περί, *c. acc.* as a genitive equivalent).

e 5 ταύτην, *istam.*

εὐήθη, 'naive', 'unsophisticated', 'artless'. The Petrie papyrus reads ἀνδραποδώδη, but that seems to be an anticipatory recollection of 69 b 8.

69 a 6 μὴ ... οὐχ αὕτη ᾖ, 'perhaps this is not —.' Cp. 67 b 2 *n.*

πρὸς ἀρετήν, 'judged by the standard of goodness.' Cp. Isocr. 4. 76 οὐδὲ πρὸς ἀργύριον τὴν εὐδαιμονίαν ἔκρινον (Riddell, Dig. § 128). We can hardly give πρός the same sense as in the next line ; for there is no question of exchanging pleasures and pains for goodness. Goodness is the standard of value, and wisdom (φρόνησις) is the only currency in which it can be rightly estimated. Nor can πρός mean 'towards', 'in the direction of'. That interpretation is a survival from the time of the vulgate text, which omitted ἀλλαγή and had to be understood as ἡ ὀρθὴ πρὸς ἀρετήν (sc. ὁδός). The disappearance of ἀλλαγή from the text is an interesting study in corruption. B has ἀλλά, and T must have had the same ; for it presents us with an erasure of four letters. The vulgate text came from a copy of T. W and Iamblichus preserve the word.

a 7 πρὸς ἡδονάς, 'for pleasures,' *contra voluptates.*

a 8 μείζω πρὸς ἐλάττω, i. e. greater pains and fears for less, and lesser pleasures for greater, e. g. the fear of slavery for the fear of death, the pleasures of the table for the pleasures of health.

a 9 ἀλλ' ᾖ, i. e. ἀλλὰ μὴ ᾖ, the construction being carried on from a 6. Pleasures and pains are to be exchanged for wisdom, which alone makes goodness truly good. If we give up the pleasures of the table, not merely to enjoy the pleasures of health, but because they stand in the way of the acquisition of wisdom, we may be said to exchange them for wisdom, and that is true σωφροσύνη. So, if we only face death to escape slavery, that is mere popular courage. To put the thing in a modern way, this is a sort of ethical mono-metallism, wisdom being the gold standard of value.

b 1 καὶ τούτου μὲν πάντα κτλ. I think it certain that this sentence is interpolated. The words τούτου μὲν πάντα clearly belong to ὠνούμενά τε καὶ πιπρασκόμενα, and their meaning must be ' all things bought and sold for wisdom ', but it is hardly credible that Plato should use ὠνούμενα as a passive, or that he should use πιπρασκόμενα at all. For ὠνεῖσθαι in a passive sense, the grammars can only quote Xen. *Eq.* 8. 2 ὅτε μὲν γὰρ ἐωνεῖτο, πειρᾶσθαι ἐκελεύομεν εἰ δύναιτο

ὁ ἵππος ταῦτα ποιεῖν, but there it is clearly active, 'at the time he
was buying it.' As to πιπρασκόμενα, Cobet's remark is true : *Neque
Iones neque Attici ea forma utuntur, sed apud sequiores protrita
est (Nov. Lect.* p. 158). It occurs only in one other place (*Soph.*
224 a 3), where also it seems to be interpolated. I believe, then,
that τούτου μὲν πάντα ὠνούμενα καὶ πιπρασκόμενα is a scholium on
καὶ μετὰ τούτου. The interpretation is wrong, as Wyttenbach saw;
for we are not supposed to buy and sell goodness for wisdom, but to
buy wisdom with pleasures, &c. If we take the sentence thus, the
simile does not break down, as Geddes and Archer-Hind say
it does.

b 1 μετὰ τούτου τῷ ὄντι ᾖ, 'when accompanied by this (i.e. wisdom)
our goodness really is goodness.' The words μετὰ τούτου are explained by b 4 μετὰ φρονήσεως and opposed to b 6 χωριζόμενα δὲ
φρονήσεως. I should like to read μετὰ μὲν τούτου. If I am right
about the interpolation, it implies this reading.

b 2 καὶ ἀνδρεία κτλ. In the *Protagoras* Socrates shows that true
courage only belongs to those who are θαρραλέοι μετ' ἐπιστήμης.
This is the way in which he interpreted the doctrine, which was
common to him and to the 'Sophists', that Goodness is Knowledge.
The distinction between 'philosophic' and 'popular' goodness
came to be of great importance. Cp. my edition of Aristotle's
Ethics, pp. 65 sqq. (where, however, I have ascribed to Plato what
I now see belongs to Socrates).

b 4 καὶ προσγιγνομένων καὶ ἀπογιγνομένων, 'whether they be added or
not.' The verbs are virtual passives of προστιθέναι and ἀφαιρεῖν,
'to add' and 'to subtract'. Cp. προσεῖναι, προσκεῖσθαι.

b 5 χωριζόμενα δὲ κτλ. As the participle agrees with πάντα ταῦτα
(b 1), i.e. pleasures, pains, &c., there is a slight anacoluthia in
μὴ ... ᾖ ἡ τοιαύτη ἀρετή. Socrates means 'the goodness which
depends upon the exchange of fears, pleasures, &c., for one another
apart from wisdom'.

b 6 [καὶ] ἀλλαττόμενα: as καί is omitted in B, it is probably an interpolation arising from failure to see that χωριζόμενα is dependent on
ἀλλαττόμενα (cp. 61 b 2 n.). The meaning will then be 'exchanged
for one another apart from wisdom' (opp. μετὰ τούτου).

σκιαγραφία τις, 'a sort of scene-painting' (Cope). Cp. Photius
σκιαγράφος ὁ νῦν σκηνογράφος. The term does not mean 'a rough

sketch', but implies the use of painted shadows to produce the impression of solid relief on a flat surface. This art has two chief characteristics: (1) it is deceptive, cp. *Critias* 107 d 1 σκιαγραφίᾳ ... ἀσαφεῖ καὶ ἀπατηλῷ, (2) it only produces its effect from a distance. Cp. *Theaet.* 208 e 7 ἐπειδὴ ἐγγὺς ὥσπερ σκιαγραφήματος γέγονα τοῦ λεγομένου, συνίημι οὐδὲ σμικρόν· ἕως δὲ ἀφειστήκη πόρρωθεν, ἐφαίνετό τί μοι λέγεσθαι. The most instructive passage is *Rep.* 365 c 3 πρόθυρα μὲν καὶ σχῆμα κύκλῳ περὶ ἐμαυτὸν σκιαγραφίαν ἀρετῆς περιγραπτέον, where the idea is that of a 'painted *façade*', on which columns, &c., are made to appear solid by skilful shading. Cp. also *Rep.* 583 b 5 and *Parm.* 165 c 7. When Aristotle (*Rhet.* 1414 a 8) compares the diction of the public speaker (δημηγορικὴ λέξις) to σκιαγραφία, he does not mean that it is 'sketchy', but that it requires the light and shade to be 'laid on thick'.

b 7 ἀνδραποδώδης: so in *Rep.* 430 b 7 Socrates opposes true courage to τὴν ... θηριώδη καὶ ἀνδραποδώδη, and in *Phaedr.* 258 e 5 he says of bodily pleasures δικαίως ἀνδραποδώδεις κέκληνται, just because they imply preceding pain (τὸ προλυπηθῆναι).

b 8 οὐδὲν ὑγιὲς ... ἔχῃ, 'has nothing sound about it.' The word ὑγιής is used of earthen or metal vessels which have no crack or flaw (opp. σαθρός). The old variant ἔχουσα for ἔχῃ gives a smoother construction, but we may easily understand ᾗ after τε in b 8. See Vahlen, *Opusc.* ii. 361.

τὸ δ' ἀληθές, 'the real thing', of which the σκιαγραφία gives a deceptive appearance.

c 1 κάθαρσις, 'purgation.' Cp. 61 a 3 *n.* In Xen. *Symp.* I. 4 Callias son of Hipponicus uses the phrase ἀνδράσιν ἐκκεκαθαρμένοις τὰς ψυχὰς ὥσπερ ὑμῖν in addressing Socrates, Critobulus, Hermogenes, Antisthenes, and Charmides. He seems to have heard something of Socrates' teaching on this point, unless he is merely drawing on the *Phaedo*.

c 2 καθαρμός: this is the specifically religious term for the initiatory ceremony of 'purgation'. The religious poem of Empedocles was entitled καθαρμοί (E. Gr. Ph.[2] pp. 256 sqq.).

c 3 τὰς τελετάς: the mystic 'initiations'. The context shows that the people referred to are the Ὀρφεοτελεσταί.

c 4 οὗτοι, *isti.* The touch of ironical condescension is characteristically Socratic (cp. 62 b 5 *n.*). It is plain that Socrates did not think much of the actual 'Ορφεοτελεσταί of his time, who are described in the *Republic* (364 e 3 sqq.) in terms which suggest the itinerant friars, pardoners, and traffickers in indulgences of the later Middle Ages.

c 4 καταστήσαντες : cp. Eur. *Bacch.* 21 κἀκεῖ χορεύσας καὶ καταστήσας ἐμὰς | τελετάς.

c 5 αἰνίττεσθαι, 'to speak in riddles' (αἰνίγματα). The word is regularly used of allegorical statements. It comes from Ion. αἶνος, 'fable', 'riddle' (cp. 61 b 4 *n.*). For πάλαι cp. 67 c 5 *n.*

c 6 ἐν βορβόρῳ κείσεται, 'will lie in the Slough.' Cp. *Rep.* 363 d 5 (of the Orpheotelestae) τοὺς δὲ ἀνοσίους αὖ καὶ ἀδίκους εἰς πηλόν τινα κατορύττουσιν ἐν ᾍδου. The βόρβορος is also referred to in Ar. *Frogs* 145 εἶτα βόρβορον πολὺν | καὶ σκῶρ ἀείνων· ἐν δὲ τούτῳ κειμένους | εἴ που ξένον τις ἠδίκησε κτλ., and Olympiodorus is doubtless right in saying παρῳδεῖ ἔπος Ὀρφικόν. Heindorf quotes a saying of the Cynic Diogenes (Diog. Laert. vi. 39) γελοῖον εἰ Ἀγησίλαος μὲν καὶ Ἐπαμεινώνδας ἐν τῷ βορβόρῳ διάξουσιν, εὐτελεῖς δέ τινες μεμνημένοι ἐν ταῖς μακάρων νήσοις ἔσονται. We must interpret *Rep.* 533 d 1 τῷ ὄντι ἐν βορβόρῳ βαρβαρικῷ τινι τὸ τῆς ψυχῆς ὄμμα κατορωρυγμένον in the light of this.

c 8 ναρθηκοφόροι μὲν πολλοί : Plato often adapts the beginning of a verse to his own prose, preferring to slip into the verse rather than give a formal quotation. The original must have been πολλοὶ μὲν ναρθηκοφόροι. The νάρθηξ (*ferula communis*) was the plant of which the Dionysiac *thyrsus* was made.

d 1 βάκχοι : the true worshippers were so called (cp. the Βάκχαι of Euripides). Schol. Ar. *Knights* 406 Βάκχον οὐ τὸν Διόνυσον ἐκάλουν μόνον, ἀλλὰ καὶ πάντας τοὺς τελοῦντας τὰ ὄργια. See Farnell, *Cults of the Greek States*, vol. v, p. 151.

d 2 ὀρθῶς, 'in the true sense of the word.' Cp. 67 b 4 *n.*

ὧν . . . γενέσθαι, 'to become one of whom', 'to join whose number'.

d 3 οὐδὲν ἀπέλιπον, 'I have left nothing undone.' The phrase states negatively what is positively stated by παντὶ τρόπῳ προυθυμήθην (cp. *Meno* 77 a 3 προθυμίας οὐδὲν ἀπολείψω), 'I have done my best in every way.'

d 5 καί τι ἠνύσαμεν : i. e. 'I and the rest of the band'. The shift from singular to plural is quite natural. To read ἠνυσάμην with Heindorf would make the plurals which follow (ἐλθόντες ... εἰσόμεθα) very awkward.

d 5   τὸ σαφές, 'for certain.'   Cp. **57** b 1 *n.*

d 7   ταῦτ' ... ἀπολογοῦμαι ὡς ..., 'this is the defence I make to show that —.'   Cp. **63** e 8.

d 8   τοὺς ἐνθάδε δεσπότας : cp. **62** e 1 ; **63** a 6 sqq.

e 1   κἀκεῖ : cp. **64** a 1 *n.*

e 3   τοῖς δὲ ... παρέχει : these words seem to have been interpolated here from **70** a 1. They break the sentence awkwardly and spoil the effect of the phrase when it comes in its proper place. Such things do not happen often in the text of Plato, but they happen sometimes.

(3) *Cebes points out that all this implies the immortality of the soul, and asks that this should be established* (**69** e 6—**70** c 3).

e 6   ὑπολαβών : cp. **60** c 8 *n.*

70 a 4   εὐθὺς ἀπαλλαττομένη κτλ.   Riddell (Dig. § 207) takes these words down to οὐδαμοῦ ᾖ as explanatory of the preceding clause ('binary structure'). I have punctuated after a 4 σώματος with Heindorf. Then καί will co-ordinate διαφθείρηται καὶ ἀπολλύηται with οἴχηται, and ἐκβαίνουσα will belong only to the second clause. It is easy to 'understand' σώματος with it.

a 5   ὥσπερ πνεῦμα ἢ καπνὸς διασκεδασθεῖσα : this is the belief assumed throughout the Homeric poems. The ψυχή is the 'ghost' which a man 'gives up', the breath which he 'expires' at death. For the καπνός cp. *Il.* xxiii. 100 ψυχὴ δὲ κατὰ χθονὸς ἠΰτε καπνὸς | ᾤχετο τετριγυῖα, a verse selected for special reprobation by Socrates in the *Republic* (**387** a 1).

a 6   οὐδὲν ἔτι οὐδαμοῦ ᾖ : Homer does not go so far as this ; for even in the House of Hades there is a ψυχὴ καὶ εἴδωλον. But it might just as well be nothing and nowhere ; for it is witless (ἀτὰρ φρένες οὐκ ἔνι πάμπαν, *Il.* xxiii. 104).

αὐτὴ καθ' αὑτὴν συνηθροισμένη : cp. **67** c 8.

b 2   παραμυθίας, 'persuasion', 'reassurance'. Cp. *Laws* **720** a 1 παραμυθίας ... καὶ πειθοῦς. The original sense of παραμυθεῖσθαι is 'to talk over' (cp. παράφημι, παρεῖπον, παραπείθω) as in **83** a 3. The meanings 'encourage', 'console', as in **115** d 5, are secondary.

πίστεως, 'proof,' not 'belief'.

b 3 ψυχή: there seems to be no rule for the addition or omission of the article with ψυχή. Where MSS. differ, the less commonplace use without the article is to be preferred.

δύναμιν ἔχει καὶ φρόνησιν: even Homer allows that souls 'are somewhere' after death, but Cebes wishes to be assured that they are not merely ἀμενηνὰ κάρηνα (this is the point of δύναμιν ἔχει), of whom it can be said φρένες οὐκ ἔνι πάμπαν. Here, then, φρόνησις is not equivalent to σοφία, but is used in its popular sense, answering to the Homeric φρένες.

b 5 'Αληθῆ, ἔφη, λέγεις, ὁ Σωκράτης: for the interlaced order (a b a b) cp. 77 c 1; 78 a 10; 78 c 5; 82 c 9; 83 e 4 (Riddell, Dig. § 288).

b 6 διαμυθολογῶμεν: cp. μυθολογεῖν, 61 e 2 n. The word is specially appropriate as introducing εἴτε εἰκὸς κτλ.

c 1 κωμῳδοποιός: Aristophanes was not the only comic poet who made fun of Socrates. Eupolis said (fr. 352) Μισῶ δὲ καὶ ⟨τὸν⟩ Σωκράτη, τὸν πτωχὸν ἀδολέσχην, | ὃς τἆλλα μὲν πεφρόντικεν, | ὁπόθεν δὲ καταφαγεῖν ἔχοι τούτου κατημέληκεν, a fragment preserved by Olympiodorus in his commentary on this passage. The charge of ἀδολεσχία ('garrulity') was commonly brought against all men of science by the practical Athenians and the comic poets who wrote to please them.

οὐ περὶ προσηκόντων, 'about things which do not concern me', 'things I have nothing to do with'. For the position of the preposition see Riddell, Dig. § 298 and cp. 110 c 2.

First Proof of Immortality (70 c 4—77 d 5).

This proof is based upon two considerations (1) the doctrine of παλιγγενεσία, (2) the doctrine of ἀνάμνησις. Neither of these taken by itself furnishes a proof, though taken together they may be said to do so (77 c 7).

With regard to the proofs of immortality, it should be observed that the first two are successively abandoned as inadequate, while even the third is said to require further examination (107 b 5). The proof which satisfied Plato himself is not one of them (cp. 94 b 4 n.). Nevertheless each contributes something to our knowledge of the subject.

(1) *The ancient doctrine of* παλιγγενεσία *is shown to rest on the law of* ἀνταπόδοσις (70 c 4—72 e 1).

c 4   αὐτό, 'the matter.'

c 5   παλαιὸς ... λόγος: cp. the way in which the same Orphic doctrine is introduced in *Meno* 81 a 5 ἀκήκοα γὰρ ἀνδρῶν τε καὶ γυναικῶν σοφῶν περὶ τὰ θεῖα πράγματα ... a 10 Οἱ μὲν λέγοντές εἰσι τῶν ἱερέων τε καὶ τῶν ἱερειῶν ὅσοις μεμέληκε περὶ ὧν μεταχειρίζονται λόγον οἵοις τ᾽ εἶναι διδόναι· λέγει δὲ καὶ Πίνδαρος καὶ ἄλλοι πολλοὶ τῶν ποιητῶν ὅσοι θεῖοί εἰσιν. ἃ δὲ λέγουσιν, ταυτί ἐστιν· ... φασὶ γὰρ τὴν ψυχὴν τοῦ ἀνθρώπου εἶναι ἀθάνατον, καὶ τοτὲ μὲν τελευτᾶν—ὃ δὴ ἀποθνήσκειν καλοῦσι—τοτὲ δὲ πάλιν γίγνεσθαι, ἀπόλλυσθαι δ᾽ οὐδέποτε. So *Epist.* vii. 335 a 2 πείθεσθαι δὲ ὄντως ἀεὶ χρὴ τοῖς παλαιοῖς τε καὶ ἱεροῖς λόγοις, οἳ δὴ μηνύουσιν ἡμῖν ἀθάνατον ψυχὴν εἶναι κτλ. For παλαιὸς cp. 67 c 5 *n.* Herodotus (ii. 123) is mistaken in assigning an Egyptian origin to this doctrine (E. Gr. Ph.² p. 95).

c 6   ὡς εἰσὶν ἐνθένδε ἀφικόμεναι ἐκεῖ, 'that they are in the other world, having come there from this.' There is no parallel to justify us in taking εἰσὶν ἀφικόμεναι together as if it were εἰσὶν ἀφιγμέναι. Note the interlaced order (*a b a b*).

c 8   πάλιν γίγνεσθαι: the regular name for this doctrine in later writers is παλιγγενεσία. The word μετεμψύχωσις, though it has found its way into all modern languages, is quite inaccurate, and is not used before Graeco-Roman times, and then very seldom (Diodorus, Galen). Cp. Servius on *Aen.* iii. 68 *non* μετεμψύχωσιν *sed* παλιγγενεσίαν *esse dicit* (*Pythagoras*). Hippolytus, Clement, and other Christian writers say μετενσωμάτωσις ('reincarnation'), which is accurate but cumbrous.

d 2   τοῦ ταῦτ᾽ εἶναι, 'of the truth of this.' For the neuter plural cp. Riddell, Dig. § 41.

d 7   κατ᾽ ἀνθρώπων: cp. *Meno* 76 a 5 κατὰ γὰρ παντὸς σχήματος τοῦτο λέγω (Riddell, Dig. § 121). Originally κατά, *c. gen.*, is quite neutral in meaning, especially in the phrase κατὰ πάντων (Isocr. 15. 189 ταῦτα ... κατὰ πασῶν λέγομεν τῶν τεχνῶν). From this use comes the Aristotelian κατηγορεῖν τι κατά τινος, 'to predicate something of anything,' and κατὰ ὅλου (*Meno* 77 a 6), καθ᾽ ὅλου, καθόλου.

e 1   ἆρ᾽: indirect questions are not infrequently introduced by ἆρα.

Cp. *Lach*. 185 d 9 σκοπεῖν ἄρα .. ., *Meno* 93 b 2 τόδε σκοποῦμεν, ἄρα .. ., *Rep*. 526 c 9 σκεψώμεθα ἄρα .. ., and just below e 4.

e 1 οὑτωσί: this is explained by οὐκ ἄλλοθεν κτλ. Cp. 71 a 9. Socrates generalizes the Orphic doctrine that the living are born from the dead, and treats it as a case of the principle, maintained by Heraclitus, of the generation of opposites from opposites (E. Gr. Ph.² p. 186).

e 2 ὅσοις τυγχάνει ὂν τοιοῦτόν τι, 'everything, that is, which has an opposite,' equivalent to e 5 ὅσοις ἔστι τι ἐναντίον.

e 3 καὶ ἄλλα δὴ μυρία κτλ. For this way of breaking off an enumeration cp. 73 d 10; 94 b 10 (Riddell, Dig. § 257).

e 5 ὅσοις... αὐτό: for the singular pronoun referring to the plural ὅσοις cp. 104 d 2 (αὐτοῦ referring to ἅ).

a 13 δύο γενέσεις: if opposites arise from one another, it follows that between every pair of opposites (μεταξὺ ἀμφοτέρων πάντων τῶν ἐναντίων) there must be two *processes* (γενέσεις), one by which A arises from B, another by which B arises from A.

b 3 αὔξησις καὶ φθίσις, 'increase and decrease.' We see from this passage that much attention had already been given to accuracy of terminology.

b 6 διακρίνεσθαι καὶ συγκρίνεσθαι, 'decomposing and combining.' These terms were used by the early natural philosophers to denote the analysis of compound bodies into their constituents, and the formation of compound bodies out of something more primitive, such as what were called at a later date *elements* (στοιχεῖα).

b 7 κἂν εἰ μὴ κτλ. The attempt to construct an accurate terminology in any language is sure to reveal gaps. In the *Ethics* Aristotle often has to say that the mean, or one or other of the extremes, is ἀνώνυμον. Cp. Bywater on *Poet*. 1447 b 9.

c 9 συζυγίαν, 'pair' (originally of oxen or horses). The word may be applied, however, to a larger number of things than two. In grammar it is a 'conjugation', i.e. a class of verbs similarly inflected.

ἐγώ σοι, ἔφη, ἐρῶ, ὁ Σωκράτης: for the interlaced order (*a b a b*) cp. 70 b 5 *n*.

e 4 τοῖν περὶ ταῦτα, i. e. τοῖν τούτων (περί *c. acc. = gen.*).

e 8 οὐκ ἀνταποδώσομεν; 'shall we not assign it an opposite process to balance it?'

e 9 χωλή, 'halt', 'lame in one foot'. Cp. the advice of Cimon μήτε τὴν Ἑλλάδα χωλήν, μήτε τὴν πόλιν ἑτερόζυγα περιιδεῖν γεγενημένην (Plut. *Cim.* 16).

e 13 ἀναβιώσκεσθαι, 'to come to life again.' Sometimes the verb is transitive, ' to bring to life again ' (e. g. *Crito* 48 c 5) ; but in that case the aorist is ἀναβιώσασθαι (not ἀναβιῶναι), as below 89 b 10.

72 a 6 ἐδόκει : 70 d 2.

a 11 ὅτι οὐδ' ἀδίκως κτλ., 'that we were not wrong either — '. Cp. 63 b 8 ἠδίκουν ἄν, 'I should be wrong.'

a 12 εἰ ... μὴ ... ἀνταποδιδοίη, 'unless there were a constant correspon‑ dence.' The verb is here intransitive, as below b 8. Cp. L. S. *s. v.* ἀποδίδωμι II.

b 1 κύκλῳ περιιόντα : the κύκλος τῆς γενέσεως is Orphic. It was just from the Wheel of Birth that redemption (λύσις) was sought by means of purgatory observances (καθαρμοί). On one of the gold plates from Thurii (E. Gr. Ph.[2] p. 88) the ransomed soul says κύκλου δ' ἐξέπταν βαρυπενθέος ἀργαλέοιο. Here, of course, the refer‑ ence is to cyclical processes generally, but that is characteristic of the way in which a scientific sense is given to religious ideas throughout the passage.

b 2 εὐθεῖά τις, 'in a straight line.' A rectilinear process is only in one direction, a circular has two.

b 3 καὶ μὴ ἀνακάμπτοι κτλ. The metaphor is taken from the δίαυλος, in which the runners turned round the καμπτήρ and came back to the starting-point (Dict. Ant. *s. v. Stadium*, ii. 693 b). Cp. Aesch. *Ag.* 344 κάμψαι διαύλου θάτερον κῶλον πάλιν.

b 9 τελευτῶντα . . . ἀποδείξειεν, ' would end by making Endymion seem a thing of naught (a ' bagatelle ') by comparison.' This use of ἀποδείκνυμι is fully illustrated in Wyttenbach's note. Cp. e. g. Plato, *Phaedr.* 278 c 6 λέγων αὐτὸς ... τὰ γεγραμμένα φαῦλα ἀποδεῖξαι, *Epist.* vii. 324 d 7 χρυσὸν ἀποδείξαντας τὴν ἔμπροσθεν πολιτείαν, 'making the previous constitution seem like gold by comparison.' Plut. *C. Gracch.* 1 ἀπέδειξε τοὺς ἄλλους ῥήτορας παίδων μηδὲν διαφέροντας, Plato, *Epist.* iv. 320 d 6 παρασκευάζου τόν τε Λυκοῦργον ἐκεῖνον ἀρχαῖον ἀποδείξων καὶ τὸν Κῦρον, ' to make them seem out of date by compari‑ son.' Wyttenbach shows too that λῆρος is regularly used in such comparisons. Cp. e. g. Arist. *Lys.* 860 λῆρός ἐστι τἆλλα πρὸς Κινη‑ σίαν, Antiphanes fr. 232 ἆρ' ἐστὶ λῆρος πάντα πρὸς τὸ χρυσίον; Xen

An. vii. 7. 41 Ἡρακλείδῃ λῆρος πάντα ἐδόκει εἶναι πρὸς τὸ ἀργύριον ἔχειν ἐκ παντὸς τρόπου. The meaning is not 'to make the story of Endymion appear an idle tale', as most editors say. On the contrary, it would be all the more credible.

c I οὐδαμοῦ ἂν φαίνοιτο, 'he (note change of subject) would be nowhere,' an expression taken, like its English equivalent, from the race-course. Cp. *Gorg.* 456 b 8 οὐδαμοῦ ἂν φανῆναι τὸν ἰατρόν, 'the doctor would come in nowhere.' Dem. *de Cor.* 310 ἐν οἷς οὐδαμοῦ σὺ φανήσῃ γεγονώς, οὐ πρῶτος, οὐ δεύτερος, οὐ τρίτος, οὐ τέταρτος, οὐ πέμπτος, οὐχ ἕκτος, οὐχ ὁποστοσοῦν.

c 3 καθεύδειν: just as τοῦτο πάσχει &c. are regularly followed by a clause in apposition (cp. **68 e 2 n.**), so τοῦτο πάσχειν (πεπονθέναι) is regularly followed by an infinitive in apposition. Cp. **73 b 7**; **74 a 6**; **78 c 2**. There is, therefore, no reason for deleting the word with Dobree.

c 4 τὸ τοῦ Ἀναξαγόρου: cp. Anaxagoras fr. **I** *ad init.* Ὁμοῦ πάντα χρήματα ἦν (E. Gr. Ph.² p. 299). There is a similar jesting use of the phrase in *Gorg.* 465 d 3 τὸ τοῦ Ἀναξαγόρου ἂν πολὺ ἦν ... ὁμοῦ ἂν πάντα χρήματα ἐφέρετο ἐν τῷ αὐτῷ.

d I ἐκ ... τῶν ἄλλων, i. e. from some other source than the dead who were once alive.

d 8 ἐκ τῶν τεθνεώτων κτλ. It is important to observe that in this passage οἱ τεθνεῶτες are simply souls existing in the other world. They are certainly not dead bodies. All through this argument γένεσις means the union of soul to body and θάνατος their separation.

e I καὶ ταῖς μέν γε κτλ. These words appear to repeat **63 c 6**, where the statement is in place.

(2) *The doctrine of* ἀνάμνησις *is shown to rest on the theory of Forms* (**72 e 3—77 a 5**).

e 3 ὑπολαβών: cp. **60 c 8 n.**

καὶ κατ' ἐκεῖνον ... e 6 καὶ κατὰ τοῦτον: the καί means 'as well as' according to the παλαιὸς λόγος of **70 c 5**.

e 4 ὃν σὺ εἴωθας θαμὰ λέγειν: it is surely very difficult to regard this definite statement as a fiction. The doctrine is also ascribed to Socrates in the *Meno* and the *Phaedrus*. It is to be noted, further, that Cebes speaks of it as one peculiar to Socrates, while Simmias knows very little about it. It did not, therefore, belong to fifth-century Pythagoreanism, though there can be little doubt of its Orphic and Pythagorean origin. The legend of Pythagoras makes a point of his remembering his earlier incarnations, and Empedocles professed to remember his (E. Gr. Ph.² p. 259, *n.* 1). The apparent contradiction is to be explained as follows. The scientific Pythagoreans of the fifth century had to some extent dropped the religious doctrines of their founder (E. Gr. Ph.² pp. 319 sqq.), and their teaching was really inconsistent with a belief in the soul's immortality (E. Gr. Ph.² p. 343). The originality of Socrates seems to have consisted just in this, that he applied the old religious doctrine of ἀνάμνησις to science, and especially to mathematical science.

e 5 ὅτι ἡμῖν κτλ., 'that our learning is really nothing else than reminiscence,' i. e. that it is simply the process of being *reminded* of what we once knew. It is important to bear in mind that the process is one of *being reminded*, not merely one of *remembering* or *recollection*.

e 6 καὶ κατὰ τοῦτον repeats and emphasizes κατ᾽ ἐκεῖνον ... τὸν λόγον above (e 3).

e 7 ἃ νῦν ἀναμιμνησκόμεθα, 'what we are now reminded of.' Cp. *Meno* 81 c 7 οὐδὲν θαυμαστὸν ... οἷόν τ᾽ εἶναι αὐτὴν (sc. τὴν ψυχὴν) ἀναμνησθῆναι ἅ γε καὶ πρότερον ἠπίστατο, d 2 ἓν μόνον ἀναμνησθέντα—ὃ δὴ μάθησιν καλοῦσιν ἄνθρωποι—τἆλλα πάντα αὐτὸν ἀνευρεῖν.

73 a 1 πρὶν ... γενέσθαι, 'before entering into this human frame.' Here εἶδος is practically equivalent to σῶμα. Cp. 77 b 7 πρὶν καὶ εἰς ἀνθρώπειον σῶμα ἀφικέσθαι. So *Symp.* 210 b 2 τὸ ἐπ᾽ εἴδει καλόν, *Phaedr.* 249 a 8 ἀξίως οὗ ἐν ἀνθρώπου εἴδει ἐβίωσαν βίον, *Rep.* 402 d 1 ἔν τε τῇ ψυχῇ ... καὶ ἐν τῷ εἴδει.

a 7 ἑνὶ μὲν λόγῳ (sc. ἀποδείκνυται) ... a 10 ἔπειτα ... We regularly find ἔπειτα (usually without δέ) in the sense of 'secondly' after πρῶτον μὲν ... 'firstly'. This fixes the meaning of ἑνὶ λόγῳ here. It does not mean 'to sum up', as it does above 65 d 13, but 'by one argument'. I think Mr. R. G. Bury is right in holding (*Class. Rev.* xx, p. 13) that the process ἐπὶ τὰ διαγράμματα ἄγειν is opposed to, rather than included in, the process καλῶς ἐρωτᾶν, and I would illustrate his point further from *Theaet.* 165 a 1 ἡμεῖς δέ πως θᾶττον ἐκ τῶν ψιλῶν λόγων (arguments without diagrams) πρὸς τὴν γεωμετρίαι ἀπενεύσαμεν. I am also inclined to accept his reading πρῶτον for ἐνί, though it is not absolutely necessary. The use of α', β', γ' as numerals has certainly affected the reading in several passages of Plato. In any case this is better than altering ἔπειτα to ἐπεί τοι with Heindorf.

a 8 αὐτοί, 'of themselves.' Cp. 64 a 5.

a 10 ὀρθὸς λόγος, 'a right account of the matter.' An ὄνομα is ὀρθόν when applied to something which we are justified in applying it to (cp. 69 d 2 n.). In the same way a λόγος or statement is ὀρθός when it expresses the truth. The rendering 'right reason' is misleading; for it suggests that λόγος is a mental 'faculty'.

b 1 ἐπὶ τὰ διαγράμματα: this seems a fairly certain reference to *Meno* 82 b 9 sqq., where Socrates questions a slave about a geometrical diagram, in order to prove that μάθησις is ἀνάμνησις. No doubt, if we hold this doctrine and its proof to be genuinely Socratic, the reference to the *Meno* is less certain; but, on the whole, Plato seems to indicate that, as he has already treated it elsewhere, he need not repeat the proof here.

b 2 κατηγορεῖ, 'it is proof positive' (Riddell, Dig. § 97), 'it is manifest' (*velut passim occurrunt* ἐδήλωσε, προσημαίνει, δείξει *et id genus alia*, Heindorf). The verb κατηγορεῖν is used just like the Latin *arguere* (L. S. *s. v.* II) and might very well take the impersonal construction of δηλοῦν, for which cp. *Gorg.* 483 d 2 δηλοῖ δὲ ταῦτα πολλαχοῦ ὅτι οὕτως ἔχει. If the verb is personal we must supply ὁ ἄγων ἐπὶ τὰ διαγράμματα, which is not satisfactory.

b 6 αὐτὸ ... τοῦτο ... παθεῖν ... ἀναμνησθῆναι, 'to have done to me the very thing we are speaking of, namely, to be reminded.' The MSS. have μαθεῖν, and παθεῖν is a conjecture of Heindorf's (not of Serranus, as Stallbaum says). The words are constantly confused; for in uncial writing Μ is very like Π, both being written without lifting the pen. This is one of the comparatively few corrections in the text of the *Phaedo* which may be called certain, though it is not adopted in the most recent edition (Wohlrab, 1908). Cp. *Gorg.* 505 c 3 αὐτὸς τοῦτο πάσχων περὶ οὗ ὁ λόγος ἐστί, κολαζόμενος.

b 7 ἀναμνησθῆναι: in apposition to τοῦτο παθεῖν. Cp. 72 c 3 n.

b 8 ἐπεχείρησε λέγειν, 'attacked the proof.' We see here the beginnings of the use of ἐπιχειρεῖν as a technical term of dialectic. Cp. also ἐπιχείρημα.

c 1   εἴ τίς τι ἀναμνησθήσεται, 'if a man is to be reminded of a thing.' Cp. 72 e 7 n.

c 5   τρόπῳ τοιούτῳ, 'in such a way as this.' Here τοιοῦτος refers forward, and the explanation of it is introduced by the question and answer 'What way do I mean? This.' For similar rhetorical interrogations see Riddell, Dig. § 325.

c 6   ἐάν τίς τι ἕτερον κτλ. Here we have a careful psychological analysis of what is meant by 'being reminded'. A modern treatise would say 'If a man, having seen A (τι ἕτερον) ... also thinks of B'. The reading τι ἕτερον is sufficiently well attested (T), and the double ἄλλο is used in the same way below 74 c 13, while the other reading, πρότερον (B), is easily accounted for and yields no satisfactory sense. Recent editors mostly adopt πρότερον and then enclose it in square brackets.

ἤ τινα ἄλλην αἴσθησιν λαβών, equivalent to ἤ τινι ἄλλῃ αἰσθήσει αἰσθόμενος, but Plato avoids the juxtaposition of cognate words. The same phrase is used below 76 a 2.

c 7   μὴ μόνον ἐκεῖνο γνῷ κτλ., 'not only apprehends A, but also thinks of B.'

c 8   οὐ μὴ ἡ αὐτὴ ἐπιστήμη : this is an important reservation. Certain things, notably opposites, must be known together or not at all (τῶν ἐναντίων μία ἐπιστήμη). It proves nothing that odd reminds us of even, or that darkness reminds us of light; for in this case the knowledge of the one is *ipso facto* knowledge of the other.

c 9   τοῦτο: internal object of ἀνεμνήσθη (cp. 72 e 7 n.) and antecedent of οὗ, 'that he was reminded of that which he thought of (B).' The words οὗ τὴν ἔννοιαν ἔλαβε refer to ἀλλὰ καὶ ἕτερον ἐννοήσῃ above.

δικαίως is used much like ὀρθῶς. Cp. 72 a 11 n.

d 6   πάσχουσι τοῦτο : followed as usual by a clause in apposition. Cp. 68 e 3 n.

d 7   ἔγνωσαν : empirical ('gnomic') aorist. Cp. 113 d 3.

ἐν τῇ διανοίᾳ ἔλαβον : equivalent to ἐνενόησαν, but with more emphasis on the ingressive force of the aorist.

τὸ εἶδος, 'the bodily form.' Cp. 73 a 1 n.

d 8   τοῦτο: pred. 'and reminiscence is just this'. Cp. 75 d 10.

d 9   πολλάκις ... ἀνεμνήσθη : empirical aorist with temporal adverb. Gildersleeve, S. C. G. § 259.

d 10   καὶ ἄλλα που μυρία κτλ. Cp. 70 e 3 n.

11 μέντοι νὴ Δία : cp. 68 b 7 *n.*

e 5 ἵππον γεγραμμένον, 'a painted horse.' This is a more complex case. We are reminded of B not by A, but by an image of A, which we may call *a*.

e 9 αὐτοῦ Σιμμίου : Simmias as opposed to the picture of Simmias. In this case we are reminded of A by *a*, or of B by *b*. This is the case described just below as ἀφ' ὁμοίων, the two first being ἀπὸ ἀνομοίων. It is for the sake of this distinction that the point is elaborated.

a 6 ἐννοεῖν : in apposition to προσπάσχειν, cp. 72 c 3 *n.* When a man is reminded of A by *a* or of B by *b*, an additional thought necessarily presents itself to his mind, the thought of the presence or absence of any deficiency in the likeness of *a* or *b* to A or B. This thought is only forced upon us when we are reminded ἀφ' ὁμοίων.

εἴτε τι ἐλλείπει τοῦτο ... ἐκείνου ... , 'whether this (*a* or *b*) falls short in any respect of that of which he has been reminded by it (A or B).' The intransitive use of ἐλλείπειν was familiar in Pythagorean geometry. Cp. Proclus, *in Eucl. I,* p. 419 (Friedlein) "Εστι μὲν ἀρχαῖα, φασὶν οἱ περὶ τὸν Εὔδημον, καὶ τῆς τῶν Πυθαγορείων Μούσης εὑρήματα ταῦτα, ἥ τε παραβολὴ τῶν χωρίων καὶ ἡ ὑπερβολὴ καὶ ἡ ἔλλειψις. The use of the words *parabola, hyperbola,* and *ellipse* in Conic Sections comes from this, but Conics are post-Platonic.

a 9 φαμέν που κτλ. Cp. 65 d 4 *n.*

We have seen already that the 'forms' (what we really *mean* when we speak of 'triangle', 'right', 'beautiful', &c.) are not perceptible by the senses, but can only be apprehended by thought.

We are now introduced to a second point in the theory. The 'forms' are *types* (παραδείγματα) to which particular sensible things approximate more or less closely. A given triangle is never what we really *mean* by 'triangle', nor a right action what we really *mean* by right.

According to this view, particular sensible things are μιμήματα or εἰκόνες of the 'forms'. There is ample evidence that a doctrine like this was held by the later Pythagoreans (E. Gr. Ph.² pp. 353 sqq.).

τι εἶναι ἴσον ... αὐτὸ τὸ ἴσον : we speak of sticks and stones being 'equal', but this is not the equality with which arithmetic and geometry deal. We only call them equal at all because they remind us of what we really *mean* by 'equal'. This is something different (ἕτερόν τι), 'over and above' all these things (παρὰ πάντα ταῦτα), which is 'just the equal' (αὐτὸ τὸ ἴσον).

b 1   μέντοι νὴ Δί(α): cp. 65 d 6 n. Simmias was not familiar with the doctrine of Reminiscence, but now he feels at home once more.

b 2   αὐτὸ ὃ ἔστιν: W adds ἴσον and so do the margins of B and T. It is, perhaps, unnecessary, but gives the full technical expression for this kind of reality, 'the what it is by itself', 'the just what it is'.

b 4   ἐξ ὧν νυνδὴ ἐλέγομεν: we certainly have an exact scientific knowledge (ἐπιστήμη) of equality, but we have seen (65 d 9) that equality cannot be perceived by the senses. These, then, are not the source of our knowledge. Sensible objects only *remind* us of equality. But we cannot be reminded of a knowledge which we never possessed.

b 8   τῷ μὲν ... τῷ δ' οὔ : there is an ancient variant τότε (i. e. τοτὲ) μὲν ... τότε (i. e. τοτὲ) δ' οὔ. Either reading gives a good sense. Sticks and stones sometimes seem equal and sometimes unequal to the same persons, and they appear equal to one person, unequal to another. This shows that the 'really equal' (αὐτὸ ὃ ἔστιν ἴσον) is something different.

c 1   αὐτὰ τὰ ἴσα: things that are 'just equal'. There is no difficulty about the plural. When Euclid says (*Ax*. 1) Τὰ τῷ αὐτῷ ἴσα καὶ ἀλλήλοις ἐστὶν ἴσα, he is not speaking of sticks or stones, but of αὐτὰ τὰ ἴσα. Cp. αὐτὰ τὰ ὅμοια, *Parm*. 129 b 1. The two angles at the base of an isosceles triangle are an instance of αὐτὰ τὰ ἴσα.

c 4   ταῦτα ... τὰ ἴσα: the sticks and stones mentioned above, not αὐτὸ τὰ ἴσα.

c 11   Οὐκοῦν ... d 3 Πάνυ μὲν οὖν: this step in the argument is not, perhaps, strictly necessary, and some critics would bracket the words. It must be observed, however, that they serve to make the proof that our knowledge of the equal is reminiscence clearer, by reminding us of the preceding discussion. The equality of sticks and stones must either be like or unlike real equality, but in either case it is different from it, and our conception of real equality therefore corresponds to the account already given of reminiscence. Socrates does not assume at this stage that the equality of sticks and stones is 'like' real equality. That is the next step in the argument.

13 ἕως ἂν . . . : *dummodo*, 'so long as' . . . For the formula which follows cp. **73** c 6; **76** a 2.

d 2 αὐτό, 'the process in question.'

d 4 τι τοιοῦτον refers forward. The fact here noted indicates that we have to do with ἀνάμνησις ἀφ' ὁμοίων. Cp. **74** a 5.

d 6 ἢ ἐνδεῖ τι ἐκείνου . . . ἢ οὐδέν; ' do they fall short of it at all . . . or not ?' For the rare use of ἐνδεῖν as equivalent to ἐλλείπειν cp. *Rep.* 345 d 4 ἕως γ' ἂν μηδὲν ἐνδέῃ τοῦ ποιμενικὴ εἶναι, 529 d 1 τῶν δὲ ἀληθινῶν πολὺ ἐνδεῖν. There is no need, then, to read ἐκείνῳ with Madvig.

d 7 τῷ τοιοῦτον εἶναι οἷον τὸ ἴσον, 'in being such as the equal.' For the dative of that in which one is deficient cp. Thuc. ii. 87. 1 τῇ . . . παρασκευῇ ἐνδεὴς ἐγένετο, Isocr. *Paneg.* 105 τοὺς ταῖς οὐσίαις ἐνδεεστέρους. Owing to a misunderstanding of this construction late MSS. insert μή after τῷ, and various conjectures have been proposed by modern critics.

d 9 βούλεται . . . εἶναι, 'aims at being.' The phrase is often used to express a *tendency*, especially by Aristotle.

e 1 [ἴσον] : this seems a clear case of an 'adscript' which has crept into the text. Though it is in W it is not translated in the version of Aristippus, who has simply *tale esse quale illud.*

e 2 φαυλότερον, 'inferior.'

e 3 ἐνδεεστέρως δὲ ἔχειν, 'but of which it falls short.' The relative οὗ cannot be repeated after ᾧ, though αὐτοῦ might have been added. Cp. **65** a 5 *n.*

e 9 Ἀναγκαῖον ἄρα . . . προειδέναι : the point of the argument is that we could not judge the equality of sticks and stones to be defective unless we were in possession of a standard by which to judge them. Sensible things could never furnish us with such a standard, therefore we must have derived it from some other source.

a 2 ὀρέγεται : equivalent to βούλεται, **74** d 9.

a 7 ταὐτὸν δὲ κτλ., 'I count all these as the same thing' (for the purposes of the present argument, as appears from the reply). Cp. *Meno* **75** e 2 πάντα ταῦτα ταὐτόν τι λέγω· ἴσως δ' ἂν ἡμῖν Πρόδικος διαφέροιτο.

11 Ἀλλὰ μὲν δὴ κτλ. It can only be from the senses that our judgement of the inferiority of sensible objects originates, and yet that judgement implies previous knowledge of the standard by which we judge them and find them inadequate.

b 1 τὰ ἐν ταῖς αἰσθήσεσιν, sc. ἴσα. The phrase is modelled on the common ἐν ὀφθαλμοῖς.

ἐκείνου . . . τοῦ ὅ ἐστιν ἴσον: for the terminology cp. **74** b 2 *n*. and below d 2 *n*.

b 4 Πρὸ τοῦ ἄρα ἄρξασθαι κτλ. The reasoning is quite sound, as we shall see if we remember that we should never call sticks or stones equal at all, unless we knew clearly what we meant by equality.

τἆλλα αἰσθάνεσθαι, 'make use of our other senses'; for τἆλλα is internal accusative (Riddell, Dig. § 2).

b 6 τὰ ἐκ τῶν αἰσθήσεων is substituted for τὰ ἐν ταῖς αἰσθήσεσιν under the influence of ἀνοίσειν. This is simply a case of the 'attraction' of prepositions with the article by verbs of motion. Cp. 76 d 9; 109 e 4.

b 7 ἀνοίσειν, 'to refer.' Reference to a standard is regularly expressed by ἀναφέρειν πρὸς . . ., *referre ad* . . . Cp. 76 d 9.

ὅτι seems to be used as if ἀναφέροντες ἐννοήσειν had preceded instead of ἀνοίσειν. Vahlen (i. 489) proposes to insert καὶ ἐννοήσειν before ὅτι.

προθυμεῖται, 'do their best,' a still more picturesque way of expressing *tendency* than βούλεται or ὀρέγεται above.

πάντα, sc. τὰ ἐν ταῖς αἰσθήσεσιν ἴσα.

b 10 γενόμενοι εὐθύς, 'immediately upon birth.'

c 1 πρὸ τούτων: before we saw, heard, &c.

c 7 εἰ . . . ἔχοντες ἐγενόμεθα, sc. αὐτήν, 'if we were born with it,' i. e. the knowledge of the equal.

c 9 τὸ μεῖζον καὶ τὸ ἔλαττον: the knowledge of τὸ ἴσον implies these: for together they make up its opposite, τὸ ἄνισον, and τῶν ἐναντίων μία ἐπιστήμη.

c 11 περὶ αὐτοῦ τοῦ καλοῦ κτλ. We see here how the theory originated in mathematics, and was thence transferred to what we call morals and aesthetics. The beautiful and the good resemble the equal in this, that they are nowhere perfectly realized.

d 2 οἷς ἐπισφραγιζόμεθα κτλ., 'on which we set the seal of αὐτὸ ὃ ἔστι.' Here again we have 'we' in connexion with a technical term, and this implies the work of a school. Cp. 65 d 4 *n*. For the metaphor cp. *Polit.* 258 c 5 (τῇ πολιτικῇ) μίαν (ἰδέαν) ἐπισφραγίσασθαι, *Phileb.* 26 d 1 ἐπισφραγισθέντα τῷ τοῦ μᾶλλον καὶ ἐναντίου γένει.

τὸ "αὐτὸ ὃ ἔστι", 'the just what it is': so I have ventured to

write for the τοῦτο ὃ ἔστι of the MSS. Iamblichus has simply τὸ ὃ
ἔστι, and it seems to me that τό must be right. The reading which
I have given accounts sufficiently for the others. Most editors
write τοῦτο, ὃ ἔστι.

d 2 καὶ ἐν ταῖς ἐρωτήσεσιν κτλ.: i. e. διαλεγόμενοι, for question and
answer are the two sides of the Socratic dialectic. We see from
78 d 1 that this phrase also was technical in the Socratic school.
Cp. *Crito* 50 c 8 ἐπειδὴ καὶ εἴωθας χρῆσθαι τῷ ἐρωτᾶν τε καὶ ἀποκρίνεσθαι, *Rep.* 534 d 9 (διαλεκτικὴ) ἐξ ἧς ἐρωτᾶν τε καὶ ἀποκρίνεσθαι
οἷοί τ᾽ ἔσονται.

d 7 Εἰ . . . ἑκάστοτε μὴ ἐπιλελήσμεθα, 'unless we forget them on
each occasion' of our birth. The doctrine of παλιγγενεσία seems to
be implied by ἑκάστοτε and ἀεὶ γίγνεσθαι ('to be born on each
occasion') below. There would be no room for reminiscence unless
birth involved forgetting. Heindorf proposed to insert γιγνόμενοι
after ἑκάστοτε to make this clear; but we may easily 'understand' it.

d 9 λαβόντα κτλ., 'having acquired knowledge of a thing, to have it
and not to have lost it.' ἔχειν καὶ μὴ ἀπολωλεκέναι is an instance of
'polar expression'. Cp. 86 a 5 ἔτι εἶναι . . . καὶ μὴ ἀπολωλέναι.

10 ἐπιστήμης ἀποβολήν, 'loss of knowledge' (ἀπόλλυμι and ἀποβάλλω
are synonyms in this sense). For other definitions of λήθη cp.
Symp. 208 a 4 λήθη γὰρ ἐπιστήμης ἔξοδος, *Phileb.* 33 e 3 ἔστι γὰρ
λήθη μνήμης ἔξοδος.

e 2 Εἰ . . γιγνόμενοι ἀπωλέσαμεν, 'if we lost it in the process of
birth.'

e 3 περὶ αὐτά: here αὐτά means simply 'the things in question'. Cp.
60 c 1 ; 76 c 2. There is no need to read ταῦτα with W ; for the
reference is plain.

e 4 πρίν: the use of πρίν as an adverb almost unexampled in prose
(except with the article).

e 5 οἰκείαν . . . ἐπιστήμην ἀναλαμβάνειν, 'to recover knowledge
which is our own.' This is the real meaning of the whole doctrine,
which can only be adequately expressed in a mystical form. The
mystery of knowledge is the same as the mystery of love. It is
a 'mystical union' with what at first seems alien (ἀλλότριον), but is in
time recognized to be our very own.

e 7 ὀρθῶς: cp. 62 b 2 *n*.

76 a 1 ἢ ἰδόντα κτλ. These participles are subordinate to αἰσθόμενον, 'whether by sight or hearing or any other sense.'

a 5 πάντες is opposed to οὖς φαμεν μανθάνειν and repeated below **b 8**. We must not, therefore, read παντός.

a 6 οὐδὲν ἀλλ' ἤ, 'nothing but.' The phrase ἀλλ' ἤ is used after negatives and treated as a single word (cp. 68 b 4). It is wrong to write ἀλλ' (for ἄλλο) as is shown by 81 b 4 μηδὲν ἄλλο . . . ἀλλ' ἤ . . ., 97 d 2 οὐδὲν ἄλλο . . . ἀλλ' ἤ . . .

b 5 δοῦναι λόγον, 'to give an account of it.' This is the mark of the διαλεκτικός. Cp. *Rep.* 534 b 3 Ἦ καὶ διαλεκτικὸν καλεῖς τὸν λόγον ἑκάστου λαμβάνοντα τῆς οὐσίας (cp. 78 d 1) ; καὶ τὸν μὴ ἔχοντα, καθ' ὅσον ἂν μὴ ἔχῃ λόγον αὑτῷ τε καὶ ἄλλῳ διδόναι, κατὰ τοσοῦτον νοῦν περὶ τούτου οὐ φήσεις ἔχειν ;

b 9 ὧν νυνδὴ ἐλέγομεν, sc. τοῦ ἴσου, τοῦ καλοῦ, τοῦ ἀγαθοῦ, &c.

b 11 αὔριον τηνικάδε, 'this time to-morrow.' It seems to me that, if Plato originated the theory, he could not possibly have put this statement into the mouth of Simmias. Cp. *Prot.* 336 b 8, where Alcibiades says τοῦ δὲ διαλέγεσθαι οἷός τ' εἶναι καὶ ἐπίστασθαι λόγον τε δοῦναι καὶ δέξασθαι θαυμάζοιμ' ἂν εἴ τῳ ἀνθρώπων παραχωρεῖ (Σωκράτης).

c 12 ἐν ἀνθρώπου εἴδει, 'in human form.' We see from the next words how close εἶδος in such phrases comes to the meaning of σῶμα. Cp. 73 a 1 *n.*

καὶ φρόνησιν εἶχον, 'and had intelligence.' For the sense of φρόνησις here cp. 70 b 4 *n.* The doctrine of ἀνάμνησις gives the first indication of the intelligence of the disembodied soul.

d 1 ἐν ποίῳ ἄλλῳ χρόνῳ ; sc. ἢ ἐν τῷ τοῦ γίγνεσθαι. The interrogative ποίῳ is not a mere equivalent of τίνι. It always expresses feeling of some sort, surprise, scorn, or incredulity. Here we may reproduce the effect by saying, 'And at what other time do we lose it, pray?'

d 2 ἄρτι : 75 d 4.

d 8 ἃ θρυλοῦμεν ἀεί, 'the things we are always talking of.' Once more we have the 'we' which implies that this doctrine was perfectly familiar to the school.

d 9 οὐσία : cp. 65 d 13 *n.*

τὰ ἐκ τῶν αἰσθήσεων : cp. 75 b 6 *n.*

ἀναφέρομεν : cp. 75 b 7 *n.*

e 1 ἡμετέραν οὖσαν : equivalent to οἰκείαν above 75 e 5.

e 2 ταῦτα, sc. τὰ ἐν ταῖς αἰσθήσεσιν.

οὕτως ὥσπερ καί, 'in just the same way that', 'just as surely as'.

e 3 ταῦτα, sc. καλόν τέ τι κτλ. There is no real difficulty in the fact that ταῦτα here and in the next line has a different reference from ταῦτα in e 2. The reference is quite plain in all three cases.

e 4 ἄλλως ... εἰρημένος, 'spoken in vain', 'this argument will go for nothing'. Cp. 115 d 5 ἄλλως λέγειν. Cp. L.S. *s. v.* ἄλλως II. 3.

e 9 εἰς καλόν: this phrase can hardly have any other than its usual meaning *opportunely*. Cp. *Meno* 89 e 9 εἰς καλὸν ἡμῖν Ἄνυτος παρε-καθέζετο, *Symp.* 174 e 5 εἰς καλὸν ἥκεις, and often. The phrase is purely adverbial, and it is not correct to say, with most editors, that it is explained by the words εἰς τὸ ὁμοίως εἶναι κτλ., which depend directly on καταφεύγει.

καταφεύγει, 'is taking refuge.' The λόγος or argument is over and over again spoken of as the thing hunted (cp. 63 a 2 *n.*, and below 88 d 9 *n.*). I take the meaning to be that it has 'taken cover' very conveniently *for us who are hunting it*. From *Rep.* 432 b sq. we see that the idea is that of a hare or other animal taking refuge in a bush (θάμνος), which the huntsmen surround so that it cannot escape (Adam's note *in loc.*). When the argument is proved, it is caught. Cp. *Lysis* 218 c 4 ἔχαιρον, ὥσπερ θηρευτής τις, ἔχων ἀγαπητῶς ὃ ἐθηρευόμην.

a 1 ὁμοίως, 'in the same way', 'just as surely', equivalent to οὕτως ὥσπερ καὶ ... οὕτως καί above (76 e 2).

a 5 ἀποδέδεικται, 'the demonstration is adequate.' The words ἔμοιγε δοκεῖ are parenthetical, and do not affect the construction. Cp. 108 d 8. The omission of δοκεῖ in TW is an attempt to normalize the construction. The answer shows that δοκεῖ is right ; for it is the only word that can be supplied after Τί δὲ δὴ Κέβητι ;

(3) *The doctrines of* παλιγγενεσία *and* ἀνάμνησις *afford an incomplete demonstration until they are combined* (77 a 6—77 d 5).

a 8 Ἱκανῶς, sc. ἀποδέδεικται. Simmias and Cebes point out, however, that the argument from ἀνάμνησις only proves the antenatal existence of the soul, not its survival after death. Socrates replies that we must take the argument from ἀνταπόδοσις and that from ἀνάμνησις together. At the same time, he admits that a more thorough discussion is required.

b 3 ἐνέστηκεν, 'there is still the objection.' This is originally an agonistic metaphor; for ἐνστῆναι is 'to stand up to'. Cp. Lysias, **3.** 8 εὐθύς με τύπτειν ἐπεχείρησεν· ἐπειδὴ δὲ αὐτὸν ἠμυνάμην ἐνστάς . . ., Isocr. **5.** 39 ἐνστῆναι τοῖς εἰρημένοις. Hence comes the technical use of ἔνστασις (*instantia*) in dialectics of an 'objection' to an argument (ἐπιχείρημα). Plutarch uses the word for the tribunes' *intercessio*.

b 4 ὅπως μὴ . . . διασκεδάννυται κτλ. For the use of ὅπως μή after verbs of fearing instead of μή cp. below **84 b 5**. There are four or five instances of this construction in Plato. The verb is subjunctive and has long υ, but the termination should not be accented -ῦται as if it were contracted from -ύηται. It is really an older form of the subjunctive (Kühner-Blass, § 281. 3). So διασκεδάννῦσιν, **77 e 1**, and the opt. πήγνυντο, **118 a 2**.

b 6 ἄλλοθέν ποθεν, 'from some other source' than from the souls in the other world which have come there from this (the ἐνθένδε ἀφικόμεναι of **70 c 6**). I formerly read ἁμόθεν ποθέν with Bekker; but, apart from the fact that the regular phrase is ἁμόθεν γέ ποθεν, I now think the meaning is settled by **72 d 1** ἐκ μὲν τῶν ἄλλων, where see note.

c 1 Εὖ λέγεις κτλ. For the interlaced order cp. **70 b 5 n.**

c 5 τέλος . . . ἕξειν, *i. q.* τελεία ἔσεσθαι, 'to be complete.' Cp. τέλος λαμβάνειν, τέλος ἐπιθεῖναι, &c. In Greek philosophy the word τέλος always implies the idea of completion or full growth. An animal or plant τέλος ἔχει when its growth is complete, when it is full grown. B has ἔχειν for ἕξειν, which would be equally correct. It is impossible to draw any distinction between the two constructions. For the fut. inf. in this use cp. e. g. *Rep.* **567 b 8** εἰ μέλλει ἄρξειν.

c 7 καὶ νῦν, 'even as it is.' The sense of νῦν is the same as in the common νῦν δέ . . ., *nunc vero . . .*, 'but, as it is.'

συνθεῖναι . . . εἰς ταὐτόν, 'to combine the present argument (viz. that the soul exists and is conscious before our birth) with the argument we assented to before it.'

d 5 ὅπερ λέγετε, 'the point you mention.' This reading comes from a late MS. and is probably due to conjecture alone. It gives, however, a much better sense than the ὅπερ λέγεται οt the oldest MSS., which is supposed to mean 'as is said', i. e. 'as I say'. We should certainly expect ὅπερ λέγω in that sense, and the confusion of -τε and -ται is common; both being pronounced alike.

(4) Practical Application.—We must rid ourselves of the fear of death at all costs (77 d 5—78 b 4).

This digression (cp. 78 a 10) marks the end of the First Argument and leads up to the Second.

d 6 διαπραγματεύσασθαι, 'to discuss thoroughly.' Cp. below 95 e 9 and the use of πραγματεία above 63 a 1.

d 7 τὸ τῶν παίδων, 'as children do.' That the phrase does not necessarily mean 'as children say', is shown e. g. by Xen. Oec. 16. 7 ἀνεμνήσθην τὸ τῶν ἁλιέων, which in the context must mean 'what fishermen do'.

e 1 διασκεδάννυσιν is probably subjunctive and to be pronounced with long υ (cp. 77 b 4 n.). The indicative would not be so appropriate; for the fear refers to the future. If the verbs were indicative, we should have to render 'lest the wind puffs it away and scatters it' on each occasion when it issues from the body.

e 2 ἐν μεγάλῳ τινὶ πνεύματι, 'in a high wind,' the regular phrase. So μέγας πνεῖ ὁ ἄνεμος. This clause is, of course, a humorous addition to the theory.

e 3 ὡς δεδιότων, sc. ἡμῶν, in spite of the fact that strict grammar would require δεδιότας in agreement with ἡμᾶς, the unexpressed object of ἀναπείθειν. The genitive absolute is often used in this way. Cp. Riddell, Dig. § 274.

e 4 μᾶλλον δέ, vel potius, 'or rather,' the regular phrase in introducing a correction.

μή belongs to δεδιότων, but is anticipated for emphasis. A striking instance of this is Crito 47 d 9 πειθόμενοι μὴ τῇ τῶν ἐπαϊόντων δόξῃ.

e 5 ἐν ἡμῖν, 'in us.' It is necessary to state this, as it has been suggested that the words mean 'among us' and refer to Apollodorus! This makes nonsense of the passage. The 'child in us' is often referred to by later Platonist writers like Porphyry, Themistius, and Simplicius (cp. Wyttenbach's note).

ὅστις differs from ὅς as qui with the subjunctive from qui with the indicative. Its use here is justified by the preceding τις.

a 6 πειρῶ μεταπείθειν was conjectured by Heindorf, and is now known to be the reading of W. It is far better than the πειρώμεθα πείθειν of BT; for it resumes πειρῶ ἀναπείθειν above with a slight variation which is quite in Plato's manner.

e 7 τὰ μορμολύκεια, 'bugbears.' Μορμώ (whose full name was Μορμολύκη) was a she-goblin used, like 'Ακκώ, "Εμπουσα, and Λάμια to frighten naughty children. Cp. Theocritus xv. 40 οὐκ ἀξῶ τυ, τέκνον, Μορμώ, δάκνει ἵππος, Xen. *Hell.* iv. 4. 17 φοβεῖσθαι τοὺς πελταστάς, ὥσπερ μορμόνας παιδάρια, Lucian, *Philops.* 2 παίδων ἔτι τὴν Μορμὼ καὶ τὴν Λάμιαν δεδιότων. According to the Platonic Lexicon of Timaeus, μορμολύκεια were masks, τὰ φοβερὰ τοῖς παισὶ προσωπεῖα. The verb μορμολύττεσθαι is used in *Crito* 46 c 4 and *Gorg.* 473 d 3.

e 8 ἐπᾴδειν, *incantare*, 'to sing charms' (*carmina*, ἐπῳδαί). Socrates makes an elaborate use of this idea in *Charm.* 155 e sqq., cp. esp. 157 a 3 θεραπεύεσθαι δὲ τὴν ψυχὴν ἔφη (Ζάλμοξις), ὦ μακάριε, ἐπῳδαῖς τισιν, τὰς δ᾽ ἐπῳδὰς ταύτας τοὺς λόγους εἶναι τοὺς καλούς· ἐκ δὲ τῶν τοιούτων λόγων ἐν ταῖς ψυχαῖς σωφροσύνην ἐγγίγνεσθαι, ἧς ἐγγενομένης καὶ παρούσης ῥᾴδιον ἤδη εἶναι τὴν ὑγίειαν καὶ τῇ κεφαλῇ καὶ τῷ ἄλλῳ σώματι πορίζειν. The ascription of this to the Thracian Zalmoxis shows it to be Pythagorean; for Herodotus tells us (iv. 95) that Zalmoxis (or Zamolxis) had been a slave of Pythagoras (E. Gr. Ph.² p. 93), and it goes well with what we know of the Pythagorean musical κάθαρσις (cp. 61 a 3 *n.*). Socrates also used the term in connexion with his μαιευτική (*Theaet.* 149 d 1).

e 9 ἕως ἂν ἐξεπᾴσητε, 'till you have charmed it out of him.' This is another conjecture of Heindorf's which has been confirmed by fuller knowledge of the MSS.; for it is actually found in a Vienna MS. and virtually in TW. The reading of B is ἐξιάσηται, and it appears from the margin of W that this was an ancient variant. It cannot, of course, be passive; but we might supply τις as its subject. 'One must sing charms . . . till one has healed him.'

78 a 3 Πολλὴ ... ἡ Ἑλλάς, wide enough, for instance, to include Southern Italy, where the Pythagoreans were once more becoming powerful. For this use of πολύς cp. the Homeric πολλὴ γαῖα, πολλὴ χώρη (*Il.* xxiii. 520), Thuc. vii. 13. 3 πολλὴ δ᾽ ἡ Σικελία, Theocr. xxii. 156 πολλή τοι Σπάρτη, πολλὴ δ᾽ ἱππήλατος Ἦλις.

a 4 τὰ τῶν βαρβάρων γένη : Socrates is no doubt thinking primarily of Thracians and Phrygians. The Orphic 'orgia' came from the former, the Corybantic 'purifications' from the latter. Plato regarded the distinction between Hellenes and barbarians as an unscientific division of mankind (*Polit.* 262 d 1 sqq.), but it was revived by Aristotle.

a 6 εις ὅτι ἂν εὐκαιρότερον : this is the reading of T and seems far better than the variant εἰς ὅτι ἀναγκαιότερον. The corruption is an extremely easy one, and the omission of ἂν in the variant is, to say the least of it, hard to justify, while the insertion of ἂν after ὅτι would spoil the rhythm. Of course εὐκαιρότερον is the comparative adverb, not the adjective.

a 7 καὶ αὐτοὺς μετ' ἀλλήλων, 'by yourselves too' (as well as by questioning Hellenes and barbarians), 'along with one another' (for joint search is the true Socratic method). We cannot take μετ' ἀλλήλων to mean 'among yourselves' as some do. Apart from the unheard-of sense thus given to μετά *c. gen.*, the pronoun ἀλλήλων excludes such a rendering. We should have had ἐν ἡμῖν αὐτοῖς.

a 8 ἴσως γὰρ ἂν κτλ. The usual hint that Orpheotelestae and Corybantic καθαρταί are not to be taken too seriously. Cp. 69 c 4 *n.*

10 ταῦτα . . . ὑπάρξει, 'that shall be done', 'you may count on that'. For the interlaced order cp. 70 b 5 *n.*

Second Proof of Immortality (78 b 4—84 b 8).

This proof is based, not upon ancient doctrines, but on a consideration of the soul's own nature, which is shown to resemble that of the eternal forms. From this we may infer that, like them, it is indissoluble.

b 5 ἑαυτούς is an emphatic ἀλλήλους.

b 6 τὸ διασκεδάννυσθαι is better attested than the τοῦ διασκεδάννυσθαι of B. We have seen (72 c 3 *n.*) that τοῦτο πάσχειν takes an infinitive in apposition. The article is added in this case because τὸ πάθος precedes.

b 7 καὶ τῷ ποίῳ τινὶ ⟨οὔ⟩ : some of the early editors deleted καὶ τῷ ποίῳ τινί as a tautology ; but the pronoun πότερον in b 8 shows that two kinds of things have been distinguished. We must therefore add οὔ with Heindorf, though it appears in no MS. and Olympiodorus did not read it ; for he tries to get rid of the tautology by taking the first τῷ ποίῳ τινί of things and the second of persons.

b 8 πότερον, 'which of the two,' not 'whether'.

b 9 θαρρεῖν ἢ δεδιέναι, 'to fear or not to fear.' Cp. 63 e 10 *n*.

> (1) *Only that is dissoluble which is composite, and the things which*
> *are constant and invariable are not composite. Further, the*
> *things which are constant and invariable are invisible. We*
> *have to ask, then, whether the soul belongs to the class of in-*
> *visible, constant and invariable, non-composite things, or to*
> *that of visible, variable, composite, and therefore dissoluble*
> *things* (78 c 1—80 c 1).

c 1 τῷ ... συνθέτῳ ὄντι φύσει: if we take these words together with
Wyttenbach, they add a fresh touch to τῷ συντεθέντι. That suggests an artificial combination; this refers to what is essentially
and from the nature of the case composite. The addition of
the participle ὄντι indicates that this is the construction and
makes it very unnatural to take φύσει προσήκει together, as many
editors do.

c 2 τοῦτο πάσχειν, διαιρεθῆναι: cp. 72 c 3 *n*. The verbs συντιθέναι,
'compound,' διαιρεῖν, 'divide,' are the regular opposites.

   ταύτῃ ἧπερ συνετέθη: e. g., if it is a compound of the four 'elements', it will be divided into these.

c 6 κατὰ ταὐτὰ καὶ ὡσαύτως, 'constant and invariable.' We see that
this is the sense from the ἄλλοτ' ἄλλως, which is the opposite of
ὡσαύτως, and μηδέποτε κατὰ ταὐτά, which is opposed to κατὰ ταὐτά.
Cp. d 2; 80 b 2.

c 7 τὰ δὲ ἄλλοτ' ἄλλως: the familiarity of the term may excuse
the ellipse of ἔχοντα and make it unnecessary to read ἅ for τά with
Heindorf.

c 8 ταῦτα δὲ σύνθετα: for the resumptive demonstrative with δέ
cp. e. g. Lach. 194 d 2 ἃ δὲ ἀμαθής, ταῦτα δὲ κακός. So below 80 d 8;
81 b 8; 113 e 5.

d 1 ἡ οὐσία ἧς λόγον δίδομεν τοῦ εἶναι, 'the reality the being of which
we give account of.' The hyperbaton of δίδομεν has misled the
commentators here. We must take λόγον τοῦ εἶναι together as
equivalent to λόγον τῆς οὐσίας or 'definition', and as governing the
genitive ἧς. For λόγος τῆς οὐσίας cp. *Rep.* 534 b 3 ἦ καὶ διαλεκτικὸν
καλεῖς τὸν λόγον ἑκάστου λαμβάνοντα τῆς οὐσίας; The meaning, then,
is simply 'the reality which we define'. When we define 'triangle',

it is not this or that triangle, but αὐτὸ ὅ ἐστι τρίγωνον, 'just what is triangle,' that finds expression in our definition.

1 καὶ ἐρωτῶντες καὶ ἀποκρινόμενοι, *i. q.* διαλεγόμενοι, cp. 75 d 2 *n.* In the dialectic process it is by question and answer that definitions are reached. When we ask τί ἐστι; the answer is a λόγος τῆς οὐσίας.

3 αὐτὸ ἕκαστον ὅ ἐστιν, 'what any given thing itself is' or 'is by itself', 'just what a given thing is'. Cp. 74 b 2 *n.*

4 τὸ ὄν, 'the real,' is added to suggest the opposition of εἶναι and γίγνεσθαι.

5 μονοειδὲς ὂν αὐτὸ καθ' αὑτό, 'being uniform if taken alone by itself.' I regard αὐτὸ καθ' αὑτό as a reservation here. The triangle, for instance, has more than one εἶδος. There are equilateral, isosceles, and scalene triangles. But none of these εἴδη enter into the definition of the triangle simply as such.

10 Τί δὲ τῶν πολλῶν κτλ. (Riddell, Dig. § 27), 'what of the many beautiful things?' as opposed to τὸ αὐτὸ ὅ ἐστι καλόν. It is clear that we cannot retain both καλῶν here and ἢ καλῶν in e 1, and most editors bracket the former. This, however, commits us to the view that there are εἴδη of men, horses, and clothes, which is a point that has not been referred to, and which raises certain difficulties which do not concern us here. It is hard to believe that ἱμάτια would have been mentioned at all except as an instance of τὰ πολλὰ καλά. I therefore take Τί δὲ τῶν πολλῶν καλῶν . . . ἢ ἴσων together, and regard 'people, horses, and clothes' as examples of the first, just as 'sticks and stones' might be given as examples of the second. It is only as instances of καλά that people, horses, and clothes can be said to be ὁμώνυμα τῷ καλῷ (cp. e 2 *n.*).

e 1 τοιούτων: i. e. καλῶν. This, I take it, has caused the interpolation of ἢ καλῶν.

e 2 πάντων τῶν ἐκείνοις ὁμωνύμων, 'all the (other) things (besides καλά and ἴσα) which bear the same name as those,' i. e. as αὐτῶν ἕκαστον ὅ ἐστι. For this way of expressing the relationship between τὰ πολλὰ ἕκαστα and αὐτὸ ὅ ἐστιν ἕκαστον cp. *Parm.* 133 d 2 τὰ . . . παρ' ἡμῖν ταῦτα ὁμώνυμα ὄντα ἐκείνοις. Observe the tendency to use ταῦτα of the 'many' and ἐκεῖνα of the 'ideas'.

πᾶν τοὐναντίον ἐκείνοις, 'just the opposite to these,' i. e. to αὐτὸ τὸ καλόν, &c. What we call 'beautiful things' or 'equal things' are constant neither to themselves nor to one another. As we have seen (74 b 8), they do not appear beautiful or equal to different people, or even to the same person at different times.

79 a 3 τῷ τῆς διανοίας λογισμῷ, 'by thinking.' There is no distinction here between διάνοια and νοῦς. The phrase means thinking generally as opposed to sense-perception.

a 4 ἀιδῆ, 'invisible.' The correct form was first made known by the Flinders Petrie papyrus, and has since been found to be the reading of the first hand of T and of W. Cp. the Homeric ἀίδηλος, ἄιστος, ἀιδνύς. The reading of B, followed by nearly all MSS. and editions, is ἀειδῆ, which could only mean 'formless', 'unsightly', and is quite inappropriate.

a 6 Θῶμεν οὖν βούλει κτλ. Olympiodorus distinguishes three ἐπιχειρή-ματα intended to prove that the soul is more like the indissoluble than the body: (1) ἐκ τοῦ ἀοράτου αὐτῆς, (2) ἐκ τοῦ διανοητικοῦ αὐτῆς, (3) ἐκ τοῦ δεσπόζειν τοῦ σώματος. The first ἐπιχείρημα begins here.

δύο εἴδη τῶν ὄντων, 'two types of things.' It is important to observe that the word ὄντα is used of both. It means 'things' in the widest and vaguest sense. Of course, strictly speaking, visible things are not ὄντως ὄντα and the things invisible are not 'things' at all.

b 1 ἄλλο τι, *nonne*, just like ἄλλο τι ἢ ... above (70 c 9). The words have become phraseological, but their original sense ('anything else') is so far felt that the affirmative answer is given by Οὐδὲν ἄλλο.

b 4 φαμὲν ἂν εἶναι: this seems better than the equally well attested φαῖμεν ἂν εἶναι. In the direct speech ὁμοιότερον ἂν εἴη would be quite natural.

b 9 τῇ τῶν ἀνθρώπων φύσει, sc. ὁρατὰ καὶ μή. It is left open for us to say that in some sense we may 'see' these things πρὶν ἐν ἀνθρωπείῳ εἴδει γενέσθαι or after the soul has left its human body. Such a beatific vision is described in the *Phaedrus*, but belongs to another aspect of the theory than that dwelt upon in the *Phaedo*.

b 13 Οὐχ ὁρατόν. 'Αιδὲς ἄρα; cp. 105 d 15 'Ανάρτιον. The inference from 'not visible' to 'invisible' seemed more necessary to the Greeks than to us.

c 2 Οὐκοῦν καὶ τόδε κτλ. The second ἐπιχείρημα (cp. a 6 n.). The soul can apprehend the invariable best apart from the body.

c 2 πάλαι, 'some time ago,' i.e. 65 b 1 sqq. For the meaning of πάλαι cp. 63 d 5 *n.*

c 8 τοιούτων, sc. πλανωμένων καὶ ἐν ταραχῇ ὄντων (Riddell, Dig. § 54). The soul fluctuates and is confused because it is in contact with objects which are fluctuating and confused.

d 3 συγγενὴς οὖσα: we have seen already that reality is οἰκεῖον to the soul (75 e 5), and this has been reinforced by the consideration that it is more alike to the invisible than the visible.

d 4 καὶ ἑξῆ αὐτῇ, sc. μετ' ἐκείνου γίγνεσθαι.

d 5 καὶ περὶ ἐκεῖνα ... ἔχει, 'and remains ever constant in relation to them.'

d 6 τοιούτων: i.e. κατὰ ταὐτὰ ὡσαύτως ἐχόντων.

τοῦτο ... τὸ πάθημα, 'this condition,' i.e. a constant relation to constant objects.

e 3 ταύτης τῆς μεθόδου, 'this line of argument.' The verb μετέρχομαι (88 d 9) and its substantive μέθοδος furnish another illustration of the metaphor from hunting. The literal sense of μετιέναι is ' to go after', ' to follow up ', especially of going in pursuit of game. As the λόγος is the game in the θήρα τοῦ ὄντος, the phrase μετιέναι τὸν λόγον is natural.

ὅλῳ καὶ παντί: the usual phrase is ὅλῳ καὶ παντὶ διαφέρειν, ' to be totally different.' Here it is used of likeness.

e 8 Ὅρα δὴ καὶ τῇδε κτλ. The third ἐπιχείρημα (a 6 *n.*). The soul rules over the body. This is the argument which comes nearest to Plato's own proof of immortality.

a 4 οἷον ἄρχειν ... πεφυκέναι, 'to be by nature such as to rule and lead ', ' to be naturally adapted for rule and leadership '. For this use of οἷος cp. 83 d 9; 94 e 4; 98 c 8. We must ' understand ' οἷον again with ἄρχεσθαι.

10 εἰ ... τάδε ἡμῖν συμβαίνει, 'whether this is our conclusion.' The results of a dialectical discussion are technically called τὰ συμβαίνοντα, and it is in the light of these that the ὑπόθεσις with which it starts must be examined. If an impossibility συμβαίνει, the ὑπόθεσις must be given up.

b 3 ὁμοιότατον εἶναι ψυχή, sc. συμβαίνει. The verb συμβαίνει in this sense is generally used personally; cp. 67 c 5 κάθαρσις δὲ εἶναι ἄρα οὐ τοῦτο συμβαίνει ...;, so there is no need to read ψυχήν. The impersonal construction also occurs; cp. 74 a 2 ἆρ' οὖν οὐ ... συμβαίνει τὴν ἀνάμνησιν εἶναι κτλ. There is no anacoluthon; for the prospective τάδε above is merely shorthand for τῷ θείῳ ὁμοιότατον εἶναι ψυχή, τῷ ἀθανάτῳ ὁμοιότατον εἶναι ψυχή, &c.

b 4 ἀνοήτῳ: a play on words is involved in making this the opposite of νοητῷ, for ἀνόητος properly means 'senseless', 'foolish'. The true opposite of νοητός, 'intelligible', 'object of thought', is αἰσθητός, 'sensible', 'object of sense'.

b 6 ᾗ οὐχ οὕτως ἔχει, 'to show that it is not so.' This meaning would be equally well expressed by ὡς which is an ancient variant and well attested. Schanz's ᾗ, however, has the advantage of explaining the readings of B (ῇ) and W (ῇ). Cp. *Theaet.* 184 c 4 ἐπιλαβέσθαι τῆς ἀποκρίσεως . . . ᾗ οὐκ ὀρθή.

b 10 ἐγγύς τι τούτου: a hint that this argument is not quite conclusive. The soul has only been shown to resemble the indissoluble.

(2) *Practical Application.—We must purify our souls and purge it of the corporeal* (80 c 2—84 b 8).

c 3 ἐν ὁρατῷ κείμενον, 'situated in the visible region.' Ast quaintly interprets : 'lying in a visible thing,' i.e. a coffin or tomb.

c 4 καὶ διαπνεῖσθαι is so well attested that its omission in B must be a slip. I cannot see that it is an inappropriate word to use of a dead body.

c 5 ἐπιεικῶς συχνὸν . . . χρόνον, 'a fairly long time.' Cp. *Crito* 43 a 10 ἐπιεικῶς πάλαι.

c 6 ἐπιμένει, 'remains as it is' (dist. περιμένει, 'waits'). Cp. 59 e 4 *n.* ἐὰν μέν τις καὶ . . ., 'indeed, even if a man . . .' For the hyperbaton of καί Schmidt compares *Prot.* 323 b 3 ἐάν τινα καὶ εἰδῶσιν ὅτι ἄδικός ἐστιν. The μέν ('indeed') is *solitarium* as in *Prot.* 361 e 3 τῶν μὲν τηλικούτων καὶ πάνυ (however it may be with others). The meaning, then, is that even if a man dies with his body in good condition, it lasts quite a long time. Of course a healthy body decomposes more rapidly than an old and withered one.

χαριέντως ἔχων, equivalent to καλῶς or εὖ ἔχων. We find μετρίως and ἐπιεικῶς used in the same sense. Cp. 68 e 2 *n.* There is no suggestion of 'gracefulness', but only of εὐεξία or 'good condition'.

c 7 ἐν τοιαύτῃ ὥρᾳ, 'at a fine season of the year' (τοιαύτῃ standing for καλῇ implied in χαριέντως, Riddell, Dig. § 54). Decomposition is more rapid in summer than in winter. Most recent editors understand the phrase to mean 'in the bloom of youth'; but (1) ἐν ὥρᾳ without τοιαύτῃ would be sufficient for this. **Cp.** *Meno* **76** b 8 ; *Phaedr.* **240** d 7 ; *Rep.* **474** d 4 ; and (2) when ὥρα is mentioned in connexion with death, it means not 'youthful bloom', but 'a ripe old age'. Cp. e.g. Eur. *Phoen.* 968 αὐτὸς δ', ἐν ὡραίῳ γὰρ ἵσταμαι βίου, | θνῄσκειν ἕτοιμος. On the other hand, one who dies in early youth (and in that sense ἐν ὥρᾳ) is said to die πρὸ ὥρας or ἄωρος. The latter word is common in sepulchral inscriptions.

C 7 καὶ πάνυ μάλα, sc. συχνὸν χρόνον, 'for quite a long time.'

συμπεσόν, 'reduced to bones and muscle', 'emaciated'. This clause justifies the preceding ἐὰν μέν τις κτλ. An emaciated body remains almost entire for an inconceivable time, and even a body in good condition lasts quite a long time. For συμπίπτειν cp. Hdt. iii. 52 ἀσιτίῃσι συμπεπτωκότα. In the medical writers σύμπτωσις is technical for emaciation.

c 8 καὶ ταριχευθέν : there is nothing unnatural in Socrates' frequent references to Egypt, which was always an object of interest to the Greeks. Socrates must have known many men who had fought there in 460 B.C. This passage has strangely been supposed to prove Plato's Egyptian journey.

c 9 ὀλίγου ὅλον μένει, sc. τὸ σῶμα, 'remains all but entire.'

d 1 καὶ ἂν σαπῇ, sc. τὸ (ἄλλο) σῶμα.

νεῦρα, 'sinews.' Cp. below 98 c 7 *n.*

d 5 ἄρα, *scilicet.* The particle indicates that we have to do with an *argumentum ex contrario* (cp. 68 a 3 *n.*) put in the form of a question. 'Are we to say, then, that the soul . . . ?'

τοιοῦτον . . . ἕτερον, 'just like itself' (cp. 58 d 8 *n.*), not equivalent to ἀιδῆ, for that is expressly mentioned besides. The meaning is that expressed throughout the preceding argument by ὅμοιον.

d 6 εἰς Ἅιδου ὡς ἀληθῶς, 'to the House of Hades in the true sense of the word.' This refers to the commonly accepted etymology of the word, for which cp. *Crat.* 404 b 1 καὶ τό γε ὄνομα ὁ 'Ἅιδης' . . . πολλοῦ δεῖ ἀπὸ τοῦ ἀιδοῦς (*sic* BT) ἐπωνομάσθαι. The denial of the etymology here shows that (rightly or wrongly) it was commonly accepted.

d 7 τὸν ἀγαθὸν καὶ φρόνιμον θεόν : in the mystic theology Hades or Zeus Chthonios is called Eubouleus, and Eubouleus is also found (e. g. at Eleusis and on the Orphic gold plates of Southern Italy) as an independent god. I suspect that Socrates is here alluding to this sacred name.

d 8   αὕτη δὲ δή resumes ἡ δὲ ψυχὴ ἄρα after the parenthesis.

e 2   ἐὰν μὲν κτλ. The protasis is interrupted at e 5 and resumed by 81 a 4 οὕτω μὲν ἔχουσα. Then ἐὰν μέν is answered by 81 b 1 ἐὰν δέ γε.

e 3   κοινωνοῦσα: imperfect participle.

e 4   ἑκοῦσα εἶναι, ' so far as it could help it' (61 c 4 *n.*). The reservation is the same as that implied in ὅτι μὴ πᾶσα ἀνάγκη 67 a 4.

e 6   τὸ δέ: this is the reading of the Petrie papyrus, and is more likely to have been altered than the τοῦτο δέ of the MSS.

81 a 1   τεθνάναι μελετῶσα ῥᾳδίως, 'practising death without complaining.' Most editors emend or delete ῥᾳδίως, which is found not only in all MSS. and citations, but also in the Petrie papyrus. The use of the perfect infinitive need cause no difficulty ; for it is often used of the moment of death which completes the process of τὸ ἀποθνῄσκειν (62 a 5 *n.*). Vahlen (*Opusc.* ii. 213) proposes to construe ῥᾳδίως with μελετῶσα, but there has been no question of complaining about the practice of death, while we have had ῥᾳδίως ἂν ἐθέλειν ἀποθνῄσκειν (62 c 10) and ῥᾳδίως ἀπαλλάττοιντο αὐτῶν (63 a 7) explained just below by οὕτω ῥᾳδίως φέρεις. The opposite is ἀγανακτεῖν ἀποθνῄσκοντας (62 e 6). All these passages are quoted by Vahlen himself.

a 8   κατὰ τῶν μεμυημένων, ' *of* the initiated.' Cp. 70 d 7 *n.* This resembles the fairly common use of κατά *c. gen.* with ἔπαινος, ἐγκώμιον, and the like.

a 9   διάγουσα : after ἀπηλλαγμένη we expect διαγούσῃ, which Heindorf proposed to read. It would be easier to write ἀπηλλαγμένη, for there is no reason why the grammatical construction of ὑπάρχει should be kept up. The general sense of the sentence suggests the nominative.

b 3   ἐρῶσα, sc. αὐτοῦ.

γοητευομένη is read by T as well as by the papyrus. It is not easy to decide between it and the equally well attested γεγοητευμένη.

τε is connective here. This is a poetical usage, and becomes increasingly frequent in Plato's later style. For a striking instance from his middle period cp. *Phaedr.* 267 a 6 Τεισίαν δὲ Γοργίαν τε.

b 4   δοκεῖν, 'to think ': cp. 64 b 2.

b 5   ἀλλ' ἤ ...: cp. 68 b 4 *n.* ; 76 a 6 *n.*

b 5   οὗ: the relative cannot be repeated in a different case (cp. 65 a 5 n.), so the ὅ and ᾧ which are logically required as the sentence proceeds, are simply omitted.

b 7   φιλοσοφίᾳ αἱρετόν: Stallbaum compares *Tim.* 29 a 6 λόγῳ καὶ φρονήσει περιληπτόν.

b 8   τοῦτο δὲ ...: cp. 78 c 8 n.

c 4   διειλημμένην, 'broken up by', 'patched with the corporeal'. The meaning of διαλαμβάνειν is best seen from 110 b 7. As applied to colours, it means 'to pick out', *distinguere*, as in a quilt or tartan. Cp. Milton, *Comus* 453-75.

c 6   σύμφυτον: though σύμφυτος and συμφυής usually mean 'congenital', that sense is excluded by ἐνεποίησε. We also find both words in the sense of 'grown together' (from συμφῦναι, 'to coalesce'), and this must be the meaning here. We also find σύμφυσις as a medical term, especially of bones.

d 1   κυλινδουμένη, 'haunting.' I have not ventured to write καλινδου- μένη, though Cobet says (*N. L.* p. 637) 'Platonica sunt καλινδεῖσθαι ἐν ἀμαθίᾳ, ἐν πάσῃ ἀμαθίᾳ, et odiose ἐν δικαστηρίοις καλινδεῖται, quem- admodum quis proprie ἐν πηλῷ aut ἐν βορβόρῳ dicitur καλινδεῖσθαι'. Very like the present use of the word is *Rep.* 479 d 4 μεταξύ που κυλινδεῖται τοῦ τε μὴ ὄντος καὶ τοῦ ὄντος εἰλικρινῶς. The suggestion is that of a restless spirit which cannot tear itself away from the body. Cicero, *Somn. Scip.* 9 says *circum terram ipsam volutantur* of such souls.

d 4   διὸ καὶ ὁρῶνται, 'which is just why they are visible.' There is a touch of Socratic playfulness in this theory. If the soul is invisible, we must give some such account of ghosts as this.

d 6   Εἰκὸς μέντοι: cp. 65 d 6 n.
     οὔ τι ... ἀλλά..., a common formula in Plato. The γε belongs to καί.

d 8   τροφῆς, practically equivalent here to διαίτης, 'way of life.' Cp. 84 b 4; 107 d 4.

e 2   ἐνδοῦνται: cp. 82 e 2 n. For similar doctrine see *Phaedr.* 249, *Rep.* 618 a, 620 sq., *Tim.* 42 b, 91 sq.

e 3   ἤθη: we can say 'bad characters' for people who have bad characters, though we should hardly use the word of the lower animals. Very similar to the English use are *Rep.* 496 b 2 γενναῖον καὶ εὖ τεθραμμένον ἦθος, 503 c 9 τὰ βέβαια ταῦτα ἤθη quoted by Bywater on Ar. *Poet.* 1454 a 23.

e 6 καὶ μὴ διηυλαβημένους: an instance of 'polar expression'; for διευλαβεῖσθαι means 'to avoid carefully' or 'scrupulously' (εὐλαβῶς).

82 a 7 ᾗ ἂν ... ἴοι, 'the way they would take,' a variation for οἵ, which some late MSS. unnecessarily read.

ἕκαστα, 'each class.' Note how the gender is varied (1) τοὺς ... προτετιμηκότας, (2) τὰς τοιαύτας (sc. ψυχάς), (3) ἕκαστα.

a 10 καὶ τούτων: i. e. καὶ τῶν ἄλλων. There are degrees of happiness even among souls which are not wholly purified.

a 11 τὴν δημοτικὴν καὶ πολιτικὴν ἀρετήν, 'popular goodness, the goodness of the good citizen.' This is related to philosophical goodness just as true belief is related to science. Socrates admits the relative value of both. For the phraseology cp. *Rep.* 619 c 7 ἔθει ἄνευ φιλοσοφίας ἀρετῆς μετειληφότα. Here πολιτική means 'belonging to citizens' (cp. *Gorg.* 452 e 4), not 'political'.

b 5 τοιοῦτον κτλ., 'a race civilized and tame like themselves.' The regular opposite of ἥμερος is ἄγριος, and both words are used of men, animals, and plants. They mean 'civilized', 'tame', 'cultivated', as opposed to 'savage', 'wild'.

b 8 ἄνδρας μετρίους, 'good men,' though of course only in the popular sense. We might have had ἐπιεικεῖς or σπουδαίους with the same meaning. Cp. 68 e 2 *n.*

b 10 μὴ φιλοσοφήσαντι ... ἀλλ' ἢ τῷ φιλομαθεῖ: the tendency to 'polar expression' here asserts itself at the expense of logic. The sentence ends as if οὐδενί had preceded. We must remember that φιλόσοφος and φιλομαθής are synonyms (*Rep.* 376 b 8 Ἀλλὰ μέντοι ... τό γε φιλομαθὲς καὶ φιλόσοφον ταὐτόν;). For ἀλλ' ἤ cp. 68 b 4 *n.*

c 3 οἱ ὀρθῶς φιλόσοφοι: cp. 67 b 4 *n.*

c 5 οἰκοφθορίαν, 'waste of substance.'

οἱ ... φιλοχρήματοι are contrasted with οἱ φίλαρχοί τε καὶ φιλότιμοι just below. Here once more we have the Pythagorean doctrine of the tripartite soul and the 'Three Lives'. Cp. 68 c 1 *n.*

c 8 ἔπειτα emphasizes the preceding participles.

d 1 μέντοι μὰ Δία: cp. 65 d 6 *n.*

d 3 σώματι πλάττοντες ζῶσι: most editors suspect πλάττοντες, and it has been emended in various ways. The true interpretation, however, was given by Vahlen long ago (cp. *Opusc.* i. 83). He pointed out that πλάττειν is used much in the same sense as θεραπεύειν in

64 d 8 and 81 b 2, and compared *Rep.* 377 c 3 καὶ πλάττειν τὰς ψυχὰς αὐτῶν τοῖς μύθοις πολὺ μᾶλλον ἢ τὰ σώματα ταῖς χερσίν, to which passage may be added *Tim.* 88 c 3 τόν τε αὖ σῶμα ἐπιμελῶς πλάττοντα. Cp. also Plut. Εἰ διδακτὸν ἡ ἀρετή 439 f ὥσπερ αἱ τίτθαι ταῖς χερσὶ τὸ σῶμα πλάττουσιν and *Coriolanus* 32. Vahlen holds further that σώματι is governed by ζῶσι, and that the meaning is 'live for the body, moulding it into shape', though the only example of ζῆν *c. dat.* in this sense which he quotes is in [Dem.] 7. 17 Φιλίππῳ ζῶντες καὶ οὐ τῇ ἑαυτῶν πατρίδι. Perhaps Eur. *Ion* 646 ἔα δ᾽ ἐμαυτῷ ζῆν με may be added. If this is not accepted, I would rather read σώματα with TW than have recourse to conjecture. The σώματι of B is, however, the *difficilior lectio*, and I believe Vahlen's interpretation to be right. His discussion (*loc. cit.*) of the use of participles with an object to be understood from the context should be read.

d 3 χαίρειν εἰπόντες, 'dismissing from their thoughts.' Cp. 63 e 3 *n.*

d 6 τῇ ἐκείνης λύσει: this, as well as καθαρμός, is Orphic. Olympiodorus quotes some Orphic verses, which at least contain some old ideas: Ὄργια ἐκτελέσουσι, λύσιν προγόνων ἀθεμίστων | μαιόμενοι· σὺ δὲ τοῖσιν ἔχων κράτος οὓς κ᾽ ἐθέλῃσθα | λύσεις ἔκ τε πόνων χαλεπῶν καὶ ἀπείρονος οἴστρου.

e 1 παραλαβοῦσα, 'taking in hand,' as a doctor takes his patient in hand for treatment. The vb. παραλαμβάνειν is technical in this sense, especially of teachers taking pupils. Cp. *Rep.* 541 a 1 τοὺς δὲ παῖδας αὐτῶν παραλαβόντες.

e 2 διαδεδεμένην: cp. 62 b 3 *n.* It is noteworthy that Socrates now adopts and expounds the very doctrine which he had put aside as 'too high'; for the εἱργμός is clearly the φρουρά. The reason is that he is now able to give a more scientific account of it.

e 4 κυλινδουμένην: cp. 81 d 1 *n.* Here the word means simply 'wallowing'. Cp. *Polit.* 309 a 5 τοὺς ... ἐν ἀμαθίᾳ ... καὶ ταπεινότητι πολλῇ κυλινδουμένους, *Theaet.* 172 c 8 οἱ ἐν δικαστηρίοις ... κυλινδούμενοι.

e 5 τὴν δεινότητα, 'the cleverness', 'the ingenuity'. So far as I can see, none of the editors take the word in this sense; but surely the point is just that the prison-house is ingeniously contrived so as to make the prisoner co-operate in his own imprisonment.

ὅτι δι᾽ ἐπιθυμίας ἐστίν, sc. ὁ εἱργμός, 'that it is effected by means

of desire,' i.e. 'that it has desire as its instrument'. As we shall
see, pleasures and pains, with which ἐπιθυμία is concerned, are the
agents by which the soul is imprisoned (83 d 4 ; 84 a 4).

e 6   ὡς ἂν ... εἴη. This is an extremely rare construction in Attic
prose, the nearest parallel being Xen. *Cyr.* i. 3. 8 καὶ διδόασι τοῖς
τρισὶ δακτύλοις ὀχοῦντες τὴν φιάλην καὶ προσφέρουσιν, ὡς ἂν ἐνδοῖεν τὸ
ἔκπωμα εὐληπτότατα τῷ μέλλοντι πίνειν. It is equivalent in sense to
ὅπως *c. fut. ind.* after verbs of 'ways and means' (the idea of con-
trivance being implied in δεινότητα). In other words, ὡς is a relative
adverb of manner, and ἄν is to be taken closely with the optative.
Tr. 'so as best to secure the prisoner's co-operation in his own
imprisonment'.

83 a 1   τοῦ δεδέσθαι : the MSS. have τῷ, but Heindorf's τοῦ restores the
normal construction of συλλαμβάνειν, 'to co-operate' (*dat.* of the
person with whom, *gen.* of the thing in which). Cp. Eur. *Med.* 946
συλλήψομαι δὲ τοῦδέ σοι κἀγὼ πόνου, Xen. *Mem.* ii. 2. 12 ἵνα ... ἀγαθοῦ
σοι γίγνηται συλλήπτωρ, ib. 7. 32 ἀγαθὴ συλλήπτρια τῶν ἐν εἰρήνῃ πόνων.

a 2   οὕτω ... ἔχουσαν go together, 'in this state.'

a 3   παραμυθεῖται : cp. 70 b 2 *n.*

b 1   ὅτι ἂν ... τῶν ὄντων : here it is once more implied that both the
objects of sense and the objects of thought are ὄντα. Cp. 79 a 6.

b 2   δι' ἄλλων, opp. αὐτὴ καθ' αὑτήν, and virtually equivalent to διὰ τῶν
αἰσθήσεων.

     ἐν ἄλλοις ὂν ἄλλο, opp. αὐτὸ καθ' αὑτό, 'that which varies in varying
conditions,' as opposed to τὸ ἀεὶ ὡσαύτως ἔχον.

b 6   οὕτως emphasizes the preceding participles. Tr. 'It is just
because she does not think it right to ... that she ...'

b 7   καὶ φόβων is omitted by T, the Petrie papyrus, and Iamblichus.
It looks as if it had been inserted to make this clause symmetrical
with the next, in which ἢ λυπηθῇ appears to have been inserted for
a similar reason. Plato avoids exact symmetry of this sort, though
his editors, ancient and modern, often foist it on him.

b 9   τοσοῦτον, here practically 'so small'.

c 1   ὧν : Iamblichus has ὡς, which would be more regular, but is to
be rejected for that very reason. The partitive genitive is used as
if only οὐδέν, not οὐδὲν τοσοῦτον, preceded.

c 3   καὶ οὐ λογίζεται αὐτό, 'and does not take it into account.'

c 5   ἀναγκάζεται ἅμα τε ... καὶ ... : the emphasis falls on ἅμα. A

belief in the reality of its object must arise simultaneously with any
strong feeling of pleasure or pain. We have really to deal, therefore, with a wrong view as to what is real, which is another way of
saying that goodness is knowledge.

c 8 ⟨τά⟩ seems necessary and could easily have been dropped by
haplography after μάλιστα.

d 4 ὥσπερ ἧλον ἔχουσα, 'with a rivet,' like Κράτος and Βία in the
Prometheus, as Geddes suggests. It is pleasure and pain that rivet
the fetters of the bodily prison-house.

d 9 οἷα: cp. 80 a 4 n.
καθαρῶς: Heindorf conjectured καθαρός, comparing 67 a 7 ; 80 e 2 ;
82 c 1 ; but the Petrie papyrus confirms the adverb.

10 ἀναπλέα, 'contaminated', 'tainted'. Cf. 67 a 5 n., and *Symp.*
211 e 1 εἰλικρινές, καθαρόν, ἄμεικτον, ἀλλὰ μὴ ἀνάπλεων σαρκῶν τε
ἀνθρωπίνων καὶ χρωμάτων. The feminine form is Ionic.

e 1 ἐμφύεσθαι : cp. *Tim.* 42 a 3 ὁπότε δὴ σώμασιν ἐμφυτευθεῖεν ἐξ ἀνάγκης
(ψυχαί).

e 5 οἱ δικαίως φιλομαθεῖς, synonymous with οἱ ὀρθῶς φιλόσοφοι, 'those
who deserve the name of philosophers.' Cp. 67 b 4 n.

e 6 κόσμιοι, equivalent to σώφρονες. Cp. 68 e 2 n.
οὐχ ὧν . . . ἕνεκά φασιν, 'not for the reason given by the mass of
men ' (cp. 82 c 5 sqq.). It is not necessary to discuss the precise
nature of the ellipse here ; for the meaning is plain. The Petrie
papyrus omits φασιν, as Hermann originally proposed to do. This
is the only case where it confirms a modern conjecture.

a 2 οὐ γάρ, 'No, indeed.' It is better to punctuate after γάρ than to
take οὐ γὰρ ἀλλά together with the older editors and Riddell (Dig.
§ 156).

a 3 τὴν μὲν φιλοσοφίαν κτλ. We must subordinate and say 'that,
while it is philosophy's business to release the soul, the soul should
hand itself over to pleasures and pains to fasten its chains once
more'.

a 4 αὑτήν, 'of itself', 'of its own accord'. Cp. 64 a 5.
παραδιδόναι (cp. 82 c 4) is the correlative of παραλαμβάνειν (82 e
1 n.). Once more pleasures and pains are represented as the agents
of the soul's imprisonment. The εἰργμός is δι' ἐπιθυμίας (82 e 5).

a 5 ἐγκαταδεῖν, sc. τῷ σώματι. Cp. 62 b 3 n.
ἀνήνυτον ἔργον . . . μεταχειριζομένης, 'to engage in the endless task

of a Penelope handling her web in the opposite way.' The vulgate μεταχειριζομένην is a late conjecture and has nothing to commend it. I formerly read μεταχειριζομένη with Peipers, which is certainly better (cp. R. G. Bury in *Class. Rev.* xx, p. 13). But μεταχειριζομένης is the reading of BTW, attested by the Petrie papyrus and Iamblichus, and would not be a natural mistake. It would be safer to write τινός for τινά if any change were required ; but the web is the real point of the metaphor, and the indefinite pronoun may attach itself to ἱστόν for that reason.

a 7   τούτων, sc. τῶν ἐπιθυμιῶν.

a 8   ἐν τούτῳ οὖσα : cp. 59 a 3 *n.*

τὸ ἀδόξαστον, 'what is not the object of belief (δόξα),' but of knowledge. The word is found only here in this sense. Cp. the similar use of ἀνόητον above 80 b 4.

b 3   ἀπηλλάχθαι, sc. οἴεται, not οἴεται δεῖν, as is shown by the nominative ἀφικομένη. The soul believes that after death she is done with all human ills.

b 4   οὐδὲν δεινὸν μὴ φοβηθῇ, 'there is no danger of her fearing.' Cp. *Apol.* 28 b 1 οὐδὲν δὲ δεινὸν μὴ ἐν ἐμοὶ στῇ, 'there is no fear of my being the last ', *Gorg.* 520 d 5 οὐδὲν δεινὸν αὐτῷ μήποτε ἀδικηθῇ, *Rep.* 465 b 8 οὐδὲν δεινὸν μή ποτε . . . διχοστατήσῃ.

b 5   [ταῦτα δ' ἐπιτηδεύσασα]: I take this to be an explanation of, or more probably an ancient variant for, ἐκ δὴ τῆς τοιαύτης τροφῆς. To change δ' into γ' with Stephanus and most editors is to hide the wound, not to heal it.

ὅπως μὴ . . . : cp. 77 b 4 *n.*

b 6   ἐν τῇ ἀπαλλαγῇ τοῦ σώματος : i. e. ἐπειδὰν ἀπαλλαγῇ τοῦ σώματος (70 a 2). The whole clause refers back to what Cebes said at 70 a.

Narrative interlude. Socrates is as ready as ever to hear objections to what he says (84 c 1—85 b 9).

This long interlude marks off the first part of the dialogue from the second, in which more serious objections have to be faced than those of οἱ πολλοί. There are scientific objections too.

c 2   πρὸς τῷ . . . λόγῳ ἦν, 'was absorbed in the foregoing argument.' Cp. *Phaedr.* 249 c 5 πρὸς γὰρ ἐκείνοις ἀεί ἐστιν, d 1 πρὸς τῷ θείῳ γιγνόμενος, *Rep.* 567 a 1 ἵνα . . . πρὸς τῷ καθ' ἡμέραν ἀναγκάζωνται εἶναι, Dem. 19. 127 ὅλος πρὸς τῷ λήμματι.

c 3 ὡς ἰδεῖν ἐφαίνετο, lit. 'as he appeared to look at', 'to judge from his appearance'. In this usage the epexegetic ἰδεῖν means much the same as τὴν ὄψιν. Cp. *Tim.* 52 e 1 παντοδαπὴν ἰδεῖν φαίνεσθαι, Eur. *Her.* 1002 εἰκών, ὡς ὁρᾶν ἐφαίνετο, Παλλάς.

c 4 σμικρὸν ... διελεγέσθην, 'went on talking in a low voice' (not 'for a little'). The opposite of (σ)μικρὸν λέγειν, &c., is μέγα λέγειν, &c. 'to speak loud.'

c 6 ἔχει ὑποψίας καὶ ἀντιλαβάς: 'it admits of, suggests, gives room for many misgivings and is open to many forms of attack' (ἀντιλαβή, like ἀντίληψις, 87 a 6, is a metaphor from wrestling, 'the opponent's grip').

d 3 εὐπορήσειν, 'that you will find a way out of your difficulty,' εὐπορία being the opposite of ἀπορία.

d 5 πάλαι, 'for some time.' Cp. 63 d 5 *n.*

e 2 μὴ ... διάκειμαι of fear for something in the present, whereas d 7 μὴ ... ᾖ refers to the future, 'lest it should prove to be'. It is incorrect to say that the present indicative implies certainty.

e 4 τῶν κύκνων: for the 'swan-song' cp. Aesch. *Ag.* 1444 ἡ δέ τοι (Cassandra) κύκνου δίκην | τὸν ὕστατον μελψασα θανάσιμον γόον | κεῖται. Aristotle, *Hist. An.* 615 b 2 ᾠδικοὶ δὲ (οἱ κύκνοι) καὶ περὶ τὰς τελευτὰς μάλιστα ᾄδουσιν· ἀναπέτονται γὰρ καὶ εἰς τὸ πέλαγος, καί τινες ἤδη πλέοντες παρὰ τὴν Λιβύην περιέτυχον ἐν τῇ θαλάττῃ πολλοῖς ᾄδουσι φωνῇ γοώδει, καὶ τούτων ἑώρων ἀποθνήσκοντας ἐνίους. Cp. D'Arcy Thompson, *Glossary of Greek Birds*, p. 106 sq.

a 1 κάλλιστα: this is Blomfield's correction of the MS. μάλιστα, and is now known to be the reading of W, though the first hand has written καὶ μάλιστα above the line. We cannot defend μάλιστα by interpreting it as 'loudest'. That would be μέγιστον, which I had conjectured before the reading of W was known.

a 2 τὸν θεόν: Apollo, as we presently learn, and, in particular, Apollo Hyperboreus who, as I have shown in E. Gr. Ph.² p. 97, *n.* 3, was the chief god of the Pythagoreans (cp. 60 d 2 *n.*). Aristophanes too was aware that the swans sang to Apollo. Cp. *Birds* 769 τοιάδε κύκνοι ... συμμιγῆ βοήν, ὁμοῦ πτεροῖς κρέκοντες, ἴακχον Ἀπόλλω ... ὄχθῳ ἐφεζόμενοι παρ' Ἔβρον ποταμόν.

a 3 τὸ αὑτῶν δέος τοῦ θανάτου, 'their own fear of death.' (Some editors wrongly take τοῦ θανάτου with καταψεύδονται.)

a 5 ἐξᾴδειν, 'to sing a song of departure.' There is some reason to believe that the last song of the chorus was spoken of as τὰ ἐξῳδικά as well as τὸ ἐξόδιον. The scholiast on Ar. *Wasps* 270 says so, though the text is generally emended to τὰ ἐξοδικά, and Plotinus, *Enn.* 6. 9. 8 (p. 1404. 10) says οἷον χορὸς ἐξᾴδων. Cp. Polyb. xxxi. 20. 1 μάτην ἐξᾴσας τὸ κύκνειον, Plut. *Symp.* 161 c (of Arion) ἐξᾷσαι δὲ καὶ τὸν βίον τελευτῶν, καὶ μὴ γενέσθαι κατὰ τοῦτο τῶν κύκνων ἀγεννέστερος.

a 7 ἥ τε ἀηδὼν καὶ χελιδὼν καὶ ὁ ἔποψ (note how Plato avoids the formalism of the article, Riddell, Dig. § 237). These are the three birds of Attic legend, Procne, Philomela, and Tereus. Procne, not ' Philomel ', is the nightingale in Athenian legend.

b 3 διαφερόντως ἥ, ' in a higher degree than,' cp. below 95 c 3. The construction διαφέρειν ἥ is as regular as διαφέρειν *c. gen.*

b 5 ἱερὸς τοῦ αὐτοῦ θεοῦ : we know from the *Apology* that Socrates regarded himself as consecrated to Apollo by the answer given to Chaerephon at Delphi. The view that Plato invented this does not merit discussion. With the expression ὁμόδουλος cp. *Apol.* 23 c 1 διὰ τὴν τοῦ θεοῦ λατρείαν.

b 6 οὐ χεῖρον . . . ἔχειν, ' that I possess the art in no inferior degree ', ' that I am not worse provided than they are with the gift of prophecy at my Master's hands'. Cp. Hdt. iii. 130 φλαύρως ἔχειν τὴν τέχνην.

b 8 τούτου γ᾽ ἕνεκα, ' so far as that is concerned.' Cp. 106 d 2.

b 9 Ἀθηναίων : the absence of the article is normal, and the position of the word suggests the official style.

The Objections of Simmias and Cebes (85 b 10—95 e 6).

(1) *The Objection of Simmias* (85 b 10—86 d 4).

c 3 τὸ μὲν σαφὲς εἰδέναι, ' sure knowledge.' As we have seen (62 b 5), Plato represents Socrates as speaking with a certain reserve as to the details of the doctrine.

c 4 μὴ οὐχὶ . . . καὶ μὴ . . . : the negatives are not co-ordinate. The first is dependent on μαλθακοῦ εἶναι ἀνδρός (which implies a negative and therefore takes μὴ οὐ). The second merely introduces a negative statement of παντὶ τρόπῳ ἐλέγχειν. Tr. ' To fail to test them in every way without desisting till one is utterly exhausted by examining them on every side, shows a very poor spirit '.

c 7 ἢ μαθεῖν ... ἢ εὑρεῖν, 'either to learn (from another) or find out (for oneself).' This contrast had an almost proverbial currency. Cp. Soph. fr. 731 τὰ μὲν διδακτὰ μανθάνω, τὰ δ' εὑρετὰ | ζητῶ· τὰ δ' εὐκτὰ παρὰ θεῶν ᾐτησάμην. So below 99 c 8.

c 8 εἰ ταῦτα ἀδύνατον : cp. *Parm.* 160 a 2 ταῦτα δὲ ἀδύνατον ἐφάνη.

d 1 ὀχούμενον: cp. Ar. *Knights* 1244 λεπτή τις ἐλπίς ἐστ' ἐφ' ἧς ὀχούμεθα. ὥσπερ ἐπὶ σχεδίας : cp. Cic. *Tusc.* i. 30 *tamquam in rate in mari immenso nostra vehitur oratio.* Simmias is thinking of the raft of Odysseus.

d 3 λόγου θείου τινός : this must refer to the Orphic and Pythagorean doctrine of the soul. It is quite in keeping with all we can make out as to the history of Pythagoreanism that Simmias and Cebes should feel regretfully that they can no longer accept the λόγος of their society. We are just about to learn that they had adopted a view of the soul which was wholly inconsistent with it. I assume that Heindorf is right in deleting ἤ; for otherwise the whole phrase must go. The conjunction ἤ is never used to introduce an explanation. Even, however, if ἢ λόγου θείου τινός is an adscript, or a question asked by some reader, it gives a perfectly correct explanation of the meaning, as is shown by c 9 τῶν ἀνθρωπίνων λόγων.

d 7 πρὸς ἐμαυτόν : cp. 95 e 7 πρὸς ἑαυτόν τι σκεψάμενος.

e 3 ἔμοιγε, sc. οὐ φαίνεται ἱκανῶς εἰρῆσθαι.

περὶ ἁρμονίας, 'with regard to the tuning of a lyre and its strings.' It is important to remember here that ἁρμονία does not mean what we call 'harmony'. It has its literal sense of 'tuning' in a certain key or mode, from which its other senses, 'scale' and 'octave', are easily derived. What we call 'harmony' is in Greek συμφωνία. Cp. 86 a 1 ἐν τῇ ἡρμοσμένῃ λύρᾳ, 'in the tuned lyre.'

a 3 κατάξῃ refers to the framework of the lyre, διατέμῃ and διαρρήξῃ ('cut and break') to the strings. Schanz (*Stud.* p. 36) regards διατέμῃ as an adscript to διαρρήξῃ. It is true that in a 7 we have only διερρωγυιῶν and not διατετμημένων, but that is just Plato's way of avoiding formal symmetry.

a 6 οὐδεμία ... ἂν εἴη : Bekker brackets ἄν, which restores the normal construction on the assumption that εἴη is indirect speech for ἐστί. But the direct speech might very well be ἂν εἴη, which would remain unchanged in *oratio obliqua.*

b 2 ἀλλὰ φαίη ἀνάγκη ... εἶναι : the original protasis εἴ τις διισχυρίζοιτο

... ὡς κτλ. is resumed, but in *oratio recta*, as is natural after the parenthesis. Of course, φαίη still depends upon εἰ in a 4, but has no effect upon the construction. It is the parenthetical φησί, *inquit*, adapted to the construction of the long protasis. We might write ἀλλὰ (φαίη) ἀνάγκη κτέ.

b 5 καὶ γὰρ οὖν κτλ.: Simmias here interrupts himself. He thinks he may as well drop the imaginary τις and state plainly that the comparison of the soul to a ἁρμονία is their own doctrine. The hesitation with which he does so is responsible for the cumbrousness of the sentence, and is the natural consequence of the feelings which he expressed in the interlude.

καὶ αὐτόν σε κτλ.: it is assumed that Socrates is familiar with the recent developments of Pythagoreanism, though he may not accept them.

b 6 ὑπολαμβάνομεν: who are 'we' this time? Most editors suppose that no particular school is meant, and that the theory under discussion was simply a popular belief. This is most improbable. It has all the marks of being a medical theory, and we now know that Philolaus was a medical writer (E. Gr. Ph.² p. 322). Further, the doctrine was held at a later date by Aristoxenus, who was acquainted with the last of the Pythagoreans (E. Gr. Ph.² p. 320), who were disciples of Philolaus like Simmias. We shall see below (88 d 3) that Echecrates, another disciple of Philolaus, had accepted it too. I have pointed out elsewhere (E. Gr. Ph.² pp. 339 sqq.) how such a doctrine would naturally arise from the attempt to adapt Pythagoreanism to the views of the Sicilian school of medicine, which were based on the Empedoclean doctrine of the four 'elements' identified with the 'opposites' hot and cold, wet and dry (E. Gr. Ph.² p. 235). Further confirmation of this view will be found in the following notes. Aristotle says (*De An.* A. 4. 407 b 27 καὶ ἄλλη δέ τις δόξα παραδέδοται περὶ ψυχῆς, πιθανὴ μὲν πολλοῖς οὐδεμιᾶς ἥττον τῶν λεγομένων, λόγους δ' ὥσπερ εὐθύνας δεδωκυῖα καὶ τοῖς ἐν κοινῷ γινομένοις λόγοις (i. e. dialectical discussions)· ἁρμονίαν γάρ τινα αὐτὴν λέγουσιν· καὶ γὰρ τὴν ἁρμονίαν κρᾶσιν καὶ σύνθεσιν ἐναντίων εἶναι, καὶ τὸ σῶμα συγκεῖσθαι ἐξ ἐναντίων.

b 7 ὥσπερ ἐντεταμένου κτλ. The body is thought of as an instrument tuned to a certain pitch, the opposites hot and cold, wet and dry taking the place of high and low (ὀξὺ καὶ βαρύ) in music.

8 καὶ συνεχομένου, 'and held together.' It is the presence of the opposites hot and cold, wet and dry which keeps the body together, so long as neither opposite prevails unduly over the other (cp. Zeno, ap. Diog. Laert. ix. 29 καὶ ψυχὴν κρᾶμα ὑπάρχειν ἐκ τῶν προειρημένων (the four opposites) κατὰ μηδενὸς τούτων ἐπικράτησιν).

ὑπὸ θερμοῦ κτλ. This was the characteristic doctrine of the Sicilian school. Cp. *Anon. Lond.* xx. 25 (from Meno's Ἰατρικά) Φιλιστίων δ' οἴεται ἐκ τεττάρων ἰδεῶν συνεστάναι ἡμᾶς, τοῦτ' ἔστιν ἐκ τεττάρων στοιχείων· πυρός, ἀέρος, ὕδατος, γῆς. εἶναι δὲ καὶ ἑκάστου δυνάμεις, τοῦ μὲν πυρὸς τὸ θερμόν, τοῦ δὲ ἀέρος τὸ ψυχρόν, τοῦ δὲ ὕδατος τὸ ὑγρόν, τῆς δὲ γῆς τὸ ξηρόν. Cp. the speech of the physician Eryximachus in *Symp.* 186 d 6 ἔστι δὲ ἔχθιστα τὰ ἐναντιώτατα, ψυχρὸν θερμῷ, πικρὸν γλυκεῖ, ξηρὸν ὑγρῷ ... τούτοις ἐπιστηθεὶς ἔρωτα ἐμποιῆσαι καὶ ὁμόνοιαν ὁ ἡμέτερος πρόγονος Ἀσκληπιὸς ... συνέστησεν τὴν ἡμετέραν τέχνην.

9 κρᾶσιν, *temperaturam.* The word was properly used of the mixture of wine and water in the κρατήρ in certain fixed proportions. This seems to have been an earlier way of describing what the later Pythagoreans called a ἁρμονία. Parmenides (fr. 16) already speaks of the κρᾶσις μελέων, and Diogenes Laertius ix. 29 ascribes the theory to Zeno (cp. above b 8 *n*). The whole doctrine of the 'temperaments' is a development of this. Eryximachus (*Symp.* 188 a 1) uses both terms in connexion with climate (ἡ τῶν ὡρῶν τοῦ ἐνιαυτοῦ σύστασις) which is good ἐπειδὰν ... πρὸς ἄλληλα ... τά τε θερμὰ καὶ τὰ ψυχρὰ καὶ ξηρὰ καὶ ὑγρὰ ... ἁρμονίαν καὶ κρᾶσιν λάβῃ σώφρονα.

2 εἰ οὖν τυγχάνει κτλ., 'if then our soul is just a tuning.' After the explanation given in the last parenthesis, the protasis is resumed (hence οὖν) in another form. For the present εἴ τις διισχυρίζοιτο κτλ. is dropped.

3 ὅταν χαλασθῇ: χαλᾶν is a regular synonym of ἀνιέναι, *relaxare*, to loosen a string. The opposite is ἐπιτείνειν, *intendere*.

6 ἐν τοῖς φθόγγοις, 'in musical notes.' In Attic the word φθόγγος is practically confined to the meanings 'note' (whether in music or the notes of birds) and 'accent'.

1 ὅρα οὖν: this introduces the apodosis, which also contains, in the words ἐάν τις ἀξιοῖ, a reminiscence of the original protasis εἴ τις διισχυρίζοιτο.

d 3 τῶν ἐν τῷ σώματι, of the elemental opposites (hot-cold, wet-dry) of which the body is composed.

(2) *The objection of Cebes* (86 d 5—88 b 8).

d 5 Διαβλέψας, ' with a broad stare ' (aor. pcp. synchronous to ἔφη). This verb occurs nowhere else before Aristotle Περὶ ἐνυπνίων 462 a 12 ἐνίοις γὰρ τῶν νεωτέρων καὶ πάμπαν διαβλέπουσιν, ἐὰν ᾖ σκότος, φαίνεται εἴδωλα πολλὰ κινούμενα, where it plainly means ' having the eyes wide open '. The words ὥσπερ . . . εἰώθει suggest that the reference is to the well-known peculiarity of Socrates' eyes described in *Theaet.* 143 e 9 as τὸ ἔξω τῶν ὀμμάτων, a peculiarity also referred to in Xen. *Symp.* 5. 5, where Socrates says that his eyes are able to see, not only what is in front of him (τὸ κατ' εὐθύ), but also τὸ ἐκ πλαγίου (obliquely) διὰ τὸ ἐπιπόλαιοι εἶναι (because they are *à fleur de tête*). That this is the meaning of τὸ ἔξω τῶν ὀμμάτων is, I think, proved by the opposition of ἐξόφθαλμος (so Plato, *Theaet.* 209 c 1) to κοιλόφθαλμος in Xen. *Eq.* 1. 9, though in itself Campbell's suggestion that τὸ ἔξω refers to the position of the eyes and the width between them is perfectly possible. It is the same peculiarity which Aristophanes intends when he makes the Clouds say to Socrates (*Clouds* 362) τὠφθαλμὼ παραβάλλεις. If this is so, δια- does not mean ' through ', but ' apart ', as in διαβαίνω, so we must not translate ' with a piercing glance '. The phrase ταυρηδὸν ὑποβλέψας below (117 b 5) means something rather different.

d 7 τί οὐκ ἀπεκρίνατο; the aorist in such questions expresses impatience. Cp. *Gorg.* 509 e 2 τί οὐκ αὐτό γέ μοι τοῦτο ἀπεκρίνω; So already Hdt. ix. 48 τί δὴ οὐ . . . ἐμαχεσάμεθα;

d 8 ἁπτομένῳ τοῦ λόγου, ' handling the argument.' Cp. *Euthyd.* 283 a 2 ἐπεσκόπουν τίνα ποτὲ τρόπον ἅψοιντο τοῦ λόγου. Heindorf's view that ἅπτεσθαι is here used *reprehendendi et impugnandi potestate* seems improbable, though adopted in L. and S.

e 1 χρόνου ἐγγενομένου, ' when we had had time.' Cp. *Symp.* 184 a 6 ἵνα χρόνος ἐγγένηται. The phrase is common in Thucydides.

e 2 ἔπειτα [δέ]: the balance of evidence is in favour of omitting δέ. Cp. 73 a 7 *n.*

συγχωρεῖν, sc. δοκεῖ χρῆναι.

e 3 αὐτοῖς, sc. Σιμμίᾳ καὶ Κέβητι.

ἐάν τι δοκῶσι προσᾴδειν, ' if it appears that they are at all in tune.'

The voice and the accompanying instrument are said προσᾴδειν or ἀπᾴδειν. Socrates gently rallies the musical terminology of the Thebans. Cp. 92 c 5.

e 3 οὕτως ἤδη, *tum demum*, 'then and not till then.' There is a slight anacoluthon, as ἤ has preceded.

e 4 ὑπερδικεῖν is a poetical word found only in late prose.

e 5 τὸ ... θρᾶττον, 'what is troubling you.' Here we have an old word (Pind., Aesch.), though with Att. -ττ- for -σσ-. Cp. the Homeric τέτρηχα. The reading τό is well attested, so ἀπιστίαν παρέχει is probably due to the same hand as the interpolation at 69 e 3. The change of τό to ὅ in later MSS. is clearly a 'conjecture'.

e 6 ἐν τῷ αὐτῷ ... εἶναι, 'to have got no further.'

e 7 ὅπερ ... ταὐτὸν ... ἔχειν, 'to be open to the same criticism as we made in our former argument' (77 b 1 sqq.).

a 2 τόδε τὸ εἶδος, 'this (human) body.' Cp. 76 c 12.

οὐκ ἀνατίθεμαι, 'I do not retract,' a metaphor ἀπὸ τῶν πεττευόντων καὶ τὰς κεκινημένας ἤδη ψήφους (' pieces ') διορθούντων (Harpocration). Cp. *Hipparch.* 229 e 3 ὥσπερ πεττεύων ἐθέλω ... ἀναθέσθαι. It takes the construction of verbs of denying.

a 3 χαριέντως, syn. εὖ, καλῶς. Cp. 80 c 6 *n*.

ἐπαχθές, 'exaggerated.' The word is applied not only to arrogant self-praise (Dem. *Cor.* 10 ἵνα μηδὲν ἐπαχθὲς λέγω) but also to 'overdone' or 'fulsome' praise of others. Cp. *Laws* 688 d 6 λόγῳ ... σε, ὦ ξένε, ἐπαινεῖν ἐπαχθέστερον. It is just this sensitiveness to τὸ ἐπαχθές which accounts for the way of speaking described in 68 e 2 *n*.

a 5 οὔ μοι δοκεῖ τῇδε, SC. ἱκανῶς ἀποδεδεῖχθαι, 'I think the demonstration is deficient in this respect.'

a 6 ἀντιλήψει, 'objection,' a metaphor from wrestling; cp. 84 c 7 ἀντιλαβάς.

a 7 τί οὖν ἂν φαίη ὁ λόγος: the argument is often personified in this way. Cf. *Soph.* 238 b 4 ὥς φησιν ὁ λόγος. For the position of ἄν cp. 102 a 1. The parenthesis was so familiar that φαίη ἄν was not consciously to the speaker a separate clause. (Riddell, Dig. § 295.)

b 4 ὁμοίως ... ὥσπερ ἄν τις ... λέγοι, 'with as much right as if.' The whole of this section is thrown into the form of a reported dialogue between ὁ λέγων and ὁ ἀπιστῶν.

b 5 ἀνθρώπου ὑφάντου πρεσβύτου, simply 'an old weaver'. It is idiomatic to add ἄνθρωπος to the names of trades. In Scots we might say a 'webster body'.

b 6 ὅτι οὐκ ἀπόλωλεν κτλ., 'that the man is not dead, but is safe and sound somewhere.' Of course this is not supposed to be an argument for the continued existence of the weaver's *soul*, but is meant to disprove the fact of his death in the ordinary sense of the word. The weaver corresponds to the soul, and the garment to the body.

b 7 σῶς: all MSS. have ἴσως, but it is difficult to reject Forster's correction σῶς in view of the next line and c 5 below.

αὐτὸς ὑφηνάμενος: this touch is not necessary to the argument, nor indeed is it strictly necessary that the old man should be a weaver at all; but Cebes has in view a theory of the soul weaving the body as its garment, which is pretty nearly the opposite of the view that it is the ἁρμονία or κρᾶσις of the elementary opposites. The latter makes the soul a resultant of the bodily organization, the former makes it the organizing principle. The view that the body is the garment of the soul is primitive (cp. the Orphic χιτών, and Empedocles, fr. 126 Diels σαρκῶν ἀλλόγνωτι περιστέλλουσα χιτῶνι, E. Gr. Ph.² p. 258, *n.* 1) ; but the theory of Simmias is essentially Heraclitean. Such eclecticism was characteristic of the time.

c 1 ἀπιστοίη is Heindorf's correction of the MS. ἀπιστῶν, which seems to involve an incredible anacoluthon ; seeing that ἀνερωτῴη must have the τις in b 4, not that in b 8, for its subject.

c 3 τινος strikes me as a not very successful attempt at botching the sentence after ἀπιστοίη had been corrupted into ἀπιστῶν. The argument surely requires that the person asked, not 'some one', should give the answer, and we can easily supply αὐτοῦ from the context.

c 6 τὸ δ(έ), 'whereas,' *cum tamen.* This is a fairly common Platonic idiom (cp. 109 d 8), though it can hardly be said that it has been satisfactorily explained.

c 7 πᾶς [γὰρ] ἂν ὑπολάβοι, 'any one would retort,' rather than 'every one would understand'. The γάρ is more likely to have been inserted in B than dropped in TW. The asyndeton is quite correct.

ὅτι εὔηθες λέγει κτλ., 'that this is a silly argument.' The verb is used twice over in order to make the construction personal.

c 8   οὗτος, *iste*, 'this weaver of yours.'

d 4   ψυχὴ πρὸς σῶμα, 'the relation of soul to body will admit of the same comparison.'

d 5   μέτρι(α) ... λέγειν: *i. q. εὖ λέγειν.* Cp. 96 d 6.

d 7   ἂν φαίη: cp. 87 a 7 *n.*

d 8   εἰ γὰρ ῥέοι κτλ., 'for, even if the body is in a state of flux and is perishing while the man is still living, yet the soul always weaves afresh the web that is worn out.' This is a parenthesis intended to justify the statement that each soul wears out many bodies. The optative is regular in the parentheses of indirect speech, and ἀλλά means *at.* For the theory (which is just that of modern physiology) cp. *Tim.* 43 a 4 τὰς τῆς ἀθανάτου ψυχῆς περιόδους ἐνέδουν εἰς ἐπίρρυτον σῶμα καὶ ἀπόρρυτον. It is essentially Heraclitean (E. Gr. Ph.² pp. 161 sqq.).

e 3   τυχεῖν ... ἔχουσαν, 'it must have at the time.'

e 4   τὴν φύσιν τῆς ἀσθενείας, 'its natural weakness.' Such words as φύσις are often used with the genitive to form a mere periphrasis for the noun which they govern, but their proper meaning may emerge more or less, as here.

e 5   ἐπιδεικνύοι ... διοίχοιτο: the construction reverts to d 5 μέτρι' ἄν μοι φαίνοιτο λέγειν, ὡς ... All this is still the speech of ὁ ἀπιστῶν. There is a much stronger instance of an oblique optative with nothing to depend on below 95 d 3.

a 1   εἰ γάρ τις κτλ. These words are addressed, not (as Heindorf and Stallbaum thought) by Cebes to Simmias, but by the supposed objector to Cebes. 'Even if,' he says, 'we were to make a still greater concession to the man who uses this argument (τῷ λέγοντι) than the concession which you (Cebes) mention' (above 87 a 1 sqq.).

a 6   αὐτό, 'the thing in question,' i. e. the soul. Cp. below 109 a 9.

a 7   ψυχήν (τὴν ψυχήν W) is added for clearness after γιγνομένην. The more regular construction would be to say either αὐτήν or γιγνόμενον.

a 8   μηκέτι συγχωροῖ: these words continue the protasis and still depend on εἰ, 88 a 1. 'If, having granted this, he were to stop short of making the further admission that . . .'

πονεῖν was technical for λυπεῖσθαι in fifth-century philosophy. Cp. Anaxagoras (quoted in Aristotle's *Ethics* 1154 b 7) ἀεὶ πονεῖ τὸ ζῷον.

b 3   εἰ δὲ τοῦτο οὕτως ἔχει κτλ.   The original protasis, εἰ ... τις ... συγχωρήσειεν, which has just been continued by b 2 φαίη, is dropped, and a new protasis, resuming the argument of τις, is begun.

οὐδενὶ προσήκει, 'no one has a right', 'is entitled'.   Stephanus reads προσήκειν.

b 4   θάνατον θαρροῦντι: as θαρρεῖν is equivalent to οὐ (μὴ) φοβεῖσθαι (cp. 63 e 10 n.) it naturally takes an object accusative.

b 6   ἀνάγκην εἶναι is dependent on b 2 φαίη.   The reported speech which is dropped for a moment at b 4 προσήκει reasserts itself here.

Dramatic Interlude.   The effect of the objections (88 c 1—89 a 8).

The importance of this break in the argument is marked by the fact that it takes us back to Phlius and Echecrates, and that the dramatic form is resumed.   It has to be shown that current Pythagorean views about the soul are inadequate and that we must go deeper.

c 4   εἰς ἀπιστίαν καταβαλεῖν: cp. *Phileb.* 15 e 4 εἰς ἀπορίαν αὐτὸν ... καταβάλλων.

οὐ μόνον τοῖς ... ἀλλὰ καὶ εἰς τά ...   The change of construction is characteristic.

c 6   μὴ ... εἶμεν ... ᾖ: the change of mood is due to the fact that the first verb refers to the present, the second to the future.   The opt. μὴ εἶμεν is the indirect form of μὴ ... ἔσμεν, while μὴ ... ᾖ means 'lest they should prove to be'.   The subj. here might also have become opt., but this would have obscured the difference of meaning.   For other instances cp. Riddell, Dig. § 89.

d 1   ἐπέρχεται, 'it is borne in upon me.'

d 2   ὡς ... ὤν: exclamations, like interrogations, may be conveyed by a participial phrase.

d 4   ἀντιλαμβάνεται: this is a different application of the metaphor from wrestling, explained 84 c 6 n.   Cp. *Parm.* 130 e 2 οὔπω σου ἀντείληπται φιλοσοφία ὡς ἔτι ἀντιλήψεται.

d 9   μετῆλθε τὸν λόγον: cp. 76 e 9 n.   The λόγος is the game which is hunted.   So *Meno* 74 d 3 εἰ οὖν ὥσπερ ἐγὼ μετῄει τὸν λόγον, *Soph.* 252 b 8 ἔτι τοίνυν ἂν ... καταγελαστότατα μετίοιεν τὸν λόγον.   That this is the meaning appears from the equivalent phrase διώκειν τὸν λόγον *Theaet.* 166 d 8.

e 1   τι is internal object of ἀχθόμενος.

e 2   ἐβοήθει τῷ λόγῳ. Here we have a different, but almost equally common, metaphor.

a 1   ἐκεῖνος : cp. Riddell, Dig. § 194.

a 2   ὡς ἡδέως κτλ. : cp. 58 e 4 *n.*

a 3   ἀγαμένως: Plato often uses ἄγαμαι of the effect produced on Socrates by his interlocutors.

Protreptic interlude (89 a 9 — 91 c 5).   *A Warning against* μισολογία.

b 1   ἐπὶ χαμαιζήλου τινός : Χαμαίζηλος· διφρίον μικρόν, ἢ ταπεινὸν σκιμπόδιον (Timaeus, *s. v.*).

b 2   καταψήσας οὖν κτλ. This is imitated in Xenophon's *Apology* 28 τὸν δὲ λέγεται καταψήσαντα αὐτοῦ τὴν κεφαλὴν εἰπεῖν κτλ. In Xenophon, however, it is the head of Apollodorus that Socrates strokes. This is pointless ; for he would hardly wear his hair long like the youthful Phaedo. It appears from the following words that Socrates wishes to see how Phaedo will look with his hair cropped as a sign of mourning.

b 8   'Ἀλλὰ τί ; 'What then?' Heindorf shows from Aristophanes that this was a regular colloquial formula.

b 10   ἀναβιώσασθαι : cp. 71 e 13 *n.* The metaphor here implied is the same as in βοηθεῖν τῷ λόγῳ, 88 e 2.

c 1   εἰ . . . με διαφεύγοι : here we have the other metaphor, the hunting of the λόγος.

c 2   ὥσπερ Ἀργεῖοι : Hdt. i. 82 Ἀργεῖοι μέν νυν ἀπὸ τούτου τοῦ χρόνου κατακειράμενοι τὰς κεφαλάς, πρότερον ἐπάναγκες κομέοντες, ἐποιήσαντο νόμον τε καὶ κατάρην μὴ πρότερον θρέψειν κόμην Ἀργείων μηδένα . . . πρὶν Θυρέας ἀνασώσωνται.

c 5   πρὸς δύο . . . οὐδ' ὁ Ἡρακλῆς : the proverb is more fully explained in *Euthyd.* 297 c 1 τοῦ Ἡρακλέους, ὃς οὐχ οἷός τε ἦν τῇ τε ὕδρᾳ διαμάχεσθαι . . . καὶ καρκίνῳ τινὶ . . . ἐκ θαλάττης ἀφιγμένῳ . . . ὃς ἐπειδὴ αὐτὸν ἐλύπει οὕτως ἐκ τοῦ ἐπ' ἀριστερὰ . . . δάκνων, τὸν Ἰόλεων τὸν ἀδελφιδοῦν βοηθὸν ἐπεκαλέσατο, ὁ δὲ αὐτῷ ἱκανῶς ἐβοήθησεν.

c 7   ἕως ἔτι φῶς ἐστιν : cp. 61 e 4 *n.*

c 10   τὸν Ἡρακλῆ : the poetical form (cp. Soph. *Trach.* 476) is purposely used to suggest a poetical reminiscence (Vahlen, *Opusc.* i, p. 485).

d 1 μισόλογοι, 'haters of discourses' or 'arguments' (not 'reason'), as appears from d 3 λόγους μισήσας. Minucius Felix, *Octav.* xiv. 4, quoted by Geddes, translates quite correctly *igitur nobis providendum est ne odio identidem sermonum omnium laboremus.*

d 2 τούτου ... ἤ ...: cp. *Crito* 44 c 2 τίς ἂν αἰσχίων εἴη ταύτης δόξα ἢ δοκεῖν κτλ. Riddell, Dig. § 163.

d 5 ἄνευ τέχνης: the meaning of this is made clear by e 5 ἄνευ τέχνης τῆς περὶ τἀνθρώπεια.

e 2 οὐδενὸς οὐδὲν ὑγιές: cp. 90 c 3, Ar. *Plut.* 362 ὡς οὐδὲν ἀτεχνῶς ὑγιές ἐστιν οὐδενός. So *Crat.* 440 c 6 καὶ αὑτοῦ τε καὶ τῶν ὄντων καταγιγνώσκειν ὡς οὐδὲν ὑγιὲς οὐδενός. For the meaning of ὑγιές cp. 69 b 8 *n.*

90 a 1 σφόδρα qualifies χρηστοὺς καὶ πονηρούς, not ὀλίγους, as is shown by a 4 τῶν σφόδρα σμικρῶν καὶ μεγάλων.

a 8 τὰ ... ἄκρα τῶν ἐσχάτων: the ἔσχατα are opposed to τὰ μεταξύ, and the ἄκρα are the extremes of these.

b 2 φανῆναι: cp. 72 c 1 *n.*

b 4 ταύτῃ μὲν οὐχ ... ἀλλ' ἐκείνῃ, ᾗ ..., 'that is not the point of comparison but this ...'

b 7 τῆς περὶ τοὺς λόγους τέχνης: the term Logic (λογική, sc. τέχνη) originated from phrases like this, though neither ἡ λογική nor τὰ λογικά are used till a far later date. Logic is thought of here as an art of dealing with arguments, just as the art of life (ἡ περὶ τὰ ἀνθρώπεια τέχνη 89 e 5) teaches us to deal with men.

b 8 ὤν, 'being so.' We cannot take ὤν here as equivalent to 'being true' with some editors. If anything, it is ψευδής that must be supplied.

b 9 καὶ μάλιστα δὴ κτλ. The protasis which began at b 6 ἐπειδάν is forgotten and never resumed.

οἱ περὶ τοὺς ἀντιλογικοὺς λόγους διατρίψαντες: the true originator of ἀντιλογικοὶ λόγοι was Zeno of Elea, who was some twenty years older than Socrates (E. Gr. Ph.[2] p. 358). From quite another point of view Protagoras maintained δύο λόγους εἶναι περὶ ἅπαντος πράγματος, ἀντικειμένους ἀλλήλοις, οἷς καὶ συνηρώτα, πρῶτος τοῦτο πράξας (Diog. Laert. ix. 51). Cp. 101 e 2.

c 4 ἀτεχνῶς ὥσπερ ἐν Εὐρίπῳ: the current in the Euripus was said to change its direction seven times a day (Strabo ix. 403). In reality the παλίρροια is more irregular, being partly tidal and partly due to *seiches*. Cp. Pauly-Wissowa, vi, col. 1283. The current is strong enough to stop a steamer. For ἀτεχνῶς introducing such expressions cp. 59 a 4 *n.*

c 5 ἄνω κάτω στρέφεται κτλ. The language of this sentence is just that which is elsewhere used of the followers of Heraclitus (E. Gr. Ph.² p. 417 *n.* 3). Cp. *Crat.* 440 c 6 αὐτοῦ τε καὶ τῶν ὄντων καταγιγνώσκειν ὡς οὐδὲν ὑγιὲς οὐδενός, ἀλλὰ πάντα ὥσπερ κεράμια ῥεῖ, καὶ ἀτεχνῶς ὥσπερ οἱ κατάρρῳ νοσοῦντες ἄνθρωποι οὕτως οἴεσθαι καὶ τὰ πράγματα διακεῖσθαι, ἀπὸ ῥεύματός τε καὶ κατάρρου πάντα χρήματα ἔχεσθαι. Now, in the *Theaetetus* Plato makes Socrates say that Protagoras justified his πάντων χρημάτων μέτρον ἄνθρωπος by basing it on the doctrine of Heraclitus. It seems, then, that Protagoras is mainly intended here. It is certain, at any rate, that Plato would not have made Socrates refer in this way either to Antisthenes or Euclides; for both are supposed to be present.

c 9 δή τινος: the particle δή follows the interrogative τίς but precedes the indefinite τις. Cp. 107 d 7; 108 c 1; 115 d 4.

d 1 ἔπειτα marks inconsistency or inconsequence by emphasizing the preceding participle.

d 9 μὴ παρίωμεν, 'let us not admit' (from παρίημι).

e 2 πολὺ μᾶλλον: we must supply ἐννοῶμεν or some such word from the context.

a 2 οἱ πάνυ ἀπαίδευτοι: here we have the beginnings of the characteristic Aristotelian use of ἀπαιδευσία for ignorance of Logic. Aristotle applies the word to the followers of Antisthenes (*Met.* Z. 3. 1045 b 24 οἱ Ἀντισθένειοι καὶ οἱ οὕτως ἀπαίδευτοι), but no such reference is admissible here. Cp. 90 c 5 *n.*

a 3 φιλονίκως: the MSS., as usual, have -ει- for -ι-, but it is very doubtful whether there ever was such a word as φιλόνεικος, 'strife-loving,' and Plato certainly derives φιλόνικον from νίκη in *Rep.* 581 b 2 (see Adam, *in loc.*). In every passage where the word occurs in Plato the meaning 'victory-loving' is appropriate. Here the sense is clearly that Socrates may seem to be arguing for victory rather than truth.

a 5 ἃ αὐτοὶ ἔθεντο, 'what they themselves have laid down,' their own θέσεις.

a 8 εἰ μὴ εἴη πάρεργον, 'except incidentally.' Cp. *Polit.* 286 d 5 πλὴν εἰ (εἰ μὴ T) πάρεργόν τι.

b 1 ὡς πλεονεκτικῶς : Socrates playfully suggests that he is taking an unfair advantage. It is 'Heads I win ; tails you lose'.

b 3 ἀλλ' οὖν... γε, 'at any rate.' The emphatic word is placed between ἀλλ' οὖν and γε in this combination.

b 4 ἦτ. v . . . ὀδυρόμενος, I shall be less likely to distress the company by lamentations.'

b 5 ἄνοια, 'folly.' Most editors follow Stephanus in reading ἄγνοια, apparently without MS. authority. B has διάνοια, a mistake due to the resemblance of A and Δ. Schanz's ἡ δὲ δὴ ἄγνοια implies a much less likely corruption.

c 3 εὐλαβούμενοι is omitted in B, but this may be an accident.

c 5 τὸ κέντρον ἐγκαταλιπών: cp. the description of the oratory of Pericles by Eupol·s (fr. 94 Kock) οὕτως ἐκήλει καὶ μόνος τῶν ῥητόρων | τὸ κέντρον ἐγκατέλειπε τοῖς ἀκροωμένοις.

Reply to the objection of Simmias (91 c 6—95 a 3).

The objection of Simmias is fully dealt with, but that of Cebes is found to raise a larger question, and leads up to the Third Proof of Immortality.

c 7 Σιμμίας μὲν γὰρ κτλ. The two views are resumed and carefully distinguished. There is (1) the view that the soul is the ἁρμονία of the body and must therefore perish even before the body, and (2) the view that the soul weaves for itself many bodies, but perishes with, or even before, the last of them.

c 8 ὅμως...όν, ' in spite of its being.' The adv. ὅμως is 'attracted' by the participle.

d 1 ἐν ἁρμονίας εἴδει οὖσα, a periphrasis which only differs from ἁρμονία οὖσα by being more emphatic. Cp. above 87 e 4 τὴν φύσιν τῆς ἀσθενείας.

d 3 τόδε ἄδηλον παντί, sc. φάναι to be supplied from συγχωρεῖν.

d 7 ἀπολλύμενον οὐδὲν παύεται, 'is unceasingly perishing.' Cp. 87 d 8 εἰ γὰρ ῥέοι τὸ σῶμα καὶ ἀπολλύοιτο ἔτι ζῶντος τοῦ ἀνθρώπου. Distinguish οὐδὲν παύεται, *finem nullum facit*, from οὐ παύεται.

92 a 1 ἐνδεθῆναι: cp. 62 b 3 *n*.

a 5 ἄλλο ποτέ τι : I now observe that Heindorf suggested this reading, though he did not print it in his text.

a 6 Ἀλλὰ ἀνάγκη κτλ. It is shown first that the view of the soul as a ἁρμονία is inconsistent with the doctrine of ἀνάμνησις which Simmias accepts. A ἁρμονία could exist before the body of which it is the attunement just as little as it could survive it. This brings out the fundamental inconsistency of the later Pythagorean doctrine.

a 8 ἐκ τῶν κατὰ τὸ σῶμα ἐντεταμένων συγκεῖσθαι, 'to be composed of' the elementary opposites, hot and cold, wet and dry, which are here spoken of as the strings of the body.

b 1 σαυτοῦ λέγοντος: for the phrase cp. 92 e 2 ; 96 e 7. It is mere superstition to read αὑτοῦ because B has αὐτοῦ.

b 4 συμβαίνει: the regular term for the consequences of a ὑπόθεσις. Cp. d 6 n.

b 5 εἶδός τε καὶ σῶμα : the two terms are synonymous. Cp. 73 a 1 n.

b 8 ᾧ ἀπεικάζεις : i. e. οἷον ᾧ ἀπεικάζεις, 'like the thing you are comparing it to.' Cp. Rep. 349 d 10 τοιοῦτος ἄρα ἐστὶν ἑκάτερος αὐτῶν οἷσπερ ἔοικεν ;

c 3 πῶς συνᾴσεται ; cp. 86 e 3 n.

d 1 ἄνευ ἀποδείξεως μετὰ εἰκότος τινὸς καὶ εὐπρεπείας, 'without demonstration, from a specious analogy.' Cp. Theaet. 162 e 4 ἀπόδειξιν δὲ καὶ ἀνάγκην οὐδ' ἡντινοῦν λέγετε ἀλλὰ τῷ εἰκότι χρῆσθε, ᾧ εἰ ἐθέλοι Θεόδωρος ἢ ἄλλος τις τῶν γεωμετρῶν χρώμενος γεωμετρεῖν ἄξιος οὐδ' ἑνὸς μόνου ἂν εἴη, Euthyd. 305 e 1 πάνυ ἐξ εἰκότος λόγου . . . οὐ γάρ τοι ἀλλὰ ὅ γε λόγος ἔχει τινὰ εὐπρέπειαν τῶν ἀνδρῶν.—Καὶ γὰρ ἔχει ὄντως . . . εὐπρέπειαν μᾶλλον ἢ ἀλήθειαν.

d 2 τοῖς πολλοῖς . . . ἀνθρώποις, 'most people' who do hold it. We cannot infer from this expression that it was a widespread popular belief.

d 4 ἀλαζόσιν, 'impostors.' Cp. Lys. 218 d 2 φοβοῦμαι . . . μὴ ὥσπερ ἀνθρώποις ἀλαζόσιν λόγοις τισὶν τοιούτοις [ψευδέσιν] ἐντετυχήκαμεν. Rep. 560 c 2 ψευδεῖς δὴ καὶ ἀλαζόνες . . . λόγοι τε καὶ δόξαι.

d 6 δι' ὑποθέσεως ἀξίας ἀποδέξασθαι : Socrates assumes that the meaning of ὑπόθεσις is familiar to his hearers from its use in geometry, which is illustrated in a well-known passage of the Meno (86 e sqq.). Even Xenophon knew the term : cp. Mem. iv. 6. 13 εἰ δέ τις αὐτῷ περί του ἀντιλέγοι μηδὲν ἔχων σαφὲς λέγειν, ἀλλ' ἄνευ ἀποδείξεως . . . φάσκων κτλ. . . ., ἐπὶ τὴν ὑπόθεσιν ἐπανῆγεν ἂν πάντα τὸν λόγον ὧδέ πως κτλ. We shall learn shortly exactly what a hypothesis is. It will be sufficient to say here that it is a statement of which the truth is postulated and from which we deduce its consequences (τὰ συμβαίνοντα). The phrase literally means 'the argument proceeded (ὁ λόγος ... εἴρηται) *by means of* a hypothesis worthy of acceptance'.

d 7 ἀξίας ἀποδέξασθαι : we are not told here, nor were we told above, why the hypothesis in question is worthy of acceptance. We only know that Cebes and Simmias accepted it at once. The position of the argument, then, is this : Simmias declares that he cannot give up the doctrine that μάθησις is ἀνάμνησις so long as he accepts the hypothesis, and this he will not give up.

ἐρρήθη γάρ που κτλ. The ὑπόθεσις is given formally above 76 d 7 εἰ ... ἔστιν ἃ θρυλοῦμεν ἀεί, καλόν τέ τι καὶ ἀγαθὸν καὶ πᾶσα ἡ τοιαύτη οὐσία ... Now it has been shown that we refer all our sensations to this standard, and that this means that our soul already possesses it and rediscovers it in the process of learning. From this it followed in turn that our soul must have existed before entering into a human body. These steps have been rigorously demonstrated (ἱκανῶς ἀποδέδεικται), and therefore, *so long as we accept the* ὑπόθεσις, we must accept the conclusion.

d 8 ὥσπερ αὐτῆς ἐστιν κτλ. : i. e. the pre-existence of the soul is as certain as the fact that the reality which bears the name of τὸ ὃ ἔστιν belongs to it (cp. 76 e 1 ὑπάρχουσαν πρότερον ἀνευρίσκοντες ἡμετέραν οὖσαν). This is the interpretation of Wyttenbach and Heindorf. Most recent editors adopt Mudge's emendation ὥσπερ αὐτὴ ἔστιν κτλ. That would, no doubt, give a correct sense ('as certainly as the reality itself which bears the name of ὃ ἔστι exists '), and would even be a more accurate statement of the ultimate ὑπόθεσις. But αὐτῆς ἐστιν serves to remind us of the point on which the whole argument turns, namely that this οὐσία is really the soul's original possession, and that what we call learning is really οἰκείαν ἐπιστήμην ἀναλαμβάνειν (75 e 5). For the form of expression cp. *Theaet.* 160 c 7 τῆς γὰρ ἐμῆς οὐσίας ἀεί ἐστιν (ἡ ἐμὴ αἴσθησις).

e 1 ταύτην, sc. τὴν ὑπόθεσιν. There is no doubt about the conclusion (τὸ συμβαῖνον) being correctly demonstrated; what Simmias says here is that he firmly believes himself to be justified (ὀρθῶς) in accepting the ὑπόθεσις which forms the major premise.

e 4 Τί δὲ ... τῇδε ; the following argument proceeds on independent lines, and is based upon the nature of ἁρμονία itself. Socrates first gets Cebes to make two admissions. These are (1) that every ἁρμονία is determined by its component elements, (2) that no ἁρμονία admits of degrees.

e 4 δοκεῖ σοι κτλ. The first ὁμολόγημα (92 e 4—93 a 10). Every ἁρμονία is determined by its component elements. The note which anything will give out depends entirely upon what it is made of. It does not lead; it follows.

a 8 Πολλοῦ ... δεῖ: the subject is ἁρμονία.

ἐναντία ... κινηθῆναι ... ἢ φθέγξασθαι, 'to move (vibrate) or give out a sound in opposition to its parts,' i. e. to the tension and relaxation which produces it, as explained below 94 c 3.

11 Τί δέ; κτλ. The second ὁμολόγημα (93 a 11–b 7). No ἁρμονία admits of degree. A string is either in tune or it is not. To use the language of the *Philebus*, ἁρμονία is a form of πέρας and does not admit τὸ μᾶλλον καὶ ἧττον.

οὕτως ... ὡς ἂν ἁρμοσθῇ, 'just as it is tuned,' i. e. according as it is tuned to the fourth (διὰ τεσσάρων), the fifth (διὰ πέντε), or the octave (διὰ πασῶν). Modern editors suppose the meaning to be just the opposite and vainly try to explain in what sense one ἁρμονία can be more a ἁρμονία than another; but the meaning is stated quite clearly below 93 d 2. Olympiodorus, representing the school tradition, is quite explicit: ὑποτίθεται μὴ εἶναι ἁρμονίαν ἁρμονίας πλείω μηδὲ ἐλάττω, ἀλλὰ μηδὲ μᾶλλον μηδὲ ἧττον.

14 μᾶλλον ... καὶ ἐπὶ πλέον: Olympiodorus refers the first term to pitch (ἐπίτασις and ἄνεσις) and the second to the intervals. If a string is in tune it cannot be made more in tune by tightening or loosening. Nor is it correct to say that the octave is more of a ἁρμονία than the fifth or the fifth than the fourth.

b 1 εἴπερ ἐνδέχεται τοῦτο γίγνεσθαι, 'supposing this possible,' a plain indication that it is not possible. Socrates is only explaining what would be implied in saying that one ἁρμονία is more a ἁρμονία than another. It would mean that it was more tuned, which is absurd; for, as we learn from *Rep.* 349 e 11 the musician, in tuning a lyre, will not be willing μουσικοῦ ἀνδρὸς ἐν τῇ ἐπιτάσει καὶ ἀνέσει τῶν χορδῶν πλεονεκτεῖν ἢ ἀξιοῦν πλέον ἔχειν.

2 ἥττων τε καὶ ἐλάττων: some inferior MSS. read ἧττόν τε, which is more symmetrical, but the evidence is against it.

b 4 ʼΗ οὖν κτλ. That being so, we must further admit that, **if the** soul is a ἁρμονία, no soul can be more or less a soul than another. Socrates does not express a view one way or the other on this point. He only wishes an admission from Simmias that, on his ὑπόθεσις, it must be so.

ἔστι ... ὥστε ... So below 103 e 2. Cp. Lat. *est ut.*

b 5 μᾶλλον ἑτέραν ἑτέρας : some editors bracket μᾶλλον here, and it is in a sense redundant. We may say that it is more fully expressed by the words ἐπὶ πλέον ... ἧττον.

b 8 Φέρε δή κτλ. Socrates now proceeds to make use of the two ὁμολογήματα, but in the reverse order. We have seen that, if the soul is a ἁρμονία, no soul can be more or less a soul than another, i. e. more or less a ἁρμονία. But goodness is also a ἁρμονία, and souls differ in that one is better than another, which would imply that one ἁρμονία is more or less of a ἁρμονία than another, which is absurd.

c 3 τί ... ὄντα ; 'being what ? ' We can say τί ἐστι ταῦτα ; and the question may be asked by a participle in Greek. We must render 'What will he say that these things are which are in our souls ? ' (εἶναι ἐν ταῖς ψυχαῖς go together).

c 6 τὴν μὲν ἡρμόσθαι κτλ. Are we to say that both the good and the bad soul *are* ἁρμονίαι, but that the good soul also *has* a ἁρμονία and **is** in tune, while the bad soul has none and is out of tune ? If we say that the soul is a tuning, we shall have to say that a tuning may be tuned or untuned.

d 2 τοῦτο δ' ἔστι τὸ ὁμολόγημα, 'this is just our admission.' Here we have an explicit statement that our admission was that no ἁρμονία can be more or less a ἁρμονία than another. Editors who do not see this are obliged to bracket ἁρμονίας in d 4, or to explain it unnaturally as ' the particular harmony which is the soul'.

d 6 τὴν δέ γε, sc. ἁρμονίαν. The application of this to ψυχή only begins at d 12. The point here made depends on 93 a 14, where it was shown that being more or less tuned would involve being more or less a ἁρμονία, which is absurd.

d 9 ἔστιν ὅτι πλέον ... μετέχει ; 'does it partake more in —?' Here ὅτι is acc. neut. of ὅστις. Cp. e 7 ἆρ' ἄν τι πλέον κακίας ... μετέχοι ;

94 a 1 Μᾶλλον δέ γέ που ..., 'yes, or rather, surely —.'

κατὰ τὸν ὀρθὸν λόγον, 'according to the right account of the matter,' 'to put the matter correctly.' It the soul is a ἁρμονία, no soul can be better than another (for no ἁρμονία can be more in tune than another). Indeed, no soul can be bad at all (for no ἁρμονία can be out of tune).

a 12 πάσχειν ἂν ταῦτα, 'Do you think this would happen to our argument if our ὑπόθεσις were right?' Here the συμβαίνοντα are inadmissible, and therefore the ὑπόθεσις is destroyed (ἀναιρεῖται). For the use of πάσχειν in dialectic cp. *Parm.* 128 d 4 τοῦτο βουλόμενον δηλοῦν, ὡς ἔτι γελοιότερα πάσχοι ἂν αὐτῶν ἡ ὑπόθεσις, εἰ πολλά ἐστιν, ἢ ἡ τοῦ ἓν εἶναι.

b 4 Τί δέ; Socrates now takes up the first of the two ὁμολογήματα and tests the hypothesis by it. It is the soul which rules the body, whereas a ἁρμονία is dependent upon that of which it is the ἁρμονία (93 a 6).

c 3 ἐν τοῖς πρόσθεν: 92 e 4.

μήποτ᾽ ἂν . . . c 6 οὔποτ᾽ ἂν . . . Both negatives are legitimate after ὁμολογεῖν. Here they are alternated for variety.

c 4 οἷς ἐπιτείνοιτο καὶ χαλῷτο . . . ἐκεῖνα : equivalent to ταῖς ἐπιτάσεσιν καὶ χαλάσεσιν . . . ἐκείνων, οἷς representing τούτοις ἅ, where ἅ is internal accusative. This is a favourite construction with Demosthenes (cp. Shilleto on *de Fals. Leg.* 415), but is not common in Plato. Observe that χαλᾶν is equivalent to ἀνιέναι (*remittere*) the usual opposite of ἐπιτείνειν (*intendere*).

c 5 ψάλλοιτο is the reading of Stobaeus and seemingly of T before correction. As ψάλλειν is the proper word for striking strings, it is very appropriate here. The vulgate reading πάλλοιτο is supposed to refer to vibrations. The verb is used of 'brandishing' weapons and shaking lots, and in the passive of the heart 'quaking', but never of strings or instruments.

d 5 ταῖς ἐπιθυμίαις . . . διαλεγομένη : the comma after νουθετοῦσα is due to Hermann and makes the construction more regular. It is to be observed, however, that such a construction as τὰ μὲν ἀπειλοῦσα, τὰ δὲ νουθετοῦσα, ταῖς ἐπιθυμίαις is not indefensible.

d 6 ἐν 'Οδυσσείᾳ: *Od.* xx. 17. The passage is quoted in a similar connexion in *Rep.* 390 d 4 ; 441 b 6.

e 5 ἢ καθ᾽ ἁρμονίαν : in such phrases κατά means 'in a line with', 'on the level of'. Tr. 'far too divine a thing to be compared with a ἁρμονία.' Aristotle made use of the preceding argument in his

Eudemus. Cp. Olympiodorus : ὅτι ὁ Ἀριστοτέλης ἐν τῷ Εὐδήμῳ οὕτως ἐπιχειρεῖ· τῇ ἁρμονίᾳ ἐναντίον ἐστὶν ἡ ἀναρμοστία· τῇ ψυχῇ δὲ οὐδὲν ἐναντίον· οὐσία γάρ. καὶ τὸ συμπέρασμα δῆλον. ἔτι· εἰ ἀναρμοστία τῶν στοιχείων τοῦ ζῴου νόσος, ἡ ἁρμονία εἴη ἂν ὑγίεια ἀλλ' οὐχὶ ψυχή.

Reply to the Objection of Cebes begun, but broken off (95 a 4–e 6).

95 a 4 Εἶεν δή κτλ. Socrates now goes back to the objection of Cebes. The transition is effected by means of a pleasantry about Harmonia of Thebes (Θηβαϊκῆς, not Θηβαίας, for the κτητικόν, not the ἐθνικόν, is used with names of women). She has become fairly propitious, and we must now tackle Cadmus (who married Harmonia in the Theban legend), i. e. the objection of Cebes. There is no need to seek a deeper meaning in the words.

a 8   θαυμαστῶς . . . ὡς are to be taken together. Cp. 102 a 4.

a 9   ὅτε : Forster's conjecture ὅ τι (or, as I prefer to write in accordance with ancient practice, ὅτι) is attractive, but it is hard to account for the ὅτε of all MSS. unless it is original. Linde proposes ὅ γε ἠπόρει.

b 1   τι . . . χρήσασθαι τῷ λόγῳ : cp. *Theaet.* **165** b 7 τί γὰρ χρήσῃ ἀφύκτῳ ἐρωτήματι ;

b 5   μὴ μέγα λέγε, 'do not boast.' Cp. μέγα φρονεῖν, 'to be proud' (the other sense 'do not speak loud' is less appropriate here). Cp. *Hipp. ma.* 295 a 7 Ἀ μὴ μέγα . . . λέγε. Eur. *Her.* 1244 ἴσχε στόμ', ὡς μὴ μέγα λέγων μεῖζον πάθῃς.

b 6   βασκανία, 'malign influence,' lit. fascination of the 'evil eye', to the effects of which those who boast of their luck are specially exposed.

περιτρέψῃ, 'turn to flight,' keeps up the metaphor of ἔφοδος above.

b 7   Ὁμηρικῶς ἐγγὺς ἰόντες, 'coming to close quarters.' The metaphor is kept up. Homer nowhere uses the phrase ἐγγὺς ἰόντες, and Herwerden would read ἆσσον ἰόντες, but Ὁμηρικῶς may mean 'like Homeric warriors', not ' in Homeric phrase '.

b 8   τὸ κεφάλαιον, 'the sum and substance.' The word is derived from the ancient practice of writing the sum of an addition at the top. Cp. Lat. *summa* (sc. *linea*).

c 7   ἀθανασίαν μὲν μή, ὅτι δὲ . . . 'not immortality, but only that—.'

d 3   ζῴη . . . ἀπολλύοιτο : the optatives are due to the indirect speech, though there is no principal verb with ὅτι (or ὡς) on which they can be said to depend. They cannot, as some editors say, depend on c 7 φῇς, for φάναι only takes *acc. c. inf.* Cp. above 87 e 5 *n*, where also the optatives occur after a clause introduced by ἀλλὰ γάρ. Riddell, Dig. § 282.

d 7 εἰ μὴ . . . εἴη : the simplest explanation of this optative is to regard τῷ μὴ εἰδότι as equivalent to εἰ μὴ εἰδείη.

Narrative Interlude. The origin of the new Method (95 e 7—102 a 2).

e 8 Οὐ φαῦλον πρᾶγμα, 'no light matter,' 'no easy task.' Cp. L. S. *s. v.* I. I.

e 9 περὶ γενέσεως καὶ φθορᾶς τὴν αἰτίαν, 'the cause of coming into being, and ceasing to be.' Περὶ γενέσεως καὶ φθορᾶς is the title of one of Aristotle's most important treatises, best known by the scholastic name *De generatione et corruptione.* Περί *c. gen.* is used instead of the simple gen. or περί *c. acc.* under the influence of the verb διαπραγματεύσασθαι. Cp. 96 e 6 ; 97 c 6 ; 97 d 2 ; 98 d 6, and 58 a 1 *n.*

a 2 τά γε ἐμὰ πάθη, 'my own experiences.' It has been strangely supposed—so unwilling are interpreters to take the *Phaedo* in its plain sense—that these are either Plato's own experiences or 'an ideal sketch of the history of the mind in the search for truth.' Besides the general considerations stated in the Introduction, there is this special point to be noted, that the questions raised are exactly such as were discussed in the middle of the fifth century B.C., when Socrates was young, and that they correspond closely with the caricature of Aristophanes in the *Clouds*, which was produced in 423 B.C., when Plato was a baby. By the time of Plato's youth quite another set of questions had come to the front at Athens.

a 8 περὶ φύσεως ἱστορίαν: this is the oldest name for what we call 'natural science' (cf. E. Gr. Ph.² p. 14 *n.* 2). Heraclitus (fr. 17) said that Pythagoras had pursued ἱστορίη further than other men, and it appears that even geometry was called by this name in the Pythagorean school (E. Gr. Ph.² p. 107 *n.* 1). The restriction of the term to what we call 'history' is due to the fact that Herodotus followed his predecessors in calling his work ἱστορίη, and his predecessors belonged to Miletus, where all science went by that name (E. Gr. Ph.² p. 28). The term 'Natural History' partly preserves the ancient sense of the word, a circumstance due to the title of Aristotle's Περὶ τὰ ζῷα ἱστορίαι (*Historia Animalium*).

a 8 ὑπερήφανος agrees with σοφία or ἱστορία and εἰδέναι is added to it epexegetically. Heindorf compares *Gorg.* 462 c 8 οὐκοῦν καλόν σοι δοκεῖ ἡ ῥητορικὴ εἶναι, χαρίζεσθαι οἷόν τ' εἶναι ἀνθρώποις; The ὑπερήφανον of Eusebius and Stobaeus would simplify the construction, but the evidence is against it.

b 1 ἄνω κάτω: we say 'backwards and forwards'. Cp. 90 c 5 and *Gorg.* 481 d 7 ἄνω καὶ κάτω μεταβαλλομένου.

b 3 ὥς τινες ἔλεγον. This is the doctrine of Archelaus, the disciple of Anaxagoras, and, according to a statement already known to Theophrastus, the teacher of Socrates (cp. *Phys. Op.* fr. 4 Ἀρχέλαος ὁ Ἀθηναῖος ᾧ καὶ Σωκράτη συγγεγονέναι φασίν, Ἀναξαγόρου γενομένῳ μαθητῇ, Diels, *Vors.*² 323, 34; 324, 26). The following are the relevant quotations and rest ultimately on the authority of Theophrastus. Hippolytus, *Ref.* i. 9, 2 εἶναι δ' ἀρχὴν τῆς κινήσεως ⟨τὸ⟩ ἀποκρίνεσθαι ἀπ' ἀλλήλων τὸ θερμὸν καὶ τὸ ψυχρόν, *ib.* i. 9. 5 περὶ δὲ ζῴων φησὶν ὅτι θερμαινομένης τῆς γῆς τὸ πρῶτον ἐν τῷ κάτω μέρει, ὅπου τὸ θερμὸν καὶ τὸ ψυχρὸν ἐμίσγετο, ἀνεφαίνετο τά τε ἄλλα ζῷα πολλὰ καὶ ἄνθρωποι, ἅπαντα τὴν αὐτὴν δίαιταν ἔχοντα ἐκ τῆς ἰλύος τρεφόμενα. Diog. Laert. ii. 17 γεννᾶσθαι δέ φησι τὰ ζῷα ἐκ θερμῆς τῆς γῆς καὶ ἰλὺν παραπλησίαν γάλακτι οἷον τροφὴν ἀνιείσης. This last touch explains the reference to putrefaction (σηπεδών). As Forster already pointed out, early medical theory made πέψις, *cibi concoctio*, a form of σῆψις, and Galen says (*in Hippocr. Aph.* vi. 1) παλαιά τις ἦν συνήθεια τούτοις τοῖς ἀνδράσιν ἄσηπτα καλεῖν ἅπερ ἡμεῖς ἄπεπτα λέγομεν. Now Aristotle criticizes Empedocles for applying the σῆψις theory to milk. Cp. *Gen. An.* 777 a 7 τὸ γὰρ γάλα πεπεμμένον αἷμά ἐστιν, ἀλλ' οὐ διεφθαρμένον, Ἐμπεδοκλῆς δ' ἢ οὐκ ὀρθῶς ὑπελάμβανεν ἢ οὐκ εὖ μετήνεγκε ('used a bad metaphor') ποιήσας ὡς τὸ γάλα 'μηνὸς ἐν ὀγδοάτου δεκάτῃ πύον ἔπλετο λευκόν'. σαπρότης γὰρ καὶ πέψις ἐναντίον, τὸ δὲ πύον σαπρότης τίς ἐστιν, τὸ δὲ γάλα τῶν πεπεμμένων. The meaning is, then, that the warm and cold gave rise by putrefaction (σηπεδών) to a milky slime (ἰλύς) by which the first animals were nourished. We are thus able to give συντρέφεται its natural sense. It is significant that Socrates should mention the theory of Archelaus first.

b 4 ᾧ φρονοῦμεν, 'what we think with.' The question of the 'seat of the soul' or sensorium was keenly debated in the first half of the fifth century B.C. The views that the soul is blood or breath are primitive, but both had just been revived as scientific theories. Empedocles had said (fr. 105 Diels) αἷμα γὰρ ἀνθρώποις περικάρδιόν ἐστι νόημα, and he was the founder of the Sicilian school of medicine (E. Gr. Ph.² p. 288 *n.* 3). The doctrine that the soul is air was as old as Anaximenes, but had just been revived by Diogenes of Apollonia (E. Gr. Ph.² p. 414), and is attributed in the *Clouds* (230) to Socrates. The Heracliteans at Ephesus of course maintained their master's view that the soul was fire.

b 5 ὁ δ' ἐγκέφαλος κτλ. The credit of being the first to see that the brain was the seat of consciousness belongs to Alcmaeon of Croton (E. Gr. Ph.² p. 224), and the same view was upheld in the fifth century B.C. by Hippocrates and his school. It is one of the strangest facts in the history of science that Aristotle, followed by the Stoics, should have gone back to the primitive view that the heart was the seat of sensation.

b 7 γίγνοιτο : the optative is due to the general sense of indirect speech.

b 8 κατὰ ταῦτα : equivalent to οὕτως.

γίγνεσθαι : note ἐστιν (b 5) ... γίγνοιτο (b 7) ... γίγνεσθαι (b 8), 'a gradual transition from the direct to the most pronounced form of the indirect speech' (Geddes).

ἐπιστήμην : Diels (*Vors.*² 102, 18) attributes to Alcmaeon this explanation of knowledge as arising from memory and belief ' when they have reached a state of quiescence '. We seem to have an echo of it in Aristotle *An. Post.* B. 19. 100 a 3 sqq. ἐκ μὲν οὖν αἰσθήσεως γίγνεται μνήμη, . . . ἐκ δὲ μνήμης ἐμπειρία, . . . ἐκ δ' ἐμπειρίας ἢ ἐκ παντὸς ἠρεμήσαντος τοῦ καθόλου ἐν τῇ ψυχῇ . . . τέχνης ἀρχὴ καὶ ἐπιστήμης. From *Gorg.* 448 c 4 sqq. we learn that Polus of Agrigentum derived τέχνη from ἐμπειρία. There is no reason for doubting that the distinction between ἐπιστήμη and δόξα is pre-Platonic. It is alluded to by Isocrates in *Helena* 5 ὅτι πολὺ κρεῖττόν ἐστι περὶ τῶν χρησίμων ἐπιεικῶς δοξάζειν ἢ περὶ τῶν ἀχρήστων ἀκριβῶς ἐπίστασθαι, and Blass dates the *Helena* before 390 B.C. Antisthenes is said to have written four books Περὶ δόξης καὶ ἐπιστήμης (Diog. Laert. vi. 17).

b 9 τὰ περὶ τὸν οὐρανὸν (i.e. τοῦ οὐρανοῦ) . . . πάθη : it is highly characteristic of the middle of the fifth century B. C. that the theory of τὰ μετέωρα is mentioned last and in a somewhat perfunctory way. For the time, the rise of medicine had brought biological and psychological questions to the front, while astronomy and cosmology remained stationary in eastern Hellas until new life was given them by the Pythagoreans. The state of science here indicated is quite unlike any we know to have existed either at an earlier or a later date. It belongs solely to the period to which it is here attributed, a period which I have endeavoured to characterize in E. Gr. Ph.[2] pp. 405, 406.

c 2 ὡς οὐδὲν χρῆμα : the Ionic χρῆμα only survives in Attic in a few phrases like this (L. S. *s. v.* II. 3.) The Athenians only used freely the plural χρήματα, and that in the sense of ' property '. Cp. *Laws* 640 c 5 ὡς οὐδενί γε πράγματι.

c 5 ἐτυφλώθην (sc. ταῦτα): cp. Soph. *O. T.* 389 τὴν τέχνην δ' ἔφυ τυφλός.

c 6 ἃ πρὸ τοῦ ᾤμην εἰδέναι repeats c 4 ἃ καὶ πρότερον κτλ. (*a b a*).

d 1 ἐπειδὰν γὰρ κτλ.: this refers to another great question of the time. Socrates means that his former beliefs were upset by the question of Anaxagoras (fr. 10) πῶς γὰρ ἂν ἐκ μὴ τριχὸς γίνοιτο θρὶξ καὶ σὰρξ ἐκ μὴ σαρκός ; This led to the doctrine that there were portions of everything in everything. Cp. also Aët. i. 3. 5 (*Dox.* 279 a) ἐδόκει αὐτῷ ἀπορώτατον εἶναι πῶς ἐκ τοῦ μὴ ὄντος δύναταί τι γίνεσθαι ἢ φθείρεσθαι εἰς τὸ μὴ ὄν. τροφὴν γοῦν προσφερόμεθα ἁπλῆν καὶ μονοειδῆ, ἄρτον καὶ ὕδωρ· καὶ ἐκ ταύτης τρέφεται θρὶξ φλὲψ ἀρτηρία σὰρξ νεῦρα ὀστᾶ καὶ τὰ λοιπὰ μόρια. τούτων οὖν γινομένων, ὁμολογητέον ἐστὶν ὅτι ἐν τῇ τροφῇ τῇ προσφερομένῃ πάντα ἐστὶ τὰ ὄντα, καὶ ἐκ τῶν ὄντων πάντα αὔξεται. (Cp. E. Gr. Ph.[2] p. 303.)

d 6 μετρίως, *i. q.* καλῶς. Cp. 68 e 2 *n.*

d 8 ᾤμην γὰρ κτλ. This refers to another set of questions, which stand in a close relation to Zeno's criticism of the Pythagoreans. Roughly, we may say that the difficulty here touched upon is the nature of the unit, whether in measuring, weighing, or numbering.

e 1 αὐτῇ τῇ κεφαλῇ, 'just by the head.' This is an example of a popular unit of measurement. Cp. *Il.* iii. 193 μείων μὲν κεφαλῇ Ἀγαμέμνονος.

e 3 προσεῖναι (TW) is virtual passive of προσθεῖναι, which is the reading of B. That is a natural slip.

e 6 περὶ τούτων ... τὴν αἰτίαν: cp. 95 e 9 *n.*

e 8 ἐπειδὰν ἐνί τις προσθῇ ἕν κτλ. The difficulty here is what is meant by the addition of units. How can it be that when one is added to one the result is two? How can either the original one *or* the one which is added to it become two; or how can the one which is added *and* the one which is added to it become two? The nature of the unit involved real difficulties which we need not discuss here; it is more important for our purpose to observe that in the *Parmenides* Plato actually represents the young Socrates as discussing such subjects with Parmenides and Zeno. The two dialogues confirm each other in the most remarkable way; for here too we are dealing with the youth of Socrates.

a 2 εἰ ὅτε μὲν . . ., ἐπεὶ δ' . . . Another instance of the disjunctive hypothetical sentence (cp. **68 a 3** *n.*) What causes surprise is that the two things should be true at the same time.

a 4 αὕτη, 'this,' sc. τὸ πλησιάσαι ἀλλήλοις, but assimilated in gender to the predicate αἰτία, and further explained by ἡ σύνοδος κτλ.

a 5 ἡ σύνοδος τοῦ . . . τεθῆναι, 'the coming together which consists in their juxtaposition.'

οὐδέ γε ὡς . . . πείθεσθαι ὡς . . . The repetition of ὡς is a colloquialism. We are still dealing here with the difficulty of conceiving a unit. In the *Republic* (**525** d 8 sqq.) Socrates refers to the same difficulty, but he is not troubled by it, for he has come to see that the unit is an object of thought and not of sense. Plato can hardly have felt it seriously at any time.

b 4 δι' ὅτι ἓν γίγνεται, 'how a unit comes into being at all.' Cp. Arist. *Met.* M. 6. 1080 b 20 ὅπως δὲ τὸ πρῶτον ἓν συνέστη ἔχον μέγεθος, ἀπορεῖν ἐοίκασιν (οἱ Πυθαγόρειοι).

b 6 τρόπον τῆς μεθόδου, 'method of investigation.' The noun μέθοδος by itself came to bear this meaning, as 'method' always does in our usage.

b 7 αὐτὸς εἰκῇ φύρω, 'I make up a confused jumble of my own.' There can be no doubt that φύρειν is 'to make a mess' (cp. 101 e 1), and εἰκῇ, *temere*, emphasizes that meaning. Cp. Aesch. *P. V.* 450 ἔφυρον εἰκῇ πάντα. Of course, Socrates has not the slightest doubt of the superiority of his new method, and this description is only a piece of characteristic εἰρωνεία.

b 8 τινός, . . . ἀναγιγνώσκοντος: it is natural to think of the Anaxagorean Archelaus, who was said to be the teacher of Socrates (cp. 96 b 3 *n.*).

c 1 ὡς ἄρα κτλ. The actual words of Anaxagoras were (fr. 12 Diels) καὶ ὁποῖα ἔμελλεν ἔσεσθαι καὶ ὁποῖα ἦν, ἄσσα νῦν μὴ ἔστι, καὶ ὁποῖα ἔστι, πάντα διεκόσμησε νοῦς. The familiar πάντα χρήματα ἦν ὁμοῦ, εἶτα νοῦς ἐλθὼν αὐτὰ διεκόσμησεν (Diog. Laert. ii. 6) is not a quotation, but a summary of the doctrine (E. Gr. Ph.² p. 299, *n.* 1).

c 7 περὶ ἑκάστου: cp. 95 e 9 *n.*

d 2 περὶ αὐτοῦ ἐκείνου: *de illo ipso,* sc. περὶ αὐτοῦ τοῦ ἀνθρώπου. I formerly bracketed ἐκείνου, which rests only on the authority of B; but Vahlen has since shown (*Opusc.* ii. 558 sqq.) that αὐτοῦ ἐκείνου is too idiomatic to be a mistake.

d 7 κατὰ νοῦν ἐμαυτῷ, 'to my mind,' as we say. I cannot believe that this common phrase involves any reference to the νοῦς of Anaxagoras. Such a joke would be very frigid.

d 8 πλατεῖα . . . ἢ στρογγύλη: this was still a living problem in the days when Socrates was young, but not later. The doctrine that the earth is spherical was Pythagorean; the Ionian cosmologists (including Anaxagoras himself and Archelaus) held it was flat, with the single exception of Anaximander, who regarded it as cylindrical.

e 3 ἐν μέσῳ: so far as we can tell, this was not only the doctrine of Anaxagoras and Archelaus, but also of the early Pythagoreans. It is important to observe that the geocentric theory marked a great advance in its day as compared, e. g., with the belief of Thales that the earth was a disk floating on the water (E. Gr. Ph.² p. 32). Plato does not commit the anachronism of making Socrates refer to the later Pythagorean doctrine that the earth revolved with the planets round the Central Fire (E. Gr. Ph.² pp. 344 sqq.). That was familiar enough in the fourth century B. C., but would have been out of place here.

98 a 1 ποθεσόμενος: this is now known to be the reading of T as well as of Eusebius. B has ὑποθέμενος, which cannot be right, and the ὑποθησόμενος of W looks like an emendation of this.

a 4 τάχους . . . πρὸς ἄλληλα, 'their relative velocity.'

τροπῶν, 'turnings.' This refers to the annual movement of the sun from the 'tropic' of Capricorn to that of Cancer and back again, which is the cause of summer and winter. The Greeks gave the name of τροπαί to what the Romans, from a slightly different point of view, called *solstitia*.

a 6 ἃ πάσχει : symmetry would require the addition of καὶ ποιεῖ, but Plato avoids such symmetry.

b 1 ἑκάστῳ . . . καὶ κοινῇ πᾶσι, 'to each individually and to all collectively.'

b 3 οὐκ ἂν ἀπεδόμην πολλοῦ, 'I would not have sold for a large sum.'

b 7 ᾠχόμην φερόμενος: this is a slight variation on the usual phrase ἀπ' ἐλπίδος κατεβλήθην, κατέπεσον, 'I was dashed down from my hope' (cp. *Euthyphro* 15 e 5 ἀπ' ἐλπίδος με καταβαλὼν μεγάλης). Socrates speaks as if he had been cast down from Olympus like another Hephaestus (πᾶν δ' ἦμαρ φερόμην, *Il.* i. 592).

b 8 ἄνδρα, 'a man.' The word expresses strong feeling, here disappointment. Wyttenbach compares Soph. *Aias* 1142 ἤδη ποτ' εἶδον ἄνδρ' ἐγὼ γλώσσῃ θρασύν, 1150 ἐγὼ δέ γ' ἄνδρ' ὄπωπα μωρίας πλέων (cp. Arist. *Ach.* 1128).

τῷ μὲν νῷ οὐδὲν χρώμενον: Plato expresses the same feeling in his own person in *Laws* 967 b 4 καί τινες ἐτόλμων τοῦτό γε αὐτὸ παρακινδυνεύειν καὶ τότε, λέγοντες ὡς νοῦς εἴη ὁ διακεκοσμηκὼς πάνθ' ὅσα κατ' οὐρανόν. οἱ δὲ αὐτοὶ . . . ἅπανθ' ὡς εἰπεῖν ἔπος ἀνέτρεψαν πάλιν κτλ. Xenophon (*Mem.* iv. 7. 6) preserves a faint echo of this criticism of Anaxagoras. Aristotle (*Met.* A. 985 a 18) simply repeats it (E. Gr. Ph.[2] pp. 309 sq.).

b 9 οὐδέ τινας αἰτίας ἐπαιτιώμενον, **sc.** τὸν νοῦν, 'nor ascribing to it any causality.' For the double acc. cp. Dem. *Phorm.* 25 τίν' ἂν ἑαυτὸν αἰτίαν αἰτιασάμενος . . . δικάζοιτο; Antipho, 1. 29 ἃ ἐπαιτιῶμαι τὴν γυναῖκα ταύτην. Aristotle (*loc. cit.*) says πάντα μᾶλλον αἰτιᾶται τῶν γιγνομένων ἢ νοῦν.

c 7 νεύρων, 'sinews,' 'tendons,' not nerves. The nervous system only became known in the third century B. C. Cp. Galen, *de plac. Hipp. et Plat.*, p. 647 Ἐρασίστρατος μὲν οὖν (*floruit* 258 B. C.), εἰ καὶ μὴ πρόσθεν, ἀλλὰ ἐπὶ γήρως γε τὴν ἀληθῆ τῶν νεύρων ἀρχὴν κατενόησεν· Ἀριστοτέλης δὲ μέχρι παντὸς ἀγνοήσας εἰκότως ἀπορεῖ χρείαν εἰπεῖν ἐγκεφάλου.

c 8 διαφυάς ἔχει, 'are jointed.' The διαφυαί are the same thing as the συμβολαί (d 3), looked at from another point of view. Cicero, *de Nat. D.* ii. 139 says *commissurae*.

d 2 αἰωρουμένων . . . ἐν ταῖς . . . συμβολαῖς, 'swinging in their sockets.'

d 5 συγκαμφθείς : cp. 60 b 2.

d 7 φωνάς τε κτλ. Cp. e. g. Diogenes of Apollonia (Diels, *Vors.*² p. 332, 14) τοῦ ἐν τῇ κεφαλῇ ἀέρος ὑπὸ τῆς φωνῆς τυπτομένου καὶ κινουμένου (τὴν ἀκοὴν γίνεσθαι).

e 4 παραμένοντα, ' not running away.' We have no English word for παραμένειν, any more than for θαρρεῖν (cp. 63 e 10 *n.*). It is the negative of ἀποδιδράσκειν (99 a 3). Cp. 115 d 9.

e 5 νὴ τὸν κύνα : such euphemisms seem to occur in all languages. Cp. *parbleu! ecod!* It is true that in *Gorg.* 482 b 5 Socrates says μὰ τὸν κύνα τὸν Αἰγυπτίων θεόν (Anubis), but that seems to be only a passing jest. A euphemistic oath of this kind was called 'Ραδα-μάνθυος ὅρκος (Suid. *s. v.*).

99 a 1 περὶ Μέγαρα ἢ Βοιωτούς : cp. *Crito* 53 b 4 where it is suggested that Socrates might escape ἢ Θήβαζε ἢ Μέγαράδε. He would have found friends in both places, as we know. This whole passage is reminiscent of the *Crito*.

a 8 καὶ ταῦτα νῷ πράττων, ' and that too though I act from intelligence,' as was admitted above, 98 c 4. The MSS. have πράττω, but Hein-dorf's πράττων is a great improvement and gives καὶ ταῦτα its proper idiomatic force.

b 2 τὸ γὰρ μὴ . . . οἷόν τ' εἶναι κτλ. is another instance of the excla-matory infinitive justifying a strong expression of feeling. Cp. 60 b 5 *n.* and *Symp.* 177 c 1 τὸ οὖν τοιούτων μὲν πέρι πολλὴν σπουδὴν ποιήσασθαι, Ἔρωτα δέ μηδένα πω ἀνθρώπων τετολμηκέναι . . . ἀξίως ὑμνῆσαι.

b 3 ἄνευ οὗ : here we see the beginning of the technical term οὗ (or ὧν) οὐκ ἄνευ, the *conditio sine qua non*. Such causes are called συναίτια in the *Timaeus*. Cp. 46 c 7 Ταῦτ' οὖν πάντα ἔστιν τῶν συναιτίων οἷς θεὸς ὑπηρετοῦσιν χρῆται, τὴν τοῦ ἀρίστου κατὰ τὸ δυνατὸν ἰδέαν ἀποτελῶν· δοξάζεται δὲ ὑπὸ τῶν πλείστων οὐ συναίτια ἀλλὰ αἴτια εἶναι τῶν πάντων κτλ.

b 4 ψηλαφῶντες, ' groping in the dark.' Cp. Ar. *Peace* 690 πρὸ τοῦ μὲν οὖν ἐψηλαφῶμεν ἐν σκότῳ τὰ πράγματα, *Acta Apostolorum* xvii. 27 εἰ ἄρα γε ψηλαφήσειαν αὐτὸν καὶ εὕροιεν.

b 5 ἀλλοτρίῳ ὀνόματι, ' by a name that does not belong to them,' which is not their οἰκεῖον ὄνομα. The vulgate ὄμματι cannot be defended, though it is the reading also of BW.

b 6 αὐτό repeats ὅ (cp. 104 d 2 *n.*).

b 6 ὁ μέν τις κτλ. Once more we have the scientific problems of the middle of the fifth century. The first theory is that the earth does not fall because of the rapidity of the revolution of the heavens. This was the western theory, and was originated by Empedocles, who supported it by the experiment of swinging a cup full of water rapidly round (E. Gr. Ph.² p. 274). Cp. Arist. *de Caelo* 295 a 16 οἱ δ᾽ ὥσπερ Ἐμπεδοκλῆς τὴν τοῦ οὐρανοῦ φορὰν κύκλῳ περιθέουσαν καὶ θᾶττον φερομένην τὴν τῆς γῆς φορὰν κωλύειν, καθάπερ τὸ ἐν τοῖς κυάθοις ὕδωρ· καὶ γὰρ τοῦτο κύκλῳ τοῦ κυάθου φερομένου πολλάκις κάτω τοῦ χαλκοῦ γινόμενον ὅμως οὐ φέρεται κάτω πεφυκὸς φέρεσθαι διὰ τὴν αὐτὴν αἰτίαν. The vortex theory of Leucippus was more subtle than this (E. Gr. Ph.² p. 399) and is not referred to here. In *Clouds* 379 Aristophanes makes fun of the αἰθέριος Δῖνος who has taken the place of Zeus.

b 7 ὑπὸ τοῦ οὐρανοῦ μένειν : these words are to be taken together, as Geddes says (after Hermann) and μένειν is a virtual passive, 'is kept in its place by the heavens.'

b 8 ὁ δὲ κτλ. This is the eastern theory, which originated with Anaximenes and was still upheld by Anaxagoras and Democritus. As Aristotle tells us (*de Caelo* 294 b 14), they said τὸ πλάτος αἴτιον εἶναι . . . τοῦ μένειν αὐτήν· οὐ γὰρ τέμνειν ἀλλ᾽ ἐπιπωματίζειν τὸν ἀέρα τὸν κάτωθεν. Its breadth prevents it from cutting the air beneath it, and it lies on it 'like a lid' (πῶμα). It is absurd to suppose that Plato was ever troubled by crude notions of this kind, and even Socrates must soon have learnt better from his Pythagorean friends. Everything points to the Periclean age and no later date.

καρδόπῳ, 'a kneading-trough'. This, however, does not seem to be a very appropriate image, and I believe we should read καρδοπίῳ from Hesychius Καρδόπιον· τῆς καρδόπου τὸ πῶμα, 'the lid of a kneading-trough '; cp. Aristotle's ἐπιπωματίζειν quoted above. The discussion of the word κάρδοπος in Arist. *Clouds* 670 has another bearing. It refers to the speculations of Protagoras about grammatical gender.

c 1 τὴν δὲ τοῦ κτλ. Constr. τὴν δὲ δύναμιν τοῦ οὕτω νῦν (αὐτὰ) κεῖσθαι ὡς οἷόν τε βέλτιστα αὐτὰ τεθῆναι. As we see from the following words, δύναμιν has its full meaning. The fact that they are in the best possible place is regarded as a force which keeps them there.

That being so, ταύτην (τὴν δύναμιν) is the subject of δαιμονίαν ἰσχὺν ἔχειν.

c 3 τούτου ... ἰσχυρότερον, 'an Atlas stronger than this one' (τούτου is masc.).

c 5 ὡς ἀληθῶς τὸ ἀγαθὸν καὶ δέον: I think these words must be taken together; for ὡς ἀληθῶς is often used to call attention to an etymology (cp. 80 d 6 n.), and here τὸ δέον, 'the fitting,' is taken as 'the binding'. The hyperbaton is of a normal type. For the etymology itself cp. *Crat.* 418 e 7 ἀγαθοῦ γὰρ ἰδέα οὖσα ('being a form of good') τὸ δέον φαίνεται δεσμὸς εἶναι καὶ κώλυμα φορᾶς.

c 9 τὸν δεύτερον πλοῦν: the paroemiographers say this expression is used ἐπὶ τῶν ἀσφαλῶς τι πραττόντων, καθόσον οἱ διαμαρτόντες κατὰ τὸν πρότερον πλοῦν ἀσφαλῶς παρασκευάζονται τὸν δεύτερον. According to this, the reference would be rather to a less adventurous than to a 'second-best' course. See, however, Eustathius *in Od.* p. 1453, 20 δεύτερος πλοῦς λέγεται ὅτε ἀποτυχών τις οὐρίου κώπαις πλέῃ κατὰ Παυσανίαν. Cp. also Cic. *Tusc.* iv. 5, 'where *pandere vela orationis* is opposed to the slower method of proceeding, viz. *dialecticorum remis*' (Geddes). In any case, Socrates does not believe for a moment that the method he is about to describe is a *pis aller* or 'makeshift.' The phrase is ironical like εἰκῇ φύρω above. Cp. Goodrich in *Class. Rev.* xvii, pp. 381 sqq. and xviii, pp. 5 sqq., with whose interpretation I find myself in substantial agreement.

d 1 ᾗ πεπραγμάτευμαι: these words depend on ἐπίδειξιν ποιήσωμαι and govern τὸν δεύτερον πλοῦν.

d 5 τὰ ὄντα like τὰ πράγματα just below (e 3) are 'things' in the ordinary sense of the word. It seems to me quite impossible that these terms should be applied to the ὄντως ὄντα, τὰ ὡς ἀληθῶς ὄντα. They must be the same as τὰ ὄντα in 97 d 7 τῆς αἰτίας περὶ τῶν ὄντων, that is, the things of the visible world. It is quite true that Plato makes Socrates use the expression τὸ ὄν for τὸ ὄντως ὄν, but I know of no place in which he is made to use τὰ ὄντα *simpliciter* of the εἴδη. Further, the whole point of the passage is that Socrates had become exhausted by the study of physical science, and what he calls the δεύτερος πλοῦς is, we shall see, nothing else than the so-called 'Theory of Ideas.'

τὸν ἥλιον ἐκλείποντα, 'the sun during an eclipse.' This is a mere illustration. Socrates keeps up the irony of the phrase δεύτερος πλοῦς by suggesting that his eyes are too weak to contemplate the things of the visible world. He had to look at them in a reflexion, he says.

e 3 τοῖς ὄμμασι καὶ ἑκάστῃ τῶν αἰσθήσεων: this makes it quite clear that τὰ ὄντα, τὰ πράγματα are the things of sense.

e 5 εἰς τοὺς λόγους καταφυγόντα, 'taking refuge in the study of propositions' or 'judgements', or 'definitions'. It is not easy to translate λόγους here; but at least it is highly misleading to speak of 'concepts' (Begriffe), nor is there any justification in Plato's writings for contrasting Socratic λόγοι with Platonic εἴδη. It is just in λόγοι that the εἴδη manifest themselves, and what Socrates really means is that, before we can give an intelligible answer to the question 'what causes A to be B', we must ask what we mean by saying 'A is B'. So far from being a δεύτερος πλοῦς, this is really a 'previous question.'

e 6 ἴσως μὲν οὖν κτλ. Here Socrates distinctly warns us not to take his ironical description too seriously. It is not really the case that the λόγοι are mere images of τὰ ὄντα or τὰ πράγματα. On the contrary, it will appear that the things of sense may more fitly be called images of the reality expressed in the λόγοι. To use the language of the *Republic*, we must not confuse διάνοια and ἐπιστήμη with εἰκασία.

ᾧ εἰκάζω: i. e. τούτῳ ᾧ εἰκάζω τὸ ἐν τοῖς λόγοις σκοπεῖσθαι τὰ ὄντα.

a 2 ἐν [τοῖς] ἔργοις, 'in realities'. The word ἔργα is equivalent to ὄντα and πράγματα, and is used here because it is the standing opposite to λόγοι.

a 3 ὑποθέμενος ἑκάστοτε κτλ., 'in any given case assuming as true.' This amounts to saying that Socrates had recourse to the method of deduction. Here it is important to remember, first, that in the fifth century B. C. geometry had advanced far beyond all other sciences, just because it had adopted the deductive method, and, secondly, that this advance was due to the Pythagoreans. The ideal is that all science should become 'exact science'.

a 4 ὃν ἂν κρίνω κτλ. We start from a proposition (λόγος) which we judge not to be open to attack. If this is admitted, we may proceed; if not, we cannot do so until we have established our ὑπόθεσις.

b 1 οὐδὲν καινόν: if Plato had been the real author of the 'Theory of

Ideas', and if, as is commonly believed, it was propounded for the first time in the *Phaedo*, this sentence would be **a** pure mystification.

b 2 οὐδὲν πέπαυμαι. 'Οὐ παύεται et οὐδὲν παύεται sic differunt ut Latine : finem non facit et finem nullum facit,' Cobet *Nov. Lect.* p. 500.

b 3 ἔρχομαι ... ἐπιχειρῶν ... ἐπιδείξασθαι, 'I am going to try to show'. In this construction ἔρχομαι usually takes a future participle ; but, as Heindorf says, ἐπιχειρῶν ἐπιδείξασθαι is 'instar futuri ἐπιδειξόμενος'.

τῆς αἰτίας τὸ εἶδος, 'the sort of causation I have worked out'. A phrase like this shows how far εἶδος is from being a technical term. When Socrates wishes to be technical, he speaks of the 'just what it is' (τὸ αὐτὸ ὃ ἔστιν).

b 4 ἐκεῖνα τὰ πολυθρύλητα : cp. 76 d 8 ἃ θρυλοῦμεν ἀεί. Here once more the doctrine of εἴδη is assumed to be well known and generally accepted. What is new is the application of it, the method of ὑπόθεσις and deduction. This time it is Cebes who assents to the doctrine without hesitation ; last time it was Simmias.

b 8 τὴν αἰτίαν ἐπιδείξειν καὶ ἀνευρήσειν ὡς : there is a curious and characteristic interlacing of words here (a b a b); for τὴν αἰτίαν ἀνευρήσειν and ἐπιδείξειν ὡς would naturally go together. Riddell, *Dig.* § 308 classes this under the head of *Hysteron proteron.*

c 1 ὡς διδόντος σοι κτλ., 'You may take it that I grant you this, so lose no time in drawing your conclusion.' Cp. *Symp.* 185 e 4 οὐκ ἂν φθάνοις λέγων.

c 3 Σκόπει... ἐάν ... Cp. 64 c 10 n.

c 5 οὐδὲ δι' ἕν is more emphatic than δι' οὐδέν.

ἢ διότι μετέχει κ.τ.λ. If we say that a, *a*, *a* are beautiful, that implies (1) that 'beautiful' has a *meaning* quite apart from any particular instance of beautiful things, and (2) that this *meaning* (A) is somehow 'partaken in' by the particular instances a, *a*, *a*. These have a meaning in common, and their relation to it is expressed in the relation of subject to predicate. This too Cebes admits at once.

d 1 χρῶμα εὐανθὲς ἔχον, 'because it has a bright colour'. The participle explains δι' ὅτι, which is the indirect form of διὰ τί. The adjective εὐανθής is common in Hippocrates, especially of the bright red colour

of blood, &c. As applied to colour, ἄνθος is 'bloom', 'brightness', and is sometimes almost synonymous with χρῶμα. Cp. *Rep.* 429 d 8 and 557 c 5 with Adam's notes. The point is that it is meaningless to say a, *a, a are* A because they are *x, y, z,* unless we have first shown that *x, y, z* necessarily 'partake in' A.

d 3 ἁπλῶς καὶ ἀτέχνως καὶ ἴσως εὐήθως as opposed to the σοφαὶ αἰτίαι mentioned above. The irony of 97 b 7 εἰκῇ φύρω is here kept up, and this should warn us against taking the expression δεύτερος πλοῦς as seriously meant. (Distinguish ἀτέχνως from ἀτεχνῶς.)

d 5 εἴτε παρουσία κτλ. The precise nature of the relation between predicate and subject may be expressed in various more or less figurative ways. We may say that the predicate is 'present to' the subject, or that the subject 'partakes' in the common nature of the predicate. Socrates will not bind himself to any of these ways of putting it; he only insists that, however we may express it, it is beauty that makes things beautiful.

d 6 ὅπῃ δὴ καὶ ὅπως κ.τ.λ. These words are an echo of the formula used in the public prayers, for which cp. *Crat.* 400 e 1 ὥσπερ ἐν ταῖς εὐχαῖς νόμος ἐστὶν ἡμῖν εὔχεσθαι, οἵτινές τε καὶ ὁπόθεν χαίρουσιν ὀνομαζόμενοι, ταῦτα καὶ ἡμᾶς αὐτοὺς (sc. τοὺς θεοὺς) καλεῖν. It seems to me, therefore, that Wyttenbach's suggestion, προσαγορευομένη for προσγενομένη, must certainly be right, though he did not adopt it himself. The manuscript προσγενομένη goes well enough with παρουσία, but not with the other terms. The whole question is one of names; for Socrates has no doubt as to the fact. Plato elsewhere represents him as making use of this formula. Cp. *Prot.* 358 a 7 εἴτε γὰρ ἡδὺ εἴτε τερπνὸν λέγεις ... εἴτε ὁπόθεν καὶ ὅπως χαίρεις τὰ τοιαῦτα ὀνομάζων, *Phileb.* 12 c 3 τὴν μὲν Ἀφροδίτην, ὅπῃ ἐκείνῃ φίλον, ταύτῃ προσαγορεύω. So *Tim.* 28 b 2 ὁ δὴ πᾶς οὐρανὸς ἢ κόσμος ἢ καὶ ἄλλο ὅτι ποτὲ ὀνομαζόμενος μάλιστ' ἂν δέχοιτο, τοῦθ' ἡμῖν ὠνομάσθω, *Laws* 872 d 7 ὁ γὰρ δὴ μῦθος ἢ λόγος ἢ ὅτι χρὴ προσαγορεύειν αὐτόν. The formula arose from fear that the gods should be addressed by the wrong name. Cp. Aesch. *Ag.* 160 Ζεύς, ὅστις ποτ' ἐστίν, εἰ τόδ' αὐ|τῷ φίλον κεκλημένῳ, | τοῦτό νιν προσεννέπω. This connexion is made quite clear in the passage from the *Philebus* quoted above, which is introduced by the words Τὸ δ' ἐμὸν δέος ... ἀεὶ πρὸς τὰ τῶν θεῶν ὀνόματα οὐκ ἔστι κατ' ἄνθρωπον, ἀλλὰ πέρα τοῦ μεγίστου φόβου.

d 6 οὐ γὰρ ἔτι κτλ., 'I do not go so far as to insist on that'. Cp.

Aristotle *Met.* A. 6. 987 b 13 τὴν μέντοι γε μέθεξιν ἢ τὴν μίμησιν, ἥτις ἂν εἴη τῶν εἰδῶν, ἀφεῖσαν (sc. οἱ Πυθαγόρειοι καὶ Πλάτων) ἐν κοινῷ ζητεῖν, i. e. 'they left it as a point for dialectical inquiry' (for this meaning of ἐν κοινῷ cp. *de An.* A. 4. 407 b 29 quoted in 86 b 6 *n.*). I think Aristotle is referring to the present passage. He is quite clear about the Pythagorean origin of the theory.

d 8 [γίγνεται] is omitted both here and below e 3 by B; and W, which inserts it in e 3, has it in a different place from T. Most likely, then, it is an interpolation, and the formula τῷ καλῷ τὰ καλὰ καλά is much neater without it.

d 9 τούτου ἐχόμενος, 'holding to this.' Cp. 101 d 1 ἐχόμενος ἐκείνου τοῦ ἀσφαλοῦς τῆς ὑποθέσεως.

101 a 5 φοβούμενος οἶμαι κτλ. The *Euthydemus* shows that Socrates is making no extravagant supposition in suggesting that the ἀντιλογικοί might make such criticisms as (1) if A is taller than B 'by a head', B is also smaller than A 'by a head', therefore the same thing is the cause of greatness and smallness, and (2) that a head, being small, cannot be the cause of greatness.

a 6 ἐναντίος λόγος: for the personification of the λόγος cp. 87 a 8 *n.*

b 1 τέρας, 'a portent.' The word seems to have been common in dialectic as equivalent to ἄτοπον or ἀδύνατον. Cp. *Meno* 91 d 5 καίτοι τέρας λέγεις εἰ ..., *Parm.* 129 b 2 τέρας ἂν οἶμαι ἦν, *Theaet.* 163 d 6 τέρας γὰρ ἂν εἴη ὃ λέγεις, *Phil.* 14 e 3 τέρατα διηνάγκασται φάναι.

b 9 τὴν πρόσθεσιν ... c 1 τὴν σχίσιν: addition of unit to unit or division of the unit into fractions. Cp. above 96 e 7 sqq.

c 2 ἄλλως πως ... ἢ μετασχὸν κτλ., 'otherwise than by participation in the proper reality of any given form (ἑκάστου) in which it participates.' The theory is thus summed up by Aristotle, *de Gen. et Corr.* 335 b 9 ἀλλ' οἱ μὲν ἱκανὴν ᾠήθησαν αἰτίαν εἶναι πρὸς τὸ γίγνεσθαι τὴν τῶν εἰδῶν φύσιν, ὥσπερ ὁ ἐν τῷ Φαίδωνι Σωκράτης· καὶ γὰρ ἐκεῖνος, ἐπιτιμήσας τοῖς ἄλλοις ὡς οὐδὲν εἰρηκόσιν, ὑποτίθεται ὅτι ἐστὶ τῶν ὄντων τὰ μὲν εἴδη, τὰ δὲ μεθεκτικὰ τῶν εἰδῶν· καὶ ὅτι εἶναι μὲν ἕκαστον λέγεται κατὰ τὸ εἶδος, γίγνεσθαι δὲ κατὰ τὴν μετάληψιν, καὶ φθείρεσθαι κατὰ τὴν ἀποβολήν. Observe that Aristotle does not ascribe this theory to Plato, but to 'Socrates in the *Phaedo.*'

c 4 ἐν τούτοις, 'in the cases just mentioned.'

c 5 μετάσχεσιν, *i. q.* μέθεξιν. The form seems to occur here only.

c 8 κομψείας: Wyttenbach points out that Socrates has in mind the words of Euripides' *Antiope* which Plato makes him quote in *Gorg.* 486 c 6, ἄλλοις τὰ κομψὰ ταῦτ' ἀφεὶς (σοφίσματα). It is part of the irony that the plain man's way of speaking is described as a 'subtlety', while the new theory of predication is called artless and naïve.

c 9 δεδιὼς ... τὴν σαυτοῦ σκιάν: Aristophanes is said to have used this expression in the *Babylonians*. It probably (like our phrase *take umbrage*) referred originally to horses shying at their shadows. We have to go warily with so many ἀντιλογικοί lying in wait for us.

d 1 ἐχόμενος ἐκείνου κτλ., 'holding fast to the safe support of the ὑπόθεσις' (cp. 100 d 9), which is regarded as a staff (Ar. *Ach.* 682 οἷς Ποσειδῶν ἀσφάλειός ἐστιν ἡ βακτηρία).

d 3 εἰ δέ τις κτλ. It does not seem possible to take ἔχεσθαι here in the sense of 'attack', and Madvig's conjecture ἐφοῖτο is the reverse of convincing. It does, however, seem possible to render 'if any one fastens on' or 'sticks to the ὑπόθεσις', that is, if he refuses to consider the συμβαίνοντα till the ὑπόθεσις has been completely established. The method of Socrates is different. He first considers the συμβαίνοντα to see whether they involve any contradiction or absurdity. If they do, the hypothesis is *ipso facto* destroyed. If the συμβαίνοντα are not contradictory or absurd, the ὑπόθεσις is not indeed established, but it has been verified, so far as it can be, by its application. When we have seen that the axioms of geometry lead to no contradictions or absurdities in their application, they are at least relatively established. Cp. *Meno* 86 e 2 συγχώρησον ἐξ ὑποθέσεως αὐτὸ σκοπεῖσθαι. For the terminology of the method cp. *Parm.* 135 e 9 εἰ ἔστιν ἕκαστον ('a given thing') ὑποτιθέμενον σκοπεῖν τὰ συμβαίνοντα ἐκ τῆς ὑποθέσεως. Cp. e. g. the example immediately after (a 5) εἰ πολλά ἐστι (the ὑπόθεσις), τί χρὴ συμβαίνειν κτλ. The method of experimental science is the same. The ὑπόθεσις is first tested by seeing whether it is verified or not in particular instances; the deduction of the ὑπόθεσις from a higher one is another matter, which must be kept distinct.

d 4 ἕως ἂν κτλ. It is doubtful whether ἄν can ever be retained with the opt. in *oratio obliqua*, though there are several examples in our texts (*G. M. T.* § 702). The better explanation is that given in L. & S. (*s. v.* ἕως I. c) that 'ἄν ... is added to the Optat. (not to ἕως) if the event is represented as conditional'. In that case, the real construction is ἕως... σκέψαιο ἄν, and ἄν is anticipated. Cp. Isocrates, 17. 15 μαστιγοῦν... ἕως ἂν τἀληθῆ δόξειεν αὐτοῖς λέγειν. The meaning, then, will be 'till you have a chance of considering'.

d 4 τὰ ἀπ' ἐκείνης ὁρμηθέντα: i. e. τὰ συμβαίνοντα. In e 2 below the phrase is τῶν ἐξ ἐκείνης ὡρμημένων, and those who regard the sentence as spurious hold that the aorist participle is incorrect. But (1) the aorist is appropriate, because it is only after the consequences have been drawn that we can compare them with one another, and (2) it is more likely that Plato himself should vary the tense than that an interpolator should do so.

d 5 εἰ ... διαφωνεῖ: Jackson holds that this clause is inconsistent with the account of the method given at 100 a 4 ἃ μὲν ἄν μοι δοκῇ τούτῳ συμφωνεῖν τίθημι ὡς ἀληθῆ ὄντα κτλ., but that is a different stage in the process. We first posit as true whatever agrees with the ὑπόθεσις, and then we test the hypothesis by considering whether the things thus posited agree with one another.

ἐπειδὴ δὲ κτλ. Socrates recognizes that the ὑπόθεσις is not established by the process described so far. That can only be done by subsuming it under some higher ὑπόθεσις, and that in turn under a higher, till we come to one which is unassailable. This is the process described at greater length in *Rep.* 533 c 7 sqq.

d 7 τῶν ἄνωθεν, 'higher,' i. e. more universal. Cp. *Rep.* 511 a 5 τῶν ὑποθέσεων ἀνωτέρω ἐκβαίνειν.

e 1 ἐπί τι ἱκανόν: i. e. to an ἀρχή which no one will question. This is not necessarily an ἀρχὴ ἀνυπόθετος (*Rep.* 510 b 7). A ὑπόθεσις may be, humanly speaking, adequate without that (cp. below 107 b 9).

οὐκ ἂν φύροιο, 'you will not jumble the two things together.' Though the middle does not appear to occur elsewhere, φύρεσθαι τὸν λόγον, 'to jumble *one's* argument,' seems very natural Greek, and it is hardly necessary to read φύροις. Otherwise we must take φύροιο as passive, comparing *Gorg.* 465 c 4 φύρονται ἐν τῷ αὐτῷ... σοφισταὶ καὶ ῥήτορες.

ὥσπερ οἱ ἀντιλογικοί: Socrates is no doubt thinking of the attacks on mathematics made by Protagoras and others. When we study geometry, we must accept its fundamental ὑποθέσεις; the question of their validity is a different one altogether, and one with which the geometer as such has nothing to do. Only hopeless confusion can result from mixing up the two things.

e 2 τῆς ἀρχῆς, 'your starting-point,' i. e. the ὑπόθεσις. Though ἀρχή is sometimes used of an ultimate ἀρχή as opposed to an ὑπόθεσις, it can be used of any starting-point whatsoever. When we are discussing the συμβαίνοντα, we take the ὑπόθεσις as our ἀρχή and decline to give any account of it.

e 5 ἱκανοὶ ... ὑπὸ σοφίας κτλ., 'their cleverness enables them ...' There is a slight redundance in the use of δύνασθαι after ἱκανοί, but it is easily paralleled. They can make a mess of everything without disturbing their own self-complacency.

a 3 Νὴ Δία κτλ. The distinction which Socrates has just made appeals at once to a Pythagorean mathematician. We are taken back to Phlius for the last time, in order that the next stage of the argument may have its full weight.

Third Proof of Immortality (102 a 10—107 b 10).

The first two proofs were based upon analogy. They both depended upon the Doctrine of Forms ; but in neither was Immortality deduced from that doctrine. The Third Proof is intended to be such a deduction.

b 2 τἆλλα : i. e. particular things.

τὴν ἐπωνυμίαν ἴσχειν, 'are called after them.' This is how Socrates expresses the 'extension' of a class as opposed to its 'intension'. Cp. *Parm.* 130 e 5 δοκεῖ σοι ... εἶναι εἴδη ἄττα, ὧν τάδε τὰ ἄλλα μεταλαμβάνοντα τὰς ἐπωνυμίας αὐτῶν ἴσχειν. Cp. 78 e 2 πάντων τῶν ἐκείνοις ὁμωνύμων.

b 8 'Ἀλλὰ γὰρ κτλ. The notion here formulated is that of the *essential attribute*. We say, indeed, as a *façon de parler* (τοῖς ῥήμασι) that Simmias is greater than Socrates ; but it is not *qua* Simmias or *qua* Socrates that they stand in this relation, but only in so far as greatness and smallness can be predicated of them. The emphatic words are πεφυκέναι and τυγχάνει ἔχων. The first expresses participation in an εἶδος which belongs φύσει to the subject, the latter participation in an εἶδος which belongs to the subject *as a matter of fact*, but not essentially. The sentence is anacoluthic; for the subject τὸ ... ὑπερέχειν is dropped and a new subject τὸ ἀληθές is substituted.

b 10 ἐπωνυμίαν ἔχει ... εἶναι, 'has the name of being.' Heindorf quotes Hdt. ii. 44 ἱρὸν Ἡρακλέος ἐπωνυμίην ἔχοντος Θασίου εἶναι. So often ὀνομάζειν εἶναι.

C 11   τοῦ μὲν κτλ., 'submitting his smallness to the greatness of A (Phaedo) to be surpassed by it, and presenting his own greatness to B (Socrates) as something surpassing his smallness.' The reading ὑπέχων is not merely a conjecture of Madvig's, as even the most recent editors say, but the best attested MS. reading (TW). The meaning of ὑπέχειν is much the same as that of παρέχειν, and it takes the same construction, the epexegetic infinite active (ὑπερέχειν), which we express by a passive. Cp. *Gorg.* 497 b 9 ὑπόσχες Σωκράτει ἐξελέγξαι.

d 2   Ἔοικα ... συγγραφικῶς ἐρεῖν, 'it looks as if I were about to acquire a prose style.' Wyttenbach took συγγραφικῶς as referring to the language in which ψηφίσματα were drafted, comparing *Gorg.* 451 b 7 ὥσπερ οἱ ἐν τῷ δήμῳ συγγραφόμενοι. Heindorf derived it from συγγραφή, a 'bond' or 'indenture', and thought of legal phraseology. On the whole, it seems to me more likely that there is a reference to the balanced antitheses of Gorgias and his followers, of which the preceding sentence certainly reminds one. The word συγγραφικός only occurs in late writers, but there it is the adjective of συγγραφεύς and always refers to prose style. This interpretation makes the fut. inf. ἐρεῖν more natural than the others.

d 7   τὸ ἐν ἡμῖν μέγεθος: the form of greatness, so far as it 'is present' in us or we 'participate' in it.

d 9   δυοῖν τὸ ἕτερον κτλ. This alternative is important for the argument, and the terminology should be noticed. If any form is 'in' a given thing, that thing will not admit (δέχεσθαι) any form which is opposed to it. The original form will either (1) *withdraw from* (or 'evacuate') the thing, or (2) *perish*. The metaphors are military throughout this discussion.

e 2   ὑπομένον δὲ κτλ. These words explain the following. 'It refuses to be something other than it was by holding its ground and admitting smallness.' Here ὑπομένειν 'to hold one's ground' is used as the opposite of ὑπεκχωρεῖν 'to get out of the way', 'to withdraw in favour of' (its opposite).

e 3   ὥσπερ ἐγὼ κτλ. Socrates can 'admit' either greatness or smallness without ceasing to be Socrates; but the greatness which is 'in' Socrates cannot 'admit' smallness.

e 5   τετόλμηκεν seems to be suggested by the military metaphor.

a 1   ἐν τούτῳ τῷ παθήματι, 'when this happens to it,' i. e. when it is attacked by its opposite.

a 4   οὐ σαφῶς μέμνημαι is probably nothing more than a touch of realism. We need not look for covert meanings.

a 5   ἐν τοῖς πρόσθεν . . . λόγοις: 70 d 7 sqq.

    ἡμῖν is the reading of W, but ὑμῖν (BT) is also possible.

a 8   αὕτη εἶναι, 'to be this,' a change of construction from τὸ μεῖζον γίγνεσθαι. Both the personal and the impersonal construction are admissible with ὡμολογεῖτο.

a 11   παραβαλὼν τὴν κεφαλήν, 'turning his head' as one naturally would to a new speaker (not 'bending').

b 3   τὸ ἐναντίον πρᾶγμα: i. e. the thing in which there is an opposite form. It is a cold thing that becomes hot and a hot thing that becomes cold; hot does not become cold, or cold hot. In the previous illustration Socrates is the σμικρὸν πρᾶγμα which may become μέγα, though smallness cannot admit greatness.

b 5   τὸ ἐν τῇ φύσει (sc. ἐναντίον) is the opposite form αὐτὸ καθ᾽ αὑτό as opposed to τὸ ἐν ἡμῖν which is chosen as an instance of the form so far as it is 'in' a thing. For this way of speaking of the εἴδη cp. *Rep.* 597 b 5 where the 'ideal bed' is spoken of as ἡ ἐν τῇ φύσει οὖσα, and *Parm.* 132 d 1 τὰ μὲν εἴδη ταῦτα ὥσπερ παραδείγματα ἑστάναι ἐν τῇ φύσει, τὰ δὲ ἄλλα τούτοις ἐοικέναι. All Greek thinkers use the word φύσις of that which they regard as most real. The Ionians meant by it the primary substance (E. Gr. Ph.[2] p. 13); Socrates means by it the world of εἴδη.

b 6   τῶν ἐχόντων τὰ ἐναντία: a clearer expression for τῶν ἐναντίων πραγμάτων.

b 7   τῇ ἐκείνων ἐπωνυμίᾳ: cp. 102 b 2.

b 8   ὧν ἐνόντων: governed by τὴν ἐπωνυμίαν (not gen. abs.).

c 1   γένεσιν ἀλλήλων, 'becoming one another', 'turning into one another'.

c 5   Οὐδ᾽ αὖ κτλ. On previous occasions (77 a 8 ; 86 e 5) we have heard of the doubts of Cebes, but 'he does not feel his doubts return on this point' (Geddes).

    καίτοι οὔτι λέγω κτλ. Here we have another hint that the doctrine is not fully worked out. Cp. above 100 d 5 and below 107 b 5.

c 10 Ἔτι ... καὶ τόδε κτλ. We now advance beyond the merely tautological judgements with which we have been dealing hitherto, to judgements of which the subject is a thing and the predicate a form. We have seen that hot will not admit cold or cold heat; we go on to show that fire will not admit cold, nor snow heat. We advance from the judgement ' A excludes B ' to ' a excludes B '.

c 11 θερμόν τι καλεῖς: cp. 64 c 2 n. It will be found helpful to keep this simple instance in mind all through the following passage.

c 13 ὅπερ is regularly used to express identity. A is not identical with a nor B with b.

e 2 Ἔστιν ... ὥστε: cp. 93 b 4 n.

e 3 τοῦ αὐτοῦ ὀνόματος, 'its own name,' the name of the εἶδος, e. g. hot or cold (ἀξιοῦσθαι, ' to be entitled to ').

e 4 ἀλλὰ καὶ ἄλλο τι, sc. ἀξιοῦσθαι αὐτοῦ, i. e. τοῦ ὀνόματος τοῦ εἴδους, e. g. fire and snow ; for fire is always hot and snow is always cold.

e 5 τὴν ἐκείνου μορφήν: i. e. τὴν ἐκείνου ἰδέαν, τὸ ἐκείνου εἶδος. The three words are synonyms. Observe how the doctrine is formulated. There are things, not identical with the form, which have the form as an inseparable predicate (ἀεί, ὅτανπερ ᾖ).

e 7 δεῖ ... τυγχάνειν, i. q. ἀξιοῦται.
ὅπερ νῦν λέγομεν, sc. τὸ περιττόν.

104 a 2 μετὰ τοῦ ἑαυτοῦ ὀνόματος, 'along with its own name,' whatever that may be. In addition to its own name we must also call it odd (τοῦτο καλεῖν, sc. περιττόν) because it is essentially (φύσει, cp. πεφυκέναι) odd.

a 3 λέγω δὲ αὐτὸ εἶναι κτλ., 'I mean by the case mentioned (αὐτό) such a case as that of the number three,' which is not only entitled to the name ' three ', but also, and essentially, to the name ' odd '. Similarly fire is not only entitled to the name ' fire ', but also, and essentially, to the name ' hot '.

a 6 ὄντος οὐχ ὅπερ κτλ. Most editors adopt Heindorf's conjecture οὗπερ for ὅπερ, which is demanded by grammar ; for ὅπερ ought to be followed by ἡ τριάς (sc. ἐστίν). On the other hand, it may be urged that ὅπερ was so common in geometry, especially to express ratios, that it may hardly have been felt to be declinable. It is a symbol like : or =, and nothing more.

a 8 ὁ ἥμισυς τοῦ ἀριθμοῦ ἅπας, ' one whole half of the numerical series.' For ὁ ἥμισυς instead of τὸ ἥμισυ see L. & S. s v. I. 2, and, for the expression, *Theaet.* 147 e 5 τὸν ἀριθμὸν πάντα δίχα διελάβομεν ('we divided into two equal parts').

b 2 ὁ ἕτερος . . . στίχος, 'the other row' or 'series'.

b 10 ἐπιούσης . . . c 2 ὑπομεῖναι: the military metaphors are still kept up. Cp. 102 d 9 *n.*

c 1 ἀπολλύμενα ἢ ὑπεκχωροῦντα, as if dependent on φαίνεται, **b 7,** the intervening ἔοικε being ignored. We are now able to say that things which have opposite forms as their inseparable predicate refuse to admit the form opposite to that which is 'in' them, but either perish or withdraw at its approach. The simplest instance is that of snow which is not opposite to heat, but melts at its approach.

d 1 τάδε . . . ἃ κτλ. We are not defining a class of εἴδη, but a class of things (c 8 ἀλλ' ἄττα) which are not αὐτὰ ἐναντία to the 'attacking' form. It has not been suggested in any way that fire and snow are εἴδη, and it seems improbable that they are so regarded. On the other hand, 'three,' which, for the purposes of the present argument, is quite on a level with fire and snow, is spoken of (d 5) as an ἰδέα. It is this uncertainty which creates all the difficulties of the present passage. That, however, is not surprising; for, in the *Parmenides*, Plato represents Socrates as hesitating on this very point, and as doubtful whether he ought to speak of an εἶδος of 'man, *fire*, or water'. This, however, does not affect the argument. We need only speak of 'things' without deciding whether they are 'forms' or not.

ἃ ὅτι ἂν κατάσχῃ κτλ. Things which, though not themselves opposite to a given thing, do not withstand its attack, are 'those which, if one of them has taken possession of anything, it compels it not only to assume its own form, but also in every case that of something opposite to it' (i.e. to the attacking form). The illustration given just below makes it quite clear that this is the meaning, though the pronouns are a little puzzling, and will be dealt with in separate notes. The verb κατέχειν keeps up the military metaphor; for to 'occupy' a position is χωρίον κατέχειν.

d 2 τὴν αὑτοῦ ἰδέαν, sc. τὴν τοῦ κατασχόντος. There is nothing abnormal in the shift from plural (ἅ) to singular in a case like this. After an indefinite plural some such subject as 'any one of them' is often to be supplied, and κατάσχῃ is felt to be singular in meaning as well as in form, as is shown by ὅτι ἄν and αὐτό, whereas at d 5 we have ἃ ἂν κατάσχῃ duly followed by αὐτοῖς. For the change of number cp. also 70 e 5 n. and *Laws* 667 b 5 δεῖ τόδε . . . ὑπάρχειν ἅπασιν ὅσοις συμπαρέπεταί τις χάρις, ἢ τοῦτο αὐτὸ μόνον (sc. τὴν χάριν) αὐτοῦ τὸ σπουδαιότατον εἶναι κτλ.

d 2   αὐτό refers to ὅτι ἂν κατάσχῃ, the thing occupied. For the slight pleonasm cp. 99 b 6; 111 c 8. The meaning is fixed by d 6 ἀνάγκη αὐτοῖς referring to ἃ ἂν . . . κατάσχῃ.

d 3   αὐτῷ is omitted by most editors, but the meaning of ἐναντίον is by no means clear without a dative. If we remember once more that we are defining a class of things which do not hold their ground before the onset of an opposite, it is not difficult to interpret αὐτῷ as 'the opposite in question' implied in τὰ ἐναντία οὐχ ὑπομένει ἐπιόντα above. This is also borne out by the illustration given below. It is the form of the odd which prevents the approach of the even to three, just as it is the form of cold which prevents the approach of heat to snow. (Cp. below e 9 τὸ γὰρ ἐναντίον ἀεὶ αὐτῷ ἐπιφέρει. This last passage is strongly against the reading δεῖ for ἀεί, which I regard as a mere corruption (ΑΕΙ, ΔΕΙ).

d 12   ἡ περιττή, sc. μορφή. There does not seem to be any other instance of this brachylogy. The normal use is seen just below in ἡ τοῦ ἀρτίου.

e 5   Ἀνάρτιος ἄρα. The precise point of this step in the argument only emerges at 105 d 13 sqq. The term περιττός, 'odd,' does not at first seem parallel to a term like ἀνθάνατος. As Wohlrab says, the point would not require to be made in German; for in that language the odd is called *das Ungerade*.

e 7   ὁρίσασθαι: W has ὁρίσασθαι δεῖν, which gives the meaning, but is probably due to interpolation. Tr. 'What I said we were to define'.

πoῖα κτλ. Fire, for instance, is not opposite to cold nor snow to heat, yet fire will not admit cold, nor will snow admit heat.

e 8   αὐτό, τὸ ἐναντίον. It is plain from αὐτὸ δέχεται in the next line that αὐτό must refer to the same thing as τινί, and, in that case, τὸ ἐναντίον can only be added if we suppose τινί to mean virtually τῶν ἐναντίων τινί, 'one of a pair of opposites,' and take αὐτό as 'the opposite in question'. I cannot attach any appropriate sense to the vulgate αὐτὸ τὸ ἐναντίον, which ought to mean 'what is actually opposite to it', which would imply e. g. that snow will not admit the cold. The same objection applies to the variant αὐτῷ τὸ ἐναντίον adopted by Schleiermacher and Stallbaum. Wyttenbach proposed either to delete τὸ ἐναντίον or to read τὸ οὐκ ἐναντίον. The former proposal would simplify the sentence; the latter shows that he understood it.

e 8   νῦν, 'in the present case.'

e 10   ἐπιφέρει is another military metaphor (cp. ἐπιφέρειν πόλεμον, *bellum inferre*, ὅπλα ἐπιφέρειν &c.). Tr. 'it always brings into the field its opposite', i. e. τὸ περιττόν. It is very important to notice that ἐπιφέρειν is always used of the thing 'attacked', while ἐπιέναι and κατέχειν are used of the thing which 'attacks' it. Ἐπιφέρειν refers to the means of defence. It is, we may say, τὸ ἀμυνόμενον which ἐναντίον τι ἐπιφέρει τῷ ἐπιόντι. Further, ἐπιέναι is not the same thing as κατέχειν, which implies a successful ἔφοδος.

ἡ δυὰς τῷ περιττῷ, sc. τὸ ἐναντίον ἐπιφέρει, i. e. τὸ ἄρτιον.

a 1   ἀλλ' ἄρα κτλ. ἀλλά resumes after the parenthesis with a slight anacoluthon.

a 2   μὴ μόνον κτλ. Taking the same instance as before, not only does cold refuse to admit its opposite, heat, but so does snow, which always brings cold (which is the opposite of heat) into the field against it in self-defence.

a 3   ἀλλὰ καὶ ἐκεῖνο κτλ. All editors seem to take ἐκεῖνο as subject of δέξασθαι and antecedent to ὃ ἂν ἐπιφέρῃ, but that leads to great difficulties, the chief of which are that we have to refer ἐκείνῳ to something other than ἐκεῖνο and to take ἐφ' ὅτι ἂν αὐτὸ ἴῃ of the thing which is being attacked instead of the attacking form. Riddell (Dig. § 19) took ἐκεῖνο (sc. ὁρίζῃ) as an accusative pronoun in apposition to what follows. I prefer to take it as the object of δέξασθαι and closely with ἐφ' ὅτι ἂν αὐτὸ ἴῃ. The subject of δέξασθαι will then be ὃ ἂν ἐπιφέρῃ τι ἐναντίον ἐκείνῳ. Then αὐτὸ τὸ ἐπιφέρον repeats ὃ ἂν ἐπιφέρῃ κτλ. and τὴν τοῦ ἐπιφερομένου ἐναντιότητα repeats ἐκεῖνο. We have thus an instance of interlaced order (*a b a b*) which is, I take it, what Socrates means by speaking συγγραφικῶς.

a 5   οὐ . . . χεῖρον, 'it is just as well.'

a 6   τὴν τοῦ ἀρτίου, sc. ἰδέαν. Cp. 104 d 14.

a 7   τὸ διπλάσιον, in apposition to τὰ δέκα, 'which is the double of five,' and therefore an even number.

a 8 τοῦτο μὲν οὖν κτλ. I formerly inserted οὐκ before ἐναντίον with most editors, but this leaves καί and the concessive μὲν οὖν without any meaning. I now interpret: 'It is quite true that this (the double) *is* itself opposite to another thing (viz. the single, τὸ ἁπλοῦν); but at the same time it will also refuse to admit the form of the odd' (to which it is not itself opposite). The reason is, of course, that τὸ διπλάσιον always ἐπιφέρει τὸ ἄρτιον, brings the even into the field to resist the attack of the odd; for all doubles are even numbers. It goes without saying that it will not admit τὸ ἁπλοῦν which is its own opposite.

b 1 οὐδὲ δὴ κτλ. The almost accidental mention of double and single suggests another opposition, that of integral and fractional. With Heindorf, I take the construction to be οὐδὲ δὴ τὸ ἡμιόλιον (3/2) οὐδὲ τἄλλα τὰ τοιαῦτα, τὸ ἥμισυ (1/2) καὶ τριτημόριον αὖ (1/3) καὶ πάντα τὰ τοιαῦτα (δέχεται) τὴν τοῦ ὅλου (ἰδέαν). If we observe the slight colloquial hyperbaton of τὴν τοῦ ὅλου, there is no need to interpret τὸ ἥμισυ in an artificial way (as 'fractions whose denominator is 2', like 3/2 and 1/2) or to delete it. No given fraction is itself opposite to τὸ ὅλον, but they all 'bring into the field' τὴν τοῦ μορίου ἰδέαν in self-defence against the attack of τὸ ὅλον.

b 5 ὃ ἂν ἐρωτῶ, 'in the terms of my question' (Church). The readings of the MSS. vary considerably, but the meaning is clear from the sequel.

b 6 λέγω δὴ κτλ., 'I say this because, as a result of our present argument, I see another possibility of safety over and above (παρ') that safe answer I spoke of at first' (100 d 8).

b 9 ᾧ ἂν τί κτλ., 'what must be present in anything, in its body (i. e. 'in a thing's body'), to make it warm?' The text is not quite certain, and it would no doubt be simpler to omit ἐν τῷ with Stephanus, thus making the construction the same as in c 3. It is possible, however, to understand ἐν τῷ σώματι as a further explanation of ᾧ ἂν ἐγγένηται, so I have let it stand.

c 1 τὴν ἀμαθῆ, 'foolish.' Cp. 100 d 3. The irony is kept up.

c 2 κομψοτέραν: κομψός is the urbane equivalent of σοφός, and ἀμαθής is the regular opposite of σοφός (cp. 101 c 8). We are taking a step towards the κομψεῖαι which we deprecated before. ἐκ τῶν νῦν: cp. b 7.

ᾧ ἂν πῦρ. It is safe to say this because θερμότης is an inseparable predicate of πῦρ, and so the presence of fire is a sufficient αἰτία of bodily heat. This does not mean in the least that fire is the only such cause, as appears clearly from the other instances. There are other causes of disease than fever, and other odd numbers than the number one (ἡ μονάς).

d 3 Ψυχὴ ἄρα κτλ. Previously we could only say that participation in the form of life was the cause of life; but, ἐκ τῶν νῦν λεγομένων, we may substitute ψυχή for ζωή, just as we may substitute πῦρ, πυρετός, μονάς for θερμότης, νόσος, περιττότης. There is not a word about the soul being itself a form or εἶδος, nor is such an assumption required. The soul may perfectly well be said to 'occupy' the body without being itself an ἰδέα. It is a simple military metaphor (cp. **104 d 1** n.), and implies no metaphysical theory.

d 10 Οὐκοῦν ψυχὴ κτλ. The point is that, though ψυχή itself is not opposite to anything, it always 'brings into the field' something which has an opposite, namely life. We may say, then, that soul will not admit that opposite (i. e. death), but must either withdraw before it or perish.

d 13 Τί οὖν κτλ. The point here is mainly verbal. It has to be shown that what does not admit θάνατος may be called ἀθάνατος.

e 1 Ἄμουσον ... τὸ δὲ ἄδικον stands for τὸ μὲν ἄμουσον, τὸ δὲ ἄδικον by an idiom of which Plato is specially fond. Cp. *Prot.* 330 a 3 ἄλλο, τὸ δὲ ἄλλο, *Theaet.* 181 d 5 δύο δὴ λέγω ... εἴδη κινήσεως, ἀλλοίωσιν, τὴν δὲ φοράν, *Rep.* 455 e 6 γυνὴ ἰατρική, ἡ δ' οὔ, καὶ μουσική, ἡ δ' ἄμουσος φύσει.

e 10 Τί οὖν κτλ. It has been proved that the soul will not admit death; but we have still to deal with two possible alternatives; for it may either 'withdraw' or 'perish'. This alternative actually exists in all other cases; but in the case of τὸ ἀθάνατον the second is excluded; for τὸ ἀθάνατον is *ipso facto* ἀνώλεθρον. Therefore the soul must 'withdraw' at the approach of death.

a 1 ἄλλο τι ... ἤ, *nonne.* The interposition of the subject is unusual, but cp. **106 e 1**. There is no contradiction in saying that 'the uneven' is perishable. If there were, three would be imperishable because it may be substituted for 'the uneven'.

a 3 τὸ ἄθερμον, though the reading rests only on the authority of the corrector of T, must be right (θερμὸν BTW Stob.). The word is coined, like ἀνάρτιος, to furnish a parallel to ἀθάνατος. Snow is to τὸ ἄθερμον as soul is to τὸ ἀθάνατον.

a 4 ἐπάγοι: another military metaphor.

a 8 τὸ ἄψυκτον: Wyttenbach conjectured ἄψυχρον to correspond with ἄθερμον, but ἄψυκτον, 'what cannot be cooled,' is a better parallel in sense, if not in form, to ἀθάνατον.

c 1 αὐτοῦ, sc. τοῦ περιττοῦ: ἀντ' ἐκείνου, sc. ἀντὶ τοῦ περιττοῦ.

d 2 τούτου γε ἕνεκα: cp. 85 b 8.

d 3 μὴ δέχοιτο: I can find no parallel to this use of μή. There are instances of μή with the potential optative in interrogations introduced by πῶς or τίνα τρόπον. We might have had πῶς ἄν ... μὴ δέχοιτο; 'how could anything else avoid receiving?' and this is virtually what the sentence means (G. M. T. § 292).

107 a 5 ἀναβάλλοιτο is an instance of the optative without ἄν often found after such phrases as (οὐκ) ἔσθ' ὅστις ..., (οὐκ) ἔσθ' ὅπως.

b 6 ἐπισκεπτέαι σαφέστερον, if the text is sound, is a very striking anacoluthon due to the parenthesis. This sentence is just like the reference to the μακροτέρα ὁδός in *Rep.* 435 d and the μακροτέρα περίοδος, *ib.* 504 b. It is clear that the πρῶται ὑποθέσεις which are to be re-examined are just those mentioned above, 100 b 5, that is to say, the 'Theory of Ideas' in the form in which it is presented to us in the *Phaedo.* Whether Socrates was conscious that the theory required revision, I am not prepared to say; but it is clear that Plato was. The re-examination of these ὑποθέσεις is to be found chiefly in the *Parmenides* and the *Sophist,* both dialogues in which Socrates does not lead the discussion.

b 9 τοῦτο αὐτό, viz. that you have followed up the argument as far as is humanly possible. If you make sure (σαφές) of this, you need seek no further. The argument ends with a fresh confession of the weakness of human arguments. Cp. 85 c 1 sqq.

οὐδὲν ζητήσετε περαιτέρω: cp. *Tim.* 29 c 8 ἀγαπᾶν χρή, μεμνημένους ὡς ὁ λέγων ἐγὼ ὑμεῖς τε οἱ κριταὶ φύσιν ἀνθρωπίνην ἔχομεν, ὥστε περὶ τούτων τὸν εἰκότα μῦθον ἀποδεχομένους πρέπει τούτου μηδὲν ἔτι πέρα ζητεῖν.

The conclusion of the whole matter. The Myth (107 c 1—115 a 8).

c 2 εἴπερ ἡ ψυχὴ ἀθάνατος κτλ. Cp. *Rep.* 608 c 9 Τί οὖν; οἴει ἀθανάτῳ πράγματι ὑπὲρ τοσούτου δεῖν χρόνου ἐσπουδακέναι, ἀλλ' οὐχ ὑπὲρ τοῦ παντός;

c 3 ἐν ᾧ καλοῦμεν τὸ ζῆν, 'for which what is called life lasts.' For this way of speaking cp. *Il.* xi. 757 καὶ 'Αλησίου ἔνθα κολώνη | κέκληται. Wyttenbach quotes several poetical parallels and Xen. *Hell.* v. I. 10 ἔνθα ἡ Τριπυργία καλεῖται.

c 4 νῦν δή, *nunc demum.* Cp. 61 e 6 *n.*

c 6 ἕρμαιον, 'a godsend,' Schol. τὸ ἀπροσδόκητον κέρδος. The word was properly used of treasure-trove ('windfall,' *aubaine*), which was sacred to Hermes. Cp. *Symp.* 217 a 3 ἕρμαιον ἡγησάμην εἶναι καὶ εὐτύχημα ἐμὸν θαυμαστόν and the expression κοινὸς 'Ερμῆς, 'Shares !' (Jebb on Theophrastus, *Characters*, xxvi. 18).

c 8 νῦν δέ, 'but, as it is . . .'

d 4 τροφῆς: cp. 81 d 8 *n.*
λέγεται, sc. ἐν τῷ λόγῳ, in the mystic doctrine. Cp. 67 c 5 *n.*

d 6 ὁ ἑκάστου δαίμων : cp. for the mystic doctrine of the guardian δαίμων Menander (fr. 550 Kock) "Απαντι δαίμων ἀνδρὶ συμπαρίσταται | εὐθὺς γενομένῳ μυσταγωγὸς τοῦ βίου. The idea that the δαίμων has a soul allotted to it as its portion appears in the *Epitaphios* of Lysias 78 ὅ τε δαίμων ὁ τὴν ἡμετέραν μοῖραν εἰληχώς, and Theocritus iv. 40 αἰαῖ τῶ σκληρῶ μάλα δαίμονος ὅς με λελόγχει. It was doubtless the common view, but is denied by Socrates in the Myth of Er (*Rep.* 617 e 1), where the προφήτης says : οὐχ ὑμᾶς δαίμων λήξεται, ἀλλ' ὑμεῖς δαίμονα αἱρήσεσθε.

d 7 εἰς δή τινα τόπον κτλ. We learn what the place was from *Gorg.* 524 a 1 οὗτοι οὖν . . . δικάσουσιν ἐν τῷ λειμῶνι. The 'meadow' of Judgement is Orphic. Note the use of δή τις in allusion to something mysterious. Cp. 108 c 1 ; 115 d 4. So ὃς δή, 107 e 1, 2. All through this passage δή is used to suggest something known to the speaker and to those whom he addresses, but of which they shrink from speaking.

d 8 διαδικασαμένους κτλ. In *Rep.* 614 c 4 we read that the Judges, ἐπειδὴ διαδικάσειαν, bade the righteous proceed to the right upwards and the wicked to the left downwards. The active is used of the judges and the middle of the parties who submit their claims to judgement (cp. 113 d 3). The meaning cannot be, as has been suggested, 'when they have received their *various* sentences,' for that would require the passive, and διαδικάζεσθαι always means ' to submit rival claims to a court'.

e 1 ᾧ δή: cp. d 7 *n.*

e 1   τοὺς ἐνθένδε : cp. 76 d 8 *n.*

e 2   ὧν δὴ τυχεῖν : cp. d 7 *n.* I have adopted δή from Stobaeus rather than the MS. δεῖ, which reads awkwardly. Cp. *Crat.* 400 c 5 ὡς δίκην διδούσης τῆς ψυχῆς ὧν δὴ ἕνεκα δίδωσιν (referring to the Orphic doctrine).

e 4   ἐν πολλαῖς . . . περιόδοις (ἐν of the time a thing takes cp. 58 b 8 *n.*). In *Rep.* 615 a 2 we have a χιλιέτης πορεία, consisting of ten περίοδοι of a hundred years each. In the *Phaedrus* (249 a) the περίοδοι are longer.

e 5   ὁ Αἰσχύλου Τήλεφος. The references to this quotation in other writers seem to be derived from the present passage, not from the original play.

108 a 4   σχίσεις τε καὶ τριόδους, 'partings of the way and bifurcations.' The reading τριόδους was that of Proclus and Olympiodorus and is much better than the MS. περιόδους, which is probably due to περιόδοις in e 4. It is the only reading which gives a proper sense to the next clause (see next note), and goes much better with σχίσεις. Cp. also *Gorg.* 524 a 2 ἐν τῷ λειμῶνι, ἐν τῇ τριόδῳ ἐξ ἧς φέρετον τὼ ὁδώ, ἡ μὲν εἰς μακάρων νήσους, ἡ δ' εἰς Τάρταρον. Virgil, *Aen.* vi. 540 *Hic locus est partes ubi se via findit in ambas.*

a 5   θυσιῶν is better attested (TW Stob.) than the ὁσίων of B, though that is an ancient variant (γρ. W). The MS. of Proclus, *in Remp.* (85. 6 Kroll), has οὐσιῶν, which explains the corruption (O for Θ). The reading θυσιῶν alone fits the explanation of Olympiodorus, ἀπὸ τῶν ἐν τριόδοις τιμῶν τῆς Ἑκάτης (cp. last note). The sacrifices to Hecate (*Trivia*) at the meeting of three ways are well attested, and Socrates means that these shadow forth the τρίοδος in the other world.

a 7   οὐκ ἀγνοεῖ τὰ παρόντα : i. e. the purified soul is familiar with the region through which it must travel.

a 8   ἐν τῷ ἔμπροσθεν : 81 c 10.
    περὶ ἐκεῖνο (sc. τὸ σῶμα) . . . ἐπτοημένη, 'in eager longing for'. The verb πτοεῖσθαι always refers to fluttering or palpitation of the heart, often, as here, caused by desire. For desire of the corporeal in a disembodied soul cp. 81 e 1.

b 4   ὅθιπερ : Cobet proposed οἷπερ, but cp. 113 a 2 οὗ . . . ἀφικνοῦνται (where, however, Schanz reads οἷ). The poetical form is not out of place here.

b 5 τοιοῦτον : i. e. ἀκάθαρτον.

b 7 ταύτην μέν resumes τὴν μέν above.

b 8 συνέμπορος : συνοδοιπόρος Timaeus. The word is poetical, like the use of the simple ἔμπορος for 'wayfarer'.

αὐτή, 'by itself', 'alone'.

c 1 ἕως ἂν . . . γένωνται, 'till they have passed.' The χρόνοι are the περίοδοι. Cp. *Prot.* 320 a 7 πρὶν ἐξ μῆνας γεγονέναι.

δή τινες : cp. 107 d 7 *n.*

c 2 ὧν ἐλθόντων, 'when they are gone,' i. e. when they have passed. ὑπ' ἀνάγκης is equivalent, as often, to ἐξ ἀνάγκης. There is no personification.

c 3 μετρίως : i. e. καλῶς. Cp. 68 e 2 *n.*

c 7 τῶν περὶ γῆς εἰωθότων λέγειν. From the time of Anaximander and Hecataeus the construction of γῆς περίοδοι had been a feature of Ionic science (E. Gr. Ph.² p. 53, *n.* 4). Aristophanes mentions a περίοδος containing the whole earth as among the furniture of the φροντιστήριον (*Clouds* 206). In this passage, as we shall see, Socrates abandons the central doctrine of Ionian geography.

c 8 ὑπό τινος πέπεισμαι. It is best not to inquire too curiously who this was. It was not Archelaus ; for he believed the earth to be a flat disk hollow in the centre. It was not Anaximander ; for he regarded the earth as cylindrical. It was not a Pythagorean ; for the 'hollows' are distinctively Ionian. The influence of Empedocles on the details of the description is well marked. Such an attempt to reconcile opposing views may well have been made at Athens during the second half of the fifth century B.C., but hardly at any other time or anywhere else. Personally, I am quite willing to believe that the theory is that of Socrates himself. It can scarcely have been seriously entertained by Plato at the time he wrote the *Phaedo* ; but it continued to have great influence. The cosmology of Posidonius, as we know it from the Περὶ κόσμου wrongly included in the Aristotelian *corpus*, is based upon that of the *Phaedo*, and it was in substance the cosmology of Posidonius which ultimately prevailed over the more scientific doctrines of the Academy, and dominated European thought till the time of Copernicus. The leading thought is that, if the earth is spherical, there must be other οἰκούμεναι than the one we know ; for our οἰκουμένη is but a small portion of the surface of the sphere.

d 4 οὐχ ἡ Γλαύκου τέχνη : Eusebius has οὐχὶ ἡ, so perhaps we should read οὐχί for οὐχ ἡ with Heindorf, who shows that later writers quote the proverb in this form. The paroemiographers give several explanations of it, the simplest of which is that it comes ἀπὸ Γλαύκου Σαμίου ὃς πρῶτον κόλλησιν ἐφεῦρε σιδήρου (cp. Hdt. i. 25). I believe, however, that the more complicated explanation is right, and that the reference is to a working model of the 'harmony of the spheres' originally designed by Hippasus, for which see Appendix II.

d 5 ἅ γ' ἐστίν, sc. ἃ πέπεισμαι, ὡς μέντοι ἀληθῆ, sc. πέπεισμαι, χαλεπώτερον, sc. διηγήσασθαι.

d 9 ἐξαρκεῖν is the best attested reading, but that of B, ἐξαρκεῖ, might stand, if we take μοι δοκεῖ as a parenthesis.

e 4 Πέπεισμαι ὡς . . . δεῖν : anacoluthon.

e 5 ἐν μέσῳ . . . περιφερὴς οὖσα : the original Pythagorean doctrine (E. Gr. Ph.² p. 345). Note the propriety with which οὐρανός is used for 'the world', i. e. everything contained within the heavens (E. Gr. Ph.² p. 31). Plato does not commit the anachronism of making Socrates adopt the later Pythagorean view, that the earth revolves round the Central Fire (E. Gr. Ph.² pp. 344 sqq.).

109 a 1 ἀέρος: the accepted Ionian doctrine (cp. 99 b 8 n.).

a 2 τὴν ὁμοιότητα, 'its equiformity.' This is another instance of historical accuracy in terminology ; for the terms ὅμοιος and ὁμοιότης were originally employed where ἴσος and ἰσότης would have been used later. Cp. Proclus' *Commentary on the First Book of Euclid*, p. 250. 22 Friedlein λέγεται γὰρ δὴ πρῶτος ἐκεῖνος (Θαλῆς) ἐπιστῆσαι καὶ εἰπεῖν ὡς ἄρα παντὸς ἰσοσκελοῦς αἱ πρὸς τῇ βάσει γωνίαι ἴσαι εἰσίν (Eucl. i. 5), ἀρχαϊκώτερον δὲ τὰς ἴσας ὁμοίας προσειρηκέναι. Just as what we call equal angles were called similar angles, so a sphere was said to be 'similar every way'. Aristotle ascribes both the theory and the use of the term ὁμοιότης to Anaximander (*de Coelo* 295 b 11 εἰσὶ δέ τινες οἳ διὰ τὴν ὁμοιότητά φασιν αὐτὴν (sc.τὴν γῆν) μένειν, ὥσπερ τῶν ἀρχαίων Ἀναξίμανδρος· μᾶλλον μὲν γὰρ οὐθὲν ἄνω ἢ κάτω ἢ εἰς τὰ πλάγια φέρεσθαι προσήκει τὸ ἐπὶ τοῦ μέσου ἱδρυμένον καὶ ὁμοίως πρὸς τὰ ἔσχατα ἔχον, ἅμα δ' ἀδύνατον εἰς τἀναντία ποιεῖσθαι τὴν κίνησιν· ὥστ' ἐξ ἀνάγκης μένειν. It is quite wrong to take ὁμοιότης as referring to homogeneity of substance or density. As we shall see, the world is not homogeneous in substance at all.

a 3 τῆς γῆς αὐτῆς τὴν ἰσορροπίαν, ' the equilibrium of the earth itself.'

Anaximander's cylindrical earth could hardly be called ἰσόρροπον like the Pythagorean spherical earth in the centre of a spherical world (οὐρανός).

a 6 ὁμοίως . . . ἔχον is equivalent to ὅμοιον ὂν (πάντῃ). Cp. Aristotle *loc. cit.* (a 2 *n.*) ὁμοίως πρὸς τὰ ἔσχατα ἔχον.

a 8 Καὶ ὀρθῶς γε. The ready assent of Simmias marks the doctrine, so far, as Pythagorean.

a 9 πάμμεγά τι εἶναι is a direct contradiction of Archelaus, who said κεῖσθαι δ' ἐν μέσῳ (τὴν γῆν) οὐδὲν μέρος οὖσαν, ὡς εἰπεῖν, τοῦ παντός (Hippolytus, *Ref.* i. 9. 3).

αὐτό, sc. τὴν γῆν. Cp. 88 a 6.

b 1 τοὺς μέχρι κτλ. The Pillars of Herakles are well known as the boundary of the οἰκουμένη on the west, and Aeschylus spoke of the Phasis as the boundary of Europe and Asia (fr. 185) δίδυμον χθονὸς Εὐρώπης | μέγαν ἠδ' Ἀσίας τερμόνα Φᾶσιν), cp. Hdt. iv. 45. So Eur. *Hipp.* 3 ὅσοι τε Πόντου τερμόνων τ' Ἀτλαντικῶν | ναίουσιν εἴσω.

b 2 περὶ τὴν θάλατταν οἰκοῦντας, 'dwelling round the Mediterranean (the θάλαττα κατ' ἐξοχήν) like frogs or ants round a swamp.' (Cp. *Et. M.* τέλμα· τόπος πηλώδης ὕδωρ ἔχων.)

b 3 καὶ ἄλλους ἄλλοθι κτλ. As Wyttenbach saw, this part of the theory comes from Anaxagoras (and Archelaus). Cp. Hippolytus, *Ref.* i. 8. 9 εἶναι γὰρ αὐτὴν (τὴν γῆν) κοίλην καὶ ἔχειν ὕδωρ ἐν τοῖς κοιλώμασιν (Ἀναξαγόρας φησίν), ib. 9. 4 λίμνην γὰρ εἶναι τὸ πρῶτον (τὴν γῆν), ἅτε κύκλῳ μὲν οὖσαν ὑψηλήν, μέσον δὲ κοίλην (Ἀρχέλαός φησιν), a view which is obviously a generalization from the Mediterranean basin. Here it is combined with the theory of a spherical earth (Anaxagoras and Archelaus believed in a flat earth), and it is assumed that there are several such basins with water in the middle and inhabited land round them. According to Posidonius, too, there were many οἰκούμεναι, but they were islands, not hollows.

b 6 τό τε ὕδωρ καὶ τὴν ὁμίχλην καὶ τὸν ἀέρα. Here again Plato correctly represents fifth-century science, according to which water is condensed air, mist being the intermediate state between them (E. Gr. Ph.² p. 79, *n.* 1). The discovery of atmospheric air as a body different from mist was due to Empedocles (ib. p. 263) and Anaxagoras (ib. p. 309); but it appears that the Pythagoreans adhered to the older view. Cp. *Tim.* 58 d 1 ἀέρος (γένη) τὸ μὲν εὐαγέστατον ἐπίκλην αἰθὴρ καλούμενος, ὁ δὲ θολερώτατος ὁμίχλη τε καὶ σκότος.

b 7 αὐτὴν ... τὴν γῆν : the true surface of the earth (called below 'the true earth'), as opposed to the basins or 'hollows'. It rises above the mist and 'air'. It is clear that we are to suppose considerable distances between the basins.

b 8 αἰθέρα : αἰθήρ is properly the sky regarded as made of blue fire. This, as we see from the passage of the *Timaeus* quoted in the last note, was supposed to be air still further rarefied. It is the intermediary between fire and air, as ὀμίχλη is that between air and water.

c 1 τοὺς πολλούς κτλ. This implies that Socrates knows the divergent views of Empedocles and Anaxagoras, the former of whom gave the name αἰθήρ to atmospheric air (E. Gr. Ph.² p. 263 sq.), while the latter used it of fire (ib. p. 312 *n*. 1).

τῶν περὶ τὰ τοιαῦτα εἰωθότων λέγειν : I do not know any other instance of περί *c. acc.* after λέγειν in Plato (*Gorg.* 490 c 8 is not one ; for πλέον ἔχειν is 'understood' and λέγεις is parenthetical). I am inclined to think the words εἰωθότων λέγειν have been wrongly added from 108 c 7. For the resulting phrase cp. *Phaedr.* 272 c 7 ὃν (λόγον) τῶν περὶ ταῦτά τινων ἀκήκοα, ib. 273 a 5 τοῖς περὶ ταῦτα.

c 2 ὑποστάθμην, 'sediment,' lit. 'lees' (τρυγία, τρύξ Hesych.). Note that air, mist, and water are the sediment of the αἰθήρ.

d 4 παρὰ σφίσι : Socrates is thinking of a whole people dwelling at the bottom of the sea. This is not inconsistent with εἴ τις above (c 4) ; for εἴ τις is continued by a plural oftener than not.

d 7 διὰ τούτου, sc. διὰ τοῦ ἀέρος.

d 8 τὸ δὲ εἶναι ταὐτόν, ' whereas it is just the same thing ' with us as with the imaginary dwellers at the bottom of the sea. For τὸ δέ cp. 87 c 6 *n*. I see no reason to suspect the text. The *asyndeton explicativum* is quite in order ; for εἶναι ταὐτόν is explanatory of ταὐτὸν δὴ τοῦτο καὶ ἡμᾶς πεπονθέναι (cp. 72 c 3 *n*.).

e 2 ἐπ' ἄκρα : the surface of the ' air ' is parallel to that of the sea (d 1).

e 3 κατιδεῖν ⟨ἄν⟩ : the δή of Eusebius is probably a trace of the lost ἄν (AN, ΔΗ), which might easily be dropped by haplography.

e 4 ἀνακύπτοντες : cp. *Phaedr.* 249 c 3 (ψυχὴ) ἀνακύψασα εἰς τὸ ὂν ὄντως. The position of the attributive participle outside the article and its noun is normal when there is another attribute. Cp. Phil. 21 c 2 τῆς ἐν τῷ παραχρῆμα ἡδονῆς προσπιπτούσης.

e 5 οὕτως ἄν τινα . . . κατιδεῖν is a good instance of a form of 'binary structure', noted by Riddell (Dig. § 209), in which 'the fact illustrated is stated (perhaps only in outline) before the illustration, and re-stated after it' (*a b a*).

e 7 ὁ ἀληθῶς . . . τὸ ἀληθινὸν . . . ἡ ὡς ἀληθῶς: observe how Plato varies the expression.

a 1 ἥδε . . . ἡ γῆ, 'this earth of ours,' i. e. the hollow in which we dwell and which we take to be the surface of the earth.

a 5 σήραγγες, σῆραγξ, ὕφαλος πέτρα ῥήγματα ἔχουσα, Hesych., Suid.

a 6 ὅπου ἄν καὶ [ἡ] γῆ ᾖ, 'wherever there is earth' to mix with the water. Though there is no good authority for the omission of ἡ, it is certainly better away.

a 8 ἐκεῖνα, the things above on the true earth which are in turn (αὖ) as superior to what we have as those are to the things in the sea.

b 1 εἰ γὰρ δὴ . . . καλόν is far the best attested reading, though B omits καλόν and alters δή to δεῖ. Olympiodorus apparently had δεῖ and καλόν, for he finds it necessary to explain why the μῦθος is called beautiful. It is to be observed that a μῦθος is only in place where we cannot apply the strictly scientific method. There is nothing 'mythical' about the εἴδη, but all we call 'natural science' is necessarily so, as is explained at the beginning of the *Timaeus*. It is, at best, a 'probable tale'. Cp. Taylor, *Plato*, pp. 50-2.

b 6 ἡ γῆ αὐτή, 'the true earth.'

ὥσπερ αἱ δωδεκάσκυτοι σφαῖραι, 'like balls made of twelve pieces of leather.' This is an allusion to the Pythagorean theory of the dodecahedron, which was of special significance as the solid which most nearly approaches the sphere (E. Gr. Ph.[2] p. 341 sq.). To make a ball, we take twelve pieces of leather, each of which is a regular pentagon. If the material were not flexible, we should have a regular dodecahedron ; as it is flexible, we get a ball. This has nothing to do with the twelve signs of the zodiac, as modern editors incorrectly say. Cp. *Tim.* 55 c 4 ἔτι δὲ οὔσης συστάσεως μιᾶς πέμπτης (a fifth regular solid besides the pyramid or tetrahedron, the cube, and the icosahedron), ἐπὶ τὸ πᾶν ὁ θεὸς αὐτῇ κατεχρήσατο ἐκεῖνο διαζωγραφῶν ('when he painted it', see next note). The author of the *Timaeus Locrus* is perfectly right in his paraphrase of this (98 e) τὸ δὲ δωδεκάεδρον εἰκόνα τοῦ παντὸς ἐστάσατο, ἔγγιστα σφαίρας ἐόν. The whole matter is fully explained in Wyttenbach's note, from which it will be seen that it was clearly understood by Plutarch, Simplicius, and others. Proclus, in his *Commentary on the First Book of Euclid*, shows how the whole edifice of the *Elements* leads up to the inscription of the regular solids (κοσμικὰ or Πλατωνικὰ σχήματα) in the sphere.

b 7 χρώμασιν διειλημμένη. The true earth is represented as a patchwork of different colours (for διειλημμένη cp. 81 c 4 *n.*). This must be the explanation of the words ἐκεῖνο διαζωγραφῶν, 'painting it in different colours' (cp. διαποικίλλω). Each of the twelve pentagons has its own colour.

b 8 δείγματα, 'samples.' In the same way our precious stones are 'pieces' (μορία) of the stones of the true earth (below, d 8).

c 2 πολὺ ἔτι ἐκ λαμπροτέρων : for the position of ἐκ cp. 70 c 1 *n.*

ἢ τούτων : the case after ἢ assimilated to that before it (Riddell, Dig. § 168). Cp. *Meno* 83 c 8 ἀπὸ μείζονος . . . ἢ τοσαύτης γράμμης, *Laws* 892 b 1 οὔσης γ' αὐτῆς (sc. ψυχῆς) πρεσβυτέρας ἢ σώματος.

τὴν μὲν . . ., sc. γῆν, 'one portion of it,' one pentagon.

c 4 τὴν δὲ ὅση λευκή, 'all the part of it which is white.'

c 6 καὶ γὰρ αὐτὰ ταῦτα κτλ. The meaning is that, as the basins or 'hollows' are full of 'air' and water, the surfaces of these produce the appearance of glistening patches among the other colours, so that the general appearance is that of a continuous (συνεχές) surface of various colours (ποικίλον).

c 7 ἔκπλεα is quite a good word, and there is no need to read ἔμπλεα with inferior authorities.

d 3 ἀνὰ λόγον, 'proportionally.'

d 6 τήν τε λειότητα : so W. B makes the almost inevitable mistake τὴν τελειότητα, and so at first did T, but erased it in time.

d 7 ταῦτα τὰ ἀγαπώμενα, 'the precious stones that are so highly prized in our world.' Prof. Ridgeway has some interesting observations on the relation between the Pythagorean solids and natural crystals in *Class. Rev.* x (1896) p. 92 sqq.

e 1 οὐδὲν ὅτι οὐ, 'every one of them.' The phrase is regularly treated as a single word equivalent to πάντα. Hence the plural καλλίω.

e 3 οὐδὲ διεφθαρμένοι κτλ. Another instance of interlaced order (*a b a b*); for ὥσπερ οἱ ἐνθάδε ὑπὸ τῶν δεῦρο συνερρυηκότων go closely together, and ὑπὸ σηπεδόνος καὶ ἄλμης goes with διεφθαρμένοι (so Stallbaum). The συνερρυηκότα are water, mist, and air (cp. **109** b 6).

e 5 τοῖς ἄλλοις, 'to animals and plants besides.' Cp. *Gorg*. 473 c 7 ὑπὸ τῶν πολιτῶν καὶ τῶν ἄλλων ξένων.

a 1 ἐκφανῇ, 'exposed to view,' not, as with us, hidden beneath the earth.

a 6 ἐν νήσοις κτλ. This is an attempt to fit the old idea of the Islands of the Blest into the mythical landscape. Cp. Pindar, *Ol*. ii. 130 ἔνθα μακάρων | νᾶσος ὠκεανίδες | αὖραι περιπνέοισιν, which is humourously paraphrased by ἃς περιρρεῖν τὸν ἀέρα, the air being the sea in which these islands are. But they are 'close to the mainland', otherwise we should see them from our hollow! The suggestion of Olympiodorus, that these men feed on the apples of the Hesperides, is therefore not so wide of the mark as might appear.

a 7 ὅπερ ... τοῦτο ..., the regular way of expressing a proportion. Cp. 110 d 5 ἀνὰ λόγον.

b 2 κρᾶσιν, 'temperature.' In Greek, however, as in French, the word has a wider sense than in English. It is not only the due *temperamentum* of the hot and cold, but also that of the wet and dry (cp. 86 b 9 *n*.). The κρᾶσις τῶν ὡρῶν is 'climate'.

b 4 φρονήσει: sight and hearing stand for the senses generally (hence πάντα τὰ τοιαῦτα), to which intelligence must of course be added. It is, therefore, wrong to read ὀσφρήσει with Heindorf. Cp. *Rep*. 367 c 7 οἷον ὁρᾶν, ἀκούειν, φρονεῖν.

b 6 ἄλση: T has ἔδη, and this reading was adopted by Heindorf from the apographa. In the Lexicon of Timaeus we read ἔδος· τὸ ἄγαλμα. καὶ ὁ τόπος ἐν ᾧ ἵδρυται, and, as the word does not occur elsewhere in Plato, this may indicate that Timaeus read it here, but ἄλση seems better. Cp. Livy, xxxv. 51 *in fano lucoque*.

b 7 φήμας, 'sacred voices.' Like φάτις and κληδών, φήμη is used of omens conveyed by the hearing of significant words. Virg. *Aen*. vii. 90 *Et varias audit voces, fruiturque deorum | colloquio*.

b 8 αἰσθήσεις τῶν θεῶν: not in dreams or visions, as some say. The point is just that they see the gods with their waking senses.

c 1 αὐτοῖς πρὸς αὐτούς, 'face to face.' Here πρὸς αὐτούς (τοὺς θεούς) belongs to συνουσίας and αὐτοῖς (τοῖς ἀνθρώποις) to γίγνεσθαι (a b b a).

c 2 οἷα τυγχάνει ὄντα, 'as they really are.' This is an astronomer's vision of blessedness.

c 6 τοὺς μὲν κτλ. Three sorts of τόποι are enumerated (1) deeper and broader (than the Mediterranean basin), (2) deeper and narrower, (3) shallower and broader. The fourth possibility, shallower and narrower, is not mentioned. Plato does not care for symmetry of this kind.

c 8 αὐτούς: Heindorf read αὐτῶν from inferior MSS., and I formerly conjectured αὖ. No change, however, is necessary. For the pleonasm cp. Riddell, Dig. § 223. It assists the shift from ὄντας to ἔχειν.

d 2 ὑπὸ γῆν . . . συντετρῆσθαι, 'are connected by subterranean openings.' This seems to come from Diogenes of Apollonia. Cp. Seneca, *Nat. Quaest.* iv. 2. 28 *sunt enim perforata omnia et invicem pervia.* The geological conformation of the country made such views seem very credible in Greece.

d 5 ὥσπερ εἰς κρατῆρας : cp. Soph. *Oed. Col.* 1593 κοίλου πέλας κρατῆρος ('near the basin in the rock', Jebb). A scholium on this passage of Sophocles runs : τοῦ μυχοῦ· τὰ γὰρ κοῖλα οὕτως ἐκάλουν ἐκ μεταφορᾶς· ὅθεν καὶ τὰ ἐν τῇ Αἴτνῃ κοιλώματα κρατῆρες καλοῦνται. Cp. such names as 'The Devil's Punchbowl' in English. It is easier to understand how the crater of a volcano got its name, if we may trust this scholium, and the rocky basins fit in very well with the present context.

e 1 ἐν Σικελίᾳ κτλ. This seems to come from the Sicilian Empedocles, who explained the hot springs of his native island by comparing them to pipes used for heating warm baths (E. Gr. Ph.² p. 277). The ῥύαξ is the lava-stream. Cp. Thuc. iii. 116 ἐρρύη δὲ περὶ αὐτὸ τὸ ἔαρ τοῦτο ὁ ῥύαξ τοῦ πυρὸς ἐκ τῆς Αἴτνης.

e 3 ὡς ἄν : the MSS. have ὧν ἄν, but Stallbaum's conjecture ὡς ἄν is now confirmed by Stobaeus.

e 4 ταῦτα δὲ πάντα κτλ. The theory is thus stated in Aristotle's Μετεωρολογικά, 355 b 32 sqq. τὸ δ' ἐν τῷ Φαίδωνι γεγραμμένον περί τε τῶν ποταμῶν καὶ τῆς θαλάττης ἀδύνατόν ἐστιν. λέγεται γὰρ ὡς ἅπαντα μὲν εἰς ἄλληλα συντέτρηται ὑπὸ γῆν, ἀρχὴ δὲ πάντων εἴη καὶ πηγὴ τῶν ὑδάτων ὁ καλούμενος Τάρταρος, περὶ τὸ μέσον ὕδατός τι πλῆθος, ἐξ οὗ καὶ τὰ ῥέοντα καὶ τὰ μὴ ῥέοντα ἀναδίδωσι πάντα· τὴν δ' ἐπίρρυσιν ποιεῖν ἐφ' ἕκαστα τῶν ῥευμάτων διὰ τὸ σαλεύειν ἀεὶ τὸ πρῶτον καὶ τὴν ἀρχήν· οὐκ ἔχειν γὰρ ἕδραν, ἀλλ' ἀεὶ περὶ τὸ μέσον εἰλεῖσθαι (*l.* ἴλλεσθαι, 'oscillate')· κινούμενον δ' ἄνω καὶ κάτω ποιεῖν τὴν ἐπίχυσιν τῶν ῥευμάτων. τὰ δὲ πολλαχοῦ μὲν λιμνάζειν, οἵαν καὶ τὴν παρ' ἡμῖν εἶναι θάλασσαν, πάντα δὲ

πάλιν κύκλῳ περιάγειν εἰς τὴν ἀρχήν, ὅθεν ἤρξαντο ῥεῖν, πολλὰ μὲν καὶ
κατὰ τὸν αὐτὸν τόπον, τὰ δὲ καὶ καταντικρὺ τῇ θέσει τῆς ἐκροῆς, οἷον εἰ ῥεῖν
ἤρξαντο κάτωθεν, ἄνωθεν εἰσβάλλειν. εἶναι δὲ μέχρι τοῦ μέσου τὴν κάθεσιν·
τὸ γὰρ λοιπὸν πρὸς ἄναντες ἤδη πᾶσιν εἶναι τὴν φοράν. τοὺς δὲ χυμοὺς καὶ
τὰς χρόας ἴσχειν τὸ ὕδωρ δι' οἵας ἂν τύχωσι ῥέοντα γῆς.

e 4 ὥσπερ αἰώραν τινά (cp. 66 b 4 *n.*), 'a sort of see-saw,' ἀντιταλάντωσις
Olympiodorus, cp. French *balancement* from *bilancem*. The term
αἰώρησις, *gestatio*, was familiar in medical practice, where it was
used of any exercise in which the body is at rest, sailing, driving, &c.
(cp. *Tim.* 89 a 7), and αἰώρα meant a 'swing' or 'hammock' (*Laws*
789 d 3). Aristotle's paraphrase has διὰ τὸ σαλεύειν. The whole
description shows that a sort of pulsation, like the systole and
diastole of the heart, is intended. The theory is, in fact, an instance
of the analogy between the microcosm and the macrocosm (E. Gr.
Ph.² p. 79), and depends specially on the Empedoclean view of the
close connexion between respiration and the circulation of the
blood (E. Gr. Ph.² p. 253).

a 1 διαμπερὲς τετρημένον, 'perforated right through.' Tartarus has
another opening antipodal to that first mentioned. We are not
told that it is a straight tunnel, but that seems likely, and we
shall see that it passes through the centre of the earth. So, too,
Dante's Hell is a chasm bored right through the earth (*Inferno*,
xxxiv, *sub fin.*, Stewart, *Myths of Plato*, p. 101).

a 2 Ὅμηρος: *Il.* viii. 14. 'The Arcadian form of βέρεθρον, scil.
ζέρεθρον, was the special name for the singular "Katavothra" of
Arcadia' (Geddes). Cp. Strabo, p. 389 τῶν βερέθρων, ἃ καλοῦσιν οἱ
Ἀρκάδες ζέρεθρα, τυφλῶν ὄντων καὶ μὴ δεχομένων ἀπέρασιν. The whole
account of Stymphalus, from which this is taken, is very suggestive
of the present passage.

a 4 ἄλλοθι: *Il.* viii. 481.

a 7 δι' οἵας ἂν ... γῆς: Aristotle (*l. c. sub fin.*) specifies taste and
colour as the characteristics the rivers derive from the earth they
flow through.

b 2 πυθμένα ... βάσιν: Aristotle (*loc. cit.*) says ἕδραν. There is no
bottom at the centre of the earth. 'On comprendra la pensée de
Platon en se rappelant que théoriquement une pierre jetée dans
un puits traversant la terre selon un diamètre irait indéfiniment
d'une extrémité à l'autre' (Couvreur). We must keep in mind

throughout this passage that everything falls to the earth's centre. The impetus (ὁρμή) of the water takes it past the centre every time, but it falls back again, and so on indefinitely.

b 3 αἰωρεῖται δὴ κτλ. Aristotle (*loc. cit.*) says ἀεὶ περὶ τὸ μέσον εἰλεῖσθαι, for which we must read ἴλλεσθαι, the proper word for oscillatory or pendulum motion. (Cp. *Tim.* 40 b 8, where I take the meaning to be the same. E. Gr. Ph.[2] p. 346 sq.)

καὶ κυμαίνει : the doxographical tradition connects this with the tides Cp. Aëtius on the ebb and flow of the tides (*Dox.* p. 383) Πλάτων ἐπὶ τὴν αἰώραν φέρεται τῶν ὑδάτων· εἶναι γάρ τινα φυσικὴν αἰώραν διά τινος ἐγγείου τρήματος περιφέρουσαν τὴν παλίρροιαν, ὑφ' ἧς ἀντικυμαίνεσθαι τὰ πελάγη. From this we may infer that there are two oscillations a day.

b 4 τὸ περὶ αὐτό, sc. τὸ περὶ τὸ ὑγρόν. The πνεῦμα is mentioned because the whole theory is derived from that of respiration. Cp. the account of ἀναπνοή in *Tim.* 80 d 1 sqq., where much of the phraseology of the present passage recurs : τὸ τῆς ἀναπνοῆς ... γέγονεν ... τέμνοντος μὲν τὰ σιτία τοῦ πυρός, αἰωρουμένου δὲ ἐντὸς τῷ πνεύματι συνεπομένου (cp. b 4), τὰς φλέβας ... τῇ συναιωρήσει (cp. b 7) πληροῦντος τῷ ... ἐπαντλεῖν (cp. c 3). Brunetto Latini ' speaks, very much in the same way as Plato does, of waters circulating in channels through the Earth, like blood through the veins of the body ' (Stewart, *Myths of Plato*, p. 103).

b 5 εἰς τὸ ἐπ' ἐκεῖνα ... εἰς τὸ ἐπὶ τάδε, ' in the direction of the further side of the earth ' (the antipodes), ' in the direction of the hither side '.

c 2 τὸν δὴ κάτω καλούμενον : the words δή and καλούμενον are a protest against the popular view that the antipodes are ' down '. It is just to avoid this incorrectness that Socrates says τὰ ἐπ' ἐκεῖνα, or τὰ κατ' ἐκεῖνα.

τοῖς κατ' ἐκεῖνα ... εἰσρεῖ, ' the streams flow into the regions on the further side of the earth,' as opposed to τὰ ἐνθάδε. I apprehend that τοῖς κατ' ἐκεῖνα must be explained in the same way as b 5 τὸ ἐπ' ἐκεῖνα, and in that case τὰ ῥεύματα must be the subject. Further, if we omit διά in c 3 with Stobaeus, we may take τοῖς κατ' ἐκεῖνα τῆς γῆς together. Even if we retain διά I have no doubt that we must ' understand ' τῆς γῆς after τοῖς κατ' ἐκεῖνα. Cp. Aristotle's paraphrase (*loc. cit.* III e 4 *n.*) τὴν δ' ἐπίρρυσιν ποιεῖν ἐφ' ἕκαστα τῶν ῥευμάτων, where τῶν ῥευμάτων is governed by ἐπίρρυσιν, and ἐφ' ἔκαστα means ἐπ' ἐκεῖνα καὶ ἐπὶ τάδε.

c 3 ὥσπερ οἱ ἐπαντλοῦντες, sc. πληροῦσιν, 'like irrigators.' The word ἐπαντλεῖν is used of raising water to a height for purposes of irrigation (*Dict. Ant. s. v. Antlia*). No stress is to be laid on the particular process by which this is done ; the point of the simile lies in the way the water rises to a point further from the centre (whether on this side of it or the other) and then flows off through the channels (ὀχετοί, *rivi*) like irrigation waters.

c 4 ἐκεῖθεν . . . δεῦρο, 'from the antipodes . . . towards us.'

c 6 εἰς τοὺς τόπους κτλ. All the streams are raised by the αἰώρα above the centre (on either side) and are drained off to τόποι on the surface of the earth, from which they once more find their way back to Tartarus by subterranean channels.

c 7 ἑκάστοις ὡδοποίηται, 'a way is made for each of them.' The simile of the irrigation-channels is kept up. The εἰδοποιεῖται of W confirms the ὡδοποίηται of Stobaeus, and T has ἑκάστοις as well as Stobaeus. The reading of B (εἰς οὓς ἑκάστους ὁδοποιεῖται) is inferior to this.

d 3 ⟨ἤ⟩ ἦ : there is some doubt as to the necessity of inserting ἤ here and in d 5. It seems safer, however, to insert it. In *Symp.* 173 a 6 B has ἦ and TW ἢ ἦ. In *Crito* 44 a BTW have ἢ ἦ.

d 4 ὑποκάτω εἰσρεῖ τῆς ἐκροῆς, 'at a lower level than the point of issue' really means nearer the centre of the earth, not nearer the antipodes.

d 5 καταντικρὺ . . . κατὰ τὸ αὐτὸ μέρος : Aristotle (*loc. cit.* III c 4 *n.*) interprets these words by κάτωθεν and ἄνωθεν, by which he clearly means ' on the other side' and ' on this side of' the earth's centre. The choice of words is unfortunate (especially as he bases his criticism on them) ; for we have been warned (c 1) that to call the antipodes ' down ' is only a popular way of speaking. In substance, however, Aristotle seems to me quite right in his interpretation. I do not see how κατὰ τὸ αὐτὸ μέρος can mean ' on the same side of Tartarus', as many recent editors suppose. The phrase must surely be interpreted in the light of e 2 τὸ ἑκατέρωθεν . . . μέρος, which certainly refers to the sections of Tartarus on either side of the earth's centre. The difficulties which editors have raised about this interpretation are purely imaginary. So long as a stream falls into Tartarus at a point nearer the earth's centre than it issued from it, it may correctly be said to fall into it ὑποκάτω τῆς ἐκροῆς, quite irrespective of whether it debouches on this side of the earth's centre or on the other.

d 5 ⟨ἣ⟩ ᾗ [εἰσρεῖ] ἐξέπεσεν, sc. εἰσρεῖ. If we omit εἰσρεῖ with Stobaeus we can take ᾗ (or ἣ ᾗ) ἐξέπεσεν together as equivalent to τῆς ἐκροῆς. It is important to observe that ἐκπίπτειν is the verb corresponding to ἐκροή, and that the reference is to the point at which the stream issues from Tartarus.

d 6 ἔστι δὲ ἃ κτλ. We have had the case of streams which issue from Tartarus in one hemisphere and fall into it in the other; we are now told of streams which come back to the hemisphere in which they started after circling round the other. They may even make this circuit several times, but with each circuit they will be 'lower', i.e. nearer the earth's centre. Their course will therefore be a spiral, and that is the point of περιελιχθέντα ... ὥσπερ οἱ ὄφεις, for ἕλιξ means just 'spiral'. As to περὶ τὴν γῆν it does not necessarily mean 'round (the outside of) the earth'. Cp. 113 b 1 *n.*

d 8 καθέντα is intransitive or rather 'objectless'. Cp. Ar. *Knights* 430 ἔξειμι γάρ σοι λαμπρὸς ἤδη καὶ μέγας καθιείς (of a wind), and συγκαθιέναι (sc. ἑαυτόν), 'to condescend.'

e 1 ἑκατέρωσε μέχρι τοῦ μέσου, 'in either direction as far as the middle,' that is to say, from either opening of Tartarus to its middle, which coincides with the centre of the earth.

e 2 ἄναντες γὰρ κτλ., 'for the part (of Tartarus) on either side (of the centre) is uphill to both sets of streams,' i.e. both to those which fall into it καταντικρὺ ἣ ᾗ ἐξέπεσεν and to those which fall into it κατὰ τὸ αὐτὸ μέρος. The πρός which B and W insert in different places is probably due to an ancient variant πρόσαντες. How old that variant must be is shown by the fact that Aristotle (*loc. cit.*) has πρὸς ἄναντες. Heindorf conjectured πρόσω, and recent editors follow him, but that is a non-Attic form and not used by Plato.

e 5 τυγχάνει δ' ἄρα ὄντα κτλ. Cp. *Od.* xi. 157 μέσσῳ γὰρ μεγάλοι ποταμοὶ καὶ δεινὰ ῥέεθρα, | Ὠκεανὸς μὲν πρῶτα κτλ., ib. x. 513 ἔνθα μὲν εἰς Ἀχέροντα Πυριφλεγέθων τε ῥέουσι | Κωκυτός θ', ὃς δὴ Στυγὸς ὕδατός ἐστιν ἀπορρώξ.

e 6 ἐξωτάτω, 'furthest from the centre.'

e 7 περὶ κύκλῳ, 'round in a circle.' There seems to be no doubt that περί can be used as an adverb in this phrase. Cp. *Tim.* 40 a 6 νείμας περὶ πάντα κύκλῳ τὸν οὐρανόν, *Laws* 964 e 4 περὶ ὅλην κύκλῳ τὴν πόλιν ὁρᾶν. The phrase is also found written in one word (*v.* L. & S. *s. v.* περίκυκλος) and this is how B writes it here. Perhaps Hermann is right in accenting πέρι to show that it is an adverb. We are not told that the λίμνη made by Oceanus is the Mediterranean, but that is doubtless so.

e 7 καταντικρύ, 'diametrically opposite,' i.e. on the opposite side of the centre of the earth (cp. 112 d 5 *n.*). Acheron is the antipodal counterpart of Oceanus, running in the opposite direction. It is fitting that the place of the dead should be in the other hemisphere. In the *Axiochus*, an Academic dialogue of the third century B.C., we are told (371 b 2) that 'the gods below' took possession of τὸ ἕτερον ἡμισφαίριον.

3 a 1 ὑπὸ γῆν ῥέων : the Acherusian Lake is subterranean.

a 2 οὗ : cp. 108 b 4 *n.*

τῶν πολλῶν : all except αἱ τῶν ὀρθῶς φιλοσοφούντων. Cp. 114 b 6 sqq.

a 5 εἰς τὰς τῶν ζῴων γενέσεις, 'for the births of animals.' Cp. 81 e 2 sqq.

τούτων κατὰ μέσον : i.e. at a point intermediate between Oceanus and Acheron. As Oceanus flows ἐξωτάτω, i.e. furthest from the centre (112 e 6 *n.*), Acheron will branch off from Tartarus nearer the centre, but on the other side. The point intermediate between these ἐκβολαί will therefore be above the centre on the same side as Oceanus.

a 6 ἐκβάλλει, 'issues', 'branches off' (from Tartarus). The word is synonymous with ἐκπίπτει (112 d 5 *n.*) and so is ἐκβολή with ἐκροή.

a 7 πυρὶ ... καόμενον. It seems to me that this may have been suggested by the remarkable statements in the Περίπλους of the Carthaginian Hanno (§§ 11–14) about the regions blazing with fire which were seen on the voyage southward from Cape Verde to Sierra Leone. If so, Pyriphlegethon is doubtless the Senegal. The Περίπλους, if genuine, would be well known in Sicily in the fifth century B.C.

b 1 περιελιττόμενος ... τῇ γῇ is generally assumed to mean 'winding round the earth', whereas it is clear that, like Cocytus (c 3), Pyriphlegethon must go under the earth after leaving the λίμνη in order to reach the Acherusian Lake, which is certainly subterranean. In the erroneous belief that Eusebius omits τῇ γῇ, most editors bracket the words; but this is quite unnecessary. They can quite well mean 'coiling itself round inside the earth' (*ambire terram intus in ipsa*, Stallbaum); cp. *Il.* xxii. 95 ἐλισσόμενος περὶ χειῇ of a serpent 'coiling himself round (the inside of) his nest' (Monro). Cp. **112** d 8 ὥσπερ οἱ ὄφεις.

b 3   οὐ συμμειγνύμενος τῷ ὕδατι : cp. *Il.* ii. 753 οὐδ' ὅ γε (sc. Τιταρήσιος) Πηνειῷ συμμίσγεται ἀργυροδίνῃ, | ἀλλά τέ μιν καθύπερθεν ἐπιρρέει ἠΰτ' ἔλαιον· | ὅρκου γὰρ δεινοῦ Στυγὸς ὕδατός ἐστιν ἀπορρώξ.

b 4   κατωτέρω τοῦ Ταρτάρου, 'at a lower point in Tartarus,' i.e. nearer the earth's centre than the Acherusian Lake, which must itself be nearer the centre than the ἐκβολή of Pyriphlegethon, though on the opposite side.

b 6   ὅπῃ ἂν τύχωσι τῆς γῆς, 'at various points on the earth's surface.' This shows that Pyriphlegethon in its subterranean spiral course passes under Etna. For the ῥύακες cp. **111** e 1 *n.*

  τούτου ... καταντικρύ : i.e. on the other side of the earth's centre, but nearer it than the ἐκβολή of Acheron, though further from it than the Acherusian Lake.

b 8   οἷον ὁ κυανός : it is not certain what substance is intended. In Theophrastus κυανός is *lapis lazuli* and that stone is probably meant here. In any case, we are to think of a bluish grey, steely colour, in strong contrast to the fiery plain of Pyriphlegethon.

c 1   ἐν δή, sc. τόπον (not ποταμόν). For δή cp. **107** e 1 *n.*

d 3   διεδικάσαντο : cp. **107** d 8 *n.*

  βιώσαντες : the Ionic participle is in place in a solemn passage like this, though in **95** c 3 we have the Attic βιούς. Later, the Ionic form became trivial, as in the λάθε βιώσας of Epicurus.

d 4   οἳ ... ἂν δόξωσιν, 'those who are found to have —,' a regular forensic expression.

  μέσως, 'middlingly,' to be distinguished from μετρίως which stands for εὖ.

d 5   ἃ δὴ κτλ. Another allusive and mysterious δή (cp. **107** e 1 *n.*). The ὀχήματα on which they embark must be boats of some kind. Charon's bark is familiar, but there are other boats of the dead besides that.

d 6   τὴν λίμνην, sc. τὴν Ἀχερουσιάδα.

d 7   καθαιρόμενοι : Purgatory is an essentially Orphic idea. Cf. Suid.

(*s. v.* 'Αχέρων) ὁ δὲ 'Αχέρων καθαρσίῳ ἔοικε καὶ οὐ κολαστηρίῳ, ῥύπτων καὶ σμήχων τὰ ἁμαρτήματα τῶν ἀνθρώπων. They are purified by fire as well as by water.

d 7 διδόντες δίκας is subordinate to καθαιρόμενοι, 'purged by punishment.'

d 8 εὐεργεσιῶν, 'good deeds,' seems to have been the regular word in this connexion (opp. ἀδικήματα). Cp. *Rep.* 615 b 6 εἴ τινας εὐεργεσίας εὐεργετηκότες καὶ δίκαιοι καὶ ὅσιοι γεγονότες εἶεν.

e 2 ἀνιάτως ἔχειν κτλ. The doctrine of the incurable sinners occurs also in the myths of the *Gorgias* (525 c sqq.) and the *Republic* (615 e sqq.). The rudiments of it are to be found in the picture of the three great sinners—Tantalus, Ixion, and Sisyphus—in the Νέκυια of the eleventh book of the *Odyssey*. From the *Gorgias* we learn that they are eternally punished as παραδείγματα.

e 6 οὔποτε, 'nevermore,' is more solemn than the everyday οὐδέποτε, 'never.' The Neoplatonists are very anxious to get rid of the doctrine of eternal punishment, but it is stated quite explicitly.

a 1 μεταμέλον: accusative absolute, *cum eos paenituerit.* Tr. 'and have lived (aor. subj.) the rest of their life in repentance'. An γ impersonal verb may take this construction: cp. *Apol.* 24 d 4 μέλα ι γέ σοι, *Rep.* 346 b 4 συμφέρον αὐτῷ, 'when it is good for him.'

a 2 τοιούτῳ τινὶ ἄλλῳ τρόπῳ, 'in some other way of the same sort,' viz. as those who have done wrong ὑπ' ὀργῆς.

a 5 τὸ κῦμα, 'the reflux.' Cp. 112 b 3 κυμαίνει ἄνω καὶ κάτω. This fits in well with the general scheme. Pyriphlegethon and Cocytus rise in opposite hemispheres. When the water in Tartarus rushes ἐπὶ τάδε it casts them out by Pyriphlegethon, when it rushes ἐπ' ἐκεῖνα by Cocytus.

κατὰ τὸν Κωκυτόν, 'down Cocytus.' Heindorf compares Xen. *Cyr.* vii. 5. 16 τὸ ὕδωρ κατὰ τὰς τάφρους ἐχώρει. In a 7 κατὰ τὴν λίμνην we have another meaning of κατά, 'on the level of', 'opposite to'. It must be remembered that the waters of Pyriphlegethon and Cocytus do not mingle with the Purgatorial Lake.

b 7 διαφερόντως πρὸς τὸ ὁσίως βιῶναι, 'to have led exceptionally holy lives,' as contrasted with those who have lived μέσως (113 d 4). We must 'understand' ζῆν or some such word with ὁσίως. For such an ellipse Stallbaum compares *Euthyd.* 281 a 5 τὸ ὀρθῶς (sc. χρῆσθαι) ἐπιστήμη ἐστὶν ἡ ἀπεργαζομένη, *Symp.* 181 b 6 ἀμελοῦντες δὲ τοῦ καλῶς (sc. διαπράξασθαι) ἢ μή, *Phileb.* 61 d 1 ἆρα ... τοῦ καλῶς ἂν μάλιστα ἐπιτύχοιμεν ; For similar brachylogies designed to obviate the repetition of the same word cp. *Prot.* 325 b 3 σκέψαι ὡς θαυμασίως γίγνονται οἱ ἀγαθοί (sc. ἀγαθοί), 344 e 1 τῷ δὲ κακῷ (κακῷ) οὐκ ἐγχωρεῖ γενέσθαι, *Meno* 89 a 6 οὐκ ἂν εἶεν φύσει οἱ ἀγαθοί (sc. ἀγαθοί). The προκεκρίσθαι added by Theodoret is an obvious interpolation.

c 2 ἐπὶ γῆς: i. e. on the 'true earth', the Earthly Paradise.

c 3 ἄνευ ... σωμάτων: cp. 76 c 12 χωρὶς σωμάτων. This is the statement which brought upon Plato the condemnation of the Church as being inconsistent with the resurrection of the body. Eusebius has καμάτων for σωμάτων, which looks like a deliberate falsification.

c 4 οἰκήσεις ... τούτων καλλίους. 'We are to think, perhaps, of the natal stars of the *Timaeus*' (Stewart, *Myths of Plato*, p. 109). In any case, those alone reach the Celestial Paradise who have undergone the philosophic κάθαρσις. The ordinary purgation is not sufficient.

c 7 πᾶν ποιεῖν, 'to leave nothing undone.' Cp. *Gorg.* 479 c 1 πᾶν ποιοῦσιν ὥστε δίκην μὴ διδόναι.

c 8 καλὸν ... τὸ ἆθλον: cp. *Rep.* 608 b 4 Μέγας ... ὁ ἀγών, ... μέγας, οὐχ ὅσος δοκεῖ, τὸ χρηστὸν ἢ κακὸν γενέσθαι, c 1 Καὶ μὴν ... τά γε μέγιστα ἐπίχειρα ἀρετῆς καὶ προκείμενα ἆθλα οὐ διεληλύθαμεν.

d 1 Τὸ μὲν οὖν κτλ. The difference between scientific knowledge and a 'probable tale' is once more insisted on. For the expression cp. 63 c 1 sqq., 108 d 5 sqq., *Meno* 86 b 6 καὶ τὰ μέν γε ἄλλα οὐκ ἂν πάνυ ὑπὲρ τοῦ λόγου διισχυρισαίμην, ὅτι δὲ ..., περὶ τούτου πάνυ ἂν διαμαχοίμην. Contrast d 4 ἐπείπερ ἀθάνατόν γε ἡ ψυχὴ φαίνεται οὖσα ('evidently is').

d 5 πρέπειν, sc. διισχυρίσασθαι.
ἄξιον, sc. εἶναι, 'that it is worth while to take the risk of thinking it is so.' Cp. 85 d 1.

d 7 ἐπᾴδειν: cp. 77 e 8.

e 3 πλέον θάτερον ... ἀπεργάζεσθαι, 'to do more harm than good.' The phrase occurs twice in the *Euthydemus* 280 e 5 πλέον γάρ που οἶμαι θάτερόν ἐστιν, ἐάν τις χρῆται ὁτῳοῦν μὴ ὀρθῶς πράγματι ἢ ἐὰν ἐᾷ, 297 c 7 ὁ δὲ αὐτῷ ἱκανῶς ἐβοήθησεν (sc. Ἰόλεως Ἡρακλεῖ), ὁ δ' ἐμὸς Ἰόλεως εἰ ἔλθοι, πλέον ἂν θάτερον ποιήσειεν. Cp. also Isocr. *Aeg.* 25 τούτον τὸν ταλαίπωρον οὐδεὶς τῶν συγγενῶν ... ἐπισκεψόμενος ἀφίκετο, πλὴν τῆς μητρὸς καὶ τῆς ἀδελφῆς, αἳ πλέον θάτερον ἐποίησαν. I do not think that, in these places, the meaning is 'to make bad worse' (Hemdorf), or that θάτερον has anything to do with Pythagorean views about 'the other'. We should hardly find the phrase in a private speech of Isocrates if it had. More likely it is a colloquialism like πλέον τι ποιεῖν, οὐδὲν πλέον ποιεῖν.

5 a 2 ὡς ... καλῇ: Hirschig for once seems to be justified in an ἀθέτησις. It is very difficult to believe that Plato should spoil the effect of his own words two lines below by anticipating them here.

a 5 φαίη ἂν ἀνὴρ τραγικός, 'as the man in the play would say'. The phrase does not occur in any extant tragedy.

a 8 νεκρὸν λούειν: for the construction cp. *Meno* 76 a 9 ἀνδρὶ πρεσβύτῃ πράγματα προστάττεις ἀποκρίνεσθαι.

Practical Application. The real Socrates will not die (115 b 1— 116 e 7).

b 2 ἐπιστέλλεις is the *vox propria* for the last wishes of the dying. Cp. 116 b 4.

b 9 ὥσπερ κατ᾽ ἴχνη: cp. *Rep.* 365 d 2 ὡς τὰ ἴχνη τῶν λόγων φέρει. The hunting metaphor once more.

c 1 οὐδὲν πλέον ποιήσετε, *nil proficietis*, 'you will do no good', 'it will profit nothing'.

c 6 Οὐ πείθω κτλ. Aelian, *V. H.* i. 16, has another version of this, which he is not likely to have composed himself: Καὶ πῶς ὑπὲρ ἡμῶν καλῶς Ἀπολλόδορος δοξάζει, εἴ γε αὐτὸς πεπίστευκεν ὅτι μετὰ τὴν ἐξ Ἀθηναίων φιλοτησίαν καὶ τὸ τοῦ φαρμάκου πῶμα ἔτι ὄντως ὄψεται Σωκράτην; εἰ γὰρ οἴεται τὸν ὀλίγον ὕστερον ἐρριμμένον ἐν ποσὶ καὶ κεισόμενόν γ᾽ ἐμὲ εἶναι, δῆλός ἐστί με οὐκ εἰδώς. This may be a fragment of Aeschines or another.

c 7 οὗτος Σωκράτης, 'Socrates here.' The omission of ὁ is idiomatic when the pronoun is used δεικτικῶς.

d 1 πῶς με θάπτῃ: indirect deliberative. Goodwin, *M. T.* § 677.

d 4 δή τινας: once more the allusive and mysterious δή. Cp. 107 d 7 *n.*

d 5 ἄλλως λέγειν: cp. 76 e 4.

d 7 ἦν οὗτος ... ἠγγυᾶτο does not refer to the offer of Plato, Crito, Critobulus, and Apollodorus, to become security for the fine of 30 minae which Socrates proposed in his ἀντιτίμησις (*Apol.* 38 b 6). We may infer from *Crito* 44 e 2 sqq. that Crito had further given security that Socrates would not run away (ἦ μὴν παραμενεῖν).

e 3 προτίθεται κτλ. The πρόθεσις ('laying out for burial') and the ἐκφορά ('carrying to the tomb') are the regular parts of the ceremony before the actual burial. The middle voice of προτίθεσθαι is justified because people lay out '*their* dead'. Cp. Eur. *Alc.* 663–4 καὶ θανόντα σε | περιστελοῦσι καὶ προθήσονται νεκρόν, Thuc. ii. 34. 2 τὰ μὲν ὀστᾶ προτίθενται ... ἐπειδὰν δὲ ἡ ἐκφορὰ ᾖ ... ξυνεκφέρει ... ὁ βουλόμενος.

e 5 εἰς αὐτὸ τοῦτο, 'so far as the thing itself (inaccurate language) goes'.

The Closing Scene (116 a 1—118 a 17).

116 a 2 ἀνίστατο εἰς: cp. *Prot.* 311 a 4 ἐξαναστῶμεν εἰς τὴν αὐλήν. οἴκημα means 'a room'.

a 5 τοτὲ δ' αὖ, as if τοτὲ μέν had preceded. Cp. the omission of ὁ μέν, 105 e 1 *n.*

b 1 δύο γὰρ κτλ. Cp. 60 a 2 *n.*

b 2 αἱ οἰκεῖαι γυναῖκες . . . ἐκεῖναι is certainly the original reading and ἐκείναις (to be construed with διαλεχθείς) is apparently a conjecture. It seems to be implied that the women of Socrates' family were well known to Echecrates and his friends. In fact, ἐκεῖναι has much the same effect as the γιγνώσκεις γάρ with which Xanthippe is introduced (60 a 2). It is surely impossible to believe with some editors that Xanthippe is not included among the οἰκεῖαι γυναῖκες. The mere fact that the youngest child is brought back seems to show that she is.

b 3 διαλεχθείς, sc. αὐτοῖς, i.e. τοῖς παιδίοις καὶ ταῖς γυναιξίν. The vulgate reading ἐκείναις would imply that he had no last words for his sons.

b 6 χρόνον... πολὺν κτλ. As the conversation recorded in the *Phaedo* began in the morning, and it is now close upon sunset on one of the longest days of the year, it is plain that Socrates spent several hours alone with the women and children. There is no trace of indifference to them. Cp. 60 a 7 *n.* Of course Phaedo can only narrate conversations at which he was present.

b 8 στὰς παρ' αὐτόν, 'stepping up to him.'

c 5 ἐν τούτῳ τῷ χρόνῳ, during the thirty days (cp. 58 a 4 *n.*) for which Socrates had been in prison.

d 6 ἀνδρῶν λῷστος, 'the best of men.' In Attic λῷστος is confined to a few phrases.

d 7 ἀποδακρύει : cp. 117 c 8 ἀπέκλαον.

d 9 ὁ ἄνθρωπος. It is to be observed that the man who administers the hemlock-draught is not the same person as the officer of the Eleven. The seeds were pounded in a mortar to extract the juice. Cp. App. I.

e 1 ἔτι ἥλιον εἶναι κτλ., 'that there is still sunlight on the hilltops.' For this sense of ἥλιος cp. Hdt. viii. 23 ἅμα ἡλίῳ σκιδναμένῳ. The meaning cannot be that the sun has not yet sunk behind Cithaeron ; for Crito says οἶμαι. He means that, though no longer visible, it is still shining on the hilltops.

a 2 γέλωτα ὀφλήσειν παρ' ἐμαυτῷ, 'to make myself ridiculous in my own eyes.'

φειδόμενος οὐδενὸς ἔτι ἐνόντος, 'sparing the cup when there is nothing in it,' a proverbial way of speaking. Cp. Hesiod, Ἔργα 367 μέσσοθι φείδεσθαι, δειλὴ δ' ἐνὶ πυθμένι φειδώ. For the Latin version of the saying cp. Seneca, *Ep.* I *nam, ut visum est maioribus nostris, sera parsimonia in fundo est,* 'Begin to spare halfway, it is a sorry saving when you reach the lees' (Geddes).

a 3 μὴ ἄλλως ποίει, 'don't refuse me,' a common colloquialism. Cp. *Crito* 45 a 3 : *Rep.* 328 a 10.

a 4 τῷ παιδί, 'to his servant.'

b 1 αὐτὸ ποιήσει, 'it will act of itself.' In the medical writers ποιεῖν is used technically of the action of drugs. Heindorf quotes Dioscorides i. 95 ποιεῖ πρὸς φάρμακα, 'it acts against poisons.'

b 3 καὶ μάλα ἵλεως, 'very cheerfully indeed.' For καὶ μάλα cp. 61 e 1 *n.* ἵλεως is the adverb.

b 4 οὐδὲ διαφθείρας : Plutarch uses φθείρειν and φθορά of mixing colours (L. S. *s. vv.*), and the expression employed here seems to be derived from that technical use. Cp. *Il.* xiii. 284 τοῦ δ' ἀγαθοῦ οὔτ' ἆρ τρέπεται χρώς κτλ.

b 5 ταυρηδὸν ὑποβλέψας. This does not seem to have anything to do with ταυροῦσθαι, ἀποταυροῦσθαι, which refer to the *glare* of an angry bull. An angry or threatening look would be quite out of the picture here. In Arist. *Frogs* 804 ἔβλεψε γοῦν ταυρηδὸν ἐγκύψας κάτω is, indeed, given as a sign that Aeschylus βαρέως φέρει, but ὑποβλέψας is quite different from ἐγκύψας κάτω, which suggests the bull about to toss. It means 'to look askance at' (ὑπόδρα), and, from its use in Hippocrates and Aristotle (L. S. *s. v.*), we see that the original meaning was to look with the eyes half open. It is, then, a 'mischievous look' rather than a threatening one.

b 6 πρὸς τὸ ἀποσπεῖσαί τινι. Perhaps Socrates thought of pouring a libation in honour of Anytus, just as Theramenes had toasted Critias in hemlock-juice. Cp. Xen. *Hell.* ii. 3. 56 καὶ ἐπεί γε ἀποθνῄσκειν ἀναγκαζόμενος τὸ κώνειον ἔπιε, τὸ λειπόμενον ἔφασαν ἀποκοτταβίσαντα εἰπεῖν αὐτόν· Κριτίᾳ τοῦτ' ἔστω τῷ καλῷ. For the use of πρός cp. *Symp.* 174 b 1 πῶς ἔχεις πρὸς τὸ ἐθέλειν ἂν ἰέναι ἄκλητος ἐπὶ δεῖπνον.

c 4 ἐπισχόμενος ... ἐξέπιεν, 'he held his breath and drank it to the last drop.' Stallbaum shows that πίνειν ἐπισχόμενος was a standing phrase. Cp. e. g. Stesichorus fr. 7 Σκύφιον δὲ λαβὼν δέπας ἔμμετρον ὡς τριλάγυνον | πῖ' ἐπισχόμενος κτλ. The rendering 'putting it to his lips', though grammatically possible, does not seem strong enough for this and other passages where the phrase occurs, so I prefer K. F. Hermann's interpretation. The sense assigned to ἐπισχόμενος is not unlike that which it has in *Symp.* 216 a 7 ἐπισχόμενος τὰ ὦτα.

καὶ μάλα εὐχερῶς, 'without the very least disgust'. As δυσχερής means 'fastidious' and δυσχεραίνειν *fastidire*, the meaning is that he drank the poison as if it was quite a pleasant drink.

c 5 ἐπιεικῶς, 'fairly', 'pretty well'.

c 7 ἀστακτί: not in single drops, but in a flood. Cp. Soph. *Oed. Col.* 1251 ἀστακτὶ λείβων δάκρυον, 1646 ἀστακτὶ ... στένοντες. W has ἀσταλακτί, which would mean the same thing, and also preserves an ancient variant ἀβαστακτί, which would mean 'unbearably'.

c 8 ἀπέκλαον ἐμαυτόν, 'I covered my face and wept for my loss.'

c 9 οἵου ἀνδρὸς κτλ., 'to think what a friend I was bereft of.' This is another 'dependent exclamation'. Cp. 58 e 4 *n.*

d 5 κατέκλασε, which Stephanus conjectured for κατέκλαυσε, is actually the reading of T. Cp. Homer, *Od.* iv. 481 κατεκλάσθη φίλον ἦτορ, Plut. *Timoleon* 7 τὸ δὲ Τιμολέοντος ... πάθος ... κατέκλασε καὶ συνέτριψεν αὐτοῦ τὴν διάνοιαν.

e 1 ἐν εὐφημίᾳ: cp. 60 a 3 *n.*

118 a 1 τὰς κνήμας: cp. Arist. *Frogs* 123 Ἀλλ' ἔστιν ἄτραπος ξύντομος τετριμμένη | ἡ διὰ θυείας.—Ἆρα κώνειον λέγεις;— | Μάλιστά γε.— Ψυχράν γε καὶ δυσχείμερον· | εὐθὺς γὰρ ἀποπήγνυσι τἀντικνήμια.

a 2 πήγνυτο: cp. 77 b 4 *n.*

καὶ αὐτὸς ἥπτετο, 'the man himself' (not Socrates). It is implied that the others had touched Socrates by the executioner's directions.

a 5 τὸ ἦτρον : ὁ μεταξὺ ὀμφαλοῦ τε καὶ αἰδοίου τόπος Timaeus, ἦτρον... 'Αττικῶς· ὑπογάστριον 'Ελληνικῶς Moeris.

a 7 τῷ 'Ασκληπιῷ ὀφείλομεν ἀλεκτρυόνα : for the offering of a cock to Asklepios cp. Herondas iv. 11 ἵλεῳ δεῦτε | τοῦ ἀλέκτορος τοῦδ' ὄντιν' οἰκίης τοίχων | κήρυκα θύω, τἀπίδορπα δέξαισθε. Socrates hopes to awake cured like those who are healed by ἐγκοίμησις (incubatio) in the Asklepieion at Epidaurus.

a 16 ἡμεῖς, ' we,' his disciples.

τῶν τότε, ' of the men of his time.' The phrase is regular in such appreciations. Stallbaum compares Hdt. i. 23 'Αρίονα ... κιθαρῳδὸν τῶν τότε ἐόντων οὐδενὸς δεύτερον, Xen. An. ii. 2. 20 κήρυκα ἄριστον τῶν τότε. Cp. Plato, Epist. vii. 324 d 8 φίλον ἄνδρα ἐμοὶ πρεσβύτερον Σωκράτη, ὃν ἐγὼ σχεδὸν οὐκ ἂν αἰσχυνοίμην εἰπὼν δικαιότατον εἶναι τῶν τότε.

a 17 καὶ ἄλλως, ' and in general.' The calm of the closing sentence is characteristically Attic. We find the same thing in tragedy and in the Orators.

APPENDIX I

DEATH BY HEMLOCK

IT is expressly stated by Xenophon (*Hell.* ii. 3. 56) that Thera-menes was put to death by a draught of κώνειον, and Plutarch says the same of Phocion (*Phoc.* 36). As described in the *Phaedo*, the drug acts by producing a gradual refrigeration proceeding from the feet upwards to the heart. Death ensues when the heart is affected, and is accompanied by a spasm or convulsion (ἐκινήθη, 118 a 12). The same symptoms are implied in the passage of Aristophanes (*Frogs* 123) quoted in the note on 118 a 1, where κώνειον is men-tioned by name, and where we are told that it was pounded, as the drug referred to in the *Phaedo* also was (117 a 6). Pliny (*Hist. Nat.* xxv. 95) speaks of the *vis refrigeratoria* of the *cicuta*, and says that the juice was prepared from pounded seeds. It is to be noted further that wine was used as an antidote in cases of such poisoning. Pliny tells us this of *cicuta* (*Hist. Nat.* xiv. 7), and Plato himself implies the same of κώνειον in the *Lysis*.[1] This agrees very well with the warning given to Socrates by the expert not to talk too much (*Phaed.* 63 d 5 sqq.). He explains that this will impede the action of the drug by heating him. Wine would act in the same way. There can be no doubt, then, that Socrates was poisoned by κώνειον, or that κώνειον is *cicuta*. That *cicuta* is 'hemlock' is shown by the use of the word in the Romance languages (Fr. *ciguë*).

In the face of all this, it is disturbing to be told, as we are by some authorities, that hemlock-juice would produce quite different symptoms. I cannot pronounce an opinion on that; but I have submitted the case to an eminent pharmacologist, my colleague Professor C. R. Marshall, who says that 'as evidence against the view that Socrates died of conium poisoning I do not think the statements' (of the authorities referred to) 'worthy of serious con-sideration. Personally I am decidedly of opinion that his death

---

[1] *Lys.* 219 e 2 οἶον εἰ αἰσθάνοιτο αὐτὸν (τὸν ὑὸν) κώνειον πεπωκότα, ἆρα περὶ πολλοῦ ποιοῖτ᾿ ἂν οἶνον, εἴπερ τοῦτο ἡγοῖτο τὸν ὑὸν σώσειν;

149

was due to conium. It is difficult to be absolutely positive on the point, as conium is somewhat peculiar in its action, and the symptoms produced vary with the dose and probably with the individual '. From this it appears that there is certainly no scientific ground for rejecting the philological evidence.

APPENDIX II

Γλαύκου τέχνη

The correct text of the scholium in Ven. T is as follows :

παροιμία ἤτοι ἐπὶ τῶν μὴ ῥᾳδίως κατεργαζομένων, ἢ ἐπὶ τῶν πάνυ ἐπιμελῶς καὶ ἐντέχνως εἰργασμένων. Ἵππασος γάρ τις κατεσκεύασε χαλκοῦς τέτταρας δίσκους οὕτως, ὥστε τὰς μὲν διαμέτρους αὐτῶν ἴσας ὑπάρχειν, τὸ δὲ τοῦ πρώτου δίσκου πάχος ἐπίτριτον μὲν εἶναι τοῦ δευτέρου, ἡμιόλιον δὲ τοῦ τρίτου, διπλάσιον δὲ τοῦ τετάρτου, κρουομένους δὲ τούτους ἐπιτελεῖν συμφωνίαν τινά. καὶ λέγεται Γλαῦκον ἰδόντα τοὺς ἐπὶ τῶν δίσκων φθόγγους πρῶτον ἐγχειρῆσαι δι' αὐτῶν χειρουργεῖν, καὶ ἀπὸ ταύτης τῆς πραγματείας ἔτι καὶ νῦν λέγεσθαι τὴν καλουμένην Γλαύκου τέχνην. μέμνηται δὲ τούτων Ἀριστόξενος περὶ τῆς μουσικῆς ἀκροάσεως, καὶ Νικοκλῆς ἐν τῷ περὶ θεωρίας. ἔστι δὲ καὶ ἑτέρα τέχνη γραμμάτων, ἣν ἀνατιθέασι Γλαύκῳ Σαμίῳ, ἀφ' ἧς ἴσως καὶ ἡ παροιμία διεδόθη. οὗτος δὲ καὶ σιδήρου κόλλησιν εὗρεν, ὥς φησιν Ἡρόδοτος.

This comes from the paroemiographer Lucillus Tarrhaeus (cp. L. Cohn, *Quellen der Platoscholien*, pp. 836 sqq.), and the reference to Aristoxenus takes us back to the time when there was a living Pythagorean tradition. Eusebius, *c. Marc.* 15 D (quoted by Heindorf), is fuller, and mentions some other versions. One says that Glaucus was drowned at sea (just like Hippasus!) before his invention was spread abroad ; another agrees with the story in the scholium ; a third refers to Glaucus of Samos and the ἀνάθημα at Delphi. The fourth is as follows : ἕτερος δὲ Γλαῦκον αὐτὸν ἀναθεῖναι τρίποδα χαλκοῦν δημιουργήσαντα τοῖς παχέως τε (τοῖς πάχεσιν ὥστε?) κρουομένου τούς τε πόδας ἐφ' ὧν βέβηκε καὶ τὸ ἄνω περικείμενον καὶ τὴν στεφάνην τὴν ἐπὶ τοῦ λέβητος καὶ τὰς ῥάβδους διὰ μέσου τεταγμένας φθέγγεσθαι λύρας φωνῇ. If this is genuine tradition, as it appears to be, it is not without significance that Socrates should allude to a distinctively Pythagorean invention.

INDEX TO THE NOTES

I. PROPER NAMES

151

INDEX TO THE NOTES

II. GREEK WORDS

II. GREEK WORDS

INDEX TO THE NOTES

INDEX TO THE NOTES

II. GREEK WORDS

III. GRAMMATICAL

ἄν, omission of 62 c 7
Aorist in impatient questions 86 d 7
Aorist participle (synchronous) 58 b 8 ; 58 e 1 ; 60 c 8 ; 60 c 9
Aorist, empirical 73 d 7 ; 73 d 9
Asyndeton explicativum 61 a 1
Attraction of prepositions 75 b 6
Crasis 58 e 3
Disjunctive question 68 a 3
Infinitive, epexegetic 84 c 3 ; exclamatory 60 b 5 ; 99 b 2
Metaphors from hunting 63 a 2 ; 66 a 3 ; 66 b 4 ; 76 e 9 ; 79 e 3 ; 88 d 9 ; 89 c 1 ; 115 b 9 ; from wrestling 84 c 6 ; 87 a 6 ; 88 d 4 ; military 104 b 10 ; 106 a 4
Optative 87 e 5 ; 107 a 5
Polar expression 59 e 5 ; 81 e 6 ; 82 b 10
Relative 65 a 5

PRINTED IN GREAT BRITAIN
AT THE UNIVERSITY PRESS, OXFORD
BY VIVIAN RIDLER
PRINTER TO THE UNIVERSITY